KNOCKNAGOW

OR

THE HOMES OF TIPPERARY

KNOCKNAGOW

or, The Homes of Tipperary

Charles J. Kickham

ANNA LIVIA

First published 1870
This edition published 1988 by Anna Livia Press, Dublin.

ISBN 1 871311 004

Cover by Bluett

*Cover illustrations from 'The Emerald' 1870,
courtesy of National Library of Ireland.*

*Printed in Great Britain by The Guernsey Press Co. Ltd.,
Guernsey, Channel Islands.*

DEDICATION

——o——

I Dedicate this Book

ABOUT THE HOMES OF TIPPERARY

TO

MY LITTLE NIECES, ANNIE AND JOSIE,

WITH MANY REGRETS AND APOLOGIES

THAT IN SPITE OF ALL THEIR ENTREATIES I WAS OBLIGED TO

" LET POOR NORAH LAHY DIE."

C.J.K.

INTRODUCTION.

———o———

KNOCKNAGOW has been out of print for a considerable time, and very many eager inquiries have been made for it. It now reappears in a new and cheap edition, which may be usefully introduced by a brief account of its Author. The secondary title which he gave to his tale was—" *The Homes of Tipperary.*" His own home was one of them.

Charles Joseph Kickham was born in the year 1825, at Mullinahone, a small town of the County Tipperary. The Anner flows past the town, and Slievenamon rises not far away—the river and the mountain which figure often in his writings. His father, John Kickham, had a large drapery establishment in that place, and was widely respected for his intelligence and probity. His mother, Anne O'Mahony, was a pious and charitable woman, whom he lovingly described in the earliest of his stories, " Sally Cavanagh ; or, Untenanted Graves." His uncle, Father Roger Kickham, was a zealous member of the Vincentian Order ; and another uncle, whose name he bore, was a priest in the Archdiocese of Cashel. But the Author of KNOCKNAGOW was probably called after his grandfather, Charles Kickham.

In his youth he was greatly influenced by *The Nation* of Davis and Duffy ; and, like his kinsman, John O'Mahony, he took an active part in the '48 movement. He was the leading spirit in the Confederate Club, in Mullinahone, which he was chiefly instrumental in forming ; and after the failure of the rising at Ballin-garry, which was not far from his home, he was forced to hide himself for a time. A little later, while still a very young man, he worked earnestly in the Tenant Right League, hoping against hope that something would be done to keep the people at home. When that failed, he lost faith in legal agitation.

In persevering in a political career, and devoting his life to what he believed to be the service of his country, Charles Kickham showed not a little of that iron will which enabled Henry Fawcett to achieve distinction as a public man, in spite of tremendous difficulties of a similar character. The Englishman, on the threshold of manhood, was totally deprived of sight by an accident in a shooting party; yet in spite of this misfortune (the more distressing because his father's hand fired the shot), Fawcett contrived to work on, to ride, to skate, to fish, to become a successful University professor, an active and influential Member of Parliament, and a most efficient Postmaster-General. Young Kickham's accident was not so tragical in its cause, nor so destructive in its effects, at least in one respect. One day, while he was drying a flask of damp gunpowder, it exploded, injuring permanently not only his sight, but his hearing. This was not (as we have seen stated in print) in his sixteenth year, but two or three years earlier. Both sight and hearing grew duller, and his frame less robust, as time went on; and the hardships of his prison life greatly increased these infirmities.

For it was to a prison that his political career conducted him. He was one of the writers in *The Irish People*, the organ of the Fenian movement. Of course, there was an informer working in the very office of the newspaper. Kickham was arrested in November, 1865. He was tried in the court-house of Green Street, Dublin, on the 5th of January, 1866. He was found guilty, and Judge Keogh, after expressing his sympathy for the prisoner, and respect for his intellectual attainments, sentenced him to penal servitude for fourteen years. His attorney announced the sentence to him through his ear-trumpet. He heard it with a smile. As he was led away to his cell, something on the ground attracted his notice, and he picked it up. It was a little paper picture of the Blessed Virgin, and he kissed it reverently. "I was accustomed to have the likeness of the Mother of God morning and evening before my eyes since I was a child," he said to the warder. "Will you ask the governor if I may keep this?"*

In prison he showed great patience and fortitude. His health, already impaired, soon gave way, but he bore up bravely. He felt deeply his sister's death in the first year of his prison life. The sister of his associate, Mr. John O'Leary, asked in after years, did he pray much while there? He answered that he said exactly the same prayers as when he was out in the world. From the solitary confinement of Pentonville he was removed to the invalid prison at Woking. Once he was set to knit stockings. The warder pointed out that he was not making much progress in this novel art. "I have time enough to learn in fourteen years," he replied. What proficiency he had attained we do not know when this particular study was interrupted. His wretched health, helped no doubt by his blameless character and gentle demeanour, shortened very considerably his term of imprisonment. He was released in March, 1869.

To somebody who asked what he had missed most in gaol, he replied, "Children, and women, and fires." He was very fond of little children, and knew how to win their hearts. "It delighted him," says one of his best friends, "when the little ones tried to talk to him on their fingers; and he was most patient in

---

* This touching incident probably comes from Kickham himself, for we take it from an affectionate memorial written "before the first bloom of daisies was dead upon his grave," by the young lady whose kindness soothed his last years and his last hours, Miss Rose Kavanagh. She recalls a "parallel passage" in his life, when almost the last use his tongue made of language after the fatal blow came, was to say aloud the Rosary of the Blessed Virgin

teaching them, taking particular care not to allow
them to speak incorrectly. Children who loved him,
were playing about his feet in the sunshine when the
stroke of paralysis came upon him at the last." There
was much of what is best in woman and in child in
his nature ; and it was impossible, says another devoted
young friend, to know him well without feeling that
he was trustful, and kindly, and sympathetic as a
woman. His slender hand was fashioned like a woman's,
too. There was a great deal of silky grey hair in curls
about his head, which was finely shaped and he was
very tall.

These last phrases are taken from a writer, who,
in her affectionate obituary, speaks thus of the tale
which we are now introducing anew to the public :—

" No writer has produced more faithful pictures of
Irish country life than Charles Kickham. For no
other writer possessed a mind quicker to see, or wider
to hold the best feelings of our people ; none other
owned head or hand more obedient to the highest
impulses of the Celtic character, and his memory was
filled with the traditions of our land and race.
' Knocknagow ' illustrates many sides of his own per-
sonality and of his ready humour, which was never
cynical. In this book, as in nearly all he wrote, tears
and laughter are close together. . . .

" ' Knocknagow ' had always been my favourite
Irish story, and when an opportunity of meeting its
Author came, it was an event in my life. I remember
giving him the sort of information he must have had
from hundreds of persons—of what a pleasure his
stories and songs were, and how dear to me and my
friends were Grace Kiely, and Mary Kearney, and
poor Norah Lahy, whom, in spite of his niece's entreaties,
he had to let die. He bore the infliction good·
humouredly and talked about his heroines as if they
had just gone out for a walk."

Besides the present novel and " Sally Cavanagh,"
and some shorter tales, Mr. Kickham left behind him

a full length novel, which was published last year, in a cheap form, under the title of " For the Old Land." His knowledge and love of the Irish character in many different phases are shown in every page of this tale, and fun and pathos are very skilfully intermingled.

Charles Kickham's poems are very few and short, those at least which he gave to print. Very many of our readers must be familiar with the pathetic little ballad about the Irish peasant girl who " lived beside the Anner, at the foot of Slievenamon." Also, " Rory of the Hills " and " Patrick Sheehan " have taken a great hold on the people.

This Introduction has now, perhaps, served its purpose by letting the reader know something beforehand about this book and its Author. With the addition of a few names and dates learned from his kinswoman, the Sister of Mercy who helped to make his death bed as holy as his life had been innocent, our sketch, as it has acknowledged more than once, has followed the published recollections of Miss Ellen O'Leary and Miss Rose Kavanagh. To the personal description cited from the latter, we may join that given by the former lady :—

" In person, Charles Kickham was tall and strongly built. He walked like a sailor, swaying from side to side. He had a fine picturesque head, on which the wavy brown hair, of late years thickly streaked with gray, grew in soft curls ; a large forehead, keen, piercing eyes, which had a strange power of reading one's very thoughts, and a rough skin, somewhat scarred by that terrible powder accident. The expression of his face when in repose was striking—a face you'd love to look upon : earnest, thoughtful, rather sad, and so good. In conversation he showed wonderful powers of observation, an intuitive insight into character. His talk, when in good spirits, was very pleasant. He had a great fund of quiet humour, and would describe a scene or a character with a few well-painted strokes. Though gentle and kind in disposition, he could be a good hater as well as a fervent 'over.'

Charles Joseph Kickham died at Blackrock, near Dublin on the 22nd of August, 1882. His body was brought home to the Tipperary graveyard where his father, and mother, and sister, and many kinsfolk were buried. In the Dublin Exhibition of 1864, he had lingered long before a painting, "the Head of a Cow," by one of the Old Masters, not on account of any subtle genius be discovered in it, but "because it was so like an old cow in Mullinahone." A quaint trait of the affectionate, home-loving nature which made it fitting that his grave should be where his cradle had been—"beside the Anner, at the foot of Slievenamon."

MATTHEW RUSSELL, S.J.

Dublin, 27th Feb., 1887.

CONTENTS.

———o———

KNOCKNAGOW;

OR,

The Homes of Tipperary.

CHAPTER I.

I T is Christmas Day.

Mr. Henry Lowe has just opened his eyes, and is debating with himself whether it is the grey dawn, or only the light of the young moon he sees struggling through the two round holes in the window shutters of his room. He has slept soundly, as well he might, after a journey the day before of some eighty miles on the outside of the mailcoach, from the metropolis to the town of —— ; supplemented by an additional drive of a dozen miles in his host's gig to his present not uncomfortable quarters.

The young gentleman knows little of Ireland from personal experience, having spent most of his life in what is sometimes oddly enough called " the sister country."

Mr. Henry Lowe is at present the guest of his uncle's principal tenant, Mr. Maurice Kearney. The visit was partly the result of accident and partly a stroke of policy on the part of the young man's mother. Her brother, Sir Garrett Butler, owned

—at least nominally—extensive landed property in the
South of Ireland; and the prudent mother was trying to
induce him to give her son the agency. And Mr. Kearney
having gone to Dublin to see the landlord about the renewal
of his lease, it was agreed that the young gentleman—whom
we intend to introduce to the reader when he gets out of
bed—should accompany him on his return home, and spend
some weeks among his uncle's Tipperary tenants.

And so we find Mr. Henry Lowe half buried in down, this
clear Christmas morning, in the best bedroom of Ballinaclash
Cottage—for so Maurice Kearney's commodious, if not handsome, residence is called.

He had just settled the question with which his mind had
been occupied for some ten minutes back, in favour of the
moon, and was relapsing into slumber, when it suddenly
occurred to him—

That he was a land agent in embryo.

That he was at that moment in the midst of a district not
unknown to fame in connection with "agrarian outrages;"
and

That his room was on the ground floor.

This train of thought gave the holes in the window-shutters
a new interest in his eyes.

He was beginning to succeed pretty well in calling up a
vision of a blunderbuss loaded to the muzzle with slugs, and
two tall figures in frieze coats and knee breeches, with crape
over their faces, when a tremendous report—as if the blunderbuss had gone off and burst—made him start to a sitting
posture.

A second bang, if possible more stunning than the first,
caused Mr. Henry Lowe to execute a jump—or rather to put
forth a degree of muscular action which, under more favourable circumstances, would have resulted in that gymnastic
feat; but which, owing to his position and the non-elasticity
of a feather-bed, must be pronounced a failure. The repetition of the sound a third, and a fourth, and a fifth time, was
followed by as many vigorous but—whether we have regard
to a "high" or a "long jump"—abortive efforts on the part
of Mr. Henry Lowe.

At this stage of the proceedings the bedroom door was
opened, and Mr. Kearney entered with a lighted candle in

his hand. He held the light above his head, and looked considerably astonished when his guest was revealed to him, performing, as he thought, the identical African dance which the Reverend Edward Wright, the missioner, had been describing to him a few days before.

The gentlemen regarded each other with looks of mutual surprise and inquiry. But Mr. Kearney, divining the cause of his guest's perturbation, said, apologetically :

" I'm sorry they're after disturbing you."

" Wha—what is it ? " gasped Mr. Lowe, who maintained his sitting position and his scared look.

" The drum," replied his host, in a self-satisfied way, as if further explanation would be altogether superfluous. " I came in to tell you not to mind it."

" Oh !—a drum," the young gentleman repeated, somewhat reassured, but evidently still bewildered. " Yes, there it is again. But what drum ? What does it mean ? "

" The Knocknagow Drum," was the reply. " They always meet at the Bush. But don't stir. They'll shortly be off, and you can have a good sleep before breakfast is ready."

" Knocknagow ! The Bush ! What o'clock is it ? "

" Not six yet. We're going to seven o'clock Mass. We'll be back to breakfast at nine. So stay where you are, snug and warm, till I call you."

" Am I to understand the whole family are going to prayers ? " the visitor inquired ; not at all relishing the idea of being left alone in the house.

" Yes ; we always go to early Mass on Christmas Day."

" Would there be any objection to my going with you ? "

" Not the least. But the morning is very cold ; hard frost."

" Well, but I'd like to witness as many of the customs of the country as possible."

" Very well. Please yourself. I'll send up Wattletoes with hot water to you."

He laid the candlestick on the dressing-table, and Mr. Lowe soon heard him shouting to Wattletoes to bring hot water to the gentleman in the " middle room."

The gentleman in the middle room lay back upon his pillow, and surveyed the bearer of the hot water with some curiosity.

The first thing that struck him was, that it would be impossible to say whether this individual were old or young or middle-aged. He was low-sized and stooped somewhat. But his face, though shrivelled and puckered in an extraordinary manner, was the face of a withered boy, rather than of an old man. He wore an old frock coat, which evidently reached to the knees of the original owner, but nearly touched the heels of its present possessor. The legs of his trousers, which were as much out of proportion as the other garment, were rolled up, and formed thick circular pads half-way between his knees and his ankles.

Before Mr. Lowe could proceed further with his inspection, this odd-looking figure was disappearing through the door.

" What is your name ? " he asked.

The grotesque figure stopped suddenly in the doorway, and, wheeling round, with his hand to his forehead, he answered with a grimace, of which it would be vain to attempt a description :

" Barney, sir—Barney Brodherick."

" Not Wattletoes," thought the young gentleman, as he pulled the blankets tightly over his shoulder. " I wonder who the devil *is* Wattletoes ! Have I much time to dress ? " he asked aloud.

" Lots uv time, sir. On'y if you don't hurry you'll be too late."

" Lots of time," Mr. Lowe repeated ; " but I'll be too late if I don't hurry."

Before he could ask for an explanation of this somewhat contradictory piece of information, Barney vanished, scratching his head and muttering something about " the boots," as if he felt himself in a difficulty.

Mr. Lowe had nearly completed his toilet when Barney returned with his boots, followed by Mr. Kearney, whip in hand, and wrapped in a frieze great-coat.

The master had evidently been " pitching into ' the man ; for Barney explained as he placed the visitor's boots on the floor :

" Blur-an-agers, have sinse, sir—have sinse."

" Have sense yourself—and that's what you'll never have, you ninny-hammer." retorted the master, in an apparently angry tone. " He was told," he continued, turning to his guest, " to bring blacking from Kilthubber yesterday ; and they desired him to get Martindale's blacking. When they found they had no blacking, and asked him why he didn't bring it—' I tried every house,' he says, ' from Gallows-hill to Quarryhole, and the devil a Martin Dale could I find."

Though no trace of a smile could be detected in Maurice Kearney's ruddy face while he spoke, his repeating Barney's explanation of the non-appearance of the blacking, twice over, showed that he enjoyed it in his own way.

When they stood within the glow of the blazing wood fire in the parlour, the host again advised his guest to remain within doors till the family had returned from Mass. But the young gentleman repeated his desire to accompany them.

The roll of the drum—the performer evidently using less force than when he so startled the stranger a while ago—accompanied by the shrill but not unpleasing music of half-a-dozen fifes, signified that the procession—which consisted of nearly the whole population of Knocknagow—had set out for Kilthubber.

Mr. Kearney and his guest were soon seated in the gig in which they had arrived the night before, and slowly following the crowd along the snow-covered road.

It was too dark to see much either of the country or the people, and Maurice Kearney could do little more to amuse the stranger than to point out the direction in which some objects of interest would be visible in the daylight. But, even with the light they had, Mr. Lowe could not help being struck with the fine outline of the mountain range in front of them.

The far-famed Knocknagow drum shook the windows of the old town of Kilthubber, as the procession marched through the principal street to the chapel, at the gate of which the music suddenly ceased.

Barney Brodherick was in waiting to take the horse to the hotel, and Mr. Lowe was conducted by his host up the gallery stairs and soon found himself in a front pew, next a lady who, he rightly conjectured, was his host's eldest daughter, but to whom he had not yet been introduced, owing to the

lateness of the hour when he arrived at the cottage the night
before, and to the fact that Miss Kearney was on her way to
church before he left his room in the morning.

Never having been in a Catholic place of worship during
divine service before, he looked around him with some
curiosity, not unmingled with a sense of awe. The altar
was brilliant with innumerable tapers and tastefully decorated with flowers and ever-greens. Three branches, suspended by long chains from the ceiling, gave light to the
congregation that filled the spacious aisle, while candles in
sconces attached to the pillars and round the walls enabled
the occupants of the pews in the gallery to read their prayer
books. The tinkle of a small bell called back his attention
to the altar, and he saw that during his survey of the church,
the priest, accompanied by a number of boys in white sur-
plices, had moved from the sacristy and now stood bowing
with clasped hands in front of the altar. As he ascended
the carpeted steps the organ pealed out solemnly ; and in
spite of his prejudices, the ceremony and the evidently
earnest devotion of the worshippers impressed Mr. Lowe
with a respect for their form of religion which he never had
felt before. This feeling, however, was giving place to a
sense of weariness, when he was startled by the suddenness
with which the people rose from their knees and pressed
forward towards the altar. He looked down with astonishment upon the swaying sea of upturned faces till it settled
into stillness as the clergyman turned to address the congregation.

A peculiar ring in the preacher's sweetly-modulated tones
at once attracted the stranger's attention. Having read the
text, he replaced the book on its stand, and, leaning back
against the altar, commenced his sermon. At first his words
came slowly and hesitatingly. But as he warmed with his
subject he moved about, now to the right, now to the left,
and sometimes straight forward to the verge of the altar-step,
which formed the platform upon which he stood—pouring
forth what seemed to the unaccustomed ears of Mr. Lowe a
torrent of barbaric eloquence, which rose into a kind of
gorgeous sublimity, or melted into pathos, sometimes homely,
sometimes fancifully poetical. Such language Mr. Lowe
would have thought ill-suited to such a crowd as he now

looked down upon, if he had not witnessed the effect it produced. And he was surprised to find that it was the figurative passages that moved the people most. For instance, when the preacher depicted the Virgin wandering through the streets of Bethlehem, seeking for shelter and finding every door closed against her, and proceeded : " The snow falls ; the cold winds blow—*and the Lily of Heaven is withered,*" a cry burst from the congregation, and the sobs were so loud and frequent that the preacher was obliged to pause till the emotion he had called forth had subsided.

The sermon was short and withal practical ; for while it comforted the poor, it impressed upon the rich the duty of alleviating their sufferings.

And as the clock struck eight, the Knocknagow drum told such of the inhabitants of Kilthubber as had not yet left their beds that first Mass was over and the congregation were on their way homeward.

CHAPTER II.

" MY ELDEST DAUGHTER, SIR."

MR. LOWE judged from the hearty " I wish you a merry Christmas, sir," which greeted his host so frequently on the way homeward, that Mr. Kearney was on excellent terms with his neighbours. They did not wait for the procession ; and, after a brisk drive of twenty minutes, the young gentleman again found himself in front of the crackling wood fire. While looking out on the snow-covered landscape, his attention was attracted by the extraordinary gait of a person approaching the house, swinging his legs and arms about in a manner impossible to be described. As he came nearer, the size and shape of the feet were particularly noticeable. And as the figure was passing the window, the fact flashed upon Mr. Henry Lowe, as if by inspiration, that after all Barney Brodherick *was* Wattletoes.

He had the curiosity to raise one of the windows to see
what Barney meant by stopping suddenly opposite the hall-
door, and holding out his hand with a coaxing wink of his
little grey eyes.

Maurice Kearney's youngest son, a fat, innocent-looking
boy, stood, with his shoulder leaning against the jamb of the
door, picking the raisins out of a great slice of plum-cake.

" I'll bring you to hunt the wran," said Barney.

" I can go with Tom Maher," the boy replied.

" I'll give you a ride on Bobby," Barney continued, in a
still more insinuating voice.

But the boy continued picking the raisins out of his plum-
cake.

" Be gob, Mr. Willie, I'll—I'll show you a thrish's nist ! "
exclaimed Barney, in a sort of stage whisper.

The boy looked from the cake to the tempter, and hesitated.

" With five young wans in id," continued Barney, pressing
the advantage he saw he had gained, " feathered an' all—
ready to fly."

This was too much. The thrush's nest carried the day ;
and Barney was in the act of taking a bite out of the plum-
cake as he repassed the parlour window on his way round to
the kitchen. But the promise of a thrush's nest, with five
young ones in it, on a Christmas morning in our latitude,
impressed Mr. Lowe with a high opinion of Barney Brodherick's powers as a diplomatist.

" Come, Mr. Lowe," said his host, as he placed a chair
for him at the breakfast table, " you ought to have a good
appetite by this time. I'm sorry you would not take something before you went out this morning."

" Oh, thank you," he replied, " but I'm all the better able
to do justice to your viands now."

As the young gentleman was sitting down, Mrs. Kearney's
portly figure caught his eye in the doorway. She at once
walked up to him, holding out her hand, and apologised for
not having been prepared to receive him properly on his
arrival " But indeed," she added, " we had not the least
notion that any one was coming. Why did you not write to
say that Mr. Lowe would be with you ? " she asked, turning
to her husband.

"Where was the use of writing, when I knew I'd be home myself before the letter," was the reply, in a rather brusque manner, which was peculiar to Maurice Kearney.

"The time," said Mr. Lowe, "is very unusual for such a visit ; but you know I am a homeless wanderer at present."

"My eldest daughter, sir," said Mr. Kearney, waving his hand towards the door, near which the young lady had stopped hesitatingly for a moment.

Mrs. Kearney took her portly person out of the way ; and her face beamed with pride and fondness as she surveyed the lovely girl, who, after courtesying gracefully, advanced, and, with a half-bashful smile, gave her hand to her father's guest.

The young gentleman was taken completely by surprise. He had felt some curiosity to know what sort was the face hidden by the thick veil next him in the chapel. He thought it would be rather a pleasant discovery to find that the face was a handsome one ; and was quite prepared for a blooming country girl in the person of his burly host's daughter. But the lady who now stood before him would have arrested his attention anywhere. She was tall, though not of the tallest. The driven snow was not whiter than her neck and brow. A faint blush at that moment tinged her usually pale cheek, which, together with a pair of ripe, rosy lips, and eyes of heavenly blue, imparted a warmth to what otherwise might be considered the marble coldness of her almost too ideal beauty.

Mr. Henry Lowe, for once in his life, felt at a loss for something to say ; but the entrance of two young girls spared him the necessity of making a speech. The taller of the two moved timidly behind her father's chair without venturing even to glance at the stranger ; while the other surveyed him from head to foot, and then turned to Miss Kearney with a look of surprise if not reproach. Miss Kearney understood the look, and said with a smile :

"Mr. Lowe, let me introduce you to my friend, Miss Gracie Kiely."

"Miss *Grace* Kiely," said the little lady, drawing herself up to her full height, and bowing with great dignity.

She was moving away, with an air of studied gravity, when Mr. Kearney said

"Come, Grace, sit here near me. 'Tis a long time since you and I had a talk together."

Her face lighted up at once, and, forgetting all her womanly dignity, she ran, with child-like glee to the chair which he had drawn close to his own. She resumed her serious look again ; but her keen sense of the ludicrous was too much for it, and one of Maurice Kearney's characteristic observations had even the effect of making our dignified young lady laugh into her cup, and spill so much of the tea that Mrs. Kearney insisted upon filling her cup again.

"How did you like the sermon, Mr. Lowe ? " Miss Kearney asked.

"It was so unlike anything I ever heard before," he replied, "that I really cannot venture to give an opinion. But he certainly moved his hearers as I have never seen an audience moved by a preacher. Some passages were quite poetical ; and these, I was surprised to find, produced the greatest effect. It is very strange."

"I believe," said Miss Kearney, "we Irish are a poetical people."

"I particularly admired that passage," Grace observed, with her serious look, "beginning, ' From the ripple of the rill to the rolling of the ocean ; from the lily of the valley to the cedar on the mountain.' That passage was very beautiful."

"Yes, I remember that," said Mr. Lowe, with a nod and a smile, which so flattered Miss Grace's vanity that she could only preserve her look of gravity by dropping her eyelids and almost frowning. But, in spite of her efforts, a glance shot from the corner of her eye which plainly showed how gratified she was.

"She could preach the whole sermon to you," said Mr. Kearney, in his emphatic way. And then, after a pause, he added, still more emphatically : "I'd rather have her in the house than a piper."

This was too much for Grace ; and Miss Kearney and her mother joined in her ringing laugh, while Mr. Lowe looked quite as much puzzled as amused, as he turned full round and stared at his host, apparently expecting some explanation of this extraordinary testimony to Miss Grace's powers of pleasing.

Mr. Kearney, however, rubbed his whiskers, contemplatively, to all seeming quite unconscious of their mirth, and added, with a jerk of his head :

"Wait till you hear her play 'the Foxhunter's Jig.' Miss Butler is a fine girl," he observed, abruptly changing the subject.

All eyes were turned upon Mr. Lowe, and he felt called upon to say something. So he said :

"Indeed yes, a very fine girl."

But the young gentleman felt that a certain opinion which he had always held regarding the respective merits of black and blue eyes, was considerably modified during the past half-hour.

"She plays the harp," said Mr. Kearney confidently to Grace, who nodded, and evinced by her look that the concerns of great people possessed a great interest for her.

"And the guitar," he added. "Though the devil a much I'd give for that, only for the singing. She has a fine voice," he remarked, turning to Mr. Lowe.

"Does Miss Kiely sing ? "

"She does, she does," his host replied, rather impatiently.

"But I'm talking of your cousin, Miss Butler."

"Oh, she sings very well," said Mr. Lowe.

"I never heard 'Savourneen Dheelish' or the 'Coulin' played better. She brought the tears to my eyes."

"She is quite an enthusiast about Irish music," said Mr. Lowe.

"Kind father for her," put in Mrs. Kearney. "He and my Uncle Dan used to spend whole days and nights together playing Irish airs. My Uncle Dan played the fid—violin," said Mrs. Kearney, correcting herself, for she liked to call things by their grandest names, particularly when they happened to be connected with her Uncle Dan, or, indeed, with any of the great O'Carrol's of Ballydunmore. "Mr. Butler," she continued, "used to play the flute." He made some beautiful songs about Annie Cleary before they were married. He was not Sir Garrett then, for it was in Sir Thomas's time. My Uncle Dan, too, had a great turn for poetry, and he used to help Mr. Butler to arrange the music for the songs. 'Twas my Uncle Dan," she added, turning to her husband, as if she were imparting a piece of information he

had never heard before, " 'twas my Uncle Dan that translated the ' Coravoth ' into English."

" I know, I know," said her husband, rubbing the side of
his head uneasily—knowing from sad experience that when
his portly better half once set off upon her hobby it was no
easy matter to pull her up.

" My Uncle Dan," she proceeded, " was the most talented
of the family, though the COUNSELLOR had the name."

Mrs. Kearney closed her lips after uttering the word
" Counsellor," and then opened them with a kind of smack,
followed by a gentle sigh, as she bent her head languidly
to one side, and rested her folded hands upon her knees.
Her husband rubbed his head more and more frantically ;
for these were infallible signs that the good lady was settling
down steadily to her work. But fortunately Mr. Lowe,
whose curiosity was really excited, averted the threatened
infliction.

" Did Sir Garrett," he asked, " really make verses ? "

" Oh, yes," Mrs. Kearney replied ; " ' Father Ned's sweet
Niece,' and ' Over the Hills,' and several others."

" I knew his marriage was a romantic business," said Mr.
Lowe. " But I was not aware that my uncle was a poet.
He was greatly blamed by his family, but Sir Thomas's
conduct was quite unjustifiable. There was nothing so
extraordinary in such a marriage, after all."

While Mr. Lowe was speaking, a robin flew round the
room, and dashed itself against the window. Miss Kearney
leaning back in her chair and shading her eyes from the
light with her hand, looked up at the bird as it fluttered
against the glass. And the picture thus presented had, we
suspect, something to do with Mr. Henry Lowe's inability
to see anything extraordinary in his uncle's marriage. She
stood up to let the robin escape, and her father and Mr.
Lowe also left the breakfast table. The latter, with
an air of easy good breeding, put back the bolt and drew
up the window ; while the graceful girl gently took the
robin in her hand, and, after looking for a moment into the
bold, bright little eyes with a smile that made Mr. Henry
Lowe swear mentally that eyes of bird or man never
beheld anything more lovely, let him fly out into the sunshine.

" As ready as he is to come in," she said, as she followed
the released prisoner with a melancholy gaze, which in the
difference her companion thought was even more killing
than the smile it succeeded—" as ready as he is to come in,
he is always impatient to get away. I believe no bird loves
liberty so well."

" If you could set all your captives free as easily it would
be well."

" I'd wish to do so—that is, if I had made any, of which
I am unconscious."

She felt conscious, however, of the young gentleman's
disposition to be more openly complimentary than she
thought quite agreeable, and to divert his attention to something else, she said :

" I fear you will find our neighbourhood very dull. But
my brothers will be home to-day, and I hope they may be
able to find some amusement for you."

This speech was calculated to have the very opposite effect
of what she intended ; but her father unintentionally came
to her relief.

" You have good snipe shooting in the bog," he said
abruptly, " and if we have a thaw, the hounds will be out."

" I am most anxious," said Mr. Lowe, " to have a day with
the Tipperary hounds."

" I can mount you well," said Mr. Kearney. " Come and
I'll show him to you. Tell Wattletoes," he continued, turning to the servant who had come in to replenish the fire
" to lead out Mr. Hugh's horse."

" He's gone to hunt the wren, sir," she replied.

Mr. Lowe saved Barney from a storm of abuse by remarking that as often as he had heard of hunting the wren he had
never seen it.

" Let us walk over toward the fort," said his host, " and
you'll see enough of it."

" We'll go too, Mary," exclaimed Grace, leaping from the
sofa upon which she had been reclining in a graceful attitude,
and in what she persuaded herself was a dreamily sentimental mood.

Miss Kearney held up her hand warningly, but her father
turned round before he had reached the door and said :

" Yes, Grace, let you and Mary come with us."

"Of course you will come too, Ellie," said Miss Kearney to her young sister, who was reading a book near the fire, and apparently afraid of attracting attention.

"Oh, no," she replied with a start, "mamma will want me."

CHAPTER III.

MAT THE THRASHER.

As the party approached the avenue gate, on their way to the fort, a tax-cart was seen coming from the direction of the village.

"Oh! 'tis Richard," Grace exclaimed; "I'm so glad."

She evinced her joy by a series of little bounds as she took Miss Kearney's arm and tried to hurry her forward. But her companion's pace was too slow for her impatience, and she ran on alone.

"She is a very interesting child," said Mr. Lowe.

"She would not thank you for calling her a child," said Miss Kearney, with a smile.

"I should scarcely have called her a child a moment ago," he replied, "for she talked and even looked like a very sensible woman. Perhaps she is older than she seems?"

"No; she is a child in years. But she really astonishes me sometimes."

"Who are the gentlemen?" he added, as the tax-cart stopped.

"My brothers."

Grace pulled open one side of the heavy gate with all her might; but as she was about exerting her strength with the other, she suddenly let go her hold, and ran out on the road. The taller of the two occupants of the tax-cart reached her his hand, and she was standing between his knees in an instant. They drove on; and Miss Kearney said, in reply to her companion's look of surprise:

"They are going round to the back gate. Grace will bring them out immediately, you may be sure."

" Is she a relative of yours ? " he asked.

" Her mother's sister is married to an uncle of mine," she replied. " Her father, Doctor Kiely, is a very eminent physician, and a man of distinguished talent."

" Oh, I believe I have heard of him. Is he not one of your great agitators ? "

" Yes ; I suppose you would call him an agitator. He does not try to conceal his patriotism ; and yet, strange to say, he is the favourite doctor of nearly all the great families of the county, and he has ever so many public appointments. Grace would say, ' quite a monopoly of them,' " she added, smiling her angelic smile—as much at her own homely phrase as at the more learned one her little friend would have used.

" That tells well for the liberality of the aristocracy."

" Perhaps it tells as well for the high character and skill of Dr. Kiely."

" About what age is he ? " Mr. Lowe asked.

" I believe about fifty," she replied. " He is the finest looking man I ever saw."

" Has he a large family ? "

" No ; two daughters. The eldest is a very beautiful girl ; but Grace is her father's idol."

" Has he. no son ? "

" Yes ; he has a son."

There was a kind of hesitation in her manner of replying to his last question that caused Mr. Lowe to look inquiringly at her. But their conversation was interrupted by a tall, brawny peasant, who stopped, as he was passing the gate, to talk to Mr. Kearney.

The peasant's name was Donovan, but he was universally known as Mat the Thrasher. He excelled in all kinds of work as a farm labourer, and never met his match at wielding a flail. As a consequence, he was in great request among farmers from October to March ; and, indeed, during all the year round—for Mat could turn a hand almost to anything, from soleing a pair of brogues to roofing and thatching a barn. His superiority as a ploughman was never questioned. As a proof of his skill in this line, we may mention that when Maurice Kearney was about running what in Ireland is called a " ditch " through the centre of the " kiln field," the difficulty presented itself—how to make the fence perfectly straight. And, as a matter of course, Mat Donovan was immediately sent for.

" Now," said Mat, after looking at the ground, " where do you want to run it ? "

" From this bush," his employer replied, laying his walking-stick on a whitethorn bush in the fence, " to the ash-tree at the left-hand side of the gap," pointing to a tree at the opposite side of the field. " In a straight line," he added, looking at Mat as if the problem were worthy to be grappled with even by his genius.

Mat walked away without uttering a word, leaving Mr. Kearney and the half-dozen workmen, who, leaning on their spades, were waiting the order to begin at the construction of the new ditch, altogether unable to conjecture how he intended to proceed ; but with unshaken faith in his ultimate success.

Mat walked leisurely back to the " gurteen " where he had been at work, and was soon seen coming through the gap near the ash-tree with his plough and horses. With one huge hand he leant on the handle of the plough, thereby lifting the irons, so as that they might glide over the ground without cutting through it, till he came to the ash-tree. Facing his horses towards the whitethorn bush at the opposite end of the field, he fixed his eye steadily on that object.

Mr. Kearney and the workmen heard his " Yo—up ! " to the horses, and on he came, nearer and nearer, slow but sure, till they could catch the air of the song which he commenced to chant with as great solemnity of look and intonation as if its accurate rendering were a necessary condition of the success of his undertaking. They soon had the benefit even of the words, and as Mat pulled the horses to one side as their breasts touched the whitethorn bush, he continued while he reined them in :—

> " Oh, had I the lamp of Aladdin.
>   And had I his geni also.
> I'd rather live poor on the mountain,
>   With coleen dhas cruiteen amo."

" There it is for you," he exclaimed, as he folded his arms

after flinging down the reins, " as straight as the split in a peeler's pole."

Mr. Kearney thrust his thumbs into the arm-holes of his waistcoat, and looked intensely solemn, which was his way of expressing extreme delight. The workmen looked at one another and shook their heads in silent admiration—Jim Dunn, as he flung his coat against " the belly of the ditch," declaring in a decided tone, as if there could be no possible question of the fact, " that nothin' could bate him." And Tom Maher, after spitting first in one fist and then in the other (if we may be pardoned for chronicling such a proceeding), firmly clutched his spade with both hands, and eyeing his hero from head to foot, devoutly wished " bad luck to the mother that'd begrudge him her daughter." By which Tom merely meant to express in a general way his belief that Mat the Thrasher was good enough for any woman's daughter, and intended no allusion to any particular mother or daughter. But the flush that reddened the honest face of the ploughman, and a certain softening of his grey eyes, told plainly enough that Tom Maher had unconsciously touched a sensitive chord in the heart of big Mat Donovan.

Some readers may, perhaps, require an explanation of Mat's allusion to " the split in a peeler's poll." The fact is, that respectable " force," now known as the Royal Irish Constabulary, have always been noted for the extreme care bestowed by them on the hair of their heads. At the time of which we write, a " crease " down the back of the head was one of the distinguishing marks of a policeman in country districts where " swells " were scarce. And to such a pitch of perfection had the " force " attained in the matter of this crease, that Mat the Thrasher could find nothing in art or nature capable of conveying a just idea of the straightness of the line he had marked out for Maurice Kearney's new ditch but " the split in a peeler's poll." We have thought this explanation necessary, lest the split in the poll should be mistaken for a split in the skull—a thing which our good-natured friend never once thought of. The " new ditch " is to this day the admiration of all beholders. To be sure, it never was and never will be the slightest earthly use—a fact of which Hugh tried to convince his father before this whim was put into execution. But Maurice Kearney was headstrong, and would have his way in such matters. The new ditch narrowly escaped being a furze ditch—or what in other parts of the country would be called a whin hedge— by a characteristic blunder of Wattletoes, who was sent by his master to sow the seed of the " unprofitably gay " shrub. In due time a drill of turnips appeared along the top of the new ditch ; while Hugh Kearney was astonished one fine morning to find a promising crop of furze in the very middle of his " purple-tops."

Miss Kearney wished Mat a happy Christmas.

" I wish you the same, and a great many of them, Miss," he replied, looking towards her for a moment, and then turned to resume the conversation with her father.

" He is a magnificent specimen of the Irish peasant," said Mr. Lowe to Miss Kearney.

" Let us wait till you hear him talk," said she. " You will be sure to hear something out of the common from Mat the Thrasher, as we call him."

Mat, it appeared, wanted to know if Mr. Kearney would sell him " a couple of barrels of the Swedes."

" No," replied the latter ; " I won't sell any turnips. I'll want all I have, and more. But I thought you had a good crop of potatoes. I never saw finer."

" They turned out bad," said Mat.

" Were those the potatoes behind your house, Mat ? " Miss Kearney asked. " Nelly pointed them out to me one day, and asked me did I ever see a flower-garden so blooming."

" The very same, Miss," Mat replied, with a sorrowful shake of the head. " I never laid my eyes on such desavers."

" I suppose they were blighted," said Miss Kearney.

" No then, Miss," he replied, with a reproachful sadness in his look and voice. " Every stalk ov 'em would make a rafter for a house the first of November. But put the best man in the parish to dig 'em after, and a duck 'ud swally all he'd be able to turn out from morning till night."

The idea of a potato-stalk making a rafter for a house made Miss Kearney smile in spite of herself ; but the duck swallowing all the potatoes a man could dig in a day, forced her to laugh outright. To make amends for what she considered her ill-timed mirth, she said to her father :

"I think, sir, you might give Mat the turnips he requires."

"Do you want to have the whole parish coming for turnips?" exclaimed her father in no amiable tone.

"Sure you can refuse the next person that comes."

"Very well," said he, with a resigned look and a shrug of the shoulder, as if there were no help for it.

Mat Donovan expressed his thanks; but in a manner that showed he was pretty sure his request would have been granted in any case. He strode up the hill with an easy, swinging gait; and as he carried a huge stick in his hand and turned in the direction of the fort, Miss Kearney remarked that he was going to join the "wren boys."

She should have known better, however, than use the words "wren boys" in the sense she did. They are only called wren boys who carry the wren in a holly bush decorated with ribbons from house to house on St. Stephen's Day; and many who hunt the wren do not join in this part of the proceedings. We may remark also that though the "king of all birds" is said and sung to be "caught in the furze" on St. Stephen's Day, he is invariably "caught," and often ruthlessly slain, too, on Christmas Day.

Mr. Lowe was beginning to feel quite at home with his fair companion—whom we shall call by her Christian name, Mary, in future—and on seeing her brothers coming through the lawn towards them, asked her to tell him something about them.

"Well," she replied, "my eldest brother, Hugh, lives at home and attends to the farm with my father. Richard is a surgeon; he has a great wish to go to Australia, but my father and mother are opposed to it."

Richard and Grace came on merrily together; while Hugh walked thoughtfully, if not moodily, behind them. He was about the middle height, broad-shouldered and strongly built. His hair and beard were black as night, and his complexion so dark that strangers sometimes asked if he had been a sailor, or had lived under a tropical sun. His dress of grey tweed betokened the farmer; but a heavy gold watch chain seemed to indicate that he was not indifferent to display. He was not popular like his father; but the respect with which he treated even the humblest day-labourer, and a certain quiet independence in his bearing towards the gentry of his neighbourhood, won for him the esteem of all classes. On the whole, Hugh Kearney was looked upon as something of a puzzle by his friends. And latterly his sister Mary, who loved him above all her brothers, used to feel uneasy at the thought that he was not happy.

Richard was a contrast to Hugh in almost every respect. He was tall, slender, fair-skinned, light-haired, gay, thoughtless, and talkative.

Maurice Kearney introduced his sons to Mr. Lowe—" Sir Garrett's nephew," and as Grace had told them all about that gentleman, and his intention of spending some days with them, Richard and he were on excellent terms immediately and had all the talk to themselves till they came up with the wren-hunters.

Mr. Lowe was astonished to see an excited crowd of men and boys armed with sticks, and running along on either side of a thick, briery fence, beating it closely, and occasionally aiming furious blows at he knew not what. After a while, however, he caught a glimpse of the tiny object of their pursuit, as, escaping from a shower of blows, it flitted some ten yards along the fence, and disappeared from view among the brambles. The crowd, among whom Mat the Thrasher and Wattletoes were conspicuous, rushed after ; and as they poked their sticks into the withered grass and beat the bushes, the poor little wren was seen creeping through the hedge, and the blows rained so thick and fast about it that its escape seemed miraculous. It did escape, however, and after a short flight had just found shelter in a low sloe-bush, when Mat the Thrasher leaped forward, and with a blow that crashed through the bush as if a forest-tree had fallen upon it, seemed beyond all doubt to have annihilated his kingship. Grace, who could only see the ludicrous side of the scene, laughed till she had to catch at Mary's cloak for support, while Mary turned away with an exclamation of pain. But though she kept her head turned away to avoid seeing the little mutilated representation of the protomartyr, even she was forced to laugh when the huge Thrasher shouted—

" I struck her ! I struck her ! and knocked my hat full of feathers out of her ! "

After a minute of complete silence, during which all eyes,

except Mary's, were fixed upon the sloe-bush, a scream of delight from Grace surprised her into looking round. When, lo ! there was the wren, safe and sound, high up in the air ! Instead of taking refuge in the briery fence it changed its tactics altogether, and flew right across the field into a quarry overgrown with brambles, followed by all its pursuers except Mat the Thrasher, whose look of amazement, as he stared with open mouth after the wren, elicited another peal of laughter from Grace, in which Mary and the young men could not help joining. Mat, however, looked at them as if to his mind it was no laughing matter, and requested some person or persons unknown to " let him alone after that." Then, after pondering deeply for a moment, with his eyes fixed on the ground, he walked slowly away ; as if, in spite of Jim Dunn's assertion to the contrary, he had met something to " bate him " at last.

" It is very ridiculous," said Mr. Lowe, " to see grown men in pursuit of a little wren, and as much carried away by the excitement of the chase as if it were—— "

" A big hare," said Mary, with an arch look that surprised Grace, and even her brother—for archness, particularly in the presence of a stranger, was not in Mary's way.

" Well," said Mr. Lowe, who was a little posed by the remark, " I believe hunting the wren is not the only kind of hunting that could easily be made to appear ridiculous."

A couple of pointers that had kept close to Hugh's heels since he left the house suggested the subject of shooting ; and Mary was relieved from the task of talking—for it often was a task to her—during their walk back to the cottage.

CHAPTER IV.

THE TRACKS IN THE SNOW.

THE window of Mary's room faced the west, and she was fond of sitting there in the evening. It was a curious little bower, up in the pointed roof of the oldest part of the cottage—which had been added to at different periods, and

presented the appearance of a promiscuous collection of odds
and ends of houses, not one of which bore the slightest
resemblance to any of the rest. The window was the only
one in the ivy-covered gable, and looked into a little enclosure,
half garden and half shrubbery. Mary sat near the window,
looking at the fast-sinking sun, while Grace stood opposite
the looking-glass arranging her hair.

"Ah, Mary," she said, with a sigh, "that's the elegant
young man."

"Who ? "

"Mr. Lowe."

"Is he, indeed ? Then I suppose Richard is to be dis-
carded ? "

"Oh, Richard is quite an Adonis. But, then, Mr. Lowe
has such an air—he is so aristocratic. He seems to admire
you," she continued. "But that's of course. They all
admire a b-e-a-u-t-y." Miss Grace dwelt upon the word,
with a curl of the lip, as if she had the most sovereign contempt for beauty. At the same time she stood upon her
toes and surveyed herself in the glass from every possible
point of view.

"Do you think yourself handsome, Grace ? "

"Well, between you and me, Mary, I do. Though not in
the usual way, perhaps."

"You mean ' handsome is that handsome does ? ' "

"Not at all ! I was not thinking of that stupid old proverb.
But there is Adonis in the garden, and—what shall we call
the other ?—Apollo."

Mary looked round and saw her brothers and Mr. Lowe
in the garden.

"And what will you call Hugh ? " she asked.

"Oh, Nabuchodonosor, if you like—or, Finn Macool,"
replied Grace, laughing. "I really don't know what to
make of him He seems to be always trying to calculate
how many thorns in an acre of furze."

Richard here called to his sister, saying :

"Can you tell us anything about these tracks in the snow ?
We are puzzled by them ? "

"No," Mary replied, opening the window, and looking
down with surprise.

"The puzzle is," said Richard, "that there are no tracks

coming towards the house The person must have jumped from your window."

" Do you think anything has been stolen ? " she asked.

" The tracks," he replied, " are those of slight high-heeled boots, such as gentlemen wear."

" I don't know on earth how to account for it," said Mary.

" And he must have been well acquainted with the place," Richard continued ; " for he faced straight to the stile behind the laurels ; and no stranger would have done that."

Mary's face flushed crimson ; but to her great relief her brothers and Mr. Lowe were looking towards the laurels and did not observe her. They followed the footprints out on the road near " The Bush "—where the lads and lasses of Knocknagow were wont to assemble—and here all trace of them was lost in the trampled snow.

The three young men returned to the house through the farmyard, Mr. Lowe having expressed a wish to see the horse of which his host had spoken in the morning.

" Really, Mary," said Grace, " it is like that one of the Melodies—

> ' Weep for the hour
> When to Eveleen's bower
> The lord of the valley with false vows came.'

Is there a lord of the valley in the case ? "

" I don't know what to make of you," said Mary, looking at her as if she thought it just possible that Miss Grace Kiely might be the queen of the fairies. " But as you really must be a witch of some kind—— "

" Not one of those ladies, I hope," Grace interrupted, " who nightly travel upon broomsticks."

" Well," Mary resumed, laughing, " anything you like. But, perhaps, you could make out the mystery ? "

" Well, let me see."

She knelt down, and resting her elbows on the low window frame, put her hands under her chin, and with knitted brow contemplated the footprints in the snow.

" The solution of the mystery is this," she gravely began. " There is nothing very extraordinary in a man's footprint

in snow. The footprint is an ordinary affair enough ; but
the wonder is, as Sydney Smith said of the fly in the amber,
' how the devil it got there.' Have you read any of Sydney
Smith's writings ? "

"No."

" Never read Peter Plymley's Letters ? "

" Never," Mary replied.

Grace shook her head, and was about proceeding with
what she called the solution of the mystery, when she again
broke off with—

" By-the-by, there was a discussion at our last literary
dinner party, as I call them when we have the poets and
editors—about Longfellow's

> ' Footprints on the sands of time.'

'Tis to be hoped when I speak of Longfellow you do not
suppose I mean your graceful brother ? "

" No," replied Mary, laughing, " I am not quite so illiterate
as you suppose. Though I dare say your poets and editors
would be apt to set me down for a fool."

" A fool ! " Grace exclaimed. " Bless your innocence, they
adore fools. No girl but a fool has the ghost of a chance of
making any impression upon them. The ' Brehon,' to be
sure, seems to appreciate your humble servant slightly, and
has perpetrated an acrostic which I will repeat for you some
time. But unfortunately the ' Brehon ' is the rummest of
the whole lot."

" The what ? "

" Oh, such ignorance ! The rummest. But ' Shamrock,'
who writes divinely, and who is really a nice fellow—I
confess to a weakness for nice fellows—is quite gone about
my foolish sister.

> ' Now, if I am, indeed, a bard,
> Immortal song, uncrowned, unstarred—
> Though gold, and friends, and rivals guard—
>   Shall win thee, spite of Fate, Jessie.'

She substitutes ' Eva ' for ' Jessie ,' and takes it all to herself.
I fear the poor child's head is a little turned," sighed Miss
Grace, with a very wise shake of her own.

Mary laughed, for the poor child was five years her senior.

But Grace, without condescending to notice the interruption, went on :

" To return, however, to the

' Footprints on the sands of time.'

It was objected that the returning tide would wash away a footprint from the sand, and therefore the idea was a bad one. But papa very properly observed that time, when compared with eternity, was nothing more than the strand between the ebbing and flowing of the tide. But to come to our footprints in the snow. We need not trouble ourselves with the notion that his Sable Majesty has had anything to do with them. Of course you read ' Robinson Crusoe ? ' "

" Yes," replied Mary, wondering what Robinson Crusoe could have to do with it.

" Very good. Well, the solution of the mystery is this : our man Friday—in a stylish pair of Wellington boots—was standing there when the snow commenced to fall ; and, like a patient savage as he was, there he remained till the snow left off—and then walked away. *Quod erat demonstrandum.* Excuse my weakness for Latin."

" I declare," said Mary, with a look of wonder, " that must be it."

" Oh," exclaimed Grace, resuming her bright look, " there are a pair of feet ' making tracks,' as our Yankee friends would say, which might well frighten John the Baptist himself if he met them in the wilderness."

And she pointed to Barney Brodherick, who was making for the stile behind the laurels, in his not-to-be-described mode of locomotion.

Mary called to him, and Barney swung round and looked up at them.

" Barney," said she, " did you meet anyone on your way from town last night ? "

" Begob, I did, Miss," replied Barney, with a start. " An' God forgive me," he continued, pulling off his hat and taking a letter from the lining, " I forgot to give you this bit uv a note."

He came under the window and threw the letter up to Grace, who caught it and handed it to Mary.

" What o'clock might it be, Miss Grace ? " Barney asked,

with the coaxing grin he always wore when speaking to
her.

"It is past four, Barney."

"Thanum-on-dioul, can it be late so early ?" he exclaimed.
"Tare-an-'ouns, I'll be kilt." And Barney "make tracks"
for the stile behind the laurels.

Grace laughed, and turned round to repeat his words ; but
checked herself on seeing Mary with the open letter in her
hand, gazing towards the distant mountains.

"And now," she said abstractedly, "he is gone."

CHAPTER V.

THE DOCTOR MAKES HIMSELF COMFORTABLE.

"I FEAR, Mr. Lowe," said Mary, "you will be put to some
inconvenience to-morrow, as we are to have the Station."

"What is that ?" he inquired.

"Oh, don't you know ? Well, Catholics go to Confession
and Communion at Christmas and Easter. And, in country
districts, instead of requiring the people to go to the chapel,
the priests come to certain houses in each locality to hear
confessions and say Mass. So that our house is to be
public property for some hours to-morrow, and I fear you
will find it unpleasant. But you can remain in your room ;
and I suppose you will have no objection to breakfast with
the priests ?"

"By no means," he replied, "it will be a pleasure.
Shall we have the gentleman who preached that remarkable
sermon ?"

"Oh, of course. He is our parish priest, Father M'Mahon.
He is a most charitable man, and almost adored by the
people. It is commonly said that when Father M'Mahon
dies he will not have as much money as will bury him. I
must warn you, however, that you will find him reserved.
and you may be tempted to think him haughty. But it is
only his manner."

"He looks awfully proud, at all events," said Grace.

"He astonished us all a few weeks ago," Mary continued, "by making this peculiarity the subject of his discourse from the altar."

"He began in such an extraordinary way," said Grace. "I was very near being obliged to laugh."

"Very near?" said Mary. "Why, you did laugh; and it was really too bad for a sensible young lady like you."

"I could not help it. Only think, Mr. Lowe, the first word he said was—'Ye say I have a proud walk.' And then he went on to explain to them in the most earnest manner, that when they thought he was walking proudly, he was, perhaps, not thinking of himself at all. 'Indeed,' he said, 'I never knew until lately that I had a proud walk. And I fear it is too late to try to correct it now. 'Tis hard to break an old dog of his trot.' Sure everybody laughed then."

"It was a most instructive discourse," said Mary.

"Oh, of course," replied Grace. "And it must have been very consoling to people who give themselves airs, as we are not by any means to infer from the said airs that they are not all humility in their hearts. But I hope it is Father Hannigan Mr. Lowe will have an opportunity of hearing to-morrow."

"Yes, I think it is not unlikely, as Father M'Mahon has not been strong for some time back, and one of the curates usually says Mass now at the Stations. You can have no idea, Mr. Lowe, what an amount of labour an Irish priest has to go through."

"I can imagine it must be very considerable from what you tell me," Mr. Lowe observed.

"Come, Grace," said Mary, "the Rosary."

Hugh stood up, and went with them to the kitchen, as he always, when at home, "headed" the Rosary.

Instead of summoning the servants to prayers in the parlour it is the general custom, among Irish Catholics of the middle class, for the master and mistress of the house with their children and guests—unless the latter should happen not to be Catholics—to "say the Rosary" in the kitchen.

In Hugh's absence the duty of beginning and ending the Rosary—the same person always "heads" and "finishes"

—fell to Mrs. Kearney or Mary ; which was looked upon as a grievance by Barney and some of the other servants.

" I'd always like to have Mr. Hugh to head the Rosary," Barney used to say. " He never puts trimmin's to id like Miss Mary and the mistress."

During the Rosary Richard and the stranger lighted their cigars in Hugh's room, and had a pleasant talk—the doctor as usual having the lion's share. His volubility was considerable ; but though people generally found it pleasant enough to listen to him—young ladies particularly—it was not easy to tell what it was all about after.

Hugh came in with a large book under his arm, and seemed unprepared for the honour that had been done him.

Mr. Lowe was standing by the fire, with his elbow on the chimney-piece. The doctor had his two heels on it, and reclined in a curious old arm-chair at the other side of the fire.

" We're just talking," said the latter, " of what we are to do with ourselves to-morrow. Mr. Lowe votes for the snipe."

" Very well," Hugh replied, " I'll have everything ready ; but you must be satisfied with a single-barrel."

" Oh, 'tis all the same, except that I can't make so much noise. Curious," continued the doctor, contemplatively, " that there are some things that some people can't do. Though I blaze away, the birds don't fall. I generally forget that there is anything required but to pull the trigger.   Or when it does occur to me that I must take aim, somehow I first think of my feet—a graceful attitude you know. And before I am all right the bird is a mile away. And then I fire."

" You can ride better than you can shoot," said Mr. Lowe.

" Pretty well at the riding ; but I never could do that either, like Hugh. The cursed attitudinizing ruins me there, too. Do you remember Kathleen Hanly ? " he asked, turning to his brother.

" Yes, I remember," Hugh replied, laughing.

" Oh, 'tis misery to think of it," the doctor continued, taking his feet from the chimney-piece, and thrusting his hands in the pockets of his shooting jacket.

" What was it ? " Mr. Lowe asked.

"The prettiest girl in the country," replied the doctor, "I'll show you where she lives to-morrow."

"Well?" said Mr. Lowe.

"Oh, you want to know all about it. Well, Hugh and I were out schooling one day, and I caught a glimpse of Kathleen walking up and down by a hedge not far from where we were. There was a wall about three feet high near where she was walking; and I thought I might as well ride down by the ditch and take a jump over the wall. I waited till she had turned at the end of her walk, and came on at the wall in a canter. I was thinking of a picture in one of Lever's novels, and my only regret was that the wall was not five instead of three feet high. Just as I was coming to the jump, it occurred to me that my left elbow was not at the proper angle. So I glanced at it and turned it more in—forgetting the necessity of keeping my seat and everything else but the elbow and Kathleen."

The doctor paused and looked at the lighted end of his cigar, as if it were the miniature of a departed friend.

"Well, what happened?" said Mr. Lowe.

"Well, I was spun," replied the doctor, with a sigh, "out between his two ears. I resolved to get out of a window in the middle of the night, and run away and enlist in a regiment under orders for India. But I changed my mind."

The doctor looked again at the ashes of his cigar, and shook his head.

"Kathleen said afterwards," he resumed, "that she always thought of me with my heels in the air. Back view, you know. And my legs are rather long."

The doctor took a last look at the ashes of his cigar, and flung the butt into the fire. He then stood up, and taking a cigar-case from the chimney-piece, carefully selected the best one in it for himself.

"Have a cigar?" said he, presenting one to Mr. Lowe; which was very civil, seeing that the case and its contents belonged to Mr. Lowe himself.

"Do you know," said the doctor, turning to his brother, after resuming his place in the arm-chair, "we may as well make ourselves comfortable."

"By all means," replied Hugh, tearing the corner off a newspaper, and offering it to him to light his cigar.

"Hold on, old boy," said the doctor.

He left the room and returned in a few minutes, with
a decanter in one hand and a sugar-bowl in the other.
Placing them on the table, he rather surprised Mr. Lowe by
producing three tumblers and a wine-glass from the pockets
of his shooting-coat. He then sat down, with his feet on the
fender, and poked the fire. While thus employed, a servant
came in with a kettle, which the doctor took with his disengaged hand, and spilled a little of the water under the
grate to see that it was boiling.

"All right, Judy," said he. "Mum's the word."

"Yes, sir," the girl replied, and left the room.

The doctor then mixed a stiff tumbler for himself, and
motioned to Hugh and Mr. Lowe to follow his example ;
which they did.

Having lighted his cigar, he turned sideways in his chair,
throwing one of his long legs over the other, and said :

"Now Hugh, your opinion is worth having on most
subjects. But I want your opinion now on a subject, of
which so far as ever I could see, you have had no personal
experience."

"What is it ? " Hugh asked.

"Love," replied the doctor, commencing to puff so vigorously that he was soon enveloped in a cloud.

"Well, what about it ? "

"Do you believe in first love and love at first sight and
all that sort of thing ? "

"Of course, if there's love at all, there must be first love
to begin with. And," he added, after a pause, "I rather
think love at first sight is not an impossibility."

"But is the first love the true love ? The 'never forget,
you know, and so forth ? ' "

"I don't think so. It may or may not."

"The fact is, you think there is no limit to the number of
times a man may be really in love ? "

"Well, I do believe a man may be really in love more
than once in his life. But I'll tell you what I believe," he
continued, after a pause. "I believe it is the destiny of
many to love once, or meet somebody whom they feel they
could have loved as they never loved before and never can
love again."

" But they *can* love again ! " said Mr. Lowe, who began to feel interested in the conversation.

" Yes, certainly," replied Hugh. " A man can love again, and be happy in the love of another. But it will not be the same kind of happiness as might have been his."

" Do you think this higher sort of happiness is the lot of many ? I fancy, in the majority of cases, people must be satisfied with the secondary kind of happiness you allude to."

" Yes, I think so, too," replied Hugh.

" And why so ? " Richard asked, as he took the kettle from the fire, and poured the boiling water carefully on the lumps of sugar in his tumbler. " Why should they not be supremely blessed ? "

And while pouring in the whiskey after the water, the doctor sang in a pleasing voice :

" Our life should resemble one long day of light,
And our death come on holy and calm as the night."

" 'Tis easily accounted for," replied Hugh. " The feeling may not be mutual ; and even when it is, how many insurmountable obstacles may be in the way ? But if it ever does happen, that a man or a woman can love only once, it is when two spirits rush together in this way, and are then parted by death, or some other cause that does not involve weakness of any kind on the part of either."

" Now, did a case of this kind ever come within your knowledge ? "

" Yes," Hugh replied. " I know of one such case. And it is what I have observed in this instance that has made me think about the matter at all."

" You seem to think," said Mr. Lowe, " that reciprocity is necessary to give immortality to the sentiment, if I may so express what I mean to convey."

" I am inclined to think," Hugh replied, " that without that it will die a natural death."

" Have you been taking large doses of poetry of late ? " said Richard. " It would scarcely surprise me to find some tender stanzas in this." And he opened the ledger which Hugh had laid on the table.

" And that would be getting blood from a turnip," said the doctor, as he turned over the leaves. " But do you really keep your accounts in this way? I thought it was only merchants did that."

" And why should not manufacturers ? "

" Manufacturers ? Do you mean that you are a butter maker ? "

" And a manufacturer of arable land," said Hugh.

" That's nonsense," said the doctor, who had a dim recollection of a lecture on political economy which he had heard some time before. " Land cannot be manufactured."

" Well if I were writing a treatise on the subject I might hesitate to use the expression ; and yet it could, I think, be defended."

" You mean a producer," said Richard, pedantically.

" No, that would not express my meaning. I'll show you an example of it to-morrow."

Richard commenced rubbing his chin with a rather serious expression of face, as he ran his eye down a column of figures. He opened his eyes and his mouth on coming to the " carried forward," and was about finding the page when Hugh glanced over his shoulder, and said :

" Come, shut it up. You will look in vain for a stanza of any sort." Saying this, Hugh shut the book and pushed it away.

The fact was the doctor had lighted upon a page where sundry sums were entered, which he himself had received in the shape of half notes and post-office orders ; and his brother good-naturedly wished to prevent him from seeing what would be a very forcible illustration of the proverb that " many a little makes a muckle."

The doctor took up a note which slipped from between the leaves of the account-book and read it. It ran thus :

" DEAR HUGH—Send me five pounds by return like ' the quintessence concentrated of a sublimated brick,' as you are. I was obliged to pop my watch last night. Particulars in my next.—Yours.   " DICK."

The author of this pithy production shook his head gravely, and, folding the paper, was about lighting another cigar with it, but changing his mind, he took a short pipe from his pocket and lighted that instead.

" I believe," said he, " I have been a little improvident in my time. But you have no idea how economical I have become. I got eleven bob from a Jew for two pair of trousers and an old coat." Here he pulled vigorously at his pipe till it was well kindled, and threw what remained unburned of the note into the fire. " And bought a second-hand clarionet at the back of the Bank," he added. " I'll give you a tune as soon as I get a new reed. Keating has given me some lessons."

He smoked on with a placid look evidently deriving, exquisite pleasure from the contemplation of his economy, as well as from the weed, which he seemed to economise, too, so tiny were the wreaths that glided from between his lips.

Hugh thought it well to take advantage of this virtuous mood, and suggested the advisability of retiring to rest. The doctor took Mr. Lowe's arm and conducted him to his room. And, after embracing that gentleman affectionately six times, he retired to his own apartment.

Hugh made an entry or two in his account book ; and after totting up a column of figures at one side, and comparing the amount with the sum total of a shorter account at the opposite side, he shook his head doubtfully, and closed the book. Opening his desk, he took out a letter and read it over. It was from Sir Garrett Butler to his father, referring him to his agent, Mr. Isaac Pender, on the subject of renewing the lease.

" I fear," he thought, as he put the letter back into the desk—" I fear that there is foul play somewhere. And yet this old man is said to be so simple and kind-hearted it is hard to suspect him. But Pender and his hopeful son are a bad pair. Well, there's nothing to be gained by brooding over it. Let me think of something else."

He was startled out of what was evidently a pleasant reverie, by a noise, which, after a moment's thought, he concluded was the death-shriek of an unlucky goose. Reynard was unusually active at that season, and he resolved upon going out and setting the dogs upon his track. But the sound being repeated in a somewhat less excruciating key, he smiled and proceeded to his brother's room.

The doctor, with his coat and one boot off, was in the act of unscrewing the mouth-piece from the second-hand clarionet.

" D—n it ! " he exclaimed, examining it with a solemn
look, " I can get no good of it."

Then putting the instrument, without the mouth-piece, to
his lips, he hummed, " Believe me if all those endearing
young charms," through it, with great feeling.

" Dick," said his brother, " have you a mind to disturb
the whole house ? Do you know 'tis past twelve o'clock ? "

" All right," said the doctor, with a jerk of his head sideways. And he dropped softly into " Nora Creena."

" Come, go to bed, and don't make a fool of yourself."

" Hugh, isn't Kathleen Hanly a devilish pretty girl ? "

Decidedly. But what's the use of freezing for her ? Go
to bed and dream about her."

The doctor was so struck with the wisdom of this suggestion that he pulled off the other boot with extraordinary
quickness and energy ; evidently bent upon following his
brother's advice without the loss of a moment.

Mr. Henry Lowe had his reveries, too.

" No, no," he thought, " it cannot be anything of that
sort."

He was thinking of the tracks in the snow, which Grace
accounted for so logically.

But even Grace's " solution of the mystery " was not
altogether satisfactory to Mr. Henry Lowe.

CHAPTER VI.

THE   STATION—BARNEY   BRODHERICK'S   PENANCE—MRS. SLATTERY CREATES A SENSATION.

EVERYTHING was so quiet about the house next morning that
Mr. Lowe quite forgot the station. But on reaching the hall
he was taken by surprise to find it filled by a crowd of people ;
and, instead of pushing his way to the parlour, he beat a hasty
retreat back to his bedroom. His attention was arrested by
Barney Brodherick, who, holding a beads between his fingers,

was kneeling in the lobby, praying with great energy and volubility. Barney sat back upon his heels and muttered his prayers in a breathless sort of way, evidently afraid of losing the clue before he had got all around the beads. When he did come to the end, it was with a rush ; and throwing himself forward, with his elbows on the floor, he performed some ceremony which Mr. Lowe was quite unable to comprehend.

After this, Barney fell back upon his heels and commenced " the round of his beads " again. Altogether, he had the look of a man walking over a river or ravine on a narrow plank, and feeling that to pause for an instant, or to swerve to the right or left, was as much as his life was worth. The manner in which he hurried on at the end and flung himself forward, completed the parallel.

" In the name o' the Lord, Barney," exclaimed the housekeeper, " what are you doing there ? "

She stood near Barney, with a silver coffee-pot in her hand, and her look of astonishment satisfied Mr. Lowe that Barney's proceedings were something out of the common.

" Salvation saze your sowl—God forgive me for cursin'—be off out uv that, and don't set me astray."

" A nice lad you are," muttered the hosekeeper, as she walked away,, " to be goin' to your duty."

Richard here made his appearance, looking as if he had not slept enough, and Mr. Lowe called his attention to the figure near the window. He, however, appeared quite as much puzzled as the housekeeper.

Barney, at this moment, was leaning forward on his left hand, and seemed to be counting something on the floor with his right. The effort was evidently too much for him, for, scratching his poll, he looked about him in a bewildered way.

" Mr. Dick," said he, on seeing the doctor, " come here and count 'em for me."

On coming near enough, the doctor and Mr. Lowe saw a pretty long score chalked upon the boards.

" How many times, Mr. Dick ? " Barney asked anxiously.

Richard stooped down and counted the marks ; and when Barney was informed of the number, he drew a long breath of relief, and got up from his knees, the effort appearing to cost him some pain.

" Glory be to God ! " he exclaimed, pressing the knuckles of his left hand against his back, as if trying to straighten it, " I have id over me."

" What is it you have over you ? " Richard asked, who had only seen the last act of the drama.

" The pinance, sir," replied Barney. " The pinance he put an me the last time ; an' I'd have no business nixt or near him if I wasn't after doin' id."

And Barney moved away as if a great load had been taken off his mind.

The two young men stood at the window and amused themselves by observing the people who loitered about the house. Mat the Thrasher stood leaning against a cart, surrounded by a group of admirers, among whom were Jim Dunn and Tom Maher. But even their admiration evidently fell short of that of Billy Heffernan, the musical genius of Knocknagow—who dreamt a piece of music entitled " Heffernan's Frolic," and played it next morning to the wonder and delight of the whole hamlet. For Billy's mother ran out to proclaim the joyful news among her neighbours ; and men, women, and children, came crowding around the inspired musician, and requesting him over and over again to play his new composition ; till Billy, fairly out of breath, put his fife in his pocket and asked them all, with an injured look, " did they think he had Jack Delany's bellows in his stumack ? "—Jack Delany being the village blacksmith. From which query it may be inferred that Billy Heffernan was under the impression that his stomach played an impor‧ tant part in the production of sweet sounds.

Billy Heffernan now took his fife from his pocket, and after examining it minutely, handed it to Mat the Thrasher.

Richard let down the window softly, to try and catch their conversation.

After looking at the instrument, Mat said :

" I'll reg'late that. I'll put a new ferl on id."

He handed back the fife to the owner, who put it to his lips and seemed to execute a pantomimic tune—for though his " flying fingers " played nimbly over the stops, no sound was audible. By degrees he breathed more and more strongly into the orifice till a lively air began to be fitfully distinguishable even to the two young men in the window. Mat the Thrasher commenced to " humour " the tune with his head ; and after a while, resting his hands on the tail-board of the cart, he performed a few steps of a complicated character. Billy Heffernan moved a pace or two backwards, keeping his eyes fixed on the dancer's feet, evidently determined not to lose a single " shuffle." Indeed, the eyes of the whole group— who had also moved back and formed a ring—were riveted on the dancer's brilliantly polished shoes. Mat's shoes presented a contrast to those of his companions in this respect ; for while his shone resplendent, theirs were only greased.

As Billy Heffernan " loud and louder blew," Mat the Thrasher's feet " fast and faster flew ! " and letting go his hold on the cart, he gave himself " ample room and verge enough," till even Mr. Lowe caught some of the enthusiasm his performance excited.

" He's a splendid fellow," he exclaimed, as Mat finished with a bound in the air, followed by a low " bow to the music."

" Take notice of him," said Richard, pointing to a man who came from the kitchen door towards the group collected round Mat and his musical admirer, picking his steps carefully, and taking long strides, as if he were walking upon ice that he feared might break under him. He was dressed in a black frock coat and dark trousers, very much the worse for the wear. His well-bleached shirt (save that the " blue-rag " had been too liberally drawn upon in its " making-up"), of which there was an unusually extensive display of front and collar, presented a striking contrast to the dinginess of the rest of his habiliments. He had come from the house without his hat, notwithstanding the coldness of the morning ; and carried a prayer-book, with his finger between the leaves, in his left hand.

" I suppose he is the clerk ? " said Mr. Lowe.

" No ; that is Phil Lahy, our tailor."

" Why, he is quite an important-looking personage. Yes," he continued, turning his head to listen, " he is remonstrating with them for their levity."

" What's the harm in a bit uv divarsion ? " said Billy Heffernan, drawing the tip of his nose, which was very blue, across the sleeve of his coat.

" That's thrue, Billy," Phil observed, gravely, " but there's a time for everything. And when a man is goin' to his duty," he added, still more impressively, " he ought to turn his mind to id."

" He's right," said Mat the Thrasher, as he sat down on one of the shafts of the cart, resting his chin on his hands, and his elbows on his knees, with a penitent look.

" Mat," said Phil, evidently satisfied with the impression he had made, " I'm not neglectin' you. I won't disappoint you. I'll do that job before Sunday."

" Faith, 'twould be time for you."

" But consider, I had two full shoots to make for Ned Brophy and Tom Brien. Ned is to be married as soon as everything is settled, an' Tom is goin' to match-make down to the county Limerick."

" An' didn't I tell you I was to be Ned's sidesman ? "

" I won't disappoint you."

And Phil, taking his pipe from his waistcoat-pocket, was in the act of catching the wooden stem between his teeth, when his hand was caught by Billy Heffernan :

" Aren't you goin' to resave ? " Billy asked with a half alarmed, half reproachful look.

" Yes, Billy ; but I have liberty to take a blast on account of my constitution."

And there was something quite pathetic in Phil's look as he pressed the spring of a small iron tobacco-box, in which an ounce of " Lomasny's " was tightly rolled up.

" Give me a light, Mat," said he, after filling his pipe, with the air of a man about performing a solemn act of duty.

Mat produced his flint and steel, and, lighting a bit of touch-paper, laid it with his own hand on Phil Lahy's pipe, while Phil commenced to " draw " with such vigour that his first " shough " frightened the sparrows from the fresh straw spread over the yard, as if a shot had been fired at them, and the sight and the fragrance of the blue tobacco smoke, as it curled in the frosty morning air, made more than one mouth water in the crowd that loitered about the yard awaiting the arrival of the priests. It may be necessary to inform some readers that a " shough o' the p'pe," without special leave from the priest, is considered a violation of the rule " to be fasting from midnight " before Communion.

When the two curates rode into the yard by the back entrance, Phil Lahy, evidently vain of his privilege, puffed away ostentatiously—which impressed upon the beholders an idea of Phil's importance, that all but placed him on a level with the priests themselves.

Father Hannigan was the first to dismount. He was a tall man, in the prime of life, and the frieze riding-coat, flung loosely over his broad shoulders, set off his manly figure to the best advantage, and gave him a homely, warm, Irish look altogether. The other curate, Father O'Neill was a very young man, with an air of refinement suggestive of drawing-rooms rather than of Irish cabins and farm-houses. They were met by the "man of the house" before they reached the kitchen door, and as he gave a hand to each, Father Hannigan's hearty "Good-morrow, Maurice," struck Mr. Lowe as being admirably in keeping with his appearance. And the words—"The top of the morning to you, Miss Grace," suggested the idea that Father Hannigan affected the phraseology of the peasantry.

"There is Father M'Mahon," said Richard, as a car passed the gate.

"Is he not to be here?"

"Yes; but he is going round to the front gate. Come into the room, and you will see him arrive."

The first thing that struck Mr. Lowe was that Father M'Mahon's servant was in livery, and that his horse and car were a decidedly handsome turn-out. When he leaped lightly from the car and walked towards the hall-door, with his shoulders thrown back, and his head raised and slightly leaning to one side, Mr. Lowe was not surprised that people said Father M'Mahon had a "proud walk."

Barney Brodherick hurried to the car, and was taking the priest's cloak, which he had let drop from his shoulders upon alighting, to hang it up in the hall; but the servant snatched it from him. He was rushing headlong to resent the affront, when the return of the priest, who had left his breviary on the seat of the car, prevented hostilities. Barney shook his fist at the man in livery, from behind his master's back; but without deigning to notice the challenge, that important functionary led the horse to the car-house and commenced unharnessing him.

The priest, without exchanging a word with any one,
walked into the drawing-room. After saying a short prayer,
he put on his stole and sat down in the arm-chair which was
placed near the fire.

The " man of the house " was already on his knees beside
the chair, and at once commenced his confession.

The door was now surrounded by a closely-packed crowd,
who went in one by one, in their turn, to be " heard "—
finding it no easy matter to push their way out again.

An almost equally large and quite as eager a throng stood
round the parlour door at the opposite side of the hall where
Father O'Neill sat.

Father Hannigan, by his own choice, remained in the
kitchen, which was filled by his penitents—principally
women—who, in spite of his loud remonstrances, would
crush and tumble almost up against his knees. He had
repeatedly to stand up and push them off by main force ;
and was at last obliged to fence himself in with two chairs
and a form.

" If ye come apast that," said he, excitedly, " except in
your turn, 'twill be worse for ye."

Things got on pretty smoothly after this, save for a suppressed scuffle now and again when two equally resolute
dames happened to meet in the front rank, and disputed the
question of precedence with an energy only second to that
which they threw into the " Hail Mary " 'or " Holy Mary "
that accompanied every shove and jostle. One of those
who had been several times pushed back at the very moment
when victory seemed certain, lost all patience, and resolved
to gain her point by stratagem. She walked along a form
and stepped from one to another of two or three chairs
ranged along the wall, with a dogged sort of determination
to conquer or die. She was in the act of climbing over
a high-backed settle behind the priest, when she missed
her footing and fell backwards, bringing down with her a
dish-cover and several other utensils with a tremendous
crash and clatter. So great was the noise that Richard and
Mr. Lowe hastened to the scene to see what could have
happened.

Father Hannigan jumped to his feet as if he thought the
house was falling about his ears, and looked all around him

but could see nothing to account for the clatter. At last he looked behind the settle, which was a few feet out from the wall, and there beheld the too eager devotee on her back, with one foot caught in something that held it high in the air. Father Hannigan released the foot, and, as he did so, shaking his head and compressing his lips, muttered a proverb in the Irish language, the best translation of which we are able to give being—" A woman would beat a pig, and a pig would beat a fair."

" Get up now," he continued, seeing her show no symptom of changing her position. " Sure you're not hurt ? " he asked, reaching her his hand.

The poor woman suffered herself to be raised up.

" Are you hurt ? " he repeated.

She seemed to think it necessary to weigh the question well before replying to it. So long did she continue to ponder over it that Father Hannigan asked again, with some concern :

" In the name of God, Mrs. Slattery, is there anything the matter with you ? "

Mrs. Slattery looked all around her, as if expecting that some one would come forward to set her mind at rest.

" What in the world ails the woman ? " exclaimed the priest.

Mrs. Slattery looked into his face anxiously, and after another long pause, spoke :

" I wonder am I killed ? " said Mrs. Slattery.

" Wisha, there's great fear of you," replied Father Hannigan. " And now go and say your prayers and take the world aisy like a Christian. Sure I'll be able to hear ye all before I go, and what more do ye want ? There's a strange gentleman from England looking at ye ; and what will he say of the Island of Saints when he goes back, if this is the way ye behave yourselves. Look at the men, how quiet and dacent they are. Can't you take pattern by the men ? But 'tis always the way with the women," exclaimed Father Hannigan, with a gesture of both hands, " to run headlong, and never look before 'em."

After this there was comparative order among Father Hannigan's penitents. But poor Mrs. Slattery made her way slowly to the hall, looking as if she were still quite

unable to settle the question whether she was " killed " or
not.

CHAPTER VII.

NORAH LAHY.—THE OLD LINNET'S SONG.

RICHARD'S proposal to take a stroll to an old castle within
about a mile of the house was readily agreed to by Mr. Lowe ;
and, as they passed through Knocknagow, the latter had
a good opportunity of seeing for himself what an Irish hamlet
looked like. Though most of the houses looked comfortless
enough, and the place as a whole had the straggling appearance
which he was accustomed to associate with an Irish village,
there was none of that unredeemed squalor and wretchedness
which certain writers had led him to expect. With one
or two exceptions every house had at least two windows.
Several had each a small out-house, and the little cart or
" car," with a high creel in it, indicated that the owner was
the proprietor of a donkey.

Mat the Thrasher's habitation, with its whitewashed walls
and elegantly thatched roof, was particularly noticeable.
Mr. Lowe remarked also the little ornamental wooden gate,
the work of Mat's own hands, that led to the kitchen-garden—
invariably called the " haggart " in this part of the world—
which was fenced all round by a thick thorn hedge, with a
little privet and holly intermixed here and there. There were
two or three small farm-houses, the owners of which held
from ten to twenty acres each. Two pipes " across " a pound
of soap, with a button of blue stuck to it, and a very yellow
halfpenny candle in the windows—if we may dignify them
with the name—of four or five poor cabins, showed that
there was brisk competition in the shop-keeping line in
Knocknagow.

The title of " shop," however, was exclusively given to
the establishment of Phil Lahy—or rather of Honor his
wife—who occupied an old slated house with pointed gables

and very thick chimneys, which had seen better days, and which tradition said had been an inn in the reign of Queen Anne. But a later tradition had fixed the name of " the barrack " on Phil Lahy's house, greatly to his annoyance. In spite of all he could say or do, however, his neighbours persisted in calling his house " the barrack."

The absence of the human face divine was easily accounted for, so far as the adults were concerned, seeing that they were all at the Station. But the fact that there was not one of the rising generation visible began to excite the surprise of the two young men as they sauntered leisurely through what seemed literally a deserted village, till a loud shout called their attention to a pretty considerable crowd in a deep quarry, near a limekiln, by the roadside—the attraction which the quarry possessed for the urchins on this occasion being a frozen sheet of water.

The shout brought a curly-headed boy in corduroy jacket and trousers to Honor Lahy's shop-door. He looked wistfully towards the sliders, as if sorely tempted to join them, when a very weak but singularly sweet voice called to him from inside :

" Ah, Tommy, don't go."

" I'm not goin' to go," he replied. " I'm on'y goin' to look at my crib."

Mr. Lowe and Richard, as if moved by the same impulse, walked into the house. Sitting in a straw arm-chair, near the kitchen fire, was a young girl, whose back was towards them. Her wasted hand, which was laid on the head of a large, rough terrier that sat near her, with its head, or rather its throat resting on her knees, at once attracted Mr. Lowe's attention. She did not seem to be aware of their presence. The dog, however, watched them with no friendly eye ; but, as if spellbound by the wasted hand on his head, he remained quite motionless save that his eyes alternately glared on the intruders and looked wistfully in her face.

" Tommy," said she, " like a good boy, will you hold the prayer-book again, till I finish the Preparation for Confession ? I won't be long."

Richard placed his finger on his lips, and beckoned to the boy to do as she desired. The prayer-book was on her knees, but she had not sufficient strength to hold it up. The boy

knelt down, and held the book open before her, so that she
could read it. His fresh, round, rosy face and laughing blue
eyes contrasted strikingly with her death-like paleness, and
the deep melancholy of her eyes, which were almost black.
She raised her emaciated hand slowly and painfully, as if the
action were almost beyond her strength, and made the sign
of the Cross. Then, with her hands clasped, and resting on
her knees, she raised her eyes for a moment, as if offering up
a short mental prayer, and commenced to read from the book
which her brother held for her.

The scene was so touching that the two young men stole
softly from the house, neither of them uttering a word till
they reached the old castle.

" I suppose that poor girl cannot live long," said Mr. Lowe.
" I never saw a human face so wasted away. It will haunt
me, I fear, for some time. There is something unearthly in
her eyes—and did you remark the long eyelashes, how they
contrasted with the pale cheeks ? I suppose she is dying of
consumption ? "

" I can't quite understand her case," replied Richard, with
an air of professional importance ; " it is rather peculiar.
She has not had the use of her limbs for several years back.
I think it is the spine, though Kiely says not."

The view from the top of the old castle was very fine,
though the breeze was too keen to allow of their dwelling
for any length of time upon its beauties. Richard, however, remained so resolutely gazing in one direction, though
the wind was directly in his face, that his companion suspected there was some object of peculiar interest in that
quarter.

" That is a pretty house on the side of the hill," he
remarked.

" Yes, the white house in the trees," said Richard, turning
his eyes in quite a different direction.

" No, I mean the house on the hill near that square grove.
Who lives there ? "

" A Mr. Hanly."

" I thought so. And have we any chance of getting a
glimpse of the beauty ? "

Richard stared at him with surprise.

" You forget," said Mr. Lowe, laughing, " that you promised

last night to show me where she lived. I dare say the wall near the paling at the end of the grove is the scene of your misadventure ? "

The doctor began pulling his moustache, and put on a grave, not to say a frowning look. He was trying to recall what he had said on the subject the night before, but apparently without success.

" Yes," he replied, quite seriously, as if he considered it no subject for jest, " that is the place where the accident occurred. Miss Hanly is a highly respectable and very superior young lady. However," he added, fixing another lingering look on the house near the grove, " this would be too early an hour to call. And, besides, we must be back before breakfast." He looked at his watch, and finding there was no time to be lost, they walked briskly back towards Ballinaclash.

As they passed through the village, Tommy Lahy was in the act of climbing up a rather tall beech tree that stood in front of the old house, the lower part of its trunk protected by a piece of mason-work which looked like a foot or two of a thick round gate pier. Tommy's laughing face looked down at them over his shoulder, as he mounted higher and higher, with the ease and regularity of a swimmer. But after reaching the topmost bough, he came tumbling down with such breakneck precipitation that Mr. Lowe started, under the impression that he had missed his hold and was grasping at the branches to save himself from being dashed to pieces. This view of the case was at once proved to be erroneous, when Tommy reached the smooth part of the tree, and slid down to the low pedestal, which he touched as lightly as a bird. Without a moment's pause he ran up the hill and into Mat the Thrasher's garden, where the thick hedge concealed him from view.

" What the devil is he up to ? " said Richard.

" I can't imagine," replied Mr. Lowe, " let us hurry up and see."

On looking over the hedge they saw Tommy standing in the middle of the cabbage plot, scratching his poll with a look of vexation and disappointment. He knelt for a moment among the cabbages, and stood up with a bird in his hand which he eyed with no friendly expression.

" What is it ? " Richard asked.

Tommy looked up, surprised at finding himself observed, but immediately answered :—

" A robineen, sir." And Tommy deliberately pulled the tail out of the robin, and then let it fly away. It perched on the square chimney of Mat the Thrasher's house—looking decidedly woebegone without its tail.

" Why have you pulled out the bird's tail ? " Mr. Lowe asked.

" What made he knock my crib ? " replied Tommy. I'd have a blackbird only for him."

Richard explained to his companion that the robin was the plague of boys who had cribs set to catch birds, as he was perpetually getting himself caught, thereby making it necessary to " set " the crib again. And, as taking the life of cock-robin was a crime from which even the wickedest urchin would shrink aghast, pulling out his tail, which was looked upon as a legitimate mode of punishment, was the only revenge they could have for all the trouble and loss he put them to.

" Did you catch much to-day, Tommy ? " Richard asked.

" No, sir ; only two wran-boys an' an aeneen."

" What have you your trap baited with ? " Mr. Lowe inquired.

Tommy opened his eyes wide, evidently not understanding the question.

" He means," said Richard, " what have you under the crib to tempt the birds to go into it ? "

" A bit of a biled pueata, sir," Tommy answered readily. " an' a shillig-a-booka, and a few skhehoshies."

Richard explained that the " biled pueata " meant a boiled potato, the shillig-a-booka a snail in its shell, and the skhehoshies the scarlet hips of the wild briar. While he was speaking, a blackbird flew across the garden and into the holly at the other side ; and Tommy knelt down to put the crib in order for his capture. But as he turned away to leave the coast clear for the blackbird, his countenance fell, for on looking at his brogues, which felt even heavier than usual, he saw the red clay clinging to them. And this fatal symptom of the awful calamity of a thaw caused poor Tommy Lahy's heart to die within him.

Remembering his promise, however, that he would not

leave his sister till his mother returned from the Station, he hurried back towards home, merely stopping to climb to the top of Tom Hogan's gate, and take a look down into the quarry. The boys shouted and waved their hats at him, but Tommy felt no way shaken in his resolution not to join them till his mother came home. But the sight of Jacky Ryan gliding over the frozen pond on one leg was so frightful a temptation, that it was only by instantly shutting his eyes and flinging himself down from the gate that he was able to resist it. He rejoined his sister in high spirits. So proud was he, indeed, of the victory he had just gained, that even the apprehended misery of finding the frost all gone next morning was forgotten.

" Mind," said he to his sister, " 'twas settin' my crib I was."

She smiled, and turned her large, sorrowful eyes towards him, but without turning her head, which rested against the back of her straw chair.

" What did you ketch, Tommy ? " she asked in her sweet, low voice.

" A robineen," he replied, " bad ——." He was going to say, " bad luck to him," but checked himself.

" Did you pull the tail out of him ? "

" I—I—did." He was on the point of saying he did not ; but, like the rough terrier, which was now coiled up at her feet, Tommy seemed under a spell in her presence. He could not curse or tell a lie while speaking to her. Wickedness of every kind seemed doubly wicked when Norah was by.

" Ah ! Tommy," said she, " I told you never to do that again. It is not so bad to kill the poor blackbirds, as we can roast 'em an' ate 'em ; but to wantonly hurt any living creature—above all, the poor little robin that hops into the house to us, an' that everybody loves."

" That was the third turn wud him knockin' id to-day," said Tommy, almost beginning to blubber, for her reproaches affected him as nothing else could. " An' sure, what harm did it do him ? On'y like Wat Corcoran, when the b'ys cut the tail off uv his bodycoat."

This logic, and the recollection of Wat Corcoran's figure on the occasion referred to made the poor girl laugh ; and

Tommy felt that his peace was made. We should mention
that Wat Corcoran was a bailiff who had received some
rough handling in the neighbourhood a short time before.

Tommy sat on a stool near the fire, to all appearances on
excellent terms with himself. He had acquitted himself to
his own entire satisfaction during the morning. The task
of " having an eye to the shop " was almost a sinecure, as
the customers were nearly all at the Station. So he took the
tongs in his two hands and built up the turf fire till it blazed
pleasantly.

The twitter of a bird made him turn round and fix his
merry eyes on a cage that hung near the window.

" Norah," said he, " I think the goldfinch will shortly be
tame enough for Miss Ellie. He's beginnin' to sing already."

" That was the old linnet," she said.

" No, 'twasn't," he replied positively. " Do you think I
don't know the call of a linnet from a goldfinch ? An' look
out at the tree—the lower branch at the right-hand side—
an' you'll see what made him call. Don't lean your head
that way. Wait, an' I'll turn the chair."

He turned her chair round till she faced the window.
Then with his chin resting on the back of the chair, and his
rosy cheek leaning against her dark hair, he pointed to two
birds in the tree.

" Do you see their yellow wings ? " he exclaimed, gleefully,
as the birds fluttered among the branches.

" Oh, they're beautiful ! " she replied, her dark eyes beaming with pleasure.

" I could ketch them two, now, if I liked," said Tommy,
" wud black buttons. But I won't, as I don't want 'em. But
I'll bring the wan I have to Miss Ellie to-day or to-morrow.
She sent for seed for him o' Saturday. But Wattletoes
brought all hemp seed instead of having it mixed—half
canary seed—as I tould him. Miss Grace said 'twas a sign
he'd be hanged."

" What sort of a girl is Miss Grace, Tommy ? Is she as
nice as Miss Ellie ? "

" She'll never see the day," said Tommy, with emphasis.
" She's as proud as a peacock," he continued. " ' Who is
that boy ? Do you speak to such boys ? ' " And Tommy
mimicked Grace's manner, and conveyed his opinion of that

proud little lady by a very expressive toss of his curly head.

" And what did Miss Ellie say ? "

" She said I was Tommy Lahy, an' why wouldn't she speak to me."

" I think, Tommy, poor Dick wants water. Look, he'll choke himself trying to put his bill down to the bottom of the gallipot. You're not taking care of him since you got the goldfinch for Miss Ellie."

Tommy immediately got upon a chair and filled the gallipot.

" And now, Tommy, put a couple of sods behind the fire, and run to the well for a kettle of fresh water, and put it down to boil, as mother will soon be home."

Tommy seized the kettle, and after whistling in a peculiar manner to his birds, with his underlip bulged out by his tongue, he trotted off to the well in the " rushy field " near the bridge. But stopping suddenly at the beech-tree he laid down the kettle and climbed sufficiently high to look at his crib in Mat the Thrasher's garden. The crib, however, was standing ; so he slid down as slowly as he possibly could with his eyes shut—after the manner of boys when left " to die " on a swing-swong—and then, suddenly regaining his wonted vigour on touching mother earth, he caught up the kettle, and set off for the well in " buck-jumps."

Norah Lahy watched the linnet as it sipped its water.

" Ah, poor old Dick," said she, " you must not be forgotten for that gay young gentleman. When will he be able to sing like you, I'd like to know ? As grand as he is with his golden wings, and his crimson-velvet head, and his pretty, sharp bill, I would not give one of your songs, poor old fellow, for all his grandeur."

The linnet, as if he understood her praises, regained his perch with a single hop, and lying down upon his breast, ruffled out his feathers. Then, with his eyes closed, the old linnet poured forth a low, sweet, wondrously varied song. She listened till her bosom began to heave, and something which we cannot call a blush glowed on her cheek. And seldom has human heart thrilled with more exquisite pleasure than that which the song of the linnet awakened in

the heart of Norah Lahy, as she sat there alone in her
straw chair; though she felt and believed that God had
willed she should never rise unassisted from that chair—
never again join her young companions in their rambles
by the hedge-rows and through the green fields, and along by
the bank of the clear, noisy little brook, to gather the wild
flowers, and listen to the lark high up in the sky, and the
"bold thrush" on the tree-top, and the blackbird's whistle
from the thicket, and, welcomest of all, the shout of the
cuckoo, proclaiming that summer was come!

Never again!

And yet, as she listened there, alone, to the linnet's song,
her whole being, every faculty of her soul, was a hymn of
praise and gratitude to God for His boundless goodness.

CHAPTER VIII.

HONOR LAHY'S GOOD LUCK.

THE kettle was just beginning to join its song to the song of
the old linnet when Mrs. Lahy—or Honor Lahy, as she was
more generally called by her neighbours—returned from the
Station. She was a comfortable-looking dame, enveloped in
a blue cloth cloak, with the hood drawn over her head, and
her hands encased in grey worsted mittens.

During the greater part of her life, Honor Lahy had found
it hard enough to make both ends meet. For honest Phil
used to "take a drop," and his earnings seldom did more
than clear off the weekly score at the public-house. His
customers dropped off one by one, the few who remained
faithful to him having often to keep their purchases for weeks
and even months till they could catch him in their own
houses; and then Phil Lahy and his goose and lap-board
were jealously guarded till the "new shoots" were finished
off, when the artist was set at liberty, looking fat and
healthy after a week or two of good fare and enforced
sobriety. His wife eked out the necessaries of life by rearing

poultry and fattening a pig; the pig going the way oi most Irish pigs—to the landlord. In spite of all her exertions, however, she grew poorer and poorer, till at last she and her husband returned one fine evening from the fair of Bally-mullin, and all the neighbours remarked that, instead of the " slip " which, as usual, they expected to see trotting before them, and which was sure to be a good one—for Phil Lahy was acknowledged to be " the best judge of a pig " in the county—Phil on this May evening carried a " bonneen ". under his arm.

When the next gale day came round—'twas an " admira-tion " how fast and sure gale days did come round in Knock-nagow—" Berky," in spite of the care lavished on her—including scratching her sides during meal times, to keep her in good humour—was little better than a " slip " ; and poor Honor looked into her sick child's face with a heart almost breaking.

One fine morning, however, Barney Brodherick tumbled himself out of the little blue donkey cart in which he made his daily journeys to town, and announced to Honor the startling piece of news that there was an American letter for her at the post-office.

Honor flung her old cloak on her head, and set off to town in a very excited state of mind, a proceeding which caused every soul of a pretty numerous female crowd, who were " bittling " in the little stream, to " wonder " where she was going. There was a feeling of anxiety among the younger girls lest it might be that Norah had got suddenly worse. and that her mother was hastening for the priest or the doctor. But a girl standing on the bridge, with a child in her arms, removed their anxiety on this point by assuring them that she could see Norah from where she stood, sitting in her straw chair under the beech tree, reading a book with " Friskey " on his haunches—" grug " was the word she used —on the " bench," snapping at the flies.

When Honor came back from the post-office she passed Norah without uttering a word. She took off her cloak and hung it on its own proper peg, and sat upon a chair, for she was rather out of breath, and waited patiently and in silence till her husband had dismissed a boy who was looking into the tailor's face, and evidently awaiting an answer of som kind to a message which he had just delivered with a pair of trousers, which, as Phil held them up to the light, seemed very suitable to drape the limbs of a scarecrow.

" Who sent this ? " Phil asked, holding up the garment with both hands.

" Mr. Andrews, sir."

" Well, tell him," said Phil, in a tone of the blandest politeness—" tell him I don't mend. I only make and repair."

The boy tucked the dilapidated garment under his arm and disappeared.

Mrs. Lahy took the letter from her bosom, and let the hand which held it drop down by her side, looking into Phil's face as if she suspected he knew all about it, and was playing off some trick upon her.

" Read it," she said at last calmly, and sat down again after handing him the letter.

Phil put on his spectacles, and studied the superscription and the post-marks with great deliberation, a proceeding which Honor seemed to consider quite necessary, for when she saw him baffled by a blotted post-mark, she stood up and pulled aside the little window-curtain to give him more light.

" 'Twas posted in Boston, United States," said Phil, " on either the first or fourth of September, eighteen hundred and —— "

" Maybe, wud the help uv God, 'tis from Larry," said she, leaning affectionately on Phil's shoulder. " Open it, Phil, in the name uv God."

Phil did so, and holding back his head, read : " My dear sister —— "

" 'Tis Larry," she exclaimed, giving Phil a shake that made him request she would " be easy."

" Thanks be to God ! 'Tis Larry. He's alive. What did I tell you ? Eh, Phil ? "

And she gave him another shake, which had the effect of making Phil deliberately push back his chair and lean against the wall, thereby preventing further assaults from behind. He glanced at the end of the letter, and said after a pause :

" 'Tis from Larry."

But on separating the leaves of the large sheet of letter-paper a slip fell from between them on his knees.

" There's ten pounds in id," said Phil, looking at the writing on the slip.

" Arra whist, Phil ! Where is id ? "

" Take this to the bank to-morrow, an' you'll get ten goold sovereigns for id."

Honor fixed her eyes upon his face, as if his words were quite beyond her comprehension.

" Phil achorra," said she, in a reproachful tone, and trying to recover her breath, " Phil, achorra, read the letter."

She drew a low stool towards her, and gently pushing the dog from between Phil's legs, sat down in front of him with her hand under her chin. Phil read the letter in a steady monotonous tone, stopping occasionally to comment upon its contents, and leaving off altogether at one place, and fixing his eyes on the opposite wall, as if he were addressing a rather numerous audience, delivered an interesting lecture on the rapid growth of American cities ; dwelling particularly on the fact that the man was still alive when the book from which he had his information was printed, who sold the ground upon which the city of Cincinnati was built for a " pony-horse "—greatly to the edification of his wife, who had a profound respect for his erudition.

" Put that in your hussif," said Phil, handing her the cheque.

She did so ; and set about preparing Norah's boiled bread and milk without speaking a word.

" Are you goin' to get that cheque cashed ? " Phil asked next morning after breakfast, as he unfolded a newspaper the schoolmaster had just given him on his way to school.

" Arra whist, Phil," was her only reply.

" Don't be makin' an oonshugh uv yourself," said Phil. " Go get yourself ready, and as soon as I finish this speech uv the counsellor's I'll go with you."

During the afternoon of that day Mat the Thrasher observed Honor and Phil from the roof of Tom Hogan's barn, which he was thatching, slowly wending their way up the hill towards the hamlet. When they came opposite the first house Honor went in, and Phil slackened his pace to wait for her. There was nothing extraordinary in this, and Mat proceeded with his work. But when he saw the same thing occur at every house they passed, his curiosity was excited ;

and instead of looking over his shoulder, he turned round
and sat upon the ladder to observe them more conveniently.
He now saw that Honor, both on entering and leaving each
house, held out her hand as if she were begging for alms.
By the time she reached Tom Hogan's there was quite a
crowd at her heels, the looks of most of whom expressed
wonder and delight; but Mat did not fail to notice a dark
scowl of envy in the faces of a few—which only showed, however, that human nature in Knocknagow was like human
nature all the world over. Mat came down from the roof of
the house to see what it was all about.

"Wisha, more uv that to you, Honor; an' didn't I always
tell you the luck 'd come when you laste expected id,"
exclaimed Tom Hogan's wife, as she followed Honor outside
the door, with the stirabout stick smoking in her hand.

And now Mat's own face assumed the look of astonishment
which it so puzzled him to account for in the faces of those
around him. For spread over the palm of Honor Lahy's
extended hand he beheld ten bright gold sovereigns shining
in the sun.

Honor and Phil spent nearly the whole of that night
discussing the important question of how their capital might
be invested to the greatest advantage. Phil was divided
between the purchase of a " new-milk's cow " and turning
corn merchant.

" As you won't agree to the cow," said Phil, " what do
you think of buying oats? The loft 'd be very handy, by
gettin' the holes mended. I always thought it a pity to see
such a loft goin' astray. An' since the new school-house was
built 'twasn't worth a penny to us—except the five shillings
from the dancing-master, an' whatever trifle Biddy Murphy
gave you for her benefit party."

But Honor had her own plan, and was resolved upon
following it.

" I'll talk to Mat Donovan to-morrow," said she, " an'
he'll tell me what things 'll be wanted to fit the place up
properly."

So Mat was consulted; and the second next day after,
Wattletoes stopped his little blue cart at Phil Lahy's door
again; but this time Phil was called out to assist in carrying
in several inch and half-inch deal-boards. Tom Carey, the

carpenter, was employed inside the house during the remainder of the week. And on a certain memorable Tuesday morning a straw basket heaped up with meal, with a bright tin measure on the top of the heap, was seen in the window of Phil Lahy's old house ; a stand of the finest salt herrings that eye ever beheld—to judge from the three that glistened on the segment of the top of the barrel that was left—stood outside the door ; and Honor Lahy stood behind her new counter, upon which was laid a huge square of salt as white as her cap.

From that day forward the world went well with Honor Lahy :—so well, indeed, that dark hints were thrown out by some people that the ten sovereigns were part of the contents of a " crock " found under the hearthstone in the " barrack," at the left-hand side of the fire. There were no fewer than five living witnesses—but four of them happened to be in America—who could bear testimony to an important circumstance in connection with the story of the crock. The circumstance referred to was this :—Three years before—the year of the big snow, in fact—Phil Lahy, while removing a projection of the hob, that encroached too far upon the fireplace, found a bad halfpenny all encrusted with mortar, which was so hard that Phil altogether failed to remove it from the coin by the application of his thumb. But when it was recollected that Phil himself had told his neighbours that the halfpenny was one of James the Second's—the truth of the story of the crock of gold was considered beyond all reasonable doubt.

CHAPTER IX.

BILLY HEFFERNAN AND HIS FLUTE.

HONOR LAHY, however, went on prospering ; and on this fine frosty morning, after returning from the Station at Maurice Kearney's, we find her a perfect picture of comfort good health, and good humour.

" How is Norah ? How is ma lanna machree ? " she asked, stooping down and looking into Norah's pale face.

" Finely, mother," she replied, with a languid smile.
" Will the priest come ? "

" He will—Father M'Mahon himself, God bless him ! He
was goin' over to Boherbeg to answer a call, but the minute
I tould him you wanted to go to confession to himself, he
said he'd send Father O'Neill to answer the call."

She pulled off her worsted mittens, and throwing back
the hood of her cloak, thereby displaying a snow-white cap,
a little crushed and crumpled by the weight of the hood,
with a gorgeous broad ribbon as a band over the crown of
her head and tied in a bow-knot under her chin, she sat on a
low stool in front of Norah.

" Give a guess what I have for you," she said, taking one
of Norah's wasted hands between her own.

" I don't know, mother."

" Somethin' Miss Mary sent you for a Christmas-box."

She put her hand into her ample pocket and took out a
pair of handsome embroidered slippers.

Norah's large eyes expressed the utmost surprise ; for such
a pair of slippers she had never seen before.

Her mother slipped the wasted hand into one of them.

" Isn't id cosy an' warm ? " she asked, looking fondly in
Norah's face, " lined with beautiful fur."

She ran to the fire and held the slippers close to the blaze
—which was purely a matter of form, for, even if they
required warming, she allowed no time for the least heat to
be imparted to them.

Gently removing Norah's shoes, she put on the embroidered
slippers, and looked up with a smile of delight. But the smile
quickly vanished, giving place to a look of amazement and
alarm. Norah's lips trembled and the tears gushed from her
eyes.

Surprise kept the poor woman passive for a moment ; but
recovering herself, she put her arm round her daughter's
shoulder.

" What is id, Norah ? " she asked. " What ails my darlin' ?"

But it was after a long struggle Norah was able to answer.

" Oh, mother," said she, " she is too good."

And, pressing her face against her mother's breast, she
sobbed so violently that the poor woman became quite
alarmed.

Phil Lahy hastened in from the shop door, where he had stopped to repeat his promise to Mat Donovan that he would not " disappoint him."

" What ails her ? " he asked.

" Oh, wisha, what but she's so thankful to Miss Mary for the slippers," Honor replied. " I don't know what in the world to do wud her."

" Have sense, Norah, have sense," said her father, gently.

She recovered herself by an effort, and resumed her usual position with her head leaning against the back of her chair.

" 'Twill do me good, mother," said she.

" Maybe so, wud the help uv God. An' Miss Mary tould me Doctor Kiely 'll be out next week, an' she'll bring him over to see you ; an' who knows, wud the blessin' uv God but he might be able to do somethin' for you. An' now," she continued, resuming her usual cheerful manner, " I'll go and get the breakfast ready. Sit down on that chair, Phil, an' talk to her, an' tell her all Father Hannigan said ; and 'tis he's the dhroll Father Hannigan. He'd have you laughin' wan minit an' cryin' the next. I wish we had Billy Heffernan to play a tune for her. That's what 'd rise her heart. An', be all the goats in Kerry, but here he is himself. Sit down there in the corner, Billy, an' play a tune for Norah. She was so lonesome all the mornin', wud no wan but Tommy and Friskey to keep her company, a tune 'll do her all the good in the world."

Billy sat down on a bench near the window under the linnet's cage, and taking the joints of an old flute from his pocket, commenced screwing them together, without uttering a word. Norah preferred " the soft complaining flute " to the " ear-piercing fife," and because she did, Billy Heffernan —though he never said so—invested the proceeds of a load of turf in the purchase of this one, and patched up his old brogues to make them last another winter ; to which last mentioned circumstance an occasional hiatus in his performance on this occasion—caused by a hurried application of the coat cuff to the nose—is, we think, to be attributed.

" Billy, a chora," Mrs. Lahy exclaimed, remonstratively, laying down her cup without tasting it—for she and Phil were now at breakfast—" Billy, a chora, stop that ! Her heart is too full to-day, for thim grievous ould airs. Play

' I buried my wife an' danced o' top uv her '—or somethin'
lively."

The musician took the hint, and delighted his audience
with a succession of jigs and planxties that might " cure
a paralytic."

So captivated were they all that Father M'Mahon was
actually standing with folded arms behind Norah's chair
before any one was aware of his presence. A sudden break-
off in the middle of a bar of " Paudheen O'Rafferty," and a
sheepish dropping of the musician's under-jaw made Phil
and Honor look around.

Father M'Mahon at once relieved them from their evident
embarrassment, by saying in a kindly way :

" So, Billy, you are playing for Norah. That's right ;
that's right. I hope she'll soon be able to come to Mass and
hear the organ." And, he laid his hand softly on her head.
She trembled as he did so, and in order to set her at ease he
sat down on the chair which Honor carefully wiped with her
apron, and said :

" Come, Billy ; ' Paudheen O'Rafferty ' is a favourite of
mine, so go on with it."

Billy Heffernan, turning his head towards the wall, gave
his troublesome nose a vigorous tweak, and obeyed.

" Thank you, Billy. Thank you. Very good, indeed,"
said the priest.

And with a gratified, though by no means cheerful, smile,
and another assault upon his troublesome nose, Billy Heffernan
left the house as silently as he entered it.

" And now, Phil," said Father M'Mahon, " I want to have
a serious word or two with you. After the promise you
made me I was exceedingly sorry to hear that you were
under the influence of drink on Thursday at the fair."

" An' you were tould I was under the influence of drink
at the fair."

" Yes."

" An' would it be any harm to ax who tould you ? "

" Oh, I am not bound to give you my authority   But it
was a person on whose word I can rely."

" An' a person on whose word you can rely tould you that
Phil Lahy was at the fair on Thursday—and that Phil Lahy
was drunk ? "

" Yes," said the priest, for Phil paused for a reply.

" An' now, will you tell me, did that person who tould you that Phil Lahy was at the fair and that Phil Lahy was dhrunk, tell you that Phil Lahy bought two pigs ? "

" Well, no ; he did not mention that."

" I'll be bound he didn't ; for the devil a thing these people, on whose word you can rely, ever think of telling but the bad thing."

Father M'Mahon rubbed his hand over his face and tried to look very grave. But thinking it best not to pursue the argument further, he turned to Honor and said :

" I think, Mrs. Lahy, I had better hear Norah's confession now."

Phil and Honor left the kitchen, and Father M'Mahon put on his stole and drew his chair close to the sick girl to hear her confession.

" Phil," said his wife, when the priest was gone, " you may as well cut out that coat for Mat. 'Twould be too bad to disappoint him, an' he goin' to be such a decent b'y's sidesman."

" I won't disappoint him," Phil replied. " But I feel too wake to do anything to-day. I think I must take a stretch on the bed."

" Well, if you don't like the work, go out an' take a walk, an' 'twill do you good."

" I can't do anything when this wakeness comes over me." And Phil did manage to look so faint, that a stranger would never have suspected that he had just eaten a very hearty breakfast.

" Tommy," he continued, " reach me the looking-glass."

Tommy brought him a small looking-glass with the frame painted a bright red, and a brass ring in it to hang it up by ; and after surveying his visage for some time, and pulling up his shirt collar, which was of the highest and stiffest, Phil exclaimed with his eyes still fixed on the glass :

" Honor, I look very bad."

" Now, Phil, don't be makin' a fool uv yourself. I never see you lookin' better in my life. Ax Norah."

" You don't look bad at all, father," said Norah.

" I feel very wake," said he, making a movement to rise, but looking as if he could not do so without assistance.

" Wisha, wisha, what am I to do wud him at all at all ? "
Honor muttered to herself. " If wance he lies down there,
he'll stay till Sunday mornin', at any rate. An' I don't
like to sind for Miss Mary the day uv the Station, an' all
—an' moreover a strange gintleman in the house."

Honor had found from experience that no one but Miss
Kearney could talk Phil out of his " weaknesses," and on
critical occasions she was in the habit of sending for her
unknown to the patient. Mary would come in, as it were,
accidentally, and after a chat with Phil about " Columbkill's
Prophecies," or some other interesting subject, she always
succeeded in convincing him that he was perfectly well, that
it was only his nerves—and that even the " inward pain "
was imaginary.

" I think, Honor," said Phil, " I'll try the spirits o' tur-
pentine. This pain is comin' at me."

This decided Honor, and she whispered Tommy—to his
great delight—to run and ask Miss Mary to take a walk
over in the course of the day if she could at all.

CHAPTER X.

" A LITTLE NOURISHMENT."

MARY, accompanied by her sister Ellie and Grace, soon made
her appearance ; and Phil jumped up from his chair with
wonderful alacrity for a man who, a few minutes before
seemed quite unable to rise without help.

Poor Norah's eyes beamed with pleasure and gratitude
and admiration as her beautiful friend bent over her and
hoped, in her low, sweet voice, that she was better.

" I am, Miss," was all Norah said. But she was so fascinated as to be unconscious of the little bunch of monthly
roses which Ellie had silently placed in her hand.

Grace cast a supercilious glance around, and seemed to

think the conduct of her friends quite absurd. But when Mary moved aside and let the light from the window fall full upon the sick girl's face, Grace's haughty look gave place to one of pity. Unlike Mary or Ellie, however, her impulse was to shrink away from that pale face, and forget that she had ever seen it.

When Mary turned round to speak to Phil Lahy, he suddenly remembered his weakness and dropped languidly back into his chair.

Mrs. Lahy exchanged glances with her visitor, and placing a chair at a convenient distance from the rapidly sinking patient, said :

" He's only poorly to-day, Miss. Maybe you could spare time an' sit down and talk to him for a start. I know he'd be in the better uv id."

" I hope, Mr. Lahy," said Mary, " it is nothing serious. I thought you looked remarkably well this morning ; and Father M'Mahon made the same remark."

" I'd want a little nourishment," said Phil.

Mary looked at his wife for an explanation ; but Honor only shook her head.

" Perhaps I could send you something," she remarked, still looking at Honor.

But another shake of the head was the only reply.

" He says," said Mary, " he requires nourishment."

" That's what I want," said Phil, turning round and looking earnestly in her face. " A little nourishment."

Mary again looked at Honor, evidently surprised that he should not have proper nourishment.

" God help you, Miss," said Honor, at last, " don't you know the nourishment he wants ? Nourishment ! " she repeated. " I never heard him call anything but the wan thing nourishment."

Mary now understood the state of the case, and changed the subject.

" You asked me some time ago, Mr. Lahy," she said, " if I could lend you Moore's ' Lalla Rookh.' I hadn't it at the time, but I can give it to you now any day you come up."

" Thank you, Miss," Phil replied " 'Tis goin' on twenty years since I read id ; an' I was wishin' to see id. What put

id into my head was seein' some lines the counsellor brought
into wan of his speeches an' I knew I seen 'em somewhere
before :—

> ' Rebellion, foul, dishonouring word,
>   Whose wrongful blight so oft has stained
> The holiest cause that tongue or sword
>   Of mortal ever lost or gained."

I disremember if them lines isn't in ' Lalla Rookh.' "

" Yes " said Mary smiling " those lines are from ' Lalla
Rookh.' "

" The Fire Worshippers " added Grace sententiously.

" Sure enough 'tis the Fire Worshippers " said Phil
looking at her with surprise.

" But " he added turning to Mary " is the wan you have
ge-nu-ine ? "

" Oh, I suppose it must be."

" 'Twas your Uncle Dan, God be good to him, that lint me
the wan I read. An' by the same token 'twas the same
day he gave me the ' Coravoth.' I was the fust that ever
sung id in those parts. But I wouldn't give a pin for them
little ' Lalla Rookhs ' that's goin' now. That wan was as
big as a double spellin' book."

Mary who did her best to keep her countenance said she
feared hers was one of the little ones ; but as her brother
Hugh had all her uncle's books she would see whether the
genuine edition of " Lalla Rookh " was among them.

Phil was by this time quite cured of his weakness and
Mary rose to take her leave.

During their conversation, Tommy was exhibiting the
goldfinch's accomplishments to its new mistress.

When the bird after much coaxing, moved sideways along
its perch, now coquettishly advancing, now timidly holding
back, at length picked hurriedly at the bunch of groundsel
which Tommy held temptingly against the wires of its cage,
Ellie's delight was only second to that of Honor Lahy herself, who gave much more attention to the little by-play at
the window than to the conversation about " books and
larnin' " between her husband and Miss Kearney.

Mary, too, stopped for a moment to contemplate the
scene.

Ellie's bonnet was hanging on her back, and her hair
fallen loose over her face and shoulders ; while the boy,
who was on his knees, looked up at her with a triumphant
smile, as the goldfinch snatched the groundsel through
the wires, and, placing its foot on it, commenced pulling it
to pieces.

Mary thought the group would be a good subject for a
pleasant picture.

But how sad was the contrast when she turned to the
straw chair, and the dark, melancholy eyes met hers. And
when she felt the love—the almost worship—for herself
that filled those melancholy eyes, Mary found it hard to
keep back the emotion that swelled up from her heart. She
turned her face away, and pulled down her veil before bidding
Norah good-bye.

" Oh, Mary," said Grace, when they had got into the open
air, " wouldn't it be well for that poor girl if she were dead,
and for her mother, too ? "

" Oh, Miss ! "

Grace started and looked around.

It was Honor Lahy who had followed them with Ellie's
gloves, which she had forgotten. The poor woman's hands
were stretched out as if begging for her child's life, and the
tears stood in her eyes.

" Oh, Miss, sure 'tis she brings all the luck to me ! "

This woman would snatch her child from the grave merely
because " 'twas she brought all the luck to her ! "

Ah, if that old house were built upon crocks of gold—
enough to purchase the fee-simple of broad Tipperary—
Honor Lahy would have flung it all into the sea, and been
content to " beg the world " with her child, if by doing so
she could keep the light in those languid eyes a little longer

Remonstrate with the heart-broken woman who paces the
floor in wordless agony from morning till night, and often
from night till morning. Tell her it is flying in the face of
Providence ; that it is time she should be reconciled to her
loss ; and she will reply : it is so sad a case. She had just
settled her in the world ; encroached upon the portions of
her other children, perhaps, in order to place her—her
darling—in a home worthy of her. And now she is gone—
the best and beautifulest of them all—and what a loss that

money is ! And she will try to make the wretched dross she had lost with her child the excuse for her sorrow. But if her darling's death had brought a queen's dowry to every other child of hers, the sorrow at her heart would be no lighter.

Say to this other one : " You should let your child go where she can better herself. Do you want to keep her a drudge all her life ? " And see, the tears are in her eyes, and she answers : " If she goes I won't have anyone to do anything for me." But give her a train of attendants to anticipate her every wish, and the tears will be in her eyes all the same.

So, again, this other one, who has lighted upon a tiny pair of red woollen stockings at the bottom of an old drawer. The little feet they encased grew tired, and a sweet, sweet little voice said : " Carry me, mamma," and a little silky head drooped like a flower, and two violet eyes grew, first brighter and brighter, and then heavy, and fixed, and glazed—twenty years ago. And when she sees you shake your head she dries her eyes, and says, with a sigh : " If I had her now how useful she'd be to me." You foolish, woman ! Look at those four healthy, blooming girls. Are they not good, and careful, and affectionate, and all that a mother's heart could wish ? On the mere score of utility you have more help than you require, more hands than you can find employment for. And yet you would cheat us with : " How useful she would be to you." But we are forgetting our story.

" Oh, Miss, sure 'tis she's bringin' all the luck to me," said Honor Lahy.

Grace turned away, with her brows knit into something very like a frown.

Mary was greatly moved, and felt at a loss for something to say that might soothe the poor woman, when Tommy's appearance relieved her from her embarrassment.

Miss Ellie is certainly an untidy girl. She forgot her gloves, and now Tommy comes running, breathlessly, up to them with a woollen ruff held high above his head.

" I hope, Mrs. Lahy," said Mary, " that Tommy continues to be a good boy."

" He is. then, Miss," she replied, wiping the tears from

her eyes with the corner of her apron, "very good at his books. An' every way—on'y for the climbin'."

Ellie looked laughingly at the delinquent, who scratched his curly poll, and returned her smile with a shrug of his shoulders and a glance of his merry blue eyes.

"Oh, but as he is so good, you must not be too strict with him," said Mary.

"But 'tis on'y the mercy uv God,' Miss," Honor exclaimed, as if her patience were tried beyond endurance, "that he don't make smithereens uv himself. An' besides, I can't keep a stitch on him."

She turned round to survey the culprit, whose bones and habiliments she considered in such constant jeopardy.

"Oh, oh, what am I to do wud him at all, at all? Look at him," she cried, catching Tommy by the shoulders and spinning him round. "How did you tear that piece out uv your breeches? An' where is it?"

Tommy looked considerably surprised; but guided by the spectators' eyes—and even Grace honoured him with a side-long glance—he clapped his hand behind and discovered that a pretty large piece was missing out of his corduroys.

It could be seen by his puzzled look that he was trying to remember where or how the accident occurred. His mind was divided between Tom Hogan's gate and Mat the Thrasher's whitethorn hedge, when casting his eyes upwards, as people will do under like circumstances (meaning no reference to Tommy's mutilated garment, but only to the operation of his mind), a ray of light seemed to break upon him from the beech tree. To Grace's profound astonishment he rushed suddenly to the tree, and, clasping his arms round it, began to ascend. Mary, too, seemed taken by surprise. But the proceeding was evidently nothing new to Ellie, who was indebted to Tommy's climbing propensities for an extensive collection of birds' eggs.

His mother shook her head, as if she had just made up her mind that Tommy's case was quite hopeless, and that reclaiming him was an utter impossibility.

Grace's eyebrows became more and more elevated as he mounted higher and higher.

But on reaching one of the highest boughs he stretched out his hand and the object of his ascent was visible to them all ; for there was the missing piece of corduroy fluttering in the breeze. Thrusting it into his pocket, he descended with a rapidity that caused Mary to put her hands before her eyes, as if she thought the catastrophe which his mother considered so imminent was at hand, and that Tommy was then and there determined to " make smithereens of himself." It was greatly to her relief, if a little to her surprise, that when she looked round, the cause of her anxiety was nowhere visible—he having scampered into the house the moment his foot touched *terra firma*, as if he were quite unconscious of the presence of the little group who had watched his performance with so much interest.

Mary said good-bye again to Honor Lahy, and went a little further up the hill to pay a visit to Tom Hogan's handsome daughter Nancy, who she suspected was pining in thought in consequence of an approaching event in which it was conjectured that one Ned Brophy was to play an important part.

Perhaps there was something in Mary's own heart, which, unknown to herself, made her sympathise with pretty Nancy Hogan.

CHAPTER XI.

FATHER HANNIGAN'S SERMON.

It is right that we should follow the two gentlemen with whom we parted some hours ago on their way back from the old castle. Mass was nearly over when they arrived at the cottage ; and Richard quieted his conscience for losing it, by persuading himself that his absence was a case of necessity.

A table in the hall, raised to sufficient height by means of two chairs, upon the backs of which it rested, served the purpose of an altar.

Mr. Lowe was again struck by the fervour of the people, who filled the hall and kitchen, while not a few knelt on the frozen ground outside the hall-door. He was not a little surprised to see Hugh Kearney, officiously assisted by Phil Lahy, " serving Mass."

Piloted by Richard, he got into the hall, the people making way for them as they went on, into the parlour, where Father O'Neill was still hearing confessions.

Mr. Lowe sat in the window seat next the door, where he could see the altar and the officiating clergyman. He saw that he was too late for the sermon he was so anxious to hear, as Father Hannigan was in the act of taking off his vestments.

But though Father Hannigan had delivered his regular discourse after the first gospel, it was his habit to address a few homely words to the people at the conclusion of the Mass, upon what we may call local and individual topics. He now turned round and began, in his deep *big* voice, with :

" Now, what's this I was going to say to ye ? "

He pressed the fore-finger of his left hand against his temple, as if trying to recall something that had escaped his memory. Mr. Lowe thought he was about giving up the attempt in despair, when he suddenly jerked up his head, exclaiming—

" Ay ! ay ! ay ! D'ye give up stealing the turf in the name o' God ! "

" Everyone," he continued after a pause, " must steal turf such weather as this that hasn't it of their own. But sure if ye didn't know it was wrong, ye wouldn't be telling it to the priest. And ye think it would be more disgraceful to beg than to steal it. That's a great mistake. No dacent man would refuse a neighbour a hamper of turf such weather as this. And a poor man is not a beggar for asking a hamper of turf such weather as this when he can't get a day's work, and the Easter water bottles bursting. Ye may laugh ; but Judy Manogue stopped me on the road yesterday to know what she ought to do. Her bottle of Easter water that she had under her bed was in a lump of ice, and the bottle—a big, black bottle that often gave some of ye a headache—an' maybe twasn't without giving more of you a heartache— before Judy took my advice and gave up that branch of her business : well, the big, black bottle was split in two with the fair dint of the frost—under the poor woman's bed. And

the Lord knows no Christian could stand without a spark of
fire to keep the life in him—let alone looking at a houseful
of children shivering and shaking, and he able and willing to
work, and not a stroke of work to be got. But ye all know
that stealing is bad, and ye ought fitter make your cases
known to the priest, and maybe something might be done for
ye. *Pride* is a good thing—dacent, manly pride—and 'twill
often keep a man from doing a mane act even when he's
sorely tempted. *Sperit* is a good thing. But, take my word
for it, there's nothing like HONESTY. And poverty, so long
as it is not brought on by any fault of his own, need never
bring a blush to any man's cheek. So, in the name o' God,
d'ye give up stealing the turf."

Here he paused, and Phil Lahy, supposing the discourse
ended, advanced with a bowl of holy water with a kind of
brush laid across it, for the purpose of sprinkling the congregation before they dispersed. But Father Hannigan
motioned him back and proceeded.

" Father O'Neill is against the beagles. He says 'tis a
shame to hear the horn sounding, and see ye scampering
over ditches and hedges on the Lord's Day. Well, I don't
know what to say to that. 'Tis the only day ye have for
diversion of any sort. And as long as ye are sure not to lose
Mass, I won't say anything against the beagles. The farmers
tell me they don't mind the loss to them to let their sons
keep a dog or two. And if ye meet after Mass—mind, I
say, *after* divine service—I don't see much harm in it. I'm
told, too, the gentlemen of the neighbourhood—that is, such
of them as *are* gentlemen—don't object to it, as ye are
honourable sportsmen and spare the hares. But then there's
the hurling. There's a deal of bad blood when ye hurl the
two sides of the river. If there's any more of the work that
was carried on at the last match, ye'll be the disgrace of the
country, instead of being, as ye are, the pride of the barony.
'Tis given up to the Knocknagow boys to be as spirited and
well-conducted as any in the county. Didn't I point ye out
to the Liberator himself the day of the Meeting, and he said
a finer body of men he never laid his eyes on. Such men,
said he, are the bone and sinew of the country. Some of
the best boys ye had are gone since that time, short as it
is ——"

Here there was a murmur amongst the women ; and a low, suppressed wail from two or three whose sons had but lately emigrated, made him pause for a moment.

" Well," he continued, shaking his head as the low wail died away ; " thank God the crowbar brigade didn't pay ye a visit like other places ; and I hope there is no danger of it, as the landlords here are not exterminators like some I could mention. I was in Cloonbeg the other day at a funeral—I was curate there six years ago—'twas the first parish I was sent to after being ordained, and it broke my heart to see the change. I could hardly believe 'twas the same place. The people swept away out of a whole side of a country, just as if 'twas a flood that was after passing over it. I married some of 'em myself and christened their children, and left 'em happy and comfortable. 'Tis little I thought I'd ever pass the same road and not find a human face to welcome me. Well, please God, there's no danger of ye that way, at any rate. And yet, sure, 'tis little security ye have—but I won't say anything that might discourage ye."

Father Hannigan turned toward the altar, and Phil Lahy was again advancing with the holy water ; but after taking a pinch of snuff he resumed his address :—

" I want ye to keep up the good name ye have. And talking of funerals reminds me of your conduct at the berrin' of that poor man ye brought to Kilree the week before last. 'Twas a charitable thing to carry him thirteen long miles through the teeming rain, and I know ye had pains in your shoulders next morning after him. 'Twas a charitable thing to lay his poor old bones alongside of his wife and children, as it was his last wish—though he hadn't a chick or child living belonging to him. I say that was a charitable, Christian, Irish act—and may God reward ye for it. But that was no excuse for the way ye behaved. The parish priest of Kilree said such a set never came into his parish. And ould Peg Naughton, that keeps the shebeen house at the church, declared to myself that, though she is there goin' on fifty-two years, 'twas the drunkenest little funeral she ever laid her eyes on. Isn't that a nice cha-*rac*-ter ye're airning for yourselves ? But I hope now ye'll remember my words. And now I have one request to ask of you. I want ye to promise me that ye'll dig the Widow Keating's stubbles for her. She hasn't a sowl to do a hand's turn for her since her boy lost his health. Will ye promise me now that as soon as the weather is fitting ye'll dig the Widow Keating's stubbles ? 'Tis short 'twill take ye if ye all join together."

" We'll do id, sir," " We will, sir, never fear," was answered all round.

" That's right, boys. And now any of ye that's very badly off, come to Father M'Mahon or myself and tell your story, and don't be ashamed. There's a little money collected for cases of distress in the town. And as the Major has subscribed ten pounds, and we're writing to Sir Garrett Butler for a subscription—and 'tisn't easy to know where to write to him "—glancing towards the parlour window —" 'tis only fair that cases of hardship on their own property should be looked after. I may as well tell ye, too, the Major sent Father M'Mahon a quarter of beef for Christmas. There's not a finer quarter of beef in Munster this minute. 'Twould do your heart good to look at it."

And abruptly seizing the brush, he dipped it in the holy water, and swung his arm round so vigorously and dexterously in all directions that even the gentleman at the parlour, window came in for a share.

The people now dispersed, and Mr. Lowe was conducted to the breakfast room, and formally introduced to the three clergymen.

CHAPTER XII.

MATRIMONY AND "MARRIAGE MONEY."—THE WIDOW'S LAST WISH.

IN the matter of breakfast, Mrs. Kearney came out in full force on the occasion of a Station. Even Mr. Lowe could not help taking notice of the display on the table. The antique silver coffee-pot was particularly conspicuous, and it was quite affecting to see the reverential gentleness with which the good woman handled this relic of the O'Carrolls. Her fingers would sometimes play softly on the lid in a manner that caused her husband visible anxiety ; for the coffee-pot had been her grandmother's, and was presented to herself at the time of her marriage by her Uncle Dan. A tall urn was equally an object of dread to honest Maurice ; and when she was heard to ask Father M'Mahon did he remember the day long ago, when he was a young student, that the urn was upset by Annie Cleary's sleeve being caught by the deer's horns on the lid, a full and true history of Ballydunmore was looked upon as inevitable. But, fortunately, the housekeeper whispered into her ear that a certain cream-jug, which, by right, should have attended the coffee-pot, was forgotten ; and the announcement so startled Mrs. Kearney as for the time to put Ballydunmore and the tea-urn completely out of her head.

Father M'Mahon spoke little, and seemed to the stranger reserved, and even haughty.

The reserve of the young curate was of a different sort and evidently arose from bashfulness.

But Father Hannigan had something to say to every one, and Mr. Lowe was not long in discovering that, with all his peculiarities, Father Hannigan was a scholar and a gentleman.

On finding that the stranger had taken his degree in one of the English universities, Father Hannigan engaged him upon some knotty points of classical learning, and the young A.B. soon began to feel not quite at his ease with so able an antagonist.

Grace paid great attention to this learned encounter, and looked so exceedingly wise with her elbow on the table and her chin resting on the little finger of her left hand, that Mary was in doubt whether she did not really understand every word.

" Really, Grace," said she, speaking so low as not to be heard by the gentleman, " one would think you are as familiar with Homer and Virgil and the rest of them as you are with Longfellow and Sidney Smyth, to say nothing of Robinson Crusoe."

" Indeed, no," she replied, with a half-displeased look, and dropping her hand on the table ; " but I was remarking that Mr. Lowe pronounces Latin like papa, and Father Hannigan like the ' Brehon.' "

" He picked up that in Trinity College," said Father Hannigan, who sat next her, and heard part of her remark. " That's not the way he pronounced it when he and I read Virgil together in Larry O'Rourke's mud-wall seminary in Glounamuckadhee."

" Oh, perhaps so," replied Grace, not at all pleased that her papa had read Virgil in a mud-wall seminary, and in a place with such a name as Glounamuckadhee.

" Ay, then," continued the priest, with a twinkle in his eye, as if he took pleasure in teasing her ; "and every one of us brought a sod of turf under his arm to school during the winter."

Grace looked quite offended, and made no reply.

" I am told," said Mr. Lowe, " that Doctor Kiely is at present writing a work on Irish antiquities."

The eyes of the offended young lady sparkled with pleasure as she fixed them with a look of pleased surprise on the speaker.

" Yes," said she, in a softened tone, " he devotes nearly all the time he can spare from his professional duties to it."

" It is a very interesting subject," he added. " I have heard Dr. Kiely's articles spoken highly of."

Grace was so delighted, that Larry O'Rourke's mud-wall seminary and the sods of turf vanished from her mind and left not a trace behind.

" Will you have many weddings this Shrove ? " Maurice Kearney asked, turning to the parish priest, who was so absorbed in thought that this sudden address made him start.

" Well," he replied, in his clear, silvery voice, " I fear not. All my boys seem bent upon going elsewhere for wives. I have already given half-a-dozen certificates while as yet I have heard of no one returning the compliment."

" Ned Brophy is getting a fine fortune," said Mr. Kearney.

" So I'm told," replied Father M'Mahon ; and Mary thought she could see a look of displeasure in his face, which she could not help connecting with the tear she noticed on Nancy Hogan's pale cheek as she was leaving the drawing-room after confession an hour or two before.

" Two hundred gold sovereigns," continued Mr. Kearney ." out of an ould saucepan."

This piece of information regarding Ned Brophy's good

luck caused a general laugh; the more readily perhaps because it was given with a look of perfect gravity.

"And you would not miss it out of it," he continued, seeming quite unconscious of their mirth.

"Out of what, sir?" Richard asked.

"The saucepan," replied his father; "Ned himself told me so."

"Do you approve of this fortune-hunting, Miss Kearney?" Father M'Mahon asked, turning to Mary.

"No, sir," she replied, blushing deeply, "I don't like it at all."

"And what do you say, Miss Kiely?"

"I really have not thought much on the subject," Grace replied. "But it is by no means unpleasant to be rich. And I'm rather inclined to think there is a good deal of truth in the proverb: 'When poverty enters the door, love flies out at the window.'"

Father M'Mahon leant back in his arm-chair, and laughed a low and somewhat satirical laugh.

"I fear," he said, "there is not much love in some of these cases. I am as much opposed as anybody to impru- dent marriages. But this buying and selling is a bad business."

"Sure you don't want them to be like the Protestants?" Mrs. Kearney observed reproachfully.

"The Protestants!" Father M'Mahon replied with surprise. "How is that?"

"I never knew a Protestant," she replied, "that would not live with a husband on a lough of water."

Father M'Mahon opened his eyes and seemed to want more enlightenment.

"There are the three Miss Armstrongs," continued Mrs. Kearney; "the youngest, to be sure, made a very good match—though she hadn't a penny—for they were after losing the property before her marriage. But the two eldest girls, with their fine fortunes, married poor men—though they were respectable, I know, and sensible, too. One of them, I'm told, is doing well in Dublin; and Mr. Armstrong tells me Fanny said in her last letter from Australia that they expected to come home and purchase an estate in Ireland yet, they are making a fortune so rapidly."

"Mr. Lowe," said Mary, "you ought to make mamma a bow. She has complimented both the ladies and gentlemen of your religion at our expense."

"And look at the Miss O'Dwyers," continued Mrs. Kearney, not heeding the interruption; "the fact is, I believe they'll never get married, as they can find no suitable matches."

"It might be better for them to be doing well in Dublin, or even making a fortune in Australia," said Father M'Mahon.

"Is it a fact," Mr. Lowe asked, turning to Hugh, "that Protestants are less hard to be pleased in the choice of wives and husbands than Catholics in Ireland?"

"It does really seem they take the plunge more courageously," replied Hugh. "I have noticed instances of it even among the humbler classes."

"Yes," said his mother, "there is George Hardford, who gave his daughter to Henry Johnson, the pensioner's son, though he hadn't a trade or anything. Took him into his house and kept him till he got a situation in the jail."

"Ah, that throws some light upon the matter," said Father M'Mahon; "situations of all kinds, high and low, are reserved for the professors of the favoured creed; landlords, too, will give farms at lower rents to Protestants than to Catholics."

"And leases," said Mr. Kearney. "I don't know a Protestant that hasn't a good lease."

"Yes," Father M'Mahon rejoined, "and it would seem the rule will soon be that Catholics will have no leases. And it is this state of dependence, this uncertainty of being able to keep a roof over their heads, that has made marriages the mercenary bargains they often are among us."

"It was not always so," Father Hannigan remarked. "I remember a time, myself, when the man looked more to the woman and less to the fortune than now."

"That is true," said Father M'Mahon. "Leases were general then, and the people were consequently more independent. Emancipation has done us harm in this respect. The sacrifice of the Forty-shilling Freeholders was a great injury to the country."

"Maybe," said Maurice Kearney, "the marriage money

has something to do with keeping people from getting married. Ned Brophy tells me the priest will charge twenty pounds for marrying him."

"Well," replied Father M'Mahon with a laugh, "that is not so much, bearing in mind that old saucepan you told us of. But another parishioner of mine tells me his match is broken off altogether on account of the exorbitant demand of the priest. The father of the girl had only fifteen acres of land, and the priest wanted fifteen pounds for marrying his daughter."

"I know all about that case," said Father Hannigan. "He went against the priest at the election."

"That makes the matter worse," rejoined Father M'Mahon. "Such practices will have the effect of making the people look upon the priest as a tyrant. But in the parish to which I refer, I am assured, as a rule, the farmer must pay half-a-year's rent to the priest for marrying his daughter."

"What do you think of the old system of public weddings?" asked Father Hannigan; "when friends and neighbours were invited, and the priest went round with a plate for his collection."

"I liked it," replied Father M'Mahon. "Indeed I was looked upon as singular because I did my best to encourage the people to keep up the old system. It made them more social and neighbourly. The priest, too, felt that what he got was given cheerfully. And besides," added Father M'Mahon laughing, "he went home with a heavier purse."

"I remember what you said at the last public wedding we had in this parish," said Mr. Kearney. "'Twas at Tom Donnelly's. The collection was larger than you expected, and when you were thanking them, you said no matter how small the sum might be, they could say, ' Go home now, sir you are paid '; but that if it was a private wedding you could charge what you liked."

"I dare say some of the bridegroom's friends have often thought of my words since. But I fear we are becoming more genteel and more selfish every day; so perhaps it is as well to make people pay for their gentility."

"I'm told," Maurice Kearney observed, "Tom Brien got the job done in Liverpool for two-and-sixpence. You were in Liverpool, Father O'Neill. How do they manage it there?"

"What you say of Tom Brien is quite true, sir," the young priest replied. "It happened it was I myself performed the ceremony ; for Tom said he'd like to have the knot tied by a Tipperary man."

"Ah, then, Father O'Neill," said Mrs. Kearney, "did you ever meet any of the poor Skehans while you were in Liverpool ? "

"I did," he replied. "One of the children knew me in the street ; and it was I prepared the old woman for death."

"I knew she would not live long," Mrs. Kearney observed ; "she was so heart-broken at leaving the 'ould sod,' as she said herself."

"Indeed," Father O'Neill rejoined, "that love of the 'ould sod' evinced itself in what some might consider a ludicrous manner at her last moment."

"How was that ? " Father Hannigan asked, seeing the young priest had relapsed into silence.

"Well," he replied, "when I had administered the Sacraments to her, and remained some time by her bedside, I thought I noticed that she wished to say something to me, but hesitated to speak. Whenever I moved, as if to go away, I saw her eyes were fixed anxiously on me ; but still she said nothing. So when I was going I asked her was there anything on her mind that was troubling her.

"'There is then, sir,' said she ; 'but maybe 'tisn't much, an' I oughtn't to be bothering you with it.'

"I assured her it was no trouble, and desired her to tell me what it was she wished to say.

"'Well, sir,' she said, looking anxiously into my face, 'I'd like to know *will my soul pass through Ireland* ? '"

Mr. Lowe looked surprised and amused ; and Grace, who honoured him with a good deal of her attention, uttered an exclamation and laughed. But all the rest were silent.

Mary stole a look at her brother Hugh, who covered his face with his brown hand, and seemed greatly moved. She knew he had special reason to be troubled, and regretted that her mother had introduced a subject which always pained him.

The fact was the Skehans had been under-tenants of his father's, and, though not exactly ejected, were induced to give up their little holding on receiving a trifling sum for the good-will and being forgiven the arrears of rent. The mere suspicion that the landlord wished to get rid of them has driven many an Irish family far away from the " old sod," who loved that old sod even as did the widow Skehan whose last earthly wish was that " her soul might pass through Ireland " on its way to Heaven.

" My God ! " exclaimed Father M'Mahon, " how they must suffer ! "

He stood up and strode across the room to a window, where he stood gazing at the white hills, with his hands clasped behind his back, for some minutes, and then left the room without taking notice of any one.

" Father M'Mahon," said Mary, " is pondering over some serious subject now."

" How can you tell that ? " her brother Richard asked. " Is it because he has forgotten his politeness ? "

" Oh, we can all tell that," Grace exclaimed ; " didn't you see the proud walk ? That's proof positive that his brains are wool-gathering."

But though Father M'Mahon forgot his politeness, he did not forget poor Norah Lahy.

CHAPTER XIII.

THE DOCTOR IN A FIX.

" Come," said Richard to Mr. Lowe, " let us prepare for the shooting."

As they passed the lobby window, Mr. Lowe glanced out into the yard, and was astonished to see Barney Brodherick in the act of rushing at Father M'Mahon's servant, evidently with the intention of doing him grievous bodily injury ; for Barney was as pugnacious as the celebrated tailor who was " blue moulded for the want of a batin.' "

Tom Maher, however, caught the wrathful Barney in his arms and held him fast.

" Let me at him ! " exclaimed Barney imploringly, after struggling and kicking to free himself. " Let me at him, an', be the livin', I'll put his two eyes into wan ! "

The tall servant regarded him with a scowl, in which scorn was largely mingled.

" Tom, for the love uv heaven, take off uv me, an' I'll brake every tooth in his head."

Here Phil Lahy appeared with his prayer-book still in his left hand ; and laying his right on Barney's shoulder, he addressed some words to him in a low voice.

" D—n well he knows that," replied Barney, almost tearfully " D—n well the blagard knows I'm in the state of grace to-day. But," he continued, through his clenched teeth, and shaking his fist at the object of his enmity, " but, please God, I won't be in the state of grace always. You Kerry b——d," he muttered, as he walked away, " from the County Limerick."

That characteristic bull was received with a shout of laughter from the bystanders. But Mr. Lowe's acquaintance with the geography of Ireland was too limited to enable him to see at once anything ludicrous in calling a man a Kerry anything from the County Limerick.

Owing to the frost the snipe were not as plenty in the bog as usual, except where there were springs.

At one of these places half a dozen rose together, but so far off that Hugh didn't fire. Richard, however, whose practice was—to use his own words—" to blaze away at everything," let fly, and down came a snipe. The successful marksman looked from one to the other of his companions with a stare of amazement, as if the result of his blazing away on this occasion were something altogether beyond his comprehension.

" You really have winged him," said Hugh.

" Yes, I think so," returned the doctor faintly.

" But," said Hugh, laughing, " you were just pulling the trigger when that one got up ten yards nearer to you than those you fired at."

But the doctor by this time had realized the fact that he had shot a snipe, and the trifling drawback alluded to by his brother did not abate his elation in the least.

He rushed forward, bounding over several bog-holes, reckless of consequences. But just as he reached the stream from which the snipe had risen, the wounded bird sprang several times a few feet from the ground ; and, finding these efforts to get upon the wing vain, it ran quickly, with a look of stealthy cunning, its long bill and neck stretched out horizontally, towards a clump of rushes some yards from the bank where it had fallen.

In his eagerness to prevent the prize from escaping, the doctor, instead of leaping the stream as he had leaped the bog-holes, rushed through it, sinking to the hips in the black mud. He managed to drag himself through the weeds and cresses to the opposite side. But when he attempted to climb up the bank, he found one of his legs caught in a bog stump at the bottom of the stream. He pulled and pulled, keeping his eyes fixed on the snipe as it made for the rushes, till he had freed his leg, and then jumped upon the firm ground. And now, being sure of his quarry, the doctor waltzed several times round the wounded snipe in a very graceful manner, brandishing the long duck gun over his head. He was rather pleased than otherwise at the loud roar of laughter by which his friends, as he thought, meant to applaud his performance.

He took up the bird and carefully examined the broken wing, as if he found in it an interesting study from a professional point of view. Then throwing off the professional air, and assuming that of the sportsman, he knocked the bird's head against his gun and put it into his pocket with a look of superhuman calmness, as if bagging snipe by dozens of braces were an everyday proceeding with him.

And now it occurred to the doctor that Hugh was rather overdoing the laughing. He took out his powder-horn to load again, feeling comfortably sure of " tumbling "—it is to *feathered* bipeds we apply the word—every bird he pointed his gun at during the rest of his life. But, on glancing at his companions, he paused, with his thumb on the spring of his powder-horn, in real surprise, for he saw them still convulsed with laughter.

" What the devil do they mean ? " he thought, putting his hand in his pocket to make sure that he *had* a snipe.

His stare of inquiry had such an effect on Hugh that he

was obliged to have recourse to his pocket-handkerchief to
wipe the tears from his eyes.

"Hang it," exclaimed the doctor, "what are ye laughing
at ? Is there anything wrong ?"

They pointed towards himself ; but after looking all around
him he could see nothing unusual.

At last he glanced at his feet ; and to his utter bewilderment discovered that one of his limbs was as bare as a
Highlander's.

The fact was, when extricating himself from the bog-
stump, he left one of the legs of his trousers behind him.

"I'd recommend you," Hugh called out, "to find the
missing article, and draw it on as fast as you can. I see a
car coming this way."

"Do you want me to dive for it ?" he asked, looking
ruefully down among the weeds and cresses.

"'Tis Hanly's phaeton," said Hugh.

The doctor looked towards the road, wellnigh petrified
with horror.

Yes, there was the phaeton coming nearer and nearer.
A bend in the road would bring it within forty yards of
where he stood—and not as much as a bush to obstruct the
view.

He turned his back to the road ; but the thought that
the view thus presented would be, if possible, more ridiculous than any other, made him quickly "about face"
again. He tried to hide the undraped limb with the single
barrel duck gun ; but the futility of the attempt became
instantly apparent. Equally hopeless was the idea of wheeling
slowly round so as to keep the presentable leg towards
the carriage as it turned the bend of the road. The sun,
too, at that moment burst through its covering of clouds,
which had the effect of bringing him out in bolder relief
before the eyes of the wondering spectators. He would
have sworn he could see the bewitching Kathleen's dark
orbs open till the white was visible all round. And then,
what was still worse, the pearly teeth flashed from between
the rosy lips, and the fair Kathleen's head was thrown back
in a manner which placed it beyond all doubt that she was
laughing at him.

He thought of flinging himself upon his face or his back,

but the bank on which he stood was just sufficiently elevated to render such a proceeding useless. The wild notion of divesting himself of what remained of the unlucky garment crossed his mind; it would be less excruciatingly ridiculous if his legs were matches. But there was no time for even this. There was the phaeton, there were the ladies, passing at the nearest point; and that mischief-loving Rose— " infernal," we regret to say, was the epithet he coupled with her name—bowing to him with fiendish politeness. And there was Doctor Richard Kearney with the nude limb stretched backwards as far and raised as high as possible— like a gander with the cramp—returning the salute with the grace for which he was famous among the young ladies of his acquaintance. He actually forgot to drop his hat upon his head, or change his position till the phaeton was out of sight.

And then he cursed his stupidity for never having thought of taking a " header " into a bog-hole, and remaining there with only his nose above water till they had passed.

He might have escaped in that way if he had thought of it in time.

He wiped the perspiration from his brow, and, as he glanced fiercely at his companions, he formed the dreadful wish that his gun were a double instead of a single barrel, that he might share the contents between them. They were still laughing at him.

Becoming more calm, the doctor made his way back to them, and Hugh, in the most unfeeling manner, suggested the advisability of getting home as fast as he could.

" Home ! " exclaimed the doctor, " and perhaps meet the Lord knows who on the way. No, I'll run over to Bob Lloyd's and borrow a trousers. Come with me," he continued, turning to Mr. Lowe, " and we'll have pleasanter shooting than here."

" Pleasanter shooting," remarked Hugh, drily. " I hope so."

" Will you come ? " the doctor asked.

" No, I'll follow the stream," said Hugh, who was a keen sportsman, and was glad to get rid of them for the rest of the day.

CHAPTER XIV.

MOUNT TEMPE AND ITS MASTER.

BOB LLOYD'S domicile was close to the bog, and rejoiced in
the name of Mount Tempe. Why Mount, it would be hard
to tell, for it was in the middle of a flat, dreary tract of
country ; and why Tempe, was a still greater puzzle. Either
taken singly might be accounted for on the " *lucus a non* "
principle ; but, joined together they are too much for us.
We must content ourselves with the fact that Bob Lloyd's
residence was known by the style and title of Mount Tempe.

Bob Lloyd was a bachelor—we cannot add, " by no choice
of his own." For if ever mortal man had the enviable
privilege to pick and choose among the fair ladies of the
neighbourhood, that man was Bob Lloyd, of Mount Tempe.
Many and ingenious were the snares laid to catch him, and
many and miraculous were his hair-breadth escapes. Mammas
manœuvred for him ; papas palavered him ; daughters'
exhausted all their arts and their patience to capture him.
But there he was safe and sound, and free as the wind that
seemed to recognise in him a congenial spirit, and took a
peculiar delight in rushing down the chimneys of Mount
Tempe House, or flinging the slates off the roof into the yard
behind, and upon the gravel plot, and out on the green lawn
in front—and particularly and especially through the roof of
what was once a conservatory at the south side, to the terror
and misery of an unhappy fox that dragged out a life of
wretchedness chained among the empty flower pots. It was
in keeping with the genius of incongruity which presided over
Bob Lloyd's establishment that the fox should be domiciled,
of all places in the world, among the flower-pots. And the
odour that assailed the nostrils on approaching the conservatory was, to speak mildly, of a kind for which strangers
were unprepared, and was usually greeted with an exclamation
indicative of a surprise the reverse of agreeable.

Mr. Lowe, on passing this delectable concern, stopped short and clapped his hand to his nose, as if he had received a violent blow on that feature ; but Richard, being prepared for the assault, passed on to the hall-door without wincing.

He knocked loudly, and while waiting for the door to be opened, occupied the time in rubbing his leg, which was fast becoming numbed. No one answered to his knock ; and, knowing the ways of the place, instead of knocking a second time, he raised one of the windows and put in his head.

" Morrow, Dick," said the gentleman of the house. " Come in."

Richard laid his hand on the window-sill and vaulted into the parlour.

" I have Mr. Lowe with me," he remarked, as he walked out to the hall to admit that gentleman by the door.

Mr. Lowe looked at the owner of the house and around the large room ; and then turned to his friend as if seeking instructions as to how he ought to act, or what was the custom of the country under such circumstances.

Mr. Lloyd was stretched on a sofa playing two jews-harps.

Richard walked deliberately to a cupboard, and taking a tall, square bottle and a couple of glasses from it, laid them on the table—having first swept a shot-belt, a bridle, a pair of horse girths, and two pairs of boxing gloves off the table on the floor.

Having filled the glasses, he tossed off one, and beckoned to Mr. Lowe to do likewise ; which he did.

The gentleman of the house at length wheeled slowly round, let his feet drop to the floor, and, sitting upright, contemplated his friend with a look of complacent admiration.

" 'Pon my soul, Dick," he said, very seriously, " you look well."

He put the jews-harp in his left hand to his mouth, and twanged it with the little finger of the same hand. Then putting the jews-harp in his right hand to his mouth, he twanged that too. Mr. Lloyd then put both jews-harps to his mouth, and played a tune, always keeping his eyes fixed on Richard's leg, as if there were some extraordinary fascination about the cap of the knee.

" 'Tisn't the latest fashion ? The newest style from the city, you know ? Eh, Dick ? "

"No. I sank in a bog-hole and tore it off with a stump or something. I want to borrow one from you. Of course, I can get it ? "

"Ay, faith," said Mr. Lloyd.

"And dry stockings ? "

"Call Jer."

Richard desired Mr. Lowe to sit near the fire, and went in search of the last-named individual.

The musician on the sofa applied himself to his instruments, and the listener began to wonder at the sweetness of the melody.

"Know the name of that tune ? " he asked.

"No ; I can't say I ever heard it before," was the reply.

"Listen again." And he repeated the tune.

"Know it now ? "

"Well, I don't. But it seems a pleasing little air."

Mr. Lloyd extended one hand, and swinging it gracefully in time to the air, sang :

> " Oh, my breeches full of stitches,
> Oh, my breeches buckled on,
> Oh, my breeches full of stitches,
> Oh, my breeches buckled on."

"This is a character," thought Mr. Lowe. "I suppose," he said aloud, "our friend's mishap has suggested it to you ? "

"Dick is a bloody clever fellow," was the not very relevant reply. "He has words at will."

The subject of this flattering remark here came to the door and called to Mr. Lowe to come with him upstairs.

The first thing that struck Mr. Lowe on entering Bob Lloyd's bedroom was, that a faded horse-rug did duty for a counterpane on the bed.

Jer appeared with the dry stockings, with a half-dozen dogs of various kinds at his heels. Over the yellow-striped waistcoat usually worn by servants, he wore a cast-off green coat of his master's, which was sadly out of keeping with his tattered corduroy small clothes and heavy brogues. Jer was a person of importance, particularly in his own estimation, and looked upon himself as a sort of senior partner in the establishment. His influence over his master was such that his good word was deemed indispensable whenever it was sought to make Bob Lloyd a party to any transaction, whether it might be the buying or selling of a horse, the granting of a lease, the paying of a bill, or the bringing about of a matrimonial alliance between the owner of Mount Tempe and any one of the many fair damsels who sighed to make him happy. For it was well known—this in reference to the fair damsels—that, though Bob Lloyd had a genius for never allowing both ends to meet by any chance, his rent-roll showed the receipt of a good eight hundred pounds a year ; and it was remarked that there " wasn't a better lot of tenants in Ireland " than his.

" Well, Jer," said Richard, " any chance of a wedding this time ? "

" We're goin' on wud a couple, sir," replied Jer, " but I don't say they'll come to anything. Everything was settled wud Miss Jane ; an', begor, there was no fear at all of the fortune they wor givin' her. She was tryin' on her weddin' dress on Saturday, when I went to tell her he couldn't marry her ; an' she tuck on terrible intirely."

Richard laughed, but evinced no surprise.

" The ould mistress an' the young ladies is tryin' to bring it on again. But," added Jer, solemnly, and as if he himself were the principal party concerned, " 'twon't do."

Richard explained to his friend that Mrs. Lloyd and her daughters lived in Kilthubber. " Devilish nice girls they are," he added ; " particularly the second."

" They're anxious to have him settled," Jer continued with a sigh, as if the settling were a great weight on his mind. " An' sure God knows so is myself. But 'tis so hard to meet a shootable woman. I'm after promisin' Tom Otway," he continued, " that we'll run down to the County Carlow in the course of the week to see his cousin. Himself is for goin' by the coach ; but I'm thinkin' 'twould look better to drive tandem. What do you think ? " he asked, as if he found it hard to decide.

" Oh, the tandem, by all means," said Richard.

" That's what I think myself," rejoined Jer, as he left the room, followed by his dogs, except two that had got into the bed for a nap.

" Is this all a joke ? " Mr. Lowe asked.

" No. Bob's wooings are always carried on in this way, and Miss Jane can hardly have been taken by surprise, for she had examples enough to warn her."

" And how does he escape the consequences ? "

" Do you mean why is he not called out ? The idea of such a good-natured fellow as Bob Lloyd shooting anybody or being shot at ! But he will tell you ' the heaviest cloutin' match '—to use his own phrase—he ever had, was with young Allcock for refusing to marry his sister, who declared that he had popped the question and been accepted in the most formal manner."

" But the law," said Mr. Lowe. " Have you no such thing as breaches of promise in Ireland ? "

" They are not quite unknown, though very rare, down here. But the immunity which Bob enjoys may in some measure be accounted for by the fact that the business is all done through Jer. Bob never writes letters ; and, perhaps, as he would say himself, that saves his bacon."

It must not be inferred that writing was not among Mr. Lloyd's accomplishments. He wrote a fair, round hand, and was fond of displaying his caligraphic skill whenever pen, ink and paper chanced to come in his way—particularly, and almost exclusively, in the execution of the words :—

" Command you may your mind from play."

which he was wont to finish off with a flourish, and seemed to derive great pleasure from the performance.

" Can we get a shot without going into that infernal bog again ? " Richard asked when they had returned to the parlour.

" Ay, faith," Mr. Lloyd replied. " If I went out to that well beyond ten times a day, I'd be sure to meet a snipe there."

" Get your gun and come with us."

Mr. Lloyd strapped a shot-belt over his shoulder, and was taking up his gun, when the door opened, and a stout, middle-sized man, with a round face, unceremoniously walked in.

" 'Morrow, Wat," said Mr. Lloyd.

" 'Morrow, kindly," Wat replied, offering him a slip of paper.

" How much is it ? "

" Fifteen pounds eleven and sevenpence."

" I'll see about it," said Mr. Lloyd.

" That'll never do for me," replied Wat.

" There's not a penny under the roof of the house," said Mr. Lloyd.

" The devil a foot I'll stir out of this till I get it," Wat rejoined.

" Have a drop of this," Mr. Lloyd remarked, filling a glass from the square bottle.

" No objection," replied Wat, sententiously.

Mr. Lloyd went to the side-board, and returned, holding a large dish in one hand with as much ease as if it were a small plate, and grasping a loaf of bread with the other.

" Come, Dick," said he, placing them on the table, " let's have a bite."

He cut some slices of bread and meat which Richard converted into sandwiches for himself and Mr. Lowe.

" Wat," said Bob Lloyd, with his mouth full, " I'll see about that."

" Pay me the money, and let me go for the cow ; that's the seein' about I want."

" What cow ? " Mr. Lloyd asked.

" A fat cow I'm afther buyin' from your father," said Wat, turning to Richard ; " and he won't let me take her wudout the money. So, shell out," he added, turning to Mr. Lloyd, with a sort of humorous sulkiness of voice and look.

Mr. Lloyd, appearing to pay no attention to this speech, bit a semicircle out of his sandwich, and holding it between him and the light, seemed to admire its regularity.

Wat, drawing an old arm-chair towards the window, thereby disturbing the repose of an old setter that had possession of it, deliberately sat down, and crossed his legs with the air of a man who was bent upon taking his ease, and had nothing on earth to trouble him. Mr. Lloyd advanced in silence, and presented a carving knife at him with a substantial slice of cold meat on the top of it.

Wat took the meat between his finger and thumb, and acknowledged the civility by uncrossing his legs and sitting upright.

Mr. Lloyd then presented a carving fork with the other hand, upon which was a chunk of bread. This Wat also accepted, if not graciously, at least without any show of

reluctance. Having emulated his host in the biting line—
with the difference that, the bread and meat being each in a
different hand, he had to take two bites instead of one—
Wat remarked oracularly :

"A pig's head ates very handsome, cowld."

"Kitty," he called out to a servant girl who was flinging
her cloak over her shoulders as she passed the window.

The girl stopped and looked at him. Whereupon Wat
raised the window and asked was she going to town.

"I am," replied Kitty. "Why so ? "

"Tell my mother to send me out an ounce of tobaccy,"
said Wat, in the calmest and most self-satisfied manner
imaginable.

"Now, Wat, what *are* you up to ? " Mr. Lloyd asked.
"Don't you know if the money was in the house there
wouldn't be a second word about it ? "

"Well, to do you nothin' but justice," Wat replied, " I
do know that. But you see two quarters of that cow are
bespoke, and I can't disappoint my customers. Moreover,
when wan quarter is for a weddin'."

"Come to-morrow."

"'Twon't do."

"Well, what do you want ? "

"D—n well you know what I want," replied Wat. " An
order on Tom Ryan. That's money any day."

"There's not a pen or a bit of clean paper in the house,"
said Mr. Lloyd.

"Ketch me ! " was Wat's comment upon this objection.
"I'm provided against accidents." And he produced an
ink bottle with a leather strap attached to the neck, and
unfolded half a sheet of paper which was rolled round a well-
worn quill pen.

Mr. Lloyd, seeing no way of escape, sat down and wrote
the letters I and C. The latter turned out such a model of
a capital letter that Mr. Lloyd held it up for the inspection
of his friends. He then slowly and carefully wrote out the
order, which ran thus :—

"I Command you to pay Wat Murphy fifteen pounds
sterling Money, which I will allow you out of your rent.

                                    " ROBERT ORMSBY LLOYD.

"To Mr. Thomas Ryan."

" All right," said Wat, as he held the document to the fire to dry. After putting it in his pocket, he pointed to the square bottle.

" Would you have any objection ? " he asked.

Bob Lloyd held up the square bottle, and, laying his hand along it, carefully measured the depth of liquor remaining. Seeming satisfied that he could afford to act on the very broad hint which Wat's question implied, he filled a glass.

" Healths apiece to ye," said Wat, tossing off the whiskey as he passed the table, without stopping. He was immediately heard whistling to his bull-dog, who, with his back against the wall outside the hall-door, was keeping at bay quite a pack of hounds of various descriptions—but among which there was not a single " mongrel " or " cur of low degree "— by the mere glare of his eye.

CHAPTER XV.

A DAY'S SHOOTING LOST.

THE snipe was at the well, as Bob Lloyd had foretold, and the moment it rose, the doctor " blazed away," But greatly to his surprise, the snipe did *not* fall with its wing broken.

" He's wounded," the doctor exclaimed, on seeing the snipe pitch in the next field. " I'll make sure of him the next time."

All three blazed away the next time ; and when the smoke cieared off they saw the snipe quietly dropping into its old quarters near the well.

Re-loading their guns they retraced their steps, and another volley woke the echoes of Mount Tempe. The snipe—as jack-snipes are wont to do—flew a couple of hundred yards, and dropped again among the rushes in the next field.

The affair now became quite exciting, and volley after volley made the unhappy fox among the flower pots shiver and creep from one corner to the other of its prison for a full hour and more.

" Hugh is doing business," said Bob Lloyd, on hearing the report of Hugh's gun from the bog.

" Ay, faith," he added, on seeing him quietly walk forward and pick up his bird.

" I'll do that fellow's job," exclaimed Richard, through his clenched teeth, as he rammed home the charge in the long duck gun with a very unnecessary expenditure of force. " Let me alone, if I don't polish him off."

We trust we need not say he did not mean his brother, but the jack-snipe.

But just as the doctor had put his gun on full cock, Bob Lloyd laid his hand on his shoulder.

" Is it a duck ? " Richard asked.

" Ay, faith," replied Bob. " The ice is broken on the pond, and he's coming about it."

The wild duck flew round and round in a circle, and so low that the chances of a shot seemed not improbable.

Bob Lloyd hurried to the corner of the field and stooped behind the fence. Richard and Mr. Lowe took up a position at some distance, and all three watched the wild duck with breathless excitement as it came nearer and nearer in each round of its flight. The doctor had his long gun to his shoulder at one time, and would have blazed away if Mr. Lowe had not stopped him.

" Why don't you let me tumble him ? " the doctor asked, in a whisper " I had him covered just when he was passing the sally-tree."

" Don't you see," Mr. Lowe replied, " that that tree is fully three hundred yards from us ? "

The duck suddenly changed from its circular course, and shot slantwise like an arrow into the pond. This move took the sportsmen by surprise ; but recovering themselves, all three hurried along the fence, with their heads on a level with their knees. On, on they crept till they reached the part of the fence nearest to the pond. There was the duck quietly swimming among the broken fragments of ice, but not within shot.

" How are we to manage ? " said the doctor.

" We're at the end of our tether, Dick," replied Bob Lloyd.

" I'll get over the ditch and take him by surprise," said the doctor.

And suiting the action to the word he climbed over the fence, and walked quickly towards the pond. The wild duck seemed really taken by surprise, for it remained hid behind a fragment of ice till the doctor reached the brink of the pond. He stood panting for a few seconds, with his gun half raised to his shoulder, but the duck never stirred. He advanced a step or two on the ice, and was beginning to think that the duck had got off in some inexplicable manner, when a tremendous splash and clatter in the water made him start. The duck rose so close to him that his first impulse was to step back. In doing this his feet slipped from under him, and he came down with extraordinary celerity on the end of his spine. The shock caused a queer sensation in his throat, and, in fact, he was much in the same state as Mrs. Slattery when she implored Father Hannigan to inform her whether she was killed.

" Why the blazes didn't he fire ? " exclaimed Bob Lloyd.

" And why doesn't he get up ? " Mr. Lowe asked, as he stood on his toes and looked over the fence.

" Faith, he's taking it easy," said Bob Lloyd. " Let us come down to him."

" What's the matter, Dick ? " he asked, on reaching the pond.

In reply Doctor Richard Kearney informed his friends in a quiet, matter-of-fact manner, and in the fewest and shortest words, that the part of his person upon which he had fallen was " broke."

" Misfortunes never come alone, Dick," said Bob Lloyd " Get up, and let us be at the jack again."

" Yes, 'tis the pleasantest," replied the doctor. " Help me up. For, hang me if I'm quite sure whether I can stand."

He found, however, that he had the use of his limbs ; and then returned to the well in pursuit of the jack-snipe.

But the jack-snipe was not to be found. In vain they tramped through the rushes, and along the drains and ditches, and everywhere that a snipe would be likely to be found. The invulnerable jack had disappeared from the scene altogether.

"He's dead," said the doctor. "I knew I peppered him the last time."

' But if he was dead," Mr. Lowe remarked, "wouldn't the dogs find him?"

They took one more round through the rushes; and then, as if moved by a single impulse, the three sportsmen grounded arms.

Bob Lloyd rested his elbow on the muzzle of his gun, and dropped his chin into the palm of his hand.

"Bad luck to that duck," said Bob Lloyd solemnly. "We lost our day's shooting on account of it."

"What is Hugh up to?" the doctor asked, pointing to his brother, who was standing on a little bridge on the bog road, and waving his handkerchief to them.

"I think it is calling us he is," said Mr. Lowe.

"Let's have another glass of grog," the doctor suggested.

"Ay, faith," replied Mr. Lloyd. "Come over."

They returned to the house; and after another application to the square bottle, retraced their steps to the bog road, where Hugh was waiting for them.

"Ye had good sport it would seem," Hugh remarked. "Game must be plenty in Mr. Lloyd's preserves?"

"Well, we didn't meet much," replied Mr. Lowe.

"And we lost our day's shooting on account of that duck," said Richard, putting his hand under his coat-tails with a look suggestive of a disagreeable sensation.

"If we cross over to the turf-ricks on the high bank," Hugh remarked, "we may get a shot or two at the plover coming into the bog. They are flying low."

"I vote for going home," replied the doctor. "I have got enough of it for one day."

"I dare say you will have a good appetite for your dinner."

"Well, rather; but we had lunch at Bob's."

"What do you say, Mr. Lowe?" Hugh asked. "Shall we cross the bog and try and add a few grey plover to our bag?"

"Well, I confess, I'm inclined to vote with the doctor for home."

"Home is the word," said the doctor. And on seeing some country people approaching he managed to let the head and neck of his snipe hang out of his pocket, and, with the long gun on his shoulder, stepped out at a quick pace, looking as if he had done wonders during the day.

CHAPTER XVI.

AN UNINVITED VISITOR.

GRACE had run to the window a dozen times in as many minutes, to see if the sportsmen were returning ; and though Mary smiled at her impatience, she could not conceal from herself that she shared it in no small degree.

" Here they are at last," Grace exclaimed, gleefully.

Mary started from her chair, but sat down again quickly. She blushed, and was glad that no one had seen her.

Grace ran to open the door ; and there was a little affectation in Mary's manner as she said, while passing through the hall :

" Grace, tell them dinner will be on the table in a few minutes."

But, as if ashamed of this " acting," she turned back and met the young men on the door-steps.

" I hope you enjoyed the shooting," she said to Mr. Lowe.

" Oh, yes," he replied, devoutly hoping that her inquiries would extend no further.

" Well, dinner will be ready immediately," said Mary. " And I need not remind you we are to have a few friends in the evening."

" Who are they ? " Richard asked.

" I thought I told you. But I am glad to have an agreeable surprise for you. It is the Miss Hanlys."

The doctor glanced at Bob Lloyd's unmentionables, and rushed up the stairs like a man bent upon throwing himself out of a window.

As Maurice Kearney took his place at the head of the table,

his first question, as he looked at the edge of the carving knife, as a matter of course, was—

" Did you shoot much ? "

" Only four or five brace, sir," replied Hugh.

" Oh, only that much," Grace exclaimed, " after all the firing we heard, I thought at one time there was a brisk skirmish going on, if not a pitched battle."

" Well, now," said Hugh, who sat next her, " how would you feel if there was really a pitched battle going on in the bog ? "

" Oh, I'd be delighted. The excitement must be so pleasant."

" And which side would you wish to win ? "

" The Irish of course. How I should like to bind up the wounds of some gallant young chief like Robert Emmet or Sir William Wallace."

" That is the Sir William Wallace whose picture you have ' drawing the fatal sword ' in the ' Scottish Chiefs ' ? "

" Yes ; I mean some young chief like that who

> " Fought for the land his soul adored,
>   For happy homes and altars free,
>   His only talisman—the Sword,
>   His only spellword—Liberty."

" Mr. Lowe says you are a rebel," said Mary.

" Oh, I don't know that," she replied, looking a little frightened. But observing that Mr. Lowe's smile indicated anything but displeasure, she added : " But I do admire a hero. And who is so great a hero as the patriot who fights and bleeds for the land of his birth ? "

" Will ye go to the bull-bait ? " Maurice Kearney inquired.

This question caused considerable surprise and some amusement.

Mary, who knew her father's talent for such surprises, could not be sure whether the bull was hauled in after his usual manner of introducing subjects that had not the remotest connection with that under discussion, or whether Irish patriots, fighting for their country, suggested to him the baiting of a bull.

" A bull-bait, sir ? " said Hugh. " Why, the practice has been entirely done away with for years."

" 'Tis to be before the end of the week ; but the place is not decided on. Wat Murphy that told me. He was here for a cow I sold him last Sunday. I gave her to him too cheap."

And Mr. Kearney rubbed his bald head, and seemed sorry too late for the bad bargain he had made with Wat Murphy.

" I wonder he told us nothing about it," Richard remarked. " We saw him over at Bob Lloyd's."

" Was that the butcher ? " Mr. Lowe asked. " I remarked that he had a very well-bred bull-dog."

" Are you an admirer of those interesting animals ? " Hugh asked, with a slight shade of sarcasm in his tone.

" Well, not exactly. But some of my English friends set great value on them. That white dog of the butcher's would, I fancy, fetch as high a price as the cow you sold him."

" I gave her to him for thirteen pounds ten," said Mr. Kearney. " 'Twas too cheap. Wat sold four pups for two pounds apiece last year."

" But what do they want them for," Mary asked, " now that there is no bull-baiting ? Surely it cannot be for their beauty they are kept. A more ill-favoured animal it would be impossible to imagine than that dog of Wat Murphy's, with his crooked legs and frightful grin. I am always quite uneasy when I see him about the place."

" Don't you see he is always muzzled ? " said her father.

" That only makes him look the more ferocious," she replied. " 'Tis a shame to have such dogs kept by any one. There was a poor beggar woman here the other day, who had her leg torn in a frightful manner by Pender's dog."

" I heard papa say," said Grace, " that such accidents are becoming very frequent. He says many farmers keep ferocious dogs now. He called to see one poor child that was attacked by a dog, and though the dog was muzzled, papa feared the child would die."

" So many robbers," said Mr. Kearney, " are now prowling about the country, people don't know what to do. But it isn't robbers Pender is afraid of, but bailiffs. He was here to-day looking for you," he added, turning to Mr. Lowe.

" For me ! Oh yes," he added, recollecting himself, " he is my uncle's agent."

" His son," Mr. Kearney replied. " And as cantankerous a cub as ever the Lord put breath in. He drove up to the door with a double-barrel gun at each side of him, and four pistols stuck in his belt. You'd be talking of bull-dogs," he added, turning to Mary, " But where will you find an uglier bull-dog than Beresford Pender ? "

" Beresford ! " exclaimed Mr. Lowe. " Is he a connection of that family ? "

" His father," replied Mr. Kearney seriously, " was a dog boy to the old marquis."

This curious sort of connection with aristocracy made the young gentleman laugh. But Hugh, feeling that it was scarcely prudent on his father's part to talk in this way of the agent and his son in presence of the landlord's nephew, changed the subject by remarking—

" But you must not suppose from what my father has said about robbers prowling through the country, that theft is one of our national vices. On the contrary, the honesty of the people, under the circumstances, is most extraordinary."

" I inferred as much," said Mr. Lowe, " from what the clergymen said the other day about stealing turf. It seems to me a very venial offence for a poor man to take a little turf in that way. And Mr. Hannigan alluded to no other acts of dishonesty."

" He had a right to say something about the turnips," said Mr. Kearney. " Only for I got a cabin in every field and had a man minding them, they wouldn't leave me a turnip these two last years, whatever is coming over 'em. And there are gangs of blackguards from the towns, besides, that will take whatever they can lay hands on."

" Unfortunately that is true," said Hugh. " Unprincipled characters go about plundering under cover of the general distress. But poor, honest people are driven to it, too, by necessity. When their houses are pulled down and they are forced to take refuge in the lanes of the next town, it is not surprising that many become dishonest. The man who would almost lie down and die of hunger in his own poor cabin, among his neighbours, rather than bring disgrace upon his family by turning thief, can easily be tempted when he finds himself in the midst of strangers in some wretched hole in the lanes or outskirts of the town.".

" I really believe what you say is true," said his mother
" Poor Molly Ryan was out here the other day, and it was
heart breaking to listen to her. Her two boys, that she
' reared honest,' as she said, got into bad company, and were
in jail for attempting to break into Murphy's store. If they
had not been turned out of their little place at the Cross-
roads, the boys, I am sure, would grow up honest and
industrious, like their poor father, who was a very decent
man, and very civil and obliging ; he used to do many little
things for us."

The cloth had been removed during the foregoing conversation ; and Maurice Kearney had just mixed his second
tumbler, and pushed the decanter to Hugh as his wife
concluded.

Richard, after waiting impatiently for a minute or two,
and seeing that his brother had no intention of applying to
the decanter, reached across the table and quietly filled his
own glass.

Mr. Lowe, we may observe, drank sherry.

" My goodness ! " Grace exclaimed, in a whisper to Mary,
" what can be the matter with Adonis ? He has not opened
his lips, except to imbibe whiskey-punch, the whole evening."

" I really don't know," replied Mary.

" His silence is positively miraculous," Grace continued,
" particularly as Father M'Mahon is not present. And he
has his dress-coat on. And," she added, opening her eyes
with surprise as the doctor wheeled round his chair and
stretched his legs towards the fire, " and his patent leather
boots. I'm lost in amazement ! "

" Do you forget that the bewitching Kathleen is coming ? "

Grace frowned awfully ; and got into a brown study
immediately.

" Are you jealous ? " asked Mary, laughing. " What a
dreadful coquette you must be. You had quite forgotten
Adonis—had only ears and eyes for Apollo—and yet you
are now up in arms against Kathleen."

" Well, now, Mary, don't talk so foolishly. Let us go to
the drawing-room."

Mr. Lowe opened the door for them, and they passed out,
Grace looking almost too grand to acknowledge the civility
by a slight inclination of the head. But before going to the

drawing-room she went upstairs, and returned wearing a necklace and other adornments, bent, no doubt, upon shining down Kathleen Hanly.

She first took up a book and, fixing herself in a becoming attitude, began to read. But her furtive glances towards the door led Mary to suspect that the book had not much interest for her.

" What are you reading, Grace ? " she asked ; and Mary laughed on seeing her turn the book round to read the title on the back.

" I guessed," continued Mary, " that you were not quite absorbed in your studies."

" You are bent upon teasing to-night. I suppose they will not favour us with their society till those ladies arrive."

" Well, we shall not have long to wait," Mary replied ; " for here they are."

The sound of wheels on the gravel was quickly followed by a knock—an unusually loud and long knock, Mary thought —at the hall-door.

The door was opened by Hugh before his sister reached the hall, and Miss Rose Hanly was explaining in a hurried and excited manner that they had brought Miss Lloyd with them.

" She came out from town with mamma in the evening," said Miss Rose ; " and, when she found we were coming to tea, she said she would come with us ; as her brother, Robert, she said, knew you all very well."

This was evidently a matter of tremendous importance in Miss Hanly's eyes ; and, though Hugh took it coolly enough, Mary seemed considerably surprised. But before anything further could be said, the lady in question, accompanied by Kathleen, made her appearance.

Mary welcomed all her visitors, and conducted them to her own room.

CHAPTER XVII.

LORY.

WHEN Hugh was closing the door, he felt some slight resistance offered from the outside ; but on looking out he could see nothing, the night was so intensely dark. On attempting to close the door a second time, the same gentle pressure prevented him.

" Who's there ? " he asked.

There was no reply ; but a rather tall young lad advanced a step or two into the hall, and looked wildly about him.

He was slight and somewhat raw-boned, and being at that moment almost blue with the cold, he presented the appearance of anything but a handsome youth.

Hugh waited, expecting him to speak ; and he waited, expecting Hugh would speak. And so they continued to stare at each other for a couple of minutes.

" I came with my sisters," said the young lad, at last, in a voice so unexpectedly deep and loud that it made Hugh start.

" Oh, Mr. Hanly," said Hugh, " I had quite forgotten you."

" No wonder for you," was the reply in the same voice, and with the same wild opening of the eyes. " I had a petticoat on me the last time you saw me. Huh ! huh ! "

He laughed a deep, hollow laugh, in which Hugh joined—not because the laugh was at all infectious, but because the allusion to the petticoat, in which his young neighbour had been kept far beyond the usual age, called up the very remarkable figure which a year or two before he occasionally saw starting from some grove or hedge, or mounted upon a gate pier, or paling, and looking, he used to think, like a young Indian in an early stage of the process of civilization.

" Come in. This is young Mr. Hanly," he added, on entering the parlour.

Young Mr. Hanly pulled off his cap, and looked round him as if he intended to bolt immediately, if he could only find an opening anywhere.

Everyone looked at young Mr. Hanly except the doctor, who was so absorbed in his own reflections, or in the shine of his boots, as to seem unconscious of what was passing.

" Good-night, Richard," said the new arrival. And the deep bass of his voice made them all start.

" Oh, Lory ! " Richard exclaimed, extending his hand to him. " How on earth did you manage to grow so fast ? "

" You're a head over me yet," replied Lory.

" Have a glass of punch ? " said Mr. Kearney.

Lory made no reply ; but the expression of his face as he drew a chair to the table was more eloquent than words.

He cast a look towards the door as if apprehending opposition from that quarter, and commenced operations in a rather hurried manner.

Mr. Kearney, who had again introduced the bull-bait, was proceeding to give them some particulars he had learned from Wat Murphy, when Lory produced another sensation by the simple remark—

" I know all about that."

Lory gulped down a mouthful of his punch, which was so hot that it brought the tears to his eyes, and hastily pushed his tumbler towards Mr. Lowe, a proceeding which rather astonished that gentleman, who seemed to think that Mr. Hanly intended to share the beverage with him.

But after looking towards the door, and finding that his sister, whose voice he had just heard in the hall, was not coming into the parlour, Lory took possession of his tumbler again, and looked at Mr. Lowe as if, on the whole, he rather thought himself in clover.

" How is your father ? " Mr. Kearney asked.

" I couldn't tell you that," replied Lory. " He's in Dublin."

Mr. Hanly the elder was an attorney ; but the nature and extent of his professional business was something of a mystery to his neighbours. He made periodical visits to the metropolis, during which he was in a manner lost to his family and friends in the country. Some inquisitive people attempted from time to time to find out his whereabouts in

Dublin, but except that he was once seen dining at a tavern in the neighbourhood of Ormond Quay, these attempts invariably proved unsuccessful. Attorney Hanly came and went like the swallows—or rather the swifts—that took periodical possession of the crevices in the old castle near his house, and no one was the wiser of where he had been, save in a general way ; for a letter to him, addressed " General Post Office, Dublin," usually reached his hands—when it suited him. He rented a not very large farm within a mile of Knocknagow, upon which he had built a handsome house, where his family always lived genteely, though somewhat economically. Attorney Hanly was eccentric, and supposed to be rich—probably because he was eccentric.

" Come, let us have a few songs from the ladies," said Mr. Kearney. " That's Miss Hanly rattling at the piano, I think."

The gentlemen followed him to the drawing-room, except the doctor, who sat with folded arms at the fire, and Lory, who waited to finish his punch.

" What's that I heard Rose and Kathleen talking about ? " Lory asked. " I couldn't get it out of them, they laughed so much. Something about you and the bog ? "

" Shut up, Lory," the doctor exclaimed, starting to his feet and filling out a glass of wine, which he swallowed with a look of distraction.

" Come," said he, after arranging his shirt-collar at the looking-glass, " finish that and let us go to them."

" Faith, I'd rather stay where I am," said Lory, looking at the decanters.

" On my honour, my dear fellow," replied the doctor, " you are not at all singular in that way of thinking. Rose and Kathleen are here ? "

" Yes, and Miss Lloyd."

" Whew ! " the doctor whistled and walked up and down the room.

" What the devil brought her ? "

" Faith, I don't know. They were all surprised when she came out with my mother on the mail-car, and walked from the cross."

" I think I understand it," said the doctor. And it was some consolation to him to reflect that Miss Lloyd's thoughts

were so concentrated upon Sir Garrett Butler's nephew, that
she probably had given no attention to his humble self and
the misadventure of the morning.

The doctor stood irresolutely at the drawing-room door,
till he heard his father say :

" Come, Grace, give us ' Who Fears to Speak of 'Ninety-
Eight ? ' "

And under cover of the song the doctor advanced and
shook hands in silence with Miss Lloyd and the two Miss
Hanlys.

Grace sang with spirit, and received the compliments of
the company with becoming dignity. She could not, however, conceal her delight when Mr. Lowe came to read the
words of the song, and ask her who was its author.

" I heard papa say," she replied, " that it was written by
one of the scholars of Trinity College. All those songs
appeared originally in the *Nation.* The airs are nearly all
old Irish airs ; but the music of that song is original."

Mr. Lowe turned to other songs in the book, and it was
with no small share of pride she told him that the writers of
some of them were " friends of her papa's."

" I should like to hear you sing this one," said he, pointing
to a song, a stanza of which he had read.

" Oh, yes ; that is one of Davis's. He was a true poet.
At first I did not admire his poetry so much. But I do
now. 'Tis so full of heart. He was an irreparable loss to
the country," she added solemnly.

" As a poet ? " Mr. Lowe asked.

" Well, yes ; but more as a patriot. You can have no idea
of how much he was beloved. I saw Mr. D——, who, papa
says, is a man of powerful intellect, burst into tears one
evening at our house, when speaking of Davis. And O'Connell,
when alluding to him after hearing of his death, said, ' I can
write no more—my tears blind me.' "

Mr. Lowe looked at her with surprise.

" Yes," she continued, as if replying to his look ; " these
are O'Connell's words."

But it was at herself he was wondering ; and Hugh and
Mary, who sat near the piano, exchanged looks and seemed
to enjoy his astonishment.

Miss Lloyd, however, was both astonished and chagrined

to find that Mr. Lowe could feel interest in the prattle of a mere child.

"I'm ashamed to acknowledge," said Mr. Lowe, still addressing himself to the little lady perched upon the stool, "that I know almost nothing about Mr. Davis. He was, I understand, a young barrister whose name seldom figured in the newspapers. But from what you tell me I must believe he was no common man."

"Papa says," she rejoined, "that his influence on the mind of the country will be felt for ever. And, young as he died, his wish was granted."

"What was his wish?"

"His wish was—

> ' Be my epitaph writ on my country's mind—
> He served his country and loved his kind ! ' "

Mr. Lowe again looked at her with surprise. But when Mary glanced at her brother this time, her glance was not returned. She saw his broad chest heave ; and a strange light, half fire, half softness, swam in his dark eyes.

Mary shook her head as she thought to herself how little they understood him who thought him cold and unsusceptible. Behind that "down look," for which Hugh Kearney got credit, there was, she was sure, a heart and a soul of no common tenderness and enthusiasm.

Miss Lloyd looked from one to the other of the group in amazement. She really could not understand what it all meant ; but there were many things which Miss Lloyd could not understand.

And besides, Miss Lloyd liked nothing half so well as the music of her own voice, which we must admit *was* musical ; so much so that it took many persons a considerable time to discover that what seemed so pleasant had nothing in it. But she had a trick of talking *to* one person and *at* another ; which was very trying to the latter—as Mr. Henry Lowe was destined to learn to his cost.

CHAPTER XVIII.

MISS LLOYD'S FOIBLES.

As we have said so much of Miss Lloyd, we shall glance at one or two more of her peculiarities.

The facility with which Miss Lloyd fell in love with every eligible young man—and occasionally with an eligible old one—that came in her way, was something marvellous, and a source of great anxiety to her family and friends. Her being still in the land of the living was a matter of daily wonderment to her sympathizing sisters—" poor Henrietta " was so often on the point of dying of a broken heart. The defection of a young ensign of nineteen produced such an effect upon her, that she spent twenty-four hours " from one fainting fit into another "—we quote the words of her own mother ; and she was known to have taken to her bed for three weeks because of the heartlessness of a widower of sixty-five who had been particular in his attentions on the occasion of his grand-daughter's marriage, Miss Lloyd being one of the bridesmaids. But Miss Henrietta Lloyd's strong point was curiosity—an all-absorbing inquisitiveness about other people and their affairs. The passion—for with her it amounted to a passion—bore down everything before it. All sense of propriety, all fear of consequences vanished like dew, in the intense heat of her desire to know what her neighbours were about. Listening at windows, dropping in uninvited at unseasonable times, stopping servants in the streets, and catechising butchers' boys, were everyday occurrences with Miss Lloyd. She had been known to rush across the street at eleven at night, and knock at Doctor Cusack's door, merely because her maid had remarked that a car had stopped there from which a man with a travelling bag had alighted. The doctor—thinking it was his assistant, whom he had sent with two bread pills to the parson's mother-in-law, who had taken suddenly ill—opened the door ; and Miss Lloyd found herself face to face with an elderly gentleman in his night-shirt, and was greeted at the same moment with a cheer from three young gentlemen of the Rev. Mr. Labart's academy, who had been making a night of it at the hotel before resuming their studies after vacation.

Miss Lloyd would slip into the kitchen for a confab with the cook during the progress of a dinner-party upstairs, her not being invited to which was meant as a deliberate slight. And we blush to say that even the apartments of single young men had no terrors for Miss Lloyd when her inquisitiveness was aroused, and could only be gratified by bearding the bachelor in his hall.

Yet, strange to say, the lady's fair fame never suffered from these peccadilloes. Her immunity in this respect, however, was partly owing to the fact that she belonged to that class of fair ones into whose " lug " the Scottish poet begged leave to whisper—

" Ye're aiblins nae temptation,"

and partly because she was a very rhinoceros to those shafts which usually wound so deeply, but which are so seldom discharged except when they can wound.

From these glimpses of Miss Lloyd's character the reader must have anticipated that two of her foibles combined to bring her this evening to Ballinaclash.

She had been on thorns during the week to get a look at Mr. Lowe ; and when Mrs. Hanly met her in the main street of Kilthubber, and casually remarked that her girls were going to tea to Mr. Kearney's in the evening, Miss Lloyd eagerly offered to accompany her home. This Mrs. Hanly really looked upon as an honour, and thought it a most unfortunate circumstance that she had come to town on the public car and was to return by the same conveyance.

" The girls," she remarked, " were returning one or two visits in the morning, and I thought it would be too late to wait for the carriage. So I took a seat on the mail car."

" Oh, no matter, my dear Mrs. Hanly," returned Miss Lloyd, " it will be quite pleasant. I know the driver of the

mail car very well. That was Mr. Labart's new servant from
Dublin that was on the car with you. I have not seen her
yet; but I'm told she has excellent discharges from her two
last places. So, my dear Mrs. Hanly, come up and I'll be
ready in a minute."

Mrs. Hanly, in the innocence of her heart, thought it would
be necessary to send an apology to Miss Kearney; as, of
course, her daughters could not think of leaving so distinguished a visitor as Miss Lloyd alone with herself during the
evening. But Miss Lloyd at once removed that difficulty by
announcing her intention of going with them.

"To be sure," said she, "I'm not personally acquainted
with them, but that makes no difference. I know their
brother, the doctor, who is a great friend of Robert's: but
I believe he is in Dublin."

"Oh, he is at home," replied Rose Hanly. "We passed
him a few hours ago in the bog. I wish you saw him."

And Rose glanced at her sister, who, so far from joining
in the laugh, looked quite huffed that her admirer should be
made sport of in such a manner.

"He is an elegant young man," Miss Lloyd observed,
gravely; "and waltzes admirably. He was at the last race
ball. I'll be delighted to meet him."

Miss Lloyd was fastening a bracelet on her wrist in a
nervous, fidgety manner, and had several pins in her mouth
while she was speaking.

"Oh, I am most unfortunate," she exclaimed, tumbling
various small articles out of her bag on the floor. "I fear I
have lost my charms."

"'Pon my word, Miss Lloyd, that is a misfortune; and
one that few would suspect you in danger of—

"' *Vacuus cantat coram latrone viator.*'"

The young lady started, and with a terrified look towards
the door, whence the sound proceeded, ran for protection to
Kathleen, and grasped her convulsively by the arm.

"Why do you come up here, sir? What business have
you in our room?" exclaimed Rose, quite in a shrewish
tone.

"To tell you that the car is at the door, and not to keep
the pony standing in the cold."

" Oh ! " gasped Miss Lloyd, with her hand pressed against her left side, " what a dreadful voice he has ! "

" I'm always at him about it," said Rose, " but I can get no good of him. And somehow you never know he's there till he speaks. He startles ourselves now as much as anybody else, as he has been at school for two years without coming home. But he's very clever," she added, evidently proud of the fact. " He took first prizes in classics. I believe that's Greek he's after talking now."

" Oh, I hope he won't talk any more Greek to me," said Miss Lloyd, drawing a long breath. " A few more such shocks would knock me up completely."

" You'll get used to it," said Rose. " In fact, it wouldn't be half so bad if you were prepared for it. But let us hurry, and not leave the poor pony to be frozen to death."

" I can't get any good of it," said Miss Lloyd despairingly.

One side of her hair was so obstinately in curl that she couldn't brush it out, and the other side was so hopelessly out of curl that she couldn't twist it in. With Kathleen's assistance, however, she fixed it somehow, and on hearing Lory rushing up the stairs again, they hurried out of the room.

" We're ready," exclaimed Rose, putting her hand on her brother's mouth, to save Miss Lloyd's nerves from another shock.

And now we find the last-mentioned lady with her elbow resting upon Mary Kearney's piano, and feeling her hair with the tips of her fingers, for the double purpose of displaying her bracelet to the best advantage, and satisfying herself as to how the refractory curl was behaving itself.

She was losing all patience at seeing Mr. Lowe throwing away so much of his time talking to " that pert little thing," while she, Henrietta Lloyd, was there for the express purpose of talking to him.

But when Rose Hanly was asked to sing, and Grace made way for her, Miss Lloyd could no longer conceal her ineffable disgust.

" Oh, really," she exclaimed, " ye are all musically mad."

To her great relief, however, the tea-tray appeared just as the song had concluded. And her good humour was quite restored when she saw they were to have tea sitting sociably round the table. Miss Lloyd shone with peculiar brilliancy at the tea table ; and she now hastened to take up a position from which she could direct her fire on Mr. Lowe through Mrs. Kearney.

"Where do you get your tea, Mrs. Kearney ? " she began. "We get ours at Phelin's," she continued, without waiting for a reply. "Mr. Hemphill recommended us to get it there."

Poor Mr. Lowe was already beginning to feel quite uncomfortable, for the lady never turned her eyes from his face for a moment.

"What strange things people will say, Mrs. Kearney ? "

Mr. Lowe looked at her inquiringly, for, from the direct stare with which she regarded him, he expected she was about accusing him of saying strange things. To his great relief, however, she continued :

"It was said in Phelin's shop that we had no fortunes."

Mr. Lowe sought relief in the bottom of his tea-cup, but failed to find it, for he felt the eyes were upon him.

"But, Mrs. Kearney, you may tell any one that asks that we have fortunes. I have two thousand, and my sisters a thousand each."

Mr. Lowe tried balancing his spoon on his finger, but the relief it afforded was only partial and temporary.

"Mr. Hemphill's son is after coming home. I have not seen him yet ; but I'm told he is an elegant young man."

Look sharp, Mr. Lowe ! Make your hay while the sun shines !

He meditated bolting from the room, but felt as if he couldn't—as if she "held him with her glittering eye," like the Ancient Mariner.

"And Robert tells me," continued Miss Lloyd, "that Mr. Hemphill is extremely intellectual."

The idea that Bob Lloyd had ever used such a phrase as "extremely intellectual" was so good a joke that both Hugh and Richard found it difficult to refrain from laughing.

But it must not be suspected that Miss Lloyd was drawing upon her imagination. She merely had recourse to a euphemism, which was her practice when quoting her brother's observations. In this instance Bob did say, in reply to a question of hers, that young Hemphill was a " bloody clever fellow," and this expression Miss Lloyd merely translated into " extremely intellectual."

" I know his brother," said Lory, from the opposite end of the table.

Miss Lloyd was in the act of putting her cup to her lips, and staring at Mr. Lowe over the brim, when Lory's remark, innocent as it may seem in print, knocked the cup out of her hand as effectually as if he had flung a projectile at it with unerring aim.

The shock was felt more or less by all present ; but when they saw Miss Lloyd with her hand in the same position as when the cup flew from it, apparently unable to move, and staring at Lory as if he had knocked the wits out of her too, a laugh that could not be suppressed went round the table. And when the nervous lady at length leant back in her chair and said faintly, " That boy is dreadful," Mr. Lowe blessed Lory in his heart for drawing her eyes upon himself.

Mrs. Kearney took the broken tea-cup in her hand ; and the good woman was inconsolable. She had not even the melancholy consolation of telling how her uncle Dan admired the pattern of this particular set ; for Richard suggested a dance at the moment, which caused a general movement among the company, and Mrs. Kearney gently laid the broken cup on the tray with a sigh.

CHAPTER XIX.

WILL SIR GARRETT RENEW THE LEASE ?

GRACE was taking her place at the piano, when Mary whispered to her that she herself would play for the dancers —an arrangement which Grace liked very well. But she looked quite offended when she saw that Mr. Lowe and the doctor had already engaged the two Miss Hanlys ; and Hugh was compelled by the exigencies of the case to offer his arm to the formidable Miss Lloyd.

"Stand up, sir," said Rose Hanly to her brother. And Lory and Grace completed the set.

"Are you long here?" Lory asked.

"Some weeks," she replied, after involuntarily moving half-a-yard away from him.

"Will you stay much longer?"

"I can't say."

"Come with me," said Lory confidentially, "and I'll show you places you never saw before."

She stared at him with unfeigned astonishment.

"I'll show you a cave," he continued, "that very few know about."

"Oh!" was her only reply. And the idea of a cave, taken in connection with her partner's voice, gave her a vague sort of impression that he lived under ground, and only visited his friends during the holidays. She looked at him more curiously than she had yet done, and thought his costume rather strengthened this notion. His coat, for instance, was evidently made for him when he was about half his present size. It was much too narrow in the shoulders ; the sleeves did not reach far below the elbows ; the buttons behind were half-way up his back ; and the skirts fell considerably short of the extremity of the spine. On the other hand, his trousers, of grey cotton tweed, was distressingly new and shiny, and very much too large ; the tailor, warned no doubt by the example of the coat, seeming to have left him " ample room and verge enough " to expand into a colossus, if he were so minded—particularly about that portion of his person which the coatskirts seemed to be straining every thread to cover, but only partially succeeded. So that Grace fancied she saw in her partner the upper half of a small boy joined to the lower half of a stout man.

She was soon struck by another peculiarity, which both surprised and distressed her. When it came near their turn to begin the figure, Lory's legs began bending and straightening at the knees. With his neck stretched forward, and staring wildly at the opposite wall, he worked up and down spasmodically to the time of the music.

Grace thought at first that the soles of his boots had, by some unaccountable means, been glued to the floor, and that he was exciting all his strength to get them free. In fact, it seemed absolutely necessary that Lory should pump himself for a minute or two before he could set off. And this getting-up of steam was more frequent than usual in consequence of Hugh's ignorance of quadrilles—and Miss Lloyd was not the sort of partner to set him right.

The doctor, who was opposite to his brother and Miss Lloyd, was greatly annoyed by these blunders; and as he seldom thought of consulting other people's wishes when his own were to be gratified, he coolly took Grace by the hand and transferred her to Hugh, handing back Miss Lloyd to Lory, who, by merely asking " did she like quadrilles ? " almost precipitated her into Maurice Kearney's lap.

This exchange of partners so bewildered Miss Lloyd, that the dance was over before she could fully realize her position.

Grace hung upon Hugh's arm, glad to escape from her late partner; and her quick eye did not fail to observe that the exchange was very welcome to Hugh too. He drew her out about Davis and other kindred subjects; but she never lost sight of the business in hand, and piloted him so deftly that there were no more mistakes till the dance was concluded.

" Wonders will never cease," said she to Mary, as she fanned herself with her handkerchief. " Fionn Macool can make himself agreeable."

" It would be strange if he could not," Mary replied, with a thoughtful smile.

The evening passed very pleasantly. Everyone who could sing, did sing—including Maurice Kearney himself, who gave them the " Cruiskeen Lawn," in excellent style. Other dances followed the first; and a polka with Sir Garrett Butler's nephew made even Miss Lloyd supremely happy.

When they reached home, the Miss Hanlys and their visitor —according to universal custom—discussed the merits of the people with whom they had spent the evening.

Kathleen was outspoken in praise of the doctor; and Miss Lloyd agreed in all she said in his praise. And Kathleen as fully shared Miss Lloyd's ecstasies on the subject of Mr. Lowe.

" Even if you separate his features," said Miss Lloyd, " he is a singularly handsome man. And what lovely hair he has ! "

" Yes," replied Kathleen, " his hair is very nice."

" And," exclaimed Miss Lloyd, clasping her hands together and turning up her eyes fervently, " did you ever see such feet with mortal ? "

" Ye may talk," said Rose, who leant on the table with her hand pressed against her forehead, as if she were suffering from headache—" ye may talk, but I'd rather have one honest smile from Hugh Kearney than all the blandishments of your elegant young man."

" 'Pon my word," replied Kathleen, opening her eyes very wide, " whatever may be thought of your taste, I cannot help admiring your candour."

" Yes, I am candid," Rose rejoined, rather crossly ; " and that's more than other people are."

The bewitching Kathleen got very red, and an angry look flashed from her eyes ; but she only stooped down, and, snatching up her lap-dog from the hearth-rug, began to fondle it assiduously.

" It really surprises me," said Miss Lloyd, " how some ladies will openly express their preferences for young men."

" *I* always do," retorted Rose. " Don't you ? "

" Well, Miss Hanly, I never forget that I am a *gentle-woman.*" And Miss Lloyd laid great stress on the word gentlewoman ; which was not very ladylike, however gentle-womanly, seeing that she meant to remind her friends that their claims to gentility—in her sense of the word—were not quite as strong as her own.

" Well," rejoined Rose, who did not want pluck. " I can't boast of much of your acquaintance. But from all I have heard of you, I am under the impression that you are in the habit of coming out pretty strong with regard to your pre-ferences for young men—and old ones too," added Rose—we fear in allusion to the widower.

Miss Lloyd turned away in disdain, and resumed her conversation with Kathleen, who became quite tender and sentimental about " Poor Richard," as she affectionately called the doctor.

And Miss Lloyd certainly did not practise what she preached, for she did come out very strong indeed in praise of Mr. Lowe.

The next day, when her s ers inquired how she liked her

new acquaintance, Miss Lloyd put her handkerchief to her eyes, and bursting into a flood of tears, declared that she was "as fond of him as she was of her life."

Before going to bed, Maurice Kearney insisted upon having a comfortable glass by the fire with his guest.

"Pender is to come again to see you to-morrow," said he. "He had a letter from your uncle."

"Indeed!" exclaimed the young gentleman, looking rather blank. It flashed upon him that he had already spent—he could not, at the moment, remember how many days—on his uncle's Tipperary estate, and knew as much about it as the man in the moon.

"I wonder," continued Maurice Kearney, "did he say anything about the lease?"

"I really cannot imagine," replied his guest, absently. And, at that moment, Mr. Lowe could imagine nothing except that Mary Kearney was the most angelic being in creation.

"Times are changed," added the host, thoughtfully. "I expect he will allow me for the drainage. I wish he'd come to see the place himself. I could show him forty acres of nice land where I found him the day he sprained his knee, with his horse sunk up to the girths in a shaky bog. I lost a hatful of money by it."

"You lost more than the fee-simple is worth," said Hugh.

"I don't know how much I lost by it," replied his father, rubbing his head uneasily ; "but when I began, I didn't like to stop and throw the men out of employment."

"I can tell you what you lost by it," said Hugh.

"Poor Mr. Butler," Mrs. Kearney observed, "suffered a great deal from that accident. We had him here for six weeks. But he was as gentle as a child, and when he began to get ease from the pain he desired me to write for my Uncle Dan ; and sure so I did, and he brought his violin, and Mr. Butler sent for his flute ; and 'twas beautiful to listen to them. 'Twas the year after he was shipwrecked coming from abroad. And when the poor dear gentleman went away, the house was quite lonesome after him. Richard was born in the month of March after. And sure, I suppose," added Mrs. Kearney, contemplatively, "that's the reason he has such a taste for music."

Hugh had left the room unobserved, and now appeared

with his ledger, and, laying it on the table, he began turning over the leaves.

"For God's sake shut that book—I hate the sight of it," exclaimed his father, with a gesture of impatience.

"I thought you wanted to know what the drainage cost," said Hugh.

"I don't want to know it. What good would it do me to know it? And sure a man couldn't do anything if he was to keep an account of every penny that way."

Hugh smiled, and put the obnoxious book out of sight.

"Good night, Mr. Lowe!" exclaimed Maurice Kearney, jumping suddenly from his chair in quite a lively manner. "I'm going to the fair to-morrow, and must be half-way to C—— before daybreak."

"Ah, then," said his wife, "will you try and get a match for that cup Miss Lloyd broke? And I'm afraid you can't. I wouldn't wish it for anything."

"I will—I will," he replied. "Tell Norry to give it to Tom Maher, and let him remind me of it."

"I'm surprised she should be so awkward," continued Mrs. Kearney, returning to her grievance. "But it was all that young Hanly's fault. I declare he frightened the life out of me."

Mrs. Kearney remained buried in thought for a minute, and then added, solemnly:

"Don't be talking; but he has a terrible throat!"

This allusion to Lory elicited so loud a laugh from Hugh, that the doctor, who had been asleep in an arm-chair, started up and rubbed his eyes.

"There's eleven striking, Richard," said his mother, "and you are tired, and ought to go to bed."

"It is time for us all to go," Hugh remarked.

And he and Mr. Lowe and the doctor retired each to his own room.

But Hugh hurried on before the doctor, and thrust the second-hand clarionet under the bed, lest the idea of the fair Kathleen operating upon that taste for music which his mother had so satisfactorily accounted for, should interfere with the slumbers of the household.

And the clarionet not being in the doctor's way, every soul under Maurice Kearney's roof was resting in peace and quietness when the clock struck twelve.

CHAPTER XX.

MR. LOWE GETS A LETTER OF WARNING.

NEXT day, as the doctor was proposing another walk to the Castle, Barney Brodherick was seen cantering from the avenue gate, mounted upon the little black donkey, Bobby, which he regarded as his own peculiar property.

" Let us wait," said Hugh, " he may have some letters."

Barney rode up to the window, and handed in the letters and newspapers he had brought from the crossroads, where, as usual, he had met the mail-car.

There was a letter for Mr. Lowe.

" I think," Hugh suggested, as he tore off the cover of a newspaper, " you had better read your letter before going out. You may want to reply to it."

The letter was from Mr. Lowe's mother, and as the contents may help us on with our story, we give a few extracts:

" I am very uneasy, my dearest Henry," the lady began, " since I have received a letter from young Mr. Pender, in which he speaks of the dreadful state of the country in that locality. He has been fired at three times during the last fortnight, and would have captured one of the assassins on the last occasion only that his horse took fright and ran away with him. The horse, unfortunately, was a borrowed one, and not accustomed to stand fire. But if he had had his own horse, there can scarcely be a doubt but that he would have made prisoners of at least two of the gang. He could not use his pistols, they set upon him so suddenly, but he felled one of the miscreants to the earth, and the other two took to flight after discharging their blunderbusses at him, but fortunately without effect, except that a slug from one of them lodged in his nose. It has been extracted, and the doctors do not think the wound dangerous. But why do I go on telling you those things when, of course, you know all the particulars of the dreadful affair. He is a very brave young man, but generous to a fault. He begs me not to tell Sir Garrett, lest he should eject all the tenants from the townland where this shocking outrage occurred. For the same reason he has only given a very guarded account of it to the local papers. But of course the whole truth must come out at the trial, when the assassins are arrested, which I think they will be, as Mr. Pender has described them minutely to the police. He thinks it a duty he owes to society to prosecute them to conviction. . . . .

" Oh, my dear Henry, I have quite changed my mind about the agency. Bad as India is, it is not so bad as a place where such dreadful occurrences could take place in the middle of the noon-day—or what is all the same, for it was not long after sunset in the evening. I will never consent to your exposing your life in such a manner. . . . . .

" Mr. P. speaks of other things which I do not like to allude to in this letter. What sort of people are the Kearneys ?— I mean the younger members of the family. The old man seems good-natured and harmless, and your uncle thinks highly of his wife, at whose hands he says he experienced much kindness long ago ; but then he was always so un-suspicious and unworldly, he is apt to view things in the most favourable light. Have you noticed anything peculiar about his eldest son ?   My dearest Henry, *be care-ful*. . . . . I understand his daughter is good-looking and has got some education. Well, I know something of the world, and, take my word for it, girls of this kind, par-ticularly when they are educated above their rank, are the most *designing* creatures in existence. Your poor uncle should be a warning to you. But I ought to beg your pardon for supposing you so simple as to require any warning. . . . . . Your cousin has not yet returned— I trust you have written to her from the country. I have discovered that there is nothing she admires so much as *daring*. So, if you want to interest her, give her an account of the perils by which you are surrounded. She is most anxious that her father should settle in that part of the country ; and as he humours her in everything, it will not surprise me if he gets possession of Woodlands again, after old Mr. Somerfield's death, as his is the last life in the lease.

You ought to call and see if the place is in good repair. It was a lovely place when I was a girl, and it was there that I spent the happiest days of my life. And if those outrages could be put down—a Coercion Act is talked of—it would be a great pleasure to me to revisit the scenes of my youth. Let me know if Mrs. Lloyd, of Mount Tempe, be alive."

The young gentleman was considerably bewildered by this production. He did not know what to think of it. He seldom gave himself the trouble of thinking about anything. But the allusion to his host's daughter made his cheek flush; and between Mr. Beresford Pender's nose and Mary Kearney's eyes, things were becoming mixed in the mind of Mr. Henry Lowe.

" Unpleasant news," said Grace in a whisper to Mary.

" What is it ? " Mary asked, looking at her anxiously.

" I'm sure I can't tell you ; but look at him."

" Oh, is it Mr. Lowe you mean ? Well, I can see nothing unusual in his look."

" Well," Hugh asked, " does your letter require an immediate answer ? "

" No, no," he replied with affected carelessness. " 'Tis from my mother ; and she wants to know," he added, glancing through the letter to hide his embarrassment, " if Mrs.—Mrs. Lloyd, of Mount Temple, is alive."

" It is Mount Tempe," said Mary, " She is mother of the lady you saw here last night."

" I ought to have remembered ; we were at Mount Tempe yesterday."

" And did you meet Mr. Lloyd ? "

" Yes, we spent some time with him, and he joined us at the snipe shooting."

" Oh, I said you must have been reinforced," said Grace, " the volleys increased so much towards evening."

He was a little afraid of Grace's ridicule, and thought it wise to turn the conversation from the shooting as quickly as possible.

" My mother also wants to know," he observed, again glancing at the letter, " whether Woodlands is kept in good repair, and she says something about old Mr. Somerfield."

" The old fellow is alive," said Hugh, " and wonderfully

strong and active for his age. He cannot be far short of ninety, and yet he is never missed from the hunt."

" And how does he keep the place ? I mean the house and grounds."

" Oh ! in excellent order—nothing could be better. In fact, he has expended a large sum of money on improvements."

" Does he not pay a considerable rent for it ? "

" Well, my father could tell you all about it. Your late uncle was, I think, in want of money, and set the place to Somerfield. I suspect the rent cannot be very high, as I heard my father say there was a large fine given."

" By the way," said Mr. Lowe, somewhat hesitatingly, " have there been any outrages of a remarkable character lately in this neighbourhood ? I find some allusion to something of the kind in this letter."

" No," replied Hugh, " there has been nothing of the kind about here. But I find a paragraph in this paper referring to a threatening notice which was found nailed to a door seven or eight miles from here."

" No one has been fired at ? "

" Not that I know of. There is an unusually large number of ejectments served this year ; and when that is the case, rumours of outrages are always flying about."

" Are any of my uncle's tenants served with ejectments ? "

" Yes," Hugh replied, gravely, " two very honest and industrious men. I believe they owe some arrears. There is a good deal of anxiety among the other tenants. But," he added, as if he wished to change the subject, " I don't know all the particulars. Perhaps it would be well if you inquired into them. Indeed, I think, the landlord ought to come and see for himself how things are going on here."

" I believe he places great confidence in the agent," said Mr. Lowe.

" It would appear so," Hugh replied. " But as he has come to Ireland, it might be no harm for him to see personally how his estate is managed. Things have gone on smoothly enough up to this ; but since the leases given by Sir Thomas have begun to drop, there is considerable uneasiness. My father will tell you that before now leases were renewed as a matter of course : but latterly there is a remarkable reluctance on the part of landlords to give leases, and your uncle's tenants are uneasy lest he should follow the example set by others in this respect."

" I don't know much about the matter," said Mr. Lowe ; " but I should think it very unlikely that my uncle would act unjustly towards any one."

" That's just what I say," replied Hugh ; " and that is why I'd like to see him using his own eyes."

" I should say this is Mr. Pender," said Mr. Lowe, who sat near the window. " At least he answers in some respects to Mr. Kearney's description of him last night. He has a gun on each side of him. Yes," he added, as the person in question alighted from his gig, " and pistols in his belt."

" It is he," replied Hugh, coming to the window.

Mr. Beresford Pender, observing that the gentleman he wanted to see had a full view of him from the window, took off his belt and handed it, with the pistols in it, to his servant. Then walking to the hall door, he knocked loudly.

" Is Mr. Lowe within ? " Mr. Pender asked in a mighty voice that seemed to come up from his chest.

" I'll see, sir," said the servant.

Mr. Pender faced round, and with folded arms glared up at the tall trees on either side of the cottage, and then looked scowlingly at the top of the mountain in front.

" This is a nice place Kearney has here," muttered Mr. Beresford Pender to himself. " A nice thing it is to see fellows of this kind in a place like this, and gentlemen in thatched houses without as much as a tree to shelter them. He has a good deal of planting done here. Nice work for farmers. By ——," exclaimed Mr. Pender, swearing almost loud enough to be heard within, " if I had to deal with them they'd have something else to mind besides planta-tions."

" Yes, sir," said the servant girl, opening the drawing-room door ; and Mr. Pender strode in, glancing round him with a look in which sheepishness and something like timidity were curiously blended.

In fact, Mr. Pender looked as if he thought it possible that he might be kicked out. But finding there was no one in the room, he got up his fierce look, and brought it to bear on the mountain-top again.

Mr. Lowe came in, and, as he closed the door behind him, the runaway look came back into Mr. Pender's eyes. Reassured, however, by the polite bow of the gentleman, Mr. Pender said :

"I called to see you because I wanted to spake to you."

"Yes," replied Mr. Lowe. "I was told you called yesterday."

"I suppose you know my father is agent over the property for the last thirty years?" said Mr. Pender.

"I'm aware he is the agent, and I intended calling on him, but have put it off from day to day."

Mr. Beresford Pender commenced patting the bridge of his nose with his fingers, and Mr. Lowe observed that there was a bit of sticking-plaster adhering to the organ, which, we may remark, was of the flexible order, as if nature intended it to be tweaked ; or it may be that it was tweaking made it flexible.

"Do you think," he asked, dropping his big voice to a sepulchral whisper, "that you are safe here?"

"Why? What danger do you suppose I have to apprehend?"

"I don't like to say much," said Mr. Beresford Pender. "But, as a friend, I came to see you."

There was something so mysterious in his look, that, between it and the sepulchral whisper, Mr. Lowe began to feel impressed with the notion that Mr. Beresford Pender was a person of consequence.

"You'll see my father," continued Mr. Pender, resuming his big voice, which still further impressed Mr. Lowe with the idea that he was talking to a great man, "and spend a few days with him."

"It is my intention to see him."

"There's to be a meeting one of those days," said Mr. Pender.

"What sort of meeting?"

Mr. Beresford Pender hesitated, as if in doubt whether Mr. Lowe was a proper person to communicate with on the subject of the meeting.

"I'll tell you about it another time ; I'll be speaking to some of the gentlemen at the road-sessions to-day."

Mr. Lowe looked at him and really began to feel uneasy.

"They're quare times," said Mr. Beresford Pender. "Good morning. I'll tell my father you'll call to see him."

Mr. Beresford Pender walked out ; and it was not till he had watched him for some time as he carefully examined his pistols and buckled the belt around him, that Mr. Lowe discovered that Mr. Beresford Pender was not a very large, stout man. In fact, he was under the middle height, and rather lank than otherwise. But, between the big voice and the big look, he really often impressed people with the idea that he was a big man.

"Good gracious, Mary !" exclaimed Grace, who was observing Mr. Pender's movements from behind the window curtain, " he is like an alderman in front. But look at him behind, and he's like a pump. He'd want to wear a bustle."

"Oh, fie," said Mary, "what would Mr. Lowe say if he heard you make such a remark ? "

"I suppose it would be quite unpardonable if I remarked also that the servant's coat, with the distressingly large and bright livery buttons, is an old frock-coat of his master's."

"Nothing can escape you," said Mary, laughing ; " I'd never have noticed it if you had not pointed it out."

It occurred to Mr. Lowe that Mr. Pender had made no allusion to the several attempts upon his life ; and he stepped outside the door to satisfy his curiosity before Mr. Pender had got into his gig.

"You wrote to my mother lately," observed Mr. Lowe.

"Yes," replied Mr. Pender. "You know she has a rent-charge on Cahirdeheen, and I see to it myself. 'Tisn't aisy to manage them fellows."

"But you spoke of being attacked by five men ? "

"They were hired," replied Mr. Beresford Pender. "But I don't like to transport him." And as he spoke he looked at the parlour window, from which Mary quickly retreated, a little vexed at being seen by him.

"I'll tell you all about it another time," he added, " but keep what I'm after telling you to yourself."

Mr. Lowe did not know what to think, and was about shaking hands with his new acquaintance, when the latter said—

"Nice girl ! "

Very inoffensive and harmless words in themselves ; but there was something in Mr. Beresford Pender's manner of uttering them, as he glanced at the parlour window, that made Mr. Henry Lowe feel an almost uncontrollable impulse to kick Mr. Beresford Pender then and there.

"Good morning," said he, turning upon his heel and drawing back his hand before Mr. Beresford Pender had touched it.

CHAPTER XXI.

FIVE SHILLINGS' WORTH OF DANCE.

"WELL, what a contrast !" Grace exclaimed. "Do come here, Mary, and look on this picture and on this. Apollo is really a divinity near that satyr."

Mary could see Mr. Lowe and Mr. Beresford Pender from where she sat at the table writing.

"You are right," said she, with an emphasis that made Grace open her eyes.

" 'Pon my honour, Mary, you *can* be energetic occasion-ally."

Mary was so absorbed in her own reflections, she took no notice of this observation. She thought to herself that Mr. Lowe was a person to be liked ; and the more she saw of him, the better she liked him. The thought even occurred to her that, if there was no difference of rank or religion between them, she could like him sufficiently well to be happy with him as his wife. There was not one among the young men who honoured her with their attentions whose character she could admire so much—that is, assuming her estimate of Mr. Lowe's character to be correct.

But Mary Kearney felt her heart sinking within her at the thought that there was a hard struggle before her—that a victory should be gained over herself before she could think of any one as a husband.

She took the note Barney had thrown up to Grace in the window, and read it over.

" I fear," she murmured—and the tears welled into her eyes—" I fear he thinks I refused to see him."

She moved away the letter she had been writing, and placed a clean sheet of notepaper in its stead. She wrote the date at the top of the sheet, and then stopped irresolutely.

There was a careworn look in her face as she leant back in her chair, pressing her left hand against her bosom.

"May God direct me what to do!" she murmured.

"Did you speak?" Grace asked.

"No," she replied, recovering herself, "or if I did it was to myself."

"To whom are you writing?"

"To Anna."

"Oh, really that young lady's head is very full of romance. 'Tis to be hoped she'll find the *beau monde* all her fancy painted it. How long is she in Belgium now? I can't remember."

"Nearly two years," Mary replied.

"And all that time in the convent! 'Tis dreadful," returned Grace, shuddering.

"Do you feel it so dreadful yourself?" Mary asked.

"Oh, I have a visit from my friends sometimes, and can come home at vacation. But even that is hard enough," she added, with a sigh.

"I thought you always liked being at school. At least you told me so when I went to see you."

Grace shuggered her shoulders, but made no reply.

"Am I to suppose that you only said it to please Mrs. Clare? Is that your sincerity?"

"No; I really was sincere," replied Grace. "I did like being at school then. But, my dear Mary," she added, with a pensive shake of the head, "'tis quite different since I got notions."

Though Mary was just then in anything but a laughing mood, she could not help laughing at this; and the laugh, she felt, did her good.

"If you got your choice," she asked, "would you remain at home and never go back to school again?"

Grace remained silent for a moment, and then said, in a low, firm voice:

" I would go back."

" And why would you go back if you think it so dreadful ? "

" Because it would be right."

" Yes," said Mary, looking at her with surprise, " we ought all to do what is right. Duty before all things."

" When I am sure it is right to do anything," said Grace " I try to do it, no matter how hard it is."

" You are a little heroine," rejoined Mary. " But," she added to herself, glancing at the sheet of paper before her, " it is not always easy to know what is right."

" I think," said Grace, coming to the table, " I'll write a few lines to Anna."

" Oh, do ; she will be delighted ; she was very fond of you."

" Why do people say that you will be a nun ? " Grace asked. " I suspect it is Anna will be the nun, in spite of her fine talk about the *beau monde*. But why *do* they say that you will be a nun ? Mrs. Xavier is quite sure that you will."

" I really don't know," replied Mary, blushing.

" Oh, 'tis because you are such a mild Madonna, I suppose," said Grace, dipping her pen in the ink. " But on second thoughts," she added, " I won't write till to-morrow. I must turn it in my head, as I want to let her see that one can do something in the way of rounded periods without going to Belgium. And, besides, I must have a few French phrases. So finish your letter, and I'll just run out to see what Apollo is going to do with himself."

" I think you ought to go to Ellie—she is all alone."

" Ellie ! She doesn't want me. Her whole soul is wrapped in her goldfinch."

" Oh, that reminds me," said Mary, " that we must go to see poor Norah Lahy to-day."

" I would like to go," said Grace, thoughtfully. " That is," she added, correcting herself, " I know I ought to like to go. But oh ! 'tis saddening to look at her. It so reminds one of dying young. And, besides, I fear I hurt her mother's feelings the other day."

" You did not do it intentionally."

" Oh, indeed, no. But you know—

> ' Evil is wrought by want of thought,
> As well as by want of heart.' "

" You do not want either heart or thought, Grace. The remark you made was natural enough under the circumstances ; and you did not know Mrs. Lahy was listening to you. Now, would you not do almost anything for that poor sick girl ? "

" I would," Grace replied ; " but I'm ashamed to confess I feel a strong wish to keep away from her, and not even think of her."

" But if it be right ? "

" I will go," said Grace in the same tone as when she said she would go back to school.

Grace went to a cupboard, and, getting upon a chair, took something from the upper shelf, and was leaving the room hastily.

" And where are you going now ? " Mary asked, with some surprise.

" To Ellie," she replied. " I have some sugar for her goldfinch."

Mary smiled approvingly, and then, resting her forehead upon the back of her open hand, with which she covered the few words she had written on the sheet of notepaper, as if she wished to hide them from herself, she fell into deep thought.

" Oh, yes," she said, raising her head, " if we could be sure what is right to be done ! But how can there be anything wrong in it ? I think it is because I so much *wish* to write that I am afraid to do it. But, though my heart says 'Yes,' the 'still small voice' says 'No.' I would consult Hugh only it would add to his trouble. I wonder might Anna meet him before she comes home. But that is a foolish idea ; she is as far out of his way as I am myself."

The idea, however, reminded her of the letter she had been writing to her sister, and she took up the pen and resolved to finish it.

" Is Mr. Pender gone ? " Hugh asked, as he came round to the front of the house, from the yard, where he had been giving some directions to his workmen ; " I thought his visit would not be so short."

" Yes, he is gone," replied Mr. Lowe, who was trying to open the gate of the little garden under Mary's window, and thinking of those mysterious tracks in the snow ; which somehow he found himself often thinking of, though the tracks were no longer there, for the snow itself had disappeared.

" There is already," he remarked, " a look of spring in the sky."

" Yes," Hugh replied, " and the snow is nearly gone from the hills."

" I am always glad," said Richard, who had joined them, "when winter is past. The bright summer-time for me ! "

" Why, every one is glad at the approach of spring," replied Mr. Lowe.

" I never see the snow fading from those hills," said Hugh, " without a feeling of sadness."

" That's an odd feeling," returned the doctor, " particularly for a farmer."

" Oh, of course, I see *reason* to rejoice at the coming of spring. But what I speak of is an involuntary feeling of sadness. 'Tis like parting with an old friend. In fact, I believe there is sadness in all partings. I can fancy a prisoner looking round his dungeon for the last time with a sigh."

" Who is this coming down the hill ? " the doctor asked, pointing to a horseman on the road.

" I think it is your friend, Mr. Lloyd," replied Hugh. " 'Tis his horse, at all events."

" Yes, 'tis Bob—I know him now." And Richard vaulted over the little gate and got out on the road by the stile in the corner of the garden with the intention of intercepting Mr. Lloyd, and having a talk with him.

" The harriers are to meet at Somerfield's," said the doctor, after vaulting back again over the gate. " We ought to go."

" By-the-by, 'twill be a good opportunity for you to see the place," said Hugh. " You can have my horse ; and I think you will like him."

" And yourself ? " said Mr. Lowe.

" Well, I find I have some business to attend to, which I cannot put off. You can ride the old mare," he added,

turning to his brother. " And you need not fear but she'll
be able to carry you—but give her head and let her have
her own way."

" All right," said the doctor, " let us go fit ourselves
out."

Mr. Lowe readily assented, glad of the opportunity to
display his horsemanship and his new breeches and boots.

The horses were led round by Barney, and while Hugh
was examining the girths and stirrup-leathers, the two young
men appeared booted and spurred, and were in the saddles
before Barney had time to render them any assistance.

" O Mary ! " Grace exclaimed, bursting into the parlour,
" do come and see Apollo. He looks splendid."

Mary came to the window and said, with a quiet smile :
" He really does."

The horse was a fine one, and the rider seemed to linger
longer than was necessary arranging his bridle rein.

" Do come out," said Grace ; " he expects it."

Mary followed her out, and dropping her arm round Grace's
shoulder, she said gaily :

" She says, Mr. Lowe, that you look splendid."

He raised his hat and smiled, as he rode slowly after the
doctor, who had set off at a gallop, and was impatiently
waiting for him at the gate.

" Mr. Hugh," said Barney, " how much do you think is
comin' to me ? "

" Why so ? " Hugh asked, as he watched the paces of his
horse up the hill.

" Begob, I want five shillings," replied Barney.

" For what ? "

" I'm afther gettin' two an' sixpence worth of dance from
Mr. Callaghan," returned Barney, looking as if, on the whole,
he was not pleased with his bargain.

" Two-and-sixpence worth of dance," Grace exclaimed,
laughing. " How is it sold, Barney ? "

" Tuppence-ha'penny a lesson for plain dance, Miss,"
replied Barney, seriously, " and thruppence for figures."

" Well, and you want five shillings' worth ? " said Hugh.

" Well, you see, sir," rejoined Barney, scratching his head,
" I was purty good at the plain dance ; but Callaghan had
such fine steps, I said to myself I'd get a few new wans

An' then they persuaded me to learn the figures ; but begob
I couldn't keep 'em in my head. And now, you know, I
don't like to see my money goin' for nothin'," Barney added
with the air of a man of business.

" Will you let us see one of Callaghan's steps, Barney ? "
said Grace.

" An' welcome, Miss," replied Barney, throwing care to
the winds—for the idea of his money going for nothing
seemed to have quite a crushing effect upon his spirits—
" I'll do a step or two in a double for you."

And Barney, after going round gracefully in a circle to his
own music, commenced battering the gravel with those
remarkable feet which procured for him the *soubriquet* of
" Wattletoes," in a style which we are not mad enough to
attempt a description of.

" O Hugh," said Grace, who could hardly speak for laughing, " you must give him the five shillings."

" Would I doubt you, Miss Grace ? " exclaimed Barney,
twisting his features in a most extraordinary manner, but
ultimately allowing them to settle into a grin of delight.

" Sound man, Mr. Hugh," he added, as Hugh presented
him with two half-crowns. " An' now give me lave to run
over to the Cross."

" What do you want there ? " Hugh asked.

" Callaghan is goin' away to-day," replied Barney.

" Then he gave you credit, and you want to pay your
debts ? "

" Oh, the devil a credit," returned Barney. " What a fool
he is ! "

" I can't make out what he means," said Hugh.

" Is not that Callaghan himself passing the gate ? " said
Mary, pointing to a little man with a bundle in his hand
walking at a brisk pace from the direction of the hamlet.

" Oh, the rascal," cried Barney, " an' all my dance in his
pocket ! "

He set off in pursuit of the dancing-master as if his very
life depended upon catching him.

" Can you solve this mystery, Grace ? " said Mary.

" Really, no," she replied, shaking her head. " 'Tis too
much for me. We must wait till he comes back."

But the dancing-master was too far off to hear Barney

shouting after him, and Barney was soon too much out of breath to continue the shouting, so that both were lost to view at the turn of the road.

"He was gaining upon him," said Grace. "I think he will catch him before they reach the fort. But what does he mean?"

About an hour later, as they were setting out to visit Norah Lahy, Grace said:

"Wait a moment till I ask Barney what he wanted with the dancing-master.. I can't make head or tail of it."

"I'm glad to hear it," returned Mary. "I was beginning to fear you had some connection with the 'good people.'"

"I must repress my curiosity," said Grace, after inquiring for Barney. "He is gone to drive home the cows."

The cows referred to were at a farm some two miles from the house, and it was near sunset when Barney returned After "bailing" them in, he hastened to the barn, where Mat Donovan and Tom Maher had been at work. Their day's work was over, and Tom was just hanging the door on its hinges. Barney began at once to practise his steps on the well-swept floor.

"Blood-an-ounkers, Mat," he exclaimed, stopping suddenly, as if a happy thought had struck him, "I believe you are able to read writin'."

"Well, I believe I could," Mat replied, as he shook the chaff from his coat before putting it on. "Why so?"

Barney pulled off his caubeen, and pulled a large crumpled document from the crown.

"Read that," said he.

Mat went to the door, and unfolding the paper, held it to the light, which was beginning to fade.

Barney watched him as if he entertained doubts of Mat's ability to read writing. After a little delay, however, Mat read the words "Haste to the Wedding," which had the effect of sending Barney with a bound to the middle of the floor.

"Go on," he shouted excitedly, crushing his hat tight upon his head. And with his arms extended, as if he were going to fly, Barney commenced whistling "Haste to the Wedding."

"What the divil do you mane?" Mat asked in astonishment.

" Read on ; read, read," said Barney, breathlessly, trying
to whistle and talk at the same time.

" Oh, I see what you're at now," said Mat the Thrasher,
as if a new light had dawned upon him.   " I see what you're
up to," he repeated seriously.   " But faith I don't know that
I could read print in ' double ' time, let alone writin'."

" Oh, if you couldn't ! " And Barney took the paper and
replaced it in the crown of his hat, with a look of a man
who had been made a disgustingly inadequate offer for some
article he wanted to sell.

CHAPTER XXII.

THE BLUE BODY-COAT WITH GILT BUTTONS—ABSENCE OF MIND.
" AULD LANG SYNE."

" MAT," exclaimed Barney, brightening up suddenly, " ye'll
have a great night uv id at Ned Brophy's weddin'. Is id at
the young woman's house the weddin' is to be ? "

" No," Mat replied, putting on his coat ; " they're on'y
going to be married there. The weddin' is to be at Ned's."

" 'Twas said there was to be no weddin'," observed Tom
Maher ; " how was that ? "

" Well, the girl's father is hard," replied Mat, " an' the
priest is chargin' a show of money for marryin' 'em, and so
the ould fellow wouldn't agree to the weddin'."

" Some people do be very cute," said Tom Maher.

" And," Mat continued, " Ned's mother stood out agin him
till I brought her round, and she gev into id at last."

" She'd skin a flint," returned Tom Maher.

" The divil a lie in that," replied Mat, shaking his head.

" Sure the divil a bone in her body I don't know," continued Tom ; " an' good raison I had, livin' in one house
wud her for two years an' three months."

" I won't contradict you," said Mat, " though she's my
own fust and second cousin."

"Do you remember what you tould her about the stir-about?" Tom asked, eyeing the Thrasher with a smile.

"What was that?" said Mat.

"You tould her to bring out the pot an' empty it on the top of Corrigeen Hill, an' the divil a greyhound in the barony would be able to ketch id afore id got to the bottom. We got betther stirabout ever afther."

"Well, to give her her due," returned Mat, "she always minded anything I'd say. Ned himself could get no good uv her about the weddin' till I persuaded her. Not that I cared about it myself, only I didn't like to have Ned get the name of bein' a screw."

"A bad right any wan would have to call Ned a screw," said Tom Maher. "There's not a dacenter man from this to himself for his manes."

"He is that," replied Mat.

"No sign of anything here this turn," Tom observed, with a motion of his thumb towards the house. "Though they say there's many an eye after her. Faith, Kitty tells me," he added, dropping his voice, "that she has the heart across in this young fellow from England. An', begor, a nice fellow he is, although he has no property, on'y what'll buy a commission for him."

"I don't say Miss Mary 'd think uv him," replied Mat, "no matther what he had."

"I don't know that," returned Tom with a wink. "She's mighty sweet on him. But Kitty tells me," he added, "she'll never think of any man but the wan."

"Who is that?"

"Begor, that's what I can't make out. What are you delayin' for?"

"I was thinkin' of waitin' till the master 'd be home to know how is pigs. If there was a stir I'd sell them two I have, male is so dear."

"I'd like to see you in a farm of your own," said Tom, "like every wan belongin' to you."

"I don't know that, Tom," Mat rejoined. "A man ought to be continted; an', thanks be to God, I was never in the want uv a shillin'. An' maybe if I had what you say, I wouldn't lie down to-night wud as aisy a mind as I have now."

" Here is the masther," exclaimed Barney, running out to take the horse.

Mat followed, to inquire about the price of pigs ; and after being satisfied on that head, he turned to Tom Maher, who was locking the barn-door, and asked him to " take a walk over."

" I can't stir till Mr. Richard and Mr. Lowe comes home," Tom replied. " I must put up the horses. An' a d—d hard job I'll have uv id, for I must have 'em like a new pin."

Mat Donovan went on his way alone. There was a feeling of melancholy upon him which he could not shake off ; and instead of " shortening the road " with snatches of old songs he fell into deep thought.

For the first time in his life he began to feel discontented with his lot. It was quite true, as he had just said to Tom Maher, that he never wanted for a shilling. He had constant employment, and as he was never a " spender," he found his earnings sufficient for his wants. His mother and sister were " good managers," and their poultry and eggs went far to keep them decently clothed—with the addition of even a little inexpensive finery for Nelly, who was a belle in her way—and a couple of fat pigs paid the rent. The little " garden " he held—by which we do not mean the " haggart " where Tommy Lahy had his crib set among the " curly "—gave him potatoes every second year, and a crop of wheat or barley in the intervals. The year he had the wheat or barley on his own " little spot," the potatoes were supplied by a half-acre of " dairy ground " or " dung ground." The dung ground, we may inform the uninitiated reader, is ground upon which the peasant puts his own manure, in return for which he has the potato crop— the farmer being repaid for the use of his land for one season by the corn crop of the next, for which the land, owing to the peasant's manure, is in proper condition. For the dairy ground the peasant pays a rent—and often an unconscionably high rent—the land in this case either being manured by the farmer, or capable of yielding potatoes without manure—generally a " bawn " or newly-ploughed pasture field.

Mat Donovan laboured cheerfully during the six days of

the week, returning generally at night to his own house, where he sat by the bright little hearth as happy as a king. But this evening we find him returning to that happy fireside with something very like a heavy heart. Let us listen to him, and we may be able to divine the cause of this :

" I know," said Mat Donovan, looking towards a hill on the left-hand side of the road—" I know she has a respect for me, an' always had ; an' she was never a-shy or ashamed to show id either. She kem and sot next to me the night at Mrs. Murphy's, an' her grandfather an' a lot uv farmers and dacent people there." And here Mat raised his head with a decidedly consequential look ; for he remembered when the reckoning was called after " the night at Mrs. Murphy's," he, Mat Donovan, flung down a half-crown, while many of the farmers gave only a shilling, and it required some screwing to get an additional sixpence out of them when it was found the collection fell short of the sum required. " She did then," continued Mat, " an' didn't mind 'em wan taste ; but talked to myself so pleasant and friendly ; and reminded me uv the time, long ago, when she was a little thing goin' to school, when I used to throw the churries over the hedge to her. An' faith," he added, " I b'lieve 'tis lookin' at her copy paper, when I'd meet her on the road in the evenin', that made me able to read writin', as Barney said I was—for 'tis little I minded id whin I was goin' to school myse'f. My heart warmed to her when she kem up to me at Mrs. Murphy's, wud such a smile, and shook hands wud me, after not seein' a sight uv her for goin' an two years, while she was at her aunt's, in Dublin. But, sure, I know a poor man like me have no right to think uv her. An' for all, her smile is before me every hour uv the day ; an' bad cess to me but I think, this blessed minit, 'tis her hand I have a hoult uv instead uv this flail that I am bringin' home to put a new gad on id. 'Tis droll," he continued, shaking his head. " I, that had my fling among 'em all, an' never lost a wink uv sleep on account uv any girl that ever was born, to be this way ! Sally Mockler called me a rag on every bush, no later than last night. Faith, I wish it was thrue for her— but for all that," he added, with another shake of the head and a sorrowful smile, " I b'lieve if I could dhrive her from my mind in the mornin' I wouldn't thry."

" God save you, Mat !" exclaimed two or three young men who came up with him.   " Faith, you're takin' your time."

" God save you kindly, b'ys.   I am takin' the world aisy."

" Any strange news ?"

" No, then," Mat replied ; " nothin' worth relatin'."

" Is Ned Brophy's match settled for certain ?"

" Well, I b'lieve so."

" Sure, you ought to know.   But there was talks uv id bein' broke."

" Well, no ; 'tis all settled.   They're to be married next Wednesday."

" People wor sayin' he was thinkin' uv Nancy Hogan— but she hadn't the shiners."

" People say many things," replied Mat, as if he wished to dismiss the subject.

" Begor, Nancy 'd be good enough for him ; she's the pur- tiest girl in the parish.   Was he long afther this wan he's gettin' ?"

" I don't say there was much coortship between 'em," said Mat.   " But as you're afther remindin' me uv id I'll run into Phil Lahy's to see have he my coat made—as I'm to be Ned's sidesman."

" Wisha, now !" exclaimed one of the young men, looking at Mat with evident surprise ; for it was somewhat unusual for a snug farmer, like Ned Brophy, to pay such a compliment to a " labouring man."

" Good night, b'ys," said Mat, on coming to the beech-tree opposite Phil Lahy's door.

" Good night, Mat—good night," they responded, cheerily, as they quickened their pace and passed on through the hamlet without stopping.

" Now, I wondher what are they up to ?" said Mat to him- self.   " I thought 'twas goin' to play for the pig's head they wor, but there they're off be the bog road.   A wondher they never said where they wor goin'.   Might id be for the lend uv long John's greyhound ?"

Guessing was no use, however ; so putting his arm over Honor Lahy's half-door, and pushing back the bolt, he passed through the shop into the kitchen, which was also the tailor's workshop.

Mat was gratified to find Phil Lahy sitting cross-legged

on his shop-board. But his smile gave way to a rather blank look of inquiry when he saw that Phil, instead of plying his needle, was poring over a soiled and dog-eared volume which rested on his knee.

" God save all here !" said Mat, looking around him as if he didn't know well what to think.

" God save you kindly, Mat," replied Honor Lahy, placing a chair for him near the well-swept hearth. " Sit down an' rest."

But Phil was too deeply absorbed in his book to take any notice whatever of the visitor.

" Phil," said Mat, after a moment's silence, " *are* you goin' to disappoint me ?"

" Is that iron hot ?" Phil asked, without raising his eyes from his book.

Tommy, who was reading too—crouching upon his elbows and knees on the shop-board—jumped down, and seizing the padding of an old coat-collar, which served the purpose of " holder," snatched the iron from the fire. Testing whether it was heated in a manner which we do not deem it necessary to describe—though we grieve to say we have seen the same test applied when the smoothing-iron was of smaller dimensions than the tailor's goose, and when the hand that held it was very much fairer than Tommy Lahy's—he brought it to his father, who attempted to take hold of the handle with its woollen cover without raising his eyes from the dog-eared volume. But his finger coming in contact with the hot iron, Phil Lahy said " hop," and commenced slapping his thigh in a rather frantic fashion. After rubbing the burned finger in the hair of his head, Phil reached to the further end of the shop-board, and to Mat Donovan's great relief and comfort pulled from under some other articles, by which it had been accidentally concealed from view, a new blue body-coat with gilt buttons. Seizing his lap-board he commenced " pressing " the coat with great energy and briskness of action.

Mat Donovan left his chair and stood close to the shop-board, trying to look unconcerned and perfectly indifferent.

We'd like to see the individual who ever *was* indifferent under such circumstances.

Mat took up the dog-eared book and made believe to be reading it—while not a twinkle of the gilt buttons escaped him, as Phil turned the blue coat over and over, smoothing every seam, and plucking out the basting threads with his teeth.

Mat at last did read a line or two of the book, and remarked :

" This is the Prophecies."

" Yes, Mat," replied Phil—and the words seemed to have been jerked out of him, as the iron came down with a thump upon the sleeve of the blue body-coat. " But," he continued—leaning his whole weight upon the iron and working with his wrist as if he were grinding something— " but 'tisn't the genuine wan afther all. I got id from Andrew Dwyer, an' as id belonged to his grandfather I thought id might be genuine. But," added Phil Lahy as he drew the lap-board out of the sleeve, " I was disappointed."

" Do you think there's any truth in 'em ?" Mat asked.

" Mat," replied Phil, solemnly, " there's a great dale,"— here he snapped viciously at a basting thread which held its ground so tenaciously that when one end was plucked from the sleeve of the blue coat, the other was stuck fast between Phil Lahy's front teeth—" there's a great dale in 'em comin' to pass, Mat."

" Now, what sinse could you pick out ov this ?" And Mat read a sentence which it would, indeed, be hard to pick sense out of.

" That's James the Second's time," replied Phil, as if it were all as plain as that two and two make four. " Come," he added, pushing away his goose and lap-board, and blowing away the yellow basting threads from the coat, which he held up by the collar as high as his hand could reach— " Come, throw off that ould coat."

Mat Donovan proceeded to divest himself of his old frieze—making desperate efforts to look grave and even sorrowful.

He got himself into the blue body-coat, and Phil Lahy, standing behind him, wrapped his arms round the Thrasher, as if he were trying to span the " big tree " at Gloonavon, and botton the coat in front.

Then feeling him all over, and rubbing him down the arms and back, Phil Lahy, slapping the Thrasher on the shoulder, said—

" Well wear !"

" 'Tis a grand fit," exclaimed Honor, moving the candle all round Mat to the imminent danger of the new coat.

Norah turned round her head and said, too, while there was something almost like humour in the sad, black eyes :

" Well wear, Mat."

" Thank'ee, Norah, thank'ee," replied Mat, as he unbuttoned the new coat.

" What way is she comin' on ?" he asked, turning to her mother.

" Elegant," was her reply, as she looked into Norah's face. And what a look that was !

" The divil a dacenter man 'll be there," said Billy Heffernan, who sat, silently as usual, in the corner, with his flute across his knees.

" 'Tis thrue for you," replied Honor Lahy ; " an' if some farmer's daughter takes a fancy to him, 'twould be no wondher in life.''

After putting on his old frieze again, Mat pulled a purse from the breast pocket of his waistcoat, and commenced unwinding the long string with which it was tied.

Phil Lahy began carefully folding the new coat, seemingly unconscious of the unwinding of the string.

Mat Donovan counted some pieces of silver and dropped them into Phil Lahy's hand. His wife fixed her eyes upon him, but Phil was so pre-occupied putting his spectacles in his waistcoat pocket, that in a moment of absence of mind he put the silver in with them.

" Mat," said Phil Lahy, " I'll want you to do a little job for me."

" What is id ?" Mat asked.

Phil looked straight in his face, but remained so long silent that Mat's face indicated considerable surprise.

" We'll talk about id another time," said Phil, at length. " Did you hear the news ?"

" No," replied Mat, bluntly. " What is id ?"

" I'm tould "—and here Phil looked so hard at his questioner that Mat began to feel alarmed, and somehow the image of " somebody " flashed across his mind, though there was no earthly reason why it should—" I'm tould," said Phil, " that—there's likely to be a change in the Ministry."

" Oh, is that all !" returned Mat with a sigh of relief.
" There's talk uv that in the papers these three weeks."

Now, the fact was, that Phil Lahy having—in a fit of
absence of mind—put the money in his pocket, wanted to
turn away his wife's attention from it, by saying something ;
and so he began with the " little job " that he wanted Mat
to do for him. But being abruptly asked what the little
job was, Phil's invention failed him ; and not being able to
name any job, big or little, he put the subject off to
" another time," and took refuge in the " news." And being
abruptly asked for particulars again, Phil grasped at " the
Ministry " as a drowning man will grasp at a straw. But
scarcely were the words out of his mouth, when he reproached
himself for his stupidity for never once having thought of the
bull-bait, which was comparatively a fresh subject. However, the Ministry did very well, and Phil felt greatly relieved when he heard his wife say, without having alluded in
any way to his forgetfulness in reference to the silver :

" What hurry are you in, Mat ? Can't you rest a start ?"

" I must be goin'," Mat replied ; " I on'y called in on my
way over from Mr. Kearney's."

" Miss Mary was here to-day, and stopped a whole hour
wud Norah."

" I partly guessed," he replied, " 'twas to see Norah they
wor goin' when I see 'em comin' in this way instead of turnin'
up to the forth."

Mat Donovan said, " Good night to ye," and walked out
with his new blue body-coat under his arm. And Phil Lahy
suddenly became very busy folding and putting away the
things on his shop-board.

" Come, Billy," said he, as he drew a chair to the fire,
" can't you give us a tune to put a stir in us these dull
times ?"

He spoke in an unusually cheerful tone, and holding his
hands over the fire, seemed disposed to be sociable, and, in
fact, mildly jolly.

Billy Heffernan immediately struck up " The Priest in his
Boots."

" A mighty purty tune that is, Billy ; but I think it goes
better on the pipes."

Taking the tongs in his hand, he built up the fire very

carefully, and seemed anxious to make himself both agreeable and generally useful. But some thought struck him, and putting his hand to his forehead, he said :

" See how I should forget telling Mat that message !"

" What message ?" his wife asked.

" About goin' to throw the sledge wud the captain," replied Phil.

" There wasn't anything said about a message," returned his wife.

" Didn't he say that out of eight hundred men in the regiment he couldn't get one he wasn't able to bate ; an' that he'd like to have a throw wud Mat the Thrasher ?"

" He did," rejoined Honor ; " but not be way uv a message."

" You don't understand these things. I'll take a walk up and tell him about id. Maybe he's out uv practice ; and 'twould be a bad job if he was called on too sudden."

Honor Lahy shook her head as if there were no help for it.

" Wisha, Billy," said she, after plying her knitting needles in silence for five minutes, " why don't you talk ?"

Billy looked into the fire, and blew C natural by way of reply. He might have said, with the poet :

> " Why should feeling ever speak,
> When thou canst breathe her soul so well ? "

Norah raised her eyes and smiled.

She looked much less sickly by the firelight than on the cold, frosty day, when her pale face so shocked Mr. Lowe and Grace Kiely.

" Play ' Auld Lang Syne,' Billy !"

Billy snatches up his old flute to comply ; but something had got into his throat which he was obliged to gulp down before he could get out a single note.

Was it the melancholy music of her voice or her look ?

Or did he know the words of the Scotch song, and remember that they had.

> ——" paidled i' the burn
> Frae morning's dawn till dine ? "

Whatever the cause was, Billy Heffernan had a struggle

with the knob in his throat before he could play " Auld
Lang Syne " for Norah Lahy.

Scotch tunes were very popular at Knocknagow, but we
have heard none played and sung so often as " Auld Lang
Syne," not the words, but the air ; for the words usually
sung to the tune were something about

> " The river Suir that runs so pure
> Through charming, rare Clonmel."

Billy Heffernan played on with his eyes shut, for a few
minutes ; and then, affecting to think there was something
wrong with his flute, screwed off one of the joints and converted it into a telescope, through which he endeavoured to
make out some object in the fire.

" How do you like the book Miss Grace lent you, Tommy ?"
Norah asked, while Billy prosecuted his researches in the
fire.

" 'Tis grand," was Tommy's reply.

" I think she's nicer than you said she was," continued
Norah.

" Well, she is," he replied reluctantly, as if unwilling to
give up his first impression. " An' a dale handsomer," he
added, as if a sense of justice extorted the admission from
him.

" I think she's very nice," returned Norah.

" She is, then, nice," said her mother, " an' a darlin' little
thing."

" She wants me to write down the ' Frolic ' for her," Billy
observed, meaning, of course, " Heffernan's Frolic," that
he composed in a dream. " But I don't know how to write
music, though I could tell her the names uv the notes wan
by wan."

" Wisha, Bifly," said Mrs. Lahy, on seeing him about to
leave, " would you take a walk up as far as Mat's, an' see is
Phil there, an' be home wud him ?—An' sure I know 'tisn't
there Phil is," she thought to herself.

Billy promised to do as she required ; and, after leaving
his flute at his own house, he walked up the hill to Mat
Donovan's.

CHAPTER XXIII.

MAT DONOVAN AT HOME.

" GOD save all here," said Billy Heffernan, as he closed the door behind him.

" God save you kindly," replied Mrs. Donovan, raising her spectacles to look at him. She was about adding the usual " sit down an' rest," but Billy had already taken possession of the bench against the partition by the fireside. So Mrs. Donovan pulled down her spectacles over her eyes and went on with her darning.

" What news ?" she asked as she opened the wick of the candle with the darning needle, to give herself more light.

" Nothing strange," replied Billy, looking round the house, " I thought Phil Lahy was here."

" He wasn't here since I was below," replied Mat, who was cutting a strip from a piece of horse-skin to make a gad for his flail.

" Faith, Billy," said Mat's sister, Nelly, " 'tis a cure for sore eyes to see you in this direction. Here, card a few rowls uv this for me."

She laid a handful of wool on the end of the bench upon which Billy sat, and then presented him with a pair of cards.

" 'Twould be time for you to stop," said her mother. " Where is the use of killing yourself that way ?"

" As soon as I have this cuppeen filled I'll stop," she replied.

And Nelly returned to her wheel—to the hum of which the grating of the wire-toothed cards was added, as Billy Heffernan went on converting the wool into rolls so soft and light that the sudden opening of the door blew some of them from the bench down upon the hearth.

The door was opened by a slatternly woman, smelling of soap-suds and snuff. After thrusting her dishevelled hair under a very dirty cap with borders that flapped backwards and forwards without any visible cause, and pulling up the heel of a man's brogue, which she wore as a slipper upon her stockingless foot, she announced the object of her visit to be " a squeeze of the blue rag."

" 'Tis there in the drawer of the dresser," said Mrs. Donovan, coldly.

She got the article she wanted, which was a small piece of flannel tied with a string into something like a rude purse.

" 'Tis button blue," she remarked, feeling what was tied up in the piece of flannel.

" No, 'tis slate blue," rejoined Mrs. Donovan, in no civil tone.

The slatternly woman took a black bottle from her pocket, and, after holding it between her and the light, and turning it in various directions, extracted the cork with her teeth. Then throwing back her head, she held the bottle, bottom upwards, over her open mouth for several seconds.

" The divil a duge," she exclaimed, replacing the cork, and striking it with the palm of her hand. " This is the second three half-pints I'm goin' for for 'em," she added ; " though they never as much as axed me had I a mouth on me."

" Who are they ?" Mrs. Donovan asked.

" Dick and Paddy Casey, Andy Dooley, and Phil Lahy," she replied. " Single-hand. Wheel out for a half-pint."

" Faith, if I'm to wait for Phil," thought Billy Heffernan, as he presented the last roll of the wool on the back of the card to Nelly, " 'tis a long wait I'll have, I'm afraid. An' if I don't wait, Honor'll think I didn't mind what she said to me. An' maybe Norah'd think it bad uv me." This last reflection decided Billy Heffernan to wait for Phil Lahy ; and he knew his man sufficiently well to be pretty sure that he would call to Mat Donovan's on his way home, and try to make his wife believe that it was at Mat Donovan's he had been all the time.

" Look at them "—here a difficulty presents itself : we are not sure whether it be possible to convey by means of the English alphabet the only name ever given to potatoes in Knocknagow. " Praties " would be laughed at as a vulgarism only worthy of a spalpeen from Kerry, while " potatoes " was considered too genteel except for ladies and gentlemen and schoolmasters. The nearest approach we can make to the word we were about writing is " puetas " or " p'yehtes."

" See if them puetas is goin' to bile," said Mat Donovan ; " 'twould be time for 'em."

Billy Heffernan anticipated Nelly before she could stop her wheel, and raised the wooden lid from the pot.

" The white horse is on 'em," said he.

Nelly now having " filled the cuppeen "—that is, spun as much thread as the spindle could carry—placed her wheel against the wall, and drew a very white deal table to the middle of the floor. Upon the table she spread a cloth as clean, but scarcely so white as itself—for it was of home-spun unbleached canvas—and upon the cloth she laid a single white plate with a blue rim, and three very old black-handled knives, with the blades worn to a point and very short. Taking a small saucepan or porringer from a nail in the wall, she half filled it with spring water and put it down to boil on a red sod of turf which she took from the centre of the fire with the tongs, and broke upon the hearthstone. Thrusting the tongs into the pot, she took a potato and felt it in her left hand, which was covered with the corner of her apron, and then laid it smoking on the table-cloth. The pressure of her hand did not break the potato, but she knew by the feel it was boiled to the " heart." Whipping the pot from the fire she emptied its contents into a boat-shaped basket placed over a tub, to drain off the water. Nelly Donovan then " threw out " the potatoes on the table, adroitly catching one or two that were rolling away and placing them on the top of the pile.

Her mother now took off her spectacles, making many wry faces as she did so, for they had got entangled in her white hair, or she imagined they had—which came to the same thing—and placed them on the upper shelf of the dresser. The dresser was of deal like the table, and scoured, if possible, into a more snowy whiteness. It was pretty well furnished with plates with blue rims, and some cups and saucers in which red and green predominated, a sturdy little black earthenware teapot, half-a-dozen iron spoons fixed in slits in the edge of the top shelf, which top shelf was crowned with a row of shining pewter-plates, and two large circular dishes of the same metal—relics of the good old times when " a pig's *head* and a bolster of cabbage " used to be no rarity to them.

Having placed her spectacles upon the upper shelf, and her darning needle and the half-mended stocking in one of the two drawers under the lower shelf of this imposing article of furniture, Mrs. Donovan smoothed down her apron, and took her accustomed place at the table. She was a quiet, decent-looking woman, with a sad, careworn face, but tranquil and contented at the same time. Her well-starched cap was scrupulously clean, and her grey hair carefully smoothed over her temples. She wore a small, yellowish shawl pinned over her dark brown stuff gown, and a white cotton kerchief under it, which was visible at the throat and round her neck. Her hand, as she rested it on the table, appeared bony and shrivelled, and it could be seen that the gold wedding ring was now too large for the finger it once fitted tightly enough—which made it necessary for her to wear a smaller ring of brass, as a guard.

" Put up that flail, Mat," she said, somewhat reproachfully, " and sit down to your supper."

Mat tucked up his cuffs ; and, after washing his hands in a wooden basin—always called a " cup "—and drying them on a strip of canvas that hung from a peg in the wall, he, too, sat at the table, exclaiming, as he pushed some of the potatoes out of the way, and laid the small iron candlestick on the middle of the table :

" Put the priest in the middle of the parish."

Then seizing a good-sized potato, he looked admiringly first at one side and then at the other. It was white and floury, and altogether a tempting object for a hungry man to look at. There was even something appetising in the steam that curled up from it. In fact, the potatoes were remarkably good potatoes, notwithstanding the bad name Mat had given them to Miss Mary Kearney when he pronounced them " desavers."

During this time Nelly Donovan was engaged in cooking a salt herring on a small gridiron, which was constructed by simply bending a piece of thin rod iron, zig-zag, into something like the outline of a hand with the fingers extended, traced with a burnt stick upon the wall, and bringing the ends of the iron together and twisting them into a handle, which might represent a very attenuated arm to the hand aforesaid. When the herring was done, she tossed it on the plate, and poured some of the boiling water out of the por- ringer upon it for sauce.

And now the repast being prepared, Nelly sat down to partake of her share.

" Won't you come an' ate, Billy," she said, turning to their silent visitor.

" No, thankee," he replied, " I'm afther my supper."

" Oh, wisha ! wisha !" Nelly exclaimed, discontentedly, as she glanced at the table, " how well I should forget." She stood up and opened the door ; but seeing that the night was dark and the wind rising, she turned to Billy Heffernan and said, " Come out wud me, Billy."

He left his bench in the chimney corner, and followed her out. They returned in a minute or two, and after washing something in a black, glazed earthenware pan, and drying her hands, Nelly laid two small leeks on the table near her mother.

The meal then commenced, but Nelly started up again, exclaiming :

" Bad cess to me, but there's somethin' comin' over me."

She selected half-a-dozen of the best potatoes and laid them in a semi-circle round the fire to roast, and again took her place at the table.

The worn knives were used to peel the potatoes—though towards the conclusion of the meal, Nelly sometimes fell into a contemplative mood and did the peeling with the nail of her thumb—but all three helped themselves with their fingers to the herring, which they took in minute pinches, as if they were merely trying how it tasted.

Billy Heffernan left his bench and sat upon a straw- bottom chair in front of the fire, so that his back was towards the table—the Irish peasant always considering it rude to stare at people while eating. And as he was turning the " roasters " with the tongs, a laugh from Nelly, clear and musical as ever rang through festal hall, made him look round. Mat, it appeared, was making great inroads upon the her- ring, the backbone of which was well nigh laid bare from the head to the tail. He had his hand stretched out to help himself to a second pinch, by way of supplement to an

unconscionably large pinch he had just taken, when his
sister snatched away the plate. Mat, finding his finger and
thumb close upon vacancy, opened his mouth, not to add
the supplemental pinch to its contents, but in blank amazement ; and as he stared at his sister, she laughed till she
was obliged to wipe the tears from her eyes with the corner
of her apron. Even her mother's sad face relaxed into a
smile ; which, however, was followed by a forced look of
reproach, as she requested Nelly to " behave herself." Mat
now rested the handle of his knife on the table with the air
of a man who had made a good meal, and was pretty well
satisfied. All three, in fact, paused as if the work in hand
were completed. But Nelly, going to the fire, took up the
" roasters," which served the purpose of a second course,
and placed three of them before Mat and two before her
mother, reserving one for herself. These being disposed of
after the manner of tarts or some such delicacies, Mat
Donovan leant back luxuriously in his straw-bottom chair
for a minute or two. Then hastily making the Sign of the
Cross, he stood up, and, dipping a cup in a pail of spring
water which rested on a stone slab under the little window,
Mat Donovan took a draught with a relish that drinkers of
champagne dream not of. He then placed the little iron
candlestick on the window, while his sister set about clearing
away the table, and joined Billy Heffernan at the fire.

Mat Donovan's house was on the top of a hill where two
roads met ; and the candle in the little window was a beacon-
light to many a splashed and weary wayfarer during the
dark winter nights. In fact, his latch was often raised not
only by the neighbours who came in for a " shanahus " of
an evening, but travellers who were accustomed to pass the
way made it a point to light their pipes at the bright turf
fire, or in the hot summer days to take a draught from the
pail under the little window, which was sure to be found at
all hours and seasons as fresh as in the well under the whitethorn in the " rushy field " near the bridge.

" Have you the flute, Billy ?" Mat asked, as he sat in the
chair which Billy had again left for the bench in the corner.

" No," was the reply ; " I left id at home."

" I'll engage he hasn't," said Nelly. " 'Tis seldom he has
a tune for *us*."

" Begor, you can't say that, Nelly. Whin did I ever disappoint ye whin ye wanted a tune ?"

" Well, that's thrue enough, Billy," returned Nelly. " You're a good warrant to play for us whenever we ax you. 'Tis jokin' I was."

" That's what you're always doin'," said her mother, shaking her head.

" 'Tis better be merry than sad," she replied, with a laugh.

The latch was here raised and the door pushed open ; but as no one came in, Mat leant backwards and peered out into the darkness. By shading his eyes from the fire-light he was able to see that some one was fastening a horse to the back-stick iron in the door-post ; and after a little delay— more perhaps than a perfectly sober man would require—a tall, broad-shouldered man turned round and advanced a step or two into the house.

" Is that Ned ?" Mat asked.

" 'Tis," was the reply, as he took off his hat and swung it downwards to shake off the wet with which the fur—for it was a beaver or " Caroline "—was dabbled.

" Is it rainin' it is ?" Mat inquired, in some surprise.

" No, but the wind whipped id off uv my head as I was passin' the quarry."

At this Mrs. Donovan made the Sign of the Cross on her forehead ; for it was generally believed that the " Good People " were wont to take their nightly journeys through the air to and from Maurice Kearney's fort over the quarry.

Nelly took the hat, and, bringing it close to the candle, gave it as her opinion that it was " spiled " ; and immediately set to work to dry the inside.

" A fine, new Car'line," said she, as she gave it back to the owner ; " take care an' don't rub the outside till 'tis dhry."

" Faith, Ned," she added, taking up the candle and viewing him all over, " I'm thinkin' I could make a good guess where you're comin' from."

Ned smiled and looked rather sheepish, as she held the candle down almost to his shoes, and then slowly raised it till she came to the " fine new Car'line," and then dropping the light on a level with his waistcoat, moved her hand

as if she were describing a circle in the air, till the little
glass buttons on the waistcoat twinkled like so many little
bright black eyes winking at her. Ned's riding-coat was that
which he usually wore, but everything else about him was
brand new, even to the black silk cravat with a scarlet
border, the bow knot of which happened to be under his left
ear, till Nelly pulled it back to its proper position.

"Tell us something about her, Ned," she began, laughingly.
"What sourt is she ? Shawn-na-match says you're bringin'
a patthern to the parish. But far away cows wear long horns,
you know."

"Go about your business, and thry an' have a little sense,"
said her mother, rising from her place in the chimney-corner.
"Sit down, Ned, an' never mind her."

"No, Nell, no ; 'tis too late, and I'm in a hurry. Take a
walk down as far as the bridge," he added, turning to Mat,
"I want to spake to you."

There was something in his voice and manner that made
Mat apprehend that he had unpleasant news to communicate, so he at once stood up, and taking the bridle from the
jamb of the door, set back the horse and desired the owner
to mount.

"No, I'd rather walk," said he, taking hold of the bridle
and leading the horse out upon the road.

They walked on in silence for some time, and at last Ned
Brophy—for it was the same Ned Brophy of whom mention
has been made more than once—said :

"I believe this business is settled."

"Is the day appointed an' all ?"

"All is settled," was the reply.

"Well, you're gettin' a fine fortune any way," said Mat
Donovan.

Ned Brophy made no reply, but walked on in silence till
they came to the bridge ; and then he stooped and looked
down at the little stream as it rushed under the ivy-covered
arch.

"Mat," said he, covering his face with his hands, "my
heart is broke."

"I don't see the use of talkin' that way now," Mat
replied, a little angrily. "I tould you to look before you.
An', begor, Ned, 'tisn't for *you* I have the compassion."

"Don't be too hard on me, Mat. You don't know the way they wor at me. Judy said she'd dhrag the red head off uv her."

"More shame for Judy to talk that way uv as dacent a girl as ever she was. But, like that, you know, she had no great harm in id. An' sure 'tis no wondher she'd be agin a match that'd lave herself wudout a fortune. But as I often said to you, you had a right to think uv all this long ago, an' not to be the manes uv setting any girl astray. But 'tis too late to talk about id now; so dhrop id in the name o' God."

"You don't know the way I do be," said Ned Brophy, "whinever I pass over this bridge. Two hundred pounds is a fine fortune, moreover, whin a man'd want id. But that bush beyand an' the bridge here that kills me."

Mat took up a stone from the road and jerked it into the stream, but made no reply.

"There now," continued Ned Brophy, with a groan, "I think I'm lookin' at her peltin' the little pebbles into the wather. Och! I do be all right till I stand on this bridge."

"Well, don't stand on id," rejoined Mat. "But you're not fit to talk to now; and if you wor itse'f, there's no use in talkin'."

Mat turned his back and then his shoulder to the wind, which was blowing in strong, fitful gusts over the unsheltered bridge.

"Come, come," he continued, pulling up his coat collar over his ears, "there's no use in perishin' here."

He held the horse while Ned put his foot in the stirrup and mounted; and after saying "safe home," was starting off up the hill, when Ned Brophy suddenly wheeled round his horse and laid his hand on Mat's shoulder.

"Mat, what way is she?" he asked.

"I didn't see her since the day uv the Station," he replied. "She wasn't at the dance o' Sunday."

"Wasn't she, Mat?" he asked in a tone of such real feeling that Mat was moved, and added:

"Nelly goes in to see her now an' then; an' she says she is purty well, on'y she can't stir herself to go among the b'ys an' girls like she used."

" I'm tould," Ned continued, " the mother is very bitther
agin me. But Tom or herse'f says nothin'."

" Nancy Hogan couldn't say a hard word uv any wan,'
returned Mat Donovan. " But I'd rather you wouldn't meet
Jemmy till his passion cools. Good night, an' safe home.
An' mind your hat goin' through the bog, if you don't want
to have id swep' where 'twon't be as aisy for you to find it as
in the quarry."

Ned Brophy rode away at a brisk trot, and Mat the
Thrasher turned toward home, remarking, as he did so, that
the light had disappeared from the little window.

CHAPTER XXIV.

" GOD BE WITH YE!"

THE disappearance of the light was accounted for when, after
shutting the door behind him, he saw Phil Lahy sitting at
the fire reading a newspaper, and Billy Heffernan holding the
candle for him.

" What's the news, Phil ?" he asked.

" 'Tis an American paper I'm afther gettin' the lend of,"
replied Phil Lahy. " But I can't see much in id that we
hadn't before, except that speech of Bishop Hughes's. That's
a great man," said Phil, solemnly. " But I won't mind
readin' the spee—spee—speech," he added, pronouncing the
word with considerable difficulty, " till to-morrow."

" Wouldn't id be time to be goin' home ?" Billy Heffernan
ventured to suggest.

" Yes, Billy. ' Home sweet home, there's no place like
home.' I have a poor wife," continued Phil Lahy, turning
round and looking straight in Mat Donovan's face, " that
wouldn't say a word to me—no matter what I'd do."

" She is a good wife, sure enough," replied Mat, as he
gently touched Phil's shin with the tongs, with the view of
inducing him to draw his foot out of the fire, into which he
had just thrust it.

" Billy," said Phil, after staring at him for a minute, " you're lookin' very bad."

This was said with a solemnity that quite frightened Billy Heffernan.

" You ought," Phil Lahy continued in a fatherly way, " you ought to take a little nourishment. You'd want it."

" The divil cut the hand uv me," returned Billy Heffernan, recovering from his fright, " if ever I take a dhrop uv anything stronger than wather. 'Tis little good id ever done me while I was takin' id."

" That is, Billy, because you didn't take it in raison. I'm not takin' anything myself now in a public-house, on account uv a little promise I made. *You'd* say now," he added, turning suddenly to Mat, " that I was fond uv the dhrop ?"

He waited for a reply, but Mat only looked into the fire.

" No ; I wouldn't give you *that* for a pun-puncheon of it." And Phil laid the top of his finger on his tongue, and after looking at it steadily as if there were a thorn in it, performed the action known as snapping the finger. " Not *that* would I give for it," he repeated, " on'y for the company."

" An' why couldn't you have the company wudout the whiskey ?" Nelly asked. " Many's the pleasant company I see where there wasn't either a pint or a glass."

" Nelly," said Phil, looking very seriously at her, but answering her rather wide of the mark, " I forgot thankin' you for the fresh eggs you sent to my poor sick daughter ; an' our own hens stopped layin' this I don't know how long."

" Faix an' 'tis the same story we'd have ourselves," replied Nelly, " if Mat could have his own way, an' keep the hens out on the roost he made for 'em in the pig-house. We're gettin' ——." Here Nelly stopped short. She was about telling him she was getting three-halfpence a couple for her eggs, when it occurred to her it would look as if she wished to let him see the extent of the favour he was thanking her for.

" Nelly," said Phil Lahy, with a politeness that was quite affecting, " I'll thank you for wan of them knittin'-needles to ready this pipe."

She plied her needles with increased nimbleness for a few seconds, and then handed him one of them.

Phil thrust the knitting-needle into the wooden stem of

his pipe, but forgot to draw it out, till it came in contact
with his nose, as he was putting the pipe to his mouth, which
made him start and look very much astonished.

" It never could be said of me, Mrs. Donovan," he proceeded—as he drew out the knitting-needle, which slipped
through his fingers several times—" it never could be said
that I "—here he paused and looked into her face as if
something had struck him in the outline of her nose that
he had never noticed before—" that I," he repeated, " ever
went to bed wudout sprinklin' the holy wather on myse'f.
An', as long as a man has that to say, he can't be called a
drunkard at any rate, Mrs. Donovan."

" Let us be goin'," Billy Heffernan suggested. But
before the hint could be acted upon—supposing that Phil
Lahy was disposed to act upon it—the latch was again
raised.

" I ran in to take my lave of ye, for fear I mightn't see
ye again," said a young girl, who stepped lightly into the
kitchen, forgetting to close the door behind her.

A gust of wind rushed in after her, and was met by another
gust that rushed down the chimney ; and both gusts joining
together, whirled round and round Mat Donovan's kitchen,
extinguishing the candle which Billy Heffernan had laid on
the end of the bench upon which he sat, and blowing the ashes
and some sparks of fire into Mrs. Donovan's lap, causing the
good woman to start to her feet and beat her apron as if it
were in a blaze about her ; and, not content with this mischief,
the two gusts of wind whirled up to the thatched roof, and so
jostled Nelly Donovan's hens about, on the roost over the door,
that their querulous screams at being thus rudely and unsea-
sonably awakened from their repose were piteous to listen to ;
and then, by way of finishing their frolic, the intruders swept
the old red cock himself from the collar-beam, where he re-
posed in solitary dignity, bringing him down straight upon
Phil Lahy's head, who had just risen to his feet and was
making an ineffectual effort to comprehend the state of affairs,
and upon whom the sudden assault had such an effect that he
staggered backward and was coming down in a sitting posture
upon the fire, when Billy Heffernan caught him in his arms
in time to prevent the unpleasant catastrophe. And the
two gusts of wind, having fulfilled their mission, went out of

existence as suddenly as they came into Mat the Thrasher's kitchen by the door and by the chimney.

Mrs. Donovan blessed herself several times. She had her own private opinion as to the nature of the two gusts of wind ; and had not a doubt that the denizens of Maurice Kearney's fort were unusually frolicsome that night—witness Ned Brophy's hat and the old red cock, who stood upon the hearth-stone looking quite dazed and foolish, as if he were just after receiving a box on the ear, which bothered him to that degree that he was deliberately walking into the fire till Nelly snatched him up in her arms.

" Faith, you wor never in Dublin, whoever you are," said Billy Heffernan, as with a vigorous swing he placed Phil Lahy in his chair.

" Oh, wisha !" exclaimed the innocent cause of the commotion, " see how I should forget to shut the doore."

" Light the candle, Billy," said Nelly Donovan. " I wondher who have we at all ? Maybe 'tis Judy Connell."

" 'Tis, Nelly," was the reply. " I'm comin' out from town, an' I didn't like to pass by wudout comin' in to see ye, as I don't know the minute or hour the captain's letter might come, an' maybe I mightn't have time to take my lave uv ye."

" Sit down, Judy," said Mrs. Donovan sadly.

" No, ma'am, thank you," she replied : " Mary is wud me, an' we're in a hurry home, as there's a few friends comin' to see me."

" An' is id walkin' ye are ?"

" No, Nelly ; Joe Burke came wud us, an' brought his horse an' car."

As she spoke she ran to Nelly, and, flinging her arms round her neck, kissed her, we might say, passionately.

She also kissed the old woman, but more calmly.

They were all now standing around her, and as she gave her hand to Mat she tried to smile.

" God be wud you, Mat," said she, " 'tis many's the time we danced together at the Bush."

The recollection of those happy times was too much for her, and the tears gushed from her eyes.

" God Almighty be wud ye all," she exclaimed in a choking voice, as she hurriedly shook hands with Billy Heffernan and Phil Lahy.

And as she turneᾳ towards the door, which Nelly ran to
open for her, she pressed one hand on her bosom and the
other over her eyes, and a cry so full of sorrow burst from
her that the tears came rolling down Mat Donovan's cheeks
before he could turn away to hide them under the pretext of
placing the candle in its usual place on the little window.
And a presentiment seized upon him at that moment that
his own heart would one day feel the pang that wrung that
cry from the heart of Judy Connell.

"I never thought," Nelly remarked, when the emigrant
girl had left, "that herself an' Joe'd ever be parted."

" 'Tisn't Joe's fault," Mat returned ; " his lase is out, an'
he's expectin' the notice every day like the rest of the tinants
on the property. As fast as their lases dhrop, out they
must go."

" An' she tould me last Sunday," continued Nelly, "that
on'y for her sisters sendin' for her, she'd never go. She has
a sore heart to-night any way," added Nelly with a sigh.

"Short she'll think uv Joe, once the say is betune 'em,"
Billy Heffernan observed, somewhat cynically.

" 'Tis more likely 'tis short Joe'll think uv her," retorted
Nelly, apparently nettled by the insinuation of female
inconstancy which Billy's remark implied.

"May be 'twould be out uv sight out uv mind wud the two
uv 'em," Mrs. Donovan observed. " An' may be not," she
added more seriously, after a pause.

"That," said Mat, who was gazing thoughtfully into the
fire, "that depends on the soart they are. The round uv the
world wouldn't put some people out uv wan another's mind.
But there's more uv 'em," he added, with a shake of the head,
" an' the cross uv a stubble garden would do id."

"Wisha, would I doubt you for sayin' a quare thing," Nelly
replied, with a mixture of surprise and contempt in her tone ;
" I wondher what put a stubble garden into your head ? An'
'tis you're the lad that'd forget a girl before you'd be the
cross uv a bosheen, not to say a stubble garden."

"The world is only a blue rag, Billy. Have your squeeze
out of id," said Mat, shaking off the gloom that seemed to
oppress him during the evening, and resuming his usual
cheerful look.

"There's more of id," returned Nelly. "Whoever called the

world a blue rag before ? I suppose 'tis because Kit Cummins came in for a squeeze of id a while ago, that put the blue rag into your head. I'd rather a man like yourself, Billy, that wouldn't mind any wan, than a fellow that'd be goin' about palaverin' every girl he'd meet."

" I don't know," retorted Mat, with a shrug of his shoulders, " I had my fling among 'em, sure enough ; but where's the wan uv 'em that ever had to say a bad word uv me ?"

Mat gazed into the fire again, with that look of his which had in it such a strange blending of humour and sadness, like the music of his country. The smile was on his lip, and the smile was in his eye. But for all that there was a melting something in big Mat Donovan's face, as he gazed into the turf fire, that made Billy Heffernan expect every moment to see the humourful eye swim in tears and the smiling lips give passage to a sigh. The sigh did come ; but not the tears. And Mat Donovan, leaning back in his chair, and with a sidelong glance up at the collar-beams, relieved his feelings, as was his wont on such occasions, by chanting one of his favourite songs.

Now, if we were drawing upon our imagination we would give Mat the Thrasher a more suitable song than he chose to sing on this not eventful night—so far as our (perhaps) not eventful history is concerned—even if we were obliged to compose one specially for him. But being simply the faithful chronicler of the sayings and doings, joys and sorrows of Knocknagow, a regard for truth compels us to record that Mat the Thrasher's song was no other than that sentimentalest of sentimental lyrics, " Oh, no, we, never mention her."

And furthermore, we feel bound to state that this song was second to none in popularity among the music-loving people of Knocknagow. How is this fact to be accounted for ? Is there some innate good hid under the lackadaisical in this renowned effort of Mr. Haynes Bailey's muse ? Or might it be that " the hawthorn tree " brought the bush near Maurice Kearney's back gate, with its host of tender associations, to the minds of the singers and listeners ? Or, to make another, and, probably, the best guess, perhaps the words—

> " Were I in a foreign land
> They'd find no change in me."

came home to many a loving heart in Knocknagow? For
some or all of these reasons, or for some reason unknown to
us, this song, as we have said, was popular in a high degree,
from the cross-roads at the foot of the hill to the cross-roads
at the top of the hill ; and indeed we might say as far as the
eye of a spectator standing on Maurice Kearney's fort could
reach all around.

> " 'Tis true that I behold no more
>   The valley where we met,
> I do not see the hawthorn tree,
>   But how can I forget ? "

So sang Mat the Thrasher. And Nelly, who at first seemed
disposed to be scornful, when he came to these words began
to accompany him unconsciously, but in an almost inaudible
voice. Billy Heffernan bent down with his elbows on his
knees and his hands covering his face. Mrs. Donovan's arms
dropped by her side, and a dreamy look came into her sad
face, as if her thoughts went back to the far past. Yes!
there was "a valley where we met" in her memory, and as
she smoothed her grey hair over her temples, Mrs. Donovan
stealthily wiped a tear from her cheek with the back of her
hand.

And Mat the Thrasher's song reminds us that at the very
last wedding we had the honour of being invited to in the
neighbourhood of Knocknagow, the two musicians, standing
in the corner appropriated to them, commenced to play a
" slow tune " during the interval between two dances ; which
slow tune so fascinated our good friend, Father Hannigan,
who was a bigoted admirer of Irish music, that he left his
place behind the mahogany table at the opposite side of the
room, and, after pushing his way through the dancers, stood
with folded arms close to the musicians, who, flattered by
the compliment, put their whole souls into their fiddles.
And when we, at the suggestion of the bride's father, went
to escort Father Hannigan back to his place at the mahogany
table, and to the little comforts " smiling " thereon—we borrow the expression from a well-known song beginning—

> " Let the farmer praise his grounds,
>   Let the huntsman praise his hounds," etc.

—he laid his hand impressively on our shoulder and said in
a whisper :

" That's a fine thing !"

" Why, that," we replied, " is the *English* sentimental song—' Oh, no, we never mention her.' " To which Father Hannigan frowned a scornful contradiction.

But we having reiterated the assertion, Father Hannigan listened again, and, suddenly turning to us a with a look of profound amazement, said :

" Begor, you're right !"

And then Father Hannigan made his way back to the mahogany table, rubbing the side of his head, and evincing all the symptoms of a man conscious of having been " sold."

So the music as well as the words of this much-abused lyric has been a puzzle to us.

And before dismissing Mr. Haynes Bailey, we must further record that another song of his, though " caviare to the general," was a decided favourite with Mat the Thrasher. He was wont to chant with great feeling how " She wore a wreath of roses the time when first we met," and a " wreath of orange blossoms " on the second occasion. And when once again they met, the widow's cap had taken the place of roses and blossoms. Mat's rendering of this last stanza was quite heart-breaking. But the great triumph was a new reading of the last line but one. In the original it is, we believe,

> " And there is no one near
> To press her hand within his own,
> And wipe away the tear."

which Mat altered, whether intentionally or not we never could discover, to

> " But there was no one near
> *To roll her in his arms,*
> And wipe away a tear."

Mat Donovan sang on, with his eyes fixed on the collar-beams, and with a continuous wavy motion of the head, which had a softness in it in harmony with the humorously pathetic look which was peculiar to him when the theme of his song, or his discourse, or his thoughts happened to be that which we are assured rules the court, the camp, the grove, and even " makes the world go round."

" As long as the fox runs, he's caught at last," said Mrs. Donovan, looking at Mat, as if she suspected he was in the toils, as long as he seemed to have kept clear of danger.

Phil Lahy had been taking a comfortable nap, with his head hanging over the back of his chair, unnoticed by everybody except Billy Heffernan, who gave him an occasional push when he showed symptoms of tumbling off.

" We must stir him up," said Billy. " Give him a shake, Mat, and tell him to come home."

" Come, Phil," said Mat, shaking him, " get up and pay for your bed."

Phil opened his eyes and stared about him as if the whole place were quite strange to him. But, on recognising Mat, who was shaking him by the collar, Phil Lahy commenced to laugh, as if he thought the proceeding the funniest and most side-splitting of practical jokes.

" Mat," said he, " you wor always a play-boy."

" The divil a much of a play-boy in id," returned Mat ; I'm on'y tellin' you to keep your eyes open."

" No doubt, no doubt," Phil replied, with the look of a man that couldn't laugh if it were to save his life. " No doubt, Mat " ; and he nodded so far forward that Billy Heffernan stretched out his hands with a start, imagining that he had taken a sudden fancy to dive head foremost into the fire.

" Let us be movin', Phil," said Billy Heffernan. " 'Tis gettin' late an' I must be off, an' we may as well go home together."

" You know, Billy, I have a poor wife that wouldn't say a word to me, no matter what I'd do."

" I know that," Billy replied, as if 'twas the most sorrowful thing he ever heard in his life.

" Poor Norah is comin' on finely," Nelly observed. " 'Tis long since I see her lookin' so well as she did to-day."

The mention of Norah's name had an instantaneous effect upon her father, who seemed to become almost sober in a moment.

Billy Heffernan expected this result, and yet he could not mention Norah's name himself.

" Billy," said Phil Lahy, looking at him as if it were he and not Nelly who had spoken, or rather as if no one had spoken at all—" Billy, I have a daughter, an' the like uv her is not in the world." He said this confidentially, leaning forward as if he were imparting a secret to him.

That affection of the throat which had prevented Billy Heffernan from at once complying with Norah's request that he would play "Auld Lang Syne," was now observed by Nelly Donovan, who was watching him very closely.

Perhaps Nelly Donovan had her own reasons for watching Billy Heffernan; and possibly his presence had something to do with her forgetfulness a while ago, in reference to the leeks and "roasters." And when she said that she'd rather a man like him that "wouldn't mind anyone" than a "rag on every bush" like Mat, she had certain misgivings that her words did not exactly apply to Billy's case; and now as she looked at him she felt sure that they did not. But though her first feeling, on making this discovery, was one of disappointment, if not of pain, it soon gave place to admiration and sympathy at the recollection of Norah's pale face. And Nelly Donovan never cared so much for Billy Heffernan as now that she believed he cared for another.

"Billy," said Phil Lahy rising from his chair, "you ought to be in your own house. A young man ought to keep regular hours."

"Well, I b'lieve so," replied Billy, getting up from the bench in the corner and stretching his arms. "Good-night to ye."

"Mat, I have somethin' to be talkin' to you about," Phil observed before he reached the door, "but it will do another time. Good-night, Mrs. Donovan."

"Good-night, Phil. Nelly, hold the candle for 'em till they get a-past the turn; I b'lieve the night is very dark."

"There's great fear of 'em," returned Nelly in her good-humoured way. "Here, take this in your hand," she continued, presenting a blackthorn stick to Billy Heffernan; "maybe you might meet the night-walkers. And 'tis the stick you ought to get," she added, giving him a blow of her open hand as he stepped over the threshold.

"'Tis a shame for you," said her mother. "You'll never have a stim uv sinse." At which Nelly Donovan laughed her ringing laugh as she closed the door and fastened it with the back-stick.

"Heigho! heart—wan here an' another in Cork," she exclaimed, as she took the broom from behind the door and tucked up her apron, putting the corner under the string behind her back.

" Wisha, Mat," she continued, " how long you're about makin' thim couple uv brooms. These sally brooms don't hold a minute. Wan birch broom'd be worth a dozen uv 'em."

" I'll desire Barney to cut the makin's uv 'em," replied Mat, " the next time he's goin' over to Ardboher. I haven't time myself, if you don't want me to go in the night—or lose a Sunday for 'em."

Mat Donovan, we are bound to confess, would not have thought it a mortal sin to cut the makings of a broom on the Sabbath, and by "losing a Sunday " he meant losing a dance, or the 'hurling, or the hunt, which he could only enjoy on the day of rest. As he spoke to his sister, he unfolded a crumpled ballad, and was just beginning to hum the chorus, when his mother reminded him that it was time to go to bed.

" Well, I b'lieve so," he replied, rolling the ballad between his hands, like a ball, and replacing it in his waistcoat pocket.

" What raison do you rowl id up that way instead of foldin' id right ?" Nelly asked, " I thought 'twas goin' to play scut wud id you wor."

" You know nothin'," returned Mat ; " if I folded id right, as you say, 'twould cut in my pocket ; an' now id won't."

He was on his knees by his bedside without requiring another hint. And by the time his mother and Nelly had their prayers said, and the house swept, and the fire raked, Mat the Thrasher was sound asleep.

And so, for the present, we wish good-night to the occupants of this humble little Tipperary home.

CHAPTER XXV.

PHIL LAHY IN THE BOSOM OF HIS FAMILY.

BILLY Heffernan, on reaching his own door, was about bidding his companion good-night, when it occurred to him that Phil might take it into his head to pay a visit to Jack Delaney's forge, from the door of which, late as it was, a gleam of light shone out at intervals, indicating that the blacksmith had some work in hand which it was necessary to finish before morning.

Billy Heffernan's suspicion proved well founded ; for, after reflecting for a minute or two, Phil said :

" Billy, I'll wish you good-night. I'll take a walk down to the forge. I want to talk to Jack Delaney about—about a little business."

" Sure you can see him to-morrow, or any time," replied Billy.

Phil put his finger and thumb into his waistcoat-pocket, and taking out the last shilling of what Mat the Thrasher had given him, he fell into a deep reverie.

" Faith, I b'lieve 'tis burnin' you," said Billy Heffernan to himself. " 'Tis gettin' late," he observed aloud ; " an' maybe if you stopped out any longer Norah might be frettin'."

This decided Phil, who walked off so quickly that Billy found himself standing alone in the middle of the road.

He was about turning towards his own door—a little disappointed, perhaps—when Phil was at his side again as suddenly as he had left it.

" Billy," said he, " you may as well come in for a minute."

This invitation was not prompted by politeness on Phil Lahy's part. Perhaps if it were, Billy Heffernan would have declined it. But he knew Phil shrank from meeting his wife alone—which may appear strange, for it was quite true that she " wouldn't say a word to him no matter what he'd do," as he said at Mat Donovan's But perhaps this forbearance was the secret of her influence.

" Norah, you ought to be in bed," said Phil Lahy in a mild, parental tone, as he laid his hat on the top of the press near his shop-board, with the air of a man who had been labouring hard since daybreak to maintain his family respectably.

For Phil Lahy really seemed to be quite satisfied that he was the prop of the household. And when he did happen to do anything useful—such, for instance, as transferring a customer's account from his wife's board, where it was chalked in the shape of " strokes and O's," to the account book, or buying a couple of " slips " at the fair—Phil Lahy had the look of a martyr who was slaving from year's end to year's end to keep a roof over the heads of his wife and children. He was apt to get those " weaknesses," too, to which he was subject on these occasions, and his hints as to the necessity of a little " nourishment " were both strong and frequent.

At certain seasons, too, he was wont to take sudden fits of industry, which usually lasted half-an-hour at a time, and evinced themselves in " digging the haggart " ; and 'twas wonderful how often the handle of his spade would get loose, and how every one would be in his way while he searched for the hammer, or sharpened a knife, to make a wedge, on the brown flag at the shop door. In reference to this pecu- liarity Mat the Thrasher was heard to declare that if Phil Lahy " on'y turned a dog up from the fire you'd think the whole house was dependin' on him."

" You know, Norah," he continued, in a tone of mild reproach, " it doesn't answer you to be up late."

" An' sure you know," replied his wife, " that she wouldn't go to bed till you'd come home ; and if she did itself she couldn't sleep."

" I was readin' an American paper over at Mat's," said he. " Billy Heffernan and myself happened to be there, an' we didn't feel the time passin'. I told Nelly how much obliged to her you were for the fresh eggs."

This was a deep stroke of Phil's ; and he began to feel that he had been discharging an important duty during the evening which placed them all under an obligation to him.

" I think," he continued, as if he thought he might law- fully allow himself a little relaxation at last, " I think I'll look over the bishop's speech."

He sat down by the end of the table next the fire, and snuffed the candle with his fingers.

There were cups and saucers and a loaf of bread cut into substantial slices on the table ; and as soon as Billy Heffer- nan observed them he was moving silently towards the door. No one noticed him but Norah, who turned round in her chair and followed him with her eyes. Such an effort was so unusual with her, that her mother looked up in surprise to see what had happened. But observing nothing but Billy Heffernan's retreating figure, she turned to Norah for an explanation ; and her look of inquiry was met by one of mild reproach from Norah's dark eyes.

Mrs. Lahy was for a moment quite at a loss to understand what had gone wrong ; but the real state of affairs suddenly flashed upon her, and starting up she seized Billy Heffernan by the shoulder before he had reached the door.

" Wisha, Billy," said she, " what did we do to you ?"

" Nothin'," he replied, quite taken by surprise. " Who said ye did anything to me ?"

" Here, go over there to the corner and sit down, an' have a cup uv tay wud us."

Billy hesitated ; but Mrs. Lahy pushed him by main force into the seat in the corner ; and a glance from Norah decided him.

" I'll first run up," said Billy, " to throw a sop uv hay to the mule, and I'll be back in a minute."

" How bad she is !" returned Honor Lahy. " She can wait till you go home."

" Well," said Billy Heffernan, scratching his head uneasily, " I haven't the flute.'

This remark made Norah smile ; and she gave him one of those looks—those melancholy, grateful looks—that always brought something into Billy Heffernan's throat.

" You're sure you'll come back now ?" said Honor Lahy, keeping her position between him and the door.

" Well, I will," he replied. And she let him pass, and returned to her stool to finish the toasting and buttering of a thin piece of bread which she had left on a plate on the hearth when she started up to prevent Billy Heffernan's exit.

Billy was soon back with his flute ; but before he had time to screw the joints together, Mrs. Lahy snatched them from him, and laid them aside with Phil's American paper. And taking the sturdy little black tea-pot from the hearth, having first placed the table in front of the fire, she poured out the tea.

Billy Heffernan reached for his cup without leaving his seat in the chimney-corner. Norah's was laid with her toast on a chair near her, and Honor and Phil sat at the table, having the full benefit of the turf fire. Altogether it was a pleasant little party.

Phil Lahy was not insensible to the comforts by which he was surrounded, and their influence lost nothing by the reflection that he himself was the source and creator of them all. He was more than half sober by the time the first cup of tea was discussed, and talked so wisely, and learnedly, and feelingly upon various subjects that his wife's admiration actually shone in her face till it rivalled the turf fire in brightness ; and poor Norah, as she looked at him with a kind of wondering fondness, said to herself :

"Ah ! if he never came home any worse than he is now, how happy we'd all be !"

Supper over, Mrs. Lahy handed Phil his newspaper, and Billy Heffernan his flute ; but just as Phil had adjusted his spectacles on his nose, and as Billy was in the act of blowing the first note of the " Humours of Glyn," the half-door opened and Mr. Beresford Pender's servant came in with one of the lamps of his master's tax-cart in his hand.

"The wind is afther quenchin' the lamp on us," said he, " as we wor passin' the quarry, and I came in for a light."

Honor Lahy made the Sign of the Cross on her forehead. She and Mrs. Donovan had more than once compared notes in reference to that same quarry, and the conclusion arrived at was that certain folk who need not be mentioned had " a passage " through it.

Honor Lahy handed the candle to the man, but as he found some difficulty in lighting the lamp, Mr. Beresford Pender himself made his appearance.

"What's delaying you ?" he asked in his tremendous voice.

The delay was not much ; but minutes seemed hours to Mr. Beresford Pender when he happened to be left alone at night, particularly in the neighbourhood of those properties with which his father had any connection as agent or assistant agent. He began at once to bluster as he examined his pistols, and muttered of murderers, and robbers, and Papists and rebels, till poor Norah became quite frightened. But the oaths with which he interlarded his blustering were so shocking that the poor girl shuddered to listen to them. One was so horribly impious that she put her hands to her ears with a low cry, which she was unable to suppress.

He turned round and glared at her, but swore no more till the servant came in to say the lamps were lighted.

After looking again at Norah, Mr. Beresford Pender said, almost in a kind voice :

"Good-night, Mrs. Lahy, I'm obliged to you. I hope I didn't disturb your daughter."

"Oh, no, sir," Honor replied in a low tone, not at all like her usual hearty good-natured way of addressing people.

And Norah looked up in surprise, as if she could scarcely believe he was the same man whose language had so shocked her.

Perhaps he was not the same man. Who knows? Be sure, however, that Norah Lahys are not sent into this busy world for nothing.

This unlooked-for intrusion cast a gloom over the little party.

Honor Lahy could not shake off the feeling that Mr. Beresford Pender's appearance was a "sign of bad luck." But, notwithstanding, Billy Heffernan played the "Humours of Glyn," with variations, and several other melodies, grave and gay, before he bade them good-night.

"Oh, wisha!" exclaimed Honor Lahy, "he put Tommy's cup out uv my head. And now," she added, after tasting it, "'tis cowld."

But, though not as hot as might be wished, Tommy relished the cup of tea very much, and smacked his lips as he despatched it, with the heel of the loaf, sitting up in bed; for Tommy had been sound asleep for a couple of hours, when he opened his eyes and commenced whistling the "Humours of Glyn" in excellent accord with Billy Heffernan's flute— till Billy came to the variations, which so aggravated Tommy Lahy that he pulled the blankets over his head, and turned round with his face against the bolster, in order to shut out the tantalizing vagaries of the musician altogether. And in this position his mother found him when she brought him his share of the feast.

"I'm afeard you'll be tired after stayin' up so late."

"Oh, no, mother, I was never so happy."

"Well, come, *alanna*."

She took Norah in her arms and carried her to her bed-room.

"Put up that newspaper now, Phil. You know 'tis all hours."

"Five minutes," returned Phil. "I have the speech finished all but a quarter of a column."

"What's that ?" Honor exclaimed in a whisper, with a frightened look.

"Don't mind," replied Phil as he read on. "'Tis on'y a slate that's after bein' blown off the house."

"'Tis a terribly stormy night," said Honor. "Listen."

"I hear it," said Phil, as he folded his newspaper. "The almanac mentioned that we were likely to have either storms or heavy rain this month, or frost and snow, unless the wind happened to be from the south, or east, or north-west, and then tolerably fine weather was to be expected, with occasional showers."

"Wisha, now," said Honor, as if her fears were quite dissipated by this explanation. "Go to bed now, Phil, an' let me ready-up the place."

"I'll kneel down here," replied Phil, "and read my penance. Hand me the prayer-book."

"Remind me to-morrow," said he, as he closed the door behind him, "of Tom Donnelly's breeches."

"I will," replied Honor ; "an' I hope you'll finish id at wance. His wife was complainin' to-day that he hadn't a stitch uv dacency."

"Well, he won't have that to say much longer," replied Phil, "so far as the breeches goes." And Phil sprinkled himself with the holy water, and lay down to sleep with a mind at peace with himself and the world.

"I tell you what," he muttered to himself, as he wrapped the blanket tightly over his shoulders, "Phil Lahy is—is—is—a fine fellow !" With which comfortable reflection Phil Lahy began to snore.

CHAPTER XXVI.

A BRIDEGROOM WHO COULDN'T DESCRIBE HIS BRIDE.

"I HOPE you enjoyed the hunt yesterday, Mr. Lowe," said Mary.

"Oh, very much," he replied. "The harriers are an excellent little pack. But I must confess I thought the country rather stiff ; particularly beyond the hill."

" But how did you get through the bog ? Grace and I
could see you all in a cluster in the wood ; and Grace said
she could see the hounds going through the heath over the
high part of the bog ; but I could not see them."

" Did they not go through the place where the heath is ?"
Grace asked, turning to Richard.

" Yes ; and into the wood at the other side ; and we don't
know what became of them after that."

" I knew I could not be mistaken," said Grace. " Though
Mary wanted to persuade me it was a flock of geese I mistook
for the hounds."

" We thought ye'd be back to dinner," said Mrs. Kearney.
" We were an hour later than usual. But Hugh said if ye
had not gone somewhere ye'd be home before then, and there
was no use waiting."

Mr. Lowe apologised ; and justly threw all the blame on
the doctor.

" The fact is," said the doctor, " Bob Lloyd insisted that
we should dine with him. He had young Hemphill and a
few more friends."

" Mr. Beresford Pender among the number I suppose,"
said Mary.

" No, he didn't ask him ; though he was with us at the
time. Lloyd doesn't care about him. I think he told me
his father overreached him in some money transaction."

" Depend your life on old Isaac for that," said Mr.
Kearney.

" By-the-by," said Mr. Lowe, turning to Grace, " your
friend young Mr. Hanly was there—I mean at the hunt.
And he is really one of the boldest riders I ever saw. He
had an unbroken colt with his tail down to the ground and
all covered over with mud—as indeed was the rider, for they
both rolled over in a muddy ditch."

Grace laughed at this description of her admirer. It was
agreed on all hands that she had made a conquest during
the short time she had been Lory's partner in the dance.

He had come back several times to shake hands with
her and bid her good-night ; renewing his offer to show her
the cave each time ; besides telling her he could lend her
Pope's Homer, or the Rambler, or Thomson's Seasons, or
Goldsmith's Poetical Works.

" I'll bring them all to you," said Lory.

But Grace assured him all those books were in her papa's library ; and Lory, shaking hands with her for the fifth time, mounted to his place in the phaeton ; but tumbled out again immediately, and thrusting his long neck inside the drawing-room door, startled Mrs. Kearney with the announcement that he had " The Devil on Two Sticks."

" And four volumes of the ' Spectator,' " added Lory, " and the second volume of ' Tom Jones.' "

So that it was agreed on all hands that she had made a conquest. And the moment Lory was mentioned, Mary looked at her, but Grace frowned scornfully—till the picture called up by Mr. Lowe of Lory mounted upon an untrained colt with a long tail and covered with mud, forced her to laugh whether she would or not.

" He certainly has pluck," said Mr. Lowe ; " and rides remarkably well."

An almost imperceptible motion of the head—something between a nod and a toss—and a certain thoughtfulness in her look, led Mary to suspect that Miss Grace was just saying to herself that a young gentleman who had pluck was not to be despised.

And in fact Grace resolved that her reception of him the next time should be more gracious than it had been on previous occasions when he came to pay his respects. She remembered his love of books, and that some of his remarks were very striking. She even began to think that there was something manly in what Mrs. Kearney called his " terrible throat." So that it was quite lucky for Lory that Mr. Lowe gave him credit for pluck.

To be sure it could be wished, Grace thought, that his coat were wider in the shoulders and longer in the skirts, and the other garment less suggestive of carrying several stones of potatoes in the rear. It was to be regretted, too, that his hair stuck out straight from his head, and that there were so many pimples on his face. But that one virtue of pluck covered a multitude of defects, and Lory was gaining ground rapidly. She recalled, too—what she did not before consider worth attending to—that Lory had insinuated that he would exert all his eloquence to induce his sister to give him her jay, which was both a pretty and an intelligent bird, and in case of success that he, Lory, would be most happy to present the jay to Miss Kiely. Grace remembered all this now, and hoped Lory would keep his word; and if he appeared mounted upon the long-tailed colt, so much the better. Her cogitations were broken in upon by Mr. Kearney asking Mr. Lowe abruptly, how did he like the Hall.

"'Tis a very fine place," Mr. Lowe replied. "I wonder how my grandfather parted with it."

"He could not help it," returned Mr. Kearney bluntly, "the property was going to be put into Chancery at that time, and Somerfield gave him a large fine. We all made up money for him. I lent him eight hundred pounds myself."

Mrs. Kearney started as if from a reverie, and was on the point of announcing that the eight hundred pounds were given to her by her Uncle Dan; but Mary suggested at the moment that Mr. Lowe would have another cup of tea, which caused Mrs. Kearney to start again. The cup of tea knocked the eight hundred pounds out of her head, and her Uncle Dan was left to rest in peace for the present.

"Has Mr. Somerfield any landed property of his own?" Mr. Lowe asked.

"Yes, he has a nice little property near the old church you were looking at the other day. And his son has two or three farms very cheap."

"How can he afford to keep a pack of hounds?"

"Oh, that's not much; they're billeted among the tenants, and the son is a good judge of horses, and makes money by 'em. He has several agencies, too, and a d—n bad agent he is. There is not a lease on any of the properties he is over. He pretends 'tis the landlords refuse to give leases; but 'tis well known 'tis himself puts 'em up to it. He's a magistrate now. The father was a good sort of an old fellow, nothing troubling him but hunting. But the son is a rogue. He's after turning more people out than any man in the county, and giving the land to Scotch and English tenants at a lower rent, and leases."

"I thought you said there were no leases?"

"I mean to the old tenants. But the Englishmen and Scotchmen are sure of leases."

"I had no idea such a system was being carried out."

"You'll probably learn more about it when you see Mr. Pender," said Hugh.

"Sir Garrett said nothing about it," replied Mr. Lowe.

"I suspect," said Hugh, "he knows nothing about it."

This was all very uninteresting to Grace and the doctor, and they were both leaving the room, after yawning several times, when the door opened, and a servant informed Mr. Kearney that Ned Brophy wanted to speak to him.

"Tell him to come in," said Mr. Kearney. "I suppose he is coming to remind us of the wedding."

Ned Brophy soon appeared with his "clothes spic-and-span new," as the song says ; but we cannot add, "without e'er a speck," for Ned's clothes were pretty well speckled with mud—and not his clothes only, for a pellet of the mud had hardened and dried on his right cheek under the eye, and two or three smaller spots were visible about his temples.

Ned was accompanied by his "best man," Mat Donovan.

"Sit down, Ned ; come, Mat, sit down here," said Maurice Kearney, placing two chairs near the window.

"Well, Ned, what's the news ?"

"A fine wet day, sir," replied Ned, who felt and looked somewhat embarrassed as he glanced at Mat to help him on.

"Ned that's afther comin' over, sir, for the lend uv the ould mare to carry home the wife," said Mat Donovan.

This request seemed to surprise Mr. Kearney, who looked at Ned as if he expected some explanation of it.

"I have Tom Bolen's side-car," said Ned, rousing himself, "an' this coult uv mine is in the habit of runnin' away, an' I don't like to venture to drive him in harness, as if he made off on the way home, 'twouldn't look well."

"An' he says I can ride the coult," Mat added, "an' as the mare was idle 'tis I put id into his head to ax the lend uv her. He was goin' to hire a car, but I tould him he needn't, an' 'twould be dacenter not, as people'd say he hadn't a horse uv his own to bring home the wife."

Mat Donovan was quite sincere in recommending this arrangement to Ned Brophy. But he might not have been so positive in urging it if the opportunity of figuring in the blue body-coat on the colt were out of the question. Yet Mat Donovan had no thought of captivating some farmer's daughter with a good fortune, as Honor Lahy prophesied he would be sure to do.

"Oh! very well," said Mr. Kearney, "you can get the mare, Ned."

"Thank'ee, sir. You needn't fear but I'll be careful uv her."

"Don't stir," continued Mr. Kearney, as they were rising to go. "Wait till the mare is ready.—Go out to Wattletoes," he added, turning to his youngest son, "and tell him to get the mare for Ned Brophy."

"And will you tell him to show me my thrush's nest?"

"You were a fool," replied his father, "to give him the cake till he showed you the nest. That was buying a pig in a bag."

"He says now," returned Willie, "that the old one was in the ivy and was listening when he promised to show me the nest, and that she took the young ones all off to Bally-daheen wood; but that he'll go after them the next day he has time; and if he can't find them he says he'll pull a grand stick for me—a holly oak stick with blackthorn knobs on it, he says."

"A holly oak stick with blackthorn knobs on it!" repeated his father. "Would I doubt Wattletoes?"

There was a silence of some minutes after Willie had gone to order the mare, which Mat the Thrasher felt a little embarrassing, particularly as he saw Grace pulling Mary by the sleeve and calling her attention to himself.

"I never see this girl yet, Ned is gettin', sir," said Mat.

"Well, maybe Ned would describe her for us now."

"Wisha, begor I couldn't, sir," replied Ned, scratching his poll and looking puzzled. "I never see her but twice, an' I was dhrunk the two turns."

All eyes were turned with laughing surprise on the speaker, who, at the moment, was anything but a picture of happiness.

"I'm tould, sir," said Mat indignantly, "she's wan uv the finest girls in the parish. How d—n well you wor able to see the two hundhred sovereigns."

"And the old saucepan," said Mr. Kearney. "Did you get the money, Ned?"

"No, sir," he replied solemnly, "but it was counted out

on the table the first day I was at the house, an' put back
again."

" An' you wouldn't miss it out of it ?" said Mr. Kearney,
who seemed to enjoy the matter immensely.

" Hardly," replied Ned. " I never see such a show uv
money together before. It reminded me uv California or the
Bank uv Ireland."

" You'd betther not lose any more time," Mat observed.
" 'Tis gettin' late."

" That's a fine new coat you have, Mat," said Mr. Kearney,
looking at him admiringly as the Thrasher drew himself up
to his full height.

" 'Tis in compliment to Ned I got it, sir," returned Mat.

" You ought to do something for yourself. Make your
harvest at the wedding—maybe you could get a haul at the
old saucepan."

" Thim times is gone, sir," replied Mat. " No chance now
of farmers' daughters an' ' five hundred pounds in goold,' as
the song says." And Mat glanced at Miss Kearney in a
manner that quite annoyed Mr. Lowe.

" He's an impertinent fellow, after all," he thought.

But so far from being offended, Mary returned Mat's
smile in a manner that made the young gentleman quite
angry.

" I don't know that," returned Mr. Kearney. " Try your
luck with one of the other sisters, an' Ned will put in a good
word for you."

" Well, I b'lieve he would, sir," replied Mat, " if there was
any use."

" I hope you'll be over wud us to-night, sir," said Ned, as
he was going. " And if Miss Kearney or Miss Kiely would
like to have a dance they'd be heartily welcome."

" I'm getting old now, Ned," Maurice Kearney replied.
" But Hugh will go. I must take care of myself or this
woman might be on the look-out one of those days."

" Indeed," said Mrs. Kearney, indignantly, taking the
matter in downright earnest, " that's what one of the name
never did. No one could ever say that one of the Ballydunmore family ever married a second time."

" Maybe 'twasn't their fault," exclaimed her husband, who
was evidently enjoying the fun.

"You're quite mistaken," returned Mrs. Kearney. "My Aunt Judith had more proposals than all the young girls of the county, and she never accepted one of them—though my Uncle Dan said she ought to marry. But she never did." And Mrs. Kearney left the room quite offended.

"Mat looks much more like the happy man than Ned," Grace observed, when they had left. "And, indeed, it would not surprise me if it was he got the two hundred pounds out of the old saucepan, and not Ned."

"If poverty enters the door," said Mary; "you know what you said to Father M'Mahon."

"Well, that's true," replied Grace, with a shake of the head. "'Twould be all very well if that view of the case could be kept out of sight."

"I fear, Mr. Lowe," said Mary as she took up her work at a little table near one of the windows, "I fear this will be a wet day."

"Yes, I fear it will continue wet," he replied, after walking to the window, and looking up to the drifting clouds. Mr. Lowe said "feared," but he meant "hoped."

"A wet day in the country is an awful bore," said the doctor, who was just then thinking how certain chums of his in Dublin would spend the day, and wondering why Keating didn't answer his last letter.

Mr. Lowe, on the contrary, thought a wet day in the country anything but a bore under certain circumstances, though he did not say so.

To the surprise of all present the door opened, and Mat Donovan advanced a step or two into the room, and stood rubbing his chin as if he had something to say, but did not know how to begin.

Mary looked round the room, supposing that he had forgotten something, and seeing a walking-stick standing in one of the corners, she took it in her hand, and said: "Perhaps this is your stick, Mat."

"No, Miss," replied Mat, whose eyes were fixed on Grace. "But I'm comin' to ax a favour of Miss Grace, if she'd have no objection."

"Oh, what is it?" Grace asked with quite a coquettish air.

"Well, Miss, there's a little delay about the harness, an' I said to myself I'd run in an' ax you to play that tune for

me you were playin' th' other evening for the masther
'Tisn't but that I know it uv ould," Mat added, " but someway I'm running into another tune in the middle uv the
succond part, an' I have a raison for wishin' to hear id agin."

" What's the name of it ?" she asked.

" It goes by the name uv ' *Nach m-baineaun sin do*,' Miss,"
replied Mat, " but 'tis many's the name id is called."

" It must be one of the Melodies," Grace observed, turning
to Mary. " But the question is, which of them is it ?"

" I can't remember," Mary replied, " but I suppose it must
be one of those you always play for my father."

Grace pressed her finger on her lip, and seemed to be seeking the solution of a mystery.

" Is the tune you want," she asked, " ever called ' Lan-
golee' ?"

" No, Miss, I know that ; an' you played it beautiful, too.
But 'twas in the same book—the large wan wud the goold
harp on the cover."

" Come and we'll look for it," exclaimed Grace, jumping
from her seat, and running out of the room.

CHAPTER XXVII.

THE JAY.

MARY stood up and asked Mat to come to the drawing-room,
where they found Grace already sitting at the piano.

" Oh, my goodness !" she exclaimed, looking round, " what
sort of gentlemen are those ?"

But before she could proceed further with her censure, Mr.
Lowe was at his post and placed the music before her.

" Well, now, let me think of all Mr. Kearney's tunes," said
she, turning over the leaves. " Listen to this one, Mat."

" No, Miss," replied Mat, shaking his head, " that's ' Moll
Row in the Morning.' "

" Well, this," and she played a few bars of another.

Mat shook his head again.

" Oh, I think I know it now," she exclaimed, as she turned rapidly over the leaves. " Why, here it is, with the very same name he has mentioned. Mr. Kearney has some words to it about—

> " I'll go to the fair, and I'll sell my old cow,
>   For twenty-five shillings, one pound and one crown,
>   I'll drink what I earn, and pay what I owe,
>   And what's that to any man whether or no ?"

" That's id, Miss !" Mat exclaimed, in quite an excited way.

" 'Tis ' They may Rail at this Life,' " said Grace, turning to Mary. " Sit down, Mat."

Mat's spirit was attentive as she played ; and after a little while he began to move his head from side to side and turned his eyes to the ceiling.

Mary watched him with a smile ; for it seemed quite evident he was mentally going through his song with all possible care. Her suspicion in this respect was confirmed beyond all doubt when Mat thrust his hand into his pocket and pulled out a sheet of paper which he hastily unfolded, and, after glancing at it for a moment, turned his eyes again to the ceiling and commenced what he would himself call " humouring " the tune.

" Good luck to you, Miss," he exclaimed, when she had stopped playing. " I think I have id purty well now."

" I think, Mat," said Mary, " you ought to sing the song for us."

" Begor, I couldn't, Miss," he replied, after some hesitation. " I'll thry an' sing id to-night for 'em. 'Tis a new song I got from the young schoolmaster over at Loughneen ; an' I said I'd get id be heart an' sing id at the fust weddin' I'd be at ; an' Ned's happens to be the fust. Though, faith, Miss Mary, I was thinkin' I might be singin' id at your own this turn."

Though the look which accompanied this last observation was precisely the same as that which so annoyed Mr. Lowe in the parlour, he now laughed and saw nothing at all impertinent in it.

" Mat is surely a *deluder*," said Grace, when he had left.

" I'm quite vexed that he never favours *me* with any of his admiring glances."

" You like to be admired, Miss Grace," said Mr. Lowe.

" Who does not, I'd like to know ?   Though some people may *pretend* not to care about it."   And she glanced at Mary.

" Take care," said Mary, " or I'll tell Mr. Lowe what you said about him the other day."

" And will you tell him that somebody else said I was right ?"

Mary got a little frightened ; and, lest she should have the worst of it in such an encounter, she hurried back to the parlour and took up her work.

Hugh was sitting at the little table near the window.   He had gone out with the intention of walking over the farm, but turned back on finding the rain was heavier than he expected.

Mr. Lowe and Grace immediately followed Mary, and there was much lively chat on the subject of the manners and customs of the peasantry, suggested by Mat Donovan's visit.   Grace had quite a fund of anecdotes, picked up at those " literary dinners " she alluded to when trying to find the " solution of the mystery " connected with the tracks in the snow.

Hugh was silent ; but to the watchful eye of his sister, it was plain he was enjoying Grace's lively sallies and merry laughter.   He leant over the back of his chair, and during a lull in the conversation seemed to have fallen asleep. Mary called Grace's attention to him, in order that she might do something to rouse him.   His long black hair hung over the table, and Grace happened to have the scissors in her hand, clipped off a lock.

Hugh started up, and seeing what she had done, snatched the scissors from her ; and twisting a tress of her hair round and round his finger, cut it off, to her consternation.

" Oh, you wretch !" she exclaimed, pulling down her hair to see what amount of damage he had done.   But finding the tress would not be missed, she resumed her good humour.

" Could you invent anything for us to do ?" the doctor asked piteously, from the sofa.

" 'Tis too wet to go out," replied Hugh

"It is too bad," said Mary, "that Mr. Lowe must remain a prisoner."

"I assure you," he replied, "I can be resigned to my fate."

"Will you go to the wedding?" she asked, turning to Hugh.

"I suppose I must. There is no getting out of it, as my father won't go."

"He is a great stay-at-home, Mr. Lowe. He will not go anywhere but when he can't help it. And you saw he does not even dance quadrilles."

"Except when he has some one to lead him like a bear," said Grace.

"Was it not customary," Hugh asked with solemnity, "when dancing bears used to be exhibited, to have the bear led by a monkey? I think I read about such a thing somewhere."

"I see what you mean, sir," said Grace. "Perhaps it is all fair."

"A hit," said the doctor, "a palpable hit. But I'd sooner have expected it from Lory. He's devilish clever at that sort of thing."

"Is he, indeed? Then I was peculiarly fortunate in getting two such clever partners."

"You are a match for them," said Mary laughing.

"A *match*—you are certainly complimentary."

"I mean you are able for them all—to give them tit for tat."

"*Quid pro quo*," replied Grace. "I should hope so."

"It would be diamond cut diamond," said Mary.

"Diamond!" repeated Grace. "Do you call him a diamond?"

And she nodded her head towards Hugh, in a way that made the doctor break into a horse-laugh, and kick up his heels on the sofa.

"Or," she continued, opening her eyes, in which there was a curious blending of astonishment and fun, "is *that* the gem?"

She pointed out into the lawn; and there was Mr. Lory Hanly doing his best to shelter himself from the rain with the collar of his scanty coat, running towards the house with his head down—the wind being in his face—as if he

intended making a battering ram of himself to drive in the
hall-door. He was covered with mud from head to foot, and
it was astonishing how high up and far behind him he
managed to fling his heels.

Grace hurried out to open the door She stood back
behind it, as if she expected to see Lory shoot past her, and
involuntarily held her breath in anticipation of a frightful
crash among Mrs. Kearney's crockery ; for a vague notion
crossed her mind that Lory would be picked up insensible
in the pantry at the end of the hall after splitting the door
of that sanctum in two with his skull.

Lory, however, had stopped himself on the door-step, and
Grace stared at him in speechless amazement.

The rain was running down in little rivers all over him—
particularly over his eyes ; which made it necessary for him
to cut off the streams at the eyebrows with the knuckles of
his thumbs before he could see distinctly. Lory, too, looked
surprised when he found who had opened the door for him.
But recovering himself before she could ask him in, he
fumbled with one hand under his coat, and then thrust out
both arms at full length towards her.

" Here he's for you now," said Lory, breathlessly.

Grace took what he presented to her mechanically, without
having the least notion what it was, and Lory instantly
wheeled round—his hob-nailed boots making as much noise
as if a horse had stumbled on the door-step—and set off for
home, forgetting that the wind would be now in his back ;
the consequence of which was that Lory was precipitated
head-foremost, and had to run on all-fours for good ten yards
before he could recover himself.   Once in an upright position,
however, he was blown back to the avenue gate without
further exertion from himself than lifting his feet and keeping one hand clapped against his poll to prevent his cap from
being swept across the bog, and, peradventure, stuck into a
crevice of the old castle, like the piece of an old petticoat—
to which it bore a striking resemblance—in the broken
window of Jack Delaney's sleeping apartment behind the
forge. It was observed, too, that the wind kept Lory's diminutive skirts stuck against his back, as if they had been
pinned up under the shoulder-blades. He had actually
reached the gate before Grace recovered from her surprise,

even so far as to think of shutting the door. But then she could not use her hands for that purpose, and as she was collecting her senses to think what was to be done, Hugh came out to know what had happened to make Lory beat so precipitate a retreat.

"What is it all about, Grace?" he asked, as he closed the hall-door. "What have you done to frighten Lory? Has he popped the question and been rejected? The effect was dreadful. I very much fear the young gentleman's body may be found, nine days hence, floating in the Poulnamuck."

But Grace returned to the parlour without noticing his banter, and was holding out Lory's gift to satisfy her own and her friends' curiosity, when a sharp pinch on the wrist made her let it go with a scream. And "with many a flirt and flutter," like the celebrated raven, Lory's jay perched upon Miss Kearney's work-box. He looked about him with the utmost nonchalance, and then winked his eyes several times and moved his neck as if he had been sleeping in an uneasy position; and then the jay opened his beak and yawned, as if he were very drowsy, and meant to go to sleep again. But just as he was burying his head cosily between his shoulders, he caught a glimpse of himself in the lid of the work-box, and the sight so far awakened his curiosity that he pecked at the rosewood, and in doing so his feet began to slip upon its polished surface : whereupon the jay extended his wings a little, and jerked up his tail. What followed we shall not venture to describe ; but Mary jumped from her place near the table with a scream almost as loud as Grace's when she got the pinch on the wrist. The doctor turned round to see what had happened ; and seeing it, flung himself on his back, and commenced cutting capers with his feet in the air.

"That Lory is a genius," said the doctor. "He has cured me of a severe fit of the blues. I'm eternally indebted to him."

Grace got into good humour, too, and after carefully pulling down her cuffs, she ventured to take the jay between her hands again. "I'll go and make Ellie happy," she said, running away, holding the jay at arm's-length above her head.

The sky began to brighten over the hills, and Hugh predicted that the remainder of the day would be fine. The

wind continued to blow ; but before evening the sun flashed
through the broken clouds, and it was agreed on all hands,
that Ned Brophy's " hauling home " would be more propitious
than could have been anticipated a few hours earlier.

" I wonder," said Mrs. Kearney, who came into the parlour
in an evidently distressed state of mind—" I wonder what
can be delaying Barney ? And he has things we want for
the dinner."

" I suppose it was the heavy rain," Mary replied. " No
one would face out in such a storm ; and I daresay Barney
waited till it cleared up."

" Even if he did, he might be here now."

" Well, you know," said Mary, " Mr. Lowe has decided on
going to the wedding with Hugh, so you need not be
particular about our dinner to-day."

" Why so ?" Mrs. Kearney asked, as if she could not see
the force of the reasoning.

" Why, of course, if they go at all, they'll be there for
dinner."

" Oh, yes, they call it a dinner, but it will be more like a
supper. I'll engage it won't be on the table before eleven
o'clock—or ten the earliest."

" Well, even so," replied Mary. " They'll go at the usual
hour, and you need not be so particular about our dinner
to-day."

" 'Tis too late already," rejoined Mrs. Kearney, with a
sigh, " to think of roasting a bit of beef. But if that fellow
was home in time, sure I could have a nice steak for them
at any rate. He's always disappointing me, and making
mistakes, bringing wrong things, and running after peep-
shows, and ballad-singers, and Punches and Judys. My heart
is broken with him," continued Mrs. Kearney, sighing deeply.
" But indeed," she added with severe dignity, as she folded
her plump hands and rested them on her knees—" but
indeed, only for the respect my Uncle Dan had for his
mother I wouldn't keep him another hour under the roof of
the house."

Mary was not at all apprehensive that Barney was in
danger of instant dismissal ; but wishing to put her mother
into good humour she observed, as if to herself, that " poor
Barney was very devoted and strictly honest."

"Well, indeed," replied her mother in a softened tone, "there's nothing to be said against his honesty. His father would lay down his life for my Uncle Dan, and, indeed, I believe poor Barney would do the same for any one of the name."

CHAPTER XXVIII.

BARNEY WINS A BET, AND LOSES MUCH PRECIOUS TIME.

THE cause of Mrs. Kearney's trouble was all this time comfortably ensconced in the chimney corner, in the little kitchen behind Mrs. Burke's shop, with his foot on the hob—which foot, by the way, the servant girl had seized with the tongs while making the fire, mistaking it for a sod of turf of the description known as "hand turf"; in the manufacture of which the moulders allow free scope to their fancy, and occasionally produce a marvel of grotesqueness.

Barney had but just reached Mrs. Burke's door, when the rain began to pour down in right earnest. So, after putting Bobby under a shed in the yard, he took possession of the corner, and kept it without flinching even when the fire was at the hottest, and the big black pot hanging over it was enveloped in the blaze—which drew from the girl who had attempted to boil the potatoes with his foot, the remark that "the divil a wan else she ever knew could stand the same corner but Dan Brit and John Roche, the lime-burners."

"An' spake uv the ould boy an' he'll appear," she added; "here is Dan himse'f."

The individual spoken of drew a chair to the fire, scowling at Barney as if he considered him an intruder. It could be seen at a glance that Dan Brit was not a model of sobriety. After eyeing Barney in silence for a minute, he was turning to the girl to order a pint of porter, when he looked again at him and hesitated. In fact, Dan Brit was debating with himself whether, if he ventured to ask Barney to take a drink, was Barney the sort of person to say afterwards, "Let us have another." And in case he was the

man to say so, Dan Brit had his mind made up to call back
the girl just as she was going for the two pints of porter,
saying, " Kitty, I'll take a glass of the old malt ; I'm not
very well to-day."   And so Dan Brit would have a glass of
whiskey, price threepence, in exchange for the pint of porter,
price three-halfpence ; which, in a social and friendly way,
and, in the spirit of a " good fellow," he was thinking of
pressing Barney Brodherick to accept at his hands.

And while Dan Brit was pondering the risks to be run in
the matter, his eye fell upon Barney's foot on the hob,
which object seemed to fascinate Dan Brit and drive all
other objects and subjects out of his thoughts for the time
being.

" The divil so ugly a foot as that," said Dan Brit, solemnly,
" *I* ever see, anyhow."

" There's an uglier wan in the house," rejoined Barney.

" No, nor in Ireland," returned Dan.   " Nor in Europe,
Asia, Africa, or America."

" Will you bet a quart uv porther ?" said Barney.

" That there's not an uglier foot in the house ?" exclaimed
Dan, staring in astonishment at him.

" Yes," replied Barney, with spirit, " I'll wager a quart uv
porther, an' let Kitty be the judge, that there's an uglier
foot in the house."

" Done !" exclaimed Dan Brit, who grasped at the certainty
of getting a drink without paying for it.   " But will you
stake the money ?"

" Ay, will I," said Barney, suiting the action to the word,
and slapping down the coppers on a chair near him.

" Take that money, Kitty," said Dan Brit, " an' decide the
bet."

" What is the bet ?" Kitty asked.

It was explained to her ; and Kitty shook her head sorrowfully, and told Barney he was always a fool.

" Stake the money, yourse'f," said Barney.   And Dan did
so.

" Come, give me back that change," said Dan ; " an' bring
in the drink.   The bet is mine."

" Wait a bit," returned Barney.   " Kitty, give us a peep
at your own."

" What   impudence   you   have !"   exclaimed   Kitty, indignantly. " Who dare say a word agin them, I'd like to know ?" And Kitty exhibited a pair of very presentable feet.

" Begob, Kitty," said Barney, with a grin, " if I was dependin' on thim, I'd lose my bet."

" An' do you mane to say you haven't lost id ?" Dan asked. " Run, Kitty, for the porther."

" Ay, will she ; but 'tisn't my money'll pay for id."

" Didn't you bet there was an uglier foot in the house than that ?"

And Dan Brit pointed to the foot on the hob.

" I did."

" An' where is id ?"

Barney Brodherick slowly and deliberately drew his other foot from under the chair, and held it up to view.

" Here's your money, Barney," exclaimed Kitty, in an ecstasy of delight. " You won the bet ; I'll go for the porter."

Dan Brit's jaw fell down as he stared with open mouth at Barney. And after swallowing his share of the porter he walked away with an expression of countenance which made Kitty observe that " wan'd think 'twas a physic o' salts he was afther swallyin'."

When the rain ceased, Barney, snatching one of his baskets from Mrs. Burke's counter, hurried off to Wat Murphy's and presented Mrs. Kearney's written order to the butcher.

" I haven't what she wants," said Wat ; " but I can send her a nice bit that will answer her as well."

He seized his knife and saw, and cut and weighed the beef so quickly that it was wrapped in the cloth and deposited in the basket before Barney could collect his wits to demur to the proceeding.

" An' now," he muttered, scratching his head as if the thing were done past recall, " an' now she'll be puttin' the blame on me, an' sayin' 'twas my fau't—an' that's the way they're always layin' everything on my shoulders. The divil may care what's done wrong—'tis Barney wud every wan uv 'em, big an' little."

" If she finds any fau't wud that," said Wat, as if he were threatening somebody, " tell her 'tis her own cow,"—which, however, did not happen to be the fact. But Wat Murphy

told lies in the way of business on principle. " For "—Wat
was wont to observe—" if I didn't tell lies, do you think I
could ever sell an ould ram ?"

" Och ! be the hokey, 'twill dhrag the arm out uv me !"
exclaimed Barney, as he raised the basket. " If I thought
'twould be so heavy, I'd bring up the ass."

" Put it on your head," Wat suggested.

" I'm d——n sure I won't. Do you want to make a
woman uv me ? Is it like a can uv wather you want me to
carry id ?"

" A purty woman you'd make," observed Wat, as Barney
stooped under the weight of the heavy basket.

" Blood-an-ouns, Wat !" he exclaimed, turning round outside the door, " when are we to have the bull-bait ?"

The question was suggested by the white bull-dog, who
walked to the street-door and back again without condescending to take the slightest notice of Barney, or anyone
else.

" I'm not at liberty to give particulars," Wat replied, in
a manner that put a stop to all further inquiries on the
important subject of the bull-bait.

Barney held on his way till he reached the corner of the
street, when he was obliged to rest his basket against the
iron railings of a genteel house, separated by a small garden
from the street.

" Oh, murther, murther !" he muttered, " I'll be kilt afore
I'm down to Mrs. Burke's. An' 'tis a good deed ; where was
I comin' wudout Bobby ? An' thanum-un-dioul ! the misthress'll murther me worse nor the basket. I remimber
now, she warned me to be home as fast as I could. I wondher
what excuse I'll have for her ? Let me see. Begob, I'll say
Bobby got the cholic after the peltin' we got comin' through
the bog. For how will she know but it was skelpin' in our
face, barrin' Judy Brien might tell her ; an' nice thanks that
id be afther givin' her a lift from the crass."

Here Barney pulled up his sleeve to the elbow and looked
at his arm, upon which the handle of the basket had left its
mark.

" Begob, 'twill cut the arm off uv me," he continued.
" An' the divil's cure to me ; where was I comin' wudout
Bobby ?"

He swung the basket on the other arm and was setting off again, when the hall door of the genteel house opened, and a lady came running towards him down the straight gravel walk.

"Wait for a minute," she called out, "I want to speak to you."

Barney stopped; but she required a minute or two to recover breath.

"You're Mr. Kearney's man," she said at last.

"Yes, Miss," replied Barney, "I'm his b'y."

"What have you in the basket?"

"Mate, Miss."

"What sort? Show it to me."

Barney raised a corner of the cloth.

"Beef!" she exclaimed. "I declare it's a round. Will that be all dressed together?"

"Begob, mese'f don't know, Miss."

"Do your people have butchers' meat every day?"

"Faith, an' they do so, Miss; barrin' Friday."

"Oh, yes, they're Roman Catholics. Are you a Roman Catholic?"

"Begob, I am, Miss—though my mother was born a haythen."

"Born a heathen! Is it possible?"

"The divil a lie in id, Miss—an' reared. But she turned afther runnin' away wud my father—God rest his sowl."

She looked at Barney as if he were a natural curiosity; and began to wonder what particular race of savages his mother belonged to.

"Of what country was your mother a native?" she asked.

"A native?" Barney repeated, as if the question were rather puzzling. "Oh, ay!" he added after a pause, "is id what counthryman is my mother? Begob, she was bred, born, an' reared in Ballyporeen. Her father was the clerk uv the church; an' my father was sarvin' the slathers whin they wor roofin' id. 'Tis of'n I heard her tellin' the ins an' outs uv id. He used to run up an' down the laddher so soople, that, be japers, she tuck a sthrange likin' to him, an' med off wud him—though her sivin generations afore her wor haythens."

"Oh, you mean," said the lady, "that your mother was

a Protestant, and she married a Papist, and became an
apostate."

"Begob, that's id, Miss," replied Barney, perfectly satisfied with her version of the affair. "But this'd never do
for me," he added, thrusting his arm into the handle of his
basket. "'Tis all hours, an' I'm in for gettin' Ballyhooly
from the misthress."

"Wait for a moment," the young lady exclaimed, quite
frightened at the idea of his escaping. "Tell me ; is Mr.
Lowe with your people still ?"

"Begob, he is, Miss ; I have letthers for him."

"Show them to me !" she exclaimed eagerly, thrusting out
her hand through the railing.

"They're in the basket, below, at Mrs. Burke's, Miss, wud
the newspapers an' things for Miss Mary."

"What things are they ?"

"The divil a know I know. I get a scrap uv writin'
mentionin' what I'm to brin'. On'y for that they'd bother
the life out uv me."

"How does Mr. Lowe spend his time ?"

"He's d——n fond uv discoorsin' Miss Mary," Barney
replied, with the extraordinary grimace which he meant for
a smile.

"Oh, I suppose he has no other amusement ?"

"Himself and the docthor goes uv an odd time over to
Hanly's," said Barney ; "an' they wor out wud the hounds
yesterday."

"I wonder," said she, as if thinking aloud, "did they
meet Robert ?"

"They didn't lave Mr. Bob's till wan o'clock last night,
Miss," returned Barney. "An' 'tis I have good raison to
know id ; for I stopped up wud Tom Maher for the horses,
an' they kep' me dancin' for 'em in the kitchen till I hadn't
a leg to put ondher me. The docthor was purty well I thank
you. An' faith there was no fear uv Mr. Lowe aither."

"Do you mean to say that Mr. Lowe was at Mount Tempe
last night ?"

"Faith, then, he was so, Miss ; an' 'tis I have raison to
remimber id."

She turned round and ran into the house, as if she suddenly discovered that Barney was not a safe companion, and

that the fate of the clerk's daughter, of Ballyporeen, might be hers if she did not instantly fly from danger. But, so far from having any such amiable intentions, Barney, as he swung his basket on his hip, ejaculated an imprecation of so extraordinary a character that we are not sure whether it would bear repeating—at least in his own words. Miss Lloyd—we hope the reader has recognised Miss Lloyd—pulled up her skirts considerably higher than her ankles as she ran back to the house ; and the glimpse thus afforded of the nymph's limbs must have suggested to Barney Brodherick the before-mentioned imprecation. For, looking after the flying fair one, and recollecting the precious time he had lost on her account, Barney prayed that a certain sable gentleman might have " her shin-bone for a flute, playing the 'Rakes of Mallow' for her sowl," into a place where it might dance to the music upon a pavement which must be pretty extensive by this time.

"O Isabella !" Miss Lloyd exclaimed. "O Isabella !" She dropped into an arm-chair and panted for breath.

Isabella ran to the window to try if she could catch a glimpse of the desperado who, she had no doubt, must have attempted to carry off her sister.

"O mamma," she continued, " Mr. Lowe has been at Mount Tempe."

"Well ; and what of that ?"

"What ! Oh, that we must have the party at once, and I am sure he will come."

"No ; I tell you he would not unless those people with whom he is staying were asked."

"And what great harm would it be to invite them ?"

"Henrietta, you astound me ! But there has been enough of that nonsense already. It is out of the question."

"But what I mean is that *they* would not come."

"No matter, it would be talked of. You know the Scotts did not ask ourselves last time ; and if they knew we had such acquaintances what would they not say !"

"But why do you think he would not come if they were not asked ?"

"Indeed, Henrietta," said her sister—a blooming, blue-eyed girl of twenty summers or thereabout—" it would be positive rudeness after your being there."

" I would not mind the rudeness," rejoined her mother.
" But when he saw you there he must be under the impression that they are recognised by the gentry. Indeed, I don't
know how you can disabuse him of this notion—you are for
ever thrusting yourself into improper places."

" Oh, I can say it was merely accidental. He knows they
are only farmers. And Robert is so intimate with their
brother."

" Oh, if there was no one but him I should have no objection. But the sister is out of the question. I really wonder
both she and her mother have not called on you. I saw them
drive by the day before yesterday. And, indeed, I'd have
no objection. Mrs. Barn tells me she's a respectable sort of
person ; and very good to make presents."

" There is Robert," said Isabella, pointing to the window.

" Oh, we must send for him !" exclaimed Miss Lloyd. " I
wonder is there a meeting of the club to-night ?"

" No, it is to be on Thursday," her mother replied.
" They are going to elect Beresford Pender."

" Robert says he'll black-ball him," said Isabella.

" I really cannot understand his prejudice against him.
He is a young man of excellent principles," replied her
mother.

" I hate the sight of him !" exclaimed Isabella. " He is
the most insufferably vulgar creature I ever saw."

Mr. Robert Lloyd, in hunting costume, and mounted upon
his well-known grey horse, had ridden quietly past his
mother's house without turning his eyes towards it. A servant, however, was sent to the hotel for him ; and he soon
strolled up the gravel walk, with his hands in his pockets.

" O Robert," said his eldest sister, " you had Mr. Lowe
last night ?"

" Ay, faith," he replied.

" Do you think you could get him to stay with you for a
few days ?"

" He's a d—d sight better off where he is. I wish I could
exchange places with him."

Miss Lloyd made a gesture expressive of the most ineffable
contempt.

" He's to be at Ned Brophy's wedding to-night," Bob
observed.

"Oh, and we are asked," exclaimed Miss Lloyd. "Are you going, Robert?"

"Ay, faith. I always go to a tenant's wedding."

"It is what the highest people do," said his mother.

"And don't you think we ought to go?" Miss Lloyd asked.

"If you wish it, I see no objection."

"Will you come, Bell?"

"If I thought there would be any chance of fun, I would. Will there be any fun, Robert?"

"Ay, faith. He has two pipers and three fiddlers."

"And an excellent dinner," said Miss Lloyd. "I saw all the things. They have three legs and two shoulders of mutton, and——"

"Don't mind the bill of fare. But can we make ourselves fit to be seen in so short a time?"

"I'll wear my blue gauze," said Miss Lloyd.

"What! Will you go in a low body?"

"Of course I will; and I'll wear my pearls. And, mamma, will you lend me your bracelets?"

"Yes, you may have them; but take care and don't lose them, as you did those trinkets the other day."

"Oh, they were only worth a few shillings."

"Yes, but it would be just as easy to lose them if they were diamonds."

"Oh, you need not fear; I'll take care of them. Come, Isabella. And, mamma, will you tell John to have the car ready?"

And Miss Lloyd hurried to her chamber, on hostile thoughts intent, so far as Mr. Henry Lowe's heart was concerned.

"Now, Robert," said Mrs. Lloyd, on finding herself alone with her son, "did you do anything in that matter yet? You know her fortune is very considerable, and would enable you to put everything to rights. So I beg you will make up your mind this time, and don't act so strangely as you have so often done."

"I'll talk to Jer about it."

"Well, Jer is sensible, and has got you out of some awkward scrapes. But this is a different thing altogether. So I request you will act for yourself now. Have you seen her?"

" Ay, faith."

" And how do you like her ? "

Mr. Robert Lloyd opened his mouth very wide and
yawned. And when his mother looked round to see why he
had not replied to her question, the gentleman was leisurely
walking out of the room with his hands in his pockets.
Whistling was one of the things that Mr. Robert Lloyd did
well ; and as he sauntered down the gravel walk, his mother
could distinctly hear the little air which he had played upon
his jew's-harp for Mr. Lowe, and of which he had become
particularly fond since Richard Kearney's misadventure in
the bog.

CHAPTER XXIX.

THE HAULING HOME.—" IS NORAH LAHY STRONG ? "

" GOOD evening, Barney," said Mr. Lloyd, as he was passing
Mrs. Burke's shop-door, where Barney Brodherick was fixing
sundry baskets and parcels in his donkey-cart. " What
news ? "

" Nothin' strange, sir," replied Barney ; " barrin' that I'm
in a divil uv a hurry."

" Barney, maybe you'd carry this as far as Honor Lahy's
for me ? " said Judy Brien, who stood by the donkey-cart
with a new cradle she had just purchased from a travelling
vendor.

" An' welcome, Judy, an' yourse'f on the top uv id."

" Oh, I must wait for Tim, an' he'll carry me behind him.
I was goin' to lave the cradle here at Mrs. Burke's, till I met
you. I thought you wor gone home hours ago."

" All right," said Barney. " Put id on top uv this hamper,
an' I'll tie id down wud this bit of coard."

" Hallo ! Bill," shouted Mr. Bob Lloyd, who watched the
fixing of the cradle with great interest, and even held it in its
place while Barney was tying it—" hallo, Bill, where are you
bound for ? "

It was Billy Heffernan upon his mule. The saddle was
very far back towards the animal's tail, and kept in its place

by a crupper. He was obliged to put both hands to one side of the rein in order to bring his steed to a stand, which he effected by very nearly riding through Mrs. Burke's shop-window. This catastrophe was only prevented by Bob Lloyd hitting the mule on the nose with his whip.

"Comin' home wud Ned Brophy, sir," replied Billy. "He sint me—wo, Kit!—on afore 'em to tell them to sind for another gallon uv whiskey an' some ginger cordial, as there's more comin' from that side than he expected."

"All right, Bill," said Mr. Lloyd, turning the mule's head towards the road.

And moving back a pace or two, Mr. Lloyd drew his hunting-whip from under his arm and deliberately lashed the mule several times under the flanks, which had the effect of making Kit fling out her hind legs as if she wanted to fling her shoes at the head of her assailant. But finding that this was impracticable, Kit put her head between her fore legs, and after a minute's debate with herself as to the proper course to be pursued under the circumstances, she clattered up the main street at a canter, with her nose to the ground, after the manner of mules and donkeys with a pack of canine tormentors at their heels.

"Begob, sir," exclaimed Barney, as if a bright idea had struck him, "I b'lieve I might as well wait an' be home wud the weddin'."

"Ay, faith, Barney," replied Mr. Lloyd.

And there being neither peep-show, nor ballad-singer, nor Punch and Judy in Kilthubber on that day, Ned Brophy's wedding was a regular god-send to Barney; for were it not for the wedding, in spite of his ingenuity in finding temptations to keep him from being home at a proper time, Mrs. Kearney might possibly have been able to have the "nice steak" for dinner.

A wedding party is always an object of interest; and Ned Brophy being well known in Kilthubber and along the whole line of march, men, women, and children were on the look-out for his.

The procession comprised some ten or fifteen "carriages of people," including jaunting cars and "common cars," and a considerable troop of equestrians, among whom Mat the Thrasher, in his blue body-coat, mounted upon Ned Brophy's colt, was the observed of all observers. They were greeted with a cheer from a considerable crowd collected at the corner of the street, which compliment was attributed to the fact that several boon companions of the bridegroom's were in the crowd. But when they got a cheer at every cross road and cluster of houses they passed after leaving the town behind them, so unusual a circumstance began to excite surprise.

Mat Donovan, however, having to alight to pick up the bridegroom's hat, which somehow had got the habit of being blown off his head every ten minutes or so, the whole procession rattled past him before he could remount ; and as he came up with them just as they were passing the cross of Dunmoyne, he discovered that they were indebted to Barney Brodherick for turning Ned Brophy's hauling home into what the newspaper reporters call " a regular ovation." Barney was standing with a foot on each shaft, belabouring his donkey to keep him at a gallop, and behind him, on the top of his load, was Judy Brien's new cradle. It was naturally supposed that Ned Brophy had provided himself with a cradle at this early stage of his matrimonial journey ; and such an instance of foresight was hailed with shouts of applause from Kilthubber to Knocknagow.

Barney stopped at Honor Lahy's to leave the cradle there.

" What is this ?" a gentleman asked, putting his head out of a chaise that stood near the beech tree while the driver was repairing a break in the harness, pointing to the cars and horsemen as they passed.

" Ned Brophy's funeral, sir," replied Barney as he pitched the cradle down on the ground.

" Don't mind him, sir," said Honor Lahy, " 'tis his weddin'."

" The difference is not much," returned the gentleman— who must have been an incorrigible old bachelor—as he pulled up the window and leant back in his seat.

Mary Kearney, and Grace, and Ellie were out walking, and on hearing the shouts, and catching a glimpse of the wedding party, they ran into Mat the Thrasher's house, where they could see without being seen, from the little window, the light from which was wont to cheer the belated traveller as he plodded along the bleak bog road.

Nelly Donovan was arraying herself in her best finery for the wedding.

"Come here, Nelly," said Mary, "and point out the bride to us."

"I never see her myself, Miss," replied Nelly, running from the room with her hair about her shoulders; "but that's Ned's first cousin on the same side of the car wud him; so, I suppose the tall wan at this side is the wife."

"The cousin is very nicely dressed," Grace remarked. "That's a very pretty bonnet she has. In fact, she is quite lady-like. What is her name?"

"Bessy Morris, Miss."

"Is that Bessy?" said Mary, looking at the owner of the pretty bonnet with increased interest. "So it is; I see her now." For Bessy Morris had turned round and looked over the clipped hedge, and up at the old cherry-tree, and then down towards the school-house beyond the quarry, with a wistful gaze that Mary interpreted into a sigh for the times that were gone.

"She has all the latest fashions, Miss," said Nelly, "after coming from Dublin. But she was always tasty."

"Ned looks as if he were going to be hanged," Grace observed. "I should not like to see such an expression as that in *my* husband's face on the wedding-day."

The matter-of-fact way in which she spoke of *her* husband made them all laugh; while old Mrs. Donovan stopped her knitting and raised her hands in wonder.

"Ah, I wouldn't say," said Nelly, as if to herself, "but that house below in the threes is after bringin' some wan to Ned's mind that put the heart across in him the night uv the party long ago."

"And did she refuse him?" Grace asked.

"No, Miss; she was fond uv the slob—but she hadn't the fortune."

"The bride is a fine-looking girl," said Mary.

"Faith, then, she's nothin' short uv id," returned Nelly with an assenting notion of the head as she stooped down and pushed back her hair to get a better view, "though Billy Heffernan tould me she was a step-laddher."

"Oh, a step-ladder!" exclaimed Grace. "What did he mean by that?"

"Long and narrow, Miss," replied Nelly, laughing, "like huxter's turf."

"Come, Grace," said Mary; "it is getting late, and we have to call at Mrs. Lahy's yet. I didn't like to go in when I saw the chaise at the door. I hope all the wedding people are after passing."

"They are, Miss," replied Nelly. "An' maybe you'd tell Phil Lahy not to delay, as I promised to wait for him."

"Is Phil to be at the wedding ?"

"Faix, 'twouldn't be a weddin' wudout him," said Nelly.

"You're in great style, Nelly," Mary remarked with a smile. "I suppose you are determined to break half-a-dozen hearts at least before morning ?"

Nelly sighed, and shook her head ; but recovering herself, she replied in her wild way :

"Well, I must thry an' do some good for myse'f among the strangers. There'll be some likely lads there to-night, an' who knows what luck I might have."

Mary was welcomed, as usual, by Norah and her mother. But Phil seemed to have a weight upon his mind, and was as full of importance as if he were about to engage in some undertaking upon which the very existence of his little helpless family depended.

"Good evening, Miss," said he in a subdued tone. He paced up and down the kitchen, as if it were a sick chamber, rubbing his newly-shaven chin, and occasionally feeling the high stiff collar of his clean shirt in a hurried way, as if the thought were continually occurring to him that he had forgotten to put it on.

"Nelly Donovan desired me to tell you, Mr. Lahy, that she was waiting for you."

Phil Lahy took down his hat, and putting it on with the air of a humane judge assuming the black cap, he left the house without uttering a word.

"Is Mr. Hugh goin' to the weddin' ?" Honor inquired.

"Yes, he and Mr. Lowe are going."

"Wisha, Miss, maybe you'd tell him to have an eye to Phil."

"How so ?" asked Mary in surprise.

"Well," replied Honor, thoughtfully, "he's afther promisin' me an' Norah not to take anything stronger than

cordial ; an' if Mr. Hugh'd have an eye on him and remind
him uv id now an' then, I know he'd be all right."

"Well, I'll tell him," said Mary, with a smile.

Grace was becoming a great favourite with Norah.   Grace
needed only to try to become a favourite with anybody.   And
how glad she was to see by Honor Lahy's smile that the poor
woman harboured no prejudice against her, after all.

"Are you glad that spring is coming ?" she asked, turning
to Norah.

"Oh, yes, Miss ; I'm longing for the fine days, when I can
sit outside under the tree."

"Are you fond of reading ?"

"I am, Miss ; an' when I'm not strong enough myself,
Tommy reads for me, an' so does my father sometimes."

"I think I have some books at home you would like.
And when I go home I'll send them to you the first opportunity I get."

Norah looked her thanks, and perhaps there was a little
pleased surprise in the look.

"You are fond of music, too, I am told ?"

"I am, Miss, very. I'm told you play the piano beautiful ?"

"Well, I do play ; but not near so well as I could wish.
I played some Irish airs for Mat Donovan this morning."

"Mat is a fine singer, Miss."

"Yes, I have often caught snatches of his songs from the
barn.   But he would not sing for us to-day when we asked
him."

Ellie here interrupted them.   She came to exhibit Tommy's
new paper ; but Grace motioned her away as if just then she
had no time for trifling.

"You showed me that before."

"No, that was his old copy-book.   But he is in Voster
now."

"In what ?"   She took the paper in her hand and read :

"THE RULE OF THREE DIRECT.
"*Commenced by Thomas Lahy, January the 8th,*
"*Anno Domini, One thousand Eight*
"*Hundred and . . . .*"

This was written at the top of the first page in the school-

master's most magnificent large hand, and under this the
page was divided by a black stroke down the middle into
two equal parts. In these double columns Tommy Lahy had
copied each question and answer fully and fairly from the
book—and the sums, fully and fairly worked out, were given
under the questions and answers. Several pages of the book
were filled in this way ; and Tommy told them proudly,
though somewhat bashfully, that he'd be " in Fractions after
Easter." At which Grace looked astonished, evidently
thinking that " fractions" and " smithereens " were con-
vertible terms.

"Show her your Voster, Tommy," said Ellie.

Tommy brought the book, and, on looking at the title page,
Grace nodded, and said :

"Oh, yes ; now I understand ; but I never saw this book
before."

"Maybe 'tis a Gough you have, Miss ?"

Grace contented herself with nodding again by way of
reply.

"Could you work the piece of plank, Miss ?"

"What is that ?"

Tommy licked his thumb, and turned over the leaves till
he came to a problem requiring the dimensions of a piece of
plank of certain length, breadth, and thickness.

Grace glanced at the problem and looked wise. But she
began to think that Tommy Lahy could teach her some
useful things of which she was altogether ignorant. She
happened, however, to glance at the fly-leaf of Tommy's
" Voster," and her pleasant laugh made Norah turn round
and look at her.

" ' Thomas Lahy, of Knocknagow, His Book,' " she read.
" And listen to this :—

> " Steal not this Book, my honest Friend,
> For fear the Gallows might be your End ;
> The Gallows is High, and you are low,
> And when you'd be up you'd be like a crow.
> If this Book be lost or Stole,
> I pray the finder will send it home
> To Thomas Lahy, of Knocknagow."

Grace laughed again and held up the book, with her finger

pointing to the bottom of the page, where Mary, by leaning forward and straining her eyes a little, was able to read :—

" Thomas Lahy, Copy Dated,"

And under this, in a different hand—

" On'y for me the pigs would ate it."

" The schoolmaster says, Miss," observed Honor, " that Tommy has a great turn for——what's that he says you have a turn for, Tommy ?"

" For science," replied Tommy.

" Oh, I always said that Tommy was a very intelligent boy," said Mary.

" On'y for he's so wild, Miss," returned Honor, with a sigh, and a glance at the beech-tree.

" I am very glad, Norah," said Mary, rising from her chair, " to see you getting on so well. When the weather gets fine I hope you will be much better. And, when the flowers are in bloom, I won't be satisfied till we get you up to show you the garden."

" Thank, you, Miss," replied Norah, with that worshipping look with which she always regarded her.

" An' sure you won't forget, Miss," said Honor, " to tell Mr. Hugh to keep Phil in mind uv the cordial ?"

" Oh, never fear. I'll tell him."

" O Mary," said Grace on their way home, " how much mistaken I was !"

" In what were you mistaken ?"

" About Norah Lahy. I believe now she is the happiest girl I ever saw."

" Have you found that out ?" Mary asked, with a delighted look. " I knew you would."

" Oh, yes ; I am sure of it."

" And so am I."

They walked along in silence for some time, till Ellie, who had lingered behind them, came running up and said there was a gentleman with a red coat riding slowly after them. It was Mr. Robert Lloyd ; and, on finding that they were aware of his proximity, he put his horse to a quicker walk in order to pass them.

" He had his hand to his hat to salute you," said Grace,

"but you did not look at him. Do you know, I always thought there was affectation in that not looking at people."

"I am not sure but you are right," replied Mary.

"It looks like vulgar pride, or sulky ignorance," said Grace.

"Oh, those are very hard words," said Mary, laughing. "But do you never turn up your nose at people yourself?"

> "'Oh wad some power the giftie gie us,
>   To see ourselves as ithers see us,'"

replied Grace. "Yes, I do plead guilty to the charge. But, my dear Mary, we can all see the mote in our neighbour's eye much easier than the beam in our own. But with regard to the gentleman on the grey horse, would you not have returned his salute?"

"I am not personally acquainted with him," Mary replied. "But I would have returned his salute, though I might rather avoid it if I could do so without laying myself open to the charge of—what's that you said it looked like?"

"I believe I said vulgar pride, or sulky ignorance."

"Well, if I could not pass the gentleman without being open to such a charge, I would, of course, return his salute. And yet," she added, with a smile, "if I were a *lady* he would scarcely have saluted me without some previous acquaintance or introduction."

"Why, what on earth do you mean by saying *if* you were a lady?"

"Oh, I see you don't know what our notions are respecting ladies or gentlemen in the country."

"Well, tell me."

"Did you never hear your papa tell what Sally Egan said to Mrs. French?"

"No, I don't remember ; but I recollect Sally Egan very well. It was she nursed me."

"Well, your papa gave her an excellent character when she was leaving you, and Mrs. French asked her what place she was in before that. 'I was with a gentleman, ma'am,' she replied. 'And was not your last master a gentleman?' asked Mrs. French. 'Oh, no, ma'am,' said Sally, 'he's only a doctor.'"

Grace reddened with indignation, and pronounced Sally Egan's conduct an instance of the basest ingratitude.

" You mistake altogether," said Mary. " She did not mean to make little of the doctor at all."

" If papa is not a gentleman," exclaimed Grace, " I don't know who is."

" That's my way of thinking, too," replied Mary; " but you see it was not Sally Egan's. It is only what are called ' estated men ' are gentlemen in Ireland, and their wives and daughters are the only ladies. Tom Maher thought he was paying me a great compliment the other day by saying that I was ' *like* a lady.' "

" What must be the reason ?" said Grace, musingly.

" Try and find the solution of the mystery," replied Mary, laughing.

Grace put her finger to her lips and knit her brows.

" It is because they are *slaves* !' she exclaimed, with emphasis.

" I believe you have guessed it," replied Mary, quietly.

They came up again with Mr. Lloyd, who had gone into a house to light his pipe. It was plain he meant to be respectful, for he took the pipe from his mouth and put it behind his back while they were passing. Mary returned his salute this time.

" Do you know, Mary," said Grace, " I think it is because he knows Richard so well."

" You are quite right," she replied, quickly; " that never occurred to me before."

" There is something good-natured looking about him," Grace observed. " And he is a fine, handsome man, though, I should say, somewhat foolish."

" You are not very flattering," said Mary.

" Well, now," said Grace after another interval of silence, " tell me candidly what you think of him ?" She pointed to Mr. Lowe, who was walking with the doctor in the lawn.

" Well, I think he improves on acquaintance," Mary replied. " The more I know of him, the better I like him."

" It is just the contrary with me. I was ready to worship him as a superior being at first. His elegant, gentleman-like manner quite fascinated me. But now I feel there's something wanting. There is something milk-and-waterish about him. He is not strong."

Mary looked at her with surprise, as indeed she often did

" And is Richard, for instance, strong ?" she asked.

" No, not strong ; but he has animation, or something that the other wants."

" And Hugh ?"

" Yes," she replied, compressing her lips, and with a movement of the head. " Yes ; Hugh is strong. He has a strong face."

" Is Norah Lahy strong ?"

The question seemed to surprise her at first, but, after a moment's thought, she replied :

" Yes : Norah Lahy is strong. There are different kinds of strength. I fear I am not strong myself. In some ways I know I am ; but if I were afflicted like Norah Lahy, I never could endure it as she does."

" You could," replied Mary, " God would give you strength."

" You could bear it," returned Grace, " just the same as she does."

" Oh, I fear I never could, with such cheerful resignation. But if it ever should be my lot to be tried with affliction, how much I shall owe to Norah Lahy !"

" Mary," said Grace, after another pause, " I am beginning to feel quite nervous. That is why I can never meditate on such things. It makes me think that I shall soon die, and that frightens me."

" It is a thought that ought to frighten us all," returned Mary. " But I need not preach to you, Grace. You understand these things very well. And I am sure you do sometimes meditate on death."

" I try—sometimes."

" I seldom talk in this way," said Mary. " I scarcely know how you managed to introduce the subject. But we must hurry in and deliver Mrs. Lahy's injunctions to Hugh before they go."

" They seem to be in no hurry," Grace remarked. " There is Adonis vaulting over the gate, and, I suppose, challenging Apollo to follow him. But Apollo prefers opening the gate. And now he sees us, and is sorry he has not bounded over it like an antelope."

" Well, let us hurry," said Mary. " They are waiting for us."

"I hope," she remarked, on reaching the gate, "I hope you will find a great deal to amuse you at the wedding to-night."

"I am all impatience to see a real Irish wedding," he replied. "And to judge from the glimpses we are after getting of the party as they drove by, this is to be a genuine affair."

"Yes, 'twill be the correct thing," the doctor observed. "By Jove! only for an engagement I have I'd be tempted to go with you. Nelly Donovan's ankles would make a saint forget the sky as she tripped by just now."

"But not a sinner forget the important duty of spending a long winter evening telling an appreciative circle what he would do with the bars of the grate," said Grace.

The doctor pulled his moustache and tried to laugh.

"What do you mean by the bars of the grate?" Mary asked.

"Oh, don't you know? 'What will you do with this one?' 'I'll ask her to sing a song.' 'And what will you do with this one?' 'I'll adore her.'"

"Oh, I suppose you are too wise," returned Mary, "for such things. But I must not forget Phil Lahy and the cordial."

She quickened her pace in order to meet Hugh, who was dismounting from his horse, after returning from the out-farms. And as Mr. Lowe gazed after her, he thought to himself that if some accident occurred to prevent their attendance at Ned Brophy's wedding, he would bear the disappointment like a philosopher, and spend the evening by the fireside.

CHAPTER XXX.

NED BROPHY'S WEDDING.

WHEN Mr. Lowe found himself knee-deep in fresh straw, after jumping from the gig in Ned Brophy's yard, he looked about him with a slight sense of bewilderment. Their drive

for the first two miles had been pleasant enough, but when
they turned off the high road into a narrow " boreen," Mr.
Lowe expected every moment to be flung over the fence,
against which the wheel almost rubbed as they jolted along.

" Have we much farther to go ?" he asked, clutching the
side of the gig, as the wheel at Hugh's side sank into the
deepest slough they had met yet.

" Only a couple of fields," Hugh replied. " We'll be in
view of the house after passing the next turn."

The couple of fields seemed five miles long at a moderate
calculation to Mr. Lowe, and it was not till he found himself
on his legs in the straw he felt satisfied they had really
arrived at their journey's end. As he gazed about him he
had a confused consciousness of the twang of fiddles, mingled
with the hum of many voices and the clatter of many feet,
on the one hand, and a combination of odours, in which turf,
smoke and roast goose predominated, on the other. The
music came from the barn, and the odours from an out-office
at the opposite side of the yard, which was converted into a
kitchen for the occasion—and there being no chimney, a
plentiful supply of smoke was the natural consequence.

Hugh shouted for some one to come and take care of his
horse ; and a workman rushed from the barn, creating considerable confusion among a crowd of beggars at the door—
for whom the fun at that side seemed to possess more
attraction than the culinary preparations and savoury odours
at the other.

Mr. Hugh Kearney's arrival was soon made known to the
people of the house ; and Mat Donovan, as " best man " and
master of the ceremonies, was at the door to receive and
welcome him.

" Is this the doctor you have wud you ?" Mat asked.
" Begor, I'm glad we have him, as I was afeard there'd be no
wan to talk to the ladies."

" This is Mr. Lowe," replied Hugh.

Mat was evidently disappointed ; for he had the highest
opinion of the doctor's powers in the matter of " discoorsin'
the ladies."

On entering the kitchen, where preparations for dinner
were also proceeding on a large scale, Ned Brophy's mother
welcomed them with a curtsey, and her daughter took their

hats and overcoats to one of the two bedrooms off the kitchen.
Mat Donovan opened the parlour door, and showed the
gentlemen in with a bow and a wave of his hand that even the
accomplished Richard, whose absence he so much regretted,
might have envied.

Two ladies who sat by the fire—one in a blue ball-dress
and pearl necklace, the other in a plain black silk, with only
a blue ribbon for ornament—stood up ; and Mr. Lowe found
himself shaking hands with the blue ball-dress almost before
he was aware of it.

" Don't you remember Miss Lloyd ?" Hugh was obliged to
say ; for it was painfully evident he did not at once recognise her.

" Oh, I beg pardon," said he, " but really the pleasure was
so unexpected."

Miss Lloyd was in fidgets of ecstasy, and called to her
sister to introduce her.

Mr. Lowe bowed again, and it was pretty clear from the
expression of his eye that he thought the plain black dress
and the blue ribbon a pleasanter sight to look at than the
blue gauze and pearl necklace.

" Sit down, sir," said Mat Donovan, placing a chair in
front of the fire.   " Or, maybe," he added, turning to Hugh,
" you'd like to have a bout before the tables are brought into
the barn ?"

" Oh, no, we'll wait till after dinner," said Hugh.

" Very well, sir," replied Mat.   " Father Hannigan 'll be
here shortly, and I'll bring him in to have a talk wud ye
before supper is ready.   I'm afeard the cook is afther takin'
a sup too much, an' if the ladies here don't show 'em what
to do, things'll be apt to go contrairy."

" Oh, you may command my services," said the younger
lady, with a laugh.

" Thank'ee, Miss," returned Mat.   " But she's takin' a
sleep, and maybe she'd be all right after id."

" Who is the cook ?" Miss Lloyd asked, eagerly.   " Is it
Mrs. Nugent ?"

" 'Tis, Miss," replied Mat.   " She was up at the castle
yesterday, preparin' the big dinner, an' she's bate up intirely."

" Oh, was she at the castle ?   Where is she ?   I'd like so
much to ask her all about it."

"She's gone into the little room there, Miss, to take a stretch on the bed."

Miss Lloyd was on the rack immediately. Even Mr. Lowe faded from her mind and was lost in the steam of that big dinner at the castle.

Seizing a candle from the table, Miss Lloyd rushed into the little bedroom off the parlour. Immediately a loud scream made them all start to their feet, and fly to her assistance. All was darkness in the bedroom, till some one brought in a candle ; and there was poor Miss Lloyd, blue ball-dress, pearl necklace, and all, sprawling on the floor, and staring wildly about her. The fat cook—who was a very mountain of a woman—was lying on the floor too, snoring sonorously ; and it at once became apparent to the astonished spectators that Miss Lloyd had tumbled over her.

Hugh Kearney stepped over the fat cook, and reaching his hand to the frightened lady, raised her up.

"O Mr. Kearney," she exclaimed, panting for breath, "what have I fallen over ?"

"Over a mountain," replied Hugh, laying his hand on the fat cook's shoulder and shaking her.

The sonorous music that proceeded from the mountain suddenly ceased ; and a second vigorous shake had the effect of causing the fat cook to open her eyes.

"O Mr. Kearney," she exclaimed piteously, looking into his face, "you know what a weak constitution I have."

This address, uttered as it was in a familiar and affectionate manner, took Hugh somewhat by surprise ; for it happened that Mrs. Nugent was a perfect stranger to him.

"Tundher an' turf, Mrs. Nugent," exclaimed Mat Donovan, "everything is roasted an' biled—an' there's open war among the women. Wan says wan thing, an' another says another thing ; an' between 'em all, everything is three-na-yhela."

Mat put his arms round Mrs. Nugent and lifted her to her feet—a feat which no man in "the three parishes" but himself would have attempted.

Mrs. Nugent steadied herself for a moment, untying her apron and turning the other side out, with great deliberation.

"You know, Mr. Kearney," said she, "how a salt herring upsets me."

Hugh felt slightly confused, and altogether at a loss to understand why Mrs. Nugent should persist in assuming that he had so intimate a knowledge of her constitution.

"Really, ma'am," said he, "I do not know. I believe this is the first time I ever had the pleasure of meeting you."

"Well, if you don't, your mother does," said Mrs. Nugent, as she stuck a pin in her cap a little over her right ear—for what purpose it would be difficult to say.

"She knows what dressing a dinner is," continued Mrs. Nugent, looking round on the company, "for she was used to nothing else in her own father's house."

Hugh felt that this compliment to the O'Carrolls would have greatly gratified his mother, and that she would have quite overlooked the assertion that she was "used to nothing else" but dressing dinners at Ballydunmore.

"And how are you to-night, Miss Lloyd?" said Mrs. Nugent. "I hope your family are well."

"Quite well, thank you, Mrs. Nugent," replied the lady addressed, who was nervously feeling her pearls one by one, to know if any of them had come to grief in consequence of her tumble.

"Come, Mrs. Nugent," said Mat Donovan, "an' set 'em to rights at the dishin', in the name o' God."

"Yes, Mat the Thrasher," replied Mrs. Nugent. "Let me alone for setting them to rights."

She moved with great dignity towards the door ; but making a sudden and quite unexpected detour before she reached it, Mrs. Nugent came plump up against Mr. Henry Lowe, who mechanically caught her in his arms, as, yielding to the momentum, he staggered backwards.

"Hands off, young man, till you're better acquainted," exclaimed the fat cook, in an offended tone. "I'm no sich sort of indivigel," she added, as she shook the young gentleman from her, to his utter confusion and dismay. But before he could collect his wits to protest he meant no harm whatever, Mat Donovan took the offended lady's arm, and conducted her to the kitchen, where her appearance, as she stood with arms akimbo in the middle of the floor, made Mrs. Brophy and her servant girls feel like delinquents, so awe-inspiring was the glance the mighty empress cast round her dominions.

" Mat the Thrasher," said Mrs. Nugent, " will you——"

" Begob, there's Father Hannigan ; I must be off," exclaimed Mat, as he hurried away without waiting to know what Mrs. Nugent required.

'' God save all here,'' said Father Hannigan, stamping his feet as he stepped over the threshold. " How are you, Mrs. Brophy ?"

" You're welcome, sir," was Mrs. Brophy's reply, as she opened the parlour door.

Father Hannigan had a hearty greeting from every one, and Mr. Lowe was particularly glad to see him.

" I beg your pardon, Miss Lloyd ; but we must put Mr. Flaherty in that corner. Sit down there, Mr. Flaherty," he continued, laying his hand on the arm of a respectable-looking man, who until now had been concealed behind the tall figure of the priest.

The old man was dressed in a decent suit of black, and as he sat down in the chair to which the priest had conducted him, Mr. Lowe was struck by the placid smile that glowed over his round, ruddy face. He wore a brown wig, curled all round from the temples, which he now caught hold of over his ear, to fasten it on his head. He then commenced playing with a bunch of seals attached to his watch-ribbon, which hung from the fob in his small clothes.

" Good night, Miss Lloyd," said he, without turning towards her.

" Good night, Mr. Flaherty," she replied.

" Ha !" he laughed, appearing to look straight before him, though the lady was on one side, and rather behind him. " I think this is Miss Isabella I have beside me," he said after playing again with the bunch of seals.

" Yes, Mr. Flaherty. It is a long time now since you paid us a visit."

He did not reply, as he was listening, with an anxious look, to the conversation passing between Father Hannigan, Mr. Lowe, and Hugh Kearney.

" This is the English gentleman ?" he observed in a whisper, leaning his head towards the young lady who had just spoken to him.

" Yes ; he is Sir Garrett Butler's nephew," she replied.

Mr. Lowe's curiosity to know something of Mr. Flaherty

was so strong that it brought him to the side of Miss Lloyd, at the other end of the room. She tossed her flounces about, and made way for him in an ecstasy of delight.

" I am curious to know," he said, " who is that old gentleman ?"

As he spoke, his curiosity was further excited by seeing a little boy come into the room and place a green bag on the old man's knees.

" That's the celebrated Irish piper," she replied. " I am surprised to see him here. I did not think he attended country weddings."

" I suppose," said Mr. Lowe, " he goes round among the nobility and gentry, as we are told the harpers used to do."

" He does," she replied; " and he has a beautiful little pony the countess gave him. But I suppose he is stopping at present with the priests, and Father Hannigan has brought him with him."

" I wish he would begin to play," said Mr. Lowe. And he was rather startled when the old man immediately said :

" Yes, I'll play a tune for you."

" Oh ! thank you ; but I really did not think you could hear me."

" Ha !" he replied, laughing ; " I can hear the grass growing."

He pulled out his watch, and after opening the glass and fumbling with it for a moment, he said :

" Twenty minutes past nine."

Mr. Lowe, who looked at him in surprise as he smiled and chuckled while putting up his watch, caught a glimpse of the old man's eyeballs, and saw that he was blind.

" Sit down here near me," said Mr. Flaherty. " I knew Sir Garrett and your mother well. I'll play one of poor Garrett's favourite tunes for you."

As he uncovered his pipes their splendour quite took Mr. Lowe by surprise. The keys were of silver, and the bag covered with crimson velvet fringed with gold ; while the little bellows was quite a work of art, so beautifully was it carved and ornamented with silver and ivory. Having tied an oval-shaped piece of velvet with a ribbon attached to each end above his knee, he adjusted his instrument, and after moving his arm, to which the bellows was attached by a

ribbon, till the crimson velvet bag was inflated, he touched
the keys, and catching up the " chanter" quickly in both hands
began to play. Mr. Lowe, who watched him narrowly, now
saw the use of the piece of velvet tied round his leg, as the
" chanter " was ever and anon pressed against it to assist in
the production of certain notes by preventing the escape of
the air through the end of the tube.

The musician soon seemed to forget all mere human concerns. He threw back his head, as if communing with invisible spirits in the air above him ; or bent down over his
instrument as if the spirits had suddenly flown into it, and
he wanted to catch their whisperings there, too.

The audience, to some extent, shared in the musician's
ecstasy ; particularly Father Hannigan, from whose eyes tears
were actually falling as the delicious melody ceased, and the
old man raised his sightless eyes, and listened, as it were, for
an echo of his strains from the skies.

" Oh !" exclaimed Father Hannigan, turning away his
head, and flourishing his yellow Indian silk pocket-handkerchief, as he affected to sneeze *before* taking the pinch of
snuff he held between the fingers of the other hand—" Oh,
there's something wonderful in these old Irish airs ! There
was a ballad in last Saturday's *Nation* about that tune, that
was nearly as moving as the tune itself. Did you read it ?"
he asked, turning to Hugh Kearney.

" Yes," he replied. " Your friend, Dr. Kiely, induced me
to become a subscriber to the *Nation*."

" I don't get it myself," returned Father Hannigan. " 'Tis
Father O'Neill gets it, and I suspect he has a leaning
towards those Young Irelanders, and dabbles in poetry himself. But I wish I had that ballad about the ' Coolin,' to
read it for Mr. Flaherty. If poetry as well as music could
be squeezed out of an Irish bagpipes, I'd say that ballad came
out of that bag under his oxter."

The old man's face brightened up, as he raised his
head, and appeared to be listening to the spirits in the air
again.

" Can you remember any of the lines, Hugh ?"

" Not to repeat them," he replied ; " but I have a general
recollection of them."

" We're obliged to you, intirely, for your general recollection," returned Father Hannigan, with his finger on his temple. " But what's that he said about ' sorrow and love'?"

" Sobbing like Eire," replied Hugh.

" Ay, ay," interrupted Father Hannigan. " Now I have it. The poet, Mr. Flaherty, described the ' Coolin ' as

'Sobbing like Eire with *sorrow* and *love*.'

Isn't that beautiful ?—and *true* ? "

The old man laughed and listened more intently, as if the spirits in the air were very far off, and he were trying to catch the flapping of their wings.

" He also said," Hugh added, " that

' An angel first sung it above in the sky.' "

This seemed to catch the minstrel's fancy more than the other line, for he nodded his head several times, with his mouth slightly open, as if he were softly repeating the interjection ha ! ha ! ha !

The wedding guests had been silently dropping into the room, which was now pretty well filled. Mat Donovan occasionally seized a bottle or decanter, and filled out a glass of wine, or whiskey, or " cordial " for some of them ; and Hugh Kearney observed that Mat was particularly attentive to old Phil Morris, the weaver, whose entrance necessarily attracted attention, as he was lame and leant upon a short stick, which he struck against the ground at every step, with a sturdy defiant sort of knock, which, taken in connection with his tightly compressed lips and keen grey eyes, conveyed the idea that old Phil Morris was a Tartar, with a dash of the cynic in his composition. And old Phil really did look upon the present generation as a degenerate race, who could " put up with anything," and altogether unworthy sons of his early youth's compeers."

As Mat Donovan pressed old Phil Morris to drink with unusual earnestness, there was a hustling heard at the door, and Ned Brophy himself was seen pushing two blind pipers into the parlour with a degree of violence and an expression of countenance that led Mr. Lowe to imagine he must have caught them in the act of attempting to rob him or something of that kind. The two pipers were tall and gaunt

and yellow—a striking contrast in every way to Mr. Flaherty.
One was arrayed in a soldier's grey watch-coat, with the
number of the regiment stamped in white figures on the
back, and the other wore a coarse blue body-coat, with what
appeared to be the sleeves of another old grey watch-coat
sewed to it between the shoulders and the elbows. Both
wore well-patched corduroy knee-breeches and bluish worsted
stockings, with brogues of unusual thickness of sole, well
paved with heavy nails. Their rude brass-mounted instruments were in keeping with their garments. The sheep-skin
bag of one had no covering whatever, while that of the other
was covered with faded plaid, " cross-barred with green and
yellow." They dropped into two chairs near the door, thrusting their old " caubeens " under them, and sat bolt upright
like a pair of mummies or figures in a wax-work exhibition.

This invasion of the parlour was caused by the expulsion
of the dancers from the barn, to make room for laying the
tables for the banquet.

" Play that tune that the angel sang again, Mr. Flaherty,"
said Father Hannigan.

Mr. Flaherty complied, and the noise and hum of voices
were at once hushed.

" Have you that ?" the piper in the watch-coat asked his
companion in a whisper, at the same time beginning to work
with his elbow.

" I have," replied the other, beginning to work with his
elbow, too.

A sound like snoring followed for a moment, and Mr.
Flaherty jerked up his head suddenly, and looked disturbed—
as if an evil spirit had intruded among his " delicate Ariels."
But as the noise was not repeated, his countenance resumed
its wonted placidity, and he bent over his instrument
again.

" I think I could do id betther myse'f," said he of the blue
body-coat, holding his big knotty fingers over the holes of his
chanter. " He don't shake enough."

" So could I," replied the grey watch-coat, giving a squeeze
to his bag, which was followed by a faint squeak.

" Turn him out !" shouted Mr. Flaherty, in a voice of
thunder, as he started to his feet, his eyes rolling with indignant anger.

There was great astonishment among the company; and Miss Lloyd jumped upon her chair and stared wildly about her, with a vague notion that Wat Murphy's bulldog—of which interesting animal she entertained the profoundest dread—had got into the room and seized Mr. Flaherty by the calf of the leg.

"Come, Shamus," said Father Hannigan, "this is no place for you. Come, Thade, be off with you," and Father Hannigan expelled the grumbling minstrels from the parlour; but in doing so he gave each a nudge in the ribs, and slipped a shilling into his fist, which had the effect of changing their scowl into a broad grin, as they jostled out to the kitchen.

"Well,. Phil, are you brave and hearty?" said Father Hannigan, when he returned to his seat.

"Purty well, I thank you, sir."

"Oh, is that Phil Lahy? I didn't see you till I looked at you. 'Tis to the old cock I was talking. How goes it, my old Trojan?" he added, turning to Phil Morris, whom Mat Donovan was pressing to drink a glass of whiskey, which the old man pushed away from him.

"Sound as a bell," was his reply, as he folded his hands and leant on his stick.

"Well, if you won't take it," said Mat, "your namesake will."

"No, Mat, I'm obliged to you. But I'm takin' nothin' stronger than cordial."

"Well, sure, we have lots uv that same," Mat rejoined. "We didn't forget the teetotallers. Which soart will you have?"

"I'll take a small drop of the ginger-cordial."

"Begor, 'tisn't aisy to know id from the wine for the ladies," said Mat, holding up two decanters between him and the light. He poured a little of the contents of one into (tumbler and tasted it.

"Oh, faith, I have id," he continued, coughing; "an' hot stuff it is."

He filled the tumbler, and presented it to Phil Lahy, who took it with a look of meek resignation, which was quite affecting.

Nelly Donovan rushed in with her face very much flushed,

and, making her way to Miss Isabella Lloyd, said in a whisper :

"Wisha, Miss, maybe you'd come out an' show us what to do. We can't get any good uv the cook ; she's like the dog in the manger, an' won't either do a hand's turn herse'f, or let any wan else do id. There's lots uv dacent women here that knows what to do as well as herse'f, but she's afther insultin' every wan uv 'em, and as for poor Mrs. Brophy, she don't know whether it is on her head or her heels she's standin', wud her."

"I'll try what I can do," replied the young lady, laughing, as she followed Nelly to the kitchen.

CHAPTER XXXI.

MR. LLOYD DOES WHAT IRISH LANDLORDS SELDOM DO.

A TABLE at one end of the barn was appropriated to the more distinguished guests, at which Father Hannigan presided, with the bride on his right hand, and an empty chair on his left ; for Ned Brophy resolutely resisted all attempts to force him into the seat which Miss Isabella Lloyd had assigned him.

Before the covers were taken off the dishes, however, Mr. Robert Lloyd strolled up to the head of the table and quietly took possession of the unoccupied chair. To his eldest sister's consternation, Mr. Lloyd appeared in his scarlet coat and buckskin breeches, and even had his hunting whip tied over his shoulder.

Ned Brophy, on seeing his landlord, hurried from the lower end of one of the two rows of tables that extended along each side of the barn, and shook him vigorously by the hand.

"Welcome, Mr. Bob," said Ned-Brophy. "Begor, I'd never forgive you if you didn't come." And for the first time since his doom was sealed, Ned Brophy was seen to smile.

"This is herse'f, sir," Ned added. And Mr. Lloyd shook hands with the bride—reaching his arm behind Father Hannigan's back—in quite an affectionate manner ; which caused the bride to smile too, apparently for the first time since *her* doom was sealed. So that Mr. Robert Lloyd chased the clouds from the faces of his tenant and his tenant's wife—a thing which, as a rule, Irish landlords are not much in the habit of doing.

Mat Donovan hurried up to make room for two other unexpected guests at the principal table, and Maurice Kearney and Lory Hanly took their places sufficiently near Miss Lloyd to call up a frightened look into that nervous lady's face when she saw Lory turning round to address her.

As soon as Lory saw his sisters wholly taken up with the doctor, who punctually kept the appointment to which he had casually referred in the evening, the bright idea struck the enamoured young gentleman that he had an excuse for paying another visit to his fair enslaver. So as Mary Kearney and Grace were sitting by the fire, and feeling rather dull and lonely, a knock was heard at the door. They listened to know who might be the unexpected visitor, and immediately after the door was opened, Lory walked into the parlour with the jay's large wicker-cage in his arms. They were very glad to see him, and so was Maurice Kearney himself. But Mrs. Kearney evidently looked upon Lory as a dangerous character, and did not consider herself quite safe so long as he was in the house. Lory, however, was asked to sit down ; and the expression of his countenance as he stared round him, and then looked at Grace, might be translated "jolly."

Ned Brophy's wedding happened to be mentioned, and the whim seized Mr. Kearney that he and Lory would go there together.

The fact was, the young gentleman's dancing so tickled Maurice Kearney's fancy the evening he first made Lory's acquaintance, that he could not resist the temptation to see him perform again.

"Come, and I'll drive you over," said he, "and you'll have a good night's fun."

"Faith, I will !" exclaimed Lory, in a voice that reminded Mrs. Kearney of her broken tea-cup.

"Will you come?" he added, turning to Grace and waiting for her reply with his eyes very wide open.

"Oh, no, thank you," she replied.

"If you do, I'll dance with nobody else. 'Pon my word
I'd rather dance with you than with anybody."

Grace expressed her acknowledgment, but regretted she
should deny herself the pleasure.

Mrs. Kearney went to the kitchen to announce to Barney
that he was to drive the car, and to warn him above all
things to take care of " Flanigan's Hole." To which injunction Barney replied by doing the "side step" in a reel very
genteelly, and in a manner peculiar to himself : it being the
usual practice to have the right foot foremost when moving
towards the right, and the left foot foremost when moving
towards the left, whereas Barney reversed this, and moved to
the left with the right foot in front, and to the right with the
left foot in front—the effect of which was very striking.

"More power, ma'am! Would I doubt you? An' all my
figure dance gone out uv my head for want uv practice.
One-two-three, one-two-three, one-two-three." And Barney,
with his head thrown back, till his poll rested on the collar
of his coat, one-two-three'd to the stable.

The safe arrival of Mr. Kearney and Lory Hanly in Ned
Brophy's barn just as the wedding guests had sat down to
dinner, is a sufficient proof that Barney had driven them
safely past Flanigan's Hole.

In spite of Miss Isabella Lloyd's exertions, ably seconded
as she was by Nelly Donovan, the arrangements were not as
successful as might have been wished. For instance, when
Father Hannigan raised the cover of the large dish before
him, he was rather taken by surprise, on seeing two very
plump geese reposing side by side on a bed of very greasy
cabbage ; and what added considerably to the astonishment
of the beholders was the unusual circumstance that while one
goose was brown, the other was quite white.

A word from Miss Isabella Lloyd, who could not conceal
her indignation at the stupidity of some one whom she designated " that wretch," sent Nelly Donovan flying down between
the two rows of tables ; and when she returned bearing
another dish, that which contained the geese was pushed out
of the way, and before he had well recovered from his

surprise, Father Hannigan found a piece of roast beef before him, which might have vied with that wonderful quarter that Father M'Mahon got as a Christmas present, and merely to look at which, according to Father Hannigan, would " do your heart good." The two geese were removed to another dish, and banished to one of the side tables ; and Mat Donovan completed the arrangements by placing a huge piece of pork on the " bolster of cabbage," originally intended as its resting place.

The roast beef became " small by degrees and beautifully less," under Father Hannigan's carving knife. Hugh Kearney and his father worked with might and main, too ; and knives and forks were soon busy all round the barn. But the white goose had aroused Miss Lloyd's inquisitiveness, and she could not rest till she knew all about it. So when Nelly Donovan was passing, Miss Lloyd put back her hand and caught her by the skirt.

" What sort of a goose is that ?" she asked, as Nelly bent over her chair.

" 'Tis wan uv their own geese, Miss. Mrs. Brophy always rears three or four clutches."

" But why is it white ?"

" Oh, is id that wan ? Ould Molly, Miss, that didn't under-stand the cook, an' popped wan uv 'em into a pot of wather an' biled id, instead uv puttin' it in the oven pot as she was tould. She did the same to a beautiful pair uv ducks, an' spiled 'em."

" What's that you have on the plate ?"

" Some bacon an' cabbage, Miss, that Wattletoes is afther sendin' me to Mr. Kearney for. An' spake uv the divil an' he'll appear," she exclaimed. " Here is Barney himself."

" Tare-an'-ouns, Nelly," muttered Barney grumblingly, " is id goin' to lave me lookin' at 'em all skelpin' away you are, an' not as much as ud bait a mouse-trap furnint me, barrin' a dhry pueata ?"

" I have id here for you, Barney," she replied, presenting the well-filled plate to him.

" More power to your oaten-male-pueata-cake—an' a griddle to bile id," exclaimed Barney, as he hurried off to his place at the lower end of the barn.

We have some recollection of a description of an English

harvest-home, from the pen of Mr. Charles Reade. The
guests were of the same class as those assembled in Ned
Brophy's barn. But the English novelist tells us that during
the whole time while the viands were being demolished, the
only words uttered were the following :—

" Bo-ill, wull you have some weal wud your bacon ?"

" That I woun't, Jock."

In this respect the Irish wedding presented a singular contrast to the English harvest-home. Jokes and laughter were
heard on every side ; and from Father Hannigan at the head
of the table to Barney Brodherick who sat upon an inverted
hamper with his back against the winnowing machine, and
his plate on his knees, at the opposite end of the barn, every
face wore a smile, and fun sparkled in every eye. The only
exceptions to this rule were two or three bashful young
women whose potatoes broke upon their forks, and filled them
with confusion. One of these bashful young women, after a
second and third failure, dropped her arms by her side, and
resisted every effort to induce her to taste a single morsel of
anything. Nelly Donovan did all she could to coax her, but
the bashful young woman rigidly refused to touch knife or
fork again—even though Nelly, with mischievous drollery,
called out to Miss Isabella Lloyd—

" Wisha, Miss, maybe you'd have a little lane bit there.
We have a girl down here that won't ate a taste uv anything
for us."

The necessity of peeling the potatoes on the fork at a wedding was regarded as a very trying ordeal ; and the remark
" that's the pueata I'd like to get at a weddin'," was one
not unfrequently heard at Knocknagow, as the speaker held
up a " white-eye " between her finger and thumb, which had
resisted a tight squeeze of the hand without breaking.

But how will Professor Huxley account for the difference
we have alluded to between the Irish wedding and the
English harvest home ?

In the matter of smiling faces, however, we should make
one more exception, besides the bashful young women whose
potatoes fell to pieces. Miss Lloyd was haunted by the
boiled goose. That doughy looking object seemed both to
fascinate and frighten her. She stared at it as a shying horse
will stare at a white wall. At last, unable to resist any

longer, she held out her plate and asked to be helped to the boiled goose. A young farmer, who sat opposite that neglected and utterly forlorn-looking bird, jumped to his feet and plunged a fork into its side ; and then sawed away vigorously with his knife, but without any regard to the bones or joints of the boiled goose. In spite of his vigorous exertions—or rather in consequence of them—the unhappy boiled goose rolled and slipt about the dish, but lost not a particle of flesh under the knife of the operator.

Now, this young farmer partook of boiled goose in his own house on an average once a week—that is to say, every Sunday—since Michaelmas. But then the goose was always dismembered before it was put into the pot with the dumplings. And a very savoury dish, too, is goose and dumplings cooked in this way.

Miss Lloyd held out her plate patiently till her arm began to feel tired, when the young farmer, becoming quite desperate, pulled his fork out of the boiled goose, and plunging it into the piece of fat pork that happened to be within arm's length of him, slashed off some two or three pounds of the same, and flinging it upon the young lady's plate, exclaimed :

" Maybe you'd rather have a bit of this, Miss ?"

Miss Lloyd stared helplessly at the mass of pork on her plate, which, in her bewilderment, she continued to hold out at arm's length. Whereupon, the young farmer added a liberal supply of cabbage, and Miss Lloyd laid down the plate before her, looking as stupified as Mat Donovan's cock when he was going to walk into the fire, after falling from the collar-beam upon Phil Lahy's head. And during the rest of the meal Miss Lloyd seemed quite as incapable of further action as the bashful young woman for whom Nelly Donovan wanted " a little lane bit."

Dinner over, the two pipers and three fiddlers struck up " Haste to the Wedding," which was the signal for removing the two rows of tables, and the floor was immediately cleared for dancing.

Mr. Robert Lloyd led out the bride ; and, after a good deal of rough shaking and pushing, Mat Donovan persuaded the bridegroom to go through the usual bowing and scraping in front of Miss Lloyd, who was roused from the stupor into which the fat pork had thrown her by the words, " I dance to you, Miss," which were uttered by Ned Brophy much in the same tone and with the same look as usually accompany the phrase, " I'm sorry for your trouble."

" Come, Mr. Lowe," said Father Hannigan, " don't you see Miss Isabella there, throwing sheep's eyes at you ? Out with you and join the fun."

" Mr. Lory, your sowl," exclaimed Nelly Donovan, clapping him on the back, " before the flure is full." And Nelly seized Lory by the hand and pulled him along till they found a place among the dancers.

Hugh Kearney walked down the barn looking to the right and left among the blooming damsels, but it was evident the object of his search was not in sight.

" You want somebody," said Mat, with a meaning look.

" Well, I do," replied Hugh. " I want a partner."

" Who is she, an' I'll make her out for you ?"

" That's just what I don't know," replied Hugh. " But 'tis the girl with the white jacket."

Mat shook his head, as much as to say, " Sure, now, I knew what was in your mind." And then looking all round for the white jacket, Mat Donovan said aloud—

" The nicest little girl !" and there was a melancholy tenderness in his voice, and a softness in his smile, which made Hugh at once suspect that the owner of the white jacket was no stranger to Mat the Thrasher.

" Who is she ?" he asked.

" Bessy Morris, sir," replied Mat, after a moment's silence, as if he were roused from a reverie.

" Is that old Phil's granddaughter ?" Hugh asked in surprise. " I know her very well, but I have not seen her for a long time."

" She was in Dublin at her aunt's, sir," replied Mat. " I think she's gone into the house now to put a stitch in the bridesmaid's gown that Wattletoes is afther dhriving his fut through—would you doubt him ? I'll run in for her."

He soon returned with Bessy Morris, who blushed and laughed as he told her how Mr. Hugh Kearney had singled her out.

" I really did not know you," said Hugh, as he shook hands with her, " till Mat told me who you were."

"They all tell me I am greatly altered, sir," she replied, "but I can't see it myself."

"We have some purty girls here to-night, sir," said Mat, looking round on every side.

"Very pretty girls," Hugh replied. "There, for instance, that fair-haired girl sitting near the musicians is about as handsome a girl as ever I saw."

"So she is, sir," said Mat. "She's called the Swan of Coolmore. But for all that," he added, with a humorous glance at Bessy Morris, "'tis the white jacket he was lookin' for."

"Oh, but Bessy and I are old acquaintances," replied Hugh, laughing.

"Nabocklish!" returned Mat. "You tould me you didn't know who she was. But I always said you had a good eye uv your own."

The two pipers and three fiddlers found the "tuning" business so difficult that Mat thought there was still time for him to look out for a partner for "the first bout."

"Now, which would you advise me to take?" he asked, stroking his chin as if he found it difficult to make up his mind. "The swan or the bridesmaid—the goolden locks or the goolden guineas?"

This question had the effect of making Bessy Morris look very earnestly at him. But she laughed when he added—

"Here goes for a shake at the ould saucepan."

"But you are forgetting," said Bessy, "that you were desired to make some punch for the ladies."

"Oh murther!" he exclaimed, "that ould saucepan put id out uv me head."

Billy Heffernan here appeared at the door with a jug of boiling water in each hand, and Mat hurried to the table to make the punch for the ladies; which punch was soon "shared" all round, and caused an immense deal of coughing and a grand display of "turkey-red" pocket-handkerchiefs.

Hugh found his partner so lively and intelligent, and altogether so captivating, that he quite overlooked the fact that the dancing had commenced, till the swinging of Lory Hanley's legs warned him that he must either retire, or join in with the rest.

The "merry din" now commenced in right earnest; but

beyond all question the happiest mortal under the roof of Ned Brophy's barn that night was Barney Brodherick, who, fenced in by a table, in a corner all to himself, rattled away through all his wonderful steps as if he thought it a sin to let a single bar of jig, reel or double go for nothing.

CHAPTER XXXII.

AN OLD CROPPY'S NOTIONS OF SECURITY OF TENURE.

FATHER HANNIGAN and Maurice Kearney, with old Phil Morris and Phil Lahy, and a few more choice spirits, drew close together round the social board, and enjoyed themselves in their own way.

" I gave my daughter to Ned Brophy," said old Larry Clancy, in reply to a question of Father Hannigan's—" I gave my daughter to Ned Brophy, because he has a good lase."

" A good landlord is as good as a good lease," said Maurice Kearney.

" I do not know that," returned Larry Clancy, slowly and emphatically. " For my own part, I'd rather have a good lase wud the worst landlord, than no lase wud the best land-lord that ever broke bread. Security is the only thing to give a man courage."

" He's right," exclaimed old Phil Morris, striking his stick against the ground. " Security is the only thing. But if every man was of my mind he'd have security or know for what."

" Hold your tongue, you old sinner," said Father Hannigan, who had often combated Phil Morris's views, as to how the land question could be brought to a speedy settlement.

" I have my old pike yet—an' maybe I'd *want* id yet !" he exclaimed, with a look of defiance at the priest. " An' the man that'd come to turn *me* out on the road, as I see others turned out on the road, I'd give him the length uv id, as sure as God made Moses."

"And swing for it," said Father Hannigan.

"Ay, an' swing for it," shouted the old Croppy ; for it was a musket bullet that shattered Phil Morris's knee in '98. "Ay, an' swing for it."

"And be damned," added the priest. "Don't you know 'tis murder—wilful murder ?"

"I don't know that," he replied. "But the prayers of the congregation would carry the man's sowl to heaven, that'd do a manly act, an' put a tyrant out uv the country, and keep other tyrants from following his example. 'Tis self-defence," he added, striking his stick against the ground ; "'tis justice."

"'Tis bad work," said Father Hannigan. "And take my word, luck or grace will never come of it."

"I agree with you," Hugh Kearney observed, who had joined them during the latter part of the discussion.

"You do !" exclaimed old Phil, turning upon him with a scowl. "An' who the divil cares what you or the likes of you agree with ? You're well off as you are, and little trouble id gives you to see the people hunted like dogs."

"You're wrong there, Phil," replied Hugh. "I'd like to see that old pike of yours taken from the thatch for a manly fight like that you fought in '98. But that's a different thing."

"Well, I know that," returned Phil Morris, letting his chin drop upon his chest, and seeming to brood over the subject for a minute or two. "But five years ago," he added, "I could count three-an'-twenty houses, big an' little, between the cross uv Liscorrig an' Shanbally-bridge ; an' to-day you couldn't light your pipe along that whole piece uv a road, barrin' at wan house—and that's my own. An' why am I left there ? Because they *knew* I'd do id," he muttered through his clenched teeth, as if he were speaking to himself.

"Let him alone," said the priest. "There's no use in talking to him."

"There's raison in what he says," says old Larry Clancy, in his slow, emphatic way. "I say," he added, looking at the priest, "there's raison in what he says."

"Don't be talking foolish," returned Father Hannigan,

who saw that the eyes of three or four small farmers were fixed inquiringly on his face. " Good never came of it."

" Do you hear him ?" exclaimed old Phil Morris, turning to Hugh Kearney.

" Well, to a great extent," said Hugh, after a short silence —for he saw they all expected he would speak—" to a great extent I agree with Father Hannigan. But there is no use in denying that the dread of assassination is the only protection the people have against extermination in this part of Ireland."

" I say 'tis justice in the eye uv God," exclaimed old Phil Morris, " to punish the bloody tyrants—the robbers and murdherers that rob the people uv their little spots, an' turn 'em out to perish. 'Tis justice to punish the bloody rob- bers !" And as old Phil struck his stick against the ground and looked around, there was a murmur of applause from the bystanders, who by this time were pretty numerous.

" The man that believes he is robbed or persecuted," said the priest, " cannot be an impartial judge. If every one was to take the law in his own hands, there would be nothing but violence and bloodshed."

" Well, what do you say to giving the exterminators a fair trial before judge and jury ?"

" What judge and jury ?"

" 'Tisn't the judge an' jury in the coort-house," returned Phil Morris, " because they're all for the tyrants, an' some uv 'em tyrants themselves ; but a fair jury uv the people, an' a fair judge."

" I know what you mean," said Father Hannigan. " But if the judge and jury in the court-house be all for the tyrant, don't you think your judge and jury would be as much for the victim ?"

" No ; they'd never condemn a man that didn't desarve id," replied Phil.

" Ignorant men," rejoined the priest, " blinded by passion— perhaps smarting under wrong themselves, or dreading that their own turn might come next—couldn't be a fair judge and jury, Phil, even if what you speak of were lawful or just in the sight of God. So hold your tongue."

" Ay, that's the way always. ' Howld your tongue ' settles id."

" There is Mr. Lloyd," continued Father Hannigan, as that

gentleman returned to his seat; "and if he put out a tenant would you shoot him?"

"The divil a hair uv his head would be touched," replied Phil. "He gives good lases at a fair rent; and the man that does that won't turn out a tenant unless he desarves to be turned out. Answer me this wan question. Did you ever know uv a good landlord to be shot, or a good agent? Answer me that."

"Well, no," replied the priest. "I never did."

"There it is," observed Larry Clancy, as if that settled the question, and Father Hannigan had thrown up the sponge.

"Well, now, Mr. Lowe," said Father Hannigan, "what's your opinion of this matter?"

"I am almost entirely ignorant of it," he replied. "But I confess I came over to Ireland under the impression that the people were lawless and revengeful, particularly in your county."

"You only saw the dark side of the picture," returned Father Hannigan. "We are not so black as we are painted."

"I believe that. And a remark made by an Irish judge, with whom I had the honour of dining a few weeks ago, made a great impression on me, I confess."

"What did he say?"

"He had sentenced several men to be hanged a short time before, and a gentleman present made some severe remarks, while discussing the subject of agrarian outrages, when Judge —— said: 'I never met an instance of a landlord being killed, who did not deserve—I won't say to be hanged, as I am a judge—but I do say, a case of the kind never came before me that the landlord did not deserve to be *damned*!'"

Old Phil Morris looked with astonishment at the speaker.

"Put id there," he exclaimed, reaching his horny hand across the table. "If you were the divil you're an honest man."

"I don't despair of old Ireland yet," said the priest. "The people are good if they only get fair play."

"Ireland will never do any good till we have trade and manufactures of our own," observed Phil Lahy. And a certain thickness of utterance indicated that Phil had forgotten his resolution respecting the cordial long ago.

"Our rulers crushed our trade and manufactures," said Father Hannigan.

"Yes," returned Phil Lahy, "but the people are too much given to farming. A beggarly sky farmer that's stuck in the mud from mornin' to night, an' don't know beef from mutton—no, nor the taste of an egg ; for if he dare look at a hen's tail, his wife would fling the dish-cloth at him. An' that poor crawler, with his head bald from the rain droppin' on it from the eave from standin' outside his honour's window, waitin' till his honour condescended to talk to him—that beggar would despise the tradesman an' look down on him. Tom Hogan comes in to me this mornin' to know was there any news in the paper. 'There is,' says I. 'I'll read one uv the best articles ever you heard for you,' says I. "Look at the markets,' says Tom Hogan. Ha ! ha ? ha !" And Phil Lahy laughed quite sardonically. "'Look at the markets.' Ha ! ha ! ha !"

"There's some truth in what you say," said Father Hannigan.

"Ay," continued Phil, "an' the big farmer will make doctors an' attorneys of his sons, instead of setting 'em up in business."

"I'm going to bind my youngest son to his uncle," said Mr. Kearney.

"For a wonder," returned Phil Lahy, tasting his punch ; and, not considering it up to the mark, adding another glass of whiskey.

"That's what I call a *double entendre*, Phil," said Father Hannigan.

"I fear you are forgetting your promise," Hugh observed.

"What promise ?" Phil asked.

"Not to drink anything stronger than cordial."

Phil Lahy stared at the speaker for half a minute ; and then stared at the *double entendre* for half a minute more.

In fact, Phil Lahy felt himself in a dilemma. Making a sudden dive, however, at the ginger cordial decanter, he filled his glass and carefully added the glass of cordial to the two glasses of whiskey in his tumbler.

"Will that please you ?" he asked, turning to Hugh, as if *that* didn't satisfy him nothing could.

Hugh rubbed his hand over his face, and did his best to keep from laughing.

"Would you doubt Phil for getting out of a promise?" observed Father Hannigan. "He'd drive a coach-and-six through any promise that ever was made—as old Dan used to say of an Act of Parliament."

"Old Dan said many a good thing," rejoined Phil Lahy, not choosing to notice the reference to the "promise." "But the best thing ever he said," he continued, casting about for something that would turn the conversation away from promises and cordial altogether—"the best thing ever he said was : 'England's difficulty is Ireland's opportunity," exclaimed Phil Lahy, as the happy apothegm suddenly flashed into his mind at the very moment that he was about taking refuge in a severe fit of sneezing. "An' you'll see Ireland yet——" Here Phil stopped short, as if he had lost the thread of his discourse ; but after a good pull at the tumbler, he seemed to find it again, and added—"when a redcoat will be as great a curiosity as a white blackbird. There's a storm brewin'," he continued, with a portentous scowl. "Columbkill's words is comin' to pass. An' the day will come when we can drive the invader out of Ireland—wud square-bottles, as Mat the Thrasher said the other day."

"But I don't like to hear you running down the farmers," observed Father Hannigan.

"I don't run down the farmers—except when they deserve id."

"Manufactures are good," continued Father Hannigan ; "and we'll have enough of them when our fine harbours are crowded with the shipping of America—and of the whole world. But for all that I'd be sorry to see the homes of the peasantry disappearing from our hills and our plains, and the people crowded into factories."

"You're right," exclaimed Phil Lahy, almost with a shout.

"'Princes or lords may flourish or may fade.'

Mat Donovan has a new song that touches upon that."

"Come, Mat, give us the new song," said Father Hannigan.

"I'm afeard I haven't id be heart right yet, sir," replied Mat.

"Oh, we'll excuse you ; we'll excuse all mistakes," rejoined the priest. "Come, Mr. Hanly," he called out to Lory—

who with a dozen others was battering the floor to the tune of "O'Connell's Trip to Parliament"—"We're going to get a song. Give the poor pipers and fiddlers a rest. Come, Mat, up with it!"

There was a general movement towards the table, and all waited anxiously for Mat the Thrasher's new song, of which many of the company had heard.

Mat Donovan leant back in his chair, and with a huge hand resting on the table, and clutching one of the gilt buttons on the front of the blue body-coat with the other, he turned his eyes to the collar-beams, and sang in a fine mellow voice :

THE PEASANT-FARMER'S SONG—FOR THE TIME TO COME.

I've a pound for to lend, and a pound for to spend—
And *céad míle fáilte* my word for a friend ;
No mortal I envy, no master I own—
Nor lord in his castle, nor king on his throne.
Come, fill up your glasses, the first cup we'll drain
To the comrades we lost on the red battle plain !
Oh, we'll cherish their fame, boys, who died long ago—
And what's that to any man whether or no ?

The spinning-wheels stop, and my girls grow pale,
While their mother is telling some sorrowful tale,
Of old cabins levelled, and coffinless graves,
And ships swallowed up in the salt ocean waves.
But, girls, that's over—for each of you now
I'll have twenty-five pounds and a three-year-old cow ; ·
And we'll have *lan na mhala** at your weddings I trow—
And what's that to any man whether or no ?

Come here, *bhean na tighe*† sit beside me a while,
And the pride of your heart let me read in your smile.
Would you give your old home for the lordliest hall ?
Ha !—you glance at my rifle that hangs on the wall.
And your two gallant boys on parade-day are seen
In the ranks of the brave 'neath the banner of green ;
Oh ! I've taught them to guard it 'gainst traitor and foe—
And what's that to any man whether or no ?

But the youngest of all is the " white-headed boy "‡—
The pulse of your heart, and our pride and our joy :

---

* "*Lan na mhala.*"—pronounced lawn-na-waula.—" Full of a bag,"—*i.e.*, abundance.
‡ "*Bhean na tighe,*"—" pronounced van-a-thee.—" The woman of the house."
: " The white headed boy,"—the favourite.

From the dance and the hurling he'll steal off to pray,
And will wander alone by the river all day.
He's as good as the priest at his Latin I hear,
And to college, please God, we'll send him next year.
Oh, he'll offer the Mass for our souls when we go—
And what's that to any man whether or no ?

Your hands, then, old neighbours ! one more glass we'll drain ;
And *céad míle fáilte* again and again !
May discord and treason keep far from our shore,
And freedom and peace light our homes evermore.
He's the king of good fellows, the poor, honest man ;
So we'll live and be merry as long as we can,
And we'll cling to old Ireland through weal and through woe—
And what's that to any man whether or no ?

There was a shout of applause at the conclusion of Mat
Donovan's song ; and some of the women were seen to wipe
the tears from their cheeks with their aprons. Bessy Morris
raised her eyes to his ; and as she laid her hand upon his arm
while turning away her head to reply to a question of Hugh
Kearney's, Mat Donovan pressed his hand over his eyes, and
caught his breath, as if he had been shot through the body.

Bessy Morris resumed her coquettish ways as she went on
talking to Hugh Kearney, who was evidently captivated by
her. If he had proposed for her on the spot, with or without
his father's consent, and if it were arranged that they were to
be married that day week, or any day before Ash-Wednesday,
it would not have surprised Mat Donovan in the least. But
while she talked and laughed with Hugh Kearney, her hand
remained resting on the sleeve of the blue body-coat. Perhaps
this little incident did not mean much. Mat Donovan never
for a moment thought it meant anything. But he kept his
arm quite still, and would not have frightened away that
little hand for a trifle.

"That's a right good song, Mat," said Father Hannigan.

"The chorus," observed Phil Lahy, who seemed in a mood
for contradiction," "is as ould as the hills."

"So much the better," replied the priest. "Are we going
to get a song from anyone else ?"

"Billy Heffernan has another new wan," said a voice from
the crowd.

"Don't mind id !" exclaimed Phil Lahy, contemptuously.
"'Tis a ' come-all-ye.' " By which Phil meant that Billy

Heffernan's new song belonged to that class of ballads which invariably commence :

"Come all ye tender Christians, I hope you will draw near,"

" 'Tis a come-all-ye," repeated Phil Lahy. "Don't bother us wud id."

The twang of the fiddles, followed by the sound of drone and chanter, however, showed that the dancers were becoming impatient, and had urged the musicians to strike up ; and Lory Hanly was immediately on his legs again with his partner, to finish the " bout " which Father Hannigan had cut short so unceremoniously.

Hugh Kearney was about asking Bessy Morris to dance again, when Nelly Donovan came up to him.

"Come into the parlour, sir," said she. " 'Tis cleared up, an' Mr. Flaherty is afther consentin' to play a few sets for the ladies."

To the great satisfaction 'of many of the boys, and not a few of the girls, the priest and the " ladies and gentlemen," with about a dozen of the more genteel among the guests, withdrew to the dwelling-house. Mr. Lowe offered his arm to Miss Lloyd, and Miss Isabella evidently expected that Hugh Kearney would conduct her through the yard. But Hugh kept possession of the piquant Bessy, and Father Hannigan gallantly offered his arm to Miss Isabella, who, in spite of her good humour, looked a little vexed. Lory Hanly refused point-blank to accompany them, declaring that he considered the barn " better value " ; in which opinion Mr. Robert Lloyd entirely concurred, and pronounced Lory a lad of spirit. And here we have to record a very curious fact. No sooner was the priest's back turned than fully half-a-score of seats round the barn might have been dispensed with ; for by some strange chance quite a number of the prettiest girls found themselves sitting on their partners' knees—an arrangement, however, which not a single " matron's glance " attempted to " reprove." And now the fun began in right earnest. But not a single dancer, during that memorable night, so distinguished and covered himself with glory, as Lory Hanly, who tired down all his partners, even Nelly Donovan, who was never before known to throw up the sponge. And Barney Brodherick, too, called down thunders

of applause by dancing a " single bout " upon the big table.
In the midst of the cheers that greeted Barney's perform-
ance, Nelly Donovan pushed her way through the crowd to
Billy Heffernan, and asked breathlessly :

" Billy, have you your flute ?"

" Why so ?" returned Billy, in by no means a cheerful
manner.

" Because they want you to play the ' Frolic,' " replied
Nelly, excitedly.

" Who wants me to play id ?" Billy asked, rubbing his
nose.

" Father Hannigan, and all uv 'em. Have you the flute ?"

" Well, I have the flute," said Billy. " But I don't know
what to say about playin' the ' Frolic' while Mr. Flaherty is
there. Maybe 'tis turned out I'd be like the pipers." Billy
Heffernan evidently stood in awe of the great Flaherty.

" Come away," exclaimed Nelly. " 'Tis he wants to hear
id. Man alive ! if you heard the way Father Hannigan praised
you to the skies. He said you wor a born janius. Come,
before they're up for the next set."

" Are they dancin' ?" Billy asked, scratching his head, as
if he sought for an excuse to put off the ordeal as long as
possible.

" They are, they are," Nelly exclaimed, impatiently. " The
strange gentleman an' Miss Lloyd is afther dancin' that new
dance they call the polka. An' faith, 'tis no great things uv
a dance. 'Tis all bulla-bulla-baw-sheen. Myse'f don't know
how they can stand id—

Tal-tal, tal-tal, tal-tal, tal-tal-la !

all the same, round an' round." And Nelly sang a somewhat monotonous dancing-tune which was then known in
those parts as " the polka."

" By my word," continued Nelly Donovan, contemptuously,
" they'd soon get tired uv id—on'y for the ketchin'."

Billy Heffernan screwed his flute together, and sounded
low D.

" Maybe id wants a dhrink," said Nelly, with whom the
old flute was evidently an old acquaintance.

" No, 'tis all right," Billy replied. " I iled id yestherday.
But sure there's no hurry ; an' if I was flusthered I'd make

a show uv myse'f Sit down awhile an' tell me who's wudin, an' how they're goin' on."

"Wisha, sure you know the whole uv 'em as well as myse'f," Nelly replied, as she sat down. "Miss Isabella is a darlin', an' she's so pleasant. I must be tellin' Miss Mary to-morrow what an eye she has afther Mr. Hugh. I'd hould my life she'd rather have him than the young landlord, or whatever he is. But bad cess to me, Billy, but Bessy Morris has'em all light about her. I think she must have a four-laved shamrock or somethin'. She bates the world. An' 'tisn't because she's so handsome. There's Alice Ryan, an' she's be odds a purtier girl—an' faith she don't want to be reminded uv that same, either. If you see the bitther look she gave Tom Daniel, just because he asked her was id long since they had a letther from her brother. An' signs on, the divil a much any wan cares about her, in spite uv all her beauty. An' look at 'em all ready, you'd think, to put their hands undher Bessy's feet."

"Wisha, begor, Nelly," returned Billy Heffernan, " you wouldn't let id go wud any uv 'em yourse'f."

"Arrah, now, Billy, what sign uv a fool do you see on me ? Don't think you can come Jack Hannan over me that way. The man that'll buy me for a fool, will be a long way out of his money."

"I'm on'y tellin' the honest thruth," replied Billy, solemnly. "I said id to myse'f when you wer dancin' wud Tom Daniel a while ago."

She looked at him with pleased surprise, but said nothing.

"What way is Phil Lahy goin' on ?" he asked. " Is he stickin' to the cordial ?"

The question seemed to cast a gloom over Nelly Donovan's face, but rousing herself, she replied laughing :

"Well, yes ; he's stickin' to the cordial, but I'm afraid he puts in a drop uv the hardware sometimes by mistake."

"He's all right," Billy remarked, " 'till he comes to the holy wather."

"Faith, then, he is afther comin' to id," she replied. "Just as I was comin' out he was tellin' Father Hannigan the ould story, how he never went to bed wudout sprinklin' himse'f wud the holy wather."

"He must be looked afther," said Billy Heffernan. " I

promised Norah I'd have an eye to him. But he has so
many turns and twists in him 'tis hard to manage him. 'Tis
'cuter and 'cuter he gets the more he has taken. No matther
what you'd say, he'd have an argument agin you."

"Well, here, come away," said Nelly, taking him by the
arm and pulling him to the door. He walked voluntarily
across the yard, but came to a stand outside the parlour
door, and Nelly was obliged again to have recourse to force
to get him in.

CHAPTER XXXIII.

BILLY HEFFERNAN'S TRIUMPH.

"OH, is that you, Billy?" exclaimed Father Hannigan.
"Come, sit down here and play that tune you made yourself,
for Mr. Flaherty. He's not inclined to believe that you
made it at all."

"Begor, I don't know whether I did or not, sir," replied
Billy, as he sat down. "'Twas to dhrame id I did, sir."

"Come, do ye sit down, and rest for awhile; we're going
to get a tune from Billy Heffernan," said Father Hannigan,
addressing those who had taken their places for the next
dance, and were patiently waiting for the music. "Sit over
here, Mr. Lowe," he continued, "and listen to this."

Mr. Lowe left Miss Lloyd's side, and sat near Billy
Heffernan.

"Maybe, sir," said Billy Heffernan, looking reverentially at
the silver-mounted bagpipes, "maybe Mr. Flaherty wouldn't
like me to play."

"Oh, play," said the old man, patronisingly.

Billy looked at his flute, and seemed to hesitate. The
rustle of Miss Lloyd's dress was plainly audible, as she left
her chair and sat on the corner of a form, intending to resume
operations against Mr. Lowe as soon as possible; and this
stillness added to the musician's embarrassment.

" Come, Billy, don't you see they're all waitin' ?   Up wud
id," said Mat the Thrasher.

" Give us a tune yourse'f," returned Billy, offering him the
flute.

" I thought Mat only understood the big drum," said
Father Hannigan.

" Faith, then, he do so, sir ; and a right good player he is,"
replied Billy.

" Don't mind him, sir," returned Mat Donovan. " I'm
on'y a whaiten garden player." By which Mat intended to
convey that his music was only suitable for the open air,
and the harvest field.

" I believe every one in Knocknagow is a musician," said
Father Hannigan.   " But what's delaying you, Billy ?   I
never saw you so long about it before."

" Well, you see, sir," he replied with another glance at
the silver keys and the crimson-velvet bag, " Mr. Flaherty is
such a fine player, I feel somewhat daunted."

" Oh, don't mind, don't mind," returned Mr. Flaherty.

Thus encouraged, Billy Heffernan commenced to play ;
and as he went on, the incredulous expression in the old
blind musician's face gave place to a look of surprise, which
quickly changed again into one of delight. He caught up his
chanter, but without inflating the velvet bag, and mentally
accompanied the performer, who soon gave his whole soul to
the melody ; and, as he concluded, Mr. Flaherty exclaimed
with emphasis, with his face turned up towards the ceiling :

" Billy Heffernan—you are a musician."

" What did I tell you ?" said Father Hannigan, who was
evidently proud of his judgment.   " I always said Billy was
a first-rate player."

Every one was delighted at Billy Heffernan's triumph—
particularly Nelly Donovan, who stood leaning against the
door with her arms a-kimbo, and could scarcely resist the
impulse to jump into the middle of the floor, and call for
" three cheers for Knocknagow, and the sky over it."

Mr. Flaherty adjusted his pipes, and Father Hannigan
held up his hand as a signal for silence. And now it was
Billy Heffernan's turn to be astonished ; for the blind
musician played the tune in a manner which almost made the
hair of the composer's head stand on end.

"For God Almighty's sake, sir," Billy exclaimed imploringly, "didn't you ever hear id before?"

"No, I never heard it before," replied Mr. Flaherty.

"Oh," exclaimed Billy, with a deep sigh, "I can't b'lieve I ever med it."

"I'll play 'Heffernan's Frolic' for Father M'Mahon tomorrow," said Mr. Flaherty. And Billy Heffernan felt that he was famous.

Miss Lloyd found it impossible to keep quiet any longer. She left her seat with a skip, and actually sat down upon Billy Heffernan's knee, who occupied the nearest chair to Mr. Lowe.

"Mamma will be so delighted," she began, resuming the conversation which Father Hannigan had interrupted, "when I tell her that Mrs. Lowe remembers her." She glanced carelessly at Billy Heffernan, who leant back in his chair; and Miss Lloyd could not help smiling at the thought that poor Billy Heffernan was quite overpowered by the honour she had done him. She even stole a look at Mr. Lowe to see if he did not envy Billy Heffernan.

"And now, Mr. Lowe, won't you promise to come and see us before you leave the country?"

"You're an inconvaniance to me, Miss," said Billy Heffernan.

"What!" exclaimed Miss Lloyd, turning round, and staring at the speaker.

"You're an inconvaniance to me," he repeated, quietly.

Mr. Lowe, in spite of all he could do, was obliged to laugh.

"Oh, really!" she exclaimed, jumping up, and retreating backwards, with her eyes fixed on Billy Heffernan, as if he had been miraculously metamorphosed into a boiled goose.

And Billy Heffernan, having got rid of the "inconvaniance," quietly unscrewed the joints of his flute and put them in his pocket.

On seeing Father Hannigan look at his watch, Mat Donovan started up and hastily left the room. He soon returned with a plate in each hand.

"Here, Mr. Hugh," said he, presenting one of the plates to Hugh Kearney, "let us not forget the music."

"That's right, Mat," said Father Hannigan; "make the

collection for the musicians before we go. 'Tis near twelve
o'clock."

Hugh took the plate and went round to make the collection,
Mat keeping close to him, and transferring to his own plate
the half-crowns, and shillings, and sixpences—we don't mind
including the fourpenny-bits, they were so few—as fast as
they were dropped on Hugh's. Each person's contribution
was thus plain to be seen, which would not be the case if the
silver were allowed to accumulate on the plate upon which
it was dropped.

" 'Tis a fine collection," said Mat. " We won't mind the
barn for another hour or two ; but what about the beggars ?"

" Don't mind the collection for the poor people," said
Nelly, " till by-and-by. Sure there's no wan goin' away but
the Miss Lloyds, an' the priest, an' the two Mr. Kearneys,
an' the strange gentleman."

The collection for the beggars was accordingly put off to a
later hour, and Mat beckoned to a genteel-looking young
man, who was serving his time to the grocery business, to
help him with the negus.

" Maybe Mr. Lowe an' yourse'f would like a dhrop uv
somethin' before goin' out in the cowld," said Mat Donovan
to Hugh Kearney, who was standing near the door with
Miss Isabella Lloyd's shawl on his arm.

" Will you have something ?" Hugh asked.

" Oh, no, no," Mr. Lowe replied. " I'd rather not."

" Let us be all together as far as the cross," said Father
Hannigan. " Come, Mr. Flaherty."

When they were gone, it was agreed upon all hands that
one of the fiddlers should be brought in from the barn, and
the dance kept up in the parlour. Jugs of punch were
" shared " round at intervals, and, on the whole, Ned
Brophy's wedding gave general satisfaction. It was somewhat remarkable, however, that the two principal *dramatis
personæ* were almost entirely lost sight of.

" Where is Ned ?" Mat asked, looking around in every
direction for the bridegroom.

" Smokin' at the kitchen fire wud Phil Morris," replied
his sister. " An' there's herse'f in the corner beyand, an'
not a stir in her."

" Bring a glass of this to her," said Mat.

" Wisha, faith I won't," returned Nelly, who was under the impression that the bride slighted her as a poor relation. " His mother tould me to have an eye about me, and lend a hand to keep things to rights ; but the new misthress, I'm thinkin', thinks I'm makin' myse'f too busy. If she knew but the half uv id !" added Nelly, with a toss of her head.

The white muslin jacket flitted by while Nelly was speaking, and Mat gazed after it ; and, catching the eye of its owner he beckoned to her.

" Come over here," said he, " an' bring a glass of wine to Mrs. Ned, an' talk to her ; and if anything will put her in humour that will."

Four young men rushed after the white jacket with a view of getting possession of it for the next dance.

" Here, be off wud ye !" exclaimed Mat. " 'Tis the laste I can have her for a minute to myse'f. How do you think she can hould dancin' always ?"

The " boys " laughed ; and scratching their heads in their disappointment, went in search of partners elsewhere.

" I didn't taste a dhrop uv anything to-night," said Mat ; " an' here, now, sweeten this for me."

She took the glass, and, with her eyes laughingly raised to his, put it to her lips.

" A little sup," he continued.

She took a sip and handed back the glass to him.

" Here is luck," said Mat Donovan. " An' that we may be all alive an' well this day twelve-months," he added, laying the empty glass on the table.

There was something in his tone which brought that serious, inquiring look we have before noted, into Bessy Morris's eyes.

" Is there anything the matter with Mat ?" she asked in a whisper, turning to Nelly.

" No ; why so ?" Nelly replied, looking surprised.

" He's not so pleasant as he used to be," said Bessy Morris.

" Why then, as you spoke uv that," returned Nelly, " I noticed the same thing myse'f this while back. He's gettin' careless about diversion an' everything. All he wants is an excuse not to go to the hurlin' or a dance, or fun uv any soart. Thanks be to God 'tisn't his health at any rate," she added, turning round to look at him, " for I never see him lookin' betther."

Bessy Morris looked at him, too, and thought that he was not only looking well, but that he was the finest and honestest looking fellow in the world. But why that scrutinizing, and at the same time melancholy glance with which she regarded him ? Did she think that she herself had anything to do with the change she noticed in him ?

"How do you like Ned's wife ?" Nelly asked.

"I on'y spoke a few words to her," replied Bessy. "She seems in bad spirits."

"I wondher is id Ned's story wud her ?" said Nelly.

"What is that ?"

"Well, I think he had an ould *gra* for Nancy Hogan."

"Oh, I see," said Bessy Morris, thoughtfully, as she looked earnestly at the bride, who was sitting alone near the bedroom door. "After all, Nelly, marrying for money is a queer thing."

"Bring her the glass uv wine," said Nelly, "an' thry an' cheer her up. If any wan can get good uv her 'tis yourse'f."

The compliment was really deserved, for it could be easily seen that Bessy Morris was a universal favourite. The only exception to this rule, so far as the present company were concerned, was a stout young lady, chiefly remarkable for yellow kid gloves, which she did not take off during dinner. This young lady regarded Bessy with sulky looks because a certain young man from the mountain would keep gadding after the white jacket, though the yellow-gloved hand and four hundred pounds were at his service for the asking. But Bessy Morris had had experience enough of the world to enable her to estimate the " warring sighs " and amorous glances of the young man from the mountain at their true value. They simply meant that the young man from the mountain was sorry—all but heart-broken indeed—that it wasn't *she* had the four hundred pounds ; and *if* it was, etc., etc., etc.

"Well, we must try what we can do for Mrs. Ned," said Bessy.

Mrs. Ned took the glass of wine and folded her hands about it, but showed no symptom of any intention to drink it.

"This is a pleasant night we have," said Bessy, sitting down next the bride.

Mrs. Ned looked straight before her, and made no reply.

"Ah," thought Bessy, " I fear it *is* Ned's storv with her."

" You'll like this place very much," she continued, " when you become acquainted with the people. They are very nice and neighbourly."

Mrs. Ned said nothing.

" To be sure one cannot help feeling lonely after leaving one's own home," said Bessy. " But it must be a great comfort to you to have your family so near you."

" What soart is the cows ?" said Mrs. Ned, turning round suddenly, and looking straight into Bessy Morris's face.

" Oh," she stammered, quite taken by surprise, " I really don't know."

" Because," rejoined Mrs. Ned, " I never see such miserable calves as them two that was in the yard when we wor comin' in. Maybe 'tis late they wor," she added, after a short silence, and looking anxiously at Bessy again.

" Perhaps so," Bessy replied, not well knowing what to say.

" I'd be long· sorry to rear the likes uv 'em," said Mrs. Ned.

" Won't you drink the wine ?" said Bessy.

Mrs. Ned did drink the wine ; and hazarded a hope that the two-year olds were not the same breed as the two *angishores* she saw in the yard.

" There's no fear of her," said Bessy Morris to herself, as she took the empty glass back to the table. " She won't die of a broken heart."

In fact, Mrs. Ned Brophy was a very sensible young woman. Matches innumerable had been proposed and rejected, and " made " and " broke off " for one reason or another, in her case ; which gave her very little concern, as she knew there was wherewithal in the old saucepan to secure her a husband—or rather " a nice place "—sooner or later. There were two competitors in the field this Shrovetide ; and, in the difference, she was better pleased that Ned Brophy was the one " settled with " ; though the fact that the other " had an uncle a priest " gained him the favour of her mother. But Ned's lease carried the day with old Larry Clancy. The circumstance which made the young woman herself incline more to Ned Brophy than to the priest's nephew, was, that Ned wore a cravat, and was more respectable-looking than his rival. Strange to say, however, the rejected wooer of the old saucepan actually fell in love afterwards with a young lady—we use the word advisedly— in his uncle's parish, who had been educated in a convent, and married her. And though she did not bring him a single sovereign, her husband was wont to declare that she was worth her weight in gold—which he persisted in pronouncing " goold," in spite of all she could say to the contrary.

" Nelly, will you be home wud Phil Lahy, an' have an eye to him ?" said Billy Heffernan to Nelly Donovan, who was busy preparing tea—or " the tay," as Nelly herself was pleased to call that pleasant beverage.

" Why so ?" she asked, rather sharply, " won't you be wud him yourse'f ?"

" I must be goin'," he replied. " I ought to be on the road an hour ago."

" You'll be kilt," returned Nelly, in a softened tone, " wudout gettin' a wink uv sleep. Couldn't you put id off for wan day ?"

" Well, as they're reg'lar customers I wouldn't like to disappoint them."

" Well, you won't go till you're afther takin' a sup uv this, at any rate," returned Nelly. " You that never dhrank a dhrop uv anything."

She filled out a cup of tea, and, after tasting it and pronouncing it, " hot, strong, and sweet," presented it to Billy Heffernan.

" The old woman," she continued, while Billy was drinking his cup of tea, " wants me to stop a day or two, and help to put the place to rights, an' pack up the borrowed things. But I'll warn Mat not to lose sight uv Phil till he laves him safe at home."

" I won't take any more," said Billy, stopping her hand as she was about filling his cup again.

" Now, Billy, don't be makin' an omadhaun uv yourse'f," she replied, pouring out the tea at the risk of scalding his hand, with which he attempted to cover the tea-cup.

" Don't you be lonesome," she continued, sitting down near him, " thravellin' be yourse'f this way every night ?"

" I don't mind id," he replied. " 'Tis some way uneasy I do be when I'm comin' near the town, an' I think every minute an hour till I'm out uv id agin."

"But sure 'tis lonesomer in the summer time," she continued, "in the bog by yourse'f from mornin' till night."

"That's what I do be longin' for," said Billy Heffernan. "I'm King uv Munster when I'm in the bog, an' the phil libeens whistlin' about me. No, begor," continued Billy, smacking his lips after emptying his cup; "when I'd sit on a bank uv a fine summer's evenin', and' look about me, I wouldn't call the queen my aunt."

"But why wouldn't you sell your turf in Kilthubber, an' not be goin' all the ways to Clo'mel, in the hoighth uv winther ?"

"The divil a betther little town in Ireland to buy turf," replied Billy, "but there's too many goin' there."

"I'm looking for you this hour, Nelly," said a voice that made her start. "I'm after tiring them all down. Come and have another dance."

"Oh ! Mr. Lory, I thought you wor gone home wud Mr. Kearney two hours ago."

"What a fool I am," replied Lory. "Come."

"Sure I'm goin' to get the tay," replied Nelly.

"Leave that to the old woman," he exclaimed, catching her hand and pulling her off to the barn.

"Come, Mr. Lloyd," said Lory, "get a partner."

But just then he discovered that the dancing was suspended, and that Mr. Lloyd, who had a good voice as well as a correct ear, was in the act of favouring the company with a song. Mr. Lloyd's song was the "Soldier's Tear," and on coming to the refrain, "and wiped away a tear," at the end of each verse, Mr. Lloyd suited the action to the word, by seeming to pluck out his left eye with his finger and thumb, and fling it on the floor, in a most moving manner.

Mr. Lloyd's song was so highly appreciated that the cheering and clapping were kept up for several minutes, during which the vocalist untied his hunting-whip, and in the calmest manner possible commenced attempting the feat of snuffing a candle at the other end of the table with the lash.

"Well, will you dance now ?" said Lory, whose knees were beginning to work involuntarily.

"Another song, Lory. Sit down near me here, Nelly."

Nelly Donovan sat down near him and Mr. Lloyd sang

" My Dark-haired Girl," casting admiring glances at her as
he went on, particularly at the lines—

> " Thy lip is like the rose, and thy teeth they are pearl,
> And diamonds are the eyes of my dark-haired girl " ;

which really applied very well to Nelly Donovan.

A still louder storm of applause followed this effort, and
Nelly exclaimed :

" Faith, 'tis no wondher that so many are dyin' about you,
sir," as she jumped up to rejoin her partner.

The bridegroom sat all this time in the corner by the
kitchen fire, listening to old Phil Morris's reminiscences of
'98, and quietly smoking his pipe.   But as the guests began
to leave, and came to bid him good morning, he would start
up suddenly to shake hands with them ; and after scratching
his head with a puzzled look, Ned Brophy would seem to
remember that he was at his own wedding, and then sit down
again and forget all about it, till another " Good mornin',
Ned, I wish you joy," would recall the circumstance to his
mind.

At last, old Phil Morris himself thought it time to go home,
and striking his stick against the hearthstone, he said :

" Mat, will you see about my ass, and tell that little girl
uv mine to get ready.   She ought to have enough uv the
dancin' by this time, at any rate."

And to be sure, how Mat Donovan did start off, and how
soon the ass was put to the cart, and what a quantity of
fresh straw—oaten straw, too, for which he had to run to the
haggard—was packed into the said cart, and then shaken up
loosely, and patted and smoothed, till a sultana might have
reclined on it !

Bessy soon appeared in her cloak and bonnet, looking, if
possible, more captivating than ever.   Half-a-dozen " boys "
contended for the honour of handing her into the car ; one
of whom contented himself with placing a chair for her to
step upon, which he held firm with all his might, as if the
slightest shake would endanger her life.   Mat handed the
reins to old Phil, and led the ass out of the yard, and a little
way along the narrow boreen.

" Why don't you ever come to see us, now ?" Bessy asked,
when he stopped to say good night.

"I don't have time," he replied, "except uv a Sunday. And the days are so short yet."

"Well, they'll soon be getting long," said she, clasping his hand very warmly; "and I'm sure grandfather would like to have a *shanahus* with you."

"Well, I'll shortly take a walk over."

"Next Sunday," said Bessy, in a distractingly coaxing tone.

"Well, the b'ys will be expectin' me to hurl o' Sunday," replied Mat. "An' besides, Captain French wants to have a throw uv a sledge wud me. He's askin' me ever since he came home to go over to the castle some week-day; but I couldn't spare time. And they're so d——n exact," he added, "about breakin' the Sabbath, that he wouldn't agree to appoint a Sunday. But, now, as the regiment is goin' abroad, he wouldn't be satisfied wudout havin' a throw wud me."

"Is the regiment going abroad?" she asked, with an interest that took Mat by surprise.

"They're not the same sogers," he replied, "that's in Kilthubber. They're dragoons."

"Oh! I know. I know Captain French's regiment."

"An' who cares where they go?" old Phil exclaimed under his teeth, as he jerked the reins and dealt a blow of his stick to the ass—for which that patient animal had to thank the English army.

Mat Donovan slowly retraced his steps to the house, feeling as if Bessy Morris's departure had suddenly turned the wedding into a wake, and singing, almost unconsciously—

> Oh! I'd rather have that car, sir,
> With B——ahem!—Peggy by my side,
> Than a coach-an'-four an' goold galore,
> An' a lady for my bride."

He turned into the barn, and stood with folded arms leaning against the wall.

"I didn't see Mat dance to-night," said Mr. Lloyd to Nelly Donovan, as she sat down after another jig with Lory Hanly.

"I'll go myse'f and haul him out," returned Nelly, who was allowed to be the best dancer among the girls at Knocknagow.

" Stir yourse'f, you big lazy fellow," she exclaimed, taking hold of his arm and leading him out to the middle of the floor.

This movement was hailed with general satisfaction, and a dozen voices at once called upon the musicians to play " The Wind that shakes the Barley."

It was really a sight worth looking at. The athletic, but at the same time lithe and graceful form of the Thrasher was set off to the best advantage by Phil Lahy's *chef d'œuvre*, the blue body-coat with the gilt buttons ; and his sister was a partner every way worthy of him.

" What is id ?" a stranger to the locality asked on finding the barn-door blocked up by a crowd of eager spectators.

" A brother and sister," was the reply ; and it could be inferred from the tone and look of the speaker that the relationship between the great dancer, Mat Donovan, and his equally famous partner added greatly to the interest with which their performance was regarded. The excitement rose higher and higher as the dance went on, and a loud shout followed every brilliantly executed step. After each step the dancers changed places, and, moving slowly for a few seconds, commenced another which threw the preceding one quite into the shade, and, as a matter of course, called out a louder " bravo !" and a wilder " hurro !" When the enthusiasm was at its height, two men carrying a large door crushed their way through the crowd. Two more quickly followed bearing another large door. And, without causing any interruption, the doors were slipped under the feet of the dancers, which now beat an accompaniment to the music, as if a couple of expert drummers had suddenly joined the orchestra. There was a hush of silence as if the spectators were spell-bound, till Mat Donovan joined hands with his sister, and both bowed at the conclusion of the dance. And while a Tipperary cheer is shaking the roof of Ned Brophy's barn, we let the curtain drop on Ned Brophy's wedding.

CHAPTER XXXIV.

LONELY.

BILLY HEFFERNAN took the key of his door from a hole under the thatch and let himself into his own house. Removing the ashes from the embers on the hearth, he knelt down, and, after a good deal of blowing, succeeded in kindling them into a flame. Then, taking a slip of bog-pine from one of several bundles that hung in the chimney, he lighted it and placed it on a block of bogwood in the corner, having first stuck it in a sod of turf in which was a hole for the purpose. He recalled the fine summer evening, when, out in the lonesome bog, he thrust his thumb into that sod of turf while it was yet soft, and by that simple process converted it into a candlestick.

Everything about Billy Heffernan's house seemed to have come from the bog. The walls, from the floor to the thatch —which was not of straw, but of sedge—were lined with turf, the side-walls with the rectangular " slane " turf, which looked like brick-work blackened with smoke, and the end wall with the rougher and somewhat shapeless " hand-turf." The table off which Billy Heffernan ate his meals was of bog-oak, as was the block upon which he sat. The mule's crib and the pegs in the wall upon which the mule's harness hung were of the same material. And Billy Heffernan's ratteen riding-coat depended from a portion of the horns of an elk— which had bounded through the forest when the table and crib were portions of the living tree—fastened to one of the rafters.

He now took his antediluvian taper from the antediluvian seat and laid it on the antediluvian table ; and then hung his riding-coat upon the antediluvian elk's horns.

" Wo ! Kit," said Billy Heffernan. And the mule, who had an antediluvian look about her, whisked her tail and thrust her nose into her antediluvian manger.

He put the harness on the mule, and after shaking up the

hay in the crib, walked out and looked at the sky, in which
there was a half moon that shone with a sickly sort of lustre.
Billy Heffernan, without being at all aware of the fact, was of
a poetical and fanciful turn of mind ; and the pale moon at
once reminded him of a pale face. So he walked down the
road as far as the beech-tree ; and, after looking up at the
windows and steep roof and thick chimneys of Phil Lahy's
old house, Billy Heffernan walked back again. Taking the
linch-pins from the hob, where they were always left for
safety, he fixed them in the axle-tree ; and then led out his
mule and put her to the car. He returned to the house to
take down his old riding-coat, and after wrapping it round
him, and blowing out the light, he locked his door, and set
out with his creel of turf, upon his long journey to the town
of Clonmel.

"Wisha, begor ! 'tis thrue for her," he soliloquised, as he
plodded up the hill, " 'tis lonesome enough. The road is
lonesome, an' the house is lonesome, an' the bog is lonesome.
An', begor, the main street uv Clo'mel is the lonesomest uv
all. No matther where I am, I'm lonesome. So that I
b'lieve 'tisn't the road, or the house, or the bog, or the town,
but the *heart* that's lonesome. And whin the heart is lonesome, the world is lonesome. Wisha, Kit, what do you want
stoppin' there above all the places on the road ? You got
your drink at the lough ; but comin' or goin' nothin' will
plase you but a sup out of that little strame any day in the
year."

While the mule drank, Billy Heffernan placed a foot at
each side of the little stream that ran across the road, and
stretching out his hands, as if he were lifting some one over
it, he uttered a low moan.

"Oh ! oh ! oh !" he cried, as his hands closed on the empty
air.

The water running over his feet reminded him that he was
standing in the middle of the stream, but he did not heed it.
With his head bent down, and his hands pressed over his
face, he continued to stand there till the mule moved on of
her own accord ; and then, dashing the fast falling tears from
his eyes, he plodded on again after his creel.

"I don't know what brought id so sthrong into my mind
to-night," said he. " But somehow I thought I see her before

me, lookin' at the wather, an' afeard to lep over like the rest
uv 'em ; an' then lookin' up at myse'f wud her eyes laughin'
in her head. I hardly had the courage to take her up in my
arms. An', the Lord be praised ! 'twas the last time evei
she crossed over the same strame. She reminded me uv id
yistherday, whatever put id into her head. But sure I never
pass the same spot wudout thinkin' uv her. I gev herse'f
an' Nelly Donovan a lift home the same evenin' ; an' a
pleasant, good-hearted girl Nelly is. But there's no wan like
Norah !"

He plodded on for some time till the mule stopped to take
breath before commencing the ascent of an unusually steep
though not very long hill, that rose abruptly from the lowest
part of the glen or hollow down which they had been
gradually descending.

" Begor, 'tis thrue for ould Phil," said he, as he looked
around him. " You couldn't redden the pipe from the bridge
to the quarry. Though I remimber id myse'f when 'twas
the pleasantest piece uv a road from Kilthubber to Clo'mel.
An', faith, if I could redden the pipe now I'd like a smoke,
as 'tis afther comin' into my head."

He put his pipe into his mouth and looked around him,
while the mule rested at the foot of the hill.

" God be wud poor Mick Brien," said he. " That sally
three always reminds me uv him. 'Tis many's the piggin uv
milk they made me dhrink, for 'tis little business I'd have
axin' a dhrink uv wather at Mick's. But sure if every house,
big an' little uv 'em, was standin'," continued Billy Heffernan,
as if he caught himself reasoning from unsound premises, " I
couldn't kindle the pipe this hour uv the night. Come,
Kit !" and catching hold of one heel of the car, and leaning
his shoulder against the creel, he helped the mule on in her
zig-zag course up the hill. The descent on the other side
was gradual, and the mule was left to shift for herself till
they got upon the level, where she showed some symptoms
of stopping for another rest ; a proceeding which Billy Heffernan thought so unreasonable that he took down his whip
from the top of the load, where it usually rested, and, without a word of warning or remonstrance, gave Kit a smart
lash under the belly, at which Kit shook her ears and whisked
her tail, and was about running straight into the ditch at the

left-hand side, that being the deepest and the most likely to swallow her up ; but changing her mind as she reached the brink, Kit set off at a brisk trot along the road. This was too much of a good thing, and her master ran forward, and, seizing the rein near the bit, gave it a check that made Kit throw back her head and open her jaws very wide ; and while still pressing on the rein, Billy Heffernan let the lash of his whip drop into the same hand that held the handle, and laid both lash and handle along Kit's back, between the hip and the butt of the tail, with a tremendous whack.

" Maybe you'd go right now ?" said he, letting the rein go with a jerk.

And Kit seemed to think it was the wisest thing she could do.

So they jogged on peacefully again, till the light shining through the open door of a house surrounded by trees—which, from their size and outline, even a stranger to the locality would have known were very old whitethorns—attracted his attention.

" Wo ! Kit." said Billy Heffernan, and the mule immediately stopped.

" They're up at ould Phil's," said he, looking considerably surprised.

" But that's thrue," he added, as if the mystery were suddenly cleared up ; " sure they're at the weddin'."

He was about ordering Kit to go on, when another thought occurred to him.

" Begob !" he exclaimed, " I might as well have the smoke as I have the chance."

He opened the gate that led to Phil Morris's house, and was closing it again behind him when he found himself caught by the skirt of the coat. He turned round suddenly somewhat frightened, but found himself held fast. After remaining still for a moment, during which his heart beat very quick, he ventured to pull the skirt of the coat, but could not free himself. As nothing stirred, however, he concluded he had merely got entangled in a branch of one of the old whitethorns blown down by the storm of the morning that blew down the end of his own turf-rick. He tried to free himself without tearing his riding-coat, when, to his amazement and terror, the long skirt was raised up and shook in his face, with which it was almost on a level. He retreated backwards, but the coat was pulled the other way ; and after a short tussle, Billy Heffernan got a sharp blow on the mouth. Moved by the instinct of self-preservation, he stretched out his hands, and boldly grappled with his assailant, whom he attempted to throttle as quickly as possible. In the struggle both rolled to the ground, and Billy loudly denounced his adversary as a coward ; for he not only struck at him while down, but aimed his blows where any one having the faintest regard for fair fighting would have scorned to strike.

" He wants to murdher me," exclaimed Billy Heffernan. " That's what he wants. Can't you spake," he added, " an' tell me who you are an' what are you up to ?"

But the only reply was a repetition of the cowardly assault.

" D——n your sowl," shouted Billy Heffernan, roused to madness by a sharp blow that affected him somewhat like the sting of a bee, " if you're a man let go my ould coat an' stand up an' see id out if you're able."

This challenge seemed to have the desired effect, for after another violent struggle he found his coat skirt free. Scrambling as quickly as possible to his feet, Billy Heffernan flung off the old riding-coat, and put himself into a pugilistic attitude.

" Turn out now, if you're a man," he exclaimed.

But to his horror and consternation there was no one to answer the challenge.

Billy Heffernan's courage oozed out, we should rather say through his toes, than the tips of his fingers, for he began to feel very weak about the knees, while the strength that was so rapidly departing from his limbs seemed in some mysterious manner to be communicated to the hair of his head.

" The Lord betune us an' all harm," he muttered ; " as long as I'm goin' this road I never see anything bad before. Though they say wan uv the sogers ould Phil kilt long ago, when they set fire to the house, used to be risin' about here."

It was a relief to him when he heard some noise close to the gate ; for at that moment he would have welcomed with rapture the most formidable foe of flesh and blood.

" In the name uv God," he called out, " who or what are you ?"

A sudden bound from behind the gate-pier made him
retreat a step backwards—when a familiar voice sent a most
pleasurable sensation through Billy Heffernan's whole frame.
And a hysterical flutter about his heart imparted a tremor to
his voice as he exclaimed :

" May bad luck to you, for a goat !"

" Meg-geg-geg-geg," repeated Phil Morris's old goat, as she
trotted along the boreen to the house.

But as Billy Heffernan took up his ratteen riding-coat, his
countenance suddenly fell.

" The divil sweep you," he exclaimed with great gusto, as
he looked at the half-moon through a rent in the skirt.
" But," he continued, " I may as well run in an' redden the
pipe at any rate. An' the Lord knows I'm afther payin'
for id. Begor, they're afther comin' home," he added, as he
approached the house. " There is the ass's car in the
yard."

As he passed the little kitchen window Billy Heffernan
stopped suddenly, with his eyes and mouth wide open.
Something upon old Phil Morris's kitchen table excited his
wonder to such a degree that there he stood staring at it,
apparently bereft of the power of motion.

" 'Tis goold," he muttered.   " I wundher is id a crock he's
afther findin' ?"

Billy's idea at the moment must have been that the
" crock itself," as well as its contents, was of gold ; for the
object which excited his astonishment shone brightly, and
flashed back the blaze of the turf fire. But, after examining
it more closely, he clapped his hand against his thigh, and
exclaimed :

" Be japers, he's afther killin' a soger !"

This idea was sufficiently terrifying, and Billy Heffernan
was about beating a hasty retreat, when, glancing involuntarily around the kitchen, he started again ; for straight before
him he beheld not a dead, but a living soldier. He was a
broad-chested, bearded dragoon ; and it was his burnished
helmet, which he seemed to have thrown carelessly on the
table, that Billy Heffernan had mistaken for a crock of
gold.

Like one awakening from sleep and gradually recovering
the use of his senses, Billy now saw that the dragoon was

holding Bessy Morris by the hand, and looking down into her face—for his tall figure towered high above hers—with a look of sadness. He could not see her face, as her back was towards him, but she bent her head as if the sad gaze of the dragoon had moved her. Before Billy Heffernan could observe further, the soldier shook the hand he held in his once or twice with a quick spasmodic jerk, and seizing his helmet, which he hung upon his left arm, rushed out of the house. Billy Heffernan turned round and stared after him as he tramped along the little boreen till he reached the gate and was hid by the whitethorns.

When Billy looked again through the window, Bessy Morris was sitting in her grandfather's old arm-chair, with one hand resting on the little table beside her, and the other pressed over her eyes. It might be supposed that she was overcome by fatigue, but for the flush that reddened her forehead, and the nervous tapping of her fingers upon the table. She raised her head, and letting both hands drop upon her lap, threw herself back in the chair. Bessy Morris was certainly excited, but what might be the nature of her emotion it would not have been easy to judge from the expression of her face. Scarcely anything but a feeling of shame or self-reproval could have kept that hot glow on her forehead so long ; but then in her eyes and about her mouth there played a smile of triumph. Bessy Morris was evidently ashamed, and proud, and perhaps a little frightened, all at the same time.

Billy Heffernan felt for a moment at a loss how to act. His first impulse was to go back to his mule ; but then it occurred to him that that would look as if he had stopped for the sole purpose of playing the spy. So, as the door still stood wide open, he decided upon carrying out his original intention of lighting his pipe at Phil Morris's fire.

" God save all here," said he, as he walked into the kitchen.

" God save you kindly. Wisha, is that Billy Heffernan ? Faith, I thought you wor dead."

" Wisha, who did you send to kill me ?" returned Billy.

It wasn't Bessy that spoke, but what Billy himself would have described as a " stout block of a girl," who stood up from the bench she had been sitting on by the fire, behind the partition which shaded the fire-place from the door, and which concealed her from view till he had advanced to the middle of the floor.

Bessy stood up also, and moved out of his way.

"Don't stir," said he ; "I on'y turned in, as I was passin', to redden the pipe. You're home early from the weddin'," he remarked, as he stooped down and took a partially burnt sod of turf from the fire.

"Yes," replied Bessy. "Grandfather is not able to stop up late. I did not expect he would stay half so long."

"Worn't you there yourse'f ?" the stout girl asked.

"I was," he replied, "but I was obliged to come home to start for Clo'mel."

"Ye had a great night's fun ?"

"'Twas a fine weddin'," he answered. "Why worn't you there yourse'f ?"

"Why wasn't I axed ? An' ye had ladies and gentlemen there too ?"

"Begor, ay," replied Billy, as he blew upon the burnt end of the sod of turf till the sparks flew from it with a crackling sound into his face. "The two Miss Lloyds, an' Mr. Bob, an' the gentleman from England."

"And Mr. Hugh Kearney," said Bessy Morris.

"Begor," returned Billy Heffernan, as he sucked his pipe, against which he pressed the sod of turf, "Mr. Hugh is a gentleman, sure enough—in his heart."

"I'll be bound Mat Donovan was there," the stout girl remarked, as she drew her kerchief over her bosom ; a proceeding which Billy Heffernan thought was not unnecessary, as the hooks-and-eyes intended to fasten her dress up the front had nearly all given way to a greater amount of pressure than they were capable of sustaining.

"Sure, he was Ned's sidesman," said Billy Heffernan.

"The poor fool !" returned the stout girl, with a scornful shake of the head, and a glance at Bessy Morris that brought the flush up to her forehead again, and caused her to bite her lip as she gazed into the fire.

"Did you see Judy Loughlan there ?" the stout girl asked.

"She was there," said Billy Heffernan.

"Indeed, I see her goin'," rejoined the stout girl, "wud her yallow mittens an' her boy-o." By which latter expression the stout girl meant that article of female attire called a boa.

" I thought you wor there yourse'f when I see Bessy."

" Oh, yeh ! she's everywhere, like the bad weather. *I* have no time for gallavantin'."

" You may as well sit down, Billy," said Bessy Morris, in her usual captivating way.

" Arra do, Billy," said the stout girl. " Sit down and have a coort. Anything, you know, to keep our hands in " ; and she glanced at Bessy, who evidently winced, though she strove to command her features.

" I must be goin'," he replied. " Good night to ye."

" Good night, Billy," returned Bessy Morris ; and there was something so winning in her way of saying it that Billy muttered to himself on his way up the little boreen :

" Begor ! 'tis no wondher she *is* every place ; for any place would be the betther uv her. But I don't know what to say about that soger."

<hr>

CHAPTER XXXV.

ON THE ROAD TO THE BIG TOWN WITH THE CLOUD OVER IT.

" Come, Kit, be lively ; 'tis long since we wor on the road so late as this. An' you know that load must be bilin' the kittles for the breakfasts in Irishtown to-day."

Kit seemed to understand the state of affairs perfectly, and set off briskly, switching her tail as if she expected the whip was about being brought into requisition, and shaking one ear approvingly—which had much the same effect as wink-ing with one eye—on finding that her apprehensions were groundless.

" God save you," said Billy Heffernan, on observing the outline of a man's figure leaning against one of those sally trees, which, at short intervals along that part of the road, marked where a peasant's cabin or a small farmhouse once stood.

" And you, too," returned a deep voice.

" God save you kindly," was the response Billy Heffernan expected ; and it at once occurred to him that the person

leaning against the sally tree was a stranger ; and a cloud
having passed from the moon at the moment, he was able to
recognise the dragoon, with his helmet still slung on his arm.
Mr. Bob Lloyd's song at once occurred to him ; and, looking
back at the light in Phil Morris's window, he could almost
fancy he saw Bessy Morris " on her knees," waving a " snow
white scarf that fluttered in the breeze."

" Do you belong to this neighbourhood ?" the dragoon
asked, on observing him look towards the house.

" I do," Billy replied.   " I was bred, born, and reared at
the far-off side uv that hill beyand."

" Do you know the people that live in the house where the
light is ?"

" That's ould Phil Morris's, the weaver's," he replied.

" Are you going far this way ?" the dragoon asked.

" To Clo'mel," was the reply.

" I'm going there, too," returned the dragoon.   " We'll
be comrades on the road."

To this Billy Heffernan made no reply ; and, after a
scrutinising look into his face, the dragoon continued the
conversation.

" Ye're wild folks down here," said he.

" So they say," replied Billy ; " though myse'f can't see
much difference betune us and other people.   Yo-up, Kit."

" The old man has a daughter," said the dragoon.

" A grand-daughter," replied Billy Heffernan.   " I b'lieve
you're thinkin' uv Bessy ?"

" Yes," returned the dragoon, " I'm thinking of Bessy."

" She's a nice girl," Billy observed.

" She is that," said the dragoon.

" Wud id be any harm to ax are you acquainted wud
her ?"

The dragoon looked scrutinisingly at him again ; and
evidently satisfied that his questioner was a harmless fellow,
he replied :

" A relation of her aunt's was a comrade of mine, and I
knew her in Dublin."

" She was in Dublin, sure enough," said Billy.   " She's
not long afther comin' home."

" Her aunt is my friend," the dragoon observed.   " And I
think the girl that lives with her is my friend, too.   But I

have not seen the old man. She says he hates the sight of a red-coat."

"Well, I b'lieve he do," replied Billy. "An' maybe 'tisn't wudout raison."

"That girl told me she was her cousin. What is her name?"

"Peg Brady—she's related to the ould man."

"She is a good-natured girl," said the dragoon.

"She's a harmless soart uv a girl," Billy replied. "Come, Kit. What! Is id goin' to get into your tantrums you are? I'll soon let you know." And Billy Heffernan took down his whip from the top of the load of turf; but Kit seemed to think better of it, and put off the tantrums for the present. "Begor," he continued, addressing himself to the dragoon, "wudout mainin' any offince, you're very hot in yourse'f."

"How is that?"

"Wud your hat, or whatever you call id, hangin' on your arm that way," replied Billy.

The dragoon laughed, and put his helmet on his head.

After walking on in silence for some time, Billy Heffernan and the dragoon stopped short at a turn in the road, both looking considerably astonished. A man with his coat off was running towards them through a field adjoining the road at the top of his speed. They thought some accident must have happened, and that he was running to call them to the assistance of some one in danger, when, to their surprise, he turned the angle of the field without seeming to notice them, and continued his race in a line with the fence. The field was a small one, and he was soon round it and passed them again.

"It must be a madman," said the dragoon.

"Begor, that's what I'm thinkin' myse'f, too," returned Billy Heffernan, who showed some symptoms of being frightened as he kept his eyes steadily on the runner. But it was not of madmen Billy Heffernan stood in awe; but the notion got into his head that there were more than one runner, and that the second was invisible to them, and consequently supernatural and a thing to be dreaded.

"Begob," said Billy, as the runner passed a third time, "'tis Mick Brien, as sure as I'm alive. I'll call him when he comes round again."

" Is that Mick ?" he called out, as the man was passing
them again.

" Is that Billy ?" was the reply, and he stopped short
opposite to them.

" In the name o' God, what are you runnin' that way for ?"

Mick Brien climbed over the fence without replying, and
came out upon the road. He looked greatly surprised on
seeing the dragoon ; for dragoons were seldom met strolling
through that part of the country at night. Mick Brien's face
darkened as he fixed his eyes on the soldier—and not without
reason, perhaps ; for the last glimpse of a " bold dragoon "
which Mick Brien had seen was when a troop of these for-
midable-looking warriors rattled through his little farmyard
the day the old house was pulled down—where Billy Heffernan
was wont to take a piggin of milk in lieu of a drink of water
whether he would or no—and Mick Brien and his wife and
children were flung homeless on the world. So that we must
excuse Mick Brien if the unexpected sight of an English
soldier brought a scowl into his face.

The dragoon observed it, and said—

" Friend, I have only been to see a friend off in that
quarter "—and the dragoon turned round and pointed towards
Knocknagow—" and on my way back I have met your neighbour here on the road ; and, as we are both bound for the
same town, we have kept together so far."

" That's the way," said Billy Heffernan, in reply to Mick
Brien's inquiring look. " An' now," he continued, " maybe
you'd tell us about the runnin' ?"

Mick Brien looked on the ground, and remained silent for
a moment.

" Well," said he, with a grim smile, " I will tell you about
the runnin', for fear you might think I was afther takin' lave
uv my sinses. But come on. I needn't delay you."

" Yo-up, Kit," said Billy Heffernan, putting his hand to
the creel, and helping on Kit with a push.

All three fell back behind the car, the dragoon and Billy
Heffernan waiting with no little curiosity for an explanation
of the running.

" You're forgettin' your coat," said Billy, looking at Mick
Brien's torn and threadbare shirt sleeves.

" No ; I hadn't id on me at all," he replied. " An' now,"

he added, as if it had cost him an effort to make up his mind to satisfy their curiosity, " if you want to know about the runnin', here is the ins an' outs uv id for you. The wind tumbled wan ind uv the cabin on us last night, an' I wasn't able to fix id till I get a bundle uv straw. An' wan uv the childher bein' sick, we wor obliged to put whatever little coverin' we had on her to keep her warm. An' as the roof was stripped, I woke in a stump wud the cowld, an' couldn't get a wink uv sleep afther. So I got up an' turned into that field, an' said to myse'f I'd have a run to put the life into me. An' begor, Billy, my sperits riz whin I found myse'f so soople, an' I purtinded to myse'f that I was runnin' for a bet ; an' the divil a stop I'd stop till I was afther goin' twelve rounds on'y for you called me."

" Begob, Mick, 'twas a quare notion. An' faith you ran as fast as ever I see you runnin' at a hurlin' match when Mat Donovan 'ud be makin' off wud the ball."

" Well, good-night to ye," said Mick Brien. " See yourse'f the way the roof was swep away at that side."

They were just opposite a miserable hovel, one side of the roof of which was entirely bare. Billy Heffernan shook his head as he mentally contrasted the wretched tenement with the warm little farm-house where he had been so often welcomed and hospitably entertained by the man who now stood before him, as unlike his former self as the wretched hovel was unlike the comfortable home that once was his. There was surprise and something like pity in the dragoon's face, too, as he looked from the cabin to its owner. But just as Mick Brien was turning away, he was seized with a violent fit of coughing, and, pressing his hand upon his side, he staggered against Billy Heffernan, who caught him in his arms. The blood gushed from the poor man's mouth, and flowed down the breast of his shirt. He had evidently burst a blood vessel.

" Mick," said Billy, as he threw his arms round him to prevent his falling, " I'm sorry to see you this way." And Billy Heffernan burst into tears.

" 'Tis nothin'," he gasped, " 'tis nothin'. Help me as far as the doore, Billy."

He leant upon Billy's shoulder, and both walked into the hovel.

Oh !—we hesitate to follow them. We wish to spare the
reader such scenes as long as we possibly can. Enough to
say that when Billy Heffernan looked around him, and felt
the cold breeze as it whistled through the uncovered roof,
and saw the once rosy farmer's wife crouching in a corner
with her sick child pressed against her bosom, and her husband's coat thrown over her shoulders, he felt that swelling
in his throat which Norah Lahy's looks and words so often
caused ; and, without uttering a word, Billy Heffernan pulled
off his old riding-coat, wrapped it round the evicted farmer,
and laid him softly down upon the wisp of straw in the
corner of the cabin, where his two little boys were asleep,
locked in each other's arms. The moon shone directly down
upon their pale faces, and Billy Heffernan could scarcely
suppress a groan as he thought of the merry, bright-eyed
little fellows who used to vie with each other to know who'd
be first to run to the dairy to tell their mother that Billy
Heffernan had stopped his mule on the road and was coming
up to the house. He fixed the straw so that the poor man's
head might be in a comfortable position, and silently returned to his mule, at whose head the dragoon was standing,
as if he had turned to poor Kit for companionship.

At first the dragoon did not recognise Billy Heffernan
when he appeared without his riding-coat. But when in a
subdued tone he addressed the usual " Yo-up, Kit,' to his
mule, the dragoon guessed the reason why his companion
had left his coat behind him in the cabin.

They walked on without speaking for a considerable distance, and then the dragoon asked how much farther had
they to go.

" You'll see the cloud over Clo'mel," replied Billy, " when
we come to the top uv that hill." And they walked on in
silence again.

" There id is," said Billy, when they reached the top of the
hill.

" What ?"

" The cloud."

" What cloud ?"

" The cloud over Clo'mel."

" And why the cloud over Clonmel ? And how did you
know there was a cloud over it ?'

" Becase Clo'mel was never wudout a cloud over id since the day Father Sheehy was hung," replied Billy Heffernan.

" For what was he hung ?"

" Begor, for killin' a man that was alive twenty years afther," said Billy. " But the rale raison was becase he wanted to save the people from bein' hunted, an' the whole counthry turned into pasture for sheep and cattle. But I'll show you the house where his blood was sprinkled on the doore when the head was afther bein' cut off uv him, and they wor bringin' his body to Shanrahan to bury him."

" And what did they want to sprinkle the blood on the door for ?"

" Becase id was the doore uv the bishop's house ; an' on'y for him Father Sheehy wouldn't be hung at all. He refused to give him a character, an' that's what settled him."

"And why did the bishop refuse ?"

" Becase he was all-in-all wud the great lords an' gentlemen ; and for fear uv offendin' 'em, he wouldn't stir hand or fut to save the life uv the poor priest that had the rope about his neck. 'Tis ould Phil Morris that could give you the ins an' outs uv id."

" Thim is the Comeragh mountains," continued Billy, breaking off abruptly, and pointing towards them.

But the allusion to old Phil Morris made the dragoon turn round and fix his eyes on the hills in nearly an opposite direction.

Billy Heffernan was obliged to keep up with his mule, and when he got to the foot of the hill he looked round and saw the dragoon still standing on the top of it, with his arms folded, looking towards Knocknagow.

" Begob," said Billy, " he's a bad case."

He soon began to overtake and pass by an occasional heavily laden dray or cart, both horse and driver travel-stained, and so worn out as to require a rest, near as they were to their journey's end ; while, on the other hand, Billy himself had often to call out " hub !" or " ho !" to his mule, to make way for a fast-walking farmer's horse, whose load was not over heavy—even though the farmer's wife was enthroned on the top of it—or a trotting donkey, whose only burden was a couple of blooming country girls, coming to town to make purchases, in view, mayhap, of an approaching wedding. And the more crowded and noisy the road became, the more lonely Billy Heffernan felt, and the more anxious to be on his way back to Knocknagow.

He found it no easy task to guide the mule through the crowd of carts that blocked up one of the streets he had to pass through. In fact, he was brought to a stand opposite a row of thatched houses, which might have been mistaken for a piece of Knocknagow, so closely did they resemble the row of thatched houses between Phil Lahy's and the bridge.

While waiting patiently for the way to be cleared, a woman ran out from one of the thatched houses and laid a basket close to the wheel of the car.

" Show us a sod uv that," said she.

He loosened a sod out of his well-packed load and handed it to her.

" Give me twopence worth uv id," said she, after balancing the sod in her hand and flinging it into her basket.

" Is that all you're goin' to give me ?" she asked, when he had stopped counting the turf into the basket.

" That's all ; an' I'd like to know where you'd get as much uv such turf as that ?"

" Well, here," said she, taking hold of one handle of the basket.

Billy Heffernan took hold of the other handle, and the purchase was immediately laid on the middle of the floor in one of the little thatched houses.

The woman put her hand in her pocket to pay for the turf, when, happening to glance through the little four-paned window, with three bull's eyes in it—which, if one of the bull's eyes happened to be in the upper instead of the lower corner, Billy Heffernan would have sworn was his own window—she seized a straw-bottom chair, that it required some faith to believe was not part of the furniture of Mat Donovan's kitchen, and ran out into the street. Billy Heffernan soon saw a well-shaped foot, encased in a well-fitting boot, touch the back of the chair, and caught a glimpse of a leg quite worthy of the foot, in a grey angola stocking tied with a red worsted garter ; of which latter, however, he saw no more than the two ends that hung down in a manner suggestive of a bow-knot. In an instant a female figure laeped lightly to the ground and ran into the little thatched house, followed by the smiling hostess, bearing the straw bottom chair. Both turned into the little room on the right-hand side of the door, and Billy saw a pretty young girl fling off her cloak, and commence arranging her hair at a diminutive looking-glass that hung near the window ; and in a minute or two quite a stylishly dressed young lady came out, drawing on her gloves, and replying to the inquiries of the woman of the house, who addressed her as " Miss Julia," for the " masther " and the " misthress."

" Oh !" exclaimed Miss Julia, as if she had forgotten something, " run out and bring in the basket that's between the bags on the top of the load."

The woman of the house did as she desired, and soon returned with a small basket.

" 'Tis something," said Miss Julia, " that mother sent you."

The woman raised the lid, and exclaimed with a start, as she held up her hands in an attitude of surprise and thankfulness :

" Oh, may God increase her store !"

Miss Julia walked out, and no one meeting her would have dreamed she was the same person that descended from the top of the load of wheat, with her gay bonnet hidden under the ample cape of her mother's blue cloak ; which blue cloak, however, seemed more worthy of admiration in the eyes of the woman in whose care she had left it, than all Miss Julia's finery put together, for she held it up to the light, and looked and looked at it, till she seemed to forget everything in the world but the blue cloak.

" Begor, ma'am," said Billy Heffernan, " I b'lieve you're forgettin' me."

" Oh, honest man," she replied, with a start, " I beg your pardon. I thought I was afther payin' you."

Billy Heffernan put the twopence she handed him in his pocket, and, finding the way now more clear, led his mule slowly up the street.

CHAPTER XXXVI.

HOME TO KNOCKNAGOW.—A TENANT AT WILL.

A HAND was laid on his shoulder, and on looking round, he saw the dragoon standing close to him.

" Come and have a drink," said the dragoon.

" I don't take anything ; thank you all the same," replied Billy Heffernan.

" Oh, d——n it," returned the dragoon, " as we were comrades on the road, don't refuse a treat."

" Well, I'm a teetotaller," rejoined Billy Heffernan ; " but if you'd have no objection to come over beyond the Weshtgate, I know a place where they have peppermint."

" All right," said the dragoon ; and they continued on their way through the drays and carts.

" Is this all corn ?" the dragoon asked.

" All whate," replied Billy Heffernan.

" I never saw so much corn at a market," returned the dragoon ; " and yet ye Irish are always talking of starving. How is that ?"

" Begob," said Billy Heffernan, " 'tis many's the time I said thim words to myse'f."

" Where does it all go ?" the dragoon asked.

" Some uv id is ground in the mills here an' up the river," replied Billy Heffernan ; " an' more uv id is sent off wudout bein' ground. But ground or not ground off id goes. If you'll take a walk down to the quay, you'll see 'em loadin' the boats wud id. They brin' id on to Carrick, and from that down to Waterford, an' the divil a wan uv me knows where id goes afther that. 'Tis ould Phil Morris that could explain the ins an' outs uv id for you. But 'tis the corn that's makin' a town uv Clo'mel ; so there's that much got out uv id afore id goes, as ould Phil says ; besides the employment uv tillin' the land and reapin' id. But 'tis the big grass farms that's the ruination uv the counthry. 'Twas on account of thryin' to put a stop to 'em that they made up the plan to hang Father Sheehy. So ould Phil Morris tells me."

The mention of Phil Morris's name seemed to have put political economy completely out of the dragoon's head, and he did not again speak till Billy Heffernan roused him from his reverie after they had passed the West Gate.

"This is the house," said he.

"Come in," returned the dragoon.

"Here's luck, any way," said Billy Heffernan, as he tossed off his glass of peppermint.

The dragoon blew the froth from his mug of porter, and took him by the hand.

"Good morning, friend," said he, laying his empty mug on the counter.

"Have another," said Billy.

"No, no," returned the dragoon. "Good morning."

"Oh, begob," rejoined Billy Heffernan, getting between him and the door, and putting his hand against the soldier's broad chest, "we don't undherstand that soart o' work in Ireland."

"Yes, yes, I understand your custom," returned the dragoon smiling. "And," he added, "I will take another."

Billy Heffernan sold his creel of turf, and, after breakfasting upon a brown loaf and a bowl of coffee in a cellar, was returning through the Main Street, thanking his stars that the big town with its noise and bustle would be soon left behind him, when his eye caught the big dragoon standing with folded arms opposite a shop window, and seeming absorbed in the examination of the articles there displayed. Happening to look round, he recognised his companion of the morning and beckoned to him. Billy Heffernan stopped his mule, and waited till the dragoon had crossed over to the middle of the street.

"Going home?" said the dragoon.

"Yes," replied Billy; "I have the turf sowld."

"Would you," the dragoon asked, after a pause, "would you bring a message from me to Bessy Morris?"

"Well, I will," said Billy; but he felt, he couldn't tell why, as if he would rather not.

"Wait for a minute," said the dragoon, and he walked quickly back to the shop.

He soon returned, and handed to Billy Heffernan what seemed a small box wrapped in paper.

" What will I say ?" Billy asked, as he put the parcel in his waistcoat pocket.

" Well, I don't know," returned the dragoon, as if he felt at a loss.

Billy Heffernan very naturally looked at him with some surprise.

" Say," said he, at last, " that it is from a friend."

" Begob," thought Billy Heffernan, " he *is* a bad case. I wondher what do she think uv him ? 'Twould be d——n dhroll if Bessy Morris, above all the girls in the parish, would marry a soger. Begob, ould Phil 'ud choke her afore he'd give her to a redcoat. Come, Kit, be lively, or they'll be all in bed afore we get to Knocknagow."

Billy Heffernan and his mule had left the busy town with the cloud over it some miles behind them when the sun was disappearing behind the hills upon which the dragoon turned round to gaze when his companion would have called his attention to the Waterford mountains—by which piece of eccentricity the reader has lost an exciting legend of those mountains, which Billy Heffernan was about relating for the amusement and instruction of his military friend. But it was all owing to Bessy Morris—who we fear has much more than that to answer for. As the stars began to peep out one by one—and there was one star that shone with a pure, steady lustre, and Billy Heffernan felt sure it was looking through the beech-tree into a face as mild and beautiful as itself— he began to wonder why he felt so tired and sleepy ; but, recollecting that he had had no rest the night before, he turned to his mule, and said, " Wo ! Kit," in a manner that made that sagacious animal not only stop, but turn round till her nose touched the shaft, and look at him. The fact was, Billy Heffernan was in the act of yawning as he pronounced the word " Wo !" and a stiffness in his jaw as he attempted to add the other word suggested dislocation, which so alarmed Billy Heffernan that his mule's name escaped from him with a cry, as if some one were choking him. And hence Kit not only halted at the word of command, but looked round to see what was the matter. And, finding that there was no rude hand on her master's windpipe, Kit expressed her satisfaction by advancing her fore-leg as far as possible, and rubbing her nose to it.

Billy Heffernan placed one foot on the nave, and then the other on the band of the wheel, and climbed up till he stood on the side of his car. He put back his hand several times, and attempted to catch the skirt of his barragain coat under his arm. But the skirt was too short ; and, after two or three unsuccessful attempts, Billy Heffernan looked down at himself with a look of drowsy surprise. He first thought of the elk's horn fixed to the rafter in his own house ; then Phil Morris's old goat came to his assistance ; and at last Billy Heffernan thought of Mick Brien, and a shake of the head signified that he was satisfied. In fact, Billy Heffernan, before climbing into his creel, was attempting to tuck the skirt of his ratteen riding-coat under his arm, and was much astonished on finding that trusty companion of his journeyings missing for the first time in his life ; for the ratteen riding-coat, its owner averred, was as good to keep out the heat as the cold, and, consequently, he was never known, winter or summer, to take the road without it. For a moment he thought he must have left it at home, but then that glimpse at the half-moon through the rent in the skirt occurred to him, and he knew he had the riding-coat as far as Phil Morris's. Then the idea of the half-moon shining through the rent in the riding-coat brought the roofless cabin to his mind, and the pale faces upon which the moonlight fell so coldly, and Billy Heffernan shook his head as he remembered how he had wrapped his riding-coat around poor Mick Brien.

Billy Heffernan climbed into his creel ; and, resting his arms on the front, and leaning his chin on his arms, waited patiently till the mule was done rubbing her nose against her leg ; and as the mule continued rubbing her nose against her leg rather longer than usual, her master began rubbing his nose against the sleeve of his coat. There was, in fact, a remarkable sympathy between Billy Heffernan and his mule in the matter of rubbing the nose.

The mule at last moved on of her own accord, for which piece of considerate civility her master resolved to give her an extra fistful of bran when they got home, for he was so tired and drowsy that he felt it would be a task to say

" Yo-up, Kit." Indeed, the mere thought of being obliged to
speak brought on another yawn, and Billy Heffernan turned
his open mouth to his thumb—which required less exertion
than moving his hand to his mouth—and made the Sign of
the Cross. To neglect making the Sign of the Cross over the
mouth while yawning would be even worse in Billy Heffernan's eyes than to forget saying " God bless us " after sneezing,
and almost as bad as going to bed without saying his prayers,
or sprinkling himself with holy water.

The mule jogged on quite briskly, as if she knew her master's good intentions regarding the additional fistful of bran,
while he leant over the creel, with his cheek resting on his
arm, as a weary traveller might rest upon a gate, and looked
lazily along the road before him in a somewhat confused state
of mind. Becoming too sleepy to maintain his standing
position, he dropped down in the bottom of the car ; and
after a pantomimic wrapping of himself in the ratteen riding-
coat, resolutely resolved to keep wide awake till he reached
home. In spite of his firm resolves, however, it occurred to
him that he must have dozed for half a minute or so, as he
opened his eyes on missing the rumble of the wheels.

" Yo-up, Kit," said he, but Kit never stirred.

He turned upon his elbow ; and, looking through the laths
of the creel, saw that the mule was drinking from a little
stream that ran across the road.

Billy Heffernan rubbed his eyes, and thought he must be
either dreaming or bewitched. But there could be no mistake about it. There was the identical little stream over
which he had lifted Norah Lahy that bright summer evening
long ago, and in the middle of which he stood the night
before and wept.

" Well, that bangs Banagher," exclaimed Billy Heffernan,
rising to his feet, and rubbing his eyes again. " I thought I
wasn't wudin tin mile uv id. I wondher what time uv the
night might it be ?"

He was wide awake now, and there was an anxious expression in his face as he looked about him, while the mule moved
on briskly, seeming quite refreshed and lively after her
draught at the little stream. An old fear, by which he was
always haunted when descending that hill on his way home,
fell upon Billy Heffernan. Most people, we suspect, have

experienced some such feeling when approaching home after a lengthened absence. But it weighed upon Billy Heffernan's heart after the absence of a single day. True, he was alone in the world. He had no father or mother, sister or brother, wife or child, to awaken that feeling of dread. Yet he never descended that hill on his way from the busy town with the cloud over it without fearing that, just after passing Mat the Thrasher's clipped hedge, the children would run out from one of the next group of houses to the middle of the road, exclaiming, " O Billy ! poor Norah Lahy is dead !"

The light shone brightly, as usual, in Mat Donovan's window, so that it could not be very far advanced in the night. And when he passed the clipped hedge, and saw Honor Lahy's window giving the hamlet quite the look of a town, Billy Heffernan's heart began to beat as pleasantly as when he discovered that his assailant of the night before was Phil Morris's old goat, and not the ghost of a Hessian. He climbed out of the creel at his own door ; and, taking the key from under the thatch, let himself in.

There was not as much as a cat to welcome him home, nor a spark upon the hearth. Yet Billy Heffernan felt that he *was* at home, and was happy in his own way. Taking the mule from the car, he let her find her way to her crib, and went himself for " the seed of the fire " to the next house. Having lighted the fire, he took the tackling off the mule and hung it on the bog-wood pegs. The elk's horn reminded him of his riding-coat ; and after a glance at the fire, which seemed between two minds whether it would light or go out, Billy Heffernan shrugged his shoulders, and, sitting down in the chimney-corner on his antediluvian block, fixed his eyes on the moonlight that shone through the open doorway on the floor. Kit seemed to find some attraction in the moonlight, too, for she left her crib and smelled that portion of the floor upon which it fell, all round, and over and over, and then Kit deliberately lay down in the moonlight and tumbled. After which invigorating recreation, Kit sat up, and, instead of going back to her crib, remained where she was, winking at the moon. And Billy Heffernan, leaning back against the wall in the chimney-corner, began to wonder what Kit was thinking of. Whatever the subject of her thoughts might be, she got up after awhile and returned to her crib; and the working of her jaws reminded her master that he could not live upon moonshine either. So, taking his old gallon in his hand, he went to the well for water, thereby frightening Kit Cummins, who happened to be at the well for water, too, almost out of her life; she, by some process of reasoning peculiar to herself, having mistaken him for "the black dog," because his barragain coat happened to be nearly white. Having convinced Kit Cummins that he was not the black dog, and disgusted her by "insinuating" a doubt of that creature's very existence—though it was a well-known fact the well was haunted by him time out of mind—Billy Heffernan returned home with his gallon of water, and, pouring some of it into a small pot which he must have filled with washed potatoes before going to Ned Brophy's wedding, hung it on the fire to boil. Then closing his door behind him, he walked down to Honor Lahy's to purchase a half-penny herring. He was agreeably surprised to see Phil Lahy sitting by his own fireside, holding serious discourse with Tom Hogan and Mat Donovan, as he had almost made up his mind that the "cordial" at Ned Brophy's wedding would have proved the commencement of a protracted "spree," which would cost Norah much anxiety and suffering. But her smiling face, as she listened to her father expounding the various political questions of the day, satisfied Billy Heffernan that his apprehensions on this occasion were groundless. Honor, too, was the very picture of happiness, and in the excess of her pride and delight was actually obliged to put away her knitting, and give herself up wholly to the enjoyment of Phil's eloquence.

"Good-night, Billy; sit down," said Phil Lahy, mildly, the words being thrown in parenthetically to the peroration of his discourse on home manufactures, which, he contended, could never be revived under a foreign government.

Billy Heffernan was about declining the invitation, but seeing it was seconded by Norah Lahy's dark eyes, he couldn't.

"I don't know," was Tom Hogan's comment at the conclusion of the speech. "I never minded them soart uv things. An' though I gave my shillin' as well as another to O'Connell, to plaise the priest, I never could see the good uv id. If people'd mind their business an' industhre, they'd be able to hould on, barrin' sich as'd be turned out be the landlord."

"Tom," said Phil Lahy, with a sort of solemn indignation, "'tis wastin' words to be talkin' to you."

"'Tis thirty years now," continued Tom Hogan, "since I came into my little spot, an' so long as God spared me my health I never lost half a day ; an' signs on, look at id, an' where would you find a more compact little place in the country ? An' what was id but a snipe farm the day I came to id. But I worked airly an' late, wet an' dhry, an' glory be to God, I'm milkin' six cows now where Billy Heffernan's mule'd perish the day I came into id. An' if others done the same they'd have the same story."

"An' Tom, what rent are you paying now ?"

"Well, 'tis a purty smart rint," replied Tom Hogan seriously. "But the land is worth id," he added proudly.

"An' who made id worth id, Tom ? Answer me that."

"*I* did," he replied, with something like a swagger. "Thim two hands did id for the first ten years, barrin' what help my wife gave me ; an', begor, so far as diggin' stubbles and work uv that sort, she done ridge for ridge wud me of'en an' of'en. But I made the dhrains, an' sunk the dykes, an' riz the ditches single hand. But now," he continued consequentially, "I can keep a servant boy, an' hire a few men. An' I ate my own bit uv butther now an' then," added Tom Hogan, with the air of a lord.

"An' what rent are you payin' ?"

"Well, thirty-eight shillin's, since the last rise."

"An' suppose the next rise puts it up to forty-eight. "

Tom Hogan stared at his questioner with a frightened look.

"If he was the divil," he exclaimed, after a pause, " he couldn't put id up to forty-eight shillin's an acre."

"An' what was id when you came there first ?"

"About fifteen shillin's an acre all round. But 'tis betther worth thirty-eight now."

"Have you a lase ?"

"No, nor I don't want a lase so long as I have a gentleman for my landlord that won't disturb any poor man that'll pay him his rent fair and honest."

"An' as fast as you improve your land, putting the whole labour uv your life into id, he'll rise the rint on ye."

" An' why not, so long as he don't rise id too high ?"

" Tom Hogan," said Phil Lahy, surveying him from head to foot, and then looking him steadily in the face—" Tom Hogan, I'll see you scratch a beggarman's back yet."

Tom Hogan looked astonished, quite unable to comprehend why he should be called upon to perform such an office for a beggarman or any one else. But Phil Lahy meant to convey, in this figurative and unnecessarily roundabout way, that Tom Hogan would be a beggar himself.

" I partly see what Phil is at," observed Mat Donovan. " Whin 'tis his own labour an' his own money made the land what id is, the rint had no right to be riz on him. Sure he has his place just as if he took a piece uv the Golden Vale an' laid id down among the rishis an' yallow clay all around id. An' because he wint on dhrainin', an' limin', an' fencin', an' manurin' for thirty years, is that the raison the rint should be riz on him, wherein more uv'em that never done anything at all is on'y payin' the ould rint ? That's a quare way to encourage a man."

" An' Tom," said Phil Lahy, " what would you take for the good-will of that farm ?"

" I wouldn't take a million uv money," he replied, in a husky voice. " My heart is stuck in id."

His chin dropped upon his chest, and his hands began to tremble as if he had the palsy.

Ah, though we cannot help sharing Phil Lahy's contempt for Tom Hogan's slavishness, we heartily wish he had a more secure hold of that little farm in which " his heart was stuck " than the word of a gentleman who went on raising the rent as fast as Tom Hogan went on with his draining, and fencing, and liming, and manuring—to say nothing of the new slated barn and cow-house.

Norah looked at him with surprise, as if she could scarcely believe he was the same Tom Hogan who, a few minutes before, seemed so full of consequence as he boasted of eating his own butter now and then. She then turned an appealing look to her father, which checked the sarcasm and the bitter laugh that Phil Lahy was on the point of indulging in at the expense of the poor tenant-at-will, who tried so hard to per-suade himself and others that he was not only satisfied with his serfdom, but proud of it.

"Good-night to ye," said Tom Hogan, rising from his chair. "'Tis time to be goin' home."

"'Tis time for all uv us," said Mat Donovan. "I'll come down to-morrow night," he added, "and lend a hand to that chair of Norah's. 'Tis sinkin' too much at the side."

Norah thanked him with a grateful look. Every little act of kindness made her happy.

"Come out, Honor, and get me a herrin'," said Billy Heffernan. "Faith, I'm afeard the spuds'll be broke. I hung 'em down to bile when I was comin' out."

"Good-night," said Tom Hogan, when he came to his own gate. His hand trembled so much that he could not raise the hasp, and Mat Donovan stopped and opened and closed the gate for him.

"God help him," said Mat, as he rejoined Billy Heffernan, "if ever it comes to his turn."

"What?"

"To be turned out."

"There's no danger uv that," Billy replied. "He's the snuggest man in the place."

"All he's worth in the world," returned Mat, "is buried in the land. He couldn't give a fortune to Nancy. An' as for Jemmy, he tells me he'll run away an' list, he makes him work so hard, and wouldn't give him a shillin' for pocket-money. An' 'tis a hard thing, Billy, to think that any man could come up to you and tell you to walk out uv the house an' place you wor afther spendin' the labour uv your life on."

"Begor, Mat," returned Billy, "I could stick the man, as ould Phil Morris says he'd do, that'd turn me out of that ould cabin there, not to say a snug house and farm like Tom Hogan's."

"Peg Brady was tellin' me," said Mat, "that you called into Phil Morris's last night when you wor passin'."

"I turned in to redden the pipe whin I see the doore open."

"She was goin' on about somethin' that I couldn't pick head or tail out uv," continued Mat Donovan. "On'y she said if I knew id I'd be surprised. She said you kem in to light the pipe afther, but I couldn't understand her. But she was dhrivin' at somethin'."

Billy Heffernan put his finger and thumb into his waist-

coat pocket, and was on the point of saying that he had
passed Phil Morris's without remembering to give the little
box to Bessy, but he felt instinctively that he ought not to
speak of it, though he had no particular reason for supposing
that it concerned Mat Donovan more than anybody else.

" Did you see Bessy ?" Mat asked, seeing that his companion had offered no remark upon what he had just said.

" I did," Billy replied ; " the two uv 'em wor sittin' at the
fire."

" What two ?"

" Peg an' Bessy."

" Wasn't there any wan else ?"

" Divil a wan—whin I wint in. The ould man was in
bed."

" Peg is sich an innocent soart uv a girl," said Mat, as if
to himself. " I suppose she wanted to take a rise out uv me.
She was hintin' at somethin' or other, but the not a wan uv
me knows what id was. She tould me," he added, after a
pause, " that Bessy was comin' over to cut a new gownd or
somethin' for Miss Mary to-morrow."

" Begor," said Billy Heffernan, putting his hand again in
his pocket, " I may as well give you a message I have for
her."

" What is id ?" Mat asked.

" I won't mind id," returned Billy, as it occurred to him
that if he gave the box to Mat, he should tell from whom he
got it.

Billy Heffernan was in the habit of making little purchases
for his neighbours in Clonmel, and Mat Donovan attributed
his change of mind regarding the message, to what he considered a very natural desire on Billy's part to deliver it to
the fascinating Bessy himself.

" Come in an' rest," said Billy, when they had come to his
house.

" Oh, 'tis all hours. My mother'll think the mickilleens
is afther ketchin' me," replied Mat, as he quickened his pace
with all the appearance of a man in a great hurry. But
Billy saw him stop almost immediately, and, after hesitating
for a moment as if he thought of turning back to renew the
conversation, walk on again very slowly towards his own
house.

"By my word," thought Billy Heffernan, as he took the "spuds" off the fire—which "spuds," to his great relief, he found were not broken, owing, perhaps, to the length of time the fire had taken to kindle—"by my word I'm afeard *he's* a bad case, too."

He lighted his bog-pine candle, and examined the little package the dragoon had given him with considerable curiosity.

"Now, I wondher what might be in id," he thought, as he tried to judge of its weight by moving his hand up and down. "'Tisn't heavy, whatever id is. But what is id to me what's in id? I'll give id into her own hands, for maybe if any wan else got id they might make harm uv id, as little as id is. An'," added Billy Heffernan, with a shake of his head, "'tis a d——n little thing some people couldn't make harm uv. Well, 'twouldn't be aisy to make me b'lieve any bad uv Bessy Morris; though she *is* the divil for coortin'."

He strained the water off the "spuds" into the pool outside the door, and leaving the pot on the floor to let them cool, he sat upon his block and shook the little box close to his ear.

"Now, as sure as I'm alive," said he, "'tis a thimble. An' sure Nelly Donovan tould me 'twas to larn to be a manty-maker that Bessy stopped in Dublin so long. But 'tis thinkin' uv my two-eyed beefsteak I ought to be."

And, considering that he had eaten nothing since he breakfasted in the cellar in Clonmel, it was not surprising that Billy Heffernan should now think of his supper. And while he is roasting his herring on the tongs, we will go back for a moment to Bessy Morris, whom we left sitting in her grandfather's arm-chair, with a flush upon her forehead, and nervously tapping with her fingers on the table.

"When did he come?" she asked, without raising her eyes.

"A little start afther you goin'," replied Peg Brady, who had returned to her seat, and was occupied in taking some of the partially burnt turf from the fire and quenching it in the ashes in the corner. "I was goin to tell him to run afther ye, an' have his share uv the fun."

Bessy looked at her with surprise, and, drawing a long breath, as if she had escaped a great danger—for she shrank from the idea of the sensation the dragoon's appearance in search of her would have created at the wedding—she said with forced calmness, " You had no right to let him stay."

" Was id to turn him out the doores I was ? 'An' how was I to know that ye'd stay so late. I thought you'd be home before twelve o'clock at the farthest. An' he afther comin' for nothin' else in the world but to see you."

" But didn't you know how my grandfather hated the sight of a soldier ? There's no knowing what he might say or do if he saw him."

" There's my thanks for sendin' him into your own room till your grandfather was gone to bed, whin I hear ye comin'."

" Peg, you are very foolish." And Bessy commenced tapping the table more nervously than ever. " What would be said if he was seen in my room ?"

" Faith, you're losin' your courage," returned Peg Brady. " I thought you wouldn't mind what any wan 'd say."

Bessy Morris closed her lips tightly and gazed into the fire.

" He said he wrote a letter to you from Dublin," said Peg Brady.

" So he told me," Bessy replied, absently. " But I did not get it. Maybe 'tis at the post-office."

" Begor, he's a fine, handsome man, anyhow ; an' he's a sergeant. He said that in all his thravels he never see the like uv you."

The compressed lips parted, and a flash of light shot from Bessy Morris's eyes ; and, bending down her head, she covered her face with her hands as if she wished to hide these symptoms of gratified vanity from her companion.

" I don't know how you manage to come round the whole uv 'em," said Peg Brady, with a sigh. " I wish you'd make up your mind an' take wan an' put the rest out uv pain. An' maybe thin some uv us might have a chance."

" Well, Peg," said Bessy, as she rose from her chair, " don't say anything about it. You don't know how hard the world is."

" Oh, yes ; that's the way. Purtend to the whole uv 'em there's no wan but himse'f, and keep 'em all on your hands."

" There it is," said Bessy, stopping, before she had reached the door of her room, as if Peg's remark was a foretaste of what she had to expect.

" Well, you may depend on me," returned Peg, " I'll say nothin'."

Bessy Morris retired to her room greatly excited.

" But what is there to be frightened at ?" she thought. " Sure he's not the first bachelor that ever came to see me. But people are so bad-minded."

Yet it never occurred to her that if she had not been such a " divil for coortin'," as Billy Heffernan had expressed it, the dragoon, in all probability, would never have heard of the existence of Knocknagow, where he found himself the previous evening, and learned from Mat Donovan's mother that he had passed Phil Morris's house and left it a mile or two behind him.

" May heaven direct me !" exclaimed Bessy Morris, as she knelt down to say her prayers. " I feel as if some misfortune was hanging over me."

" I wish to the Lord," said Peg Brady, as she raked the ashes over the embers on the hearth, "that he was afther whippin' her away. An' sure what betther match could she expect ? An' who knows but—well, there's no use in countin' our chickens afore they're hatched. What a fool poor Mat is !" And Peg Brady broke off with a sigh as she put the back-stick to the door.

CHAPTER XXXVII.

DISCONTENT AND RESIGNATION.

TOM HOGAN grasped the gate with his trembling hand, after Mat Donovan had closed and fastened it, and resting his forehead upon his arm, remained standing there for some minutes like a man overcome by fatigue or weakness. Rousing himself, he looked round the yard—at the stacks in the haggard, and the snug thatched dwelling-house, and the new slated barn, of which he was particularly proud. There was a look of blank anxiety, if we may use the expression, in his

face, till his eyes rested on the new slated barn ; and then
pride seemed to gain the ascendency over every other feeling,
and Tom Hogan stood erect and looked more like a man than
he had done since Phil Lahy placed his helpless dependence
so vividly before him. From that moment, until his eye
kindled with pride as he took in the outline of the slated
barn—which was equal in every way to Attorney Hanly's,
and superior, except in size, to Maurice Kearney's—Tom
Hogan was the very picture of a crushed and spirit-broken
slave. He tried to banish from his mind the dread thought
that so unmanned him, and crossing the yard, went into the
cowhouse, and laid his hands upon the cows, one by one, as
if to assure himself that they were safe, and that he was in
very deed the owner of six cows—" as good milkers," he
muttered, " as you'd find in the parish." He lifted the latch
and pushed against the barn door to see that it was locked ;
and after paying a visit to the old brown mare and the colt,
which he intended putting to the plough that spring, Tom
Hogan pushed in the kitchen-door, and entered with a show of
haste and bustle, as if he were in capital spirits, and in quite
a hearty mood that evening. His wife, who was as thrifty
and hardworking as himself, was " scalding tubs," and his
daughter drying a pail, which she had just scoured, opposite
the fire, turning it round and round, and occasionally rubbing the iron hoops with a woollen cloth till they shone like
bands of bright steel. His son, Jemmy, lay upon his back
on a form, with his hands clasped over his face ; while Ned
Carrigan, the servant boy, was driving a few " pavers " in the
toe of his old brogue, by the light of the fire—for candles
were made to go far by Mrs. Hogan. Tom Hogan sat down
and commenced holding his hands to the fire, and drawing
them quickly through the blaze, and rubbing them together
—as if he thought it very pleasant to sit by one's own fireside on a winter's night. No word, however, was spoken by
any one, except the short sentence, " Get up, Spot," which
Tom Hogan himself, who was evidently casting about for a
pretext for conversation, addressed to the dog, and which
that drowsy animal, lying at full length upon the hearth,
responded to by lazily wagging his tail, thereby causing the
ashes to fly up into Ned Carrigan's eyes, who, at the moment,
was stooping to admire the row of nails he had driven into the

toe of his brogue, the sole of which seemed one sheet of
iron, that shone quite as brightly as the hoops on the pail.
The tubs having been scalded and rubbed dry, and the pail
laid upon the stilling, and Ned Carrigan having put his foot
into his brogue and retired to his sleeping apartment—for
it was after supper when Tom Hogan had walked out for a
chat with Phil Lahy—Mrs. Hogan lighted a candle, remarking that it was "time for honest people to be in their beds."
But no sooner had she lighted the candle and snuffed it, and
carefully removed a little ashes that adhered to it with a
large brass pin by which her shawl was fastened, than she
exclaimed in accents of surprise and alarm—

"Tom, what's the matther wud you?"

Jemmy flung himself off the form, looking quite frightened,
and Nancy turned quickly round and fixed her eyes upon her
father's face.

"Nothin' is the matther wud me," replied Tom Hogan,
looking up at his wife as if he wanted an explanation of her
question.

"Tom," said she, "you're as white as the wall. Maybe
you're not well. Or might id be anything you're afther
seein'? God betune us an' all harm."

"I didn't see anything worse than myse'f," he replied.
"An', glory be to God, I was never in betther health in my
life."

"Well, you must be afther gettin' a change, an' let me
give you a drop out uv the bottle; there was some left
since the last night James was here." Mrs. Hogan alluded
to a visit her brother had paid them some months before, when
Tom Hogan partook not only of "a bit of his own butter,"
but of a stiff tumbler of whiskey punch in his own house.

"I don't want anything,' he answered impatiently, as he
took the candle from her hand.

"Maybe 'tis nothin', wud the help uv God," Mrs. Hogan
observed; "but I didn't see him look so bad since the cow fell
in the dyke. Jemmy, what are you doin' there? You ought
to be in bed an hour ago. Get him a bit uv a candle, Nancy.
An' don't be stayin' up yourse'f, makin' a fool uv yourse'f.
'Tis no wondher for you not to be fresh an' sthrong."

Nancy assured her she would make no unnecessary delay,
and Mrs. Hogan followed her husband to the bedroom.

"I think you ought to go to bed, Jemmy," said Nancy Hogan, in a sweet low voice.

"I don't know what I ought to do," he replied fretfully, as he dropped his chin on his hand, and stared into the fire.

He was a singularly handsome young man, with a fresh, clear complexion and light blue eyes. His crisp golden curls, like his sister's, had a tinge of red in them, and it was a common remark among the neighbours that Jemmy Hogan was "too handsome for a boy." He certainly appeared delicate and effeminate to strangers ; but such a thought never occurred to his acquaintances, for it was well known that he could do as good a day's work as any man in the parish except Mat Donovan ; and that at the hurling he was often the first, and always among the first, to be "called" when the match was making. He was generally good-humoured and amiable ; but it was remarked that when strongly moved, all colour would fly from his lips, which were of so bright a red as to make the paleness of his face more striking, and his white, regular teeth seem literally of pearl.

His sister, who bore a strong resemblance to him, looked at him now with the deepest sympathy, the tears welling into her gentle eyes, and seemed at a loss for something to say that might cheer him. She approached him almost timidly, and laid the tips of her fingers lightly on his shoulder. He took no notice, and after a moment's hesitation, she pulled one of his hands from under his chin, and, sitting in his lap, looked playfully into his face.

"Tell me something about the fair," she said. "Did you meet many people you knew ?"

"I didn't meet any wan you'd care to hear about," he replied.

"Did you call into Mrs. Burke's ?"

"I did ; an' I don't know what business I have to call in anywhere."

Her countenance fell at this, but forcing a smile, she said, "How is Alice ?"

"She's very well," he replied, with assumed indifference.

"Oh, yes ! pretend you don't care which !"

"You know very well, Nancy," he said, after a short silence, "'tis no use for me to be thinkin' uv any wan."

"Well, maybe you're too young to think uv gettin' married yet awhile, but that's no raison why you wouldn't be thinkin' uv somebody. An' if you knew how light they are about you," she added laughingly.

"That's all nonsense," he replied, trying to look displeased, while a smile of gratified vanity played upon his red lips.

"Nancy," said he, after a pause, "I have my mind made up."

"For what?"

"Not to stay here any longer."

"O Jemmy, don't talk that way."

"Where is my use in stayin' here? My father don't want me. An' what am I betther than a common labourer?—nor so good. So there's no use in talkin'; go I will. An', for God's sake, don't say anything to throuble me, for 'tis throuble enough that's on me."

"O Jemmy!" she wailed, resting her head upon his shoulder, and trembling violently. "O Jemmy! I'd rather be dead."

"That's all foolishness," he replied, encircling her waist with his arm. "'Twill be the best for all uv us. You know yourse'f you never could be settled if I stopped at home, unless I got married and got a fortune to give you; an' the Lord knows when that might be. So 'tis betther for you to have the place; an' then there'll be enough comin' to look for you."

"I'll never marry, Jemmy. All I'd ever ask is to have us all live together as long as God spared us to each other. An' oh! how happy we'd be. An' wouldn't you take a delight in improvin' the place, like my father? An' afther a time you'd have some money uv your own. You might have a few heifers or cows—I'll give you my lamb!" she exclaimed suddenly, as if she were sure that the lamb, beyond all doubt, would banish discontent from his mind for evermore.

"You'll never have sinse," he replied, smiling. "But why do you say you'll never marry? Is id on account of that blackguard, Ned Brophy? I don't know what kep me from—well, no matther."

"Don't blame him, Jemmy. Maybe he couldn't help it."

"Didn't he know all along what he had to expect?" Jemmy

asked, indignantly. "An' when he knew he couldn't marry wudout a fortune, where was he keepin' gaddin' afther you, an' makin' you the talk uv the counthry ?"

"I don't care about the talk of the counthry," his sister replied, with tears in her eyes. "Let 'em talk away."

"But why do you say he's not to be blamed ?"

"Well, I don't say he's not ; only not so much as a person might think. I think," she continued, with a sigh, "it was partly my mother's fault. She was so anxious for him that the minute she saw he took notice of me, she was always huntin' him, an' pressin' him, an' nearly makin' him come whether he'd like it or not. I know I was foolish myse'f. But when every one used to be jokin' about him, an' when I see him so fond of me, I couldn't help it," poor Nancy added, blushing deeply, and struggling to keep down the sob that swelled up into her throat. "'Tis all over now," she continued, plaintively, but more calmly, "an' my mind is at rest, an' I'm satisfied. But I don't think I could ever care for any wan again—that way. Miss Kearney stopped a whole hour wud me to-day, an' 'twould do any wan good to talk to her. She says that, no matter what our lot may be, we all have duties to do ; an' so long as we don't neglect 'em, an' if we do our best to be contented, we can be happy. An', as she said, what, afther all, is this world, that we should set our hearts on it ? We ought to think of eternity ; an' that needn't keep us from enjoyin' whatever of the blessings of this life God is pleased to bestow on us. I couldn't explain it as she did ; but every word she said went to my heart. 'Tis a shame for us to be frettin' about every disappointment, an' so much terrible misery in the world."

"Well, that's thrue," returned her brother. "But, for all ——." And he continued gazing into the fire.

"Are you there, Jemmy ?" Tom Hogan called out.

"I'm just goin'," he replied, imagining that his father meant to order him to bed. But instead of that Tom Hogan continued, "Run out, Jemmy, and see who is afther stoppin' outside the gate. I hear a step." It was said that Tom Hogan knew by instinct when a strange foot, of man or beast, approached that little farm in which "his heart was stuck." Jemmy went out to the gate, and returned in a minute or two, saying that it was "only Mick Brien."

"Mick Brien," returned his father, apparently both surprised and troubled—for Mick Brien had a larger and a better farm than his own only a few years ago—and "look at him now," thought Tom Hogan, beginning to tremble.

"God help him," his wife remarked ; "his poor wife tould me this mornin' that she was afraid 'twas the faver her little girl had, and she was goin' for a ticket for the docthor, to Mr. Kearney. An' where was he goin', Jemmy, this hour uv the night ?" she asked, raising her voice so as to be heard by her son, who was in the act of kicking Spot into the yard, before barring the kitchen door.

"He didn't well know that himse'f, when I axed him," Jemmy answered ; "but he said he b'lieved he was goin' over the short-cut to Pender's."

Tom Hogan started up in his bed, to the great bewilderment of his wife, who fancied he was going to start off in pursuit of Mick Brien.

"To Pender's !" gasped Tom Hogan, whose breath seemed quite taken away by the intelligence. "An' Darby Ruadh tould me to-day they wor goin' to throw down the cabin. An' Wat Corcoran remarked he didn't like the job at all." Tom Hogan was quite a confidential friend and crony of the two bailiffs, who were wont to assure him that the master— meaning Mr. Isaac Pender—had more respect for him (Tom Hogan) "than for any man in the parish."

Nevertheless, it was not *fear*, but *hope* that took Tom Hogan's breath away.

"I know, Jemmy," his sister murmured, "'tis that young man of Captain French's that's puttin' these notions in your head."

"No," he replied, "I'm thinkin' uv it this long time. Don't be a fool. Sure I can write to ye, an' maybe I might come home afther a few years in flyin' colours."

"Is it to America ?" she asked.

"Well, no," said Jemmy, stopping to gaze into the fire again, though he was half-way to his own room when she asked the question—"my father would never give me what would pay my passage."

Nancy bowed her head in sorrow, perhaps in shame—for she felt that he had spoken only the truth—and remained silent.

CHAPTER XXXVIII.

ARE YOU IN LOVE, MARY?"

" MARY," Grace asked, " do you ever hear from Arthur O'Connor now ?"

She was sitting at the window in Mary Kearney's little room, precisely in the same attitude as when she set about solving the mystery of the footprints in the snow. The snow was gone now ; but it was evident those mysterious footprints were still visible to her mind's eye, and she followed them across the gravelled walk, and the box-bordered flower-beds, and through the laurels, and over the stile in the corner, and out upon the road to the Bush, and—*where* then ?

Grace was puzzled.

A letter she had from her brother Edmund that morning, in which he spoke of his friend Arthur O'Connor—whom he called " M. l'Abbé "—had set Grace thinking. There was a mystery about her brother, too, in which his friend Arthur was somehow mixed up. Edmund was what Grace called a " jolly good-hearted fellow," and he used to tell how he and Arthur were, by some fatality, always involuntary rivals in their boyish days ; and declared it was quite fortunate that Arthur had decided upon becoming a priest, as otherwise there would be no knowing what might happen. He also often alluded to a certain romantic adventure at the seaside, a year or two before, in which Mary Kearney played a pro-minent part ; and any allusion to which would be sure to bring a glow into Mary's pale cheek to this day. And so Grace could not help connecting either her brother or his friend with those provoking tracks in the snow.

" But why on earth ?" she asked herself, " should either one or the other of them stand there under the window till he must have been half froze to death ?" For Grace held fast to her own "solution of the mystery," and dismissed the idea altogether that the person, whoever he was, had been in Mary's room and dropped into the garden from the window. If she could only find out who wrote the note that Barney threw up to her, it might enlighten her; but Mary laughingly refused to tell her anything at all about it. And so Grace went on puzzling her brains, till the old grey cat, stealthily picking his steps close to the ivied wall under the window, startled a blackbird that had been hopping fearfully among the flower-beds; and the harsh cry of the blackbird startled Grace from her reverie; and turning round, she asked:

"Mary, do you ever hear from Arthur O'Connor now?"

"No," Mary answered, looking surprised. "Why so?"

"No reason in particular," she replied. "But you saw what Edmund said about him; and it just occurred to me that he was looking quite pale and thin when I saw him last —and so old. I think he must be unhappy."

Mary bent her head over the sewing she was doing, but remained silent.

"And yet," Grace continued, "*you* are not unhappy, Mary."

"Indeed I am not," returned Mary, looking up in surprise. "Why should I be unhappy?"

"Oh, you are one of those angelic beings who are always contented with their lot. But I doubt very much that *he* is contented. I never could like him much, he is so proud and so cold."

"You told me the other day that Miss Hanly pronounced me 'as cold as ice,' and you said she is mistaken."

"She certainly is. But if you would try to appear warm towards people you do not care about, it would be a decided improvement."

"I try to *be* warm," she replied, "but I cannot always succeed. Now, would you say that Hugh, for instance, is cold?"

"Not cold," returned Grace thoughtfully. "He may be reserved, or dark; but he is certainly not cold. Of course I know Arthur can be hot as well as cold. But a genial warmth is what I like."

"Are you glad to be going home, Grace?" Mary asked sadly.

" I believe I am always glad to go home—but I'll be sorry, too."

" If Richard and Mr. Lowe were going before you, you'd find this place very dull."

" Well, it would be dull ; but I don't think I ever feel *very* dull when I am with you, though I confess I do like society very much.   And after all, Mary, there is a magic in polished society which can scarcely be found anywhere except among the upper ten.   Don't you feel it in the case of Mr. Lowe ?"

" Well, I like his manner, certainly ; but I have seen quite as good manners in my time, though I know very little of your ' upper ten.' "

" Well, *I'll* never be satisfied till I set foot within that magic circle."   And Grace walked to the looking glass with " a hundred coats of arms " in her glance.

" If you wished to lead a life of usefulness," returned Mary, " to promote the happiness or alleviate the sufferings of others—if you even wished to distinguish yourself as a writer or an artist, I could understand you.   But the ambition *merely* to belong to the upper ten, as you call it, is what I can't understand at all.   Where can you have got such notions ?   Not from Eva—and surely not from your papa."

" Oh, papa is a democrat—that is, in theory.   For, between you and me, Mary, I can see that in his heart he ' dearly loves a lord.'   I have heard them discuss the question at one of the literary dinners, and though the ' Brehon ' gave the aristocrats some hard knocks, I was not convinced. What a pity it is that Mr. Lowe is not rich.   This black-eyed cousin of his, I suspect, is in love with him.   And I really think you have to answer for turning him from his allegiance.   There *must* be something unpleasant in the letters he gets from his mother.   And the interest he takes in hearing about his uncle's romantic marriage looks as if he were thinking of doing something of the kind himself.   He is quite a treasure for your mamma, he affords her so many opportunities of talking of her Uncle Dan in connection with Sir Garrett and his music and poetry.   But then comes the siren with the black eyes, whose singing of the ' Coolin ' brought the tears to Mr. Kearney's eyes, he says.   Do you feel afraid of her, Mary ?   I hope she is not revengeful."

" You are altogether mistaken," returned Mary.

" Why, he is the picture of misery ; and 'tis as plain as a pike-staff he admires you."

" So do several others."

" Well, how that modest remark would make some of our mutual friends stare. But, candidly now, *are* you in love with *any one* ?"

" I am *not*," Mary answered, very positively.

At which Grace turned round, and resting her elbows on the window, followed the tracks in the snow across the flower-beds, and out to the bush, through the laurels—and over the hills and far away ; perhaps over the sea.

" Come, Grace," said Mary, who began to feel afraid of her, " we have had quite enough of idle chat for one morning. I wonder what is delaying Bessy Morris ? Is this she coming down the road ?"

" Yes," Grace answered ; " and that's Billy Heffernan stopping his mule to shake hands with her," she added, on seeing Billy reach his hand to Bessy Morris, over his creel, in which he was standing.

" And there is Mat Donovan strolling up to the Bush to meet her," said Mary. " I suspect Bessy is turning the heads of all the boys since her return from the city."

" She is very nice,' Grace observed. " And I really think the rustics know how to appreciate refinement."

" I always remarked," returned Mary, " that it is the smartest and most intelligent girls that are most admired."

" The tastiest," said Grace, " as Nelly Donovan would say."

" Nelly herself is tasty," returned Mary, " but she is not like Bessy Morris. Even before she went to Dublin there was something refined about her. She was always borrowing books from me."

" Then Mat has no chance ?"

" I don't know that. With all his queer ways, Mat Donovan has something superior about him. And he is such a fine, manly, good-natured fellow ; and such a hero with the people as the best hurler and stone-thrower. He has made the name of Knocknagow famous."

" Did you remark that roguish glance of his ?" Grace asked. " It must be very effective under favourable circumstances."

" He only glances roguishly at roguish people," returned Mary, laughing.

"Pray don't be personal. But it strikes me you innocent-looking people have just as much mischief in you as your neighbours."

"You are quite right," said Mary, rather earnestly. "What are called quiet, steady people, are often as full of mischief as those who have a turn for saying satirical things, and are consequently the terror of their acquaintances."

"That reminds me," returned Grace, "of what the 'Brehon' said in defence of a literary lady of his acquaintance, of whom people were saying hard things. The 'Brehon' is dreadful when, as papa says, he takes to wielding his battle-axe."

"And what did he say ?"

"I get his speeches off sometimes," returned Grace, pressing her forefinger against her forehead. "Yes, it was something to the effect that a cultivated woman who happens to have brains and is of a lively disposition—has, in fact, 'the flash of the gem' in her—is apt to be set down as heartless, and insincere, and designing, and all that sort of thing ; while malice, duplicity, and all uncharitableness will pass for goodness and sincerity, and so forth, when they are found kneaded into a good big lump of the commonest clay, particularly if it be cast in an ugly mould. So you see, my dear Mary, wit and beauty have their disadvantages ; particularly," added Grace, with another glance at the looking-glass, "when they happen to be combined in the same unfortunate individual."

"Well," returned Mary, laughing, "I suppose I am pretty safe ; for at worst I can only be charged with one of these disadvantages."

"I don't know that. In the difference, I think beauty without wit is a greater sin than wit without beauty. It is easier to forgive a woman for being clever than for being handsome. I heard a gentleman, not long since, praising some ladies he had met to a lady from their neighbourhood ; and when she said, 'Margaret is a good, sensible girl, she was always my favourite,' I made up my mind that Margaret was the plainest of the lot ; and such I found afterwards was the case."

"Well, as I often said, I don't know what to make of you, and I am puzzled to know how much of what you say you have heard from your literary friends, and how much is the result of your own observation. But what can be keeping Bessy ?"

" Come and see," returned Grace. " Wouldn't they make a picture ?"

" They really would," said Mary, smiling. " Is there not something graceful in Mat's attitude ?"

" And how coquettishly she looks up into his face," returned Grace. " And the old hawthorn tree, with Billy Heffernan and his mule in the distance. I wish I could make a sketch of it."

Mat Donovan was leaning against the Bush, talking to Bessy Morris, who carried a small basket in her hand, and looked up at him, as Grace remarked, with a very coquettish air.

" Mat has been coming out in his unual style," said Mary, as Bessy turned away from him, and ran laughing towards the gate.

" There is the horse for Mr. Lowe," Grace observed. " He was only waiting for Barney with the letters. We ought to see him before he goes."

" Oh, it is not necessary," returned Mary. " He is only going to call on Mr. Pender."

" And on some of the tenants," Grace added. " And, by the way, I think he is afraid he is to be made a target of."

" Why should *he* be afraid of that ?" Mary asked.

" Well, you know he thinks we Irish are a peculiar people, and as the rumour has gone about that he will be his uncle's agent at some future time, he fancies it would be quite in character to shoot him beforehand."

" Bessy Morris is below," said Ellie, who had come in unobserved.

" Oh, send her up," returned Mary, spreading out the material for the new dress on the table, and assuming an air of business. " Let us lose no more time, Grace."

Ellie hurried back before she had reached the stair-head, and, with her hand on the door-handle, the following short dialogue passed between her and Grace :

" Grace, we are going to play hide-and-go-seek in the stacks. Will you come ?"

" I'd look well."

" Oh ! my dear !"   And Ellie turned away with a scornful toss of the head.

" We may as well see Mr. Lowe," Mary observed.

" I thought so," returned Grace, with a meaning smile.

The young gentleman was reading a letter, which so entirely engrossed his attention that he did not observe their entrance. On looking up, and seeing Miss Kearney, he crushed the letter into his pocket, and stammered something by way of apology for his apparent rudeness.

" Oh, by no means," said Mary. " I'm glad you will have a fine day for your ride."

" Yes," he replied, glad of an opportunity to look another way, " it is very fine. The mountain has quite a summer look."

" It is more like an autumn evening look," said Grace. " Those little white clouds remind me of the last time I was on the mountain. Edmund and Arthur O'Connor were with us that day, Mary."

" I remember," she replied, quietly. " But let us not detain Mr. Lowe."

Mr. Lowe bowed ; and, after assuring Mrs. Kearney that nothing could induce him to dine anywhere but with herself, he mounted the horse that Barney held for him, and rode slowly up the avenue.

" He certainly is in a sad way," Grace observed. " And there *must* be something strange in those letters, too."

" Maybe it is something about the tenants," returned Mary. " There are two of them to be ejected."

" That is quite a natural explanation," said Grace. " I wonder it never occurred to me."

" I hope 'tis nothing about my lease," observed Maurice Kearney, who had just come in, looking troubled and uneasy. " That rascal Pender'll never stop till he makes Sir Garrett as great a tyrant as Yellow Sam. I'm after giving that unfortunate man, Mick Brien, some straw to thatch his cabin that was stript the night before last by the storm, and he tells me they are going to pull it down on him. I wouldn't stand in Pender's shoes this minute for the wealth of Damer. But," added Maurice Kearney, suddenly becoming cheerful, " if we could get Sir Garrett himself to come down for a week

or two, all would be right.—Wattletoes," he shouted, as he
reached the hall, " get the ass, and tell Mat to bring up a
bag of the seed-wheat to Raheen to finish that corner. Jim
and Ned are gone with the horses."

" There is knavery in every lineament of that old Pender's
face," Grace observed. " He is even more odious than his
ugly son. I declare Mr. Kearney is quite a judge of character ; he described the pair to the life."

" Yes, he must be a good judge of character. I know a
young lady he considers quite a treasure."

" Better than a piper in the house," added Grace, laughing.
" Between Mr. Kearney and my friend, Lory, I have some
excuse for being a little vain—which, of course, I am not,
however."

" Of course not," returned Mary.

CHAPTER XXXIX.

THE HOOK-NOSED STEED.

" HERE is Beresford ! Here is Beresford ! Here is Beresford ! Going to dine at Woodlands ! Going to dine at
Woodlands ! Going to dine at Woodlands ! Well, Beresford ! Well, well, Beresford, do you expect much company ?
Do you expect much company to-day ?"

" I think not to-day. Only the family," replied Mr.
Beresford Pender, in his mighty voice.

Old Isaac stood in the lawn in front of his own house,
talking to three or four poor men, evidently belonging to the
class of small farmers—for they looked too spirit-broken for
" labouring men "—who pulled off their hats as Beresford
strode past, and kept them off while he turned round for a
minute on reaching the door, and stared at nothing in particular straight before him.

" Going to dine at Woodlands !" muttered the old gentleman, contemplating his son with a sort of wonder, as if his

greatness were something altogether bewildering and unfathomable.

He was *not* going to dine at Woodlands—and old Isaac knew it ; but old Isaac seemed haunted by the idea that Beresford was going to dine at Woodlands at all hours and seasons, because Beresford did dine at Woodlands once in his life. It might be supposed that he had recourse to this fiction in order to impress his hearers with a due sense of his son's importance ; but if old Isaac were quite alone, he would have muttered to himself three times that Beresford was " going to dine at Woodlands."

Mr. Isaac Pender did not at all resemble Mr. Beresford Pender outwardly. He was nervous and fidgety, and seemed perpetually on the look-out for some threatened danger ; to escape from which, judging from appearance, he would go through an auger-hole ; while Beresford looked a very daredevil, who would glory in finding himself in a den of lions, and seemed always defying creation in general to mortal combat.

After scowling defiance at the avenue gate, Mr. Beresford Pender turned into the parlour and commenced pacing up and down the uncarpeted floor.

" No, no, colonel !" he muttered ; " that will never do. The scoundrels must be kept down, by ——." We will omit Mr. Beresford Pender's oaths.

Mr. Beresford Pender was as fond of holding imaginary conversations with this " colonel " as his father was of sending him to eat imaginary dinners at Woodlands.

" I don't think," said Isaac, closing the door carefully behind him, and looking under the table for a concealed assassin, " I don't think Mr. Lowe wants to have anything to do with the property. I don't think he does. I was afraid he came down to see about these complaints some of the fellows are making. But he never went near any of the tenants. So that it was only Maurice Kearney asked him down for a few days' shooting. That was all. I know that must be the way."

" But you wouldn't know what them Kearneys might put into his head," returned Beresford.

" Well, well," rejoined old Isaac in his nervous, anxious way, " I don't think they can take any advantage of us. I don't think Sir Garrett would be bothered with stories. You see he didn't renew the lease for Kearney when I explained to him that the gentlemen of the county were opposed to giving leases. And when Mr. Lowe will be after talking to them at the meeting he will understand how it is. But, on the other hand, if I was sure he had nothing to do with the management of the property, I'd rather he wouldn't go to the meeting at all. It might only put things into his head. And he might set Sir Garrett astray."

" I think," muttered Beresford, " he ought to know the danger of being in this part of the country. He ought to be made see it is no joke to collect rents with the muzzle of a blunderbuss looking into your face at every turn."

Old Isaac started, and, closing one of the shutters, placed his back against the wall between the two windows, and commenced rubbing his hand over his face as if a swarm of midges were persecuting him.

" Well, if that could be done," he replied, " it might be no harm. But I don't see how it could be managed."

" I was talking to Darby about it," rejoined his son, " and I think we can manage it."

" Well, Beresford, be cautious. Don't do anything rash. Easy things are best."

" That's a fine place Kearney has," Beresford observed, after opening the shutter his father had closed, and looking out on the unsheltered fields around Wellington Lodge. " Do you think he can hold ?"

" I don't know," his father replied. " He was always extravagant. Always extravagant," he repeated, as if he were very sorry that so good a man as Maurice Kearney had not more sense. " But 'tis time enough to think of that. 'Tis the Ballyraheen business that's making me uneasy." And Isaac rubbed his face as if the midges began biting him again.

" I'd hunt 'em," returned Beresford, " like rats."

" Now, Beresford—now, Beresford, don't be rash. These things should be done quietly. There's no use in making a noise when it can be avoided. If I had my own way I could manage them. But I don't like making a noise and exasperating people when it can be done in a quiet way."

" No surrender !" muttered Beresford.

" Now, Beresford ! There is Stubbleton has his property cleared out to a man without even bringing out the Sheriff. I know 'twas rather expensive at first, but he got it back on the double after a little time ; besides avoiding talk."

" How did he do it ?"

" Well, he let them run into arrears first, and then 'twas easy to manage them. They gave up one by one. Then he commenced extensive drainage and improvements, and gave employment to all the small tenants on condition that they would give up possession, and they could then remain as care-takers. Some of them were earning thirty shillings and two pounds a week for their horses. They were never so well off in their lives, and were always praying for their land-lord. But when the work was finished, they saw whatever they had spared would soon be gone ; and as they were after giving up their land—some of them thought they would get it back again, for his steward is a knowing man, and when he saw any of them unwilling to give up possession he used to give them a hint that if they did not give any trouble they might get back the farms, and larger farms—but when they saw they should leave even the houses at a week's notice, they went to America while they were able. So that Stub-bleton had his whole property cleared without as much as a paragraph in the newspapers about it. He divided it into large farms, then, and got heavy fines and a good rent that more than repaid him for what he lost. The parish priest denounced him as an exterminator ; but Stubbleton gave a farm to the priest's nephew, and it put a stop to that. I'm told he's thinking of standing for the county on Liberal principles at the next election. So you see, Beresford, easy things are best."

" And do you mean to say," Beresford asked, " that you'd let the Ballyraheen fellows run two or three years in arrears ?"

" No, no ; that would be too much. But I'd put out only a few at first and give their land to the larger tenants. Then others would be expecting the same, and they'd offer money to the small holders for their good-will. In fact they'd evict one another. The great point is to divide them ; for when they pull together 'tis dangerous," added old Isaac, rubbing his face as if he were bent upon rubbing the shrivelled skin off.

" And what are you going to do with Kearney ?"

" Well, he owes about a year's rent, but I don't think Sir Garrett will press him. We'll try and let him alone for a while. Maurice Kearney is a good sort of man, and his lease is nearly expired. I'd like to have him let run on till the lease drops, and then we could see what would be best."

" Why couldn't you press him and make him pay up ?   I'd be down on him the very day the rent fell due."

" Now, Beresford, I wonder at you. Just think, if he had his rent paid up when the lease dropped, how much harder it would be to get him out than if he owed a couple of years' rent. He's an open-hearted sort of man that never looks before him ; and I don't think Sir Garrett would like to press him at present."

" Is Hanly threatening still to come down on you for that bond ?" Beresford inquired.

Old Isaac shambled all round the table, and was again attacked by the midges.

" I'm afraid," he replied at last, " I'm afraid, if we can't manage to get him a farm, he'll do something. The two Donnellys are giving up possession ; and there will be no trouble about the Widow Keating ; but without Tom Hogan's farm there is no use offering their places to Hanly."

" An' sure Hogan has no lase ?"

" I know that—I know that. But he has improved the place so much, and pays such a high rent, and is so well able to pay it, I'm afraid 'twill make a noise if he can't be induced to go of his own free will. He's a headstrong kind of a man and I'm afraid he can't be got to listen to reason."

" But if nothing else will satisfy Hanly ?"

" That's true—that's true, Beresford. 'Tis a hard case. A very hard case." And Isaac fell to rubbing his face again.

The fact was Mr. Isaac Pender had speculated in railway shares, and burnt his fingers, and Attorney Hanly held his bond for a considerable sum. But if Attorney Hanly could get about a hundred acres of land adjoining his own, including Tom Hogan's farm, he would be accommodating in the matter of the bond. To be sure he never said so—but a nod is as good as a wink from an eccentric attorney to an old land agent. And between these two worthies it will, we fear,

go hard with poor Tom Hogan ! Particularly as his " heart
is stuck " in the little farm, which has cost him the labour of
thirty long years to make it what it is now,—like " a piece of
the Golden Vale dropped among the rushes and yallow clay
all around it," as Mat Donovan said.

" But do you think Kearney can hold long ?" Beresford
asked again, putting his flexible nose against the window so
that he could see the fine old trees and young plantations
around Maurice Kearney's cottage.

" Indeed I don't think he can," his worthy father replied,
as if in the charity of his benevolent heart he wished to
believe that Maurice Kearney was not quite devoid of Christian principles. " I don't think he can. He lost too much
by draining that bog ; and he met with many disappointments
from time to time. He lost his cattle by the distemper, and
I don't think the sheep pay so well. He has the Raheen
farm all under tillage, too, and if prices continue low he
must lose by it. So that I don't think he is likely to hold
long."

" Here is Lowe," said Beresford. " I just want to spake
to Darby. I'll be back in a few minutes."

" My worthy sir," exclaimed old Isaac, as he shambled out
to receive his visitor, " I'm proud to welcome you to my
humble residence—proud to welcome you to Wellington
Lodge. Come in, Mr. Lowe—come in. Darby, take Mr.
Lowe's horse—take Mr. Lowe's horse."

Mr. Lowe glanced at the " humble residence," and thought
that Wellington Lodge, with its unplastered walls—for the
house was unfinished, though not new—was by no means an
inviting domicile.

" Sit down, Mr. Lowe—sit down. Here is Beresford—
here is Beresford."

" A fine day, Mr. Lowe," said Beresford, advancing with
his arm stretched out like a pump-handle. " I hope you
will dine with us to-day," he added ; and immediately the
runaway look came into his countenance, as if he expected
to be forthwith ordered out of the room, for his assurance.

" I promised Mrs. Kearney to be back to dinner," returned
Mr. Lowe quietly. " I had a letter to-day, and it appears
Sir Garrett is returning to the Continent immediately. I
must be in Dublin early next week."

"I knew Sir Garrett would not stay long in Ireland. I knew he would soon go back to the Continent," exclaimed Mr. Isaac Pender in a voice almost as big as his son's—the midges which seemed hovering above his head at the mention of the letter, vanishing when he heard that the landlord was about leaving Ireland without visiting Tipperary.

"I think we had better go," Mr. Lowe observed, laughing. "It would be too bad if I went back without at least looking at the houses of some of the tenantry."

Mr. Isaac Pender laughed too, and shuffled about the room, rubbing his hands instead of his face, like a very pleasant old gentleman.

"Why, Beresford—why, Beresford—is it going to ride that old horse you are? Where is your own horse?" old Isaac asked, in real surprise, as one of the poor tenants who remained hanging about the house in the hope that something might turn up for their advantage, led the two horses round from the stable.

"My own horse is after casting a shoe," Beresford replied.

"But is it safe to ride that old horse? Look at his knees —look at his knees."

The animal referred to was a tall, raw-boned, hook-nosed, ill-conditioned brute, both morally and physically.

"There's no danger," replied Beresford, climbing into the saddle, in which he sat quite perpendicularly, with his elbows as far as possible from his ribs.

"Where is Darby, to open the gate?" his father called out.

"I sent him of a message," Beresford answered, as he rode off upon the hook-nosed steed, who, it may be remarked, rejoiced in the name of "Waterloo."

Two of the poor tenants before alluded to ran to open the gate, dividing the honour equally between them, as one raised the latch, while the other pulled up the long, perpendicular bolt. There was some delay and a little jostling, as in their hurry the two took hold of the same side of the gate, and then both let that side go and took hold of the other—after the manner of people who meet suddenly at a street turning; but at last each took his own side, and the gate stood wide open, the men pulling off their hats and looking, we are ashamed to say, as if they were ready to lie down and let

" Waterloo " trample upon them, if Mr. Beresford Pender so desired. But, it must be remembered, they were conceived and born under a notice-to-quit ; it took the light out of their mother's smile, and ploughed furrows in their father's face while he was yet young ; it nipped the budding pleasures of childhood as a frost will nip the spring flowers, and youth's and manhood's joys withered under its shadow ; it taught them to cringe, and fawn, and lie ; and made them what they are now, as they stand there with heads uncovered while Mr. Henry Lowe and Mr. Beresford Pender ride through the gate of Wellington Lodge.

They rode for half-an-hour in silence up a narrow road that led into a rather wild looking glen among the hills. Mr. Lowe was busy with his own thoughts ; and his companion, not being largely gifted with conversational powers, confined himself to staring at nothing but between the ears of the hook-nosed steed.

" That's Kearney's farm," he observed at last, " where the ploughs are at work."

" I believe that's Mr. Kearney himself at the further end of the field," returned Mr. Lowe.

" He has that place for twenty-five shillings an acre," continued Beresford. " It ought to be two pounds, but he has a lease."

" Oh, is that you, Mat ?" Mr. Lowe exclaimed, on coming up with Mat Donovan, who was striding along in advance of Barney Brodherick's donkey-cart—Barney himself having disappeared down a ravine by the roadside to cut a black-thorn stick which had caught his fancy, leaving Bobby to tumble after him if anything happened to catch *his* fancy at the bottom of the ravine.

" Yis, sir, I'm goin' to scatther this grain o' whate," Mat answered, pointing to a bag in the donkey-cart. " An' where the divil is Wattletoes gone ?" he exclaimed, on finding the driver missing. But Barney soon appeared with his black-thorn under his arm, and Mat walked on with the horse-men.

" I'm told," said Mr. Pender, who seemed to have recovered the use of his tongue, " I'm told Mr. Kearney wants a horse ?"

" Well, he was talkin' uv buyin' a horse, as the spring

work will be heavy ; and he don't like to be hard on the ould mare—he's so fond uv her."

"I'd sell him this horse I'm riding cheap," said Mr. Pender.

Mat eyed the hook-nosed steed, and shook his head.

"He's a first-rate horse for the plough," continued "Waterloo's" owner, patting him on the shoulder.

"He's a legacy," returned Mat Donovan, sententiously.

"What would you say he's worth ?" Mr. Lowe asked, laughing.

"He's an ould Bian, sir," replied Mat.

"What is that ?"

"Wan uv them broken-down jingle horses," Mat answered.

"He means one of Bianconi's car-horses," said Beresford, in reply to Mr. Lowe's look. "They call 'em Bians. But you are mistaken," he added, "this fellow belonged to the lancers."

"Well, now that you remind me uv id," returned Mat, seriously, "he *has* a warlike look. But the divil a far you'd ride him before you'd be axed, 'What tan-yard wor you bound for ?'"

"He'd do the spring work well for Mr. Kearney," rejoined Beresford, reining up his steed as they reached the gate of the farmyard.

Mat moved back a pace or two and surveyed "Waterloo," from his apology for a tail to his Roman nose.

"He'll never hear the cuckoo," he observed oracularly.

Mr. Lowe had become sufficiently acquainted with Mat the Thrasher's figurative mode of expression to understand from this that Mat was of opinion the warlike steed would not live till the middle of April.

"I'll turn in to speak to Mr. Kearney," he observed.

"I'll ride on and you will overtake me," returned Beresford.

"This is a fine day for seed-sowing, Mr. Kearney," said the young gentleman, after riding round the headland ; "and this land seems to be in very good condition for it."

"I drained and subsoiled all this place," returned Maurice Kearney, waving his hand to indicate the extent of his improvement. "And brought the water all down to the river by that lead. You see it would turn a mill."

" I should not have expected that land on the side of a rather steep hill like this would require draining."

" The subsoil was like a flag, and all the water oozed through the surface," replied Mr. Kearney. " Look all along there beyond and you can see the difference."

" I certainly do see the difference," replied Mr. Lowe. " There, for instance, that field where the man is digging is not at all like this. Even the colour of the soil is quite different."

" He's preparing that for oats," said Maurice Kearney. " I don't know how that poor man is able to live and pay the rent at all."

The man looked up and touched his hat, and they saw Mr. Beresford Pender passing within a little distance of him.

Suddenly he stuck his spade in the ground and started forward towards the road. But, stopping short, after running some ten or twelve yards, he hastened back and commenced digging again with his head bent over his spade.

" By Jove !" exclaimed Maurice Kearney, " Pender is down !"

Mr. Lowe put spurs to his horse and galloped to the assistance of Mr. Beresford Pender, who was lying motionless upon the road. " Waterloo " was down, too, but was exerting all his strength in a straggling effort to gather his bony carcase out of the puddle.

" I hope you are not hurt," Mr. Lowe observed, for by the time he had reached the scene of the accident, Mr. Pender had risen to his feet, and was scraping the puddle off his left cheek with the nails of his fingers.

Beresford only glared all around him, by way of reply. He was thinking, as far as the confused state of his wits and the singing in his head would allow, whether the affair could be turned into an " outrage."

" Didn't you see me fall ?" he muttered, addressing the man who had been digging in the field, and who now came up leading Mr. Pender's horse, and carefully wiping the mud from the bridle with the sleeve of his coat—for " Waterloo " had set off for home at, for him, a very respectable trot— " Didn't you see me fall ?"

" Begor, I did, sir," he answered, " but when you worn't

stirrin' I thought you wor dead—an' you bein' such a bad
cha-rac-ter I was afeard to have anything to do wud you."

"Nice people to live among," muttered Beresford.

"What does he mean?" Mr. Lowe asked, turning to
Maurice Kearney, who had just come up panting for breath,
and wiping his face with his pocket-handkerchief.

"He means," was the reply, "that if Pender was killed
he might swing for it. And, as it is, he may be thankful
that you and I saw it all. Many a man was transported for
less."

The smoke from the chimneys of Knocknagow attracted
Mr. Lowe's attention—for dinner hour was approaching—
and from the pointed gables of Phil Lahy's old house he
turned to a pointed gable in the trees, a little to the right;
and thought it would be pleasanter to spend the afternoon
in that quarter than riding with Mr. Beresford Pender up
among those wild hills.

"Of course you won't venture to ride that horse again?"
he said.

"No, I'll lead him," replied Mr. Pender.

"Oh, we'll go back," said Mr. Lowe. "I couldn't think
of asking you to walk."

"But I'd like you'd come as far as that place of my own."

"How far is it?"

"About a mile. There it is above where you see the
three poplar trees."

"Oh, 'tis very far," returned Mr. Lowe. "I'd much
prefer returning."

Mr. Beresford Pender ground his teeth, and commenced to
kick "Waterloo" in the ribs.

"Could I leave him here?" he asked, "and would you send
one of these men for my servant?"

"Yes," replied Mr. Kearney, not very graciously, "put
him under the shed in the yard, and I'll tell Wattletoes to
run up for your man. As you're going back," he added,
turning to Mr. Lowe, "I'll go with you."

"Oh, don't leave your business on my account."

"I have no more business here; Mat will see everything
right—Mat," he called out, "when you have that seed
scattered, bring your own plough-irons to the forge, as I'm
going to break the kiln-field."

"Goin' to break the kiln-field !" exclaimed Mat in amazement ; "begob, it is a shame for you !"

Mat Donovan seemed so thunderstruck by this intelligence, that Mr. Lowe thought breaking the kiln-field must be a heartless and an altogether unjustifiable proceeding—something like turning out a widow and nine young children to perish on the roadside.

"An' there is the whole winter gone now," continued Mat, looking at Mr. Lowe, as much as to say, "Was the like ever known before in any civilized country under the sun ?"

"Why so ? " his master asked.

"Why so ?" retorted Mat, almost gruffly. "An' not a field about the place that a goal could be hurled in wud any satisfaction. We couldn't finish the match between the two sides uv the river in Doran's moon-thaun on account uv the disputes about the fall. An' there was the kiln-field, that ud put a stop to all bother, goin' for nothin'. An' you never let us know you wor goin' to break it."

"I didn't make up my mind about it till last night," replied Maurice Kearney, as if he were really ashamed of himself ; for when a large field is intended to be broken, it is customary to give it for hurling matches, and even horse races during the winter months.

"There's no help for id now," rejoined Mat Donovan, with resignation. "But I'll send word to Tom Cuddehy this evenin'," he continued musingly, "an' we'll have wan Sunday out uv id at any rate."

He filled the long, narrow straw basket out of the bag, which now stood on the ground beside the little blue cart, and commenced scattering the seed before the two ploughs. Jim Dunne and Tom Maher both remarked that Mat stopped very often to gaze towards the three poplar trees on the hill, for which Barney Brodherick was now making at the top of his speed—muttering curses on Mr. Beresford Pender and his hook-nosed charger for being the cause of sending him upon a journey, that would be sure to entail "Ballyhooly" upon his devoted head when he got home, for being away so long.

> "If ever I marry, I solemnly vow,
> I'll marry young Roger that follies the plough."

Tom Maher chanted, as he passed by Mat in order to attract his attention. But Mat gave no heed to him.

He was thinking how, one summer evening some years before, he was standing upon the little bridge upon which Ned Brophy's heart was wont to fall to pieces, and seeing the bright face beside him become pensive, he inquired the cause. "I always feel sad," she replied, "when I look at the Three Trees. I love that old place better than any place else in the world." And ever since that summer evening, so surely as he looked at the three poplar trees, so surely would Mat Donovan commence to build a castle in the air.

"God save all here ! Where is Darby ?" exclaimed Barney in a breath, as he burst into Mr. Beresford Pender's farmhouse.

"Wisha, is that Barney ?" returned the old woman who acted as a housekeeper. "An', Barney, what way are you ? An' have you any strange news ? An' is id thrue ye're goin' to have a weddin' at the cottage ? An' what soart is the young man ? I always said that Miss Mary was a lady ; an' Barney, is my words goin' to come thrue in earnest, an' no mistake ?"

This torrent of questions bewildered Barney considerably ; but he grappled with one of them, and answered:

"Very well, I thank you, Poll."

"An' 'tis yourse'f that is lookin' brave an' hearty, sure enough," returned Poll. " 'Tis of'en your mother tould me you wor the very moral uv your poor father, God be good to him. ' Poll,' siz she, ' look at Barney runnin' up the road. I can hardly b'lieve the sight uv my eyes that id isn't his father is in id.' "

A striking proof, it may be remarked, of the truth of the proverb, " Every eye forms a beauty "—bearing in mind the clerk's daughter of Ballyporeen.

"Where is Darby ?" Barney asked again.

" ' Maurice Kearney's daughter is a fine girl, Poll,' siz Mr. Beresford. ' 'Tis a pity she hasn't a fortune.' ' 'Faix an' sure 'tis she that will have the fortune, and the fine fortune,' siz I ; ' for isn't her father wan uv the richest men in the parish ?' siz I. ' The divil a stiver she'll get,' siz Mr. Beresford, ' he's too extravagant, an' he lays out too much

on his place, drainin' an' plantin',' siz he, ' an' more d——n fool
Kearney is,' siz Mr. Beresford."

"Do you think a Kearney would marry one of his breed ?"
exclaimed Barney, indignantly. "Tell me where is Darby,
an' don't keep me here all day, an' all I have to do."

"Is id Darby ? Well, Darby kem in that doore a while
ago, an' tuck down the gun off uv the rack. ' Darby,' siz I,
' where are you goin' ?' ' Ax the divil,' siz Darby. But it
might be betther for Darby if he kept a civil tongue in his
head. I do have my eyes an' my ears open, though they think
I don't. An' maybe I could tell some things that 'ud get
some people into a nice hoult if I liked. So 'twould be
betther for Darby to keep a civil tongue in his head."

"Blur-an'-ouns, Poll, tell me where he is an' let me go."

"Well, I see him loadin' the gun in the stable," the old
woman answered. "An' maybe I didn't notice 'twas a lead
ball he put in id," she muttered, "though 'twas little Darby
suspected I had my eye on him. An' maybe 'twould be
betther for Darby if he kep a civil tongue in his head."

This speech, except the first few words, was a soliloquy,
for by the time it was concluded Barney was running from
one to the other of the out-offices in search of Darby Ruadh
—or Darby the "Red-haired."

"Begob," Barney soliloquised, as he ran from one empty
and ruined outhouse to another, looking up at the sky
through the broken roof, and at the patches of grass growing
through the floor—" begob, this is a quare soart uv a place.
The divil a cow or a calf, or a sheep or a goat, put a fut in
there this five year. Nor a pig, nor a slip, nor a bonnive,"
he added, running in and out of two or three other offices in
the same condition as the cowhouse. "Nor a goose, nor a
goslin, nor a duck, nor a cock, nor a hen, nor a chicken—nor
a wranneen, nor anything !" he shouted, as he stopped short
after finishing his round, and gazed in amazement on the
ruined concern, from the thatched dwelling-house to the
roofless pig-sty. "This is not the soart uv place id was
afore poor Dick Morris was turned out, an' Pender on'y
keeps grazin' stock in the summer and nothin' at all in the
winther. Oh ! be the hoky ! he has a big windy broke out
here !" exclaimed Barney, as he turned the corner of the
house and found himself face to face with a large window.

which certainly was not in keeping with the old thatched house, but which, according to Mr. Beresford Pender's notions, had the advantage of proclaiming to all passers-by that the place was in the possession of a "gentleman."

"I'll run over to the double-ditch," continued Barney, "an' if he's about the place I can see him—bad luck to him for bringin' me up here."

Not a living thing did he see from the double-ditch, but two carrion crows on a little island in the middle of a field covered with water. He felt a sense of desolation as he looked all round the dreary spot. And observing a single magpie— which all the world knows is a sign of bad luck—pitching upon one of the rafters of the tumble-down barn, Barney resolved to get away from the ill-omened place as fast as his legs could carry him. He made for a pile of stones at a point of the road, where the engineer had to turn short at a right angle to avoid a level stretch of country, and carry his road over the sharpest point of the hill—by which ingenious manœuvre the engineer added considerably to the length of his road, besides avoiding three miles of a dead level.

But as Barney approached the landmark by which he steered his course, it suddenly occurred to him that it marked the spot where "Black Humphrey" was found one winter's morning with his skull broken—and Barney immediately wheeled to one side, so as to avoid the pile of stones at the turn of the road. For, though it was the middle of the noon-day, and not "the witching hour of night when churchyards yawn," Barney Brodherick felt by no means comfortable, and had a secret misgiving that, in a back-of-God-speed spot like that, Black Humphrey might be met with, looking for the fragments of his cranium, any hour of the twenty-four. He faced now to an old sandpit near the road a little lower down, and was climbing up the embankment on the brink of it, when he suddenly started back and fell down upon his hands and knees.

"The Lord betune us an' all harm !" he muttered through his chattering teeth, while big drops of perspiration ran down his face. "That flogs all ! 'Twas well Billy Heffernan said there was somethin' bad about the ould sandpit since the night the mule got into a cowld sweat an' she passin' id. But in the middle of the noonday to think he'd be out uv his

warm grave is a show entirely !" For Barney was quite sure
he had just caught a glimpse of Black Humphrey himself,
with his head all bloody, lying in the old sandpit.

" If I could get round to th' other side," he continued,
" maybe I might be able to cut off before he could see
me."

He crept round the embankment till he came to a gap in
it, by which he saw he could not pass without exposing himself to the object of his terror. Glancing round fearfully,
he discovered, greatly to his relief, that Mat Donovan and
the ploughmen were within view, though too far off to hear
his cry for help if the owner of the bloody head should lay
violent hands upon him. He took courage, however, to peep
over the embankment again ; and to his utter horror the
bloody head started up at the same moment, and seemed to
be looking along the road, attracted, no doubt, by the sound
of horses' hoofs, which Barney could now hear approaching
at a brisk trot. This last-mentioned circumstance gave him
further courage, and he looked more steadily than before at
the figure in the sand-pit.

" Be the hoky !" exclaimed Barney, " 'tis Darby Ruadh !"

And sure enough, there was Darby Ruadh's red head plain
to be seen, as he peered stealthily through a brake of briars
over the ravine that divided his hiding-place from the road.
A stream gurgled down the hill at the bottom of the ravine ;
and to its hoarse music, Barney discovered, was added the
cawing of a flock of crows, that whirled round and round
overhead, sometimes swooping down as if they would precipitate themselves into the pit, but suddenly stopping short
in their headlong descent, and after a moment's silence
and confused clapping of wings, shooting upwards again,
till their angry voices were softened and almost lost in the
distance.

" Id must be a fox that's about here," Barney thought,
" or else they smell powdher. An', begob, Darby has a gun.
I wondher is id rabbits he's watchin' ?"

The horsemen came nearer and nearer ; and Barney opened
his eyes in astonishment and terror, when he saw Darby
Ruadh drop upon one knee and thrust the muzzle of his gun
through the briars, resting his elbow on the brink of the sand-
pit, evidentlv with the intention of taking steady aim.

"Be cripes!" Barney mentally ejaculated "he's, goin' to let the daylight through some wan!"

On came the horsemen, nearer and nearer. But just as he had the gun to his shoulder, Darby Ruadh drew back, as if something unlooked-for had presented itself; and, instead of firing off his gun, he dropped upon his knees and let the horsemen pass. And, as they got higher up the hill, Barney could see by their shining accoutrements and clanking sabres that they were two mounted policemen—probably bearing a dispatch to the nearest military barracks for a troop or company of soldiers to protect the sheriff while clearing a townland of its human inhabitants.

When Barney looked again into the sandpit, Darby was sitting in an easy position, quietly filling his pipe, with his gun on the ground beside him.

"Id must be rabbits," thought Barney, "though the divil a hole I can see. Bless your work," he added aloud.

The man in the pit was so startled that his pipe dropped from his mouth, as he scrambled to his feet at the risk of cutting himself with the open knife he held in his hand.

"In the divil's name what brought you here?" he growled on seeing who it was who had spoken to him.

"Your own blessed masther," Barney answered, "an' his ould broken-winded horse that fell ondher him, an' I was sint up to tell you to carry him home. He's below ondher the shed in Raheen."

"Aren't they comin' up this way?" Darby asked.

"The divil a up," returned Barney. "He's gone home on shanks' mare."

"Sweet bad luck to him! afther all my trouble," growled Darby Ruadh. "I must lave this gun at the house,' he added, as he walked off without condescending to take any further notice of Barney, who set off for home muttering that he'd want to be able to change himself into a crow, the way he was ordered from one place to another and expected to be back again "while a cat'd be lickin' his ear"—and what was worse, that blackguard Tom Maher would be sure to steal his blackthorn out of the ass's car, where in an evil hour he had left it.

It was to "Waterloo" that Darby Ruadh wished "sweet bad luck." And we, too, have reason to be indignant with

that unlucky quadruped. Had he but kept upon his legs till
he reached the sand-pit, even he, " Waterloo," might have
been the making of us. We'd have something to tell that
would make the reader's breath come and go. The scene of
our story would have been immortalised to our hand ; half-a-
dozen " specials " would have done it. For, had that ill-
favoured and in every way disreputable brute not fallen with
his rider, Mr. Beresford Pender's horse would have been shot
under him—or, what would have answered as well, the horse
would have been shot when the rider had dismounted and
moved to a safe distance ; and Mr. Beresford Pender, after
discharging all his pistols, would have pursued the intended
assassin into the fox cover in the glen—and heaven only
knows what would have happened after.

It is a comfort to know that the old " legacy " *was* " bound
for a tanyard " ; and that he never *did* " hear the cuckoo "
again. For before that day week his ribs were well polished
by old Somerfield's beagles ; and for many a day after, his
shin-bone might be seen under a little boy's arm at the
gable-end of the school-house, behind the quarry, as the little
boy glanced over his shoulder at the passing traveller—while
another little boy was thrusting out his head, impatiently,
at the door, and dancing upon his heels.

CHAPTER XL.

THE DRAGOON'S PRESENT.—THE BEAUTY RACE.

DURING all this time Bessy Morris's tongue and fingers were
very busy. She talked and plied her needle incessantly ;
but ever and anon she would pause for a little while and
take to thinking. During those moments of abstraction,
Grace remarked that Bessy invariably slipped her hand into
her pocket ; and in this little circumstance Grace saw a
" mystery " which she resolved forthwith to set about unravelling. And as a pocket naturally suggests money, Grace

concluded that it was of money Bessy Morris was thinking every time she stopped working and slipped her hand into her pocket. So, by way of a beginning, Grace said :—

" Just before you came in Miss Kearney was lecturing me because I allowed my mind to dwell sometimes on so vulgar a subject as wealth. Now, don't you agree with me that poverty must be a very disagreeable thing ?"

" Indeed I do," Bessy answered, looking surprised. " I was always wishing to be rich."

" Did you ever think it would be pleasant to get a rich husband ?"

" Well, I believe that used to cross my mind sometimes," replied Bessy with a sad sort of smile. " But what I most desired was to be able to do something for myself."

" I suppose it was that made you learn dressmaking ?" Mary observed.

" It was, Miss," she replied. " Though I pretended to my grandfather that it was on account of my aunt's health I was obliged to stay so long in Dublin. Only for that he would not consent to have me away so long."

" And were you able to get money ?"

" Well, I was able to lay by a little during the last year. But 'tis very hard to make a fortune, and only that I was stopping with my aunt, I'd find it hard enough to live. My ambition was to earn as much as would make me independent."

Grace thought that this was a higher ambition than her own.

" But you seem to have enjoyed the attractions of the city very much, and I wonder how you could come back to the country," she observed musingly.

" Well, I could not leave the old man alone," Bessy replied. " And there were others reasons to induce me to come home."

" And used you not ever wish to be back in the country ?" Mary asked. " I fancy I'd pine away and die longing for the green fields if I were shut up in a city."

" Well, an odd time I would," Bessy replied. " When I'd be alone of an evening I'd find myself wishing for the old place and the old friends. But I like excitement, and I think it very dull and lonesome now, having no one hardly to converse with, and no change, but the same thing over and over every day."

" I can understand that feeling very well," said Grace. " I am dying to plunge into the gaieties and excitement of Dublin. I am to go next winter, and it puts me in a fever to think of it."

" I never could be tired of the country," said Mary.

Bessy Morris made no reply. Her hand was in her pocket again, and her tongue and her needle at rest.

" Here is a letter that Wattletoes had in his hat, and he forgot it," said Willie as he opened the room-door.

Mary started in a way that was unusual with her, and snatched the letter eagerly from her brother. Was she thinking of another letter which Barney had put in his hat and forgotten ?

" It is for you," she remarked, handing the letter to Bessy Morris, who took it without evincing any surprise, and was putting it in her pocket with a quiet smile when Grace said :

" Oh, you need not stand upon ceremony. Read it."

Bessy cut open the envelope with her scissors, and read the letter.

" Not a love-letter at all events," thought Grace, who was watching the expression of her countenance. " Oh, it is only a habit she has," she added, as Bessy's hand glided into her pocket the moment she had finished reading the letter.

Grace was wrong in both conjectures.

" Is it a love-letter ?" Mary asked.

" It is, Miss," replied Bessy, laughing.

Both Mary and Grace looked at her in surprise, for neither expected such a reply.

" Maybe you'd like to read it, Miss," she said, turning to Grace, who eagerly accepted the offer, remarking that it was the first love-letter she had ever seen except in a novel.

" ' DEAR MISS MORRIS,'—Oh ! that's a shockingly bad beginning. I am quite disappointed—' I take the present favourable opportunity of writing these few lines to you, hoping that you are in the enjoyment of good health, and free from all the ills that flesh is heir to, as Byron says. Dear and best beloved '—Ah ! that is something," Grace observed, with an approving nod—" ' words are inadequate to convey an idea of the state of my mind since that fatal Sunday afternoon, when I called at your highly respectable female relative's, at twenty minutes past one P.M., according to appointment, for the purpose of escorting you to the Zoological Gardens, and the harrowing intelligence fell upon my soul like the war of elements, the wreck of matter, and the crash of worlds—as Byron says—that you had vanished like a star from the horizon when the storm-lashed barque of the mariner is tossed upon the foaming breakers, and he paces the deck alone, and mourns the hopes that leave him, while his life is a wilderness unblest by fortune's gale, and his fevered lips are parched on Afric's burning sand, and no one near to whisper hopes of happiness and tales of distant lands— as Byron says. It was then, for the first time in the course of a chequered existence, that I fully realised the truth of the sentiment that absence makes the heart grow fonder, as the sunflower that turns on its god when he sets the same look that it turned when he rose—as Byron says. But, dear Miss Morris, I cannot by any possibility endure my present state of mind, which sleeping or waking 'tis all just the same, so I have applied for leave of absence for a few days ; and, borne on the pinions of affection, I hope to steer my barque to your native locality, the situation of which I have learned from your highly respectable female relative, who has on several occasions poured the balm of hope into my lacerated bosom, and given me all necessary information for finding the whereabouts of the object of my pilgrimage through the valley of the shadow. For truly may I say that the kiss, dear maid, thy lips have left shall never part from mine till happier hours restore the gift untainted back to thine—as Byron says. Till then farewell, and give a thought to one who never can cease to think of thee.' "

" What do you think of it, Miss ?" Bessy asked, as Grace was trying to make out the signature, which was dashed off in a manner betokening the distracted state of the writer's mind.

" Oh, 'tis very fine indeed," she replied with a wise look.

" But I don't know what to think of that kissing," Mary observed. " Was there really anything of that sort, Bessy ?"

" Well, not much, Miss," returned Bessy, laughing.

" Take care, Bessy. If he is not a person you really care

for, there may be something not quite right in it. It is quite possible he feels as he says he does; and if so, what would you do?"

Bessy looked grave, but said nothing.

"Don't mind her preaching," said Grace. "For my part, I'm determined to 'break all hearts like china-ware'—as Byron says," she added with her ringing laugh.

Bessy Morris continued to look grave, and slipped her hand into her pocket, as she had so often done during the day. But this time she drew out the little box Billy Heffernan had given her, when Grace thought he was only shaking hands with her over his creel. She would have opened it at once, but seeing Mat Donovan approaching, she thrust it hurriedly into her pocket, looking so frightened for a moment, and so very innocent and unconscious immediately after, that Billy Heffernan shook his head as he drove on after the usual "Yo-up, Kit!" to his mule, and mentally came to the conclusion that Bessy had "the two ways in her."

"But where is the wan uv 'em that *haven't*?" Billy Heffernan philosophically observed, as he untied his whip, and gave Kit—who was deliberately bent upon bringing the wheel of his cart into contact with that of an approaching dray—a touch upon the shoulder that made her wince, and keep her own side of the road.

Mat Donovan escorted Bessy to the house, and she had no opportunity to examine the dragoon's gift alone afterwards, though her curiosity was sufficiently strong every time her thoughts recurred to it.

Removing the paper in which it was wrapped, she hastily took off the lid of the little box. She started on seeing what it contained, and after looking at it for nearly a minute with her eyes wide open, handed it to Miss Kearney.

"They are very handsome," she observed.

"Oh, they are just the same as Eve's," exclaimed Grace, snatching the box from Mary's hand, "just the same."

"Do you think are they gold, Miss?" Bessy asked.

"Oh, yes, I am quite sure they are gold," returned Mary.

Bessy Morris seized the box, quite agitated with pleasure, and taking from it one of a handsome pair of earrings, fixed it with a trembling hand in her ear

" Is it the gift or the giver you are thinking of ? " Grace asked, as she marked the flush deepen upon her cheek.

Bessy looked as if she did not comprehend the question, but after a minute's reflection she understood it very well.

" I believe," she replied thoughtfully, " I was thinking of nothing but that I had a pair of gold earrings. I was often wishing to have them, but they were too dear for myself to buy them."

" You seem to be very candid," returned Mary.

" It is too much that way I am," she replied.

" Some wise man has said," Grace observed, " that the proper use of language is to conceal our thoughts ; and, to a certain extent, I agree with him."

" Indeed you do not," said Mary. " You know nothing is more odious than duplicity and deceit."

" But a little diplomacy is necessary to get on smoothly through the world. You have told us nothing about your admirer," she added, turning to Bessy Morris. " Who and what is he ? "

" If they are real gold," Bessy observed, contemplatively, as she looked at the earrings, " his love must be true."

" I am not sure that is quite correct reasoning," said Mary, with a smile. " I fear real gold is not always a proof of true love."

" But sure he would not go to such expense," returned Bessy.

" Oh, I have no doubt but he admires you very much," replied Mary ; " and unless he is rich, so costly a present may be a proof of the ardour of his regard for you."

" Well, he's only a sergeant in the army, Miss," replied Bessy.

" Oh, it is quite romantic ! " Grace exclaimed.

Bessy Morris suddenly became very industrious, and Miss Kearney thought she was trying to make up for the time lost on account of the gold earrings. But Bessy's mind was busy as well as her fingers. Miss Kearney's warning, though given half in jest, startled her, and she began to examine her conscience in reference to her conduct towards the soldier. She could not conceal from herself that she had done her best to attract him, and was flattered by every evidence of her success. She had tried to " get inside " other girls, and it gratified her vanity to see herself preferred to them. She even thought her heart was touched, she felt so pained when she fancied her admirer was wavering in his allegiance. But when she became quite sure he loved her, she found that she did not really care for him ; and, perhaps, to get rid of his attentions was one reason for her leaving Dublin. The intensity of his passion was so evident when she met him in her grandfather's house, after returning from the wedding, that it quite frightened her, and, in spite of the candour upon which she had just plumed herself, she shrank from telling Miss Kearney that her martial suitor had already "steered his barque" to Knocknagow ; for she devoutly hoped no one in the neighbourhood would ever know anything about it, as Peg Brady had promised faithfully to keep the dragoon's visit a profound secret, and Billy Heffernan said nothing about him except that he had met him in Clonmel.

She stopped sewing, and, resting her hand upon the table, commenced tapping it nervously, just as she had done while sitting in her grandfather's chair, after the soldier's passionate farewell. Happening to glance through the window, a sad, wistful look came into her face ; and it was so evident that this look was called up by some object upon which her eyes rested, that Grace followed their direction to see what it could be that made Bessy Morris look so sad, and, as she thought, yearningly. Grace could see nothing in the direction of her gaze but three tall trees standing all alone upon the bare hill.

" I often remark those lonely-looking trees," she observed, " and when the wind is drifting the snow or the cold rain over the hill, I quite pity them. I fancy they must feel the cold. And they sometimes remind me of three tall nuns."

" They are more like round towers, or something of that sort," said Mary.

" Their shadow is now on the house where I was born," said Bessy Morris.

" Indeed !" said Grace. " I thought you must feel interested in something up there ; you looked so earnestly in that direction."

" My mother was the daughter of a respectable farmer," Bessy continued. " And though my father was the son of a

tradesman, he was considered a good match for her, as his
father was able to give him three hundred pounds, which was
given as a fortune to my mother's sister. I suppose you know,
Miss, a weaver was a good trade in Ireland long ago. But
the rent was raised and crops failed, and my father was
ejected. 'Twas a cruel case, every one said, and no one ever
offered to take the farm since ; so that it comes into my mind
sometimes that I'll live there again."

"Is your mother dead ?" Grace asked.

"She is, Miss. The day the sheriff was there to turn
them out she clung to the door, and one of the bailiffs, in
dragging her from it, threw her upon the ground, and it was
thought the fall killed her ; but I believe it was her heart
that broke."

"And is your father alive ?"

"I hope he is, but I don't know."

Grace looked at her with surprise.

"When he heard my mother scream," continued Bessy,
"and saw Darby Ruadh fling her upon the ground, he lost
all control over himself, and taking hold of one of the policemen's guns, he dragged it from him and knocked the bailiff
down with the butt end of it. He then swore he'd shoot
the first man who would lay a hand on him ; and they were all
so much taken by surprise that they let him walk out of the
yard, and he had a good start before they ran after him."

"Did they catch him ?" Grace asked eagerly.

"No, Miss," returned Bessy, "he hid himself in an old
sandpit on the farm and escaped."

"Do you remember your father and mother ?" Mary asked.

"I do, Miss, well," she replied. "My mother was a beautiful young woman. She died the next night at my grandfather's. And I remember my father coming to take his
leave of her though the soldiers and police were scouring the
country after him, for 'twas thought Darby Ruadh would
not recover, as his skull was fractured. There was nothing
but meetings of magistrates, and rewards offered, and houses
searched, and people arrested to give evidence. You'd think
it was war that was in the country. My grandfather advised
my father to go to America, ' an let me see the man,' said
he, ' that'll offer to take your farm. You were robbed, and
no man but a robber will offer for your land. This trouble

about the bailiff will blow over, and you can come home again. And I'll be a father and mother to little Bessy,' says he, when he saw my father taking me in his arms and kissing me. And he kept his word," she added, wiping the tears from her eyes.

" And did you never hear from your father after ?"

" Never," replied Bessy, " except once a man from the colliery mentioned in a letter that he saw him out west, and that he had carpets on his floors. But though we made every inquiry, we could get no tidings of him."

" And do you wish very much to see him ?"

" 'Tis the strongest wish of my heart," she replied. " Only that I could not leave my poor old grandfather, I'd go in search of my father. That was another motive that induced me to become a dressmaker ; for I said to myself I'd get employment in the different towns in America, and could travel the whole country."

" Don't do anything hastily," said Mary. " While you would be looking for him, he might come back to look for you."

" That's true," returned Bessy. " But I'd keep up a correspondence with Judy Brophy, or some one. I don't think I can ever have an easy mind till I am sure of what happened to him, at any rate. I am always thinking he is poor and neglected, and was ashamed to write to us."

She looked again towards the trees ; but her thoughts recurred to the dragoon, and her brow flushed as she recollected that she had replied to one or two of his letters. He might, she thought, accuse her of faithlessness ; and her conscience told her the charge would not be altogether without foundation.

" I will request of him not to come again," she said to herself ; " and if he be a man of spirit he will respect my wishes."

" Surely this is Apollo in the garden with Adonis," Grace exclaimed. " I wonder where are they going ? I thought he was to be away on business all day—what do you think, Mary ?"

" If that is not his *fetch*, it seems he has come back," replied Mary. " But as to where they are going, I wonder you should think it necessary to ask."

" Oh, yes," returned Grace with a toss of her head, " the attraction in that quarter must be very strong indeed. But they might at least have the politeness to inquire whether we would go."

Mr. Lowe turned back before he and the doctor had reached the stile, and Grace threw open the window.

" Going to pay your devoirs to the beauty of Castleview ?" she exclaimed.

" Yes, the doctor is going to call at Mr. Hanly's ; and perhaps you and Miss Kearney would come out for a walk as the day is so fine ?"

" She is such a model of industry, I don't think you can induce her to go out—but let her answer for herself."

After a little hesitation Mary came to the window, saying, " Well, if you have patience to wait for a few minutes we will go."

Mr. Lowe bowed, and went to tell the doctor, who was standing with folded arms near the laurels, and looking intensely sentimental.

" Well, now," said Grace, as she went on arranging her hair—on observing Bessy Morris move her chair so that she could see the two young men in the garden—" which of those two gallant gay Lotharios do you think the best-looking ?"

" I think Mr. Richard has the advantage," Bessy answered.

" He is particularly well got up just now," returned Grace, glancing over her shoulder through the window, " and does really look handsome."

" 'Twas always given up to him, Miss," rejoined Bessy, " to be the handsomest young man in the parish. 'Tis often I heard it said that he was the handsomest boy, and Miss Mary the handsomest girl going into the chapel of Kilthubber. Though some would give Miss Hanly the palm."

" Why, Mary, you are quite famous ! And do they never talk of those who go to church ?'

" Oh, yes, Miss. Miss Isabella Lloyd has a strong party, who says she is by odds a finer girl than either of them. I'm told she is to be married to Captain French—and a fine couple they'll be. He's to throw the sledge with Mat Donovan next Sunday. But, talking of handsome men," continued Bessy, while her eyes sparkled with admiration, " there is a handsomer man to my mind than any of 'em."

Mary ran to the window with quite an excited look. Was there some one who, to her mind, was a handsomer man than her remarkably handsome brother ? She smiled at what she mentally called her foolishness, and the flush faded from her cheek. But her eyes sparkled, too, when she saw the person to whom Bessy alluded.

"Why," exclaimed Grace in astonishment, "'tis Fionn Macool !"

"Who is that, Miss ?" Bessy asked.

"Oh, that's what I call *him*," she replied, pointing to Hugh, who had just come into the garden.

"You couldn't call him a grander name," returned Bessy. "He was the great chief of the Fenians long ago. The top of Slievenamon is called Shee-Feen after him. My grandfather would keep telling you stories about him for a month."

"What way does he tell the story of the Beauty Race ? Is it that he had all the beautiful women in Ireland assembled in the Valley of Compsey, to run a race to the top of the mountain, and the first up would be his wife ?"

"Yes, that was the way, Miss," replied Bessy.

"The longest-legged or the longest-winded was to have him. Do you call him a hero ? The man was a savage, and the poor girls that came to grief in the race were most fortunate."

"Yes, Miss, but several great kings wanted him to marry their daughters, and it was all a plan to keep them from falling out with him. And there was one little girl he would rather have than the whole box-and-dice of them. So he told her to go fair and easy round by the Clodagh, and take her time, and not run with the rest at all. They all took to pulling and dragging one another the minute they started, and Fionn had Grauna in his arms on the top of Shee-Feen before one of them was half-way up the first hill."

"The moral of which is," said Grace, as she swung her pretty little cloak over her shoulders, "in running for a husband, 'take your time,' and 'go fair and easy,' and don't take to 'pulling and dragging' your rivals and get yourself pulled and dragged in return, besides losing the prize into the bargain. What's that you called the 'little girl he'd rather have than any of them ?'"

" She was called the Fair-haired Grauna—she was a namesake of your own—for Grauna is the Irish of Grace."

" Oh, I am quite proud to be the namesake of a lady so distinguished. And who knows but it may be an omen, and I may, like her, be clasped in a warrior's arms. Oh, those brave days of old, when one might win the love of some noble knight *sans peur et sans reproche*. When I think of it I am sick of your Apollos and your Adonises. In fact Bessy, I could almost envy you your ' sergeant in the army.' "

" Whether you joke or no, Miss," replied Bessy, laughing, " 'twas something like that was in my mind when I met him first."

" I wonder at you, who are such a patriot, Grace," said Mary, " to talk in that way."

" Oh, I was only thinking of the soldier in the abstract," replied Grace, with a frown. " And will not Mr. Lowe be an English soldier one of these days ?"

" So I understand," returned Mary. " And how would you like," she added, turning to Bessy, " to have your husband with those soldiers who passed this way the other day to shoot down the poor people whose houses were going to be levelled if they offered any resistance to the crowbar brigade ?"

" That's true," Bessy answered thoughtfully. " And I thought, too, how my grandfather was flogged in '98."

" But, Bessy," said Grace, as she drew on her gloves near the window, " how *can* you say such a black-looking fellow as that is handsome ? I always set him down as the ugliest fellow I ever saw. And though I have modified that opinion somewhat latterly—particularly since I saw Mr. Beresford Pender—still it does make me wonder to hear him called a handsome man. Where, in the name of goodness, is the beauty ?"

" Well, I don't know, Miss,' she answered, laying down her work and looking earnestly at Hugh Kearney, " but see how strong, and manly, and honest, he looks. If a lion was rushing to devour you, or a ship sinking under you, wouldn't you feel safe if his arm was around you ?"

" There is really something in what she says," Grace observed seriously. " If a lion leaped over that hedge and were about seizing you, Fionn would have him by the throat

instantly. Apollo, too, would stand his ground in his cool
way. But I strongly suspect Adonis would cut and run.
Not out of cowardice exactly, but he always thinks first of
his precious self, and would only remember poor me when I
was already gobbled up."

" Are ye going to keep us waiting all day ?" the subject of
this not very flattering criticism called out.

" He is not inclined to go ' fair and easy,' " Grace observed.
" Are you ready, Mary ?"

" I'll be ready in a moment. I merely have to direct this
letter to Father Carroll."

" By the way," returned Grace, " you did not show me
that note Barney threw up to you the other evening. It has
just occurred to me that Barney put Bessy's letter in his hat,
too', and forgot it ; and as hers was a love-letter, perhaps so
was yours."—" That's all' nonsense," said Mary.

" Did you ever see my brother Edmund, Bessy," Grace
continued, " and what did you think of him ?"

" He's a fine pleasant fellow, Miss," returned Bessy. " He
used to be fishing with Mr. Hugh at the river, and they sometimes called in to have a chat with my grandfather."

" I thought he would come home at Christmas," said
Grace, " but something turned up to prevent him. I wrote
to him to say that he has no business here any more." And
she nodded her head towards Mary, and then looked out at
Mr. Lowe, in a way that made both Mary and Bessy Morris
laugh.

" And did you tell him that Anne sent her love to him ?"

" Yes, but that's nothing. I am quite sure Anne will end
her days in a convent."

" I thought Edmund would be sure to win that prize for
which so many are contending."

" You mean Minnie Delany ? No, it will never come to
anything. He has something in his head that I cannot make
out. I heard Father Carroll and Arthur O'Connor jesting
about it. Edmund says that he and Arthur always fell in
love with the same lady by some fatality ; and only that
Arthur is to be a priest they would be sure to run foul of
each other. Only think of a duel between two such bosom
friends, about some beauty that didn't care a pin about either
of them."

" Come away," exclaimed Mary, " unless you want to have Richard vowing vengeance against us." And she ran so precipitately out of the room, that Grace shook her head and knit her brows, as if she thought that between her brother and Arthur O'Connor and Mary Kearney there was most certainly a mystery, which, as yet, she could make nothing of. She followed Mary to the garden, leaving Bessy Morris in the little room alone.

CHAPTER XLI.

MISS KATHLEEN HANLY THINKS IT ADVISABLE TO BE " DOING SOMETHING."

" Ask Hugh to come." And Mary's somewhat anxious look brightened as she saw Hugh submitting to be led on with them by Grace, who seemed to take his compliance as a matter of course. Mary was a little afraid of being left alone with Mr. Lowe. His admiration had risen to such a height that it was really no vanity in her to consider a downright declaration of love within the bounds of possibility. Her good sense enabled her to see the folly of such a proceeding, and her good nature—to say nothing of the real liking she had for him—made her shrink from wounding his feelings in any way. She said to herself that he would soon forget her in the bustle and excitement of the gay world. And if he passed on with nothing more definite than a bow and a smile—or she might have no great objection to a sigh—it would be better for both. So that Hugh's docility was a great relief to her, and she talked cheerfully, and even gaily, as they passed on through the hamlet, stopping occasionally to say a kind or pleasant word to the women and children, who always greeted her with smiles and sometimes with blessings. Nelly Donovan was examining one of her beehives, which had barely escaped being overturned by Kit Cummins's cat in endeavouring to escape from its deadly enemy, ' Friskey Lahy " (in Knocknagow the patronymic of

the owner was invariably bestowed upon his dog)—and Nelly
became so eloquent in detailing the injuries and vexations
brought upon her by Kit Cummins's cat, that Mr. Lowe
forgot his own woes, and stopped to listen to Nelly Donovan's
harangue with a more cheerful expression of countenance
than he had been seen to wear for several days before. Then
old Mrs. Donovan appeared, smoothing her white hair over
her temples, after removing her spectacles, and had a word
to say in private to Miss Kearney ; so that a quarter of an
hour was lost before the party came up with the doctor, who
was waiting at the corner of the clipped hedge, and gazing
pensively towards the old castle. Catching a glimpse of the
redoubtable Kit Cummins herself, with arms akimbo inside
the threshold of her own door, evidently prepared with a
defence of her persecuted cat, the doctor thought at this rate
they'd never reach the house on the hill ; and, to avoid
further interruptions, he proposed to turn in by the short-cut
through Tom Hogan's farm. Whereupon Kit Cummins
thrust her hair under her cap, and tried to bottle up her
wrath for a more favourable opportunity ; but finding the
effort too much for her, she relieved her feelings by a long
and well-sustained invective upon her next-door neighbour
and all belonging to her. And the never-varying response
on such occasions—" Gir-r-r-r out, you bla'guard !" fell with
such piercing distinctness upon Mr. Lowe's ear, that he stood
still in the middle of Tom Hogan's field, and gazed around
in amazement—though the partition between Kit Cummins
and her next-door neighbour was so thin that the purring of
the vagabond cat could easily be heard through it.

Attorney Hanly laid down the newspaper and left the
room so abruptly that his wife stared after him for a minute,
and commenced rubbing her eyebrow. Mrs. Hanly had
dropped an occasional hint during the morning, intended to
lead up gradually and naturally to a certain subject with
which her mind was occupied. But the abrupt and unexpected exit of Mr. Hanly seemed to have hopelessly dis-
arranged her plans. Looking through the window she saw
Mr. Isaac Pender shambling up the avenue ; and the attorney
soon appeared wrapped in his great-coat, and met the old
agent half-way between the gate and the house.

" Run, Lory !" exclaimed Mrs. Hanly, as if she saw there

was but one chance left her, "and tell him I want some money."

Lory started off without his cap, and quite terrified old Isaac by simply pronouncing the word "money" and holding out his hand. It seemed to have a stand-and-deliver effect upon Lory's father too; for he at once thrust his hands into his trousers pockets, and then into his waistcoat pockets, and then into the pockets of his great-coat. The result appeared in the shape of two or three pound notes, two or three shillings in silver, and two or three pence in copper. Rolling all these into one bundle, Mr. Hanly thrust them into his son's hand, who ran back to the house rejoicing.

"Well, it is better than nothing," said Mrs. Hanly, after counting the notes.

"But I wonder why did he mind giving me the odd coppers?" Lory asked, dropping them into his pocket, and resolving to have a game of pitch-and-toss with Barney Brodherick and Jack Delany's apprentice, the first convenient opportunity.

"Ah, you don't know all the plans he has," observed his mother. "Don't you see I am now to suppose that he has given me all the money he has, and left himself penniless?"

Lory uttered that startling two-fold sound he intended for a laugh, and evidently looked upon his father as a clever fellow. "I may as well keep this for myself," he remarked, looking at the silver in his open hand.

Scarcely had he uttered the words, when his hand was struck, and the money sent rolling about the floor.

"You must *not* keep it, sir. I don't know what you want of money. Come here and hold him, Kathleen."

There was a tremendous struggle between Rose and Lory for the money; but Kathleen, who was reclining with her lap-dog on the sofa, contented herself with holding the little animal fast, and trying to stop its barking. Mrs. Hanly quietly picked up one shilling which rolled against her foot. Rose seized another. But in spite of all she could do, Lory caught hold of the third and thrust it into his pocket. In vain did Rose exert herself, till she seemed in danger of bursting a blood-vessel, to pull Lory's hand out of his pocket. And finding the hand and arm quite immovable, she paused to parley and take breath.

"Now, what do you want that money for ?" Rose asked, as she twisted up her hair.

"For the novelty of it," added Lory, jingling the coppers, which were all safe in the other pocket.

"No, sir ; it is not for the novelty of it. I have found you out. Miss Lloyd, who hates you, because she thinks 'tis purposely to frighten her you talk loud, told me that she saw you call for three pints of beer at Bourke's ; and that you drank one yourself, and gave one to Joe Russel and another to Brummagem ; and that you talked and swaggered in a most awful manner. She could not understand half what ye said ; but it was plain to her ye were steeped to the lips in iniquity, she said."

"And where was she ?" Lory asked.

"She went in through the yard gate when she saw you in the shop, and remained behind the door while ye were there."

"I'm sorry I didn't know she was there," returned Lory ; "I'd put Brummagem up to kiss her, and pretend he thought it was Kitty, the servant girl."

"O mercy !" exclaimed Rose. "What am I to do with him ?"

"Who is this person you call 'Brummagem' ?" her mother inquired.

"That horrid fellow with the black face," Rose answered. "They call him 'Lovely Delany,' too. I suppose because he is such a monster of ugliness."

"Don't mind her," said Lory. "He's Jack Delany's nephew. His face is black because he's a blacksmith ; and they call him "Brummagem," because he was born in Birmingham, in England. I suppose they call him 'Lovely' on the same principle that you are called 'Rose,' " said Lory, with a laugh that would have been the death of his enemy, Miss Lloyd, if she were within reach of it.

"Don't be impertinent, sir," retorted Rose. "And didn't I see you playing pitch-and-toss at the end of the grove with this person and Joe Russel, and your other interesting friend, Barney Brodherick *alias* Wattletoes "

"I suppose it was he gave poor Joe the black eye," Mrs. Hanly observed

"Oh, no," said Rose, "that happened the last day he drove us into town   Grace Kiely can tell you all about it."

" The Kearneys are coming up through the fields," Lory observed—reminded of the fact by his sister's last remark.

" How do you know ?" Rose asked.

" Because I'm after seeing them," returned Lory.

" I suppose Richard is with them ?" Kathleen inquired with a yawn.

" Yes, he was on before the rest. He was looking back at them, or I would have spoken to him."

" Is Grace with them ?"

" She and Hugh were talking to Tom Hogan, who is making drains in the field next the grove."

" Kathleen !" exclaimed Mrs. Hanly, bustling about the room to put everything in its proper place, " throw away that wretched little dog, and be doing something."

Kathleen started up, and flung her favourite from her—whose doleful whine was suddenly changed into a yelp, Lory having accelerated its exit with the toe of his heavy boot, as he hurried out to meet the visitors. Kathleen looked about her, at a loss as to the " something " she ought to " be doing." She had a vague idea that her sleeves should be tucked up above her elbows ; but as there was not a moment to be lost, she snatched a bunch of keys from the table and ran up stairs ; with a view to coming down when called, with the keys at her girdle, and looking greatly surprised on finding her friends in the parlour.

The doctor's devotion was always looked upon by Mrs. Hanly as a means to an end ; and we very much fear the fair Kathleen herself had come round to that way of thinking also. A lecture from her father—illustrated by divers examples within his own personal knowledge, of what the worthy attorney called " genteel beggary "—made a deep impression upon his charming daughter. And a question casually put by her mother, apropos of Dr. Richard Kearney, to the effect, " was it in his pocket he'd put her," helped also to give Kathleen's thoughts a practical turn. So that she only yawned and went on pulling her dog's ears as she asked " was Richard with them." But the moment she heard that Hugh was coming, Kathleen started up to " be doing something."

But it must not by any means be inferred that Hugh Kearney had won the heart of the beauty of Castleview ;

except in a general way. She had come to connect the very
opposite of that dreaded " genteel beggary " with the idea of
an extensive farmer, and lost no opportunity of recommending herself to that class of wooers. She had on one occasion
all but made sure of a wealthy young farmer from the county
Limerick, who had purchased some cattle from the attorney,
and spent the evening at Castleview. The knowledge she
displayed of everything connected with farming—and particularly the wisdom of her views as to the making of
butter—made such an impression upon the gentleman from
Limerick, that, over and over again (as he afterwards confessed), he found himself repeating the words, " This is the
girl for me." And as Kathleen talked and talked in her
bewitching way, the only question that troubled the young
man's mind was, whether he would then and there ask the
attorney off-hand to give him his treasure of a daughter, or
put it off to the first Wednesday in the ensuing month, which
was the fair-day of Kilthubber. But in the very moment of
her triumph, Kathleen asked, with a look of the profoundest
wisdom—" How many *hundreds* of butter do you put in a
firkin in your part of the country ?"

The young man stared ; but Kathleen repeated her question
with a look of self-satisfied experience that absolutely appalled
him. In vain her mother made signs to signify that she
had blundered ; in vain her father's sarcastic laugh ; Kathleen
would know how many hundred-weight of butter went to a
firkin in his part of the country. And she smacked her lips
and sighed, and looked as if she had thought of nothing but
filling firkins for the best part of her life, as she paused for
a reply. To her astonishment, however, the young county
Limerick farmer suddenly rose and took his leave ; looking
as if he found himself in a place where his pockets might be
picked if he delayed another instant.

" O Lord !" exclaimed the young farmer, looking back at
the house on the hill when he had gone some distance from
it—as if to assure himself that he was safe—" O Lord,
there's no depending on any of them. I was d—d near being
taken in. I wonder did she ever see a firkin in her life ?
' How many HUNDRED of butter do you put in a firkin ?'
'Tis my opinion she don't know a firkin from a herring-stand.
Oh, and the way she talked ! I thought she was the best

manager in Munster. The fact is," he added, as if he had quite made up his mind upon the point, "they're *not* to be depended on."

For nearly a year after, the young county Limerick farmer lived in perpetual dread of being "taken in"—the sight of a delicate white hand affecting him like a snake in the grass— and to put an end to his misery, by effectually guarding against the apprehended danger, one fine morning married his dairy-maid; the dairy-maid, in the innocence of her heart, attributing her good fortune to her blooming cheeks and a pair of soft brown eyes—never dreaming that she owed it all to Miss Kathleen Hanly's Brobdignagian ideas of firkins of butter.

And now Kathleen tripped down stairs with the keys at her girdle, and, stopping in the middle of her song, looked so surprised to find that Rose was not all alone. She recovered herself sufficiently to welcome her visitors in the prescribed fashion. But as she looked around, and caught something like a malicious smile in Rose's eyes, Kathleen bit her lip, and immediately became intensely amiable.

The keys were a mistake; for Hugh did not come in at all. The lap-dog on the sofa would have done much better under the circumstances.

But that unhappy little lap-dog! How dearly he paid for these little mistakes and disappointments! The Brobdignagian firkin had well-nigh proved the death of him. For when his mistress flung herself on the sofa, after being informed that a firkin was never known to contain even *one* hundred of butter, she squeezed the poor creature's windpipe till its eyes seemed starting out of its head. And—as if the application of Lory's "blucher" were not enough punishment for one day—the fair Kathleen, on resuming her place on the sofa after seeing her visitors part of the way home, commenced knocking the persecuted little animal upon his skull with the bunch of keys; as if she were determined to practically test the truth of the proverb, "There's many a way of killing a dog besides choking him with butter."

CHAPTER XLII.

A HAUNTED FARM.

WHEN Attorney Hanly had delivered up the contents of all his pockets to his son, and left himself penniless, he fixed his eyes on Mr. Isaac Pender, who was immediately assailed by the midges, and rubbed his face all over, as if those imaginary tormentors threatened to set him out of his wits. Still Attorney Hanly kept his eye upon him, and Mr. Pender turned upon his heel for relief, and looked towards the three poplars on the hill.

" A little outlay," he said, " would make that farm of Beresford's a nice place. Look at Maurice Kearney's farm a little below it, and draining would make the other place superior to it, for it is better situated. I think," he added, venturing to look at the attorney, " I think Beresford would give it up."

" 'Twouldn't suit me at all," replied Mr. Hanly.

" If the presentment for the new road passes," Mr. Pender ventured to observe, " 'twill be as convenient to the market as your own house. And I know we could manage a satisfactory lease."

" I wouldn't take a present of it," said Mr. Hanly.

" So I thought. So I said. I knew you wouldn't care for it," rejoined Mr. Pender, as if he quite approved of his friend's view on the subject, or, at all events, fully appreciated his motives for not wishing to have anything to do with the farm. " I know you only want some land adjoining this place. And 'tis a pity your farm is not larger, when you have such a good house and offices built on it. I know you only want what will make the farm suitable for such a house and offices."

To some extent Mr. Isaac Pender was right. It was land adjoining his own that Attorney Hanly was most anxious to get. But a farm even some distance from Castleview would have suited him very well. And when Mr. Pender first spoke of "that farm of Beresford's," Mr. Hanly looked up towards the poplar trees as if they possessed considerable attraction for him; quite as much, one would have supposed from the expression of his face, as the same three trees seemed to possess for Mat Donovan. And, curiously enough, Attorney Hanly, standing in the middle of his own lawn, and gazing at the poplar trees, did precisely what Mat Donovan had done, after gazing at them from the middle of Maurice Kearney's wheat field an hour or two before. That is, Attorney Hanly turned quickly round and fixed his eyes on a cluster of whitethorn trees near the foot of another hill behind Maurice Kearney's fort. And it was after looking in this direction that Attorney Hanly said abruptly he would not "take a present of it," meaning the farm where Bessy Morris was born—as she told Grace and Mary—and which looked so desolate in the eyes of Barney Brodherick as he stood on the double-ditch trying to catch a sight of Mr. Beresford Pender's servant, to send him to take charge of the hook-nosed steed. It was a rather remarkable coincidence that Mat Donovan and Bessy Morris and Attorney Hanly were all looking towards the three poplar trees at the same time.

"Who knows?" said Mat Donovan, as he went on castle-building; "greater wonders come to pass every day." And then Mat turned round and looked towards the whitethorns at the foot of the hill beyond the pit.

"Something tells me that I will live there yet," said Bessy Morris, as she stood upon the rustic seat in the little garden under Mary Kearney's window, in order to have a better view of the poplar trees over the hedge. And then she, too, turned round and looked towards the whitethorns.

"Yes, it would do very well," thought Attorney Hanly, as he looked up at the three trees; "but—I would not take a present of it!" he added aloud, as he turned round and looked towards the cluster of whitethorns at the foot of the hill.

Since the day Dick Morris left the bailiff for dead who had flung his fair, delicate young wife from the door, and made his escape, the place had been left without a tenant. Many and many a greedy eye was turned to the three tall trees; but no one ventured to send in a proposal for the farm. Mr. Beres-

ford Pender undertook to manage it for the landlord to the
best advantage by taking in grazing stock and meadowing so
much of the land as was fit for it ; and so long had this state
of things continued, that his worthy father always spoke of
the farm as " that place of Beresford's." Yet even Beresford
would not have ventured to formally become the tenant. He
was even occasionally heard to declare that his keeping the
place was a disagreeable necessity, and that nothing would
please him better than to hand it over to any one who would
be acceptable to the landlord. The fact was, that lonesome
farm, with no living thing visible upon it that bright winter
day but two carrion crows in the midst of a sheet of water,
and a magpie upon the roof of the tumble-down barn, was
haunted. Not by the ghost of Black Humphrey, whose fate
was commemorated by the cairn near the sand-pit, but by an
old lame man, who usually kept his lips closed very hard, and
whose grey eye gleamed in a piercing sort of way that made
some people feel uneasy as he stumped about the place at
regular intervals, marking the ravages that time was making
in it, and seeming to derive particular satisfaction from the
grass growing through the floors of the out-offices. Old Phil
Morris was never accompanied by his granddaughter on these
occasions, though she often asked to be let go with him.
" No," he would say in reply to her request, " you will never
go till you can call it your own home again." And this is
how Dick Morris's farm was haunted, and remained tenant-
less in consequence. This is why Attorney Hanly would not
" take a present of it."

" I'm going to tell Tom Hogan," said Mr. Isaac Pender,
" that his rent is raised."

" Is Tom Hogan's rent raised ?" Attorney Hanly asked,
while his eyes almost flashed with pleasure and surprise.

" Only a trifle ; only a trifle," replied the agent, sorrowfully. " 'Tis not easy to get Sir Garrett to understand these
things. Sir Thomas was a great loss to the country. He
understood the proper system ; but Sir Garrett knows no
more about the management of a property than a child. He
spent nearly all his life abroad. And his nephew tells me
he's going again immediately. Why, I believe this is Mr.
Lowe coming across the field with those ladies," Mr. Pender
added in surprise. " I thought he was with Beresford. But

I suppose he didn't mind seeing many of the tenants. Mr.
Lowe is a nice young fellow—a very nice young fellow;
and doesn't want to meddle in the affairs of the tenants at
all. His mother wrote to Beresford to have an eye to him
and keep him out of harm's way. She understands the state
of the country much better than Sir Garrett. And still she
thinks she ought to get her rent-charge without any delay.
Her eldest son is in India, and he ought to be able to send
his mother something. His pay is high, and he ought to be
able to do something for his mother. She's always writing
for money."

The doctor, who thought Mr. Hanly was away from home,
looked considerably put out on discovering his mistake. In
fact, the doctor was never able to reason himself out of a
very unreasonable and absurd feeling of awe of Miss Kathleen's papa. The attorney had a habit of accosting him
with, "Well, lad?" whenever he happened to encounter him
about the house; and no amount of pulling his moustache
and looking down at his long legs, could altogether satisfy
the doctor that he was a middle-sized boy on those occasions. He felt so disgustingly young in the attorney's
presence, that he made it a point to avoid him as much as
possible. A short time before he was strolling up through the
same field, when the attorney called out from the grove at
the opposite side—"Well, lad; the girls are out." Whereupon the doctor replied, pointing to the castle—"This is a
very interesting old ruin up here. And the view from the
top is very good." "Ay, ay, very interesting old ruin!"
replied the attorney; and his dry laugh made several workmen about the place grin from ear to ear, and Dr. Richard
Kearney redden up to the eyes. And now the doctor reddened again, lest Kathleen's papa should treat him as a small
boy before his friends. It was a slight relief to him that
Grace was so far behind, as he dreaded her more than any
of them. He walked back under the pretence of helping her
over the fence, but in reality to keep out of Mr. Hanly's
reach as long as possible, and until Mr. Lowe and Mary could
have engaged his attention. Grace was highly gratified on
seeing him ready to hand her over the fence, and immediately
forgot Hugh's existence, though he had not allowed as much
as a bramble to touch her all the way, while the doctor

thought of nothing but his own boots and Kathleen Hanly, Hugh was taking her hand to help her up when she raised her eyes and saw the doctor. She had no notion that it was care for his dignity, and sheer terror of finding himself suddenly metamorphosed into a schoolboy, that drove the doctor back to her. And as she tripped on gaily by his side to overtake Mary and Mr. Lowe, Hugh thought her a very pleasant sight to look at, even though she had deserted him so unceremoniously.

" Oh !" Grace exclaimed, looking back with surprise, " what has become of Hugh ?" And she looked so sad for a moment, that Mary felt alarmed, imagining that some accident might have happened to him. But seeing him emerge from a clump of trees and go towards a stile which she knew led to the lower part of their own farm, Mary laughed at her own fears, and asked Grace why she looked so sad.

" Well, then," Grace replied, " I fear I may have offended Hugh."

" Offended Hugh ! How could that be ?"

Grace told what had just occurred, and Mary laughed so heartily that the doctor turned sharply round, under the impression that she was laughing at himself.

" What are you laughing at ?" he asked.

" Oh, I can't help it. This young lady is so full of humility. She attaches no importance to herself at all ! Ah ! poor Hugh ! I have no doubt he is quite miserable !"

" Oh, you may look at it in that light if you choose. But I feel that I have been ungrateful, and must really do something to make it up with him."

The doctor was in the act of snapping his fingers, and in fact showed some symptoms of cutting a caper, when his sister's laugh made him turn round under the impression that he himself was the occasion of it. The attorney and the agent were walking away by a footpath that led to the road, apparently as if they had not seen him or his friends. And this was such a decided piece of good luck in the doctor's eyes, that he really might in the joy of the moment have executed one of " Callaghan's steps," *a la* Barney Brodherick, had not Mary's laugh checked him.

" That is Mr. Hanly walking with the agent," said Mary. " They seem to be going to Tom Hogan's."

" Fair weather after them," returned Grace. " I'm glad they did not see us."

" If all the tenants were like Tom Hogan," the agent remarked, " 'twould be a nice property. 'Tis a pity his farm is so small. But when these three other farms will be added to it, 'twill be easy to make a nice place of it."

" Two thousand pounds," returned the attorney, " wouldn't make the rest of it like that." And he pointed to what really looked like " a piece of the Golden Vale dropped among the rushes and yellow clay all around," to quote Mat Donovan again.

" That's true ; that's true," old Isaac muttered. " But if they did like Tom Hogan," he added, half reproachfully, half sorrowfully, " they wouldn't feel it. There is Tom at the drains."

Tom Hogan got that trembling in his hands when he saw the agent and his neighbour, Attorney Hanly, coming towards him, to such an extent that the spade dropped from them ; and not caring that this should be observed, he looked about him for some excuse for having left off his work. Seeing a solitary crow pitch in the middle of his wheat-field —which looked as if a veil of green gauze were flung over the red-brown ridges—and fearing that the marauder would commence pulling up the young blades for the sake of the grains of wheat at the roots, he got out of the drain and hurried away.

" One would think he was afraid of us," said the attorney.

" No, no," returned Mr. Pender. " He knows nothing, unless Darby told him about this trifling rise in his rent, and that would not frighten him. He's only going into the house for something he wants."

" There was a very suspicious-looking fellow," Mr. Hanly observed, " lying in the grove there early this morning, and if I'm not much mistaken 'twas a pistol he thrust into his breast when he saw me coming towards him."

" What sort of looking fellow was he ?" the agent asked, rubbing his face nervously.

" A tall, wild-looking fellow, with his clothes all in rags."

" 'Twas that unfortunate man, Mick Brien," returned the agent. " I'm sorry now we ever held out any hopes to him. Darby tells me they don't like at all the way he is going on.

He got straw from Maurice Kearney to-day to thatch his
cabin, though they told him 'twas to be thrown down."

"Well, to come to business," said the attorney ; "you're
sure there'll be no difficulty in getting a renewal of my lease,
without any increase of rent ?"

"Let us walk this way," the agent suggested. "I think
I saw some one moving behind those trees in the corner.
Yes, I'm almost sure we can manage the lease of your own
place. But what hurry are you in ? If Maurice Kearney
knew just now you were getting a renewal, there's no knowing what he might do."

"I think the man has a right to a renewal," said Mr.
Hanly—who possibly was thinking of settling one of his
blooming daughters comfortably.

"Well, well," muttered old Isaac, taken quite aback, "just
let us walk this way."

"'Tis a pity Tom Hogan is so unreasonable. He can't be
got to see that his farm is too small, and that he ought to
give up peaceable possession like the Ryans and Tom Donnelly. And his son," added the agent, rubbing his face, and
looking around, as if he feared some one was about pouncing
upon him to tear him to pieces—"his son is a wild young
fellow."

"Is it of a beardless boy you are afraid ?" the attorney
asked contemptuously.

There was something in old Phil Morris's grey eye that
struck terror to the heart of Attorney Hanly. But he would
have entered into possession of Tom Hogan's farm without
the slightest misgiving !

"Afraid of a beardless boy !" he muttered. "Bah !"

CHAPTER XLIII.

TOM HOGAN BOASTS THAT HE NEVER FIRED A SHOT.

MR. ISAAC PENDER and Attorney Hanly got over the stile
and walked towards the place that Tom Hogan had just left.
They looked into the deep drains as they went on, and by

the time they got to the end of the field Tom Hogan had gone into his own house.

Attorney Hanly looked at his watch, and seeing that the mail car would not pass the cross for some time, he thought of returning home, but changed his mind on recollecting that if he did it would be necessary to show some civility to the visitors from whom he had just escaped. So he walked with Mr. Isaac Pender up and down by Tom Hogan's quickset hedge, talking about business.

"What is that?" the agent asked, staring and looking terrified.

"It was not a shot," replied the attorney. "The report was not sharp enough for a shot from a gun or pistol. Yet it seemed to be an explosion of some kind. I'll get up on the ditch and see."

"Better not," replied the agent, catching hold of him. "Keep quiet, and don't let us be seen."

"Why, what is it you are afraid of?" the attorney asked. "Your life must be anything but pleasant if every sound half frightens it out of you at this rate. Let us go on to the stile."

They walked by the quickset hedge till they reached the stile that led into the next field. What we have called the quickset hedge was not merely a hedge planted on the ground. There was a tolerably high embankment of earth —a "ditch" in fact—and on the top of this the hedge. There were two or three long stone slabs fixed in the "ditch" as steps, and some two feet of wicker-work woven between stakes on the top. Mr. Isaac Pender had one hand on the wicker-work and a foot on each of the two stone slabs, when he suddenly uttered a cry and fell back into the arms of the attorney. The attorney looked up, and he, too, was so startled, that he let old Isaac fall to the ground; and, retreating a step backwards, Attorney Hanly himself fell upon his back into one of Tom Hogan's newly-made drains. The old agent had fallen upon his back too, but raising himself upon his hands he looked up at the stile, while every feature gave evidence of the most intense terror.

The attorney had disappeared altogether in the drain, and seemed in no hurry to get out of it.

It was only Tom Hogan. who had suddenly popped his

head over the stile. But his face was blackened ; and a braver man than Mr. Isaac Pender might well have been startled by such an apparition.

Attorney Hanly got upon his hands and knees in the drain, and waited for the shot. He thought Tom Hogan must have overheard them plotting his ruin, and determined to wreak instant vengeance upon the plotters ; and the thought was a natural one enough under the circumstances.

Mr. Hanly was not by any means a coward. He would not have thrown himself designedly into the drain at the sight of Tom Hogan's blackened face. But, having fallen accidentally into it, he thought it wise to turn the accident to advantage. He was safe under cover ; and resolved to keep quiet till Tom Hogan's gun or blunderbuss had exploded and riddled Mr. Isaac Pender. Then Mr. Hanly would start to his feet and run or fight for his life. He had no notion of staying where he was till Tom Hogan had guillotined him with his spade, perhaps.

But why does he not fire ?

The attorney's heart ceased to beat as he waited for the shot. Seconds seemed hours as he crouched there in the damp, narrow drain, which was so like a grave ! He felt his flesh creep as, on turning his head to listen, his cheek touched the cold clay. And now the terrible thought occurred to him that the agent had been slain, not with a gun, but with a spade or pick-axe, and that the weapon, hot and bloody, was in the very act of crashing through his own brain. He felt, in that brief moment, the agony of dying a violent death. It was only a moment ; but to him it was an age. He tried to rise, but could not. He felt as if the heavy clay had been heaped upon him, and that he was buried alive !

The sound of voices fell upon his ear. Some persons were speaking near him in a quiet, unexcited tone. The words were :

" I hope you are not injured ?"

" Bogor, I don't know. Id tuck a start out uv me, at any rate. An' look at the way my hand is."

Mr. Hanly tried again to stand up, and succeeded. He had not been more than a minute in the drain ; but he looked about him as if he expected to discover that the face

of Nature had undergone some wonderful transformation
since last he looked upon it. But the trees, and the fields,
and the mountains, as well as his own house, and the old
castle, and Knocknagow—from Mat Donovan's to the cross ;
Phil Lahy's pointed roof and thick chimneys, and the beech
tree inclusive—were precisely in their old places. And Mr.
Isaac Pender was still in a half-sitting position, propped up
by his two arms, with his under-jaw hanging down, and his
eyes as wide open as it was possible for such eyes to be. He
was still staring up at the stile ; but the black face was turned
away, which seemed some little relief to him, for his mouth
closed, and a slight movement about the eyes indicated
that, in course of time, they, too, might recover the power of
shutting.

" Why, Mr. Hanly, what has happened ?" Hugh Kearney
asked, looking at the attorney with unfeigned astonishment,
as he emerged from the drain, like a grave-digger, Hugh
thought, which idea was probably suggested by Mr. Isaac
Pender, who, in his suit of rusty black, looked very like a
withered old sexton.

" I merely stumbled, by accident, into this drain," replied
the attorney, trying to remove the yellow clay from his
shoulders and arms.

" And Mr. Pender ?"

" I—I—I stumbled, too," that gentleman replied, but
showed no symptom of any intention to rise.

Tom Hogan looked over his shoulder at the speakers, and
his blackened face seemed to astonish them as much as at
first. The surprise was mutual. Tom Hogan was quite as
much puzzled to see his agent sitting upon the ground and
staring at him as the agent was to account for Tom Hogan's
black face.

Tom Hogan's wife and daughter appeared upon the scene.

" O Tom !" exclaimed his wife, " what happened you ?"

" Are you hurt, father ?" Nancy asked, looking anxiously
into his face.

" 'Tis nothin'—'Tis nothin'," he replied. " 'Twon't signify
a pin."

" I think it would be as well if you run up to Mr. Hanly's
and tell the doctor to come and see him," said Hugh Kearney,
turning to Nancy Hogan.

" I will, sir," she replied eagerly, flinging back her auburn hair from her face, and running with the fleetness of a frightened fawn towards the house.

" I think, Mr. Pender, you had better get up," Hugh suggested.

" I think so ; I think so ; I think so," replied old Isaac, as he turned round upon his hands and knees and struggled to get upon his feet. But his joints appeared to have become either too stiff or too weak ; and Hugh, catching him by the collar with one hand, placed him on his legs, as if he were a rickety old chair.

The doctor and Mr. Lowe were soon seen hurrying down the lawn, followed by Nancy Hogan. She had first started off in advance of them, but a feeling of delicacy made her hold back and let them pass.

" I don't think the eyes are injured," said the doctor, as he examined Tom Hogan. " There is a slight burn on the left cheek, but it will not signify. Ha ! yes ! the hand must be looked to. But I'll have you all right in a day or two," added the doctor, as he laid his finger on Tom Hogan's wrist and felt his pulse. " The system seems to have sustained a shock," he continued gravely. " That is the serious feature in the case." And the doctor pulled out his watch and counted Tom Hogan's pulse for a minute.

The two Miss Hanlys, with Mary and Grace, joined the group ; and Mary, taking Hugh by the arm, questioned him about what had happened. But before he could reply, they were startled on seeing Jemmy Hogan clearing the hedge at a bound close to where they stood. His eyes flashed fire, as he demanded breathlessly, " What happened his father ?"

" Did any one do anything to him ?" he continued, almost choked with passion, as he looked from one to another of those present.

" No, Jemmy, no," his sister exclaimed, flinging her arms round him. " No one did anything to him. 'Twas an accident."

His hands were clenched, and he looked as if he would have sprung like a tiger upon any one who would dare to hurt his father.

" No, Jemmy, no," Tom Hogan repeated—and he laughed in a strange hysterical way. " No, Jemmy ; no wan done anything to me."

His sister clung to him, and all present were struck with their extreme beauty, and the resemblance they bore to each other, notwithstanding the pleading gentleness of her look, and the passionate defiance of his.

"O Mary," Grace whispered, "did you ever imagine Jemmy Hogan had such fierceness in him ? But what *has* happened to his father ? The poor man is a perfect fright, with his hair singed and his face blackened. Perhaps he rushed into a fire to save some one—but then there is no sign of a fire anywhere.'

"I was just asking Hugh," Mary replied.

Mr. Lowe came also to inquire of Hugh what had happened.

"I think I understand the matter," replied Hugh. "I was on my way to the bottom of our farm, and on hearing a noise I turned round, and observed a thick puff of smoke in the middle of that wheat-field. I saw Tom Hogan stagger back with his hands to his face, and as it was evident an accident had occurred, I turned back. He hurried on in this direction, and was just getting over the stile when I came up to him. Those gentlemen," he continued, lowering his voice and laughing, as he nodded his head towards the agent and Attorney Hanly, "seem to have been rather startled, for I found Mr. Pender on the broad of his back on the field there, and Mr. Hanly emerging from that drain."

Grace laughed, and even Mr. Lowe could not help smiling as he turned quietly round and looked at old Isaac, who had only partially recovered from his fright.

"But still," said he, turning again to Hugh, "I don't know what the nature of the accident was."

"Tom," said Hugh, "Mr. Lowe wishes to know how the accident occurred.'

"Frightenin' the crows," replied Tom Hogan, turning to Mr. Lowe.

"How ? I really don't understand."

"Wud a grain uv quarry-powther, sir," returned Tom Hogan. "I put id into a hole, an' in the way 'twould make a report I was goin' to lay a flat stone on id before I'd set fire to the bit of touch. But some way my hand wasn't studdy, an' a spark fell on id, an', begor, id blasted up into my face. An' that's the way id happened, sir."

"And why would you not frighten the crows with a gun ?

" Is id me, sir ? No, sir," said Tom Hogan, looking
reproachfully at Mr. Lowe, as if he had done him a great
injustice. " I'm not that sort of a character, an' never was.
I never fired a shot in my life, an' plase God I never will.
No, sir," continued Tom Hogan proudly, " no wan could ever
say a bad word uv me."

Mr. Lowe looked in astonishment at Hugh Kearney, as if
he wished him to explain what all this meant.

" Don't you know it is a crime to have arms in Ireland ?"
said Hugh, sarcastically. " No one can have arms without a
licence, and men like Tom Hogan would not get a licence.
So poor Tom has come to look upon never having fired a shot
as a proof of his honesty and respectability."

" We met a man on the road," said Mr. Lowe, " who had
pistols."

" That was Wat Corcoran the bailiff," returned Hugh.
" He is a great man on the strength of his pistols. In such
a case as his, arms are the marks of the gentleman, and the
man in power."

" Tom Hogan," put in Mr. Isaac Pender, " was always a
quiet decent man. He never had anything to do with fire-
arms."

" Nor never will, sir," said Tom Hogan.

But if Tom Hogan that very hour provided himself with a
good serviceable musket and bayonet, or a rifle or carbine—
or even an old duck gun like that with which Dr. Richard
Kearney so distinguished himself, it might have been lucky
for Tom Hogan, and lucky, too, for Mr. Isaac Pender.

" Tom Hogan never had anything to do with fire-arms,"
said Mr. Isaac Pender again. " Nor his son. Nor his son.
Nor his son," he repeated, glancing furtively at Jemmy, who
was now quite calm, except for a little flurry and confusion,
which was 'perhaps less the result of his late excitement than
of the presence of so many young ladies, all of whom were
favouring him with a good deal of notice.

" A very well-conducted, industrious young man," said Mr.
Isaac Pender. " A very well-conducted young man."

Attorney Hanly, seeing the mail-car approaching, moved
away to meet it at the cross-roads.

" Pender was right," he muttered to himself. " That
young Hogan is a different sort of character from what I

thought. There was a devil in his eye. That chap would do anything if driven to it. 'Tis true for old Isaac. The case is a difficult one. But that's his business. If his part was done I'd be able to manage the affair in such a way that it would not appear that I had anything to do with it. Hallo !"

The driver pulled up, and Mr. Hanly got upon the car ; and was not seen or heard of in that part of the country till he jumped off the same car at the same place that day three weeks.

" Which way shall we go back ?" Grace asked.

" By the road," replied the doctor, who hoped Kathleen would accompany them as far as the bridge.

" By the road," said Mary, who feared that Norah Lahy might feel disappointed if she returned home without calling to see her.

CHAPTER XLIV.

HUGH KEARNEY THINKS HE WILL GET HIS FISHING-ROD REPAIRED.

HUGH KEARNEY changed his mind. He said to himself, instead of going to the lower part of the farm, he would go look at the hoggets on the hill above the fort. Somehow he found that white jacket which had so caught his fancy at the wedding running very much in his mind. But this, in some degree, might be accounted for by the fact that Grace had just been telling him the flattering things Bessy Morris had said of him. And as he had to pass close to the house on his way, he began to think of some excuse for running up to his sister's room, and having a laugh and a few words of conversation with his agreeable partner in the dance at Ned Brophy's wedding. It required a good deal of reasoning to satisfy him that there was nothing objectionable in the step he was about taking ; and the mere fact that it did take such an amount of argumentation to satisfy him ought of itself to

have been enough to convince so steady a young man as Mr.
Hugh Kearney that it might be just as well to go on up the
hill, and not mind that curious little room up in the pointed
roof, in the oldest portion of the old cottage, for the present.

" She is a remarkably intelligent girl," thought Mr. Hugh
Kearney. " If she were a beauty, like Nancy Hogan, I
shouldn't be surprised at the admiration she inspires. And
surely intellect can have nothing to do with it ; for what do
those young fellows I saw crowding about her know about
intellect ? And sure she attracted my own notice before I
spoke a word to her, or even knew who she was. It would
be quite an interesting study to discover the secret of her
attraction." And he got over the stile behind the laurels
with the intention of commencing the interesting study at
once.

He started on entering the garden, for while his eyes were
turned to the window in the ivied gable, he found himself
face to face with Bessy Morris, who was just passing the
laurels with her head bent over her sewing. Possibly she
had seen him coming, from the window.

Hugh Kearney made a few commonplace remarks, and
asked one or two commonplace questions as he walked by
Bessy Morris's side towards the house. But when she turned
round at the end of the walk, somehow he could not bring
himself to turn round with her. Perhaps it was pride that
prevented him, and he wanted an *excuse*. So far, he was
merely on his way to the house. He found an excuse, however, for delaying her a minute at the little gate to inquire
whether her grandfather ever went to fish now ? There was
a little trout stream not far from Phil Morris's house, and
the old man, notwithstanding his lameness, was an expert
angler. Some years before, Hugh cultivated the gentle craft,
and the old weaver occasionally supplied him with a cast of
flies, when the contents of his own fishing-hook failed to lure
the trout to rise and get themselves hooked. Sometimes,
too, the rain would drive him from the stream for shelter to
the little house among the hawthorns ; and he would listen
for hours to the old " croppy's " reminiscences of '98, while
the shuttle was allowed to rest as he shouldered his crutch
to show how fields were won. Mr. Hugh Kearney used not
to be quite oblivious of the presence of old Phil Morris's

lively little granddaughter ; yet now he wondered why he
had not taken more notice of her at that time, and began to
admire her retrospectively, as she moved about the house or
sat reading or sewing near the window while the old man
talked, and the rain poured down till the young ducks swam
up to the very threshold, and seemed to consult among themselves whether they would have long to wait before they
could sail into the kitchen and explore every nook and corner
without setting foot on dry land. And the glances—for
Bessy Morris was a coquette before ever she saw a bold
dragoon—that went for nothing at that time, strange to say,
began now to produce the desired effect on Mr. Hugh
Kearney's heart, as memory brought them back again, while
he leant over the little gate to ask Bessy Morris whether her
grandfather ever went to fish now.

She had seen him looking over his flies and tackle a few
days before, and Hugh resolved to send his rod to Mat
Donovan to be repaired, and said to himself that he would
pay an occasional visit to the river during the spring and
summer. It would be very pleasant. Old Phil was as
entertaining as ever, and told him some capital stories at Ned
Brophy's wedding !

Hugh Kearney, as he walked alone up the hill, acknowledged to himself that he would rather have remained in the
garden with Bessy Morris than with any girl he knew—if he
had an excuse.

It was generally said and believed among his friends that
Hugh had never been in love. Yet he had a tinge of romance
in him, after a fashion. He was a capital builder of castles
in the air ; but be his castle never so stately, never so gorgeous
and glittering, it was to him cold and unattractive till love
shed its rosy light upon it. But in spite of all this, he never
was in love in downright earnest. He had met some—one
or two, perhaps—whom, under favourable circumstances, he
might have loved. But he had got a habit of weighing possible circumstances, and looking very far before him, which
made him keep clear of actual danger, and content himself
with castles in the air. His solitary rambles over the moors
and mountains were very favourable to castle-building ; while
his close attention to the management of the farm—with
which his rambles did not interfere at all—was calculated to

give a practical business-like turn to his mind. He found health and relaxation among the moors and mountains, and never thought the time lost which was spent with his dogs and his gun, or upon horseback, clearing stone walls and double ditches, after the foxhounds or the harriers. He read more, and derived more pleasure from books than his acquaintances suspected, and was far better informed than he himself knew. He did not parade his knowledge, and consequently got credit for knowing nothing. No day passed that he did not add to his store. But he read solely for the sake of the pleasure it afforded him ; and yet he almost shrank from opening a new volume unless he had some previous knowledge of the author or the subject. He felt no craving for novelty, and liked so well to return again and again to some cherished favourites that he often thought it would scarcely be a matter for regret if the art of bookmaking were lost, and he were henceforth obliged to limit his reading to the contents of his own shelves, the greater part of which he owed to that paragon of uncles, his mother's Uncle Dan. So that Mrs. Kearney could credit her Uncle Dan with Hugh's taste for reading as well as with Richard's taste for music.

After walking among the sheep and counting them, and even catching one and feeling its ribs, he put his hands in his pockets and looked about him. He could see two figures leaning over the little bridge ; and supposing them to be the doctor and the beauty of Castleview, Hugh smiled. He always sympathized with lovers. He considered Kathleen, too, singularly handsome ; and he thought Rose an exceedingly pleasant girl to spend an hour with. Yet he turned back at Tom Hogan's boundary a while ago, and had determined to do so from the first—though Miss Grace was quite troubled to think that it was because he was " huffed " by the way she " treated him " that he left them so abruptly. In fact he felt inclined to keep aloof from the house on the hill ; and there can scarcely be a doubt that the habit of looking before him had a good deal to do with producing this somewhat odd frame of mind for a young man who admired beauty and sympathized with lovers in general, and was so given to building castles in the air. Yet he never thought of looking before him in the case of the little house among the hawthorns. Was it because it was so humble a little house ? or was it because there was more attractive metal in it ?   Perhaps both these considerations helped to make Mr. Hugh Kearney forget his usual habit of looking to possible consequences in this instance.   And besides, he had an *excuse*. He would certainly send his fishing-rod to Mat Donovan to have it repaired.   And poor Mat Donovan !—had *he* nothing to do with the affair ?   Was he in no way concerned ?   Was it nothing to him who came or went to and from that little house in the whitethorns ?

At the present moment, however, nothing sublunary seems to be troubling Mat Donovan but how best to convey, with the greatest certainty and expedition, to Tom Cuddehy, of the Rath, the important intelligence that the long disputed hurling match could be decided to the satisfaction of all concerned in Maurice Kearney's kiln-field on the following Sunday.

"Maybe," said Mat to himself, as he trudged homeward after finishing the seed-sowing, "maybe I might meet some wan from that side of the forge.   If not I don't know how best to manage ; an' Tom is likely to be at the fair to-morrow."   He saw two horsemen riding towards him, and on looking more closely he observed that there had been a funeral in the little graveyard near the castle, for, besides the two horsemen, there were two or three cars on the road, and a group of people, mostly women, standing in the church-yard.

"I didn't hear of any wan bein' dead about this place," said Mat Donovan to himself, "so I suppose it must be some stranger.   Begor, I'm all right," he exclaimed, quickening his pace ; "that's ould Paddy Laughlan, an' he'll bring word uv the hurlin' to Tom Cuddehy."   He hurried on and came out upon the main road before the horseman had passed.

"A fine evenin', Mat," said old Paddy Laughlan ; "what way are you afther the weddin' ?   The divil a betther bout uv dancin' I see these fifty years than that last bout ye danced. Have you any news ?"

"Not a word strange.   Is id a funeral ye're at ?"

"'Tis," was the reply ; "a son uv William Maher's."

"Wisha, now," exclaimed Mat in astonishment.   "I didn't hear a word uv id."

"Oh, 'tis on'y the youngest little b'y.   I b'lieve he wasn't

more than about fifteen months ould. Where are ye comin'
from ?"

"Well, we wor finishin' the seed-sowin' at Raheen ; and
I'm goin' to give some directions to Jack Delany about the
plough-irons, as we're goin' to break a field. An' now as I'm
afther meetin' you, maybe you'd ——." Here Mat Donovan
stopped short. The second horseman, who had loitered behind,
rode up ; and as soon as Mat Donovan recognised him he
ceased speaking, and looked as if he had made a mistake.
The horseman was the young man from the mountain, who
kept gadding after a certain white jacket at Ned Brophy's
wedding, when his allegiance was lawfully due elsewhere.
Was Mat Donovan jealous of the young man from the mountain ? On the contrary, his discrimination in the matter of
the white jacket made Mat Donovan feel as if he were the
sworn friend of the young man from the mountain. Yet
Mat Donovan looked grave, and stopped short in the middle
of a sentence, the moment he recognised the young man
from the mountain in the horseman who now rode up and
resumed his place at old Paddy Loughlan's side.

"What's that you wor sayin', Mat ?" old Paddy Laughlan
asked.

"Nothin' uv any account," Mat replied. "I was thinkin'
uv sendin' a message to a friend up in that direction ; but I
won't mind id."

"I'll brin' a message, an' welcome, for you," returned the
old farmer. "Maybe 'tis to Ned Brophy ? If it is, I won't
mind turnin' down an' tellin' him, if I don't happen to meet
any wan on the road to send id by. He's a cousin uv Ned
Brophy's," he added, turning to the young man who rode by
his side, as if he thought it necessary to explain why he was
so civil to a poor man like Mat Donovan.

The young man only looked at his spurs, which were very
large and very bright—first at one and then at the other—
and seemed to think that old Paddy Laughlan was on the
whole too condescending—Ned Brophy's relationship to the
contrary notwithstanding.

"I won't mind id now," returned Mat. "Good evenin'
to ye."

"Bad luck to id for money," said Mat Donovan to himself
when Paddy Laughlan and his intended son-in-law had

ridden forward, " 'tis doin' harm here an' there. Well, she'll
have her twenty cows milkin' at any rate ; ay, begor, an' a
good-lookin' young fellow, too, though he's a gag itse'f.
But if ever a woman was fond uv a man Judy Laughlan was
fond of Tom Cuddehy. An' poor Tom'd marry her if she
hadn't a cross to bless herself wud in the mornin' ; an' he
tould me he would. An' all on account uv her four hundhred
pounds fortune they're to be separated. I don't know ; she
might be a happier woman wud Tom, though he has on'y a
small farm, an' that tillage, than ever she'll be in her fine
slate house wud her twenty cows comin' into her yard.
Well, I was near playin' the divil by axin' the ould fellow to
tell Tom Cuddehy about the field. The not a wan uv me
ever thought uv how id was betune 'em till the son-in-law
reminded me uv id. An' sure I might 'asy know, whin Tom
himse'f tould me she daren't look at him for the last twelvemonth. Now, if Tom dhraws her down, as he always do, the
next time I meet him, I know the first word that'll come to
my mouth is, that there's as good fish in the say as ever was
caught. An' cowld comfort that same ould sayin' is. Well,
he'll soon be out uv pain anyway. An' maybe 'twould be
well for more of us if we had the same story." He looked
up at the three poplar trees on the hill, and then at the
little house among the hawthorns. " Well, I must see about
the plough-irons," he added, rousing himself ; " an' who knows
but wan uv these cars at the church might be from Tom's
side uv the counthry, an' I can send him word about the
hurlin'."

CHAPTER XLV.

TOM CUDDEHY BIDS HIS OLD SWEETHEART GOOD-BYE.

BESSY MORRIS, too, had her reflections as she walked round
and round the little garden. But she had not much time to
indulge in them when Miss Kearney's return brought her
back to the little room, into which the sun was now shining
so brightly, that Mary seemed in its rosy light a being too
ethereally beautiful for a mere mortal.

" Now I wonder what that girl on the car is thinking of,"
said Grace.   " And why has she stopped there ?"

It was a farmer's cart, well stuffed with straw, over which
was spread a blue woollen quilt.   The young woman who
sat on the quilt, with the skirt of a rather showy gown spread
over the greater part of it, had turned quickly round, and
laying her hand on the shoulder of the driver, desired him
to stop.   It was just at the part of the road nearest to the
house, and Grace was able to see the young woman so distinctly, that the expression of her face suggested the remark
she had just made.

" Really," she continued, " there is something awfully
sullen about her.   She certainly has about as unprepossess-
ing a face as ever I saw."

" I know her, Miss," said Bessy Morris.   " She was at the
wedding ; and she's to be married to one of the richest men
at the mountain-foot."

" I can't approve of his taste," returned Grace.

" But she has four hundred pounds fortune, Miss."

" I suppose this is the intended," Grace remarked, pointing
to a man who was just walking by the Bush, with his horse's
bridle hanging over his arm.   " He is a rather good-looking
fellow."

" This is not the man, Miss," returned Bessy.   " I saw
him pass with her father a few minutes ago."

The young woman in the car was now observed to become
restless, and floundered about upon her quilt, as if trying to
fix herself in a more comfortable position ; and opened her
cloak and hooked it again ; and knocked her bonnet back
upon her poll when intending to push it the other way and
fasten it on her head ; and pulled from around her neck—
and immediately flung it back again with a swing—that
particular piece of finery which, even more than the yellow
gloves, seemed to have excited Peg Brady's indignation when
" indeed she see her goin' " to Ned Brophy's wedding, and
which Peg designated her " boy-o."   And, after exhibiting all
these symptoms of uneasiness, she bent her head and pressed
her gloved hand over her eyes, and then looked up.

" My goodness !" Grace exclaimed.   " Did ever any one see
such a metamorphosis ?   She is positively beautiful now."

It was really so.   The face that seemed a minute before

so dull and sullen was now radiant and all aglow with smiles.

" I never thought Judy Laughlan was so handsome a girl," said Bessy Morris, wonderingly. " Look at her teeth, Miss and her eyes ! I never saw such a change all in a minute."

'Twas all Tom Cuddehy's doing ; though he had not the least notion such was the case. He walked on with the bridle on his arm, and his eyes bent on the ground. He was just conscious that there was a car on the road before him, and on looking carelessly up, was startled, and did not know whether to be glad or sorry when he saw Judy Laughlan holding out her hand to him, laughing and blushing, and on the very brink of crying. Well, why should he not shake hands with her ? Why should they not be friends ? Of course there was no reason in life why they should not. So Tom Cuddehy stepped up close to the tail-board and shook hands very warmly with his old sweetheart. And it was such a long, long time since he had done the same thing before—though they were near neighbours. But she had been forbidden to speak to him ; and her father was heard to say that Tom Cuddehy was no match for his daughter ; and Tom Cuddehy was not the sort of person to put himself in the way of being insulted by a purse-proud old *boddagh*. And so the meadow between his house and old Paddy Laughlan's might as well have been the Great Sahara, so far as he and his old sweetheart were concerned. And now as she was going to be married to a rich man—the thought crossed his mind that she'd be driving in her jaunting-car the next time again he'd see her—she wanted, he supposed, to part friends with him. And, like a manly fellow that he was, he shook hands with her in a manly and friendly way.

" I know him now, Miss," Bessy Morris remarked. " He is the leader of the hurlers at the other side of the river, the same as Mat Donovan is at this side. But he got so stout since I saw him last I did not know him till he smiled." He waited, expecting that Judy Laughlan would speak ; but she only smiled and blushed, and kept back the tears as well as she could. " Oh, go on !" said she at last to the man who drove the car, as if she were really surprised, and could not by any means understand why he should have stopped and remained standing there in such a ridiculous manner for

nothing at all ! And then she said, " Good evening," with
another smile to Tom Cuddehy, and turned her head round
very quickly, as if she feared the horse was going to run
away. And while she watched every step the horse made,
she was all the time feeling in her pocket for her handkerchief, and, drawing it out in a slow, stealthy way, Judy
Laughlan bent her head and had a good cry. Tom Cuddehy
did not see this, as she was too far off. He only saw the
smile ; and as he caught hold of his horse's mane, and placed
his foot in the stirrup, Tom Cuddehy muttered to himself,
" God be wud ould times."

A hand was laid on his shoulder, and on turning round he
saw Mat Donovan at his side.

" I'm glad I met you," said Mat. " We can get the kiln
field for the match on Sunday."

" All right, Mat. I'll give notice to the boys to-morrow."

" I was thinkin' you might be at the fair to-morrow."

" No, I'm not goin'. You may depend on me for Sunday."

He rode off, and Mat Donovan turned into the back gate.

" I should not have thought that he was a leader, as you
say, like Mat," Mary observed, in reference to Bessy Morris's
last remark. " He's not a powerful-looking man like him."

" Oh, he has the name of being the best hurler in the
country ; but Mat was never beaten at throwing the sledge
and things of that kind ; though I'm told some people are
saying that Captain French will beat him. There is a great
deal of talk about it ; and you'd think it was a great battle
that is to be fought if you heard my grandfather talking
about it."

" If Mat were beaten," said Mary, " Tom Maher would
surely die of a broken heart."

" And Billy Heffernan," returned Bessy.

" As for that," Mary observed, " he is quite an idol with
them all. His defeat would be looked on as a dreadful
calamity. But I have not the least fear but that Mat will be
victorious in this instance, as he has always been."

CHAPTER XLVI.

" MAT DONOVAN IS KILLED !"

THE whole family were assembled in the parlour ; and Bessy
Morris, with her pretty bonnet and cloak on, and her little
basket on her arm, was talking to Miss Kearney near one of
the windows. The sun was just setting, and the shadows of
the trees on the grass were beginning to disappear, when a
flash of light through the branches of a large elm tree out in
the lawn made Mary start.

" Was it lightning ?" she asked.

" I thought so, Miss," Bessy replied.

But, on looking in the direction from which the flash
seemed to have come, they glanced at each other and smiled.
They saw Mat Donovan near the top of what remained of a
large hay-rick in the lawn. The rick had been cut away till
it looked like a rectangular tower, and had quite a picturesque
effect, its brown hue contrasting agreeably with the fir grove
behind. " Old hay is old gold," was a stereotyped phrase
with Maurice Kearney's visitors when they stood at the hall-
door and looked around the handsome lawn. Mat Donovan
was about commencing to cut away another slice of this old
gold, and it was the hay-knife he held in his hand, flashing
in the last rays of the sinking sun, that Mary and Bessy
Morris had mistaken for lightning. As he buried the sharp,
broad blade in the hay, and, bending over it, commenced to
cut away vigorously, Bessy Morris almost laughed outright ;
for she caught a snatch of a well-remembered air, which
rolled down from the rick in the same old, mellow voice she
often loitered to listen to on her way from the school beyond
the quarry long ago. Even then, child as she was, she used
to fancy it was of *her* Mat Donovan was thinking whenever
he sang—

> " Hi ! for it, hi ! for it still,
> And hi ! for the little house under the hill."

And what a world of drollery was in Mat's face while he
sang these words, and tossed the cherries over the hedge to
her ! The recollection of this came back so vividly now that
Bessy could not help laughing. She knew he could see her
grandfather's house from the hay-rick ; and the consciousness
that he was thinking of herself now, as of old, may have
had something to do with the laugh that leaped up to her
eyes as she turned to say " Good evening !" to Mary Kearney.
She intended to run away without speaking to any one else,
as the window at which they were standing was near the
door ; and Mary was just in the act of shaking hands with
her, when a cry from outside caused every one in the room
to start. It was the cry of a woman, and was followed by
the words, " Mat Donovan is killed !"

Mary looked instinctively to the hayrick. But, to her
utter amazement, it was gone ! There was the elm tree ;
and the grove beyond ; and the blue mountain ; and the sky.
But the tower-like remnant of the hayrick, upon which, one
short minute before, she saw Mat Donovan standing, had
vanished like a vision !

Everything without seemed calm and still ; and the last
thing she noticed, as she sank almost fainting into a chair,
was that the sheep were quietly cropping the grass.

" Oh ! Mat Donovan is killed !"

The cry was not very loud ; but the words were strangely
distinct, and no one could say from what particular direction
they had come, or whether the person who uttered them was
near or far off.

Hugh leaped through the window, and Mary saw that he
and Tom Maher rushed against each other near the elm tree
and fell. In an instant they were on their feet again, and
wildly flinging the hay about in armfuls. They were soon
joined by others ; and immediately the whole place was alive
with men, women, and children, who seemed to have sprung
up as if by magic from the ground. They were climbing
over the gate, and over the fences, and running wildly
through the lawn. Mrs. Kearney, who stood trembling at
the window, burst into tears ; not because she had, at the
moment, any distinct idea of what had occurred—but there
was that in the eager, anxious faces of the crowd that might
well have moved a harder heart than hers. Yet Bessy

Morris stood still, without moving a muscle, her lips apart, and her eyes fixed upon the mass of hay that now lay flung along the field. The constant falling of a drop of water will wear away a rock, and the constant nibbling of a flock of sheep will undermine a hayrick.

Hugh Kearney and a few others continued to fling the hay from the place where he judged Mat must have fallen; and his voice was heard shouting to the people to keep back.

After a while the hay was seen to move, and the tall form of the Thrasher rose out of it as from a heaving sea. There was a moment of breathless silence, and then with a wild cheer the crowd pressed upon him and threatened to smother him a second time. His sister Nelly flung her arms about him, and, with her face pressed against his bosom, sobbed violently. But his mother, pushing her way back till she got outside the crowd, sat down under the elm tree and rested her head upon her knees. Phil Lahy came close to Hugh Kearney's side and solemnly suggested a " little nourishment." And Billy Heffernan was seen running faster than ever he was known to run before, to bring the joyful news to Norah Lahy that Mat Donovan was alive and well.

But, notwithstanding that wild cheer, there were many faces there as pale as Mat Donovan's own, and several women were seen wiping the tears from their eyes.

" I knew something was to happen," said Phil Lahy—who, on the strength of picking up Hugh Kearney's hat that had fallen off, and saying to Barney Brodherick, " Barney, you are in the way," was pretty well satisfied that Mat the Thrasher owed his life principally to his, Phil Lahy's, individual exertions to save him—" I knew something was to happen," said Phil Lahy, wiping imaginary drops of sweat from his brow with his pocket-handkerchief. " A mad bull hunting me all night over ditches and hedges, till I thought my heart was broke." And Phil bent down his head and finished off the wiping with the skirt of his coat.

" And didn't I know something was to happen," exclaimed Kit Cummins. " That robber next doore to me to make off wud my fine new cloak while I was goin' to the well for a can uv wather." And Kit Cummins put her arms akimbo and poured out a torrent of invective against her next-door neighbour for stealing her " fine new cloak." 'Twas only a dream to be sure, and the cloak was at the time hanging safely over the wash-tub where she had flung it before going to bed, with the hood in the suds ; but that made no difference in life to Kit Cummins, and, with arms akimbo, she continued her harangue till her breath and her vocabulary seemed to be exhausted at the same moment, and she stopped short. Then from the outskirts of the crowd came the shrill response, " Gir-r-r-r-r out, you bla'guard !" and Kit Cummins turned round with a bounce, and was beginning again, when she was struck dumb with surprise on hearing a voice from the clouds right over her head.

" Mat," said the voice, " will I throw down your coat ?"

All eyes were turned upwards ; and Honor Lahy was seen to raise her hands as if imploring Providence to take pity on her ; for there was our friend Tommy as much at his ease on one of the highest boughs of the elm tree as if he lived in the old magpie's nest, into which he was just after peeping, and had run out merely to throw Mat Donovan his coat, which he had hung upon a branch of the tree before he commenced cutting the hay.

The little episode seemed to some extent to remove the gloom that hung over the crowd. And when Barney Brodherick walked round and round the Thrasher, surveying him from his shoes to the crown of his head, and from every possible point of view, with a look of the profoundest wonder ; and pushing back his hat on his poll, exclaimed solemnly— as if the miracle he had just witnessed was too great for his comprehension—" Begob, Donovan ! you'll never be killed ! —be a cock uv hay " ; there was a shout of laughter, in which Mat himself joined ; and all was gladness and congratulation as the people dispersed and moved towards home— some returning as they had come, through the fields, and others going out by the gate near the Bush and on by the road to the hamlet.

" Did you remark Bessy Morris ?" Grace asked.

" Yes ; and it has occurred to me she must be cold-hearted," replied Mary. " She was not in the least moved."

" That was because she was stunned," returned Grace.

" I don't think so. She said ' Good evening,'" quite calmly.

" Remark what I say," said Grace, with a knowing nod of

the head. " I was watching her. She can control her feelings. And you see she has forgotten her basket."

To some extent Grace was right. When the flash of the hay-knife called her attention to Mat Donovan, and she caught the words of the well-remembered song, Bessy's thoughts flew back to the old happy times. He was the hero of the district. Wherever she turned, she heard his name mentioned with praise. The old people who smoked their pipes round her grandfather's fire, and the boys and girls at school, were equally proud of him. And when he had accepted the challenge of some renowned champion from another parish, or even another county—for Mat Donovan's fame had gone far beyond the boundaries of his native district—with what nervous anxiety the result of the contest was looked for ! And with what a thrill of joy the news of their hero's victory was welcomed ! And then he was such a warmhearted, good-natured fellow—so gentle and so strong—without an atom of the bully or the braggart in him. Yes, Bessy Morris remembered the time when she was very proud and happy to think that she was one of Mat Donovan's first favourites. And how soon she came to think that she was a greater favourite than anybody else. Though how she arrived at this conclusion she would have found it difficult to explain. He never spoke of love to her, except in jest ; just as he was accustomed to do with every lively girl who was willing to carry on the joke. But somehow Bessy Morris was satisfied that in her case Mat Donovan's palavering was " half joking and whole earnest." He certainly did single her out at the dance, and escorted her from Mass, and dropped in with his " God save all here !" to the little house under the hill pretty often. But her winning ways, and their mutual relationship to Ned Brophy, and her grandfather's stories of '98, ought to have been enough to account for this, without jumping to the conclusion that Mat Donovan was " gone " about her, To this conclusion, however, Bessy Morris did jump ; and she was certainly very proud of Mat Donovan's regard for her. But she was not slow in discovering the power of her attractions elsewhere ; and when one or two young farmers began to show decided symptoms of being smitten, the thought began to occur to her that Mat Donovan, in spite of all his good qualities, and notwithstanding the esteem in which he was held, was only a poor labourer. But as time rolled on, and even the most ardent of her wealthier admirers dropped off one by one and took unto themselves wives, the unpleasant conviction forced itself upon her that, however easy she found it to catch a rich admirer, catching a rich husband was a different affair altogether. And at the time she left the country to reside with her aunt in Dublin she was beginning unconsciously to lean more and more upon the affection of her old lover—as she believed him to be—than she had done since her girlhood. But the novelty of the change, when she found herself in the midst of the city, with all its wonders and attractions, and the different sort of people with whom she came in contact, all but completely obliterated her rustic admirer from her thoughts. For a while she was quite intoxicated by the pleasures of the city. She was brought to the theatre, and the different places of Sunday and holiday resort, and flattered and courted, till the simple, but at the same time keen-witted and ambitious peasant girl had her head turned by the brilliancy of this new world. The value of money, too, became more apparent than ever ; and she felt a strong desire, not only to be able to afford to dress well, but to be beyond the danger of want—to be independent. But sad experience soon told her that making a fortune in the city was just as difficult as catching a rich husband in the country. And an " odd time," as she told Mary Kearney, when left alone with her own thoughts, she would think of her native place and the friends of her childhood. And, on returning to her old home after an absence of two years, and meeting Mat Donovan again, his fine, manly, honest face revived in a great degree the admiration she used to regard him with when she was little more than a child ; and her heart did warm to him that " night at Mrs. Murphy's," as she reminded him of the time he used to throw the cherries over the hedge to her—though well she knew he did not require to be reminded of it ! There was another consideration which helped to raise him in her esteem. She had seen some instances of misery and suffering in homes where there were more of the comforts and luxuries that money can procure than ever she herself dared to hope for. In fact, Bessy Morris was beginning to see that a poor man's wife might be very happy, and a rich man's very wretched.

The soldier's visit had greatly disturbed her; and she wished, though she scarcely knew why, that Mat Donovan should never know of it. No light matter, she was sure, could weaken his love for her. He would go on loving, without a hope that his love would ever be returned. But if he once thought her unworthy, she felt he would tear her from his heart for ever. And since her return from Dublin, the feeling that she could not afford to lose his regard was daily growing stronger. And when the cry, "Mat Donovan is killed!" struck upon her heart, and for some minutes she thought his was stilled for ever, a sense of desolation fell upon her, and she felt as if she were alone in the world. She was really stunned, as Grace said. And when that wild cheer announced to her that he was safe, she felt like one just rescued from drowning, and too exhausted to experience the full sense of joy and gratitude which one ought naturally to feel on being snatched, as it were, from the dark grave back to the bright world, with all its life and sunshine— never so bright, never so full of life, and light, and gladness, as when it is on the point of being lost to us for ever. Grace, then, was mistaken in supposing that only self-control had anything to do with Bessy Morris's calmness when she mechanically bade them "Good evening" and left the parlour to go home.

He *was* thinking of her while he sang the old refrain —when was it he was not thinking of her?—and when he felt the rick coming down with him, and expected in another second to be flung lifeless on the ground below, the last thought that swelled his heart was a "God be with you," to Bessy Morris. He then became insensible. Consciousness, however, soon returned, and he felt that he was being suffocated to death. Then he thought of his grey-haired mother and his sister, and how desolate their little home would be when he was gone; and feeling that he was relapsing into unconsciousness, he prayed fervently that God would have mercy on his soul. At this moment he fancied that the weight that was crushing him became lighter, and, exerting all his strength, he raised himself upon his hands and knees, and pulling the hay from about his mouth he found that he could breathe. But the weight of those who were pulling away the hay, when they happened to stand directly over him,

threatened to crush him down again; and seizing a moment
when they had stepped aside, and the pressure was lightest,
he made a vigorous effort, and emerged into the light like a
lusty swimmer through the breakers.

Bessy Morris's first impulse was to get home without
meeting Mat Donovan. She was hurrying through the
kitchen in order to get out to the road by the back gate,
when she almost knocked against Nelly Donovan, who was
running into the house for a drink of water for her brother.
Their eyes met, and the looks of surprise and inquiry with
which they regarded each other, seemed to have something
of distrust or suspicion in it. Their looks were not alike,
however, for while Nelly's expressed reproach, Bessy's seemed
to indicate a dread of being detected. If Nelly Donovan
had spoken what she thought, she would have said, " Is that
all you care about him, you heartless thing ?" And if Bessy
Morris gave utterance to her thoughts she would have said,
" I wonder has she found out how much I care for him ?"

Bessy, however, recovered quickly from her surprise, and
at once decided upon making the best of the situation.

" I saw all from the window, Nelly," said she. " Thank
God he is safe. It must be a great shock to your poor
mother."

" An' what raison are you runnin' away ?" inquired Nelly,
who was the soul of candour.

" Well," replied Bessy—who was not quite so candid—
" I thought it would be only troublesome to you and your
mother if I went to talk to him. I knew ye'd rather have
him all to yourselves. And, besides, poor Mat himself might
rather be left quiet after such a shock. So I said to myself
I'd slip out by the back gate and run home, when I saw he
was safe."

This seemed natural enough to Nelly Donovan, and she
was satisfied.

" Well, maybe you're right," said she. " But, for all that,
I believe he'd be glad to see you, no matter what way he'd
be."

" Well, Nelly," returned Bessy, after some hesitation,
" I'd rather meet him when there would not be so many
people about him."

" Call in when you're passin'," rejoined Nelly, " an' my

mother an' all uv us will be glad to see you. Though they say," she added, shaking her head, " you're too proud now for your ould friends."

" That's not true, Nelly."

" Well, I don't say it is. But I must run out wud the dhrink of wather to him ; an' as you don't like to get into the crowd, I hope I'll find you sittin' in the little chair you wor so fond uv long ago."

The allusion to long ago had a decidedly softening effect upon Bessy's heart ; which, perhaps, wanted softening a little. But Mat Donovan's heart—which did not want softening at all, but rather the contrary—felt very heavy indeed, when he caught a glimpse of her as she tripped lightly by the gate, seeming not to give a thought to himself.

He raised the cup of water to his lips, and as he looked into his sister's face, and glanced at his mother sitting at the foot of the tree, the pain which the thought of Bessy's indifference had caused left his heart ; and the old smile came back into Mat Donovan's face, as he looked from one to another of the friends who still lingered about him. There was Phil Lahy, holding the coat which Tommy had dropped from the tree with an expression of countenance suggestive of woolsacks, and benches of bishops, and colleges of cardinals, and holy fathers, and martyrs and confessors in general, all rolled into one. And there was Honor, such a picture of hearty, homely good nature, that it did him good to look at her, thinking, in her own mind, whether she could by any means take forcible possession of him, and bring him home with her to rouse him, after his smothering, with a cup of tea of fabulous strength, out of the little black tea-pot. And there was Mary Kearney, as beautiful as an angel, coming from the house, and giving him her hand, with such a heavenly smile, and telling him how glad she was he had escaped unhurt. And there was Grace following her example in her own way ; and, strange to say, Mat held Grace's hand so tightly and so long, that she at first felt pleased and amused, and then looked up in surprise, and almost snatched away her hand ; for there was something about Grace that reminded Mat of throwing cherries over a hedge and other little incidents of bygone days—and so, unconsciously he held her hand and squeezed it ; and Grace laughingly submitted.

Perhaps Grace would have frowned and thought it no compliment at all if she knew he was thinking all the time of Bessy Morris. And yet to Mat's mind the greatest compliment a human being could be paid was to be thought like Bessy Morris.

Then Mrs. Kearney herself came out, and, wiping the tears from her eyes, declared that her heart she thought had broken, the shock she got was so great—particularly as it reminded her of the day the horse ran away with her Uncle Dan and broke his collar-bone—and insisted that Mat should come in and take something ; a request which Maurice Kearney seconded by seizing Mat by the collar, which he was induced to let go when Mat requested permission to put on his coat. And as Mat Donovan put on his coat, he looked round him again, and wondered that there was one particular face which he could not see anywhere. He looked again and again, and tried to think of a plausible reason for the absence of this particular face as he walked towards the house. And turning round on reaching the door-step, he took another look all round, and rubbing his poll with his open hand, Mat Donovan called out :

" Do any uv ye know where is Billy Heffernan ?"

No one could tell where Billy Heffernan was. And as he had been seen watering his mule at the " lough " half-an-hour before, every one wondered what had become of him. And, in spite of all the kindness and congratulations showered upon him, Mat Donovan felt as if a screw were loose somewhere, when Billy Heffernan's face was nowhere visible.

CHAPTER XLVII.

BILLY HEFFERNAN WONDERS WHAT IS " COMING OVER " NORAH.

BILLY HEFFERNAN had run off over ditches and hedges in a straight line, with his eyes fixed upon the chimney of Phil Lahy's old house, and never stopped till he stood behind Norah's straw chair. And then Billy Heffernan did stop very suddenly, and made a foolish pretence of having walked in very slowly and carelessly, and with no object in the world except to pass away the time. The instantaneous change from break-neck speed and breathless haste to a lazy lounge, as he moved towards Phil Lahy's shop-board, caused Norah to smile. He took up a piece of chalk and commenced writing the letters of the alphabet in round-hand on the lap-board very carefully and deliberately till he came to the letter *g*, and then Billy ventured to glance sideways at Norah, sitting in her straw-chair, with her wasted hand on the head of the rough terrier.

Now, it occurred, at the last moment, to Billy Heffernan, that to communicate the joyful news of Mat Donovan's safety too abruptly to Norah might give her a shock that would prove injurious to her. And, in his own way, he set about correcting the mistake he had made. But, as he glanced at Norah, and saw how calm and collected she was, he thought she must not have heard of the accident to Mat Donovan at all, and resolved to go on with his writing till her father and mother arrived. To his great surprise, however, before he had got half-way to the end of the lap-board, Norah said :

" Well, Billy, why don't you tell me all about Mat ?"

He turned quickly round, and to his great astonishment saw not the least symptom of anxiety or agitation about her ; but, on the contrary, she seemed as if trying to suppress a smile.

" She knows nothin' about id," thought Billy Heffernan. " Begor, I'm glad uv id ; for I was afeard it might frighten the life out uv her. An' 'twas well she tuck no notice uv the way I ran in. 'Twas well I didn't tumble up against her, I was in such a pucker to make her mind 'asy about Mat."

" Billy," said Norah, " why don't you tell me all about what's after happening to Mat Donovan ? Nelly was here with me when the report went about that he was killed, and she was terribly frightened."

Her apparent indifference about the matter astonished Billy Heffernan beyond expression ; and he stared at her with open mouth for nearly a minute before he was able to reply.

" He's all right," said Billy at last.

"Oh, yes, I know that," returned Norah quite calmly. "But he was in danger."

Billy Heffernan's astonishment now took a different turn; and, as he looked into her dark eyes and pale, spiritual face, he began. with that proneness to superstition for which he was remarkable to fancy that she had supernatural knowledge of events passing beyond the ken of mere bodily senses. She seemed to know what was passing in his mind and the covert smile about her lips and in her eyes tended to strengthen Billy Heffernan's half-formed suspicion that she must be in communion with those invisible beings of whose existence in earth and air he had no more doubt than he had of his own.   But, notwithstanding the plenitude of his faith in such matters, it is worthy of remark that Billy Heffernan always held out stoutly against the " black dog "—which piece of infidelity procured for him the undying enmity of Kit Cummins.

"You're wondering at me, Billy," said Norah, giving the smile full play at last, and revealing her ivory-white teeth; which somehow had the effect of imparting a deeper shade of melancholy to her look. "You think I'm a witch or something of that kind."

"Begor, if you're anything at all id must be somethin' good," he answered, seriously.

"Well, I was frightened, Billy," said Norah. "Poor, brave, honest Mat Donovan, with every one so proud of him, and fond of him ! But I said to myself that God was good, and that I'd offer up a few prayers for him. Then I heard the shout, and I knew he was safe. And I said to myself, too, he must be after escaping some danger, or the people wouldn't shout that way. And Billy," she added, smiling again, " I knew you'd be the first to remember me and to relieve my mind. So when I saw you rushing in, I was sure all was right."

Billy returned to his chalking and went on carefully till he came to *m*—which letter was so well executed that he stopped to admire it—but said nothing.

"Tell me what happened, Billy," said Norah, leaning her head against the back of her chair, as if, after all, she felt weary and exhausted.

Billy told her how a high rick, that was higher than the top

of the chimney, and, in fact, as far as he could judge, as high
as the beech-tree, had fallen while Mat Donovan was " cutting
a bench " up near the top of it. And how some thought he
was " made bruss of " on the ground ; and others that it was
only smothered he was by the hay on top of him ; while a
few asserted positively that Mat was " ripped open " by the
sharp hay-knife. But Billy was able to bear witness that he
had seen Mat with his own eyes, quite whole, neither
pulverised nor embowelled, and, to all appearances, having
the free use of his lungs.

" I'm very glad he's not hurt," said Norah. " But if he
was," she added thoughtfully after a pause, " he'd have a
good nurse in Nelly to take care of him."

" So he would," returned Billy Heffernan ; " and his
mother, too."

" Nelly is very good," continued Norah. " She's the best-
hearted poor thing in the world. And she's very fond of
me. She and me were always great friends, Billy."

" So ye wor," returned Billy. " Always."

" And if Mat met with an accident, he'd have some one
to take care of him," rejoined Norah, as if thinking aloud.

" But, Billy," she continued, " if anything happened you,
you'd have no one. And what would you do ?"

" I'd take my chance," Billy answered. " God is good."

" That's true," she replied fervently ; " God is good. But
'tis hard for you to feel happy all alone by yourself. And
you are going on very well, by all accounts, and getting more
comfortable every year."

" I know who I have to thank for that," he replied.

" Who ?" she asked in surprise.

" Yourse'f, Norah," returned Billy Heffernan, leaning on
his elbow upon the shop-board and proceeding with his
chalking. " You know what I was before you made me take
the pledge ; and that's what I couldn't do for the priest himse'f. An' I know I'd never be able to keep id on'y for you
prayin' for me, as you said you would. I do be wondherin'
now at myse'f. I can hardly b'lieve I'm the same unfortunate Billy Heffernan that every wan used to have compassion
for, when I see the respect they all have for me now. Begor,
I think sometimes 'tis humbuggin' me they do be, the way
they talk to me an' ax my advice about this or that, when I

think how the smallest child in the place used to have a
laugh at me before."

"Well, if I gave you a good advice at that time, Billy,
sure you ought to listen to another good advice from me
now ?"

"What is id ?'

"Well, you know what I mean," she answered, as if she
wished to avoid being more explicit. "I often think of id
this while back, when Nelly Donovan and myself do be talking about old times."

"Norah," said Billy Heffernan. quite agitated, as he hurriedly wiped out the letters he had chalked with such pains
on the lap-board, "for God's sake don't talk to me any more
that way. I'm well enough as I am. I want for nothin'.
An' if I am lonesome idse'f, 'tis lonesome I'd rather be."

Norah smiled. She smiled a little while before, because
she was amused. But this was a different kind of smile
altogether. Yes ; Billy Heffernan's refusal to listen to what
she was about proposing to him gave her pleasure. Yet, if he
did listen to her advice and followed it, it would have given
her pleasure too—pleasure sweetened by self-sacrifice. She
would be glad to see Billy Heffernan and Nelly Donovan
happy. Yet she was glad that Billy Heffernan would not
listen to her plan for his happiness. Self-sacrifice is sure of
its reward either way.

"Well, Billy," said Norah Lahy, "you will remember my
words hereafter."

Oh ! that "hereafter"—how heavily it fell upon his heart !
His back was still turned to her ; and with one elbow on
the table, and shading his eyes with his hand, he went on
with the chalking again ; but instead of carefully formed
letters, he covered the board with mere dots and shapeless
figures. He felt almost angry with her. "Sure she has no
right," he said to himself, "to be talkin' that way. Don't
she know I'd as lief be dead as the way I do be when id comes
into my head ?" And Billy held the lap-board near his
eyes—for it was now nearly dark—and seemed to be trying
to decipher the hieroglyphics he had traced upon it. "I
don't know what's comin' over her this while back," he continued, glancing stealthily at Norah ; "every wan used to be
remarkin' that you'd never hear a word from her that'd look

as if she was thinkin' uv dyin' at all. Even her mother says she never heard a word about id from her. But this is the third turn wud her dhrawin' id down to me these days back. She began t'other night about the evenin' I carried her over the sthrame. There's some change comin' over her I'm afeard, or she wouldn't be goin' on this way."

He was interrupted in his reflections by the entrance of Honor Lahy, who—rather to the surprise of Billy—was immediately followed by her husband.

" Wisha, is id there you are, Billy ?" exclaimed Honor. " Mat is after axin' where you wor ; an' not wan uv us could tell him. We wor all wonderin' what happened you."

" I ran down to tell Norah, whin I see he wasn't hurt. I thought she might be unaisy."

" Well, well," returned Honor, as if she felt quite ashamed of herself, " see how not wan uv us ever thought uv that. An' sure I might 'asy know her mind'd be throubled ; an' for all I never thought uv id." She knelt down as she spoke, and arranged Norah's shawl more comfortably about her shoulders. " We had no right," she continued, as she pinned the shawl, " to run away an' lave you by yourse'f. But I got such a start thinkin' poor Mat was killed, that I didn't know what I was doin'. An' sure on'y the mercy uv God 'tis killed he'd be."

Phil had flung himself in a chair in an almost gasping condition after his exertions. He fixed a severe glance on his wife, and even on his daughter, and then shook his head and looked into the fire. There was no sign, not the shadow of a symptom of a " little nourishment," and Phil Lahy seemed to have made up his mind that all Christian charity had vanished from the world, and that there was nothing left for him but to be resigned. And he *was* resigned ! He did not complain in the least. No murmur would ever escape his lips. He was never a grumbler ; never " a man for complaining." And in a spirit of resignation and self-abnegation, Phil Lahy dismissed all thought of his own sufferings from his mind, and only thought, as a patriot and philanthropist, of the grievances of his fellow-men.

" Billy," said he, addressing himself to Billy Heffernan, who had turned round and now stood with his back to the shop-board, resting against it, " these are quare times."

" How so ?" Billy asked.

" Well, I'm afther havin' a talk wud that poor crawler, Tom Hogan ; and the fact is I'm not the betther uv id."

" How so ?" Billy asked again.

" I was never a man of extreme views," returned Phil. " I admire some of the extreme party for their genius, and I never took part in the cry against them. But I'm a man of moderate views, and always was. Old Phil Morris and I could never agree on some points. But, Billy, 'tis enough to knock moderation out of any man to talk to a crawler ! You heard the conversation I had with that man sitting at this fire ?"

" I remember," replied Billy Heffernan. " An' Mat re- marked as we wor goin' home, that all he was worth in the world was sunk in his little spot—that he hadn't a penny ; on'y as fast as he'd have id lettin' id all go in dhrainin' an' buildin'."

" Well, that same Tom Hogan calls me over an' I passin'. ' Phil,' says he, ' I couldn't help laughin' a while ago when I thought uv you. Faith, a person 'd think,' says he, ' that you knew what they wor goin' to do.'   ' What do you mane, Tom ? says I—speakin' as civil as I could to him, because Norah here begged uv me not to be severe on him, since the way he began thremblin' when I spoke about risin' his rent from thirty-eight to forty-eight shillin's an acre. So I asked him civilly what did he mane. ' Well, my rint is riz,' says he, ' just as you said id would.' I thought 'twas humbuggin' me he was, till I remembered I see Darby Ruadh turnin' into his gate a start before. ' Tom,' says I, ' are you in airnest, or is id jokin' you are ?' ' He is in airnest, Phil,' the wife makes answer. ' Darby is afther given us notice of another rise." I looked at him," continued Phil, turning round in his chair and resting his elbow on the back of it, so as that he could look up into Billy Heffernan's face, of which, however, there was not light enough to afford more than a dim outline—" I looked at him ; and there he was, breakin' his heart laughin' ; ' 'Tis on'y two shillin's an acre, Phil,' says he, ' to make id the even money. A couple uv pounds a year won't make much difference. But whin Darby walked in an' spoke uv another rise, begor, I thought of what you wor sayin' to me last night. An' wasn't id dhroll,' he says, laughin', ' that

your words come to pass all at wance?' ' Tom,' says I, ' I
have nothin' to say to you.' ' Darby tould me,' says the wife,
' that Mr. Pender was sorry, but that he couldn't help id
whin the ordher came down from the landlord.' But 'tisn't
Tom Hogan that's throublin' me," continued Phil, after a
pause ; " but I fear we're goin' to have some bad work in the
counthry !"

" What bad work, Phil ?" his wife asked in alarm.

" Well, that blessed bird," he returned, " that came in to
light the lamp t'other night—honest Darby—and Wat
Corcoran wor overheard makin' some remarks to-day about
bein' near stirrin' times about here. An' we all know what that
manes. Mat Donovan is likely to lose his little garden, too.
An' that's a bad sign. An' there's poor Mick Brien that they
beggared. Kept him hangin' on expectin' they'd give him a
little spot somewhere, if 'twas on'y a skirt uv the bog, till
every penny he had was gone uv whatever thrifle he was able
to make by sellin' the few things he had left afther bein'
turned out uv the nice little farm that his people lived in for
hundreds uv years. Well, Maurice Kearney gave him a
couple uv bundles uv straw to cover the roof over his wife
an' childher. An' just when he had id finished, the guardian
angels come to tell him he must go out ; that the cabin is to
be pulled down, as such cabins can't be allowed on the
property any longer. I'm tould he's out uv his mind. The
wife is thought to be in a decline, an' two uv the childher
have the faver. An' the thought uv the poorhouse sets him
mad."

At these last few words the tears began to fall silently
from Norah's eyes ; and Billy Heffernan, on seeing them
dropping down one by one, began to be angry with some
one or other, and felt a strong desire to relieve his feelings
by beating Darby Ruadh and Wat Corcoran black and blue.
Indeed at that moment Billy would have faced a whole
legion of " guardian angels," and done heaven knows what
desperate things, if he had the chance.

" So you see, Billy," said Phil Lahy, " that thinkin' of
such things is enough to make any man violent."

" 'Tis thrue !" replied Billy Heffernan, almost fiercely.

" I of'en think uv Mick Brien's wife," Honor observed, as
if she were thinking aloud, while, with her chin on her hand

and her elbow resting on the shop-board, she gazed at the moon through the branches of the beech-tree. " She was sich a good, charitable woman. 'Tis too good she was. Of'en Father M'Mahon said 'twas a pity she wasn't as rich as Damer."

" 'Tis many a piggin uv milk she made me dhrink," said Billy Heffernan, " when I'd be passin' comin' from Clo'mel. An' Mick brought home my ould coat that I put about him the last night I was passin'. I'd rather he'd keep id," added Billy, " for the divil a much harm a wettin' ever done me. But Mick wouldn't be satisfied. An' whin he was comin' for the straw to Misther Kearney's, he brought home the coat. Ould Phil Morris gave him the lend uv his ass to brin' the straw. An' sure if he kem to me for the mule I'd give her to him an' welcome. But he says he thought I might be on the road. An' he knew Phil Morris's ass was idle."

" Were you talking to Bessy Morris since she came home ?" Norah asked, after an interval of silence. " She ran in to see me, but she had no time to delay."

" She was at the weddin'," returned Billy; " an' I called——. An' I met her above the Bush "—he broke off—" this mornin', as she was comin' to Misther Kearney's to make a dhress for Miss Mary."

Norah raised her eyes quickly when Billy hesitated and seemed embarrassed after saying he " called in." And when he turned the " calling in " to meeting Bessy on the road, she did not know what to think. She admired Bessy Morris very much, and liked her pretty well ; though she never did warm to her so much as to Nelly Donovan and one or two more of her schoolfellows.

She saw how much superior to them all Bessy was in many respects ; but in spite of her cleverness and winning ways, Norah could not help thinking that Bessy Morris wanted heart. She often accused herself of being unjust, but she could not reason herself out of this impression. Many little instances of selfishness on Bessy's part would occur to her ; but it was Bessy's love of conquest and admiration that tended most to prejudice Norah Lahy against her.

And now, on observing Billy Heffernan's embarrassment, she thought Bessy might have been trying the power of her fascination upon him, too. It was but the thought of a moment, dismissed almost as soon as formed. But Norah did say to herself, after a moment's reflection, that she " would not like it."

Billy Heffernan's embarrassment, however, was simply caused by remembering his resolution to say nothing about the dragoon.

" I think," Phil Lahy observed, " I ought to take a walk up to see Mat."

" Give him time to be done his supper, at any rate," returned his wife.

" Very well," he rejoined. " But what I'm afraid uv is that this fall may come against him in throwing the sledge with the captain. I'll advise Mat not to venture. 'Tis too serious a matter. And—and," added Phil Lahy, in a dignified way, " a man should not forget his duty to the public. That's Mat's weak point. He can't be got to see that he's a public character. The people at large are concerned. The credit of Knocknagow is at stake. So I must explain this to Mat. The captain, too, though a good fellow, is an aristocrat. That fact cannot be lost sight of. So I must explain matters to Mat. An' if he's not in condition, he's bound to decline throwing the sledge with Captain French on the present occasion."

" Do you think there's any danger he might be bet ?" Billy Heffernan asked, with a blending of terror and incredulity in his look.

" There's no knowin', Billy," returned Phil. "A man 'd want to be careful upon important occasions ; particularly when the public are—are——the fact is," said Phil, at a loss for a word, " I must have a talk with Mat."

" Begor," returned Billy Heffernan, " you're afther makin' me someway uneasy. Good evenin' to ye."

" Good evenin', Billy," returned Phil Lahy, benevolently. " Don't let anything I'm afther sayin' prey on your mind. Let us hope for the best."

" I'll never b'lieve," returned Billy Heffernan, stopping before he reached the shop door, " I'll never b'lieve the man was ever born that's able to bate Mat Donovan at the sledge."

" You are right, Billy—unless he does himself injustice— an' what I want to prevent is that. You know yourse'f Mat

is a soft soart of a fellow ; and requires a friend to advise him.
Are you goin' up that way yourse'f ?"

"No," Billy replied. "I have to mend the mule's
breechin', an' to fill the load, as I'm to be on the road to-
night."

"Billy," said Mrs. Lahy, "maybe you'd take a walk down
again, as I want a box of candles an' a few other things that
I'm nearly out uv."

"Very well," he replied. "I'll take a walk down before
I go to bed." And as Billy, after lighting one of his antediluvian tapers, sat down upon his antediluvian block, to
repair Kit's harness, he felt so oppressed and nervous, thinking of the strange change he had noticed in Norah Lahy, and
of the possibility of Captain French beating Mat Donovan at
the sledge, he heartily wished for the long summer days,
when he could stretch upon a bank in the lonesome bog and
listen to the whistle of the plover.

CHAPTER XLVIII.

THE " DEAD PAST " AND THE " LIVING PRESENT."—MRS.
DONOVAN'S SAD FACE.

BESSY MORRIS tripped lightly up the hill, till she came to the
clipped hedge. And then she began to walk more and more
slowly, with her eyes bent on the ground. After passing
the little gate and the neatly thatched house, she stopped,
and, turning round, looked at the clipped hedge and up at
the old cherry-tree. And while she looked, the hedge grew
green, and the bare branches of the cherry-tree were covered
with leaves, through which the cherries peeped, and seemed
to whisper above the hum of the bees—" 'Tis for *you* we have
grown red and ripe and juicy ; for you we are kept here so
long ; for you and nobody else, little Bessy Morris !"—just as
the cherries used to whisper long ago. The trees flung their
shadows across the white and dusty road ; the birds twittered
among the branches ; the swallows skimmed over the bright
little river ; the distant lowing of the cows floated upon the

clover-scented air ; the thrush's evening song rang out bold
and clear from the bushy glen ; the blue smoke stole up
through the grey sally-trees : and she was a happy, innocent
school-girl.

The deepening shadows and the bleak, wintry landscape
called her back from the dead past to the living present ; and
after a moment's hesitation, she turned in from the road, and
raised the latch of Mat Donovan's door.

There was no change. Everything was as it used to be.
The little chair of which Nelly spoke was in its old place ;
and she could almost fancy she saw the Bessy Morris of the
old time sitting in it. And how fond they all were of her
then ! A shadow seemed to fall upon her face as the thought
struck her that she had let these true friends drop almost
completely out of her memory, except Mat himself ; and if
she gave him a thought, it was only in some moment of disappointment or mental suffering, when the recollection of his
unchanging love would cross her mind. Her cheek flushed
as she reflected how little she had prized that love ; and for
a moment she felt as if she had been not only ungrateful but
false. She looked again at the familiar objects around. The
dresser—the wheel upon which Mrs. Donovan had given her
her first lesson in spinning—Mat's hurly over the fire-place
—everything just the same ! As her eye rested on the famous
Knocknagow drum, hung so high up that none but Mat
himself could reach to it, she smiled, and her thoughts seemed
to take a more cheerful turn. Seeing a slate upon the little
window—a blue slate without a frame, and having only one
side polished—she took it in her hand, for it reminded her of
the old school days. A little to her surprise, she saw there
was a sum carefully worked out upon the slate, and some
sentences correctly and fairly written. The fact was, Mat
Donovan had taken to study of late. He endeavoured to
induce a sufficient number of pupils to pay half-a-crown in
advance, to make it worth the schoolmaster's while to take a
lodging in the village—instead of sleeping at a farmer's house
two miles away—and open a night-school for the winter. But
a sufficient number of half-crowns not being forthcoming,
Mat Donovan set about teaching himself—greatly to the distress of his mother, who could see no possible explanation of
so strange a proceeding, but an intention on Mat's part of

" going to join the peelers " ; which, to her mind, was as bad
as going into the poor-house, and infinitely worse than going
to be hanged. For poor Mrs. Donovan got that sad face of
hers one bright summer day in the year '98, when her
father's house was surrounded by soldiers and yeomen, and
her only brother, a bright-eyed boy of seventeen, was torn
from the arms of his mother, and shot dead outside the door.
And then a gallant officer twisted his hand in the boy's
golden hair, and invited them all to observe how, with one
blow of his trusty sword, he would sever the rebel head from
the rebel carcase. But one blow, nor two, nor three, nor
ten, did not do ; and the gallant officer hacked away at the
poor boy's neck in a fury, and was in so great a passion, that
when the trunk fell down at last, leaving the head in his
hand, he flung it on the ground, and kicked it like a foot-
ball ; and when it rolled against the feet of the horrified
young girl, who stood as if she were turned to stone near the
door, she fell down senseless without cry or moan, and they
all thought she too was dead. She awoke, however, the
second next day following, just in time to kiss the poor
bruised and disfigured lips before the coffin-lid was nailed
down upon them. But the sad look was in her face, and
never wholly left it from that hour. It was beginning to
clear away in after years ; till once again the house was surrounded by soldiers. They came with the sheriff and bailiffs.
It was not a bright summer day, but a bitter cold day in the
bleak December this time. Yet, as she and her father and
mother passed through the glittering bayonets and shining
accoutrements that filled the yard, that fatal summer day in
'98 came back with such strange vividness that she thought
she felt her brother's head strike against her foot ; and again
she fell down senseless without cry or moan. After that the
sad look became fixed and permanent, and she was destined
to carry it with her into her coffin. It was the shadow of a
curse.

So Mat Donovan's slate and pencil made the sad look in
his mother's face a shade sadder, lest by any chance he should
be qualifying himself for the " peelers." She would rather a
thousand times see him dragged out and shot like the bright-
eyed boy whose head rolled against her foot in '98, or hanged
from the old cherry-tree in the garden.

It strikes us that statesmen might learn something from the sad look in Mrs. Donovan's face.

Bessy Morris carelessly turned over the slate, and as she looked at the unpolished back, a strange light came into her eyes. Every inch of the back of Mat Donovan's slate was covered with B's.

She laid the slate down quickly on hearing his footstep, and looked along the road, as if she had been brought to the window by the braying of Mr. Beresford Pender's tin-horn, which he had just put to his lips to warn all whom it might concern to keep out of the way of the wheels of his tax-cart, and clear the road for a " gentleman." And how Mat Donovan did start when he saw her ! For a moment he could scarcely credit the sight of his eyes, that it was really Bessy Morris, all alone in his own house. Recovering, however, from his surprise, he advanced a step or two and held out his hand.

" You're welcome !" said he, with that odd smile of his. He thought there was something very cold in her manner as she placed her hand in his. Not the faintest pressure could he feel from that dear little hand.

" You're welcome !" was all he could say. And as he said it a second time, for want of something else, there was a very little pressure upon his fingers, just as if she couldn't help it.

" You had a narrow escape," said she ; " I hope you are not hurt."

" 'Tis nothin'," he replied, letting her hand go suddenly, for he felt that she was trying to withdraw it. But the withdrawing of the hand would not have caused that pain he felt coming about his heart again, if he knew it was done simply because she saw his sister Nelly coming towards the door.

" 'Tis nothin'," said he, " on'y a tumble in the hay."

He was surprised and displeased to see that Nelly took scarcely any notice of Bessy Morris ; but he did not know they had met a few minutes before. He watched with some anxiety to see if his mother's greeting would be as cold as his sister's ; and when the old woman came in, with her sad face seeming sadder than ever, and looked first surprised, and then glad, and then held out her hand to Bessy and said,

"You are welcome," in such a kind way, Mat felt quite happy.

"And won't you sit down?" said Mrs. Donovan, with a brighter look than Mat had seen in the sad face for many a long day.

" 'Tis getting late, ma'am," returned Bessy; sitting down at the same time in the little old chair.

Mrs. Donovan sat down too, and, putting her hand under her chin, looked into Bessy's face for a full minute. It was plain she was thinking of the bright little girl who used to sit in that old chair a few years before, and so delight them all with her merry laugh and her ready wit, and her quaint, half-childish, half-womanly ways.

"Is id yourself that's in id at all?" said Mrs. Donovan.

Bessy laughed; but she was moved by the kind tone of the old woman's voice, and still more by her look. She felt it was in such a tone and with such a look her own mother would have addressed her.

"An' how is the old man?" she continued. " 'Tis a long time since he stopped to talk to me now about the year uv the hill, an' the hangin' an' the floggin' an' all. An' Bessy, avoorneen, had ye any account of your father since? Or is there any tale or tidin's uv him?"

"Not a word, ma'am," Bessy answered.

"Well, Bessy, as sure as you're sittin' in that chair a man from near the colliery met him in America, an' was talkin' to him in his own house. An' he had carpets on his flure, he says. The man he was tellin' was in here wud me."

"Well, we heard about that, ma'am; but 'twas a long time ago since the man you speak of saw him, or rather thinks he did. For all he could remember was his surname, and that he made inquiries about my grandfather."

"Well, from what the man from the colliery said, I'm a'most sure 'twas your father he was talkin' to," said Mrs. Donovan, beginning to rock herself softly from side to side as she looked kindly into the young girl's face.

The desire to find her father was a redeeming trait in Bessy Morris's character. It helped to guard her heart against the worldliness, and vanity, and discontent which sometimes threatened to take possession of it. And sitting there in that little chair, her heart began to warm to the

kind old woman, whose look was so like a mother's; and
Bessy Morris felt that at that moment she had more of good
in her than at any other time since the innocent days of her
childhood.

Mat Donovan sat on the bench, which Billy Heffernan was
wont to take possession of whenever he paid them a visit.
Mat chose this seat rather than the " sugán-bottom " chair,
because from it he could watch the play of Bessy's expressive features without attracting attention. And how his
heart did swell as he looked and looked, and asked himself
how or when she managed to get into it—a question which
for the life of him honest Mat could not answer satisfactorily.
But there she was, and no mistake; and Mat sighed such a
big, heavy sigh at the thought of how hard it would be to
eject her—when that proceeding would become an absolute
necessity and a duty—that Bessy Morris looked at him with
a melancholy sort of look, as if she knew exactly what he
was thinking of. Whereupon Mat Donovan assumed an
exceedingly humorous expression of countenance, and wanted
to say something in his usual style; something very droll
and extravagant—as became a " palaverer " and a " deluder "
and "a rag on every bush." But somehow his drollery had
quite deserted him; and not a single " quare thing " could
he remember, that would convince Bessy Morris that he,
Mat Donovan, commonly called Mat the Thrasher, was the
rollickingest, rovingest blade in all Tipperary, whom it was
not given to woman born of woman to capture and hold
captive. So Mat Donovan could do nothing better than lean
the back of his head against the partition, and look up the
chimney.

" An' what way did you lave your aunt ?" Mrs. Donovan
asked.

" She was very delicate for a long time," Bessy replied;
" but she's better now. The doctor advised her to come to
the country. And if her son comes home from England, as
he promised, I think she'll spend part of the summer with
us."

" Well, I'd be glad to see her," returned the old woman.

" We all thought she made a fine match—he was such a
grand elegant young fellow. But I b'lieve the poor woman
met with her own share uv the world."

"Indeed she had her trials," replied Bessy.

"'Tis little any wan thought he'd turn out as he did," rejoined the old woman. "But 'tis hard to judge uv people by their looks. Id might be betther for her if she married some honest b'y she knew always. But 'tis 'asy to talk now when we see the difference; but no wan'd think so at the time."

"I'll call in again to-morrow, or after, Mrs. Donovan," said Bessy, as she stood up and rested her hand on the little old chair. "But I promised my grandfather to be home early; and he might be sending Peg Brady to know what is delaying me."

"Go wud her a piece uv the road, Mat," said his mother, looking reproachfully at him, as if she thought he ought to have at once volunteered his services.

"Oh, no," Bessy exclaimed; "'tis a fine bright night. An' sure I ought to know the road well."

"I'll put you apast the sthrame," said Mat, stretching out his arms and yawning, as if he felt very tired and lazy, and would much prefer being left to doze upon the bench with his poll against the partition, and a bright little star looking down through the chimney at him from a patch of blue sky.

"See—I was near forgettin' to tell you," said Mrs. Donovan, as Mat and Bessy were going out, "to tell your grandfather about the soger."

Bessy Morris looked at her with surprise, not unmingled with alarm. And Mat, too, stopped in the doorway, seeming at a loss to understand what she meant.

"Bad cess to him," continued Mrs. Donovan, "he tuck a great start out uv me, when he walked in, an' nobody wud me but myse'f, as they wor at the weddin'. I was hardly able to answer him whin he axed me where Phil Morris lived. Id brought the time uv the Coercion Act to my mind."

"Oh, wait till you see himse'f," said Mat, who evidently thought the story was an old one.

This mistake was a relief to Bessy, and she brightened up on seeing him walk out without waiting for further particulars; but as she walked quickly after him, her mind became troubled. The dragoon, it seemed, had been as far as the hamlet ; and the object of his visit she feared might become a subject for gossip and even scandal.

Mat Donovan looked up at the little star that was looking down at him through the chimney ; and then Mat Donovan looked at the moon, which was tolerably bright. But star and moon failed to inspire Mat Donovan with a suitable topic for conversation. And failing to find it among the heavenly bodies, he bent his gaze on the muddy road, and seemed to search diligently for it there, as he walked on, with Bessy Morris by his side. Greatly to his surprise, he found himself at the stream before he had spoken one word to her. He strode across and reached her his hand. She placed her foot on the single stepping-stone, and leaped lightly over.

" 'Tis a fine night," said he, still holding her hand.

" Very fine," she replied.   " Good-night."

He was looking at the moon again, and seemed to forget that he had hold of her hand, when they were both startled by the words :

" Wisha, is id there ye are ?"

It was only Peg Brady, who had been sent by Bessy's grandfather to meet her. And Peg laughed, as if Mat Donovan holding Bessy Morris by the hand and looking at the moon were the best joke in the world. But there was something in the laugh which Bessy did not like. And for an innocent, good-natured, " harmless sort of a girl " like Peg Brady, her glance was very sly indeed, as, turning to Mat, she said :

" The little house undher the hill, Mat ?"

" God be wud ould times," returned Mat, with a shake of the head and a smile, in which there was something so sad that Bessy Morris fixed that thoughtful, inquiring look upon him, and then looked down at the moonbeams shimmering in the little stream.

What did he mean ? Might it be that he had been told something about her, and that he was sorry she was no longer the Bessy Morris of " old times ?"

" What's comin' over me at all ?" he thought, after bidding them good-night. " Sure I never expected she'd ever think uv me except as a friend and a neighbour. An' she's as friendly an' plasin' in every way as ever I see her. But, for all that, I feel quarer than ever I felt in my life. She

looks some way sorrowful at me sometimes, just as if she
knew what was in my mind. I must take care an' not let
her know, for I know id would throuble her. An' sorry I'd
be to give her throuble. Well, God bless her ! anyway," he
added, stopping, just where she had stopped an hour or two
before. " The like uv her is not within the walls uv the
world."

He looked at the clipped hedge, and up at the old cherry
tree, and down towards the school-house, behind the quarry.
And the hedge grew green, and the ripe cherries peeped from
among the leaves, and he, too, heard the twitter of the birds,
and the song of the thrush, and the lowing of the kine ; and
he waited for the shout of the children " just let loose from
school." The candle was, just then, laid in its usual place
in the little window, and its light recalled him to the living
Present. The " living Present ?" And the " dead Past ?"
We hold that the Past is the more living of the two, sometimes.

Mat Donovan looked at the outline of the mountains, and
all around the horizon.

> "Hi ! for it, hi ! for it, hi ! for it still,
> And hi ! for the little house under the hill."

—he sang, as he closed the little gate of the " haggart,"
which, no doubt, Nelly had left open when she came to pull
the leeks for her mother's supper.

Mat Donovan's house was not " under," but rather on the
top of a hill. But Peg Brady had her own reason for her
allusion to a little house that was under a hill. And we fear
Peg's reason was not a very amiable one ; for she shook her
head and repeated the phrase, " the poor fool !" several times
on her way home, glancing at the same time from the corners
of her eyes at Bessy Morris.

The light in the little window recalled another dreamer
besides Mat Donovan from the dead Past to the living
Present. This dreamer was a woman. She sat alone at a
window. Her face was pale and very beautiful ; and her white
arm gleamed like snow in the moonlight through her abundant dark hair, which had fallen down and flowed in glossy
waves over the little table upon which the arm was leaning.
Her lips were parted, and her face wore a look of sadness, as

she gazed intently at the moon. She was dreaming. She was walking by the sea-side—not alone. She leant upon the arm of one whom she regarded as a very dear friend ; one who to her mind was a superior being—something higher and nobler than ordinary mortal men—but whom to regard as more than a friend she would have thought a crime. The waves stole in softly over the smooth sand. The wide expanse of waters was calm as her own soul. They stood still, neither looking at the other, and gazed along the tranquil main. And she was happy, and thought he must be so too. But how rudely was she awakened from that happy dream ! It is the thought of this awaking that has brought that look of pain into her face, upon which the cold moonlight falls like spray upon a lily. And while her mild blue eyes are raised to the pale moon, a gleam of light, as if a little star had peeped over the brow of the hill, shines through the branches of the elm tree —and Mary Kearney is recalled to the living Present ; for she knows it is the light in Mat Donovan's window. She looks around her, as if fearful of being observed ; but she is alone, and the light laugh of a girl from the next room assures her that her absence has not been remarked upon, or Grace would have come to seek her. She ties up her hair with a steady hand ; and joins the laughing circle with a face so calm and unruffled that no one could for a moment have suspected that it ever wore a look of pain.

CHAPTER XLIX.

IN THE LONESOME MOOR—MEDITATING MURDER—DARBY RUADH THINKS HIMSELF BADLY USED—TOM HOGAN HAS AN ARGUMENT AGAINST PHIL LAHY.

THE light in Mat Donovan's little window called a third dreamer back from the dead Past to the living Present. He, too, was gazing on the moon, which shed its silvery light upon him as softly as upon the pale face and mild eyes of the lovely girl who at the same moment sat alone at

the window of the old cottage among the trees. His
dream is of a golden autumn evening. He is standing in
the shade of a row of elders, at the back of a thatched
farmhouse, looking out upon the stooks in a newly reaped
corn-field. His hand rests on the shoulder of a blushing
girl; and he tells her that the field is his, and points out
how thickly it is studded with stooks, and what a rich
harvest it will prove. The scene changes to a bright fireside. The blushing girl is a happy wife with an infant at
her breast, listening to the prattle of three rosy children
who crowd about their father's knees as he takes his
accustomed place by the hearth after the day's toil. And,
though his toil was hard, he did not grudge it so long as
he could keep that hearth warm for those happy prattlers,
and feel that at least the dread of want would never cast a
shadow upon that dear face bent so sweetly over the sleeping
infant. But the gleam of light from Mat Donovan's little
window makes him start to his feet. The bright hearth is
quenched for ever. The mother and children are cowering
over a few embers in a wretched hovel. The fields which his
toil had made fruitful are added to the broad acres of his
wealthy neighbour, whose gold induced the irresponsible
absentee landlord to do the deed that left him a pauper, with
no prospect in the wide world before him but a pauper's
grave. He had been leaning against a bank out in the lonesome bog—one of those banks upon which Billy Heffernan
loved to recline, and revel in bliss till he would scorn to claim
relationship to royalty itself ! But far different from Billy
Heffernan's visions were those of him who now, kneeling upon
one knee, and with one hand resting upon the black mould,
looked cautiously around the desolate moor. There scarcely
could have been any necessity for this caution ; for at that
hour, and in that place, it was extremely unlikely that any
human eye could observe his movements. He took a gun from
where it lay beside the bank, and after carefully examining
the lock, placed it at half cock. As he was about letting down
the hammer again, a sound like a sigh, or a deep breathing,
close to his ear, made him pause, and a sensation of fear
crept through his frame. A shadowy object passed over his
head, and, on casting his eyes upwards, he beheld something
between him and the sky which filled him with amazement

and terror. In shape it was a bird; but of such monstrous
dimensions, that it seemed like a great cloud hanging in the
air. For a moment he thought it was only a cloud; but the
slow, regular waving of the huge wings satisfied him that it
was a living thing. The long snake-like head and neck were
thrust out towards him, and in his terror he let the gun fall
from his nerveless grasp. The head was quickly drawn back,
and the monstrous bird waved its huge wings, and sailed
away through the moonlit air. He followed it with his eyes
till it dropped on the brink of the water that covered a large
portion of the bog like a lake. And now he saw it was only
a heron that had lodged for a moment on the bank above
his head. While he thought it high up in the air, the bird
was within a few feet of him; and hence the illusion by
which he was so terrified. With an exclamation of scorn at
being frightened like a child, he stooped to pick up his gun.
But he had been lying near the brink of a square bog-hole
filled with water, and the gun had fallen into it, and, of
course, sunk to the bottom. He knew the hole was eight or
ten feet deep, and that to attempt recovering the gun would
be useless. He ground his teeth with rage; but after gazing
round the silent moor, and up at the peaceful moon, it
occurred to him that the weapon had been snatched, as it
were, by the hand of Providence, from his grasp; and the
thirst for vengeance ceased to burn within him, and he felt
as if God had not abandoned him.

"I must see about gettin' id up anyway," he observed to
himself, "or poor Barney might get into throuble about id.
He tould me he was bringin' id to Mat Donovan to put a
piece on the stock, where the doctor broke id when he fell
on the ice. But he's such a fool he won't remimber the bush
he stuck id in when he med off afther the hounds. I don't
know what put id into my head to take a fancy to such an
ould Queen Anne, when this is handier and surer." And he
took a horse-pistol from his breast and clutched it firmly in
his hand. He looked down into the square bog-hole, and
touched the smooth black surface of the water with his
hand. The action reminded him of the holy water with
which he used to sprinkle himself on entering and leaving
the chapel before his clothes had become too ragged to allow
him to appear with decency among the congregation; and

involuntarily he sprinkled his forehead, and made the sign
of the Cross.

" There's some great change afther comin' over me," he
thought. " My mind is someway 'asier ; an' the madness is
gone off uv me."

And looking at the pistol again, he replaced it in his breast.

" I'll do nothin' to-night," he continued with a deep sigh,
like a man overpowered by fatigue. " If I could lie down
here in the heath an' fall asleep, an' never waken again—I'd
be all right. But," he added, rousing himself by an effort,
" but—I mustn't forget poor Mary !" He walked towards a
road which looked like a high embankment, the surface of
the bog having been cut away at both sides of it ; and as he
climbed up this embankment, the light in Mat Donovan's
window again caught his eye.

" 'Tis long since I exchanged a word wud any uv the ould
neighbours," he continued, " till Billy Heffernan chanced to
come on me th' other night, an' I makin' a show uv mese'f.
An' sure 'tis little wish I had to talk to any wan. But
someway I think now I'd like to hear a few friendly words
from some wan. An' that light in Mat's window reminds
me how I used hardly ever pass by wudout callin' in to light
the pipe."

He looked wistfully towards the light, and then looked
down upon his tattered habiliments.

" I'm a quare object," he muttered with a bitter smile,
" to go anywhere. But as 'tis afther comin' into my mind
I'll turn back."

Instead of following the road or " togher " upon which he
stood, he crossed an angle of the bog till he came to the
stream or canal in which Dr. Richard Kearney left the leg of
his nether garment, and following it for a few hundred yards
came out on the public road.

The road was quite deserted. He reached the hamlet
without meeting a living thing ; and as he stood at the
" cross," and looked up along the silent street, he felt a
strange wish to steal through it without being seen by any one.
He moved on like a spectre, treading lightly as he passed
those houses the doors of which were open, and glancing
furtively to the right and left at the lights in the window
panes. On coming to the beech-tree he stood still and looked

up at the pointed gables and thick chimneys of the " barrack ";
and happening to glance through the kitchen window, he
caught a glimpse of Norah Lahy's pale face. She was praying,
with clasped hands and eyes raised to Heaven ; and there was
something in her look that moved him instantly to tears.

"I wondher is id dhramin' I am?" he said to himself,
"I can't remember what's after happenin' to me, or what
brought me here, except like a man 'd feel afther the faver,
or somethin' uv that soart. On'y I'd be afeard I'd frighten
her, I'd go in an' ax her to pray for me, an' I know 'twould
do me good. An' as id is I feel I'm the betther of lookin'
at her ; for no wan could see such a look as that an' not
know there was another world besides this. I could kneel
down on the road here an' pray myse'f ; what I didn't do this
many a day—right, at any rate. I might go on my knees
an' say the words ; but id wasn't prayin'. The curses used
to choke the prayers ! I could hardly keep from tellin' God
that He was a bad God ! But I'm not that way now at all ;
an' maybe 'twas the Lord that sint me round this way. No
wan lookin' at her could doubt there was a heaven. The
angels are talkin' to her this minute ! An' someway I think
'tis for unfortunate sinners like me she is prayin'. For sure
she don't want to pray for herse'f. Oh, an' look at her now,"
he exclaimed in surprise, " an' how she smiles an' laughs
like a child whin her mother came in. She wants to cheer
up the poor mother that knows she won't have her long.
The Lord save us ! I feel my heart laughin' wud her ! But
I'd betther not let anyone see me standin' here," he observed,
as he walked on, on hearing Kit Cummins calling to her husband to come home to his supper, and judged from the pitch
of Kit's voice that Jack was down towards the forge, and
must necessarily pass by the beech-tree on his way home.

Mat Donovan was humming " The little house under the
hill " by the fireside, while Nelly was turning the " quarters "
of a griddle of whole-meal bread that was baking over the
fire, when the latch was raised, and a tall, gaunt figure stood
between them and the candle in the window. The fire, being
covered with the large griddle, did not afford sufficient light
to enable them to recognise the new-comer ; and the candle
being behind his back only showed the outline of his figure,
in which Nelly fancied she saw something wild ; and she felt

and looked somewhat frightened as she thought of the
" gang," which, according to common report, were just then
prowling nightly about the neighbourhood.   Mrs. Donovan,
too, seemed alarmed, as she dropped her knitting on her
knees, and stared over her spectacles at the man, who stood
looking at them for nearly a minute without speaking.

" God save all here," said he, at last.

" God save you, kindly," returned Mat, starting from his
chair, and moving towards him till he was able to see his
face.   " Is id Mick Brien ?"

" The very man," was the reply.

Mrs. Donovan and Nelly exchanged looks of the deepest
pity, but remained quite silent.

" Sit down," said Mat, placing a chair for him.

" I don't know," he replied, irresolutely.   " I just see the
candle in the windy, an' id reminded me to come in."

" Sit down and take a hate uv the fire," said Nelly, in a
subdued tone, and as if it required an effort to address him.
" I hope herse'f an' the childher is in good health ?"

'' They're on'y middlin', then, Nelly," he replied.   " The
winther was very hard."

He sat down, however, and said.more cheerfully :

" I'm glad to see you lookin' so well, Mrs. Donovan.
You're as young-lookin' this minute as you wor the night uv
poor little Sally's wake ; God rest her sowl.   But sure I
needn't pray for her ; for she had as little sin on her as an
infant, though I b'lieve she was goin' on thirteen years when
she died."

" She was a beautiful child," returned Mrs. Donovan.
" But God is good ; and maybe 'twas for her good, and your
good, and her mother's good, that she was taken from you.
God knows what is best for us all."

" That's thrue," rejoined Mick Brien.   " An' 'tis of'en I
think 'twould be well for the whole uv 'em if they went too."

" Don't say that, Mick," returned Mrs. Donovan.   " Ye
had yer own share uv sufferin' and throuble ; but there's no
knowin' what might be in store for ye yet."

" I'm afeard," said he in a hollow voice, " 'tis gone too far
for that."

While his mother was speaking, Mat was hurriedly filling
his pipe, which, after lighting, he presented to Mick Brien,

who took it eagerly, but checked himself as he was putting it to his mouth.

"No, Mat, I'm obliged to you," said he, handing back the pipe. "'Tis a good start since I tuck a blast; an' maybe 'twould be betther for me not to mind id."

Nelly and her mother exchanged looks again, and the old woman shook her head sorrowfully.

Drawing his chair to the fire, he held the backs of his hands close to the blaze that struggled from under the griddle.

"Was id in the bog you wor?" Mat asked; "your hands are black wud the turf-mould. An', begor, there's enough uv id stuck to your old brogues, too."

Mick Brien was taken by surprise, and seemed embarrassed. He could have had no legitimate business in the bog at that late hour, and felt at a loss what reply to make.

Mat noticed his embarrassment, and, with instinctive delicacy, appeared to forget the question altogether; and turning to his sister, he said:

"Are you goin' to let that bread be burnt?"

She turned the four quarters of bread, and finding them properly baked, placed them standing on their ends on the griddle, so as that the thick edges cut by the knife in dividing the circular cake into four quarters might be fully baked. While she was thus employed, the door was opened, and two men walked in with an apologetic grin, holding their pipes in their hands."

"God save ye!" said the foremost, as he approached the fire to light a piece of paper which he held between his fingers.

"God save you kindly!" returned Mat, in a manner that plainly showed they were no welcome guests.

The second man was advancing to light his pipe at the fire also. But the moment their eyes fell upon Mick Brien, both wheeled quickly round, and, lighting their bits of paper at the candle in the window, hurriedly applied them to their pipes as they made for the door, where they encountered something which drove them backwards into the kitchen again.

It was only Tom Hogan, who walked slowly after them; and, after glancing at Mick Brien—who never raised his head all the time—and looking wildly about them, the two

men, with a sneaking sort of " Good-night to ye," left the
house.

" Wisha, is that Tom Hogan ?" said Mat—for Tom was not
a frequent visitor there. " Sit down."

" I was down at Phil Lahy's," returned Tom Hogan, " an'
Honor towld me he was up here. So I tuck a walk up."

In fact, Tom Hogan had got quite a mania for talking
about landlords and agents, and kindred subjects, since that
conversation with Phil Lahy when his hands began to tremble
in so strange a manner. Before that, he only cared to know
about " the markets " ; but now nothing that bore on the
land question, or, indeed, upon any social or political question,
from Columbkille's prophecies to the latest missive ornamented with a skull and cross-bones, came amiss to Tom
Hogan. And he felt so restless and ill at ease all the evening, he walked down to Phil Lahy's the moment he was done
his supper, for the sole purpose of getting himself abused as
a " crawler."

Mick Brien continued warming his hands, and never raised
his head. Nelly took up the quarters of bread and laid them
on the dresser, and, whipping the griddle off the fire, raked
up the lighted turf that was spread out under it till it blazed
so brightly that he was obliged to draw back his chair and
close his eyes, as if the light dazzled him.

Tom Hogan was quite as much astonished as the two men
who had come in to light their pipes, on seeing Mick Brien
sitting before Mat Donovan's fire ; but, instead of retreating
like them, Tom Hogan seemed fascinated by the gaunt and
ragged figure over which the firelight flickered ; and as the
hollow eyes were turned towards him, he mechanically drew
near and sat down on the chair from which Mat Donovan had
risen when he recognised him.

" Mick," said Tom Hogan, keeping his eyes fixed on the
worn, emaciated face, " did they rise the rint on you ?"

Mick Brien seemed surprised, and evidently did not understand the question.

" Did they rise the rint on you ?" Tom Hogan repeated
anxiously.

" Is id the rint of the cabin ?" he asked.

" No," returned Tom Hogan, " but the rint uv the farm,
before they put you out ?"

" Well, no," replied Mick Brien ; " when the lase dhropped they said I should go, as my houldin' wasn't large enough. An' no matther what rint I'd offer 'twouldn't be taken."

" So they never riz the rint ?"

" No."

" What did I tell you ?" exclaimed Tom Hogan excitedly, turning to Mat Donovan, his eyes lighted up with joy. " What did I tell you, Mat ?" he repeated triumphantly.

Mat was greatly astonished ; for it happened Tom Hogan had never spoken a word to him on the subject.

" What did I tell you, Mat ?" he exclaimed a third time, apparently in the greatest glee.

" Begor," returned Mat at last, greatly puzzled, " you never tould me anythin' about id at all, so far as I can remember."

" They never rise the rint, Mat, when they're goin' to put a man out. Never. Don't b'lieve any wan that tells you anything else. Never. Such a thing was never known."

" Oh, maybe so," said Mat, quite unable to comprehend his meaning, but wishing to be civil.

" You may be sure uv id, Mat," rejoined Tom Hogan.

" Make your mind 'asy on that p'int," he continued, laying his hand on Mat's knee, as he sat down on Billy Heffernan's bench. " No, Mat. There's nothin' so incouragin' to a poor man as to have the rint riz on him. For then he knows they're not goin' to disturb him, Mat. Look at this poor man that held, I b'lieve, as good as fifteen acres more than I have mese'f ; an' see what a loss it was to him that the rint wasn't riz on him. There's nothin' like a rise to give a poor man courage. I must go an' find Phil Lahy, an' have a talk wud him. He thinks there's no wan able to argue these p'ints but himse'f. But let me alone if I don't open his eyes for him. Good-night to ye." He turned round at the door and asked : " Ah, thin, Mat, what was Wat an' Darby doin' here ?"

" They on'y came in to redden their pipes," Mat replied.

" Oh, is that all ? Well, I must go look for Phil Lahy to open his eye for him."

" An' I wondher where them fellows wor ?" Mat muttered, after appearing to brood over the question for some time. " They passed up this way late in the evenin'."

" wisha, how do I know ?" his sister replied, as if the

question were addressed to her. " But wherever they wor,
'tisn't in the betther uv them, you may be sure."

The two worthies of whom she spoke walked quickly and
in silence down the road, seeming wholly absorbed with their
pipes.

" 'Tis an admiration," said Wat Corcoran, at last, " how
long he stuck about the place. I thought he'd be gone uv
his own accord long ago."

" So did we all," returned Darby Ruadh. " But whin we
found him thatchin' the cabin, the masther said he should
get notice. He's not safe ; an' begob, we'd want to keep an
eye on him."

" 'Tisn't you or me he'd mind," replied Wat.

" You wouldn't know," rejoined Darby Ruadh. " When
they're in that soart uv way, whoever comes next to hand
'll meet id. They're d—n fools," continued Darby mildly.
" They seldom or ever knock down the right bird. Now,
he'd as soon stretch you or me, as the man that sent us ;
an' that's foolish."

" What about Tom Hogan ?" Wat asked.

" Well, from all I can see, he must go."

" There'll be no great throuble wud him. He'll get a
thrifle uv money, an' he'll go away quiet an' 'asy."

" I don't know that, Wat. Men uv his soart is the worst
of all."

" He knows nothin' about firearms, nor nothin'," returned
Wat Corcoran. " He's always braggin' he never fired a
shot."

" Thim's the men, Wat, that'll get a fellow to do the job.
I met some coves uv that soart in my time."

" Faith, be all accounts, you done some quare things yourse'f in your time, Darby."

" Well, maybe I did, an' maybe I didn't. An', by ——!"
he added fiercely, " maybe I would agin, if id was worth my
while. 'Tis enough to dhrive a man to anything to think uv
the beggarly way we're paid. They want you to put your
life in danger every day in the year—an' to swear anything
they ax you besides ; an', by ——, you're not paid betther
than a cowboy afther."

" 'Tis a hard life," returned Wat Corcoran ; " an' 'tis of'en
I do be wishin' to give id up, an' turn to somethin' else.

But when wance you get into id, 'tis hard to get out uv id."

"Unless a man could make a haul," returned Darby Ruadh, "an' make off to America. Good night, Wat."

"Good night, Darby; an' safe home."

They parted at the cross-roads; Wat Corcoran turning to the right towards his own house, and Darby Ruadh going on straight to Wellington Lodge.

Mick Brien drew his chair still further back from the blazing turf fire. The heat seemed too much for him, for the perspiration stood in large drops upon his face; and when he took off his hat, they remarked that his hair was damp and clammy. Yet it was not the heat that so affected him. *It was the smell of the newly-baked bread.* He was fainting; but by a great effort he roused himself, and asked for a drink of water.

Nelly dipped a cup in the never empty pail under the window, and handed it to him. He gulped down the clear spring water hurriedly; and, as he handed back the cup, he turned to Mat, and, with apparent cheerfulness, asked:

"What news, Mat? is there anything at all goin'?"

"No, then," replied Mat. "I don't know uv anything."

Mrs. Donovan, who had kept her sad eyes fixed upon Mick Brien's haggard face, while her knitting rested upon her knees as if she had forgotten it, now rose from her chair, and, going to the dresser, poured something from a jug into a saucepan, which she placed upon the fire. Her daughter looked inquiringly at her as if this proceeding had taken her by surprise; but the old woman resumed her seat without speaking.

"I think," said Mick Brien, "the weather is likely to hould up."

"This was a fine day," returned Mat. "But I'm afeard 'twas on'y a pet day. Phil Lahy tells me we're to have a change uv the moon to-morrow; an' he says the almanac talks uv broken weather, wud cowld showers, an' aistherly winds."

Mick Brien made no reply. His head drooped, and he seemed to be falling fast asleep.

"Nelly," said Mrs. Donovan, "hand me that white bowl." She filled the bowl with warm milk from the saucepan she had placed on the fire ; and Nelly looked quite frightened on seeing her mother present the bowl to Mick Brien.

" Here, Mick," said she, " dhrink this. I know by you there's somethin' the matter wud you. An' if id be a touch uv an inward pain you're gettin', there's nothin' like a dhrop uv hot milk for id."

On opening his eyes and seeing the bowl held close to him he started like one suddenly awakened from sleep. He looked at the milk and then into Mrs. Donovan's face, upon which he kept his eyes fixed for several seconds. Then taking the bowl between his hands, he looked at her again with a bewildered stare.

" Drink id while 'tis hot, Mick," said she, " an' 'twill do you good."

'Twas a great relief to Nelly to see him lift the bowl to his lips and drink ; not swallowing the milk hurriedly, as he had swallowed the cup of water, but slowly and continuously, as a child will do.

Mick Brien had been one of the most comfortable and respectable small farmers in the neighbourhood ; and he and his handsome wife used to call in on their way from town for a rest and a chat with Mrs. Donovan, who was much respected by them—as indeed she was by all who knew her. And now that he was reduced to poverty, Nelly was quite afraid the offer of the milk, under the circumstances, might hurt his feelings, and be taken as an insult.

Mick Brien handed the bowl to the kind old woman, and buried his face between his hands. He remained so long in this position they all began to look embarrassed, and did not well know how they ought to act—fearing that to rouse him might look as if they wished him to go away.

After some time, however, he raised his head, and stretching out his arms, but without venturing to look at any one, said with assumed cheerfulness :

" Faith, I b'lieve 'twas fallin' asleep I was."

" What hurry are you in ?' said Mat, on seeing him rise ; " sure you may as well rest yourse'f."

" I must be goin'," he replied ; " herse'f 'll be wondherin' where I was all the evenin'."

He had been lying many hours by that bank in the bog, maddened by hunger and the thought of the cruel wrongs inflicted upon him and his. He lay there waiting for the night, and bent upon having revenge. He lay there hour after hour, meditating a deed of blood ; till the mild moon called up visions of the " *dead* Past." And then the light in Mat Donovan's window recalled him to the " *living* Present," and to his purpose. And it was only the waving of a bird's wing saved his soul from the guilt of murder !

No word has ever escaped our pen intended to justify such a deed as that contemplated by this poor maddened victim of tyranny Yet when we think of his blameless life of patient toil ; of his cheerful unquestioning surrender of the greater part of the fruits of that toil to the irresponsible taskmaster to whose tender mercies the rulers of the land had handed him over body and soul ; of the pittance which he was content to retain for himself ; of his terror and anguish on discovering that a felon hand was determined to tear even that pittance from him, and fling the wife of his bosom, and the little ones that were the light of his eyes, homeless outcasts upon the world ; of the roofless cabin, the cold, the fever, the hunger,—when we think of all this, we find it hard to brand Mick Brien as a MURDERER. And surely no one will for a moment class him with the human wild beasts with whom the writer of these pages was doomed to herd for years, and among whom at this hour Irishmen, whose only crime is the crime of loving their country, are wearing away their lives in the Convict Prisons of England ?

Mat Donovan stood up to open the door for Mick Brien and see him out to the road.

" Good-night to ye," said Mick Brien, as nearly as he could in the same tone as he used to say it in after a chat and a smoke on his way from Kilthubber on market days.

Nelly ran to the dresser ; and then followed them to the door. " Mr. Brien," said she.

He turned round, but Nelly seemed to have forgotten what she was going to say. She stood with her hands behind her back, and looked into his face. At last, while the blood mounted to her forehead, she quickly brought her hands round to the front, and pressing two of the quarters of bread against his breast, she wrapped his coat over them, placing his own hand so as to keep them from falling, and looking anxiously into his face all the time. He remained quite

passive, gazing with a vacant stare straight before him. Seeing
no sign of displeasure in his look, she cautiously withdrew
her hand as if in doubt whether he would continue to hold
the bread where she had placed it. He did continue to hold
it, however, and followed Mat outside the door without
speaking a word.

Nelly leant over the back of the chair he had been sitting
on, and rested her cheek on her hand.

" God help him !" said she.

" God help him !" returned her mother, whose head was
also resting on her hand.

So they continued gazing into the fire.

" God help him !" said Mat Donovan, as he resumed his
seat by the fireside opposite his mother.

These were the last audible words spoken under Mat
Donovan's roof that night.

Yet poor Mick Brien had unconsciously laid the train of
much suffering for those kind hearts that sympathized so
deeply with him.

" Tom," said Phil Lahy solemnly, " I wish you would not
be introducin' these subjects to me. I don't want to hurt
your feelin's, or say anything offensive or insultin'. But
indurance has its limits. An' now I tell you what, Tom
Hogan, 'tisn't in human nature to have patience wud you !"

" Ha, ha, ha !" laughed Tom Hogan. " I knew I'd open
his eye. I knew I had an argument that'd put him down.
Ha, ha, ha ! Begor, Phil, you're bet ! Good-night to ye.
Good-night to ye. There's nothin'," muttered Tom Hogan,
as he closed the door behind him, " there's nothin' to give a
poor man courage like a rise in the rint—now an' then.
Look at that unfortunate man, Mick Brien, an' wouldn't id
be a lucky day for him if his rint was riz ? What signifies a
few pounds a year ? I'll let Jemmy go sell that grain uv
oats, as my face is marked afther that powdher. Jemmy is
a good boy. An' how wild he was whin he thought 'twas
any wan was afther touchin' me ! I'm very fond uv that
fellow ! Aye, an' I'll give him lave to spind a shillin' in
Clo'mel ; unless he'd rather keep id for the races. Ha, ha,
ha ! the divil a word I left Phil."

" Father," said Norah Lahy, " I'm afraid poor Tom Hogan
is not right in his mind."

CHAPTER L

rOM CUDDEHY FEELS " SOMEWAY QUARE."—A GLANCE BACK-
WARDS TO CLEAR UP THE MYSTERY OF THE TRACKS IN THE
SNOW.

TOM CUDDEHY took down his hurly from the hurdle over the
chimney corner, and examined it carefully, as a soldier might
examine his sword before the battle. His eye could detect
no crack or flaw ; but to make assurance doubly sure, Tom
Cuddehy let his hurly drop several times against the hearthstone, holding it by the small end as loosely as possible in
one hand, in order to test its soundness by the ring it gave
out. The great match between the two sides of the river
was to come off next day in Maurice Kearney's kiln-field, and
Tom Cuddehy's twenty picked men had reported themselves
ready in all respects to meet the Knocknagow boys on their
own chosen ground. The excitement at both sides of the
river was at its height ; and it was known that Mat Donovan
had despatched a messenger all the way to Cloughshannavo,
for Tom Doherty, whom Mrs. Kearney had induced to go as
servant to her cousin, Father Carroll, when he was appointed
administrator of that parish—to the great grief and sorrow
of the Knocknagow boys ; for Tom Doherty was one of their
best hurlers. If Tom Doherty failed to put in an appearance
it was the general opinion that victory would fall to " the
farmers "—for Tom Cuddehy's men were all farmers' sons—
while Mat Donovan's were all " labouring men." But, in
spite of these favourable omens, Tom Cuddehy put back his
hurly in its usual resting-place with a heavy sigh.

That accidental meeting with his old sweetheart the day
before had awakened a curious feeling in his breast, which
he described as " someway quare." The young man from
the mountain had spent the night at old Paddy Laughlan's,
and Tom had just been told that the old man and his
intended son-in-law had ridden away together after breakfast
to get the marriage articles drawn by Attorney Hanly, if they
were fortunate enough to catch that eccentric limb of the

law at home. So Tom Cuddehy sighed, and wished that dreary Saturday were well over ; for nothing less, he thought, could rouse him to shake off that " someway quare " state of mind than the excitement of the hurling match between the two sides of the river. He was throwing his riding-coat over his shoulders to go out, when the half-door was flung open, and Lory Hanly in a fearful state of excitement stood before him.

" I have a message for you," he exclaimed.

Lory's voice was sufficiently startling in itself, and his manner of opening his eyes very wide added considerably to the effect. But, in addition to the voice and the look, the unusual circumstance of Lory's wearing an old straw hat of the rudest description suggested to Tom Cuddehy that his sudden and unexpected appearance could only be the result of some very startling occurrence, of the nature of which he could not form the remotest conjecture.

So he stared at Lory, and Lory—as was his wont after causing a sensation—stared at him. While waiting to hear the expected " message," which Lory seemed on the point of projecting every moment from his half-open mouth, but which did not come for all that, Tom noticed that his visitor wore the immense straw hat in a peculiar fashion—that is, the broad leaf was turned back into the high and somewhat conical mould in front, so that the straw hat looked like a bonnet put on wrong side foremost. It just occurs to us, however, that this attempt to convey an idea of the manner in which Mr. Lory Hanly was pleased to wear his hat on this occasion, will be quite thrown away upon most of our readers, including (as a matter of course) *all* our fair readers ; for it is not for a moment to be supposed that one of them could remember what a bonnet was like, when a bonnet *was* a bonnet.

" What is id ?" Tom asked at last.

" Miss Laughlan desired me to tell you "———— Here Tom Cuddehy's bitch, Venom, took it into her head to start up from her place in the corner with a vicious snarl, misled, no doubt, by that peculiarity of Mr. Hanly's which Mrs. Kearney designated his " terrible throat," into the belief that his " message " was anything but " a message of peace."

" Down, Venom !" said Tom Cuddehy, who got very red

in the face at the mention of Miss Laughlan's name, and somehow connected Lory's appearance with the marriage articles which Tom supposed Lory's father was busy in drafting at that moment. "Well, what is id you wor goin' to say ?" he added meekly, as he lifted Venom up in his arms and flung her over the half-door.

But here we must leave Lory to deliver his message, and Tom Cuddehy to act upon it or not, as he thought fit. We must even leave the great hurling-match in Maurice Kearney's kiln-field undecided—to which the message had no reference whatever, and in which we openly avow our sympathies are with the "labouring men "; and if Tom Doherty fails, let him not hope for mercy at our hands. We must also leave the reader in suspense concerning the result of the contest between Mat Donovan and Captain French—and here again we are heart and soul against the "aristocrat "; though we by no means approve of Tom Doherty's knocking down old Major French's steward for confidently predicting the captain's victory, and offering to lay a gallon of beer thereon. But we were about to say that we must leave these exciting events undecided, and interrupt the regular course of our chronicle, in order to throw light upon certain circumstances of which the reader may have caught fitful glimpses in the foregoing chapters, and which, perhaps, ought to have been made clear long before now. And for this purpose the courteous reader will please to go back with us a year or two, and take a rapid glance at one or two new faces and scenes ; after which we shall return to our old friends, and follow their fortunes, through gloom and through gladness, over oceans and into strange lands, till we kneel by the graves of some, and—God be praised !—feel our heart beat quick while we tell of the happiness of others.

A young man in the garb of an ecclesiastical student was pacing up and down in front of a long, low, thatched house, which might be taken for an ordinary farm-house of the humbler sort were it not for its green hall-door—the fanlight of which was quite hidden by the eave—and the three good-sized windows of twelve panes each, two at one side and one at the other of the door, which was not exactly in the middle, and suggested the idea that the room at one side of the hall was twice the size of that on the other side.

The field in which the house stood—and there was no
gravelled space before the door or round the house, and no
avenue but a pathway from which the grass had been worn
off—would be by no means a favourable sample of the
"emerald isle," for it was dry and dusty-looking, and so
bare that the old white donkey who had leave to roam at
will, without let or hindrance, over the whole two acres,
seemed to have given up as hopeless the task of gathering a
belly-full—there being no thistles within the enclosure—and
philosophically resigned himself to that state of existence
which it is said the canine species either affect or are doomed
to, and which is popularly supposed to consist in "hunger
and ease." The country, as far as the eye could reach in
front and rear, and on one side of the house, was treeless and
without hedges, the fences being either of stone or clay, and
presented generally that sterile appearance which we have just
noticed in the old donkey's paddock. But though this was
the general aspect of the landscape on the right and left, and
in front of the young student as he closed his book on reaching the low wall of loose stones that divided the lawn from a
potato-field to the right of the cottage ; far different was the
picture he had before him when he turned full round, and
the rich green slopes of Hazelford met his gaze. The demesne
was only divided from the field in which he stood by a little
river that seemed to belong more to the poorer than to the
more favoured portion of the landscape, from which it was
shut out by the hazels which grew so thickly along the bank,
that, except at a few places, narrow and far apart, the existence of the stream could be known to the denizens of this
paradise only by its dreamy murmurings as it wound round
the roots of trees, and coiled into hollows and caverns, or
dashed itself fretfully against some little promontory of rock,
as if it sought, or would make for itself, an entrance into
the shady woods and sunny meadows of which it had caught
glimpses as it hurried down the furze-covered hill in the
distance, where it ceased to be a mere brook, and was first
honoured with the name of river. But strive and murmur
as it would, the cool groves and sunny meadows were forbidden ground, and the river went its way to the great ocean
without ever once reflecting the fair scenes around Hazelford
Castle in its bosom.

There was something in the deep-set eyes of the young student as they dwelt upon these fair scenes, that might suggest the thought that he, too, felt that he was excluded from them. There were fair forms gliding backwards and forwards upon a terraced walk under the ivied wall of the castle, and his pale face flushed on observing a field-glass, or telescope, directed towards himself, and handed from one to another of a group of ladies, who had evidently suspended their promenading for the purpose of surveying him. He mechanically looked around him for some less exposed place where he could continue his walk, but there was not a tree or bush near the cottage to screen him, except two old grey sally-trees, that served the purpose of piers to the wooden gate at the road. His first impulse was to walk down to the river, where he would be screened by the bushes on the opposite bank; but this, he thought, would look as if he wanted to get a nearer view of the group on the terrace, who seemed to concern themselves so much with his movements; and throwing back his shoulders, and holding his head very high, he faced towards the cottage, and pushing in the green hall-door, with the fanlight up in the thatch, turned into the parlour and sat down by the window.

Father Carroll was lying on a very stiff-looking straight-backed sofa, after a long ride to the farthest-away part of his parish. He was mentally contrasting his uncomfortable couch with the soft velvety loungers in the dean's well furnished rooms, when the young student entered.

" Well, Arthur," he asked, " has Edmund made his appearance yet ?"

" No," was the reply, " though he ought to be here before now."

" And why have you come in ?"

" Those women at the castle are so unmannerly, I couldn't stand it."

" What did they do to you ?" the priest asked, smiling. for the student's sensitiveness was a source of amusement to his friends.

" They looked at me," he replied in a tone of displeasure.

A hearty laugh from the priest prevented his finishing the sentence, and he turned to his book without attempting any further explanation.

The priest looked round his scantily furnished room, with
its bare walls and uncarpeted floor. The least bit of mould-
ing on the ceiling would, he thought, be a relief to his eyes—
to say nothing of hangings to the windows, or a more
modern article of furniture in lieu of the old mahogany concern called a desk, with its eight or ten drawers, and their
brass handles like the mounting of a coffin ; though this same
desk was the especial pride and glory of Mrs. Hayes, the
housekeeper, who always watched the faces of visitors when
she flung open the parlour door to see the effect produced by
the mahogany desk and its brass handles. " But there's
nothing like independence," said Father Carroll to himself.
" I wouldn't go back again as curate for a good deal. And
I'll be economical for a while, and will soon be able to furnish
the old cottage comfortably. I'm sorry now I never thought
of laying by a little money."

" Do you think," the young student asked, " I ought to
go back to the college for another year ?"

" I certainly think you ought," returned the priest. " You
may have a vocation, though you fancy you have not. Or it
may come in good time, if God wills it. I was at times
myself perplexed and in doubt as you are now ; but it all
passed away."

" But I never had a wish to be a priest from proper motives.
Since I was born, my mother's daily prayer has been that
she would live to see me a good priest, and I cannot bear the
thought of disappointing her hopes, particularly since the
failure of this unlucky bank has left us in rather straitened
circumstances. Nearly all that was left by my father to
educate me for a profession is gone ; and 'tis fearful to think
that so much has been thrown away upon me ; and here I
am now and don't know what course to take, even if I had
the courage to tell my mother the state of my mind. But
will it not be like acting a lie to go back again ?"

" I don't think so," returned Father Carroll, " unless you
take the loss of more time and money into account."

" The time, and the money, too, would be lost even if I did
not return to college, for I could not make up my mind what
to do next, for some time at least. Indolence and pride are
my besetting sins. My only idea in reference to becoming
a priest was that it was the easiest way to become a gentle-

man, and have people putting their hands to their hats for me."

" I don't know that most of us have not some such notion as that," returned Father Carroll, laughing. " I think you will be a priest yet."

" Here is Edmund," exclaimed the student, his sad face lighting up with pleasure as he hurried out to welcome his friend, who had just leaped off a car on the road, and vaulted over the gate, leaving the driver to open it and follow with his portmanteau to the cottage.

Edmund Kiely looked the very opposite of the pale, slightly built student whose thin hand he grasped in his warm palm, while his blue eyes and fresh, laughing face beamed with hearty good-nature. Edmund, as his little sister Grace used to say, was a " jolly fellow," never by any chance out of spirits for more than five minutes at a time. And yet the two friends whose society he most loved were Arthur O'Connor and Hugh Kearney. His father wished him to commence the study of the law, as he had a strong dislike to his own profession. But the young man had set his heart upon an open-air life, and in order to prevent his flying away to the antipodes, or to hunt buffaloes on the prairies of the West, Doctor Kiely promised to purchase some land for him in Ireland when a favourable opportunity presented itself. And Mr. Edmund Kiely is now one of those enviable mortals who have nothing on earth to trouble them. He and Arthur and Father Carroll have made several tours together, which proved such out-and-out pleasant affairs, that he is now bent upon adding one more to the number.

" I like the look of your house," he said, as he shook hands with the priest at the door of his thatched domicile. " There is something suggestive of the romantic about it. I have no doubt many a runaway couple dismounted at this door in the good old times, to demand the services of Father Cleary. Oh," he exclaimed on entering the parlour, " surely that armchair in the corner must have belonged to him. I can almost fancy I see the venerable old *soggarth* sitting in it at the present moment."

" Yes ; it and all the rest of the furniture belonged to him," Father Carroll replied. " I bought them all at the auction ; and though, as you see, they are not over elegant or expensive articles, I am in debt on account of them for the first time in my life."

" And talking of romance," Edmund went on, " of course, it was in this room Sir Thomas Butler's brother was married. I'd like to know all about it. Did you ever see his wife ?"

" No ; but Arthur can tell you all about it. She was his cousin."

" So she was, sir," old Mrs. Hayes, the housekeeper, who was laying the table, quietly observed—somewhat to Edmund's surprise. " You'd think he'd break his heart crying after poor Miss Annie. ' O uncle,' he used to say, ' what made you let that old man take her away ?' An' sure he wasn't an old man, though he was stooped and delicate-looking. We all thought he was only a painter, or an artist, as he used to say ; but he told Father Ned who he was, an' when he saw poor Miss Annie so given for him, though she thought he was only a poor painter, he gave his consent to the marriage. The poor thing got delicate soon after, an' when she found that his brother and family were makin' little of him, I know it used to fret her. He took her away to Italy for the air, for he was as fond of her as of his life. But she only held two years, an' her last letter to her uncle would bring tears from a rock, 'twas so movin'. Her husband she said, was as kind an' lovin' as ever, an' she was sure he'd be kind an' lovin' to her little Annie when she was gone."

" How did they happen to become acquainted first ?" Edmund asked, as Mrs. Hayes took her bunch of keys from her pocket, and ostentatiously shook them, preparatory to unlocking one of the drawers of the brass-mounted desk.

" Well," Mrs. Hayes replied, as she selected the key she wanted from the bunch, " herself an' Father Ned gave three weeks that year at the water. An', it seems, Mr. Butler spent all his time abroad learning the paintin' business—an' sure, I never see a man so fond of anything as he was of makin' pictures. He painted all Major French's children while he was here, an' 'tis little they thought 'twas a near cousin of their own was paintin' 'em. There is the three of 'em beyond—fine young women now," said Mrs. Hayes, pointing to the ladies who so annoyed the over-sensitive student a few minutes before. " But the pictures are all there still, an' if ever you are at the Castle 'twould be worth your while to look at 'em—you'd think they wor alive. But he was always practisin'. That an' playin' the flute was all that troubled him."

"So, 'twas while he was at the Castle he saw Miss Cleary?"

"Yes, sir; but he was shipwrecked, an' a'most dhrowned, an' Father Ned took him to the house where he lodged, an' Miss Annie nursed him; for 'twas thought he'd never get over it. An' afther that, he went about paintin' at the great houses. An' that's the way it came about. Poor Miss Annie was an orphan, you know, sir, an' lived wud her uncle ever since she came from the convent where she was educated. I'm told they had nothin' to live on but what he was able to earn, an' his brother an' all his family turned against him. 'Tis said now that Sir Thomas is near his end, an', as he never got married, Miss Annie's husband, I suppose, will come in for the property."

"And the title," added Father Carroll. "By the way, I trust it may turn out well for our friends at Ballinaclash."

"Why, what difference can it make to them?" Edmund asked.

"Oh, 'tis a matter of no little anxiety to a farmer to know what sort his new landlord will be. But any change is likely to be for the better in this case; for the present man is a rack-renter."

"I never heard Mr. Kearney say anything against him," returned Edmund. "Though he is by no means sparing of censure," he added, laughing. "'Tis a treat to listen to his comments sometimes."

"Yes, but he has a lease," replied Father Carroll. "But numbers of his tenants have been smashed trying to pay impossible rents. I should not wonder if his agent, old Pender, is urging him on in this course. But I'm inclined to think his brother will be a kind landlord, unless he is led astray; and it is said, too, Sir Thomas will leave the property greatly incumbered."

"Why, Arthur," exclaimed Edmund, "as your cousin's black eyes made so deep an impression on your boyish heart, I can't help thinking, if her daughter be at all like her, you had better keep out of her way, or she will spoil your vocation."

" I am not likely to come in contact with her," returned Arthur. " Though, for her mother's sake, I should like to know her."

" Of course, if he succeeds to the property, he will return to Ireland."

" I think not," Arthur replied. " It is said he is a complete Frenchman in his tastes and habits, and I suspect he will always live on the Continent. But where are we going to go ?"

" To Tramore," Edmund answered.

" Nonsense," returned Arthur. " Let us go somewhere where there will be no crowds. I detest the class of people you meet at these bathing places."

" Oh, yes," rejoined Edmund, laughing. " I remember your notions in this respect. You used to say you could imagine yourself marrying a peasant girl or a high-born lady ; but that you could not abide the *bourgeoisie.*"

" That is my idea still," replied the student. " They are a compound of ridiculous pride and vulgarity. But a peasant girl is seldom vulgar to my mind."

" Well, I have seen something of all classes," Father Carroll observed, " and I must say I have met some women of the class you condemn, who certainly were neither ignorant nor vulgar."

" He's a humbug," said Edmund Kiely, as if his friend's remark had nettled him a little. " 'Tis sour grapes with him, because a certain lady had the bad taste to prefer me to himself, once upon a time. You know we were always sure to be smitten by the same divinity, and though I gave him every fair play, he was never able to win a single smile the moment I entered the lists against him. And that's why he detests the sort of people one meets at the seaside. But what do you say to Tramore ?"

" I vote for it," Father Carroll replied. " I suppose old associations have something to do with it, but I can enjoy a stroll along the ' Great Strand,' more than I can the grandest cliffs and finest scenery we have. And then we'll be sure to meet some old friends there."

" Hear, hear," Edmund exclaimed. " We start to-morrow. I'll introduce you," he continued, turning to Arthur, " to the brightest and most fascinating little being that ever turned a wise man's head. And an heiress, too, for she is an only child, and her father is as rich as a Jew."

"I don't want to be introduced to her," was the reply. "The less I see of such people the better I like it."

"I suppose it is Miss Delany?" said Father Carroll. "I heard something about her. She has got an immense deal of polishing at all events."

"And it has not been thrown away—nor has it spoiled her in the least," returned Edmund. "But, by the way, I'm told Mary Kearney has turned out a downright beauty. My little sister Grace says I must marry her. She is twenty times handsomer, Grace says, than Minnie Delany. But I always thought her sister Anne would be a finer girl."

"I have not seen them for a long time," said Father Carroll. "I'm in the black books with their mother, it is so long since I paid her a visit. Father Hannigan told me she was saying to him that the world was gone when one's own flesh and blood will forget you and pass by your door without inquiring whether you are dead or alive. In fact, I got what Barney Brodherick calls 'Ballyhooly' from her. 'After getting him the best servant in the three counties,' said she, 'never as much as to say "Thank you!"'' I'm quite afraid to show my face to her. I suppose you have met Richard in Dublin?"

"Yes, we had some pleasant evenings at his uncle's. He will soon be a full-blown surgeon. I am promising myself a few days' shooting with Hugh shortly, and, if you could manage to come while I am there, I'll make your peace with Mrs. Kearney, as I am a great favourite of hers."

"Do you know any of them, Arthur?" Father Carroll asked.

"No, I never met any of them," he replied. "But I often heard of them."

"Come," said Edmund, pushing away his plate, "let us go out and look about us. Do you ever venture into Major French's grounds? I'd like to get a nearer view of those nymphs I caught a glimpse of as I was coming in. Unless it be that 'distance lends enchantment to the view,' they are worth looking at.'

"Yes, we can cross the river by the weir," returned Father Carroll. "There is a place there in a grove of large fir-trees

called the Priest's Walk. Poor Father Cleary was accustomed
to read his Office there for more than forty years ; and it is
even whispered that he may be met there still on a moonlight night. It was there his niece and her husband always
walked, too, Mrs. Hayes tells me. But, according to Tom
Doherty, there are other associations of not quite so innocent
a character connected with the Priest's Walk ; particularly
one in which a French governess figures."

" Oh, let us go to the place at once," exclaimed Edmund,
tossing his white hat carelessly on his brown curls, " and you
can tell the story of the governess ; and who knows but we
may catch a glimpse of the old priest and his beautiful niece ?
I wish I could believe in such things."

" Just wait till I tell Tom Doherty that we are to start
early in the morning. But what do you say to a glass of
punch before going out ?"

" Oh, wait till we come back, and sitting in that old chair
I'll drink the health of all true lovers, and sympathizing
uncles, who, like kind old Father Ned, will let them be
happy."

CHAPTER LI.

MAT DONOVAN IN TRAMORE.—MRS. KEARNEY AND HER " OWN CAR."—THE " COULIN."

TRAMORE—the " Great Strand "—is a household word in
very many Tipperary homes. There the child gets the first
sight of those waves, whose singing had been so often listened
to in the sea-shell on the parlour chimney-piece ; and there
the grandsire, leaning upon his staff, gazes for the last time
upon the same waves with wonder and delight more childish
than the child's. Few married couples will you meet along
the Golden Vale, and for many a mile to right and left of
it, who have not wandered over that level, velvety strand,
or reclined upon the sloping turf above the steep shore,
while the bay flashed in the autumn sun, when life's journey

seemed to them a very " path of rays." And when the corn is " drawn in," and the orchard " shook," and October frosts make it pleasant to come within the glow of the farmer's fire, see if the mention of " Tramore " will not call a dreamy look into the eyes of stalwart youths and blushing maidens !

Yes, pleasant memories of the sea are cherished in the homes of Tipperary. Yet who could ever look upon the sea without a sigh for the homes of Tipperary—and the homes of Ireland ?

Father Carroll and his two young friends were walking down the steep street towards the beach, when Edmund exciaimed :

" Surely, that is Mat Donovan with the spade in his hand. What on earth can have brought him here ?"

Mat was greeted as an old acquaintance by both Edmund and Father Carroll, but Arthur O'Connor had never seen him before, and contented himself with admiring the broad shoulders and sinewy limbs of the young peasant.

" Miss Mary, an' Miss Ann, an' the Misthress, sir," said Mat, in reply to a question from Father Carroll. " We're goin' home to-morrow, an' the misthress wouldn't be satisfied to have anyone dhrive 'em but myse'f, an' she sent for the car the week before last, so that I'm here now nearly a fortnight."

The fact was, Mrs. Kearney found that her neighbour, Mrs. O'Shaughnessy, had her own car at the seaside, and discovered at the same time that she herself was by no means well, and required " the sea air " to bring her round. Mary pointed to the window-curtain, which was fanning her mother's face at the moment, as she watched the breakers leaping up to clasp the dusky cliffs in their white arms, and then slide down and hide themselves in the bosom of the blue waves that rolled in as if to call back the truants to their proper home.

" What do you mean ?" says Mrs. Kearney with severity, on observing the laugh in Mary's blue eyes.

" Is there not sea air enough here ?" returned Mary. " And sure you can sit on the rocks, or on one of the seats on the Doneraile Walk. You have the sea air wherever you go."

But Mrs. Kearney had made up her mind that the sea air

could only be taken in its purity while driving in " her own
car " down to the Rabbit-burrow and back again. And so the
car and the old mare and Mat Donovan were sent for ; and
every day after their arrival Mrs. Kearney might be seen, with
her plump hands folded over her stomacher, jogging slowly
by the tide—which ever and anon glided under the old
mare's feet and startled the two young ladies on the other
side of the car, whose exclamations were utterly ignored by
their mamma, as she gave her whole mind to the " sea air " ;
with Mat Donovan " in an *ezad* "—to borrow his own expression—on the driver's seat. For Mat's legs were long and
the driver's seat was low, and he always descended from his
throne after a long drive, vowing that he was metamorphosed
into the last letter of the alphabet.

This jogging by the tide was a severe penance to Mary
Kearney and her sister, who often turned round to gaze with
longing looks at the promenaders on the " Doneraile Walk " ;
and we fear Miss Anne sometimes wished that the wheel
would fall off, or that the old mare would obstinately refuse
to walk or trot upon sea sand for love or money.

But really, young ladies, you must have patience. The
moon will be bright to-night ; and—don't you see the
O'Shaughnessys driving behind you ?

" 'Twould be worth your while, sir," said Mat Donovan,
" to go out in a boat to the Metal-man's Cave, an' fire a shot
in id. Such an ai-cho you never heard in your life ! I'd
give a crown to get wan box at the Knocknagow dhrum in
id. 'Twould be like the end uv the world ! Mr. Richard
fired a shot in id a few days ago, an' id made the hair stand
on my head. But I knew a box uv the big dhrum would be
a show intirely !"

" So we have Richard here," said Edmund ; "that's
fortunate."

" No, sir " ; returned Mat, " he cut away home. All they
could say couldn't stop him. The minute he laid his eyes
on that bit uv paper stuck on that windy above," continued
Mat, pointing to a window they were just passing, " nothin'
could keep him. You'd think that little scrap was a latitat,
he was so frightened when he see it."

" Do you mean the label with ' Lodgings ' on it ?" Father
Carroll asked.

"Yes, sir," replied Mat, "the Miss Hanlys wor lodgin' there ; but their father came to bring 'em home unexpected."

"Oh, I understand," said Edmund, laughing. "He is now rambling under the shadow of the old castle with the fair Kathleen."

As they walked along the beach by the "storm wall" they were obliged to cross to the other side of the road, as some hundred yards of the footway were enclosed by a high paling with a gate at each end. This arrangement puzzled Arthur O'Connor a good deal, and he wondered what was the object of locking out the public from this portion of the walk.

"The gates will be open by-an'-by, sir," Mat Donovan observed. "That palin' was put up to keep the men from speculatin' on the ladies."

"Speculating on the ladies?" Arthur repeated, inquiringly.

"Yes, sir," replied Mat seriously. "They're here from all parts—they're here from *London*," he added, with emphasis, as if London were at the other end of the world. "There's a Lady Elizabeth, an' a Lady Mary, an' ladies the divil knows what here."

"How did you happen to learn the names of those distinguished visitors, Mat?" Father Carroll asked with a smile.

"Well, sir," Mat answered, with a very solemn expression of countenance, "Phil Morris is here, an' he's lodgin' at a mantymaker's up near the chapel, an' their women do be in there. You might as well thry to understand a turkey-cock as to understand wan uv 'em," added Mat with a blending of astonishment and indignation in his tone.

"But about the speculating?" asked Arthur O'Connor, who was able to make nothing of Mat Donovan's explanation of the paling along the storm wall.

"He means that the paling is intended to keep the men from looking over the wall at the ladies bathing," returned Edmund. "That's what he calls speculating on the ladies. But, Mat, what are you going to do with the spade?"

"To bury Phil Morris, sir," Mat answered.

"Is old Phil dead? I'm very sorry to hear it. It was a treat to listen to him telling of his adventures when he was 'out' in '98."

"He's as stout as a buck," returned Mat. "I'm on'y goin'

to bury him for his pains. If you walk down as far as the mast of the ship that was wracked last winther you'll see him buried in the sand, wud on'y his head above ground, and the sweat runnin' down his face from the weight on him. He says wan buryin' is betther than twenty baths."

"Was there a vessel lost in the bay last winter ?"

"There was, sir. Wanst they get in apast them two white pillars they're done for. Though the fishermen at the Boat-cove tells me there's not an honester bay in Ireland, if the captain would on'y run the vessel in on the strand, instead uv tryin' to get back again."

"By the way, Mat," said Edmund, "has old Phil Morris his pretty granddaughter with him ?"

"He has, sir," returned Mat ; "he couldn't live wudout her, I b'lieve. An', begor, she'd surprise you. She's able to talk to the best uv 'em, an' to undherstand what they'd say. An' she was able to show the dressmaker how to manage some turns an' twists in a new-fashioned gown that she wasn't able to come at herself, afther takin' id asundher. I was standin' by mese'f ; an' she might as well thry to make a watch as put id together, on'y for Bessy."

Mat did not mind telling that he spent a good deal of his time picking shells with Bessy Morris—which shells, in after days, he could never catch the slightest glimpse of, on the fire-board to which they were glued, in Bessy's own little room, without a sigh and mental " God be with old times."

The bathers were now flocking up from the strand, and Edmund Kiely, recognising a light-footed nymph among them, with her silky tresses hanging down her back, was about giving instant chase, when Arthur caught him by the arm, and requested that he would take the world easy.

"It is Minnie Delany," exclaimed Edmund, keeping his eyes on the shining tresses. "Just let me see where she is stopping."

"I'll show you the house," said Mat Donovan, who seemed to be a walking edition of that interesting weekly sheet, ' The Tramore Visitor.'

"She's too damp yet," Arthur observed ; "and possibly her nose is blue, for the water must be rather cold to-day. Let us get a boat and go to the cave, and you can see your friends in the evening."

"They'll be out in all the colours uv the rainbow, by-an'-by," Mat Donovan observed. "But I can't see wan uv 'em to equal Miss Mary."

"Then this lady Mr. Kiely was about running after does not come up to Miss Kearney, in your opinion?" asked Arthur, who was greatly amused by Mat's free-and-easy remarks on things in general.

"Not at all!" returned Mat indignantly. "She's a nice lively little girl, an' she has so many bows, an' feathers, an' goold chains, an' sich things, that people take notice uv her. But she's on'y an Ally Blasther near Miss Mary. But I see Phil Morris waitin' for me, an' I must be off to bury him."

"But who is Ally Blaster?" Arthur asked.

"Ha'penny dolls are called Ally Blasters," replied Father Carroll. "I suspect it is a corruption of 'alabaster.'"

"I hope you will introduce me to your Ally Blaster," said Arthur.

Edmund Kiely was too disgusted to reply, and, buttoning up his "zephyr," he strode on towards the Boat-cove in advance of his friends, looking as if he considered their observations quite beneath contempt.

"This is really a nice bathing place," Arthur O'Connor remarked as he sat at the window of his room in the evening. "But is it not a wonder that the people who build these handsome houses never plant a tree?"

"Come, brush yourself up and be ready to come out," said Edmund, who had run up to his friend's bed-room to protest against his shutting himself up for the evening. "The belles you see, are just about to appear in all the colours of the rainbow, as Mat Donovan said." And Edmund pointed to a young lady at a door a little lower down the street, opening and shutting her parasol.

The evening was calm and sultry, and as Edmund ran his eye along the row of houses opposite, he remarked that all the windows were thrown open and pretty faces were visible at more than one; but for some reason or other none of them as yet emerged into the open air.

"What are they waiting for?" the young gentleman thought to himself, as the parasols at the doors became more numerous. "By Jove, Arthur, I'm in luck!" he exclaimed, aloud. "There she is in the bow-window just opposite!"

" What are you talking about ?" returned Arthur.

" But I must warn you to take care of your heart and vocation," Edmund ran on, " for I am positively haunted by the thought that sooner or later you will come to look upon me as the destroyer of your happiness."

" In the name of common sense what *are* you talking about ?"

" Look at that dazzling little being in the bow-window."

" I see her but can see nothing wonderful about her."

" But, my dear fellow, don't you see it is sweet little Minnie Delany." Here Edmund Kiely bowed and smiled, but the young lady seemed quite unconscious that the eyes of her admirer were on her. She had leant out of the window and looked up at the sky, and Edmund Kiely, following her example, saw that a heavy cloud was hanging like a pall above them. The bay, which an hour or two before looked so sunny, was now almost black. The fringe of white along the strand had become broader, and little eruptions of foam were bursting up here and there far out between the Metal-man and the two white pillars on the opposite side of the bay, marking where those treacherous rocks, so dangerous to the mariner, lifted their iron foreheads almost to the surface of the heaving billows, which now seemed roused from sleep by some mysterious agency ; for

> " There was not wind enough in the air
> To move away the ringlet curl."

from Minnie Delany's cheek, as, with her chin resting on her gloved hand, she leant out of the bow-window and glanced up at the great black cloud hanging in the sky.

" I fear the evening is likely to be wet," Edmund observed ruefully. " I'll ask Father Carroll to step over to see Mrs. Delany, and manage to have us all asked to tea. There will be no walking. There is Somerfield's carriage going back to the stable-yard, too. A splendid pair they are ; Mat Donovan pointed them out to me as we were coming up, and I was honoured by a nod of recognition from one of the ladies."

" Who are they ?" Arthur asked.

" Sam Somerfield's daughters, of Woodlands," returned Edmund. " It is he, or rather his father, keeps the harriers.

Hugh Kearney and I have often had a good run with them."

Arthur O'Connor gave very little attention to what his friend was saying. He was listening with a look of surprise to the soft sweet tones of a flute, which he could hear distinctly through the hoarse chant of the breakers. The circumstance which excited his surprise was, that the music suddenly stopped almost as soon as it had commenced, and then began again, to cease as suddenly as before. This was repeated over and over till Arthur's surprise began to change to something like irritation ; for the strain seemed familiar to him, and affected him strongly, as will often happen

> " Should some notes we used to love
> In days of boyhood meet our ear."

" Can you recognise the air ?" he added, turning to Edmund, who was pensively contemplating the movements of Miss Minnie Delany's fingers, as she twisted up her ringlets after taking off her bonnet—and it would be no violent stretch of the imagination to suppose that Miss Delany had at least a slight suspicion that Mr. Edmund Kiely was so engaged.

" Yes," he replied, after listening for a moment, " 'tis an Irish air." But it stopped again before he could be sure what particular Irish air it was.

Those snatches of melody were becoming fainter and fainter, as if the performer were moving farther away from them ; but they soon noticed them becoming more distinct again, till every note of the few oft-repeated bars could be plainly heard.

" I see how it is," said Arthur. " He began to play at this side of the street, and now he is coming back at the other side."

" Yes, there he is," returned Edmund, " and a most picturesque-looking figure he is, with his cloak and long white hair. He must be a foreigner, I should say."

The musician commenced his melody for the twentieth time ; but the window before which he stood was pulled down, and he let his flute drop into the hollow of his arm, and, hesitating for a moment, walked a few steps, and commenced again—but only to meet with the same reception.

He tried again and again with no better success, till he came within a door or two of the house at the window of which Miss Delany stood toying with her curls.

" He must be new to the business," said Edmund, " or it would not be so easy to shut him up. Did you remark the way his hands trembled when that window was pulled down with such unnecessary violence ? And, by the way, what thin, delicate hands they are. And there is something striking in his pale, melancholy face, too. He certainly must have seen better days."

" 'Tis a shame !" exclaimed Arthur O'Connor, as the poor flute-player met with still another repulse. " What sort of people must these be ?"

" I know the air," said Edmund. " It is the ' Coulin.' "

For the poor musician had walked on to the next house without taking the flute from his lips.

" Hang her !" muttered Arthur, as Miss Minnie Delany, too, pulled down her window ; though she did it so slowly and hesitatingly, that the old minstrel played on seemingly unconscious of this last repulse. Or it might be that he was borne away to other scenes by the sweet melody—

" The home-loving Coulin,
That's sobbing, like Eire, with Sorrow and Love "—

and that poverty and sorrow and humiliation were all forgotten. This, indeed, must have been the case, for the two friends observed, as he turned his mild, melancholy face sideways, towards the sea, that his eyes were closed.

Edmund Kiely reddened, and bit his lips.

Yet pretty Minnie Delany had done only what she had seen others do. She had not the courage to do as her own heart prompted. And, perhaps, the same excuse, such as it is, may be pleaded for some of the others who so rudely spurned the poor flute-player from their doors.

When the Misses Somerfield, of Woodlands, would not listen to the " Coulin "—for the splendid pair of bays champing their bits before the Miss Somerfield's door induced the old musician to begin with them—how could those who had no carriages-and-pairs at all venture to listen to it ? But if the Misses Somerfield, of Woodlands, had the faintest suspicion of who that poor flute-player was, they would have been charmed with the " Coulin," or any other tune he might choose to play, even though it were as Irish as " Garryowen " itself.

He played on now with his face towards the " melancholy ocean," as if he were playing in a dream.

> " Though the last glimpse of Erin with sorrow I see,
> Yet wherever thou art will seem Erin to me.
> In exile thy bosom shall still be my home,
> And thine eyes make my climate wherever we roam."

Edmund had murmured the words softly to the air, and was commencing the next verse, when the sweet tones of the flute were drowned by the shrill voices of a couple of ragged urchins, who accompanied themselves with a most unmusical rattling of bones as they sang, or rather yelled—

> " Out of the way, old Dan Tucker,
> You're too late to get your supper."

The window was thrown up again by Miss Delany's mamma, who seemed quite charmed by the hideous din ; and even Minnie stopped twisting her curls, and beat time to it with her little rosy fingers upon her shoulder. But still the old musician played on, with his pale face turned towards the sea.

A hand—an exquisitely fair and delicate hand—was laid upon his arm, and a pair of large dark lustrous eyes were raised to his. It could be seen at a glance that she was his daughter. The old man started as his eyes met hers ; and after casting a bewildered look around, a painful smile passed over his pale face, as he hid his flute hurriedly in the folds of his cloak. The girl was tall, and, in spite of her worn and faded apparel, singularly graceful. Her lips trembled and her eyes filled with tears as she drew her father away from the crowd of idlers that began to collect around the boys, who " yah, yahed," and rattled their " castanets," till Mrs. Delany seemed to be getting quite faint from the excess of her delight. They had not moved many steps from the crowd when Arthur O'Connor stood by the young girl's side and pressed a piece of silver into her hand. She blushed deeply ; and before she could recover from her surprise, a second piece was placed in the same hand, and, on looking round, the fairest face and the heavenliest blue eyes, she thought, she had ever beheld, met her gaze. For a moment all three seemed spell-bound. The musician's daughter looked from one to the other of her benefactors, while they looked at each other. Arthur O'Connor thought, too, that the young girl who, like himself, had run after the poor flute-player, was the loveliest creature he had ever seen. She was the first to recover presence of mind, and turning quickly round hurried past the grinning vocalists, who were becoming alarmingly black in the face from the vigour of their exertions, and entered a house within a few doors of Mrs. Delany's. The musician's daughter gazed after her with eyes brimful of admiration and gratitude ; but observing that her father had walked on without appearing to miss her from his side, she thanked the student with a smile, and hastened after him.

Edmund Kiely was a spectator of all this ; but he saw nothing distinctly but the musician's dark-eyed daughter. He watched her till she was out of sight, and then seizing his hat started off in pursuit.

Half-an-hour after Edmund Kiely found himself looking down a steep, almost perpendicular wall of rock, into a little cove, where the white surf was swaying backward and forward over the round pebbles with a sharp crashing noise that pierced through the deep rolling of the waves like the rattle of musketry amid the roar of cannon upon the battlefield. To his surprise the old man and his daughter hurried on, and on, keeping close to the shore for more than a mile. He suddenly lost sight of them at this point, and on coming up to the place, he looked over the cliff with a curiosity not unmingled with alarm, for the thought occurred to him that they might have missed their footing and been precipitated into the seething waters below. His heart beat quick as he looked in vain for some trace of them ; and a cry almost escaped from him, on seeing some dark object rising and falling with the waves some fifty yards or so from the shore. He soon, however, saw that the dark object was a mass of seaweed, and his eyes wandered again in every direction in search of the old musician and his daughter.

" Surely," he thought, " it was just here I saw them last ; and where can they have gone ? So old a man would scarcely have ventured down that narrow pathway, where a goat might run the risk of breaking its neck. By Jove!" he exclaimed with a start, "there she is on the top of that black cliff, with the waves tumbling and twisting around its base. What a corsair's bride she would make!"

After standing upon the rock for a minute or two, she waited till the receding wave allowed her to leap upon the strand, and in another moment Edmund watched her climbing, or rather bounding, up the steep pathway, with a step as light as the wild goat's. The path led up close to the rock behind which he was standing, and as she came nearer, her silvery tones fell upon his ear.

"And that's the place where you first saw my dear mother?" said she, stopping a little below where he stood.

"Yes," returned the old man, who sat upon a ledge of the cliff, concealed from Edmund's view. "When consciousness returned, she and the good old priest were standing over me by the side of that rock."

"And they took you to the same house where we are staying. I'm so glad you have brought me to see the place!"

"But I fear I have acted imprudently. It is strange I have got no reply to my letter before now. I very much fear some accident of which I have not heard must have occurred to the friend to whom I have written; for he never failed me before."

"Oh, I am sure you will have a letter to-morrow; and this money the beautiful girl and the young abbé have so kindly given to me will be quite enough for us until then. I only wish I could keep it as a souvenir of them. He is so very handsome; and she so exquisitely lovely! Did you notice them?"

"No, I noticed nothing," he replied. "My *debut* as an itinerant musician has not been encouraging."

"I asked the name of those ladies for whom you first played," returned his daughter. "I thought it very unkind of them to close their window as they did, and they such stylish people. I was told their name is Somerfield."

"Somerfield," repeated the old man, musingly. "I am acquainted with that name."

"The Somerfields of Woodlands," she added.

"The same," returned her father. "It is a strange coincidence."

" How is that ?" she asked.

" I'll tell you another time," he answered. " Let us go
now. The fisherman promised to inquire for a letter in
Waterford, and I am not without hopes that he may have
one for us when he comes back. I scarcely expected your
uncle would write, but it will surprise me much if the friend
to whom I have written do not send the small sum I asked
of him. I am determined to put my case in the hands of a
lawyer at last, and see whether I cannot compel my unkind
brother to do me justice. It is a duty I owe to you, my
child."

" My dear father," she returned, " don't be so anxious
about me. Thanks to the care you have bestowed on my
education, I feel I can earn my bread respectably whenever
it is necessary."

" I trust it will not come to that," replied the old man.
" You do not know how bitter a thing it is to be dependent
upon strangers. But see, those heavy clouds are about to
burst, and we must hasten back, or we shall get well drenched
before we can reach the cottage."

They retraced their steps for some distance along the path
over the cliffs, and Edmund, climbing to the top of the rock
against which he had been leaning, saw them turn to the left
up a steep narrow road, and enter a small thatched cottage a
couple of hundred yards from the shore.

If we ventured to turn Mr. Edmund Kiely's thoughts, as
he stood with folded arms upon that rock high above the
surging sea, into plain prose, we fear some at least of our
readers would not readily set him down for the sensible
fellow he really was. He was startled from his reverie,
however, by a vivid flash of lightning, followed quickly by a
terrific thunder-clap that seemed to shake the rocks around
him. Then, as the old musician had foretold, down came the
rain in a hissing torrent ; and Mr. Edmund Kiely leaped from
his elevated position, and pulling the collar of his zephyr up
over his ears, made straight for the fisherman's cottage, with
the fleetness of an arrow ; persuading himself that his only
earthly object was to escape getting wet to the skin.
Raising the latch, he flung the door open, and standing
inside the threshold, shook the rain from his hat and coat
without even looking about to see who or what the inmates

of the house might be. It was quite plain the young gentleman only sought shelter from the thunder-shower ! The
woman of the house, however, placed a chair in front of the
fire, and invited him to sit down ; and then he saw an old
man with white hair sitting by the fire, and a young girl
with dark hair at a table near the small window, writing or
making a sketch upon the blank leaf of a book.

" I have just run in to escape from the shower," Edmund
remarked. " It has come down very suddenly, but I do not
think it will last long."

The door was again opened before the old man could make
any reply, and the fisherman entered with the water running
down from his " sou'-wester," and over his oil-cloth jacket, as
if he had just emerged from the waves. Thrusting his hand
inside his waistcoat, he produced a letter, and presented it
without speaking to the old musician, who snatched it
nervously from his hand, and retired into an inner room,
followed by the young girl.

" Who is that old gentleman ?" Edmund asked.

" I couldn't tell you, sir," the fisherman answered. " He
says he lodged here the year the French vessel was lost in
the bay. That was in my father's time, and I was in New-
foundland myself. So I have no recollection of him. There
wasn't near so many houses in Tramore then, and people
used to come and lodge here in the summer. But, though
poor he is, he's a gentleman. I'd take my oath uv that any
day."

" Ay, an' his daughter is a born lady," added his wife.
" An' they're welcome to stop for a month if they like before
I'd ax 'em for a penny. 'Twould rise the cockles uv your
heart to hear her singin' the ' Coulin,' an' her father playin'
id on the flute. I thought I was in heaven listenin' to 'em
last night."

The old man or his daughter did not return to the kitchen,
and the rain having ceased quite suddenly, Edmund stood
up to leave, resolving that he would find some pretext for
returning to the cottage next day. Seeing that the young
girl had left her book, with the pencil in it, on the table,
curiosity impelled him to take it up and look at it. It was
a well-worn copy of Moore's Melodies. Glancing at the blank
leaf between the " Irish " and " National Melodies," his face

betokened the utmost astonishment ; for on the blank leaf
he beheld Arthur O'Connor's handsome profile done to
the life. The sensations created by this discovery were not
altogether of the pleasurable sort ; and he remembered with
some satisfaction that she spoke of Arthur a little while
before as " the young abbé." There was also an unfinished
female head, the contour of which reminded him of some
one, though just then he could not say of whom ; but he had
no doubt it was meant for " the beautiful girl ' mentioned in
connection with " the young abbé."

" 'Tis most extraordinary," thought Edmund. " Arthur
and I will most certainly be at logger-heads some day."

He wrote with the pencil on the leaf—" Don't be offended.
I am a friend of the young abbé." And slipping a pound-
note between the leaves, he replaced the book on the table.

" It is quite fine now," he remarked. " There is the
moon rising out of the bay. I shall have quite a pleasant
walk back." And bidding the fisherman and his wife
" Good evening," he proceeded on his way back to the town
by the " Doneraile Walk." Minnie Delany was among the
moonlight promenaders on the walk—for one of the advan-
tages of this pleasant seaside resort is that five minutes after
the heaviest fall of rain, the daintiest feet can venture out
without fear of wet or mud—but alas ! Mr. Edmund Kiely
deliberately turned from the smooth gravelled walk, and,
descending to the brink of the steep shore, stood there for a
good hour and more, watching the shimmering of the moonlit bay.

Edmund Kiely did not sleep as soundly as was his wont
that night, and in the morning he was pacing up and down
by the storm-wall long before there were any fair nymphs to
" speculate " upon among the breakers. He saw Mat Donovan at some distance purchasing cockles from a barefooted
woman on her way from the Black Strand ; and it occurred
to him that Mat would be able to learn something about
the old musician and his daughter for him. But Mat, with
his purchase tied up in his red cotton pocket-handkerchief,
was gone before he could come near enough to speak to him,
and he put it off till he should fall in with him in the course
of the day. But during the morning and afternoon he looked
about in vain for a sight of Mat Donovan. In the evening

he recognised Bessy Morris and her grandfather among the
rocks at the Boat-cove, and leaving Father Carroll and Arthur
O'Connor to comment upon Tom Steele's remarkable speech
at the last " usual weekly meeting " of the " Loyal National
Repeal Association," made his way over the slippery seaweed, and, after congratulating the old weaver on his good
looks, inquired of Bessy whether she had seen Mat Donovan
during the day.

" I saw him buying cockles on the strand early in the
morning," he added, " but I have not seen him since."

" He went home to-day, sir," Bessy answered, looking very
innocent and unconscious.

And the fact was, at that identical moment, Willie
Kearney and Tommy Lahy, sitting by the side of a hay-cock
in the kiln-field, were grinding those same cockles one against
another and greedily devouring them ; while Ellie was rolling
the most beautiful " pair ' of jackstones (consisting of five)
ever seen, between her hands ; and Jack Delany's twins
were making desperate efforts to choke themselves with two
monstrous lobster-claws—cockles and jackstones and lobster-
claws being presents from Mat the Thrasher, who was just
then expatiating upon the virtues of a peculiar kind of sand,
a small bag of which he was the happy possessor of, for
sharpening a scythe, and holding forth in his own expressive
and felicitous manner upon the wonders of the mighty deep,
to the amazement and delight of Tom Maher and Barney
Brodherick. And at that moment, too, Kit Cummins left
off abusing her next-door neighbour, and pushing her dishevelled hair under her cap of dubious hue, stood outside
her own door, and addressing all Knocknagow, gave it as her
private opinion that Mrs. Kearney looked younger and rosier
than her own daughters " afther the wather "—an opinion
which no one in Knocknagow ventured to contradict, unless
a suppressed " gir-r-r-out, you bla'guard," from the next
door neighbour, might be taken as an expression of dissent.

" It seems Mrs. Kearney is gone home," said Edmund,
after returning to his companions. " I'm sorry I did not
see them."

" They were wondering why you did not make your appearance anywhere last evening," returned Father Carroll. " I
wanted to persuade Arthur to spend the evening with them as

you could not be found, but he would not. And, by the way,
I see Sir Thomas Butler's death announced in this paper."

"What has that to do with my refusal?" Arthur asked.

"He was Maurice Kearney's landlord," returned Father
Carroll. "It may be a matter of some consequence to them."

Edmund, seeing the fisherman, in whose house he took
shelter from the rain the evening before, coming up from
the cove with a boat-hook on his shoulder, hastened to meet
him. The man immediately presented him with a letter.

"Are they gone?" Edmund asked, after glancing at its
contents.

"They went early this morning, sir," replied the fisherman.

"Where?" Edmund asked eagerly.

"The Lord knows," returned the fisherman. "An' the
Lord bless 'em wherever they go; for they behaved well to
us, any way. There was some great news in that letter I
brought from Waterford yesterday, but when my wife made
the same remark they said nothin'."

The pound-note was enclosed in the letter which Edmund
now held in his hand. But there was no signature, no clue
by which he could hope to trace them; only the words:
"Many, many thanks—but we do not *now* require it. May
God bless you for your kindness. We shall never forget it."

"And so ends my dream!" thought Edmund. "But
something tells me I shall meet her again. She thinks
Arthur is already a priest; it may be better for his peace of
mind not to be told of that sketch. It was a wonderfully
true likeness. I wonder has she made a sketch of *me*?—Did
you remark that girl with the old flute-player yesterday?"
he asked aloud as he came up with Arthur, who seemed to
have his own fancies at the moment.

"She was very beautiful," he replied absently.

"Beauty 'like the night,'" rejoined Edmund.

"No," said Arthur, looking surprised. "She was singularly fair; and her eyes were blue."

"There must have been something the matter with *your*
eyes," returned Edmund. "I never saw such a pair of black
eyes in all my life."

"Oh, you mean the girl that seemed to be his daughter?"

"Of course I do. Did you ever see such eyes?"

"Well, yes. They reminded me of my cousin Annie, of whom we were talking the other evening."

"Then, by all means keep out of their way—if you would not endanger your vocation," said Edmund, laughing.

Arthur O'Connor looked grave, and made no reply. He knew he had no vocation for the church. But he thought of his mother, and resolved to strive and pray for it.

"This place is infernally dull, after all," yawned Edmund Kiely. "I'm tired of it already."

One gloomy day in the following winter, Arthur was "pounding" for the examinations, in his room in —— College, when Father Carroll was announced.

"Come over to the Ursuline Convent with me," said he after shaking hands with the student. "I'm going to see Sister Clare."

Sister Clare received her reverend brother and his friend with bright smiles of welcome, and after innumerable inquiries about friends at home and abroad, she exclaimed in reply to a question of Father Carroll's—"Oh, I'll bring her down to you," and left the room.

Arthur was so occupied examining a painting of the Virgin, copied, Sister Clare had just told him, by one of the nuns from an original of one of the old masters which a gentleman in the neighbourhood had lent to them, that he was not aware of Sister Clare's return to the room till he heard Father Carroll say—

"She is keeping up the beauty, I see."

"Oh, she'll be quite spoiled," returned the nun. "Every one talks of her beauty."

Arthur turned round; and if the picture he had been examining had moved its lips or its eyes, his look could scarcely have expressed greater astonishment. Yet there was nothing in the least miraculous to excite his wonder.

"Don't you know Arthur O'Connor?" Father Carroll asked.

"No," was the low, hesitating reply.

"What is it all about?" exclaimed Father Carroll. "Ye both look as if ye had seen a ghost. This is my cousin, Miss Kearney; so don't be afraid."

"I saw Miss Kearney once before," returned Arthur; "but I did not know who she was."

"I remember," said Mary, with a smile and a blush.

" Where was it ?" Father Carroll asked.

" In Tramore," Mary answered.

" Would you like to hear her play ?" said Sister Clare.

" Do give us a tune, Mary ?" said Father Carroll.   " Though
I don't know I'll care much for your music after Flaherty.
He was at Major French's a few weeks ago, and did me the
honour of coming over for an hour or two occasionally—but
it was in compliment to your mother and her Uncle Dan,
who, next to Sir Garrett Butler, he says, was the best friend
ever he had."

Mary went to the piano, and after a little hesitation and
embarrassment commenced an Irish melody, and played it
with such feeling that Father Carroll exclaimed—" You
really play very well, Mary.   And one would think you
wanted to rival Flaherty.   That is his favourite tune ; and
you play it in his manner.   Did you ever hear him ?"

" No, I never heard Mr. Flaherty play, though I often
wished to hear him," Mary replied.

" She ought to play that air well," Sister Clare observed,
" for she is continually practising it.   Edmund Kiely was
here lately, and he would not let her play anything but the
' Coulin,' the ' Coulin,' over and over."

" Ha ! is that the way the wind blows ?" said Father
Carroll.

Mary bent her head and laughed, but made no reply.

After this Arthur O'Connor and Mary Kearney became
great friends.   He spent a week at Christmas at Ballinaclash,
and two weeks in the summer—besides meeting her at the
seaside.   Oh, those seaside musings and communings !   But
then Arthur's mother openly accused Mary of trying to lure
her son from the high and holy path he had entered upon ;
an accusation which so pained and shocked the gentle girl
that she insisted upon breaking off all further intercourse
with him.   Her brother Hugh approved of her resolution,
and ever Arthur himself admitted that she was right.   He
pursued his studies industriously, and was among the students
of —— College chosen to be sent to Maynooth at the examinations which took place a week or two before Sir Garrett
Butler's nephew did Maurice Kearney the honour of becoming his guest.   Arthur, however, preferred the Irish College
at Paris to Maynooth, and was on his way to spend a day or

two with Father Carroll before leaving Ireland, when he chanced to see Barney Brodherick and his black donkey in the main street of Kilthubber. There was some delay about the car he had ordered; and, as he would have to pass by the cottage on his way to Father Carroll's, the wish to see Mary Kearney once more, and bid her good-bye, became so strong, that he wrote a hasty line, asking her to be at the little window in the ivied gable to shake hands with him. If she had no objection, he said, he would like to see her father and mother, and all of them, before he left. But, if she feared whispering tongues might be busy if he called in the usual way, he would be satisfied with a good-bye from the garden. He gave the note to Barney, who thrust it into his hat, and, as a matter of course, forgot to deliver it till Mary's question, the evening after, reminded him of it, when she was wondering whose could be those mysterious footprints in the snow from under her window to the stile behind the laurels.

" And now he is gone !" said Mary, after reading the note. Yes, he was gone ; and in by no means a happy frame of mind.

And now the reader knows more of the tracks in the snow than Mr. Henry Lowe ; to whom we will return, just to see him safe out of Tipperary ; that is, so far as his bones are concerned. But we do not by any means vouch for the wholeness of the young gentleman's heart.

CHAPTER LII.

THE BULL-BAIT.—THE CARRICK-MAN AND HIS DOG "TRUE-BOY."—LORY PUNISHES BERESFORD PENDER, AND RIDES HOME BEHIND MR. BOB LLOYD, ON THE GREY HUNTER.—MISS LLOYD INVOLUNTARILY SITS DOWN.

MR. HENRY LOWE is pacing slowly and thoughtfully up and down the box-bordered walk in the little garden at the end of the cottage. He stops occasionally to gaze upon the blue mountains ; and once or twice he stood upon the stile behind the laurels, and looked along the road towards the hamlet.

But, whether gazing at the mountain, or looking along the
road, or pacing the box-bordered walk, Mr. Henry Lowe's
mind's eye is ever turned to the little window in the ivied
gable. As the day of his departure drew nearer and nearer,
he had been watching for an opportunity to speak to Mary
Kearney alone. But whether it happened by accident or
design, he never could find the opportunity he sought. She
was always accompanied by Grace or Ellie ; and once or
twice, when he met her by herself, she found some excuse
for going away before he could screw his courage to the
sticking place. There was nothing to hinder him from
saying at once and in plain words that he wished to have a
minute's private conversation with her ; but he couldn't
make up his mind to take what he considered so decided a
step. He wished to feel his way a little, and would prefer
a casual meeting. But the fates seemed to be against him.
He had observed that Mary was in the habit of walking alone
in the garden about this hour every day ; but until this
morning the doctor or Hugh was always with him at the
time, and he could find no excuse for leaving them.

 " Now," he thought—looking at his watch and finding that
it was past the hour when she was accustomed to take her
walk—" now if she does not come out as usual, I must con-
clude she is purposely avoiding me." The thought at first
gave him a twinge of pain ; but on reflection he said to himself that, if she were indifferent about him, she would not
keep out of his way at all. He found consolation in this
last-mentioned reflection, and continued his walk and his
reverie. He thought that, if he were a man of property, he
would, beyond all doubt, marry the beautiful daughter of his
uncle's principal tenant, or that if he had not given up his
intention of becoming a clergyman—and if Miss Kearney's
religion were not an awkward stumbling-block in the way—
what a happy quiet life he could live with her in some snug
parsonage upon as many hundred pounds a year as he could
get ! But as both the property and the parsonage were out
of the question, he could see nothing better, that was at all
practicable under present circumstances, than a very sentimental love affair, involving voluminous correspondence, with
a dim vista of something turning up in the distant future,
that might prove a substitute for the property which he

had not, or the parsonage which it was now too late to think of. His reveries were interrupted by the opening of the garden gate, and Mr. Lowe looked up quickly ; but it was not Mary, but her young brother, Willie, bearing the accomplished jay in its wicker cage in his arms, followed by Ellie with her goldfinch. The day was sufficiently soft and sunny to suggest to Ellie that both the goldfinch and the jay would like a little fresh air and sunshine. Grace was just then practising a new song, and Ellie knew it would be useless asking her to trouble herself even about her own jay—" My dear !"—and Willie's services were engaged. He laid the wicker cage on a rustic seat near the laurels, while Ellie climbed upon the back of the seat to hang her little green cage upon a nail which she had driven into the trunk of an ash tree, sufficiently high, as she thought, to save her bird from the old grey cat, who sometimes came prowling about that way. Tommy Lahy had offered to catch the old grey cat and rub his nose against the wires till it bled freely, by way of warning ; but this Ellie positively objected to, as there was no overt act to prove that the old grey cat entertained any felonious intentions whatever against her goldfinch.

At first Mr. Lowe felt annoyed when he saw they intended making an indefinite stay in the garden ; but then it occurred to him their presence would not interfere with his conversation with their sister, but, on the contrary, would make her feel more at ease. So he looked at his watch again, and took another turn up and down the walk. And now those tantalising tracks in the snow came into his head for the thousandth time. What *could* they mean ? The idea that there was a " lord of the valley," who came with "false vows," as Grace suggested, was, he thought, utterly preposterous. Yet it was not quite so clear that there might not be some one who was not a lord of a valley and whose vows were not false vows. He could not, however, look upon any of the young men whom from time to time he had seen trying to make themselves agreeable—and to all of whom she was equally gracious—as likely to prove a very dangerous rival. Not one ; not even the stylish young man in top-boots, with the horse-shoe pin in his scarf, who so astonished him by touching his hat and addressing him as " your honour." It scarcely

amounted to coxcombry in Mr. Lowe to feel pretty well satisfied that he himself held a high place in Miss Kearney's
esteem, and that in fact if any one held a higher, it was her
brother Hugh. He wondered at her taste in regard to Hugh ;
but of course he was not going to be jealous of her brother.
Yet a brother may sometimes prove a more formidable rival
than lovers dream of ; particularly when the world in general
is so stupid as not to recognise his super-excellent qualities—
which happened to be the case in this instance. She was
angry with her lady acquaintances that they did not fall
down and worship him. And it must be admitted she was
sometimes angry with Hugh for not being as enthusiastic
as he ought to be about one or two dear friends of hers
who, she thought, had the good taste to appreciate him.
There was one in particular with whom she was sure he
ought to have fallen in love. On one occasion this young
lady, when presenting Mary with a bunch of flowers, ran to
the end of the lawn for a little sprig of hawthorn and secured
it in the nosegay ; a rather odd proceeding, seeing that both
sides of the road nearly all the way from the residence of
the young lady to Ballinaclash were white with hawthorn
blossoms. But the mystery was cleared up in the most satisfactory manner when she whispered into Mary's ear that the
hawthorn was for Hugh ; for all the world—except Hugh
himself—knew that hawthorn blossom was " emblematic of
hope." Hugh, however, took the blossom with a smile ; and
Mary said gravely, " She was in earnest." To which Hugh
just as gravely replied, " Of course." Whereupon Mary
became indignant, and told him she did not know " what to
make of him," and that no one could know " what was in his
mind " ; and that she did not see why people should be
" bothering their heads about him," with more to the same
effect.

Nevertheless, Mr. Lowe was not far wrong in suspecting
that Miss Kearney made her eldest brother the standard by
which she measured other men.

He was glancing again at the window when his olfactory
nerves detected the odour of the fragrant weed, and on looking towards the gate he saw the doctor leisurely approaching
with his hands in his pockets.

" What a fine day it is for this season !" the doctor

observed, waving away a little blue cloud that almost stood still before his face, and then stopping to admire his hand, which was sufficiently white and slender. " By Jove, there is quite a glow in the air."

Mr. Lowe replied with a sigh ; for he saw all hope of the looked-for interview was gone for that day at least. And, what was particularly irritating, Mary made her appearance at the same moment, and with that smile of hers, which more than anything else about her tended to turn his head, said—

" What a lovely day this is, Mr. Lowe ! I wish you could see the country about here in the summer. But the mountains at least are beautiful at all seasons."

" Very," he replied, somewhat sulkily.

" I hope you enjoyed the evening at Woodlands ?" she asked.

" Well, not much."

" Because you had not the ladies, I suppose."

" No, not exactly that. But the conversation was not interesting. It was all about landlords and tenants, and leases and ejectments, and that sort of thing. The party seemed got up specially to discuss such matters. I expected something rollicking, but it was nothing of the kind."

" Had you Mr. Lloyd there ?"

" No, but his name was introduced several times. He was strongly condemned for the way he manages his property. He gives leases, and has no objection to small farms ; and is, it would appear, in bad odour on that account. It seems they all feel bound to abide by a resolution adopted at some meeting of landlords a long time ago not to renew leases when they expire. Mr. Somerfield thinks the more independent the tenantry become, the harder it will be to manage them. He says Mr. Lloyd's tenants don't care a rush for him, as they have all long leases at a low rent."

" Oh, if all landlords were like Mr. Somerfield," returned Mary, " Ireland would soon be a desert. There is not even one house now left on his whole property."

" Yes," her brother observed, " and you can count the number of houses he has levelled if you have any curiosity about it ; for he has left a gable of each standing as a monument of all the good he has done. But of course you know I allude to Sam ; for the old fellow had nothing to do with it. On the contrary, I'm told it grieved him to see his old tenants hunted away. Hugh tells me, too, it was a dead loss to him, and that they are head and ears in debt, stocking the land was so expensive."

" I'm heartily sick of the whole subject since last night," returned Mr. Lowe. " I think much of what they said was meant specially for me. But the more I hear about the relations between landlord and tenant, the more I am bewildered."

Mr. Lowe did feel bewildered at the moment ; for Mary's blue eyes would bewilder a sage, as she watched her young sister chasing the old grey cat, who had come slyly prowling about her goldfinch.

" There's something up," the doctor exclaimed, on observing Phil Lahy and half-a-dozen others crossing the lawn by the short-cut from Knocknagow to the cross of Rosdrum.

" Perhaps they are going to a funeral," said Mary. " They always go to funerals in that direction by the short-cut."

" Judging from their looks and the hurry they are in," returned the doctor, " it must be something more exciting than a funeral."

He stood upon the rustic seat in order to have a better view, and saw a man with a dog at his heels, accompanied by two boys who were making desperate efforts to take sufficiently long strides to keep up with him, but were obliged to get into a sling trot every now and then, so rapid was the pace at which he swept along, with his hat so far back on his poll that it seemed as nearly at a right angle as if it were hanging against a wall. The boys managed to get a little in advance of him occasionally, and looked up in his face, evidently reverencing him as an oracle, and wishing to observe the expression of his countenance, which was very red and excited, while he uttered his words of wisdom, all the time keeping his eyes steadily fixed on the hill over Rosdrum, straight before him.

" He is a stranger to me," said the doctor. " And these two young scamps with him do not belong to this neighbourhood, either, I think."

" I never saw any of them before," returned Mary. " And there is Barney off after them," she added, " leaving the ass in the middle of the lawn to go wherever he pleases. I wonder——" Here Mary uttered a cry of terror, and grasped Mr. Lowe by the arm ; which so astonished the young gentleman that the agreeable sensations the proceeding was calculated to awaken were quite lost. The cause of her alarm was nothing more or less than Wat Murphy's bull-dog, who stood wagging his tail, and holding up his muzzled snout as he looked into her face, evidently doing his best to be as amiable and fascinating as possible, but, like some others of her admirers, with only indifferent success.

" Morrow, Wat," said Maurice Kearney, who, stick in hand, was standing near the half-dozen small cocks into which the fallen remnant of the hay-rick had been hastily converted in order to save it from the weather.

" Five pounds," was the butcher's reply to the salutation.

" I won't give it to you to-day," returned Maurice Kearney brusquely.

" To buy the bull," Wat added ; and then whistled to his dog.

Maurice Kearney rubbed his poll contemplatively for a moment, and then walked leisurely into the house to procure the money.

" O Richard, Richard !" exclaimed Mrs. Kearney, hurrying into the garden in a state of distraction. " There is the ass running off, and he'll be sure to run down into that pit, and all the things will be in pieces—the wine and all. Oh, what's to become of me with that fellow ? I suppose that man with the dog must be a ballad-singer, and there he's off after him."

The doctor jumped from the rustic seat over the hedge, and set off across the lawn at the top of his speed in pursuit. Coming up with the runaway donkey before he reached the pit, the doctor seized the little blue cart behind, and commenced pulling it back with all his might. But Bobby trotted on, quite regardless of his efforts. The doctor pulled and pulled till the struggle became quite exciting. But, just as he reached the brink of the pit, and as Mrs. Kearney raised her hands in despair, Bobby, without giving the slightest notice of his intention, stood stock still, and the doctor sat down much in the same manner as he had done

upon the ice on Bob Lloyd's pond, with his legs stretched out
under the donkey-cart, his nose touching the tail-board, and
his heels almost in contact with the donkey's. After reflecting for a moment, he found it was necessary to lie upon his
back and turn himself over before he could get up ; a
manœuvre which he executed with great precipitation ; for it
occurred to him that Bobby might take a fancy to set back,
and trample upon him.

"Come on, sir," said the doctor, catching the donkey's
winkers, and pulling him on.

But Bobby never stirred a foot.

He called him " poor fellow," and patted him on the neck,
and, putting his closed hand to his mouth, blew an imaginary
horn, as Barney was wont to do when he would encourage
Bobby to put forth all his speed.

But Bobby refused to budge.

Losing all patience, Richard looked round for a stick
wherewith to punish the aggravating little brute, when
another expedient occurred to him. Seizing the reins, he
got up and sat upon the front of the cart with a foot on each
shaft. Scarcely had he fixed himself comfortably in this
position when Bobby bounded forward at a gallop, flinging
the doctor on his back in the cart with his legs in the air.
Baskets, and parcels, and bottles began bumping and tumbling about his head in a most bewildering manner ; for Bobby
had taken a sweep round to a part of the field where there
were a number of open drains, and, after clearing them all in
excellent style, ran straight for the hall door, where he again
stopped short, looking as meek as a lamb.

" O Richard," cried his mother, " are you killed ?"

The doctor tumbled himself out of the cart, and looked
wildly about him.

" Are you killed, Richard ?" Mrs. Kearney asked again.

The doctor stared at his mother with a look of the most
profound astonishment ; and then stared at Bobby ; and then
at the hall door, and the windows, and up at the chimneys,
and all around him. Then he fixed his eyes on the ground,
and seemed plunged in some mental effort that taxed his
powers of thought to the utmost. It was evident that the
little misadventure had proved confusing in a very high
degree to his faculties—which was not at all surprising, as

the clearing of the last drain had brought a bottle of port wine out of the hamper straight upon his forehead—and that, on the whole, he was not quite sure of his whereabouts or how he happened to get there.

"Are you hurt, Richard?" his mother asked again, laying her hand upon his arm.

"Blazes!" muttered the doctor, clapping his hand against his forehead.

What blazes had to do with the matter, or whether he thought "blazes" a rational and suitable reply to his mother's anxious and oft-repeated inquiry, is more than we can venture to say. But "blazes" was the only word uttered by the doctor up to this stage of the proceeding.

Mr. Lowe took the doctor's hat from among the straw in the donkey-cart and presented it to the owner, who accepted it in surprise, and honoured Mr. Lowe with a stare of surprise, as if he had not the least idea who that gentleman was.

"Morrow, Dick," said Mr. Bob Lloyd, who had turned the corner of the house, mounted on his grey horse, unobserved except by Grace, who was sitting at the drawingroom window, and whom he had already honoured with a few admiring glances.

"Good morrow," returned the doctor, who seemed to be slowly recovering his senses.

"Are you coming to the bull-bait?" Mr. Lloyd asked.

"What do you say?" said the doctor turning to Mr. Lowe.

"Well, I'd like to see what it is like," he replied.

"So would I," returned the doctor, somewhat sulkily. "But unfortunately the horses are all ploughing to-day, and I don't see how we can manage."

"'Tis only a pleasant walk by the short-cut," rejoined Bob Lloyd.

"Are you going the short-cut?" Mr. Lowe asked.

"Ay, faith," replied Mr. Lloyd, smiling at Grace in the window. "But, Dick, what the devil fancy did you take to lying on your back in the cart with your legs stuck out? I thought you were a plough with a breeches on it."

"Come and let us get ready," said the doctor, darting an angry glance at Grace, whose ringing laugh called his attention to her.

"Positively, Grace," said Mary, half-an-hour after the

gentlemen had left, " you have made a conquest of Mr. Lloyd. He never took his eyes off you all the time."

" Yes, I remarked him," returned Grace, with her wise look. " He is much more intelligent-looking than I thought. And that idea of comparing Richard's legs to a plough was really good."

" And then he is a man of property," returned Mary, with a smile.

" That fact is by no means to be lost sight of," rejoined Grace, " whatever you innocently romantic people may say. But surely," she added with a look of surprise, " those are Lory's legs careering at such a tremendous rate across that field ; but, what, in the name of wonder, is that on his head ?"

" It is a straw hat," replied Mary, seeing the article in question blown from Lory's head as he was about jumping from the top of the " new ditch."

" Yes, I see how it is," Grace observed. " Rose has locked up his cap to keep him from going to the bull-bait ; and Lory has taken Joe Russel's huge straw hat, and broken loose from his captor. That boy's energy is wonderful ; and I have no doubt he will yet distinguish himself in some way. But Rose does rule him with a rod of iron. And yet the trouble she takes brushing his hair, in the vain hope of keeping it from sticking out like the quills of a porcupine, cannot be too much admired. But I decidedly disapprove of the big bow-knot into which she insists on tying his cravat."

" There is the hat off again," said Mary.

" By the way," rejoined Grace, " did I tell you of the little drama I had the pleasure of witnessing the other day when I drove to town with Rose, on account of that same hat ?"

" No, you did not tell me."

" Well, Joe Russel was our coachman, and the big straw-hat, however becoming on the driver of a cart or dray, was not in keeping with the phaeton. But, however, while Rose was in at Quinlan's getting some note-paper, a youth on the pavement asked Joe what would he take ' for the fur of his hat.' ' Will you hould the reins for wan minute, Miss ? says Joe. Of course I could not refuse, particularly as the request was made in a tone of the blandest politeness. Well, Joe got down, and, walking over to the inquisitive youth, commenced pummelling him in the most awful manner. He struck back vigorously, however, and there was a tremendous fight, till Mat Donovan happened to be passing and put them asunder. Joe came back and resumed the reins, evidently quite satisfied in his mind, notwithstanding that his left eye was shut up. I saw the inquisitive youth after at the pump trying to stop his nose from bleeding; and he certainly looked as if he had made up his mind not to trouble himself again about the value of the fur of Joe Russel's straw hat."

On went Lory "as the crow flies," clearing everything in his way till he came to Mr. Beresford Pender's gate at the three poplars, which was secured by a broken gig wheel that leant against it.

"Go back out of that," shouted Mr. Pender from the big window that so astonished Barney Brodherick the day of his visit to that interesting concern. "Don't dare to climb over that gate."

"I passed through a good many places in my time," returned Lory, as he deliberately climbed to the top of the gate, "and this is the first time I was ever told to go back."

"You may pass through farmers' places," rejoined Mr. Beresford Pender in his big voice, "but this is a gentleman's demesne."

"A gentleman's fiddle-stick," replied Lory, pulling Joe Russel's straw-hat tightly over his ears—having first hit upon the ingenious contrivance of bending the leaf back in front into the inside to keep the hat from flying off, thereby giving it the appearance of a bonnet put on the wrong way, to which we have before likened it.

"I'll summon you before the bench," roared Beresford.

"Summon your grandmother," retorted Lory, jumping off the gate and resuming his race.

This was quite a random shot of Lory's, but it put Mr. Pender into a fury; for the venerable lady alluded to had really been brought before "the bench" for making free with certain articles of wearing apparel, drying on a hedge, which did not belong to her. This was a mere tradition, however, only remembered by Poll the housekeeper and a few others; but it had been thrown in Beresford's face once or twice, and he now swore he would "make Hanly pay for his insolence."

Lory dashed on, however, caring little for Mr. Beresford

Pender's threatened vengeance, till he came to the narrow
boreen leading to Ned Brophy's house.

"Morrow, Ned," cried Lory, seeing him fencing a gap at
some distance. But, to his astonishment, instead of returning his salutation in his usual friendly way, Ned flung the
spade out of his hand, and ran as if it were for his life, never
once glancing behind him.

"He thinks I'm a process-server," said Lory to himself.
"Or," he added, with his sepulchral laugh, pulling off his hat
and holding it at arms' length before him, "maybe 'tis Joe
Russel's hat that frightened him." He walked through the
yard, intending to follow Ned into the house, and assure him
that he had nothing to fear, when he encountered Mrs. Ned
at the door.

"I want to ask Ned to show me where the bull-bait is,"
said Lory, with another laugh at what he supposed Ned's
mistake as to his identity, or his intentions.

"Ned knows nothin' about id," returned Mrs. Ned, standing in the middle of the doorway, and with a look that made
Lory think she, too, must have formed some erroneous idea
about him. "They're over beyond the sallies, I b'lieve,"
Mrs. Ned added.

The fact was, that, since his marriage, Ned Brophy ran and
hid himself from every acquaintance who happened to come
near the house. For his wife declared that the business of
all visitors was solely and simply "to fill their craw," as she
expressed it. And Ned, seeing her "so bitter" on his friends,
felt so ashamed that he thought it best to shun them altogether. He tried to console himself with the reflection that,
at least, he'd soon have an old saucepan half filled with
golden sovereigns, Mrs. Ned was such a "fine housekeeper.'
But he sometimes thought, not of golden sovereigns, but of
Nancy Hogan's golden hair, and sighed.

Lory looked at Mrs. Ned Brophy with unfeigned surprise,
and set off for the nearest house—which happened to be old
Padly Laughlan's—to seek the information he required.

Paddy Laughlan's blooming daughter not only told him
where the bull-bait was, but walked to the end of her father's
farm with him, in spite of his protestations that her doing
so was quite unnecessary, and that he could not allow her to
go to so much trouble on his account.

" You see that little boy on the tree," said Miss Laughlan. " They are in the hollow just under him." But though pointing with her hand to the boy on the tree, Miss Laughlan kept her eyes fixed very earnestly upon a small farm-house on her left.

" Thank you," said Lory, starting off again.

" I beg your pardon, sir," said Miss Laughlan.

Lory stopped.

But Miss Laughlan only blushed and hesitated.

" I thought you spoke to me," said he. And it occurred to him at the moment that she was by far a handsomer girl than he had thought—there was such a light in her eyes !

" If you'd bring a message for me to that house—to Tom Cuddehy," said Miss Laughlan, " I'd be very thankful to you."

" Of course I will," replied Lory. " I know Tom Cuddehy well. He's the best hurler in the county, except Mat Donovan."

" Well, will you tell him I am waiting here, and that I want to speak to him just for one minute," returned Miss Laughlan, falteringly. And Lory fancied her eyes filled with tears.

" Certainly I will," he replied. " Why not ?"

This was the " message " Lory took so long to deliver when we left him in Tom Cuddehy's kitchen—when, some chapters back, we thought it necessary to interrupt the regular course of this history, in order to guard against the possibility of disturbing the equanimity of our readers here-after by anything that might bear even the faintest resembl-ance to a surprise.

" Good morning," said Lory, " I'm going to the bull-bait."

" I promised to go myself," returned Tom Cuddehy, " to thry the little bitch, for I think she has the right dhrop in her. Wait for a few minutes an' I'll be with you."

After exchanging a few words with his old sweetheart through the hedge, he returned to Lory, who was rapidly getting into the good graces of Venom, looking very solemn, and indisposed for conversation.

Miss Laughlan, it may be remarked, returned home, look-ing very serious, too—the young man from the mountain and his fine slate-house and jaunting-car notwithstanding—

and looking at one of her hands which was bleeding. For
during the few minutes' tete-a-tete with Tom Cuddehy, Miss
Laughlan made such violent attempts to break off a sprig of
blackthorn from the hedge, as if she mistook it for a bunch
of thyme or the spearmint under her window in the garden,
that when she looked at her hand she found several deep
scratches upon it. Ladies under such circumstances should
keep clear of thorn hedges.

Two or three dogs had been conquered and driven from
the lists by the bull, when Tom and Lory arrived ; and the
man with the hat back on his poll was leading his dog to the
encounter in a state of intense excitement, which was fully
shared by the two boys.

"Come, Trueboy !" said the man with the hat on his poll.

"Come, Trueboy !" shouted boy No. 1.

"Come, Trueboy," bawled boy No. 2.

And boys One and Two danced wildly about Trueboy, who
was a lank, long-legged animal, and seemed greatly at a loss
to guess what it was all about.

"Soho ! Trueboy," said his owner softly, patting him on
the head.

"Soho ! Trueboy," repeated boy No. 1.

"Soho ! Trueboy," echoed boy No. 2.

And both boys patted Trueboy on the head.

But the cry, "Here is Tom Cuddehy," caused Trueboy's
proprietor to start and look round with an expression of
intense dismay and disappointment. He had been told that
Tom Cuddehy's bitch should be let at the bull before his dog,
and great was his anxiety lest the bull should be worn out
before Trueboy had an opportunity of exhibiting his prowess.
Great was his joy, then, when some one announced that Tom
Cuddehy would not put in an appearance at all ; and now
proportionally intense was his disappointment and anguish of
spirit when on looking round he beheld Tom Cuddehy and
his white bitch, Venom, on the bank above him, just at the
foot of the tree upon a branch of which Tommy Lahy was
swaying up and down with a gentle motion, and quietly
trying to extract a thorn from his big toe with a pin.

The bull was tied by a rope round his neck in the centre
of a large hollow or pit, which answered the purposes of an
amphitheatre very well ; the crowd, which was select, but not

numerous, standing round the sloping sides. He was not at all a lordly bull to look at ; but a small, red, rough-coated hardy, sturdy, good-tempered animal—in fact, what might be called a peasant bull. He was very much at his ease, and not at all excited, having made short work of his three or four assailants—as Wat Murphy prophesied he would ; for not one of them, Wat averred, " knew that a bull had a nose on his face," or, knowing it, had the slightest idea of what that nose was intended for.

Trueboy's owner and master looked at Tom Cuddehy's bitch, and was struck speechless with despair ; for Venom, though not large, was broad in the chest, and had a lurking devil in her eye, that made it plain to the most ignorant that she was a tough customer.

Recovering himself, however, by an effort, he approached Tom Cuddehy, and implored of him, as a " decent man " and a man of spirit, to let his dog go in first, dwelling upon the fact that he had walked fifteen miles that day, and would have to walk the same distance back again ; that it was the first time he had the honour and the pleasure of coming amongst them, though he had long known them by reputation ; that his, Tom Cuddehy's, name was a household word far and near ; that " Venom " was a beauty all out, and won his heart the moment he set eyes on her ; that she was " undershod " in a manner that would make a Turk warm to her ; and, above all, that he, the petitioner, was a " Carrick-man," and 'twas an old and well-known saying that " wherever you go, you'll meet a Carrick-man " ; and that he, the Carrick-man, might have it in his power to do as much for Tom Cuddehy another time.

" Very well," says Tom Cuddehy, with an indifference that astonished his friends ; " have at him."

" Sound man !" shouted the Carrick-man.

" Sound man !" exclaimed boy No. 1.

" Sound man !" repeated boy No. 2. And Trueboy was again seized by all three and pulled into the ring.

" Good dog, Trueboy," says the Carrick-man. " Grapple him."

" Good dog, Trueboy ; grapple him," muttered the two boys under their teeth.

Thus encouraged, Trueboy leaped into the ring, and ran

all round the bull, who remained quite calm and still, pretending not to see him.

" Grapple him, Trueboy !" cried the Carrick-man, dropping upon one knee, as if he were going to take aim with a rifle at the bull's eye.

" Grapple him, Trueboy !" repeated the two boys, dropping upon their knees, too, like sharpshooters waiting the order to fire.

There was a moment of breathless silence, and Trueboy looked about him in all directions, evidently at a loss, and having no idea of what he was expected to " grapple."

" Grapple him, Trueboy !" repeated the Carrick-man, savagely.

Trueboy looked about him quite wildly now, but could not make up his mind who or what the " him " was meant to apply to ; till, glancing upwards, some object overhead caught his attention, and Trueboy commenced barking furiously at it. The eyes of the spectators were turned in the same direction, and there was a loud roar of laughter when Tommy Lahy was discovered in the tree, looking at first surprised and then delighted at finding himself the object of their attention. Tommy laughed down at the open mouths below him, and for a moment the Carrick-man and his dog were forgotten.

But the Carrick-man rushed at Trueboy, and, seizing him by the throat, knocked him down and stamped his foot upon him.

Boy No. 1 then danced on Trueboy ; and boy No. 2 went and did likewise. Then boy One struck boy Two with his clenched fist in the right eye ; and both boys were immediately " in grips," and fought fiercely for five minutes to relieve their feelings.

The Carrick-man pulled Trueboy into the ring again, and hallooed him at the bull ; but Trueboy again wheeled round and barked furiously at Tommy Lahy in the tree.

" He don't undherstand," said the Carrick-man ; " but wait till I bring him close to his head, an' ye'll see something."

He threw a leg over Trueboy, as if he were going to have a ride, and seized him by the neck with both hands with a view to wheeling him round, when the bull quietly advanced to the end of his rope, and gave the Carrick-man a playful touch of his horn under the coat-tails ; which so astonished the Carrick-man that he cleared Trueboy's head at a bound as if he were playing at frog-leaps with him, falling flat upon his face and hands some three yards beyond him. At this Trueboy, as if conscious of his disgrace, rushed over his prostrate master and up the side of the pit, uttering a dismal howl, and scampered off over ditches and hedges, as if a score of old kettles were tied to his tail; and was never seen or heard of afterwards—save that a gaunt hound was sometimes observed prowling among the rocks in the loneliest recesses of the mountains, like the ghost of the last Irish wolf; and it was conjectured by some that this unhappy animal was the Carrick-man's dog, Trueboy.

The Carrick-man himself pulled his hat over his eyes, and walked away without a word or a look to any one, followed by the two boys wiping the bitter tears of vexation and disappointment from their noses, and, it is to be feared, with the seeds of scepticism and misanthropy sown in their young bosoms.

Tom Cuddehy's " Venom " was next led into the arena. We will spare the reader a detailed description of how she acquitted herself. It was admitted on all hands that Venom was " blood to the eyes '; but still she never once "took a right hoult." And there was something so vicious and viperish and spitfirey in her mode of attack, that when, at last, she was carried away maimed and bleeding, no one was sorry for her.

"Well, now," says Wat Murphy, " *are* ye all satisfied ? Or is there any wan else that wants to thry his dog ? If there is, say the word; for I'm in no hurry in life. Down, Danger !"

There was no one else to be accommodated; and Danger's muzzle was taken off.

Danger walked slowly towards the bull, wagging his tail and locking his lips, as if his intentions were quite amicable. But the bull saw that he had a formidable foe before him now, and with his head bent down and his eyes rolling—no longer looking the mere plebeian animal he had seemed before, but a real lordly bull—prepared to receive him.

Here again we shrink from attempting a minute description of the exciting, but, we fear, revolting encounter between " Danger " and the stout-hearted little bull. Enough to say that, in spite of his gallant efforts to fling his fierce assailant

from him, or pin him to the ground, he was pulled upon his
knees at last and held there as if his nose were in an iron vice.
Then he plunged forward once more, and tried to shake his
foe from him by dragging him along the ground. But all in
vain ; the dog clung to the poor brute's nose as if he grew
there. Then the wretched bull raised his head in the air,
and uttered a low plaintive moan as if his very heart were
broken.

For the first time every one present seemed struck with the
cruelty of the " sport " they had been watching so eagerly.

" D—n it, Wat," said Mr. Lloyd, with tears in his eyes,
" loose him."

" Yes, Wat," added Phil Lahy, solemnly, " loosen his hoult."

Wat Murphy advanced, and, scientifically pressing his
thumb upon the dog's windpipe, waited quietly till want of
breath forced him to gasp, and then Wat snatched him
quickly up in his arms, and carried him off ; the dog keeping
his eyes fixed sullenly upon the poor bull, who dropped
down, sobbing, upon the ground, his rough coat all wet and
dabbled with the sweat of his agony.

" I think we had better start for home," said the doctor.

" Yes, I think so," returned Mr. Lowe, who had kept
behind a clump of bushes, as if he felt rather ashamed of
being seen at such a place.

As they were turning away, a roaring, louder than any
bull's, startled them ; and on looking up to the place whence
it proceeded, they beheld, to their amazement, Lory Hanly
" punishing " Mr. Beresford Pender most severely. Beresford
retreated backwards as Lory continued to " plant " the right
and left alternately upon his mouth and nose, until he got
his back to the tall ash tree, a bough of which Tommy Lahy
had converted into a reserved seat, from which he could
enjoy the spectacle in the pit below with ease and dignity.
This proved a most injudicious move on Mr. Pender's part,
for Lory struck higher, about the eyes and forehead, and at
every blow Tommy Lahy distinctly felt the shock, as
Beresford's poll came in contact with the tree.

" Oh ! oh ! oh-o-o-o !" roared Mr. Beresford Pender, working
his elbows up and down like wings, and lifting, now one leg,
now the other, as if he insanely hoped to defend his face with
his knees. At last a well-aimed blow so completely shut up

one of his visual organs, that Mr. Beresford Pender dropped down upon his knees, his face buried in both hands, and loudly proclaimed several times, to all whom it might concern, that his " eye was out."

At this stage Darby Ruadh came to his master's assistance.

" Here, get up," said Darby Ruadh, seizing him by the collar.

Beresford did stand up, and clapping his hand over one eye, and finding that, after all, he was able to see Darby Ruadh and several other objects, both near and in the distance, with the other, became re-assured, and muttered, " No surrender !"

To account for this little episode, it should be mentioned that Mr. Pender, after Lory's impertinent allusion to " his grandmother," mounted his horse and started in pursuit ; and Lory, finding himself suddenly collared and " arrested in the queen's name," and seeing that his captor was Mr. Beresford Pender, at once shook himself free, and brought the knuckles of his right hand into contact with the bridge of Mr. Beresford Pender's nose, which immediately produced the bellowing that so surprised Mr. Lowe and the doctor.

Bob Lloyd walked deliberately up the side of the pit and shook Lory vigorously by the hand.

" I think I gave him enough of it," Lory observed.

" Ay, faith," returned Mr. Lloyd.

" Nice work to see a gentleman encouraging the violation of the law," muttered Mr. Beresford Pender.

" Hold your tongue, you whelp," retorted Bob Lloyd, " or I'll give you a greater cutting than ever your father gave a hound."

" Bailiffs about your house !" he muttered again—but so as to be heard only by those who stood close to him—in allusion to Mr. Lloyd's occasional difficulties with his creditors, when even Jer's ingenuity could not ward off an execution, and Tom Ryan and most of the other tenants had their rents paid in advance.

Here Tommy Lahy came sliding down the tree with considerable rapidity of motion ; and, without in the least intending it, came with a very violent bump straight upon Mr. Beresford Pender's head. This mysterious assault brought him down upon his marrow-bones again, and caused him to roar louder than ever.   And, what added considerably to the mirth of the spectators, Tommy Lahy seemed to have been quite as frightened by the shock as Mr. Pender, and remained clinging to the tree at the spot where his descent had been so unexpectedly stopped short, staring over his shoulder, with his eyes wide open, till his father advanced, and, gripping him firmly by the corduroys, dragged him down by main force.

Mr. Bob Lloyd shook hands with Tommy Lahy also, and gave him a sixpence—to Tommy's utter amazement, for he could not see what he had done to deserve it.

And then Mr. Lloyd insisted that Lory Hanly should mount behind him on his grey hunter and ride home with him—an honour that not only made his peace with Rose for having escaped to the bull-bait, contrary to her express injunctions, but so puffed up that young lady with consequence, that Johnny Wilson, the bank-clerk, was received quite coldly the next time he called, notwithstanding his new "Albert chain" and silk umbrella.

And that same evening, when Kathleen was drawing the pony's rein at Maurice Kearney's gate, Rose tossed her head and said, "Don't mind," and they drove on without stopping.   But all this did not prevent Lory from having his revenge for being obliged to wear Joe Russel's hat at the bull-bait ; and he deliberately made up his mind to sit, by accident, the very first favourable opportunity, upon Rose's new bonnet—the one with the feathers—and "make a pancake of it."

Lory now found himself quite a popular character, and was greeted with looks and words of admiration wherever he went.   Barney Brodherick, in particular, became his sworn friend, and hugged himself in the hope of having a quiet set-to with Mr. Lory some fine evening in the grove, while Bobby was left to roam at will among Miss Hanly's flower-beds.   For Barney dearly loved the man or boy who would fight him ; and his implacable enmity towards Father M'Mahon's servant was solely owing to the fact that that unaccommodating individual could never, for love or money, be induced to knock him down.

Wat Murphy kept his purchase of the bull a secret from his customers, and even satisfied some of them that the flesh of that animal was by far the primest beef he had ever killed in his life before. But Miss Lloyd found him out; and arraying herself in her lavender silk dress, sallied forth to denounce him for selling such meat "to the gentry," and to proclaim his wickedness all over the town. Wat took her abuse rather coolly, however, and even put some rude questions to her on the subject of her complaint.

But her harangue threatening to be of longer duration than he thought agreeable, Wat quietly opened the back door, and the white bull-dog quietly walked in. And Miss Lloyd, seeing the white bull-dog looking up into her face, lost her speech and her breath, and the use of her limbs, and dropped down helplessly upon Wat Murphy's block, that happened to be behind her, thereby ruining the lavender silk dress for ever. When she had recovered somewhat, Wat Murphy politely offered to wipe the grease and blood off the silk dress with a coarse cloth, but Miss Lloyd declined his services.

"Let me scrape it wud the knife at any rate," said Wat, sorrowfully.

But Miss Lloyd gathered up her skirts and ran home, creating great astonishment along the street—men, women, and children crowding to every door to look after her; and frightening her mother and sisters—who at first thought she was dangerously wounded—almost out of their lives.

CHAPTER LIII.

THE HURLING IN THE KILN-FIELD.—CAPTAIN FRENCH THROWS THE SLEDGE AGAINST MAT THE THRASHER.—BARNEY IN TROUBLE.—FATHER M'MAHON'S " PROUD WALK."

"WHAT a pity it is," said Mrs. Kearney, "that Mr. Lowe is not a Catholic. 'Pon my word he's good enough to be one. And 'tis often my Uncle Dan said the same of his uncle."

Grace, who sat with Mr. Kearney on one side of the car, laughed as she turned quickly round and looked at Mary, who was with her mother on the other side.

They were returning from last Mass, and Mr. Lowe stood
outside the door to hand the ladies off the car.

" I wonder Richard would be making such a fool of himself about that Kathleen Hanly," continued Mrs. Kearney ;
" walking by the side of their old phaeton all the way from
Kilthubber, instead of driving home with Hugh in the gig,
and leaving poor Mr. Lowe by himself all the morning."

" Where is Wattletoes ?" Mr. Kearney called out as he got
off the car.

" This was his day to be at first Mass," Mrs. Kearney
observed, " and he ought to be at home an hour ago."

" He wasn't at first Mass, then," said the dairymaid, who
ran out on hearing her master's voice, and who had a grudge
against Barney for a reason of her own. " He spent his
mornin' at Kit Cummins's, card-playin' wud the lads."

Mrs. Kearney raised her hands in horror and amazement at
this damning proof of Barney's wickedness. Running after
ballad-singers, peep-shows, and Punches-and-Judys, were mere
venial offences compared with losing Mass on Sunday ; and
spending the time with " the lads " deepened the offence to
the darkest hue of guilt. A certain little club or fraternity, of
whom one Andy Dooley (*alias* Andy Meeawe) was the leaser
and oracle, who frequented Kit Cummins's, were universally
known as " the lads " or " the school " ; and with them, we
grieve to say, Barney was tempted to spend the morning,
sitting upon a skillet, and playing " scoobeen " upon the
bottom of Kit Cummins's wash-tub, which was turned upside
down for the purpose. Barney, however, was hurrying home
early enough to escape detection, counting his coppers on the
way, when, in an evil hour, he espied Brummagem (who,
owing to early impressions, could never be persuaded that
anything more was required to keep holy the Sabbath-day
than washing his face in the pool in the quarry, and drying
it with his cap) placing a small stone on the smooth part of
the road, and, after moving backwards half-a-dozen yards,
pitching a penny at it. Barney pitched a penny at the
" bob " too. It required a critical eye to judge which was
the better pitch ; but Brummagem, taking a bit of iron hoop
from his pocket, used it as a rule, making it plain that
his penny was the eighth of an inch nearer to the " bob."
This Barney admitted by a nod of assent in reply to a look

from Brummagem. The hopeful youth then laid a half-penny on the bit of hoop and held it towards Barney, who placed another halfpenny beside it ; and Brummagem, after solemnly spitting upon them for good luck, whirled both half-pence into the air with a peculiar movement of the wrist. They came down " heads," and Brummagem pocketed them in silence and pitched again. So the pitching and tossing went on with varying luck till Tom Maher announced to Barney that the family were home from Mass " this hour," and that the mistress had found out how Barney had been engaged during the morning.

" Begob, I'm done for now for ever," exclaimed Barney. And he began to debate with himself whether it was to his mother's cabin above Glounamuckadhee, or to his relations near Ballydunmore, he had better fly to escape Mrs. Kearney's wrath.

But the roll of the big drum reminded him of the great hurling match that was to come off in the kiln-field that day, and of the sledge-throwing between Mat Donovan and Captain French, and of the " high-gates" and " hell-and-heaven" ; and, above all, of Peg Brady, whom Barney pronounced to be " tuppence a pound before any girl in the parish "—and a kiss from whom, he assured Tom Maher in confidence, was " eating and drinking " ; and Barney was a happy man once more !

" Begob, Tom," he exclaimed, his eye glistening with delight, " there'll be no show but all the b'ys an' girls we'll have in the kiln-field to-day. Look up thowar's Bohervogga. The road is black wud 'em."

" 'Twill be a great gatherin'," returned Tom Maher.

" Do you think will Mat bate the captain ?" Barney asked, anxiously. " I'd rather we'd lose the hurlin' than have Mat bet at the sledge."

" There's no danger, wud the help uv God," Tom replied, " though Phil Lahy is unaisy. An' the captain *is* a powerful man. I never see such a pair uv arms. An' Tom Doherty tells me he never stopped practisin' for the last week. But, never you fear, but Mat'll open his eye for him. An' we're purty sure uv the hurlin', too, as we have Tom Doherty. I never knew Tom to fail on a p'int. He says he'll depind upon Miss Mary to get his pardon for him from Father Carroll, as he had to stale away at the first light, an' he's afeard Father

Carroll couldn't find any wan to serve Mass. An' Miss Mary promised, for she's as anxious about the hurlin' as any uv us."

This was quite true ; and when Tom Doherty told her how, every evening, when he went to water Father Carroll's horse to the weir, he was sure to see Captain French in the Priest's Walk, with his coat off, throwing a sledge " for the bare life," and that he'd give " a twenty-pound note " to beat Mat Donovan, Mary became quite nervous lest the laurels were at last about to be snatched from Mat Donovan's brows.

" What *is* it in that letter," Grace asked, " that brings that happy look into your eyes ? This is the third time you have read it within the past half-hour ; and you always look so glad."

Mr. Lowe had remarked, too, that he had never seen her look so animated—though it was the last day of his stay !

" Read it yourself," said Mary, offering her the letter—which was from her sister Anne.

" I read it before, and couldn't see anything to account for your delight. It scarcely can be this piece of news about Arthur O'Connor."

But it was the piece of news about Arthur O'Connor. And every time Mary read it she felt (or fancied she felt) a great load taken off her heart, and said to herself that " now she could write to him," and explain why she was not at the window that snowy Christmas Eve when he waited so long and so patiently for her.

" I'm so glad," said Grace, " that Richard and Mr. Lowe are to leave the same day I am going myself. It is quite a coincidence."

" And why are you so glad ?"

" Oh, I have a plan."

" What is it ?"

" Well, I'll get papa to ask them to spend the evening with us ; and we'll have Minnie Delany and the ' Brehon ' and ' Shamrock ' and a few others, and I think it will be very pleasant."

" I suppose Eva will take them by storm."

" Well, I rather think not. She requires time in spite of her beauty and her golden ringlets. You are far more striking."

" And does no thought of me enter into your plan ?"

" Didn't you say there was no use thinking you would come ?" Grace asked in surprise.

" Yes ; but does it not occur to you that I'll be very lonely when you are all gone ?"

Grace was silent for a minute, and then said—

" Mary, I am the incarnation of selfishness. That is the essential difference between you and me—I think of myself first, and you think of yourself last. You will be dreadfully lonely without a soul with you. And now that I see it I'd gladly stay if I could. But why did it not occur to me before ? Because I am selfish—that's the why."

" You are too severe upon yourself," returned Mary. " But why do you say I'll be ' without a soul '? Do Hugh, and my father and mother, and Ellie and Willie, count for nothing ? And that reminds me that I have left Ellie altogether to her story-books and her birds for some time ; and you know she is to be sent to school when Anne comes home in summer."

" Oh, you'll be all right when Anne comes home. She is so blessed with animal spirits. I expect she'll go wild after the jail-like discipline of that convent. I'm sure she'll be as great a flirt as Bessy Morris."

" Why do you suppose Bessy Morris is a flirt ?"

" Well, that soldier's letter was pretty strong circumstantial evidence ; and, besides, I heard them discussing her character in the kitchen last night, when I was helping your mamma with the pudding."

" What did they say of her ?"

" Barney said she'd court ' a haggart o' sparrows ' ; but the general opinion was that she was ' a nice crack '—whatever that means."

" A ' crack ' is a person who dresses too stylishly. But Bessy's taste is so exquisite, it is impossible to find fault with her in that respect."

" Yes, that brown stuff dress is perfection," returned Grace. " I must get one like it. And how Mat Donovan worships her ! But I suppose she would not have him."

" Oh, Mat is what might be called a universal lover," said Mary. " He has quite a number of sweethearts."

" Ah, but there's something more than that in Bessy's case,

But I can hardly reconcile myself to the idea of her becoming the wife of a labourer. Yet the little house is very pretty. The garden and the beehives would do very well. But Bessy ought to have a nicely furnished little parlour, with white curtains to the window, and some books, and a bird in a cage to sing for her all day long."

" Like Norah Lahy's linnet," Mary added.

" No," rejoined Grace, " he is too grave and sober for Bessy. Ellie's goldfinch would be more suitable, or a canary. But Mat himself would be for a thrush that would awaken the Seven Sleepers. Bessy, however, has, I think, more ambitious views than to be the mistress of that little house."

" I'd be sorry to think you are not mistaken," returned Mary, thoughtfully. " Mat is just the sort of man who would feel such a disappointment deeply. I can't help laughing at myself," she added, " I am so anxious about the hurling, and this trial of strength with Captain French. I would not wish for anything that Mat should be beaten. And yet of what consequence is it ?"

" The reason is, you sympathise so strongly with those around you," Grace observed. " I have often noticed it. There, now, your eyes light up because that bevy of girls crossing the lawn are showing their white teeth—and very white teeth they have, and very beautiful and luxuriant hair. But why do they all prefer scrambling over the ditch to going through the gate a few yards lower down ? Oh, yes ! Those youths will pull them up, and I suppose they like that. There goes the big drum and the fifes. And, my goodness ! what a number of people ! 'Tis like a races."

" And is it not pleasant to see them all so happy ?" said Mary, with sparkling eyes. " But to my mind the prettiest sight of all is that long line of children, joined hand in hand, and winding round and round in that way."

" You might call them a wreath of rosebuds," returned Grace ; " though that play they are at is known by the unpoetical name of ' thread the needle.' You see the two tallest hold up their joined hands like an arch, through which the whole line runs. The ' Brehon ' told me there is a most poetical description of the same game in an old Irish manuscript, in which the king and queen are at the head of the line of youths and maidens, who glide under their majesties' arms to the music of the harp. But I hope it was not called ' thread the needle ' in those happy days. But mind the wide circle of children of larger growth at the upper end of the field."

" That's ' high-gates,' " said Mary.

" And behold Barney Brodherick in full chase after some fair one of large dimensions, who, I fancy, is too fat to hold out long," Grace continued. " Yes, there : he has the prize captured already."

" That is Bessy Morris's cousin, Peg Brady," said Mary, laughing. " Barney is a great admirer of her."

" There go the next pair," continued Grace. " Ha ! *she* won't be caught so easily. She's as fleet as a deer."

" I think it is Nelly Donovan," said Mary.

" So it is," returned Grace. " There is something gazelle-like about Nelly. I often think what a huntress she would make. She is like one of Diana's nymphs. There, she has distanced her pursuer, and is now walking at her leisure, till he comes nearer. But he is trying to get her into the corner and catch her as she doubles back. What a happy, light-hearted girl Nelly is !"

" And a good girl, too," returned Mary. " It is quite affecting to see herself and poor Norah Lahy together ; one so strong and healthy, and the other so weak and helpless. They love each other like sisters. But surely that is Nancy Hogan's golden hair ! I'm so glad to see poor Nancy out among them again."

" Yes ; and she is evidently not indifferent to the conversation of her companion," Grace remarked.

" That is her old admirer, Tom Carey, the carpenter," returned Mary. " I am really very glad."

" I thought you'd go in for dying of a broken heart in such a case ?" said Grace.

" No, not when a man proves unworthy," Mary answered. " And Ned Brophy acted very badly."

" I'm trying to find out Bessy Morris among them," said Grace ; " but I don't think she is there. Perhaps she is too grand ? But look, there is Mr. Lloyd riding backwards and forwards over the new ditch ; and I suppose that is Captain French with him."

Here we are reminded that we owe an apology to the " new
ditch." When we first had occasion to refer to this freak of
Maurice Kearney's, we stated that it never was and never
would be of the slightest earthly use. But, in justice to the
" new ditch," we feel bound to admit that it was the best,
and the " firmest," and in every way the most suitable ditch
in the neighbourhood for training a horse to " topping," and
was availed of for that purpose by professional and amateur
trainers for miles around. And few equestrians could, when
passing the way, resist the temptation of taking a few jumps
over the " new ditch " ; so that a strip of the field at either
side of this admirable fence generally presented the appearance of a race-course between the ropes after the last heat
for the " consolation stakes." Most humbly do we beg the
" new ditch's " pardon for asserting that it was of no earthly
use.

"I think we ought to go out, and get near them," said
Grace. " I see the hurlers falling into battle array. And
there are the Hanlys on the road above the grove, and
Richard holding the pony by the head, lest he should set off
for home backwards, as he sometimes does, by way of a
practical joke."

"I have no objection to a walk," returned Mary. " But
you never thought you were not near enough till you saw
Captain French and Mr. Lloyd."

" Well, I have some slight curiosity in that way," rejoined
Grace, putting on her bonnet. " I want to see what sort of
looking person he is."

" And to be seen," Mary added, laughing.

" Certainly."

" Well, come then. I see Hugh and Mr. Lowe are going,
and we may as well join them."

By the time they reached the phaeton—the occupants of
which bowed condescendingly to them—the high-gates and
other games were suspended, and the children and young
girls stood upon the fences round the field out of the way of
the hurlers. There was a hush, and an eager, anxious look in
every face, as Mat Donovan moved from the crowd towards
the middle of the field, followed by his twenty picked men.
He pulled the ball with some difficulty from his pocket, and,
throwing it with his hurly on the field, took off his coat

slowly, and with a quiet smile. The others pulled off their coats, too ; but some of them were quite pale, while their teeth chattered with excitement.

" What's delayin' ye, boys ?" Mat called out, seeing with surprise that the hurlers at the other side were not taking their places.

The party whom he addressed made no reply, but they whispered among themselves, and one or two got upon the " new ditch " and looked towards the Three Poplars.

" Is there anything wrong, boys ?" said Mat, after leaving his place at the head of his men, and mingling with the crowd, from which " the farmers " had not yet separated.

" Tom is not here," was the reply, slowly and reluctantly given.

" Tom Cuddehy not here !" exclaimed Mat Donovan, as if a thunderbolt had fallen at his feet. " Where is he ?"

" We don't know," was the reply. " We thought he'd be here before us. But we're afther sendin' for him."

" Here they are," cried the young men on the ditch ; and three swift-footed youths were seen hurrying down the hill.

" Is he comin' ?" a dozen voices asked together.

" He's not," the foremost of the three scouts replied, gasping for breath and dashing the perspiration from his face.

" Well, if I hadn't the sight uv my own eyes," Mat Donovan observed with the deepest sorrow, " I'd never b'lieve Tom was the man to do a mane act. Afther givin' me his hand an' word on id !"

" He couldn't help id," said one of the messengers.

" Maybe, 'tis to break a leg or an arm he did ?" returned Mat, somewhat anxiously. " For, if I'm not mistaken, nothin' less'd keep Tom from his post on such an occasion as this."

" Well, no," the youth replied, with a grin. " But I don't know but he might be afther injurin' wan uv his ribs."

" How so ?" Mat asked.

" Begor, bekase he's afther gettin' a new wan," was the reply. " Ould Paddy Laughlan's daughter is afther runnin' away wud him."

" Well, I'm not sorry to hear that," said Mat. " But when I tould him the field was to be broke this week, he had a right to put id off for another time."

" Mat," said Phil Lahy, " human nature is human nature. Where is the man that hasn't his wakenesses ? So don't be too hard on Tom. Make it your own case."

And Mat happening to look towards the little group on the road—for he had noticed with pleasure that Miss Kearney had got upon the fence in her eagerness to see the match begin—his eye caught sight of a figure on the fence at the other side of the road, dearer to him than all the world beside and he forgave Tom Cuddehy.

" Will ye hurl wudout him ?" he asked.

" We'd rather not," was the reply.

" Well, I'd rather not myse'f," returned Mat. " There'd be no satisfaction. I suppose we may as well put on our coats."

" I think, Mat," Phil Lahy suggested, " you ought to make a promiscuous match."

" Do you mane over and hether ?" Mat asked.

" I do," replied Phil. " Make a match, you and Mister O'Donnell, wudout any regard to the two sides."

" Very well ; I'm satisfied," said Mat, whirling his hurly up in the air, and calling out, " Right or left for first call."

" Left," cried Mr. O'Donnell.

" You lost," returned Mat, as the hurly fell upon the field with the handle towards the right. He ran his eye along the line of hurlers, and said quietly, " Come here, Jemmy Hogan."

Jemmy Hogan's eye flashed with pride as he advanced and stood beside Mat Donovan.

Captain French's servant pointed to him, and whispered something into his master's ear that made his eye flash almost as bright as Jemmy Hogan's. Captain French was a soldier, and the son of a soldier, and, as one by one the hurlers stepped forward as their names were called, and pulled off their coats, he thought what a sin and a shame it was that such splendid " material " should be going to waste in that way.

" There is Bessy Morris and Judy Brophy," said Nelly Donovan. " I wonder why don't they come into the field ?"

" She tould me she wouldn't come at all," returned Peg Brady, with something like a scowl. " But I suppose Judy Brophy called in for her, and she came wud her."

" I'll go call 'em over," said Nelly, starting off at the top of her speed. Now, Billy Heffernan happened to be standing all alone not far from the corner of the grove near which the ladies had taken their places, and whether it was that Nelly looked at him instead of looking before her, or whatever else might be the cause of her carelessness, her foot was caught in a bramble, and she was flung forward upon her face and hands with such violence that both Grace and Mary uttered an exclamation and looked frightened.

" O Nelly, did you fall ?" said Billy Heffernan. " Come here till I take you up."

" Well, Billy Heffernan is a provokingly ungallant young man," Grace exclaimed with her ringing laugh.

Nelly Donovan, who was quickly on her feet again, laughed too, and flinging back her dark hair and twisting it into a knot behind, came towards them more slowly, and called to her friends to come into the field. Judy Brophy, who was radiant with smiles—and well she might, for since Ned's marriage she had had no less than three proposals—came down from the fence, and crossing the road at a run, climbed over the other, and was immediately shaking hands vigorously with Nelly Donovan. Bessy Morris seemed half afraid to descend from the fence, which was unusually high, and Kathleen Hanly's frown was even darker than Peg Brady's, when she saw Hugh Kearney hand her down as carefully as if Bessy Morris were a lady.

" Thank you, sir," said Bessy ; and after returning Mary's smile with a little bow, she got over the other fence without Hugh's assistance, pretending not to notice that it was proffered.

Captain French's servant called his attention to Bessy Morris, and he immediately came towards her and commenced talking to her.

Mary Kearney seemed surprised on observing this ; and she looked grave, if not pained, when she saw that Bessy's face was crimson and her eyes cast down, while the captain's white teeth gleamed—unpleasantly, Mary thought—through his dark beard.

" He is a splendid-looking man, ' said Grace.

" But what can he be saying to Bessy Morris ?" Mary asked.

" Oh, flattering her, of course," replied Grace. " And

really I never thought she was so very bashful. But she is
strikingly—not handsome, but some way fascinating. If I
were Miss Isabella Lloyd I might be jealous."

Mat Donovan felt himself pulled by the sleeve, and, on
looking round, saw Peg Brady by his side.

" Well, Peg, what's the matter ?" says Mat Donovan.

She pointed to the captain and Bessy Morris.

" Oh, ay, 'tis Bessy," he remarked. " I didn't know she
was here till I see her on the ditch a minute ago."

Peg Brady kept her eyes fixed upon his face, but she saw
nothing there but a smile of admiration and pleasure, as he
watched them.

" Bessy always had a great respect for you, Mat," says Peg
Brady.

" Well, I b'lieve she had," says Mat Donovan.

" As a friend," returned Peg Brady.

" As a friend," Mat Donovan repeated. " What else ?"

" But she's not the same since she was in Dublin," said
Peg Brady. " I must tell you somethin' wan uv these days.
Mind the captain, how pleasant he is."

Bessy Morris turned away to seek Judy Brophy—who was
taken possession of by one of her new admirers, and seemed
quite intoxicated by his high-flown compliments—when the
word " sojer " fell upon her ear, and on looking up she saw a
group of Peg Brady's special cronies regarding her with meaning looks, and whispering among themselves, keeping their
eyes fixed upon her all the time. It was plain they knew her
secret ; and wherever she turned she fancied she met looks of
suspicion and malice. This was mere fancy ; but, perhaps, it
was conscience made a coward of her. She wished she had
remained at home, and a pang shot through her heart at the
thought of how people would talk of her. She brightened up
as she passed Mat Donovan, for the same honest smile as ever
met her scrutinising glance. She could almost have thrown
herself into his arms for shelter from the poisoned arrows
which she fancied were about being launched at her.

" Come, boys," said Mat, " up wud the ball."

The ball was thrown up, and there was some good play,
and running, with a friendly fall or two ; but as it was only a
few goals " for fun," there was little or no excitement, and
the " high-gates," and " hell-and-heaven," and " thread-the-

needle" were resumed, the players merely running away like a flock of frightened sheep whenever the ball came bounding in among them.

"Mat," said Phil Lahy, when two or three goals had been hurled, "I think you might send for the sledge."

"Well, sure I'm agreeable at any time," replied Mat, "but 'twouldn't do to send for id until the captain proposes id first; you know 'twas he sent the challenge."

"Well, Donovan," said Captain French, "are we going to have the sledge? I can't stay much longer."

"Uv coorse, sir, as you came to have a throw we wouldn't like to disappoint you," returned Mat. "I'll send down to Jack Delany's for the sledge—Barney!" he shouted, as Wattletoes was passing hot-foot after a young girl, who was evidently bent upon leading him a long chase.

"You lost, Mat," said Barney, as he stopped and wheeled round, with a grin of intense enjoyment lighting up his face.

"How is that, Barney?" Mat asked.

"Oh, if you wor wud me at the high-gates," returned Barney, "you'd get your belly-full uv kisses."

"All right, Barney," rejoined Mat. "But I want you to run down to the forge for the sledge, as the captain 'd like to have a throw before he goes."

"Begob, an' I will so," exclaimed Barney, becoming suddenly quite serious, on finding himself entrusted with so important a commission.

"Take up that ball," said Phil Lahy, in a tone that quite frightened Jackey Ryan; for it reminded him of the bishop's "Come down out of that window," the day that he, Jackey, and two other aspiring youths climbed to one of the high windows in Kilthubber chapel, to hear His Grace's sermon in comfort, and, as Jackey said, without having the life "scroodged" out of them. "An' Brummagem," added Phil, "do you folly Wattletoes, for fear he might bring the wrong wan."

"I think I'll go down to the forge after 'em," said Billy Heffernan, "as they'll be apt to box about id, an' delay ye too long." But Billy Heffernan's real motive was to tell Norah Lahy that Tom Cuddehy had "disappointed," as it occurred to him that Norah might think the Knocknagow boys were beaten because there was no cheering.

Barney soon appeared with the sledge upon his shoulder, and Mat Donovan, after balancing it in his hand, laid it at Captain French's feet.

The captain stripped with the look of a man sure to win, and handed his coat and vest to his servant. A murmur, partly of admiration and partly of anxiety for the result of the contest, arose from the crowd of men, women, and children around, as he bared his arms ; for compared with them Mat Donovan's appeared almost slight and attenuated.

" I never saw the like of him," some one was heard to exclaim in a low, solemn tone, but which was distinctly audible in the dead silence.

He took the heavy sledge, and placing his foot to the mark, swung it backwards and forwards twice, and then wheeling rapidly full round, brought his foot to the mark again, and, flying from his arm as from a catapult, the sledge sailed through the air, and fell at a distance that seemed to startle many of the spectators.

It was then brought back and handed to Mat Donovan, who took it with a quiet smile that somewhat re-assured his friends. Mat threw the sledge some three feet beyond the captain's mark, and many of those around drew a long breath of relief ; but there was no applause.

But the captain's next throw was fully six feet beyond Mat Donovan's, and several of his father's tenants and retainers cried, " More power, captain !"

Mat Donovan, however, cleared the best mark again by three feet.

The captain now grasped the sledge, clenching his teeth, and looking so fierce and tiger-like, his eyes flashing from under his knitted brows, that the women at the front of the crowd involuntarily pressed back appalled. With every muscle strained to the utmost, he hurled the huge sledge from him, falling forward upon his hands ; and as the iron ploughed up the green sward far beyond Mat Donovan's throw, the shout of the captain's partisans was drowned by something like a cry of pain from the majority of the spectators.

" Begor, captain," said Mat Donovan, surveying his adversary with a look of thoroughly genuine admiration, " you're good !"

Taking his place again at the stand, he laid down the sledge, and, folding his arms, fell into deep thought. Many a tear-dimmed eye was fixed upon him, for all imagined that he was beaten.

" His heart'll break," Bessy Morris heard a girl near her murmur.

" The captain is a good fellow," thought Mat Donovan ; " an' I'd like to lave him the majority—if I could do it honourable."

He looked on the anxious faces around him ; he looked at Bessy Morris ; but still he was undecided. Some one struck the big drum a single blow, as if by accident, and, turning round quickly, the thatched roofs of the hamlet caught his eye. And, strange to say, those old mud walls and thatched roofs roused him as nothing else could. His breast heaved, as, with glistening eyes, and that soft plaintive smile of his, he uttered the words, " For the credit of the little village !" in a tone of the deepest tenderness. Then, grasping the sledge in his right hand, and drawing himself up to his full height, he measured the captain's cast with his eye. The muscles of his arms seemed to start out like cords of steel as he wheeled slowly round and shot the ponderous hammer through the air.

His eyes dilated, as, with quivering nostrils, he watched its flight, till it fell so far beyond the best mark that even he himself started with astonishment. Then a shout of exultation burst from the excited throng ; hands were convulsively grasped, and hats sent flying into the air ; and in their wild joy they crushed around him and tried to lift him upon their shoulders.

" O boys, boys," he remonstrated, " be 'asy. Sure 'tisn't the first time ye see me throw a sledge. Don't do anything that might offend the captain afther comin' here among us to show ye a little diversion."

This remonstrance had the desired effect, and the people drew back and broke up into groups to discuss the event more calmly. But Mat's eye lighted up with pride when he saw Miss Kearney upon the fence with her handkerchief fluttering in the breeze above her head, and Hugh waving his hat by her side. Even the ladies in the phaeton caught the enthusiasm and displayed their handkerchiefs ; while Grace ran to the doctor and got him to lift her up in his arms in order that she might have a better view.

"Donovan," said Captain French, "your match is not in Europe. I was never beaten before."

"Well, it took a Tipperary-man to beat you, captain," returned Mat Donovan.

"That's some consolation," said the captain. "I'm a Tipperary-boy myself, and I'm glad you reminded me of it."

"Mat," said Billy Heffernan, with the tears standing in his eyes, "can you forgive me?"

"For what, Billy?" asked Mat, in surprise.

"For misdoubtin' you," replied Billy, gulping down his emotion.

"How is that?" returned Mat.

"Whin I see you pausin' an' lookin' so quare," said Billy Heffernan, turning away to dash the tears from his face, "I said to Phil Lahy that Knocknagow was gone."

"Knocknagow is not gone, Billy," exclaimed Mat, shaking him vigorously by the hand. "Knocknagow is not gone."

"Knocknagow is not gone," repeated a clear mellow voice behind them; and on looking round they saw Father M'Mahon close to them, mounted on his bay mare.

"Knocknagow is not gone," Father M'Mahon repeated, while his eye wandered from one to another of the groups of youths and maidens who had again returned to their sports over the field. "But how long can it be said that Knocknagow is not gone?" he added dreamily.

The good priest was just after kneeling by poor Mick Brien, stretched upon his wisp of straw in the miserable cabin; and as he counted the houses that had been levelled along the way, his heart sank within him, and he asked himself were the people he loved, and who loved him in their heart of hearts, doomed indeed to destruction?

He rode back again, seeming to have forgotten the purpose for which he had turned into the field. But seeing Barney Brodherick making a short-cut to the forge, with the sledge on his shoulder, Father M'Mahon called to him.

"Oh, bloodan'ouns!" muttered Barney, "I'm goin' to get id now for ever, for losin' Mass—God help me."

"Barney," said the priest, "do you remember anything about a gun of Mr. Kearney's you hid in a bush?"

"Be cripes! your reverence," returned Barney with a start, "id wint out uv my head till this blessed minute. The masther tould me to brin' id over to Mat to mend the stock that Mr. Richard broke, an' the beagles chanced to be passin' hot fut afther a hare, an' I thrust the gun into a brake uv briars there above, an' cut afther the hunt.   An' God help me ! I never thought uv id, to carry id to Mat, but I'll go for id now."

" 'Tis not where you put it," returned the priest. " 'Tis in the square bog-hole in Billy Heffernan's turbary. I was desired to tell you so, lest you should get blamed ; but say nothing about my telling you."

" The square bog-hole," muttered Barney, as the priest rode on. " Sure the divil a bottom the square bog-hole have.   In the name uv the Lord I'll ax lave uv the masther to go see my mother, an' keep out uv harm's way till Sathurday, at any rate."   And Barney, dropping the sledge from his shoulder on the field—where it remained till Tom Maher broke his scythe against it the next summer—hurried off to ask leave to go to see his mother.

" I'm comin' to ax you to give me lave to go home for a couple uv days, sir," said Barney, with quite a broken-hearted look.

" Home !" returned his master, " what business have you home ?"

" My mother that's ill-disposhed, sir," réplied Barney sorrowfully.

" More d—n shame for her," said his master.

" Good luck to you, sir," exclaimed Barney, brightening up with extraordinary suddenness, and setting off for the little cabin above Glounamuckadhee, where he found his venerable parent in excellent health and spirits.

" I wish we had some place for a dance," remarked Mat Donovan, " to put the girls in good humour."

" I'll give you my barn for a dance," said Tom Hogan proudly ; " the best barn in the parish."

" More power, Tom," exclaimed a dozen voices.   " Up wud the music."

Mat Donovan threw the strap of the big drum over his head, and a succession of loud bangs reminded Mr. Lowe of his fright on Christmas morning, when he thought a blunderbuss had been discharged through his window.   Billy Heffernan and the other musicians produced their fifes, and a

loud cheer greeted the announcement that they were to have
a dance in Tom Hogan's barn.

The sound of the drum seemed to rouse Father M'Mahon
from his gloomy reverie, as he rode on through the village.
" No ; they are not gone yet," he thought, as he stopped
under the beech-tree—looking up among the boughs, as if he
wanted Tommy Lahy to hold the bay mare, and thought the
top of the tree the most likely place to find him—" let us
trust in God, and hope for the best."

Honor Lahy appeared at the door with a curtsey ; and
verily that wholesome, honest, smiling face of hers seemed to
say, even more plainly than the big drum itself, that Knocknagow was safe and sound—a little old or so ; but hale and
hearty and kindly, withal.

" Well, Mrs. Lahy, how is she ?"

" Finely, your reverence," Honor replied.

Father M'Mahon cast his eyes up through the boughs
again.

" He's gone wud the drum, sir," said Honor.

" Oh, yes, that's quite right. I'll just step in to see
Norah," returned Father M'Mahon, alighting and hanging the
rein on an iron hook in the beech-tree.

And how Honor Lahy's face did light up as she curtsied
again ! And how poor Norah's eyes beamed with pleasure
and thankfulness ! After inquiring how she felt, and hoping
she would be better when the fine weather came, he was
going away, when a long roll of the drum softened by distance
made him pause.

" Do you feel sorry that you cannot join them ?" he asked,
looking pityingly into the poor girl's pale face.

" Oh, no, sir," she replied—and there was gladness in her
low, sweet tones. " 'Tis just the same as if I was with
them."

" Ay, then," added her mother, "an' she makes me go out
to see which side uv the field the girls do be at, an' then she
thinks she do be wud 'em from that out."

" That's right, that's right," said Father M'Mahon, hurrying out as if the bay mare were trying to break loose and run
away. And as he took the rein from the hook, Father
M'Mahon flourished his crimson silk pocket-handkerchief and
blew his nose loudly.

Throwing the rein over his arm, and thrusting his thumbs in his waistcoat, Father M'Mahon then walked down the hill, with his head so high, and looking so awfully proud, that Jack Delany's wife snatched up the twins from the middle of the road, seizing one by the small of the back and the other by the left arm—which, strange to say, was not dislocated that time—and ran with them into the house, not even venturing to stop to pick up the " rattler " and wooden " corncrake " which Brummagem had bought for the twins at the fair after winning one-and-fourpence at " trick-o'-the-loop ;" Mrs. Delany being fully persuaded that in his then mood Father M'Mahon would think nothing of crushing the twins—one under each foot ; and then turn round and ask her how dared she bring such nuisances into the world, two at a time !

" God bless us !" exclaimed Jack Delany's wife as she stooped to pick up the " rattler " and " corncrake," when the priest had passed, " did any wan ever see a man wud such a proud walk ?"

" Mother," said Norah Lahy, " I'm as sure as I'm alive that I know two saints who are still walking the earth."

" Who are they ?" her mother asked.

" Father M'Mahon and Miss Kearney," replied Norah.

" Why, then, I know a saint," thought the poor woman, with a sorrowful shake of her head, " I know a saint, an' she's not able to walk at all." And Honor Lahy turned away her face and wept silently.

Great was Phil Lahy's astonishment when he heard that Tom Hogan had given his barn for the dance even without being asked. And, after pondering over the extraordinary circumstance for a minute or two, Phil declared that, " after that, we'd get the Repeal of the Union." He could talk of nothing, however, but Mat Donovan's triumph, which he attributed in no small degree to certain " directions" which he had given Mat ; and even when Judy Brophy's new admirer beckoned him aside, and wanted to know " what part of a woman was her contour," Phil answered shortly that he never " studied them subjects much " ; so that the young man, who thought he had hit upon a new compliment, went back to Judy's side no wiser than he came, muttering, as he rubbed his poll with a puzzled look, that he " didn't like to venture the ' contour,' though he was nearly sure 'twas all right " ; and he had to go over the old compliments again ; to which Judy Brophy listened with as much delight as if she had not heard them all fifty times before. And now it is only fair to say that there was not a warmer admirer—that is, a warmer female admirer—of Nancy Hogan's beauty at the dance that night than Judy Brophy ; and in protesting against her brother's bringing home a penniless bride, perhaps Judy Brophy did no more than a good many tolerably amiable young women might have done under similar circumstances. And, furthermore, we feel bound to admit, that were it not for those two hundred sovereigns out of Larry Clancy's old saucepan, that somewhat pedantic young man, who is so assiduous in his attentions, would not be puzzling his brains about her " contour," as he is at this moment.

" Bessy Morris's is the only sad face I can see," Grace remarked to Mary, as the joyous crowd left the field. " I wonder what can have happened to her."

Mary beckoned to Bessy as she was passing, and after saying something about the alteration of a dress, asked carelessly what was it Captain French had been saying to her.

" Well, he was humbugging me about the sergeant," Bessy replied, with a look of pain.

" Oh, yes, yes," returned Mary, brightening up. " I understand. Good evening. And tell Mat Donovan how delighted I am at his victory."

Norah Lahy sat in her straw-chair looking into the bright turf fire, and deriving as much pleasure from the dance in Tom Hogan's barn as if her foot were the fleetest among them all. But she hoped, when the dance was over, that Billy Heffernan would come down and play " Auld Lang Syne " for her—or " something lively," if her mother put her veto upon " grievous ould airs."

CHAPTER LIV.

BOB LLOYD IN DANGER.—MAT DONOVAN'S OPINION OF " DESAV-
ING" PEOPLE IN THE WAY OF COURTSHIP.

THE last straggler had left the field, and hurried on after the
fifes and drums. The Miss Hanlys had shaken hands with
Mr. Lowe and the doctor, and driven up the hill, disappearing round the angle of the road like a vanishing rainbow, or
anything else very bright and beautiful, from the doctor's
gaze. Maurice Kearney was pointing out the wonderful
straightness of the new ditch to Mr. Bob Lloyd, and telling
him how Mat Donovan had marked out the line for it with
his plough. And Mr. Lloyd, stooping forward and shutting
one eye, had looked along the new ditch between the ears
of his grey hunter, and said, " Ay, faith." Mr. Lowe had
turned into the avenue gate to overtake Mary and Grace—
when Grace, who looked round to see whether the pony would
take it into his head to play one of his practical jokes and
return to the gate backwards, uttered an exclamation and
stood still, with sparkling eyes and flushed cheek. Then
Grace ran forward a few yards and stopped again ; and then
retreated backwards, holding out her hand to feel for Mary,
and keeping her eyes fixed upon a carriage that had just
topped the hill and was coming slowly towards them. Having
found Mary without the help of her eyes, she grasped her by
the arm, holding on as if some unseen force were pulling her
away, and panting like a startled greyhound. For a minute
or so she seemed uncertain as to the occupants of the carriage ;
but all doubt was soon removed, and, regardless of consequences or appearances, Grace sprang forward and flew up
the hill as if she had wings. The old coachman, allowing his
solemn face to relax into a smile, reined in his horses, and in
another instant Grace was in the carriage.

" It is Dr. Kiely," exclaimed Mary. " It is her father."

And Mary looked so excited, that a new idea got into Mr.
Lowe's head ; and when he saw a tall man of noble presence
alight from the carriage holding his little daughter by the
hand, Mr. Lowe felt sure that Dr. Kiely was the rival he had
most to dread. He remembered how Miss Kearney had described him as the " finest man she ever saw " ; and he could
see by her look that she almost worshipped him.

" Oh, he has Eva with him," she exclaimed again, and hurried quickly back to the gate, as Richard handed a graceful
girl with very long golden ringlets out of the carriage.

When the greetings and introductions were over—and Dr.
Kiely did not fail to shake hands with Mr. Lloyd, whom he
had met before—the party all walked through the lawn, the
carriage going round to the back entrance ; but Maurice
Kearney observed that Mr. Bob Lloyd remained outside the
gate, as motionless as any equestrian statue.

" Come, Mr. Lloyd, and have pot-luck with us," said
Maurice Kearney, going back and pulling the gate open.

Mr. Lloyd rode in like a man in a dream, till he came to
the hall-door.

" Take Mr. Lloyd's horse to the stable," said Mr. Kearney
to Tom Maher. " Come in, Mr. Lloyd."

Grace never let go her father's hand all this time ; but she
glanced at Eva occasionally as if she feared some harm might
happen to her, and thought the " poor child " required looking
after. Mary was obliged to come down from her room to
remind her of the necessity of preparing for dinner, and
Grace returned with her ; but instead of taking off her
bonnet, she sat on a chair near the window, looking quite
bewildered.

" What on earth has come over you, Grace ?" Mary
asked. " You have never once opened your lips since they
arrived."

To which Grace replied by rushing at her sister, and flinging her arms round her neck. Eva stooped down and gently
submitted to a choking.

" You have lost your senses," said Mary, laughing.

" Here now, Mary," returned Grace, in a business-like
manner, " sit down and write a note which I will dictate."

" To whom ?" Mary asked.

" To Castleview. Papa likes a dance, and I can't see that

we can get on quite well by ourselves. So ask them to spend the evening."

"Very well," returned Mary; "I suppose I'm to include Lory?"

"Yes, of course."

"Who is Lory?" Eva inquired, as she tried to re-arrange her curls.

"Oh, he's one of my admirers," Grace replied.

"Shall I say, by way of inducement, that we have Mr. Lloyd?"

"Well, I think not. It would look as if we regarded that fact as a great matter. I'll send Adonis with the note, and he can just mention Mr. Lloyd incidentally. And, by-the-by, don't be too sure of Mr. Lloyd. Here is his man Jer in pursuit of him, and you know what Richard told us about him."

Mr. Lloyd was soon seen, without his hat, in the garden.

"Well, Jer?" said he.

"Aren't we goin' to the County Carlow?" returned Jer. "Afther gettin' the new traces for the tandem an' all."

"Ay, faith," replied his master. "To-morrow."

"Well, sure you may as well come away home so," rejoined Jer.

"I'm staying for dinner with Mr. Kearney," returned his master.

Jer looked at him in silence for a minute. "God help you," he muttered, with a pitying shake of the head. "You never had a stim uv sinse, since you wor the hoighth o' that." And Jer held his hand two feet from the ground.

"No danger, Jer," said Bob Lloyd, walking back to the house with a good-humoured smile.

"No danger," Jer muttered to himself, as he glanced at Miss Kearney in the window. "How mild an' innocent she looks. An' she's always quite an' studdy, an' stays at home, an' keeps her mind to herse'f But thim's the dangerous wans," added Jer, with a look of deep wisdom, "an' 'tisn't the little cockers that's always runnin' about waggin' their tails and givin' tongue from mornin' till night. But id can't be helped, an' he can't say that he wasn't warned, at any rate." And Jer returned to Mount Tempe full of sad forebodings, and almost regretting his promise to Tom Otway to go down to the County Carlow to have a look at his cousin.

The dinner was equal to anything that Mrs. Kearney had ever seen even in " her own father's house." It imparted an epicurean pout to Dr. Kiely's under lip, and threw a sort of " dim religious light " over the spirits of the whole company, which checked everything approaching to levity till the dishes were removed. Grace's laugh was hushed, and even the brilliancy of her eyes toned down. In fact, her face merely reflected her father's, and she even unconsciously imitated his movements, until after a graceful flourish of the hand she leant back in her chair and attempted to stick her thumb in an imaginary waistcoat—which reminded her that she was not six feet high and the finest gentleman in all the world. But then she was his daughter, and maintained her dignified deportment accordingly.

Dr. Kiely had the gift of drawing people out ; and the true politeness to exercise it impartially. Mr. Lowe acquitted himself so entirely to his own satisfaction, that his prejudice against his new acquaintance vanished like mist before the sun. A question or two about his professional studies gave Richard an opportunity of airing a whole vocabulary of hard words, which quite frightened his mother— so stupendous, she thought, must be his learning. Even Mr. Bob Lloyd talked so well that Grace was impressed with quite a high opinion of his good sense ; and wondered why he looked so seldom towards her side of the table. Hugh alone was left in the background ; and she thought it too bad that her papa should treat him as if he were a mere boor. But she soon noticed that Hugh and her papa exchanged looks now and then, and seemed to understand each other very well ; which was quite a " mystery " to her, but just then she could not turn her mind to unravelling it.

But Mr. Lloyd soon took to sighing so deeply, and with so melancholy an expression of face, that Mrs. Kearney became quite distressed—'twas so like her poor Uncle Dan after the marriage of his first love, for whose sake he remained all his life a bachelor, and took to writing poetry and playing the fiddle. Mr. Lloyd, she thought, must surely have been crossed in love, and her heart melted in compassion for him. She thanked goodness *she* had never made any one unhappy in that way. Though, to be sure, their neighbour, Mr. Sweeny, who was "rolling in riches," fell in love with her when she was only nineteen, and offered to marry her "without a penny." And though her father thought it would be a most fortunate match for her, and even her Uncle Dan said she ought not to be too hasty in refusing, and poor Mr. Sweeny was "so fond of her"; still she couldn't bear the thought of marrying him—on account of his nose. Not that the nose, though somewhat long, was by any means an ugly nose. But it was a *cold* nose! That's what did the mischief. Mr. Sweeny arrived unexpectedly at Ballydunmore one winter's night—it was the night after Twelfth Night, for all the world—and the light happening to be blown out in the hall, Mr. Sweeny, in an evil hour for himself, attempted to kiss her, and the contact of his nose with her glowing cheek, sent a cold shiver to her heart, and quenched the incipient combustion that was beginning to take place there, from the mingling of her own good nature with her Uncle Dan's approval; and which would inevitably have burst into a flame, were it not for that unlucky icicle of a nose. It was all in vain that she tried to reason with herself that the coldness of the nose was merely accidental, and the result of the cold rain and sleet, which the east wind had been blowing straight in Mr. Sweeny's face since he had left his own house. Unhappily reason is a mere bellows without a valve in such cases. No matter how hard you work with it, it won't help in the least to get up a blaze. And in spite of all she could do, the rosy-cheeked Miss O'Carroll of Ballydunmore found herself singing, involuntarily, twenty times a day—

> "You're too old and you're too cold,
> "And I won't have you, I won't have you,"

greatly to her own distress. And after those little snatches of melody she would accuse herself of "ingratitude," and the valveless bellows would be brought into requisition, but to very little purpose. Yet there was no knowing how it might have ended, as Mrs. Kearney was wont to say with a sigh, if young Maurice Kearney, of Ballinaclash, had not dropped in with her Uncle Dan on their way to the fair of Limerick, and stopped for the night. It was rumoured at the time—but there was no positive evidence of the fact—that a similar

proceeding to that of the night after Twelfth Night took
place on this occasion also ; but with a precisely opposite
result. And the truth of this rumour was strongly confirmed
by Mrs. Kearney's avowal afterwards that Maurice's
impudence in those days "went beyond anything."

Mrs. Kearney thought of all this as she watched the
heaving of Bob Lloyd's chest, and his languishing looks across
the table—across the table, of course, because his face happened to be turned in that direction, and not with any
reference either to the golden ringlets or the wavy tresses
of dark brown, with their accompaniments, that happened to
be straight before him. And as Mr. Lloyd continued to get
worse, Mrs. Kearney felt quite unhappy, and said to herself
that she did not "envy her, whoever she was," who could
cause such suffering as that, particularly in the case of such
a "fine, gentlemanly-looking man" as Mr. Lloyd.

Once in the drawing-room Grace emancipated herself from
the spell that so subdued her during dinner, and instead of
reflecting the mellow light of the star of her idolatry,
sparkled and scintillated with her own peculiar brightness.
Even Mr. Lloyd followed her movements with a plaintive
smile ; as a mourner over a grave might be startled into a
momentary forgetfulness of his sorrow by the flitting of a
humming bird, like a winged gem among the tombs. Mary
was far more animated than Mr. Lowe had ever seen her
before. But Eva was shy, and looked as if she would hide herself behind the golden ringlets—which made Hugh whisper
in Grace's ear while he called her attention to her sister—

> "My Mary of the curling hair,
> The laughing teeth, and bashful air."

Whereupon Grace started up from her seat with her hands
upon her knees, and then sat down again, as if she could
scarcely resist flying across the room and repeating the
strangling process over again.

The entrance of the Miss Hanlys in their new flounced
dresses created quite a sensation, and even Grace acknowledged that Kathleen was gloriously handsome. In fact, the
little improvised party was as perfect in every detail as if
it had been planned and pondered over for weeks and months
before ; and even Dr. Kiely, who was somewhat fastidious,

was charmed. And when Miss Rose Hanly ran her fingers over the keys of the piano, and the dancing commenced, it would be difficult to say whether the actual performers or the lookers-on were most delighted—always excepting Mr. Lory Hanly, whose ecstasy, in either capacity, like Maurice Kearney's impudence when he went a-wooing to Ballydunmore, "went beyond anything."

When, however, the "poetry of motion" was suspended, and poetry proper, in the shape of Moore's Melodies, introduced, Dr. Kiely began to resume his sway over the company, as he called Mr. Lowe's attention to the beauties of each song, occasionally repeating a stanza in such a mellow tone and measured cadence, that Mr. Lloyd called out at last, " Give it all to us, doctor," to the great amusement of every one, for these were the first words uttered by Mr. Lloyd since he took to sighing at the dinner-table. And when Lory, who was concealed behind the window curtains—with only one eye visible, which he kept steadily fixed upon Grace— blurted out with that " terrible throat " of his, " You took the words out of my mouth, Mr. Lloyd ; I was just going to ask him myself "—there was a burst of laughter that broke the spell under which the doctor was fast bringing them like some powerful necromancer.

Hugh thought how fortunate it was that Miss Lloyd was not present, as the voice from behind the curtain would inevitably have necessitated the burning of feathers under her nose.

Grace suggested that Mr. Hanly himself ought to favour them with a recitation ; and, with the agility of a harlequin, Lory sprang from his hiding-place upon a chair—for, as he afterwards confessed, he'd do anything she'd ask him. Mrs. Kearney took advantage of the clap with which he was received to bolt out of the room, with her two hands over her ears, as if she were flying from a shower of brickbats.

Doctor Kiely complimented Lory upon his rendering of " The Spanish Champion," and prophesied that Mr. Hanly would one day be a great orator ; by which compliment Grace was as gratified as Lory himself. Indeed, she knew his appreciation of herself was a proof that Lory had something in him.

" Well, Grace," said her father, " are we to have any more

songs ? It would not be fair to trespass too much on Miss
Hanly, so I think you ought to sing that beautiful little song
of Edward Walsh's for us."

Grace searched for her own music book—music and words
copied by herself, as she was wont to remark carelessly to her
new acquaintance—and Mr. Lloyd was roused again when
she came to the words—

> " My girl has ringlets rich and rare,
> By Nature's finger wove "—

and evinced such admiration of her singing, that Grace
requested a song from Mr. Lloyd himself. And Mr. Lloyd
complied so readily and acquitted himself so well that the
ladies all exchanged looks of wonder. The song was " Norah
Creina," and Grace saw plainly enough that she was the lady
of " the beaming eye " and the " wit refined " ; but which of
the other ladies was Mr. Lloyd's " gentle, artless Norah
Creina," was not so evident, as they all sat close together at
the opposite side of the room, and she could not be sure for
which of them the singer's melting glances were intended.

" That's an admirable song," said Dr. Kiely ; " and I never
heard it better sung in my life. In fact, I think most of
Moore's songs are best sung by men. The ladies don't attend
sufficiently to the sentiment ; they think only of the music."

" That does not apply to Miss Grace's singing," Mr. Lowe
observed.

" Oh, you are thinking of the ' cold-hearted Saxon,' " said
Mary, laughing, " when she sang the ' Coulin ' for you the
other evening."

" What about the ' cold-hearted Saxon ?' " Dr. Kiely asked.

" Mr. Lowe heard Mr. Flaherty play the air at a wedding,"
returned Mary, " and Grace sang Moore's words to it for him,
and he says the bitter hatred she threw into her look and
voice, as she fixed her eyes on himself at those words, quite
frightened him."

" Oh, 'twas dreadful !" exclaimed Mr. Lowe.

Grace laughed, and ran off to Ellie and Willie, who had
induced Lory to join them at a game of forfeits in a corner
of the room.

Rose Hanly and Eva fell in too, and after a while Hugh
and Mr. Lloyd joined in the game ; and Mr. Lloyd " loved
his love with an A because she was an angel," but solemnly

declared he could find no reason for hating her with an A, or any other letter, and preferred forfeiting his buckhorn-handled knife to attempting such an impossibility. But he soon had the satisfaction of seeing Hugh " get down " as well as himself ; and before long every one had to pay a forfeit except Grace, who volunteered to decree what the owners of the " very fine things " and the " superfine things " were " to do." The releasing of the forfeits created much merriment ; but while Lory was acquitting himself to admiration in a hornpipe, Mr. Lloyd pushed his chair close to Richard Kearney, who was making the most of the golden hours that were flying on angel's wings over him and Kathleen, and whispered—

" Dick, what the devil am I to do ?"

" Why ?" the doctor asked.

" I never made a rhyme in my life," replied Mr. Lloyd.

" Oh, any nonsense will do," returned the doctor, turning again to Kathleen.

" But, sense or nonsense," rejoined Bob Lloyd, " I can't do it unless you get me out of it while they're not minding us. And I'll do as much for you, Dick, another time."

" Well," said the doctor, rather crossly, " here is a rhyme for you :

" The man that's rich may ride in stages—

Stages, wages, rages, cages—wait, let me see,"

Dr. Kiely had just been talking of one of his aristocratic patients who had travelled by slow stages from Dublin in order to be under his care ; and this suggested the line which Dr. Richard Kearney repeated for his friend, Bob Lloyd. But to complete the couplet was not so easy.

" Well, Dick ?" said Mr. Lloyd, holding his ear close to him.

" The man that's rich may ride in stages—

" What's to come after that ?"

" ' But the man that's poor ' "—

the doctor continued.

" ' But the man that's poor ' "—

repeated Bob Lloyd.

" Must walk, by jacus "—

added the doctor, impatiently.

" Say it all together for me, Dick," said Mr. Lloyd.

> " The man that's rich may ride in stages,
>   But the man that's poor must walk, by jacus "

" Now have you it ?"

" Wait a minute," returned Bob.   " Is this it ?—

> " The man that rich may ride in stages,
>   But the man that's poor must walk, by jacus."

" That's it. Remember it now, and don't bother us any
more about it," rejoined the doctor, stroking his moustache
and throwing his arm on the back of Kathleen's chair.

" Well, Mr. Lloyd, now for your rhyme," said Grace, when
Lory had finished his hornpipe, and regained possession of
his necktie, which Rose snatched from him again, and, after
folding it carefully, chopped him under the chin, and tied
it on in that great bow-knot which Grace thought so
ridiculous.

" Silence for Mr. Lloyd's impromptu," Dr. Kiely called
out ; and all eyes were at once turned upon Mr. Lloyd, who
hemmed, and looked round upon his audience with a confident smile.

" Silence !" Dr. Kiely repeated.

> " The man that's rich——"

Mr. Lloyd began in a steady sonorous voice, and suddenly
becoming very serious—

> " The man that's rich may ride in stages,
>   But the man that's poor—by jacus, he must walk !"

And Mr. Lloyd resumed his smiling look again, and gazed
round upon the company as if quite sure of their applause.
For a moment there was a dead silence, interrupted only by
one or two slight coughs. Pocket-handkerchiefs were in
requisition, and there was some biting of lips ; but Grace
could not stand it. She threw herself upon Hugh's shoulder,
and screamed with laughter, which exploded again and again,
whenever she ventured to glance at the poet, who continued
to look round upon the company with a beaming smile of
triumph.

" Will you decide a very important question, Dr. Kiely,"
said Mary, " which these ladies have been debating for some
time back ?"

" What is it ?" he asked.

" They are talking about flirting," returned Mary. " Eva says it is a shocking practice, that nothing could justify. It is nothing less, in her opinion, than downright deceit. But Rose says she likes it, and can see no harm in the world in it. 'Tis quite fair, she thinks, to humbug the gentlemen, and she has no objection to be humbugged in return. She is just after saying that if Eva's notions were acted upon, not a soul would she have to pay her a compliment from one end of the year to another, but Mr. Johnny Wilson, who, it appears, is always quite in earnest."

" Well, and what is Miss Kathleen's opinion !"

" Oh, she seems to think the gentlemen should be always in earnest, but the ladies need not be so at all. And now I want you to pronounce judgment on the case."

" Oh, it is too serious, too important a subject," returned the doctor, " to decide upon without due deliberation. I think——"

" Poor old Mr. Somerfield is very bad," exclaimed Mrs. Kearney, who had just entered the room. " They are after sending for you, Mat Donovan says."

" Indeed ! Do they want me immediately ?"

" I don't know," replied Mrs. Kearney. " I'll call in Mat."

" Well, Mat, what is this about old Mr. Somerfield ?" the doctor asked, when Mat was ushered in.

" I was standin' at Phil Morris's gate, sir," Mat returned, " as I went home a piece uv the way wud a couple uv girls from the dance—a cousin of mine, an' another young woman ; an' just as I was afther bidden' 'em good night at ould Phil's gate, I hear a horse comin' powdherin' along the road, an' when he come up I knew 'twas Rody the huntsman, an' called to him, an' axed him where he was goin' at that hour uv the night. ' The ould masther that's afther gettin' a fit,' says he, ' an' I'm goin' for Docthor Kiely.' ' Begor thin,' says I, ' you're turnin' your back to him, for he's over at Misther Kearney's,' says I. ' Do you tell me so ?' says Rody, ' I'll go back an' tell Mr. Sam.' So he wheeled round an' galloped back again ; an' I said to myse'f I'd step over the short-cut an' tell you, fearin' that you might be in bed."

" Thank you, Mat ; you have done quite right. I suppose if I am required at once he will be here soon."

"He often got that fit before," said Maurice Kearney.
"He'll be out with the hounds to-morrow or after, as well as
ever. Sam wouldn't be so easily frightened about him only
that his life is the only hold he has on the place. Do you
think Sir Garrett will leave it to him when the old fellow
drops ?"

"I really don't know," replied Mr. Lowe, to whom the
question was addressed.

"Wait, Mat," said Dr. Kiely, who liked to draw Mat
Donovan out whenever the opportunity presented itself.
"I want to have your opinion upon a subject those ladies
are discussing."

"What's that, sir ?" Mat asked, casting one of his "de-
ludering" looks across the room.

"Well, some of them say it is very wrong for young men
to be flattering and deceiving young women ; while Miss
Rose Hanly says it is rather pleasant and she sees no harm
in it."

"In the way of coortship, sir ?" Mat inquired.

"Yes, in the way of courtship," replied the doctor, laughing.

"Begor, sir," returned Mat, rubbing his chin contemplatively, "I b'lieve 'tis like puttin' the small whate in the
bags."

"How is that ?"

"Somethin' that Father Hannigan said to a friend uv mine,
sir," Mat replied. "An' faith he'll have a harder dish to
wash now wud Father M'Mahon, for he's afther runnin'
away wud a wife, an' Father M'Mahon is mighty hard agin'
that soart uv work."

"I suppose 'tis Tom Cuddehy ?" said Mr. Kearney.

"'Tis, sir," replied Mat. "But there's every excuse for
him, as she was an ould sweetheart, an' her match was made
wud a young buck from the mountains that she didn't care
a straw about, though he's milkin' twenty cows."

"But what did Father Hannigan say about putting small
wheat in the bags ?" Dr. Kiely asked.

"'Tis what every wan do, sir," replied Mat. "The small
whate that runs through the screen is put in the middle uv
the bag, a few fistfuls in each, an' all is passed off on the
merchant, accordin' to the sample. But the merchant knows
'tis there as well as the man that put id in id."

" Well," said the doctor, "what has that to do with deceiving young women ' by way of courtship ' ?"

" Well, you see, sir, Tom Cuddehy scrupled id wan time, and tuck id into his head that it was a sin, an' tould id to Father Hannigan when he went to confession. An' sure Father Hannigan was in a hoult, an' didn't know what to say, for he knew the whole world used to put the small whate in the bags. But for all, he didn't like to say 'twas right, for fear he might be encouragin' fraud, as he said. But, on the other hand, if he said 'twas wrong, he should tell Tom to make restitution for all the small whate he passed off on the merchant all his life. So he was fairly puzzled. But afther thinkin' for a start, he says to Tom : ' Well, Tom, sure enough there's nothing like fair an' honest dealin',' says he. ' An' 'tis wrong to desave any man, Tom—even a corn merchant. But—*do your best, and they'll be up to you,*' says Father Hannigan. An' begor, sir," added Mat, with another glance across the room, " I'm thinkin' 'tis the same way in regard to desavin' the young women. Do your best, and they'll be up to you."

Dr. Kiely leant back in his chair, and laughed loud and long. Every one else laughed, too, except Mr. Lloyd, who looked quite lost in astonishment, and averred that " the divil a better thing than that he ever heard in his life."

There was a single knock at the hall-door, and the old huntsman's voice was heard asking for Dr. Kiely. And in reply to the doctor the huntsman said, with the tears in his eyes, that the old master was never so bad before, and that Mr. Sam begged that Dr. Kiely would not " lose a minute."

The gentlemen all came out to the hall to see the doctor off, and, when the doctor was off, the gentlemen walked into the parlour as if by preconcert, and each commenced brewing a tumbler of whiskey punch in silence ; to which beverage Mr. Lowe had become so reconciled by this time that he never drank wine, except a little at dinner to please Mrs. Kearney.

" Ah ! Dick !" Bob Lloyd exclaimed, in a heart-broken tone.

" What's the matter ?" the doctor asked, tasting his punch, and adding another squeeze of lemon.

"They're all fine girls," returned Mr. Lloyd. "Your sister is more like a queen than a woman."

"More like a queen than a woman?" the doctor repeated. "Hugh, the decanter."

"Ay, faith," rejoined Mr. Lloyd. "And Kathleen is a dazzler, and no mistake."

The doctor swallowed the glass of punch he had just ladled out at a gulp, as if drinking the dazzler's health.

"But," continued Bob Lloyd with a shake of his head that seemed to say that wonders would never cease—"but the little one flogs all !"

"Faith, she does !" Lory blurted out, holding his glass to his lips untasted, as he stared at Mr. Lloyd, who was standing with his elbow on the chimney-piece.

Hugh looked up, too, with surprise ; for Mr. Lloyd had all the marks and tokens of a man desperately in love, and Hugh could scarcely imagine how a mere child could be the cause of so severe a fit—for he as well as Lory thought the "little one" that "flogged all," could be no other than Grace.

"What little one ?" he asked.

Mr. Lloyd replied by putting the tip of his fore-finger to his temple, and twisting it round, and round, and round, letting the hand down lower and lower, till he could go no further without stooping.

"Oh, I see," said the doctor. "You have got entangled in Eva's golden ringlets."

"There's nothing I'd rather look at than a nice head of hair," returned Mr. Lloyd, with another deep sigh ; which was echoed from the opposite side of the fire-place, where Mr. Henry Lowe sat brooding over the thought that this was the "last night," and wondering would they have another set of quadrilles. The doctor, too, sighed heavily, and thought what lovely arms Kathleen had—for the "dazzler" had the cruelty to come in ball costume. And Lory Hanly, as he swallowed his punch, looked all round at the three sighing swains, and said to himself that he "wouldn't let it go with any of them." By which Lory meant that he was himself as bad a case as the best of them. In fact, Hugh seemed the only whole-hearted individual among them ; for which we do not mean to insinuate for a moment that he was at all to be envied.

Grace came in to ask the gentlemen to come to the drawing-room. They jumped to their feet with extraordinary alacrity ; but every one stopped to finish his punch, standing, except Mr. Lowe, who left his tumbler more than half full on the chimney-piece. (It was emptied by Kit Cummins, in the kitchen, before it was entirely cold—she having run up to try whether Dr. Kiely could do anything for the " Burgundy in her back " ; by which it is to be supposed Kit meant lumbago. And Mat Donovan remarked that the doctor would be wanted to cure every ailment ever known, " from a bone-lock to a galloping consumption," before he'd be let sit down to his breakfast next morning.)

" Dick," said Bob Lloyd, as they were crossing the hall, " stop a minute."

" What's the matter ?" the doctor asked.

" I'm a gone coon," replied Mr. Lloyd. " Go ahead." And he waved his hand solemnly towards the drawingroom door.

" Why, aren't you coming in yourself ?" said the doctor.

" Ay, faith," returned Mr. Lloyd. " Go ahead, Dick." And they walked into the drawing-room, like a pair of innocent lambs to the slaughter.

We could sit in a corner of that old room for another hour or two, without feeling at all tired. But we must say good-night—and all the more reluctantly, because it may be many a long day before we meet so many happy hearts under Maurice Kearney's roof again.

CHAPTER LV.

BILLY HEFFERNAN MAKES DR. KIELY A PRESENT, " AS A FRIEND OF PHIL LAHY'S."

MAT DONOVAN was right. Maurice Kearney's kitchen next morning seemed to have been turned into a hospital for incurables. But Dr. Kiely was an early riser, and had sent away most of the patients, with prayers and blessings on their lips, before the family had assembled in the breakfast-room. One poor man was so ill, it was necessary to carry him into the out-house where the workmen slept, and lay

him upon one of the beds. After examining him, the doctor
glanced round the apartment. There were several rude bedsteads, and two or three wisps of straw upon the ground, with
something in the shape of bedclothes flung in a heap upon
them. A bit of broken looking-glass stuck to the wall attracted his attention, and on going towards it he saw that
the wall above and below and on either side of it was plastered
with tallow, with bits of burnt wick stuck in it—proof positive
that a candlestick was an unknown luxury to Mr. Kearney's
workmen once they retired to their dormitory.

"I wonder they don't burn down the house," muttered the
doctor.

As many pairs of brogues as ever were seen in a kish at a
fair, were scattered about in all directions, some new and
some old, some patched and some ripped and broken beyond
all hope of mending ; while not a few were grey or green
with the mould of time. More pairs of dirty stockings were
flung about, too, than would be agreeable either to the visual
or olfactory organs of most people. A few suits of clothes
hung from pegs over a corn bin at the farthest end of the
room—the gilt buttons and drab silk ribbons at the knees of
Jim Dunn's Sunday breeches looking so intensely new and
brilliant, that people were tempted to come close to them
and feel them with their fingers, as something very rare and
curious. And the skin of the fat sheep—the leg of which
Dr. Kiely praised so highly at dinner the day before—
dangled from a beam over his head ; that being a safe and
convenient place to keep it from the dogs. All this and
more the doctor took in at a glance ; and feeling the air of
the place heavy and unwholesome, he pointed to the window,
which was at the back, opposite the door, and ordered Tom
Maher to open it.

Tom Maher looked very much surprised, and felt all round
the sash, thereby disturbing a whole legion of spiders—
making them run wildly over the walls and the window—and
carrying away divers layers of cobwebs upon his fingers.

"Begor, sir," said Tom Maher, as he tried to shake the
cobwebs from his hand, which they covered like an old glove,
"it don't open. I remember now wan uv the hinges was
broke, an' 'twas nailed up, as the horses was althered into
the new stable."

"What has the new stable to do with this place?" the doctor asked.

"Sure this was the ould stable, sir," Tom answered. "An' when the new one was built we came to sleep here."

"Yes, I see," returned the doctor. "Horses, of course, require to be better lodged than men! Who sleeps on that heap in the corner?"

"Wattletoes, sir."

"That's Barney. Where is he? I have not seen him."

"He went to see his mother yisterday, sir, and didn't come back yet."

The doctor turned up the covering of one of the beds, and stooping down seemed to smell the musty straw. He shook his head, as he took a last survey of the "den," as he called it, and walked out, leaving Tom Maher to look after the poor sick man.

Dr. Kiely strode into the parlour without even bowing to the ladies, which greatly astonished Mary, for the doctor was usually a model of politeness.

"I am really shocked," he exclaimed, turning to Maurice Kearney, "to see the way you treat your workmen and servants. It is disgraceful. If I had the making of the laws I'd punish such conduct."

Maurice Kearney opened his eyes and rubbed his head as if the doctor's words were utterly incomprehensible to him; while Mrs. Kearney looked the very picture of amazement and consternation. Mary, too, seemed quite frightened, not so much by the doctor's words as by his look and the tone of his voice.

"My workmen never complained of their treatment," said Maurice Kearney, when he had collected his wits. "They are well fed, and I let them have their own way except in the harvest, or when we are in a hurry to get down the seed. And show me the man that pays better wages. You're after being told lies."

"I'm after being told nothing," returned the doctor. "I allude to what I have seen with my own eyes. It is shocking! Seven or eight men huddled together in one of your out-offices, lying upon rotten straw, and covered with old blankets and quilts that I verily believe were never washed. The place looks as if it were never swept out,

and not as much as a current of fresh air to carry away its
impurities. I wonder how you have escaped fever and
pestilence."

Mrs. Kearney crossed herself at the mention of the fever,
and muttered that 'twas " their own fault," as they could get
fresh straw if they liked.

" You astonish me," continued the doctor   " It should be
your business to see to it. It would be better if you turned
them into your barn to sleep upon the ground than leave
them in such a nasty den as that."

" Whatever you'd do for them," rejoined Mrs. Kearney,
" they wouldn't thank you."

" I don't think that is the fact," the doctor replied. " But
you should not look for thanks for simply doing your duty.
Have you never thought of this ?" he asked, turning to Hugh.

" Well, I have," he replied, " but I see so many things
that require amendment, I left this as I found it."

" Oh, yes ; you would be a reformer on a great scale. But
it would be much better to attend to small things and be
practical. It must have a bad effect morally as well as
physically. Let the poor people about you feel that you respect
them. They may have their faults ; but Heaven knows the
wonder is that there is any good at all left in them."

" Well," said Mrs. Kearney, who began to show symptoms
of shedding tears, " I'll get the place cleaned out and whitewashed. And I'll give them sheets and blankets, and make
one of the girls keep it in proper order for the poor men ; for
what time have they to attend to it after their day's work ?
I'm very much obliged to you, doctor, for calling our attention to it."

" I promised to see old Somerfield again on my way home,"
said the doctor, somewhat mollified, as he glanced at his
watch. " So I think we had better walk down immediately
after breakfast," he added, turning to Mary, " to see this poor
girl that you and Grace are so interested in."

" Oh, yes," said Grace, " we'll all go. I'd like to have one
more walk through Knocknagow, and see poor Norah Lahy
again."

They found Norah sitting in her straw chair as usual.
Dr. Kiely had seen her once before, and he remembered
how nervous and frightened she was when he placed the

stethoscope to her chest. But now she was quite calm, and looked at Mary and Grace with a smile while he was listening to her breathing. A deeper sadness fell upon her face for a moment as she fixed her eyes upon Grace; and Grace knew that Norah Lahy felt that she would never see her again in this world. The doctor spoke kindly to her, and said he would send her medicine by Mr. Kearney's man, which he hoped would do her good, and desired her mother to keep up her spirits and have everything about her as cheerful as possible. Honor declared when he was gone that he made her feel "twenty years younger"; and Norah thought he "made her better," and said he was a good man.

Then Phil broke in with a full and true account of the doctor's speech at the great Repeal Meeting, and how he was the finest looking man on the platform, dressed in the green-and-gold uniform of the 'Eighty-two Club. All of which Honor drank in with eager delight, feeling confident that the man who made a speech at a Repeal Meeting in a green-and-gold uniform would surely cure her darling.

Billy Heffernan emerged from his antediluvian domicile; and, accosting Dr. Kiely, ventured to present him with an archæological treasure, in the shape of a bronze bodkin found in his own turbary.

"Will you sell it?" the doctor asked eagerly. "I'll buy it from you."

"I won't sell id, sir," he answered. "I don't want anything for id."

"Why, what use can it be to you?" the doctor asked, looking quite disappointed. "Perhaps it is worth more than you think."

"I knew you wor always on the look-out for a thing uv that soart, sir; an' I made up my mind to give id to you for nothin'; as a friend of Phil Lahy's," added Billy after some hesitation.

The doctor looked inquiringly at Mary; and, with her face half turned away, lest Billy should suspect she was talking about him, Mary explained the real state of the case.

"Ha," said the doctor; and he seemed to fall into a reverie for a minute or two. "I accept your present," he said at last. "I am very much obliged to you, and I'll always be glad to do whatever is in my power for you or your friends."

"Thank'ee, sir," said Billy Heffernan.

"I never got a fee that gave me so much pleasure," said the doctor, as they walked on after Mr. Lowe and Grace, who were a little in advance of them.

"I never saw anything like his affection for Norah," returned Mary. "It is wonderful."

"The Irish peasant is a being of sentiment," said the doctor. "The millions of money they have sent from America to their relations at home is a wonderful proof of the strength of their domestic affections."

"Indeed, yes," returned Mary. "Mrs. Lahy is just after telling me that her brother, who has often sent her money, is now offering to bring out her son and provide for him. In fact, I do not know a single family about here who have not got money from America."

"I was sorry to see so many houses pulled down since I was here last," the doctor remarked. "If it goes on, Ireland is lost."

"There were only two houses pulled down here," said Mary, "and the people gave up possession voluntarily."

"As for giving up possession, they do so because they see no hope before them. But I allude to a place a couple of miles further on."

"Oh, that's the place cleared by Sam Somerfield. He has not a single tenant now—nothing but sheep and cows."

"What a comfortable, substantial little farm-house that is," said the doctor, stopping to admire it. "What a pity it is that the people have not security, to encourage them to build such houses as that."

"Every one remarks Tom Hogan's place," returned Mary.

"And very little encouragement Tom Hogan got," said Hugh, who had come to meet them. "His rent is up to two pounds an acre now; and if all I hear be true, he must quit."

"Does he owe much rent ?"

"Not a shilling. But those three farms lower down are about to be given up by the tenants, who say they may as well go first as last. The three are to be joined into one, and as Tom Hogan's runs between two of them, I fear he is doomed."

"Is it part of Sir Garrett Butler's property?"

"It is. Notwithstanding all we heard of his kindness of heart and his simplicity, things go on just in the old way since he came in for the property. He leaves it all to the agent; and, so long as he sends him whatever money he requires, Sir Garrett seems not to care for his tenants or trouble his head about them. We are very awkwardly circumstanced ourselves. He refuses to renew my father's lease upon some frivolous pretext or other. It is hard to say how it may end. Conceal it as we will," Hugh added, clenching his hand, "it is serfdom. It is rumoured now that the greater part of the property must be sold to pay off the old debts; and the uncertainty is horrible."

Mary looked frightened, and, on observing it, Hugh changed the subject. "Is not that," he asked, "a model peasant's cottage?"

"Oh, yes; I know Mat Donovan's," replied Dr. Kiely.

"Here is Mat himself coming from the forge with his plough-irons," said Mary. "You, too, Mr. Lowe," she added, "are admiring Mat's house."

"Yes; Miss Grace is drawing a pretty picture of love in a cottage for me. But why have not all the rest such neat houses as this?"

"Ask Mat Donovan himself," said Hugh.

"He deserves great credit," Mr. Lowe remarked.

"I on'y kep' id as I found id, sir," said Mat. "'Twas my grandfather done all."

"But why didn't your neighbours' grandfathers do the same?"

"Well, sir," replied Mat, "I b'lieve 'twas all owin' to the freehould."

"How the freehold?" Dr. Kiely asked.

"Well, you see, sir," Mat commenced in his somewhat roundabout way, and laying down his plough-irons, "he was comin' home from the fair of Kilthubber—'twas the Michael-mas fair, 'tis of'en I heard him tellin' the story when I was a little boy—ridin' a young coult belongin' to Mr. Kearney's father, an' happening to meet my grandmother on the road at the Cross uv Dunmore, he axed her to get up behind him' an' he'd give her a lift home. She was a good-looking lump uv a girl at the time, but mv grandfather never had any

notion uv her, an' 'd as soon think uv flyin' as uv gettin'
married, he bein' a wild soart uv a young fellow wudout house
or home, or anything to throuble him. Anyway she tucked up
her cloak an' got up on the ditch, an' come uv a bounce on
the coult's back behind my grandfather ; an' no sooner was she
settled on his back, than away wud the coult ! An' as he
had on'y a halther on him, the divil a stop my grandfather
could stop him ; an' every wan thought the two uv 'em would
be kilt at the turn near the quarry, as the wall wasn't built
at that time. But, whin my grandfather see that pullin'
the ould halther was no use, he let him have his own way,
an', instead uv tryin' to stop him, laid into him wud a hazel
stick he happened to have in his hand. My grandfather was
always for a hazel stick, because, as he said, there was no
stick handier to knock a man down if occasion required id
wudout hurtin' him ; an', though he was as given for a fight
as any man, my grandfather was ever an' always for batin' a
man wudout hurtin' him, an' till the day uv his death no wan
ever see a bit uv lead melted into a stick uv his, or even a
ferl uv any account on id. Thim was quare times," added
Mat, shaking his head, " whin people'd whale at wan another
wudout rhyme or reason at fair or market."

"Well, but what about the runaway horse ?" Dr. Kiely
asked ; for Mat seemed lost in thought upon those extraordinary times he had referred to.

" Begor, sir," he resumed, " the horse got enough uv id,
an' stopped uv his own accord at the back gate, an' my grandmother slipped down fair an' asy, an' went home. But my
poor grandfather was done for," added Mat, sadly.

" How ?" the doctor asked.

" She took such a hoult uv him, sir, when the horse made
off ; he never had an 'asy mind afther, till they wor married,"
returned Mat solemnly.

" Take care, Mr. Lowe," said Dr. Kiely laughing, " how
you venture to take a Tipperary girl on horseback behind
you, lest she should take such a *hoult* of you as would rob
you of your peace of mind. But come to the freehold, Mat.
Did he get this house and garden with the wife ?"

" Neither uv 'em had house or home, sir," returned Mat.
" An' there was a lough uv wather between the two roads
where you see the haggart there now. Sure you see the

quare shape uv id, wide in the middle, an' narrow at each end. An' where the house an' yard is was a soart uv a quarry. So my grandfather built a cabin on the dhry part, an' in coorse uv time he made a couple uv dhrains, an' began fillin' up the lough wud road stuff an' bog mowld, an' clay from the quarry, an' planted quicks about id, till by degrees he turned id into a little haggart, where he could have a few hundred uv cabbage, an' a ridge or two uv preates. At last the agent thought to put him under rent, but he refused ; an' id came out that the two estates joined at the cross uv the road there, an' no wan could tell which uv the landlords the little spot belonged to. So my grandfather was let alone. An' wan day a gentleman happened to tell him that he had a freehould while grass grows or wather runs, in spite uv law or landlord ; an' he got so proud an' had such courage that he never stopped till he made the place what you see id. An' that's how it was that the freehould made Mat Donovan's house an' haggart what every one says it is, the purtiest house an' haggart in the county Tipperary, for a poor labourin' man's."

" It is a remarkable illustration," said the doctor, " of the saying, ' Give a man a rock with security, and he'll turn it into a garden.' It is a striking argument in favour of a Peasant Proprietary."

" I often thought so," said Hugh.

" I hope we may live to see the day, Mat," Dr. Kiely observed, " when freeholds will be more numerous than they are in Ireland."

" Sure you don't think the English Parliament would do that for us, sir ? "

" I'd rather have it done by an Irish Parliament," replied the doctor. " But it is getting late," he added, looking at his watch, " and I must call at Woodlands."

The hour of parting came all too soon. Richard and Mr. Lowe had driven off in the tax-cart. Dr. Kiely and Eva were already seated in the carriage ; while Grace had run back to comfort Ellie and Willie, who were sobbing violently upon the stairs. Mrs. Kearney wiped the tears from her cheeks ; and, though Mary smiled, it was plain that tears were threatening to suffuse those mild blue eyes, as Grace kissed Ellie, and told her somewhat reproachfully not to cry, for didn't she know they'd soon meet again at the convent. And, in the meantime, wasn't she leaving her the jay ? But the allusion to the convent, however comforting to Ellie, had a precisely contrary effect upon her brother, and changed his blubbering into a loud roar.

" Come, Grace," said her father, " we have no time to lose."

She had her foot upon the step, when she stopped, looking quite sad, with her lips compressed, and her eyes bent on the ground. They were all surprised ; and her father asked what was the matter. But Grace made no reply. Turning round she walked slowly to Hugh, who was standing with folded arms beside the door, and held out her hand to him. She had forgotten him. She had said good-bye, over and over, to every one else, but never thought of Hugh. And now he looked at her as if he did not know what she meant.

" Good-bye, Hugh," said she.

" Oh, good-bye," he replied with a start, taking her extended hand. And there was something in his tone that made Mary look at him with surprise. She observed, however, that he laughed as he led Grace back to the carriage, and handed her in.

They are gone—Grace, Richard, Mr. Lowe, and all. And Mary does feel lonely ; and feels, too, that she must try hard to keep up her spirits, or they will inevitably break down. Well, that intelligence in her sister Anne's letter has removed one indefinite uneasiness from her heart at all events. The way is clear before her now, and not *clouded* by *hope*—a hope from which she shrank as from a sin, and strove to banish from her heart ; but which would, nevertheless, return again and again to disturb and trouble her. Thank God ! *that* is all over now.

" How I should like to be able to call such noble old trees as those my own," Grace observed.

Eva admired the trees, too, and the undulating lawn, and the woods around, but she could not see what good it would do her to be able to call them her own.

" It must be that Mr. Kearney was right last night when he said the old gentleman would be out with his hounds to-morrow or after. There is the horn sounding," said Mr. Lowe.

" Yes, I can see the pack, and the huntsman mounted

before the door, from where I am," returned Richard Kearney, who had walked on a little further than the rest.

They were in the avenue at Woodlands, waiting for Dr. Kiely, who had walked on to see his patient, leaving his carriage at a turn in the avenue not far from the house, though not in view of it. Richard and Mr. Lowe walked in from the road, and were now chatting with the ladies in the carriage.

"I wonder, if he be recovered, why papa is delaying so long," said Grace. "Can you see papa coming, Richard?"

"No, he's not coming," returned Richard. "There's something going on I can't make out. The doctor is standing with several others near the hounds; but I see no one mounted but the huntsman."

"I'll walk down and see," said Mr. Lowe. "And perhaps I ought to bid Mr. Somerfield good-bye after accepting of his hospitality."

Dr. Kiely was astonished to find his patient in a chair on the lawn, propped up with pillows. His son, a tall, cadaverous-looking man with grizzled hair and beard, stood on one side of the chair, and a saintly looking though somewhat spruce young clergyman at the other. Two graceful young ladies stood a little apart, looking very sad and interesting, but not altogether oblivious of the handsome young clergyman's presence.

"Blow, Rody, blow," muttered the poor old invalid. And the horn sounded, and the woods gave back the echo.

"O sweet Woodlands, must I leave you?" exclaimed the old foxhunter in tones of the deepest grief.

"You're going to a better place," said the clergyman, impressively.

"Yoix! Tallyho!" cried the invalid, faintly. "Blow, Rody, blow."

"Don't ax me, sir," returned the huntsman, after putting the horn to his lips and taking it away again; "my heart is ready to burst."

"O sweet Woodlands, must I leave you?" his master exclaimed again.

"My dear sir," the clergyman repeated, stooping over him and placing his gloved hand gently upon his shoulder, "my dear sir, you are going to a better place."

The invalid turned round and looked earnestly into the young clergyman's face, as if he had until then been unconscious of his presence.

" You're going to a better place ; trust me, you're going to a better place," the clergyman repeated fervently.

" Ah ! " replied the old foxhunter, with a sorrowful shake of his head, and looking earnestly into the parson's face— " ah ! by G——, I doubt you ! "

The parson's look of consternation brought a grim smile into the hard features of Mr. Sam Somerfield, as he adjusted his father's night-cap, which was displaced by the effort to turn round to look at his spiritual director.

The dying foxhunter seemed to drop suddenly into a doze, from which a low fretful whine from one of the hounds caused him to awake with a start. " Poor Bluebell ; poor Bluebell," he murmured. The hound named wagged her tail, and coming close to him, looked wistfully into his face. The whole pack followed Bluebell, waving their tails, and with their trustful eyes appeared to claim recognition, too, from their old master. But his head drooped, and he seemed falling asleep again. He roused himself, however, and gazed once more upon the fine landscape before him, and again called upon the huntsman to sound the horn. The huntsman put it to his lips, and his chest heaved as he laboured for breath ; but no sound awoke the echoes again.

" God knows I can't, sir," he cried at last, bursting into tears. The huntsman's emotion moved the two young ladies to tears, and they came nearer to their grandfather's chair, and looked anxiously into his face. Dr. Kiely laid his finger on the old man's wrist, and turned to whisper something to his son, who was still standing by the chair. But the doctor drew back, as if the eye of a murderer were upon him. Mr. Sam Somerfield's face was ashy pale and his lips livid, while a baleful light glared from under his shaggy brows, which were dragged together in puckered folds. His daughters, too, were terrified, and wondered what could have brought that shocking expression into their father's face. But guided by his eyes they turned round and saw that Mr. Lowe was standing near them : then they understood that terrible look.

The young girls gazed upon the woods and groves and undulating meadows, just as their grandfather had done.

And the expression in the bright eye of youth and in the dimmed eye of age was the same.

"Ah," said the younger girl, as her sister's eyes met hers "it is a sweet place."

Turn, round, young ladies, and look through that arched gateway to yon sloping hillside, speckled with white sheep, upon which the sun shines so brightly. There were many happy homes along that green slope not many years ago. There is not one now. You remember the last of them—the old farm-house in the trees, with its cluster of corn-stacks; and the square orchard, that looked so pretty in the spring-time; and the narrow boreen leading to the road between tangled wild roses and woodbines! You remember the children who peered shyly at you from under their brown arms when you rode by upon your pretty ponies! You remember what a rage your papa was in when the man who lived there refused to give up the old lease; and how he swore when the old lease had expired, and the "scoundrel" —that was the word—refused to go until the sheriff and the police and military drove him away!

To be sure, his father, and grandfather, and great-grand-father had lived there before him. He paid your papa fifty gold guineas every year, and was willing to pay half as many more if he were allowed to toil on there to the end of his days; though old people remembered when that productive little farm was covered with furze and briers, with patches of green rushes here and there in the marshy places. Well, he should go; and the children—but what do you care for such things? We merely meant to remind you that, to that poor man and his wife and children, their place, too, was "a sweet place."

"I suppose," thought Mr. Sam Somerfield, "he came here purposely to watch till the breath is out of him, in order that I may be hunted without an hour's delay." Then fixing his eyes upon the old man with a look in which pity and hatred seemed blended, he continued, "What right had he to take such a lease? He cared only for himself. Why wasn't it *my* life he got it for? He might have died, and died an old man, twenty years ago. And I wish to heaven he did die twenty years ago, before my heart was rooted in it "

An old blind hound, lying on a mat near the door, raised his head, and uttered a long dismal howl. The whole pack took up the cry; and, as it passed like a wail of sorrow over the hills, the old foxhunter fell back in his chair—dead!

The huntsman threw himself from his horse; and, with the help of two or three other servants, carried his old master into the house.

"O papa, poor grandpapa is gone!" the young girls exclaimed, flinging their arms round their father's neck.

He bent down as they clung to him, looking quite helpless and stupefied. But, when he saw the horse from which the huntsman had dismounted, walk to a square stone near the end of the house, and stand quietly beside it, and thought that "old Somerfield" would never mount his hunter from that stone again, the tears ran down his hard, yellow cheeks, and fell upon his children's hair.

The doctor and Mr. Lowe walked back to the carriage in silence, much affected by what they had seen.

"Do you think her handsome?" Richard asked.

"Not very," was Mr. Lowe's languid reply. "I could never admire girls like her. The girl that called you to see her father the other day is by far a prettier girl."

"Yes, Nancy Hogan is decidedly handsome. Yet Hugh thinks Bessy quite captivating. Curious how tastes will differ."

They had stopped to send Tom Maher into old Phil Morris's for a light, and Bessy came to the door with her sewing.

"Grace is wondering why we have stopped," said the doctor. "She will break her neck trying to look round at us. But I'll blow a cloud," he added, as Tom Maher presented him with a bit of burning stick, "that will enlighten her."

Grace had her head out of the carriage, but it was not of them she was thinking at all. She caught the outline of a man's figure on the hill above the fort, and guessed it was Hugh, watching the carriage as long as they were within view.

"Ah! it came from his heart," said she with a sigh.

"What are you saying?" Eva asked.

"Nothing," was the careless reply. She was thinking of Hugh's "Good-bye."

And Hugh did watch the carriage as long as it was in sight ; but then he had come up the hill to look at the hoggets. And as his eye rested upon the little house among the old whitethorns, he wished he had another excuse to follow the winding footpath, and have a chat with old Phil Morris about the year of the Hill, and listen to his speculations on the chances of having " anything droll " in the country before he died. And as Hugh thought of the old " croppy," he saw in fancy his bright little granddaughter, as she flitted like a fire-fly about the house, when he used to run in for shelter from the rain, some years before. And as he went on admiring Bessy Morris retrospectively, he happened to put his finger and thumb into his waistcoat pocket, and feeling something soft and silky, took it out and looked at it in great surprise. It was a long shining lock of hair. After thinking for a moment, he laughed ; but that soft light which his sister Mary sometimes noticed came into his dark eyes. And Mr. Hugh Kearney began now to call up a vision in the future, as a moment before he had called up one of the past. So long as he goes on looking " before and after " in this fashion he is safe enough. But if one day he should find " the fancy true," how will it be ? He tore off the blank leaf of a letter, and after counting backwards on his fingers, " Monday, Sunday, Saturday," wrote the day of the month and the year upon it.

" I wonder what sort she will be in a few years more ? " he thought, looking again at the shining tress which he had playfully cut from Grace's head the morning of Ned Brophy's wedding. Then, *à la* the Dean of St. Patrick's, he wrote the words, " Only a *girl's* hair," and, folding it up carefully, placed it in his pocket-book, and returned home without thinking again of the old rebel and his fascinating granddaughter, who at that moment was just after being made miserable by a good-natured friend, who had walked three miles for the sole purpose of telling her that she was " in a show " on account of the dragoon's visit.

Poor Mrs. Kearney was so nervous and depressed that day that she left even the dinner to Mary's sole superintendence. But Mrs. Kearney always wished to have a natural and rational reason for her sighs and tears, whenever she felt disposed or constrained to indulge in them. And on this occasion the cause of her trouble was her favourite son, who was a " very soft boy," and, like her poor Uncle Dan, required egg-flip very often to set him all right of a morning ; and to think that he hadn't a soul to look after him in " that Dublin," was enough to break her heart. Honest Maurice, who, like the Vicar of Wakefield, found pleasure in happy human faces, rushed in desperation into the pantry, and cutting several substantial slices from the remains of that glorious leg of mutton which Dr. Kiely praised so highly, placed them in a small basket with as much bread as there was room for, and walking off to the kiln-field, peremptorily ordered Mat Donovan to let the horses rest, and " sit down and eat that "—deriving much comfort and peace of mind from Mat's performance as he dutifully obeyed the injunction and set to work in a very business-like manner.

Mary took her sister's letter and read, for the twentieth time ; " Gretta H—— has just returned from Paris. Arthur O'Connor is ordained. She saw him in his vestments, and says he is the handsomest priest she ever saw."

" Thank goodness," thought Mary, " no tongue can ever wound me again on that score."

" What is the matter with you, Mary ? " Ellie asked.

" Why so ? "

" If you saw yourself ! I thought you were Aunt Hannah."

" Oh, my goodness," exclaimed Mary, in affected alarm. " Am I a faded old maid already ? "

" Well, you had her look," returned Ellie. " And Aunt Hannah was crossed in love."

" And do you suppose that I, too, have been crossed in love ? "

" Well, I was thinking how Grace used to be at you about Mr. Lowe."

" I am very sorry after Mr. Lowe," returned Mary. " Are not you ? "

" Not much. It is Grace I am sorry after."

" You'll have Grace with you in the convent."

" But will I be let bring my goldfinch ? "

" Oh, I fear that would not be allowed."

" Well, I'll give him back to Tommy Lahy to keep for me till I come home. I'd be afraid you would not take care of him."

" Oh, yes, I'll take care of him. And don't you know Tommy will be soon going to America ? His uncle is very rich, and his mother says Tommy will be a great man yet."

" Oh, I'm sorry Tommy Lahy is going to America," said Ellie. " And what will his poor mother and Norah do ? "

" That's true," returned Mary. " It will be a sore trial to them ; but it will be for his good, and they will make the sacrifice."

But Mary could not help smiling, when she remembered that the very climax of Honor Lahy's trouble seemed to be the thought, that Tommy would surely take to climbing to the top of " them masts," which, she understood, were standing in the middle of the ship, and would of course be a perpetual temptation to him. " The best chance he'd have," Honor added, " would be to stay at the top of it always, an' keep quiet, an' not to be peltin' himself down, the Lord save us ! like a bag from the top loft of the mill, takin' the sight uv your eyes from you, an' bringin' your heart into your mouth." And as the comparatively re-assuring picture presented itself of Tommy keeping quiet on the top of the main-mast while crossing the Atlantic, Honor brightened up and said, " she'd trust all to the mercy of God." Mary smiled as she thought of this. Then she began to think of Norah ; and Ellie would look in her face in vain for the slightest resemblance to Aunt Hannah, who was crossed in love.

CHAPTER LVI.

THE WHITE JACKET.

THE Sunday afternoons were growing longer and longer, and Mat Donovan's visits to the little house under the hill were more frequent than they had been for a long time before. He saw Hugh Kearney's fishing-rod, which he had repaired for him in " first-rate style," on the wall with Phil Morris's own old rod, which was never taken to pieces, and stretched its tapering length nearly the whole cross of the kitchen, with the wheel line wound up till the knot on the end just touched the ring on the top of the rod. So that, while Hugh Kearney was screwing his rod together and passing the line through the rings, old Phil's flies would be dropping as natural as life, on the currents and eddies of the little stream, and a shout from him would sometimes call Hugh away to secure a good-sized trout with his landing-net. But Hugh Kearney's rod and landing-net over the old weaver's loom never gave Mat Donovan the slightest trouble. We cannot say as much, however, concerning the horse which he now sees standing at Phil Morris's door. And when the young man from the mountain came out of the house and rode away, Mat Donovan felt a sinking of the heart in spite of all he could do. And when he walked in with his " God save all here ! " there was Bessy with that killing white jacket, which he had not seen since the night of Ned Brophy's wedding, sitting in her grandfather's armchair, and looking very grand indeed, as she said without rising, and almost without turning her head, " How are *you* this evening ? " The white jacket, as Peg Brady afterwards told him, had been taken from the box where it had lain for months, and hastily put on, when Bessy caught sight of the young man from the mountain turning in at the gate ; in proof of which Peg produced a little bunch of lavender which fell from the folds of the white jacket on the floor.

" I think," says Peg Brady, with that sly look of hers, " you may take off your jacket now."

Bessy reddened and bit her lips ; but said, carelessly, " Well, I believe so," and walked into her room—looking handsomer than ever, Mat thought when she came back in her brown stuff dress. Then old Phil stumped in, and Bessy took his fishing-rod and leaped upon a chair to hang it in its usual place. And how graceful she looked with her arms raised as far as they could reach, for the hooks upon which the rod rested were up near the loft. Though the house was a one-storey thatched house, there was a loft to it, upon which, in days gone by, yarn, and pieces of flannel and frieze, and blankets, to a fabulous amount, used to be stowed away. Then Bessy jumped down again, and, looking into the angler's basket, said that Mat should bring the trout to Miss Kearney.

" You have two good red trout there," said old Phil, " but

the rest are no great things. The river is not what id used to be, any more than the people. Everything is goin' to the bad. Hugh lost the finest trout I see this many a day, the last day he was over, an' all on account of not takin' his time. You'd think 'twas an elephant he had, he gave him such a dhrag—whin he had a right to give him line, an' take him 'asy. There's no fear at all uv Hugh, on'y that when he don't be mindin' himself, an' is took sudden, he's apt to pull too hard an' break his line. An' he depinds too much on the fur flies. He thinks a hare's-ear-an'-yallow ud kill the divil."

Bessy laid the speckled trout into her own basket, having first put in some of the fresh green grass the old angler had wrapped about them.

" I know," says she, " she'd like to send a couple of them to Norah Lahy. And how is she getting on, Mat ? "

" I'm afeard she's stalin' away unknownst to the world," Mat replied " She was never so late in the year before wudout sittin' outside the doore. An' though fine an' soft this week was, she was not sthrong enough to venture out, Honor tells me."

" Is id thrue for certain," old Phil Morris asked, " that Tom Hogan is to be put out ? "

" No mistake," Mat answered, " an' 'tis afther knockin' the good out uv every tenant on the property. The rent is riz again on every wan uv 'em except Misther Kearney, an' his laise is not up yet. An' they all say, what chance have they when Tom Hogan is served."

" Did them fellows near you pull down their own houses for a pound a piece, as 'tis said they did ? "

" They did then—exceptin' Billy Heffernan ; an' he towld Pender he wouldn't knock the cabin where his mother rocked him in the cradle if a fifty pound note was laid in his hand. Billy has great sperit though he hasn't much talk. They say Tom Hogan would get a thrifle uv money, too, if he'd give up ; but I don't think he'd take Maurice Kearney's farm this minute for his own little spot ; for, as he says himself, his heart is stuck in id. An' he's goin' on dhrainin' just as if he was as firm as the Rock uv Cashel in id. They must bring the sheriff any way. An' I won't plase 'em either to give up my garden, till I must."

"Are you going to be ejected?" Bessy asked, looking alarmed.

"They can't touch the house an' haggart," returned Mat, "id bein' a freehould. But they're takin' the garden from me to join id to the big farm that's to be med out of Tom Hogan's an' the other three. A man has no chance in Ireland, an' I suppose I must cross the salt wather myse'f as well as another."

"What hurry are you in?" said Bessy, as he rose to go. "Sit down an' tell us all the news."

"I was over lookin' at a horse uv Tom Cuddehy's that got a hurt," he replied, "an' just walked in on my way back."

"And how is Mrs. Cuddehy going on?"

"Very well," Mat replied. "An' her father is givin' every penny of her fortune to Tom, when he seen him act so manly, an' get married, an' pay the priest, an' all, wudout sayin' a word about money. An' ould Paddy is in wud 'em every night in the year, they're always so pleasant. An' so is Ned Brophy. An', faith, Ned can go where he likes, the wife is so well able to look to everything. An' so he walks over to Tom's to have a talk wud the neighbours."

"Is there any truth in the report about Miss Kearney and young Mr. Kiely?"

"I don't say there is. The same talk was about her and Mr. Lowe, an' there was nothin' in id. Mr. Edmund is a fine pleasant young fellow, an' a right good boy," added Mat, emphatically. "I don't know a smarter fellow, to take him at general exercise. The masther made me put two big rocks in the kiln-field to mark the throw again Captain French, an' Edmund has the pueata stalks all thrampled thryin' to put the sledge up to the captain's mark. An' faith he's not far at all from id. But as for Miss Mary, I don't say they have any notion uv wan another. An' so far as goin' on goes, I'd say 'tis Miss Anne an' himself that's pullin' the coard."

"And how is Nancy Hogan?" Bessy asked.

"I never see her in betther spirits," he answered, readily. "On'y for frettin' afther Jemmy an' the way her father is she'd be as pleasant as ever she was. I b'lieve her ould sweetheart Tom Carey is afther her again."

"He's a mane dog," Phil Morris exclaimed, "afther her father tellin' him a tradesman was no match for his daughter.

Bad luck to his impudence, the beggar ! the crawler, as Phil Lahy called him. *I'm* a tradesman, though 'tis little I do at my trade now, an' sorry I'm for id. An' I suppose I could call myself a farmer because I have a spot uv land. But I call myself a tradesman, because I'm proud uv my trade. I gave her father," turning to his granddaughter, " three hundred pounds that I made at my trade. An' if Tom Carey wants a wife let him come for her, an' he'll get her before a farmer any day "

" An' would you give her to a labourin' man ? " inquired Peg Brady, who was sitting on the settle, smelling the bunch of lavender that fell from the folds of the white jacket

" No, I wouldn't," replied the old weaver, turning sharply round, and scowling at her. " What business would a labourin' man have wud her ? "

Peg Brady bent her head and laughed.

" You ought not to be so hard against Tom Hogan for his prejudices," Bessy remarked " for you have your pre-judices too."

" But a tradesman is as good as any man," returned old Phil.

" And why should not a labouring man be as good, if he is equally honest and intelligent ? " Bessy asked.

" Faith," said Mat Donovan good-humouredly, " 'tis like the ' Town in danger ' in the spellin' book. There's nothin' like leather wud the whole uv 'em."

" I'll go home the short cut, an' give those to Miss Mary," said Mat Donovan, when he and Bessy Morris had reached the gate without exchanging a word.

" Tell her I'll call for the basket myself," said Bessy.

Mat looked up at the old whitethorns, which were now all in their glory, filling the air with perfume, and, after another interval of silence, held out his hand with a smile.

" Good evenin'," said he. " Why don't you ever take a walk down to see my mother ? They all say 'tis too proud you're afther gettin'."

" Mat," returned Bessy, holding his hand, and fixing that sad, inquiring look upon him, " are you really thinking of America ? "

" Well, I am," he replied. " There's many raisons for id. But I have nothin' decided on yet."

" You won't go without telling me at all events ? "

" Well, if I go at all, I b'lieve I'll slip away wudout takin' my lave uv any one. 'Twould break my heart."

" If you do go, you won't forget to write to me, if you hear anything about my father ? "

" Begor, Bessy," he replied, " I'd walk from wan end uv America to the other if I thought I could find your father for you."

" Good evening," said she, with her eyes still fixed upon his face.

He opened the gate, and, bending down her head, with a smile and a slight blush, she passed in, and returned to the house without looking back.

Peg Brady was strolling along the road with her hands clasped behind her back, looking up at the clouds.

" Are you comin' down ? " Mat asked.

" No," she replied. " I on'y took a walk out thinkin' I might meet some uv the girls goin' the short cut to the dance."

" Peg," said Mat, after a pause, " is there anything the matter wud Bessy ? She looks paler and thinner than ever I see' her lookin' before."

" Maybe she has raison," returned Peg.

" Raison ! " he repeated   " For God's sake, what do you mane ? "

" Oyeh ! You needn't be so frightened. Maybe she's thinkin' uv changin' her condition."

" Oh, is that all ? " he asked, with a sigh of relief.

" Did you hear her bachelor is after comin' in for a legacy ? "

" Sure I did," he replied. " He tould me himse'f. He's no man to be goin' on as he is, when he knows she don't like him."

" Don't be too sure uv that," returned Peg Brady. " He's not a sojer now ; he's out uv the army altogether. An' ax Kit Cummins about the fistful uv goold he pulled out uv his pocket t'other evenin'. Faith Kit has fine times while he's lodgin' wud her. The pan is never off uv the fire, an' he sends for a dozen uv porther together."

" He's a fool," returned Mat.

" You don't know what id is to be fond uv a girl," said Peg.

" Well, maybe not," rejoined Mat, " but I'd tear the heart out uv my body before I'd fret the girl I'd be fond uv, an' makin' her the talk uv the counthry, as he's doin'."

Peg Brady laughed, and, wheeling round, continued her stroll back again towards the house.

" Give my love to Barney," she called out.

" All right," returned Mat, as he jumped over the fence to make a short cut to Maurice Kearney's. He started on seeing a man sitting, or rather lying, behind the fence. It was the dragoon. However, he walked on without pretending to see him ; but his face flushed crimson, and, clenching his hand, he muttered :—

" The divil a thing I'd rather be doin' than whalin' the mane dog. When he knows she hates the sight uv him, what right have he to be persecutin' her this way ? "

When he reached the hill from which Hugh Kearney watched Dr. Kiely's carriage as it disappeared in the distance, Mat Donovan turned round to take another look at the " little house under the hill," and started on seeing the dragoon in conversation with a woman near the gate.

" Oh ! " he exclaimed, after looking at them for some time, " she has a light-coloured gownd on her. 'Tis Peg Brady."

CHAPTER LVII.

A GREAT EVENT.—TOMMY LAHY'S ACCOMPLISHMENTS.—ARTHUR O'CONNOR.

A GREAT event has happened in Knocknagow this still summer day. Nearly all the men, and most of the women, are out in the meadows mowing and " saving " the hay ; or cutting and " footing " turf in the bog. There is a drowsy silence over the hamlet, only broken by the ring of the blacksmith's anvil, or the occasional shrill crowing of a cock, filling the heart with an oppressive sense of loneliness, if not with forebodings of evil. Mrs. Donovan is sitting at the foot of the cherry tree watching her bees. She has had no

less than four swarms within the past week, every one of
them so considerate and accommodating as to lodge within
the bounds of the clipped hedge, not following the example
of the earliest swarm this year, which swept away like a
cloud over Tom Hogan's farm, never stopping till they
passed Attorney Hanly's grove, and to the great delight of
Miss Rose—who, in common with all the world, looked upon
such a visit as a sign of good luck—precipitated themselves
into a rose-bush under the drawing-room window. And
when Nelly Donovan came up out of breath, making a
frightful clatter, by means of an old kettle and a poker—
for Nelly was keen of eye and swift of foot, and never lost
sight of the truants till they dipped beyond the fir grove—
Rose ran out to show her where they were all in a lump in
the middle of the rose-tree. Joe Russel was despatched for
the new hive, which Mrs. Donovan had already smeared
with honey on the inside, and fixed peeled sally switches
across it to keep the new combs from falling down ; while
Lory brought a sieve from the barn to place under the hive
when the bees were shaken into it, and Rose produced a
white table-cloth to wrap around it ; and Nelly Donovan
went home rejoicing with the swarm, which her mother had
given up for lost.

And now Mrs. Donovan sits under the cherry-tree, watching her fifth swarm, hanging like a great sheep's grey stocking
from the branch of a currant-bush ; though when they broke
away from the parent hive, they whirled round and round in
the wildest commotion, as if henceforth bent upon leading a
life of lawlessness and anarchy, but suddenly changed their
minds and dropped into the currant-bush, clustering about
their lawful queen, and showing every symptom of spending
their days in harmony and industry within the four hedges
of Mat Donovan's little garden—of course taking frequent
excursions to the purple-heather on the bog, and to Maurice
Kearney's clover-field, and to the yellow " bouchelauns "
that flourished so abundantly upon Mr. Beresford Pender's
farm, and even raised their heads at the very threshold of
cowhouse and barn, to the great delight of old Phil Morris,
who chuckled over this pleasant prospect when he paid his
periodical visits to the three poplar trees on the hill.

Some children have what they call a " cobby " under the

hedge at the roadside. But the place being quite dry, and the grass green and fresh, and no mud within reach, a little girl has been dispatched for a saucepan of water to manufacture dirt—without which enjoyment is out of the question. The pool outside Kit Cummins's door is so dried up, that the pig by the hardest rooting and rubbing and crushing, has only been able to bear away a single patch of an inky composition about a foot in diameter upon a prominent part of his person ; so the saucepan had to be filled from Kit's wash-tub, the contents of which were the most suitable for the purpose intended, next to the pool outside the door. And the little girl, coming back with her saucepan full, announced to her companions the event which we have referred to at the beginning of this chapter. Nelly Donovan heard the child's words, and flinging down the bee-hive which she was making ready for the reception of the swarm in the currant-bush, ran out upon the road, and turning the corner of the clipped hedge, looked down the hill. And then Nelly Donovan flung up her arms as high as she possibly could, and clapped her hands above her head. Her mother rose from her seat under the cherry-tree and went out upon the road, too, and, looking down the hill, raised her hands, but not in a wild way like Nelly, while a smile lighted up her sad face. Kit Cummins stopped short in the very middle of an oration, which she was delivering for behoof of her next-door neighbour—to whom she could address herself at any moment through the thin partition, without inter-rupting her ordinary avocations. The next-door neighbour not possessing the gift of eloquence, usually contented her-self, when the orator paused for breath, with a " Gir-r-r-out, you bla'guard ! " in a key more or less shrill according to the sharpness of the attack, and rising to a shriek after a home-thrust more stinging than usual. On the present occasion, she was in the act of drawing a long breath pre-paratory to throwing an extra amount of defiance into the exasperatory response, when she raised her head and looked about her in complete and utter bewilderment. Kit Cummins had stopped short in the very middle of a scorching sentence, having reference to the next-door neighbour's grandmother, and there was a dead silence !

" Is she afther dhroppin' in a fit ? " thought the next-door neighbour,

She ran to the door ; and there was Kit Cummins looking down the hill, her face radiant with pleasure. The next-door neighbour advanced a step or two into the road, and immediately seemed to catch the radiant look from Kit, who turned round and began talking to her in the most affectionate manner imaginable ; and both returned to their respective domiciles like turtles. The anvil was silent for a moment, and Brummagem's begrimed face was seen at the forge door, shining with delight and surprise. In fact, there was at least one smiling face at every door of the hamlet that had not a padlock upon it, betokening that the inmates were all in the meadows or at the bog.

Norah Lahy was out ! That's what the little girl announced to her companions under the hedge.

And Nelly Donovan ran out upon the road and clapped her hands ; and her mother followed her ; and Kit Cummins and her neighbour forgot the fierce war they were waging, and exchanged friendly words of mutual joy and thankfulness ; and Brummagem grinned ; and every face from the cross to Mat Donovan's was lighted up with gladness ; and Norah, sitting in her straw chair under the beech tree, saw it all, and, bending down her head, wept tears—happy tears—of gratitude.

God bless them, every one ! Whatever be their faults, the want of loving hearts is not one of them.

And the news has somehow reached Maurice Kearney's meadow on the side of the hill ; for the sweep of the scythes has suddenly ceased, and the row of mowers, with Mat Donovan at their head, have turned quickly round, like so many tall pikemen at drill, and looked down towards the beech-tree. And three girls who were turning the hay threw down their forks, and ran headlong to the double-ditch, and standing on the top of it, waved their straw bonnets in the air. Then there was a shrill shout of laughter from the girls, and a deep roar from the mowers. For Barney Brodherick was plain to be seen, on his way from Kilthubber, standing with a foot on each shaft of his blue cart, and keeping Bobby at full gallop—there being no occasion whatever for hurry to-day. And on coming to the beech-tree, Barney uttered that sound with his lips, which, when addressed to a donkey, signifies " stand," so loudly and so suddenly, that Bobby stopped up as if he had come in contact with a stone wall ; and Barney executed an involuntary somersault out over Bobby's ears.

" Thanum-an-dioul, Norah ! " exclaimed Barney, gathering himself up, as if his ordinary and usual mode of alighting was upon the crown of his head, " is id there you are ! "

" Yes, Barney," she replied with a smile ; " I felt so much better to-day I thought I might venture to sit outside for a while, 'tis so fine."

" Begob, I thought I'd never see you there agin, Norah," returned Barney. " When May-day, an' all the fine weather passed over, an' I never see you out, I gev you up. Would you like pig-nuts, Norah ? "

" I don't think I could eat them, Barney."

Barney scratched his head, quite puzzled to think what he could present her with, or do for her, as a proof of his regard. " Begob," he exclaimed at last, " if Tommy was at home I'd show him a thrish's nest an' five young ones in id."

" Ah, poor Tom," said Norah—and her eyes glistened as she looked up at the beech-tree, " I wonder where is he now, or what is he doing."

Her mother, who had just come out, with the book Norah had been reading, glanced up through the branches, too, and then, sitting down on the bench at the foot of the tree, buried her face in her apron, and burst into tears.

" Och ! where is he now," she cried, " an' what is he doin '? Where is his rosy cheeks, an' his curly head, an' his laughin' blue eyes ? I'm afeard I used to scowld him too much, Norah, on account uv the climbin'. But, sure, 'twas for his good I was ; for, the Lord betune us an' all harm, 'tis of'en an' of'en I thought I'd find him in a pancake on this flag I'm sittin' on. But what's breakin' my heart is the way I used to shut my fist an' hit him on the bare skull, when I'd be rightly vexed. I don't mind the wollopin's at all, Norah ; 'tis the knuckles rappin' on his curly head that's killin' me. Oh, if I had him now, 'tis I'd be glad to see a piece of his breeches flyin' on the top uv every three in the parish ; an' 'tis I that wouldn't scowld him, or wollup him, or put dead bells in his ears wud a clout, as I know I of'en done. An' above all, Norah, I'd never knock cracks out uv his curly

head wud my knuckles ; for nothin' ever med him roar but
that. An' where is he now ? An' what is he doin' ? Oh,
Norah, avoorneen, whatever made me lay a hand on him ?
For 'twas he was the good warrant to have an' eye to the
shop, or run uv a message, an' to mind his book an' his
Catechism. An' 'twould do any wan's heart good to hear him
whistlin'. Billy Heffernan never played a tune that he
couldn't whistle afther him. An' I see him wud my own
eyes bringin' the birds down out uv the sky."

This recital of Tommy's accomplishments made Norah
smile through her tears, and she said cheerfully—

" Well, mother, sure we ought to be glad that he is landed
safe, and that Uncle Larry is so good to him."

" That's thrue, alanna," returned Honor, rising from her
seat, and drying her eyes with her check apron. " 'Tis
thankful we ought to be to have such fine prospects before
him. Is that the right book I'm afther bringin' you ? Or
maybe 'tis the wan wud the goold letters on the cover you
want ? "

" No, mother, this is the right one."

" Begob, I must hurry an' tell Miss Mary you're out,
Norah," exclaimed Barney. " An' 'tis she'll be ready to lep
out uv her skin."

" Thank you, Barney," said Norah. " And tell her I
won't be sure I'm out at all, or that the sun is shining on
me, till I see her."

" Come, Bobby," shouted Barney, " don't let the grass
grow ondher your feet " ; and he ran on by the donkey's
side, blowing an imaginary horn, and in as great a state of
excitement as if he had descried a ballad-singer or a Punch
and-Judy in the distance.

But surely Billy Heffernan must have taken leave of his
senses ! At least his mule must think so. For while she
was jogging on quietly, with a great pile of bog-stumps
heaped upon her car, her master rushed at her, and jerked the
rein, and told her to " come on out of that," just as if she
had been setting back into Flanagan's Hole, instead of
jogging on at a steady pace by the beech-tree opposite Phil
Lahy's door. And Billy kept hold of the winkers, and pulled
Kit on till he came to his own door, never giving a second
look towards the beech-tree, and making believe that he

had not looked towards it at all. Then taking the key from the hole under the thatch, he let himself in, and sitting on the antediluvian block by the fireless hearth, buried his face in his hands.

"Glory be to God!" he exclaimed, with a deep sigh, "I thought I'd never see her there again. My heart leaped up into my mouth when I see her sittin' in the ould place, an' her hair hangin' down over the book she was readin'. I don't know how I can make up my mind to talk to her at all. But I'll purtind to nothin', just as if I thought she was out every day. But who are those coming down the road?" he continued, on reaching the door. "Begor, ay; 'tis Miss Mary, an' Miss Anne, an' Miss Ellie, an' Mister Hugh. Ay, faith, an' that's Father Carroll an' Misther Edmund Kiely wud 'em. I have no business down now, as they'll be sure to stop and talk to her. So I may as well haul in the stumps."

Not only were they sure to stop and talk to her, but they had come out for no other purpose. For when Barney announced that Norah was sitting under the beech-tree, and that she couldn't be sure the sun was shining on her till Miss Mary saw her, Mary started up quite in a flurry, and would hardly wait for Anne and Ellie, who were tying on their bonnets as fast as ever they could. They met Hugh and Edmund and Father Carroll coming from the meadow— where Edmund had jumped over a pitchfork laid on the shoulders of Tom Maher and Jim Dunn—and, as they all felt an interest in Norah Lahy, they turned back with Mary when she told them where she was going.

And when Norah looked up from her book and met Mary's mild glance, what a picture it was! Poor Norah had a hard struggle to keep back the tears; and Mary, in order to give her time to recover herself, took up Norah's book and handed it to Edmund with a smile. Edmund smiled and nodded his head after looking at the title-page; and then Mary handed the book to Hugh. And Hugh looked and looked at Norah Lahy's book, while a smile lighted up that "strong" face of his, and the soft light came into his dark eyes. Norah's name was written in the book, and under it—"From her friend, Grace Kiely."

Ellie stole into the house for a quiet talk with the old linnet. She wanted to know did the old linnet remember

Tommy, and whispered the question softly through the wires of his cage. And the old linnet held his head knowingly on one side, and muttered something down his throat, which Ellie interpreted into " To be sure I do. Do you think I could forget poor Tommy ? " And then Ellie fixed a bit of sugar between the wires, and turned round to jump down from the chair upon which she was standing, when she saw Honor Lahy's face all aglow with pleasure and affection— notwithstanding the tears in her eyes—looking up at her. And before Ellie could jump down, she was caught round the waist and folded in Honor Lahy's arms.

" My own darlin' child," exclaimed Honor, " that poor Tommy would lay down his life for. For 'twas of'en he said there wasn't wan uv 'em like Miss Ellie."

" The poor fellow ! " returned Ellie when she was set free, " he was so generous and good."

" His uncle," returned Honor, " sent him to a great school, and he says if he has sinse he has fine prospects before him."

" He will have sense," rejoined Ellie seriously ; " for I don't think he ever did anything wrong, except pulling the tails out of the robins."

" Yes, Miss," returned Honor, " an' Father M'Mahon couldn't get him down in the General Catechism, though ' the best method ' was the first question he axed him. But if he was at him for a month he couldn't get Tommy down, from ' Who made the world ? ' to ' so be it.' Then he tackled at him wud the ' Christian Doctrine,' but Tommy was able for him at that too. An' thin Father M'Mahon said he was the best boy in his parish. That was the day they wor gettin' their tickets for Confirmation ; an' what do you think but I went into the chapel afeard uv my life that Tommy might be cast. An' more fool I was, for he was the best uv the whole uv 'em. Jacky Ryan passed, though he gev a wrong answer. ' What is Matrimony ? ' says Father M'Mahon An' as bould as you plase, Jacky makes answer, ' A place or state of punishment where some sowls suffer for a time before they can go to heaven.' Faith I thought 'twas the right answer, he spoke up so independent, till I see the schoolmaster thryin' to keep from laughin'. ' What is Matrimony ? ' says Father M'Mahon agin, very slow an' solemn. ' A place or state of punishment where some sowls suffer for a time before they can go to heaven,' says Jacky again. 'Give Jacky Ryan his ticket,' says Father Hannigan. An' whin Father M'Mahon held up his hand to stop the schoolmaster that was writin' the tickets, Father Hannigan said the boy was right, that he see no difference between Matrimony and Purgatory, and 'tis many a sinsible man would agree wud him. So Jacky Ryan got his ticket. I'm afeard," added Honor, with a sigh, "the same Jacky will come to no good. He put a red poker on Kit Cummins's cat's nose for comin' about his maggidy. An' whin Frisky jumped over the half-door wud an ould gallon tied to his tail t'other evenin', I said it was Jacky Ryan's work—though indeed I can't say I'm sure uv id."

Mrs. Lahy was interrupted by Mary, who came in in search of Ellie.

"My goodness, Ellie," she said, "I thought you were lost. They are all half-ways home, and I have come back to look for you."

Father Carroll was alone when she came up with him, Hugh having gone to the forge to see about the pointing of some pitchforks for the haymaking, and Edmund and Anne being wholly occupied with what Mat Donovan called "going on."

"This is a letter I got this morning from Arthur O'Connor," said Father Carroll. "I had some conversation with his mother about him; but she is very unreasonable."

"Why does he not come home?" Mary asked.

"Why should he?" returned Father Carroll, looking at her in surprise.

"Is it not for this diocese he is ordained?"

"Ordained? He's not ordained at all, nor can he be for some time."

"Why, Anne mentioned to me in one of her letters that he was," said Mary. "One of her school-fellows saw him in Paris."

"Oh, 'tis a mistake," Father Carroll replied.

Mary called to her sister and asked her for an explanation. But Anne could only repeat what her friend had said to her.

"The students wear vestments and assist at some ceremonies before they are ordained," said Father Carroll. "That's how the mistake arose. His health has broken down and though he says now he has his mind made up to be a priest, it is still doubtful, I think, whether he ever will be one."

" Oh, I am so sorry," Mary exclaimed, with something like a wail of pain. " But hadn't he his mind always made up to be a priest ? "

" Well, no," he replied. " He always had doubts and scruples about his vocation. His ideas of the mission of a priest are very high, and he feared his motives were not the true ones. But why do you appear so distressed ? He is not the first ecclesiastical student who has changed his mind ; and surely you don't think there would be anything wrong in it ? "

" Oh, but don't you know what they said ? " And she put her arm in his, as if asking for his support.

" Yes—that it was your doing," he replied with a smile. " Well, you may set your mind at rest on that point, for he often discussed the subject with me before he ever saw you. And 'tis only since he went to Paris that he even thought it at all likely that he could ever be a priest. He says now his scruples are nearly all removed. But I fear his health must have broken down. I am very anxious about him."

It was a relief to her to think that she was not, even innocently, the cause of turning any one from what she deemed so high and holy a mission. But then came the thought that Arthur O'Connor was not a priest, and never might be a priest at all ; and Father Carroll felt her arm trembling within his. And as he glanced at her face, which was deathly pale, and saw the quick heaving of her bosom, he was convinced that the happiness of Mary Kearney's life—perhaps her very life—depended upon either of two contingencies—that Arthur O'Connor should become a priest, or her husband. And as her arm pressed more and more heavily upon his, Father Carroll resolved that he would be her friend, though he did not betray, even by a look that he noticed her agitation.

" Anne is a great flirt," said he, nodding towards that lively young lady, who was keeping up the " going on " at a tremendous rate.

" Oh, she's awful," returned Mary.

" You are not bad yourself, either."

" I was obliged to try. People were setting me down as stupid. And you know 'tis as good to be out of the world as out of the fashion." She spoke quite cheerfully ; but immediately fell into a reverie again.

" But has your heart never been really touched ? "

She bent her head, and a carnation flush suffused her pale cheek. " Well, I think not," she answered hesitatingly. " Though Grace," she added more cheerfully, " was always insisting that I was in a sad way about the gentleman we had here at Christmas."

" I'd rather expect it was Edmund she would be throwing at you ; and you had him at the same time, I believe."

" Oh, no ; Mr. Lowe was gone before Edmund came. And, strange to say, Grace scarcely ever talked about Edmund in that way. I suspect she wanted him to be an admirer of mine, and found he was thinking of somebody else."

" Well, I know when I asked him to come here with me he jumped eagerly at the offer. So take care that you do not get inside Miss Delany."

" Is there anything serious in that ? "

" Well, she is a great prize in every way, but I doubt whether Edmund is very anxious to win her."

" I saw her once or twice, and thought her quite fascinating ; though I ought to be very prejudiced against her."

" Why so ? "

" Well," replied Mary, laughing, " she described me as a plain country-girl, very shabbily dressed."

" Oh, she was only jealous. She thought you had designs on Edmund."

" That's the gentleman," said Mary, after returning Mr. Bob Lloyd's salute, as he rode past them, " who proposed for Eva. Every one was astonished when she refused such a grand offer ; and no one so much as his own family. They insisted at first that all sorts of traps were set for him by us ; but, strange to say, they were quite indignant when he was rejected. It was a real case of love at first sight, for he only saw her the evening she and the doctor came for Grace. Grace likes him," she added, " and says that a young poet has turned Eva's head. But I am almost sure Eva will be a nun. She is too good and gentle for the rough world."

" I saw Grace last week," said Father Carroll, " and was

surprised to see her so changed. She was a little woman when I saw her before ; but now she is quite girlish. She blushed and seemed quite timid and confused when · I reminded her of some of her sayings."

" So Hugh told me," said Mary. " He saw her when he went with Ellie to the convent. But he says she is not so pretty as she was. Ah, Grace is very good," Mary added, with a sigh. " She kept us all alive ; and she did not forget to send the book to poor Norah Lahy, though at first she could scarcely bear to think of her. Grace is very sensitive. She feels either joy or grief intensely ; but she can conquer her feelings from a sense of duty."

" She will never be happy unless she has a mission," said Anne, who had waited for them at the gate.

" Every one can have that," returned Mary. " But who is that talking to my father ? "

" It is that old Mr. Pender, the agent," her sister answered.

Mary looked grave. She feared that old Isaac's visits, which were unusually frequent now, boded no good. She had questioned Hugh about them, but he evaded the subject. It was plain to her, however, that some heavy trouble was weighing upon Hugh's mind ; and at times she even feared his health was giving way, he looked so weary and worn. In one sense these apprehensions did her good, for they kept her from dwelling upon her own unhappiness. But when she felt her heart sinking at the thought that a great calamity was hanging over them, she would remember Norah Lahy, and be strong.

CHAPTER LVIII.

FATHER CARROLL'S HOARDINGS.

" You look dreadfully cut up," said Father Carroll, as he looked into Arthur O'Connor's pallid face. " Have you read too hard ? Or is there anything on your mind ? "

" Dr. Kiely asked me the same questions," Arthur replied.

" And what does he say about your health ? "

" Well, he says 'tis not gone too far ; but that I must take care of myself."

His face, always pale, was now fearfully emaciated, and of a wax-like whiteness that contrasted painfully with his long black hair and dark grey eyes. But the fretted look—the " oldness " which Grace had remarked—was gone ; and a bright happy look had taken its place. The mental struggle that had so long racked him was at an end. He was resolved to become a priest ; but the doctors had insisted upon his suspending his studies, and returning for some time to his native air. His mother was filled with remorse when she saw him so changed, and now ran into the other extreme, and declared that he should never return to college again. But Arthur smiled—a sweeter smile, she thought, than she had seen upon his lips for years—and said he would be all right in a few weeks. He had brought a letter from the president of the college to an eminent ecclesiastic in Dublin, by whose counsel he was to be guided. He delivered the letter, and, after a long conversation, this eminent divine said his case was a peculiar one, and that he would give him his opinion by letter in a few days. The letter had not yet come, and Father Carroll awaited its arrival more impatiently than the student himself.

" Let us have a stroll to the Priest's Walk," said Arthur. " I feel quite strong this evening."

" Are you not afraid of the opera-glass and the ladies ? " Father Carroll asked.

" Oh, I don't mind it," replied Arthur smiling. " I can stand any amount of ' the light that lies in woman's eyes ' without wincing now."

They passed over the weir, through which the clear water leaped, with almost the swiftness of light ; having suddenly changed its gently gliding motion into a bound, as if it feared the slanting walls of moss-covered stones would close together like a gate, and bar its way to the ocean. They passed through the meadow by the river-side and into the Priest's Walk. The rooks were cawing in the tall trees over their heads, and a rabbit popped now and then from their path into the cover at either side. It was a lonely, dreamy sort of place, calculated to fill the mind with romantic or religious musings. And the robust, sun-ruddied priest, and the pale, sickly student paced up and down for fully a quarter of an hour without exchanging a word.

"A call," said Father Carroll. "Here is Tom Doherty."

But, to his great relief, Tom Doherty only handed a letter to Arthur, and walked back to the weir, without speaking.

"No bad news, I hope?" said the priest, on remarking the troubled look—the old fretted look—come into the student's face.

"It is from Dr. ——," he replied, handing him the letter.

"I agree with him," said Father Carroll, after reading it.

"But I told him my scruples were all gone," said Arthur.

"No matter; as he says you were driven by the force of circumstances to it. You were always hoping for some means of escape. If, at any time in your life, you felt a real desire to be a priest, independently of circumstances, it would be different. But you never did. So, in God's name, give it up, and think of something else."

"But what can I think of now?"

"Well, the medical profession is the best for you. It is a noble profession, and will, at worst, secure you an humble competence. But I warn you," he added, laughing, "you will have to work hard for your bread. And, perhaps, so much the better."

"Indolence and pride were always my besetting sins," the student replied. "I never could work without an immediate motive."

"And surely the motive is not wanting now?"

"That's true," he answered, with a weary sigh. "I owe it to my mother and family."

Father Carroll thought of Mary Kearney's pale face and trembling hand, and was on the point of asking whether it ever occurred to him that there might be even a stronger motive for exertion than that he had just mentioned; but any reference to the subject yet awhile might, he thought, be premature, and he was silent.

They continued to walk up and down in silence, while the rooks crowded thicker and thicker in the trees, and the white tails of the rabbits twinkled more frequently among the withered grass, as the sun shot his last red rays through the wood.

There was such a rush and scamper among the rabbits a little in front of them that both looked up in surprise. Two beautiful girls wearing broad straw hats turned into the walk from a footpath through the wood, and as they bowed to Father Carroll, and then glanced at his companion, the laughing light in their " eyes of most unholy blue," changed suddenly to an expression of mingled surprise and sorrow. They had often inquired of Father Carroll for the student—whom they called St. Kevin, he took so much pains to avoid them in his walks. It is possible they had come through the wood for the sole purpose of seeing him ; but the alteration in him filled them with pity and sympathy.

" Those are Major French's daughters," Father Carroll observed when they had passed. " It is their pictures Sir Garrett Butler painted when they were children, as Mrs. Hayes told you."

" I remember," returned Arthur, coldly. " But I thought they might be the steward's or gamekeeper's daughters."

" Do you still hold to your old prejudice against farmer's daughters ? " Father Carroll asked, laughing.

" Well, not exactly," Arthur answered. " At least I believe there are some exceptions to the rule." A slight flush suffused his pale face as he spoke, and his friend was about rallying him upon it, but again checked himself.

As they repassed the weir, the trout were leaping at the flies, and they loitered for a few minutes to watch them.

" What an evening this would be for Edmund Kiely," Arthur observed. " He is a genuine disciple of Isaac Walton."

" Or Hugh Kearney," returned Father Carroll. " I have been trying to induce him to spend some days with me, but it is impossible to pull him away from home. He is like his sister Mary in that respect."

" Does not she go much from home ? "

" Scarcely ever. I sometimes wish I had a big parish and a big house, and I'd insist upon her spending some time with me occasionally."

" The woman that can be happy in her own home is the best woman," said Arthur.

" That is quite true. But it might be carried too far. I'm inclined to think a discontented spirit may keep young people too much at home, as well as drive them too much from it. But I'm far from suspecting that to be the case with Mary Kearney. She so loves every one and everything about her, I am sure she is really happy at home. But don't you wonder that so remarkably beautiful and superior a girl is not snatched at as a prize? She would adorn any station."

" How do you account for it ? " Arthur asked.

" Well, men generally require some encouragement before they will run the risk of being refused ; and Mary does not give the encouragement. And she really has declined two very good offers. I think she is likely to become a nun."

" I'm told her sister intends going into a convent, too."

" Yes ; she always intended it ; though she seems fitter for the world than Mary. Do you think is Edmund Kiely engaged in any way ? It has even occurred to me that he is actually married, but wants to keep it private."

" No, he is not," Arthur replied. " But he has some romantic business on hands that I can't make out."

" Come—the grass is quite wet, and it would not do for you to remain out under the dew."

During the evening they discussed Arthur's plans for the future ; and, before retiring to his room, he all but had his mind made up to take his friend's advice, and commence the study of medicine at once.

" But there is another difficulty in the way," he said, " which it is unpleasant to reflect upon."

" What is that ? " Father Carroll asked.

" Money," returned Arthur. " After the sacrifices my mother has made on my account, I don't know how I can encroach farther upon her narrow means ; particularly as I have disappointed her hopes. And you know what importance she attaches to keeping up appearances."

" Well, I have not overlooked that," rejoined Father Carroll. " But I think we can manage." He stood up, and, opening the mahogany desk with the brass handles, took a small drawer from the inside, and emptied its contents upon the table. There were a few sovereigns and half-sovereigns and several rolls of bank-notes, some worn and faded, and some white and crisp, appearing at first sight to represent quite a formidable sum, but being all one-pound and thirty-shilling notes, Father Carroll found to his disappointment that his hoardings scarcely amounted to one hundred pounds. He had not given himself a holiday since his short visit to Tramore with Arthur and Edmund Kiely, and had taken to hoarding with two objects in view—the furnishing and fitting-up of his cottage, and a visit to Rome. Rolling all the notes into one bundle, he tossed them across the table.

" It is only ninety-three pounds," said he ; " but it will do for awhile. And before that is spent, Fortune may prove more liberal of her favours."

Arthur O'Connor stared in amazement at his friend. He knew Father Carroll was a good fellow, in the best sense of the word. But so great a sacrifice as he knew this must be he was unprepared for. Arthur O'Connor was particularly sensitive on the score of pecuniary obligations, and his whole nature revolted against the acceptance of the money. He never could bear to be in debt. Even in his boyhood he could not take money from the kind old priest with whom he used to spend a few weeks of his vacation in that old cottage. He was deeply moved by his friend's generosity. But he glared at the bundle of notes upon the table before him, almost with a feeling of loathing.

Father Carroll, guessing his thoughts—which it was easy enough to do—said, " It is your duty to take it."

" But I may never be able to repay you," returned Arthur, almost angrily.

" You will. And your desire to get out of debt will be an additional incentive to exertion. Don't think so much about it. You must sometimes do violence to yourself if you mean to get on. I believe over-sensitiveness of that sort has prevented much good from being done in the world—has been the one fatal obstacle to many a useful and brilliant career."

There was a silence of some minutes ; and the student, resting his elbows upon the table, clasped his slender hands over his pale forehead.

" Don't think I am merely acting upon impulse," said Father Carroll ; " on the contrary, if I did not do what I have done, I might regret it all the days of my life."

He took one of the candles and went to bed. The second was burning low in the socket when the student raised his head. He took the bundle of notes and put them in his pocket. But he said nothing about the matter that night, or next day, or for years after. Neither shall we.

CHAPTER LIX.

ANOTHER EVENTFUL DAY.—" MAGNIFICENT TIPPERARY."

ANOTHER eventful day for Knocknagow. But there are no smiling faces, and no clapping of hands—except in grief—this time. The sheriff is out. Darby Ruadh is at the head of the bailiffs, crying down tears as he hands out articles of furniture to his assistants, telling them to " take 'em 'asy " and not break them ; and actually obliged to turn away his head and have recourse to a dirty cotton pocket-handkerchief, which he carries in his hat, when he comes to a cradle with an infant in it, or a sick woman too weak to rise from her bed. Honest Darby's grief is only second to that of his master, who declares over and over that it is " a very painful duty. A very painful duty. A very painful duty. But what can I do ? What can I do ? What, what can I do ? " old Isaac asks. And many of the poor victims believe him. Mat Donovan was almost the only person who uttered an angry word. Mat Donovan's grandfather, as we have seen, pitched his tent on a heap of stones and pool of water cut off by the road from two adjoining estates belonging to different landlords. And here now is Mat Donovan's house, and the little garden with its clipped hedge, a warning to Irish landlords to look sharp to heaps of stones and pools of water, lest by any chance Irish peasants should convert them into houses and gardens, and then have the hardihood to call them their own.

But Mat Donovan's little field which supplied him with potatoes and oats, and for which he paid a high rent, was not a " freehold," and the sheriff has just handed Mr. Isaac Pender a twig from the fence and a bit of stubble from the ground ; and old Isaac declares how sorry he is to be obliged to deprive Mat Donovan of his " little garden." At which Mat loses all patience and denounces the agent as a robber and a hypocrite, and gives it as his opinion that 'twas all old Isaac's own doing, and not the landlord's. An unlucky speech for Mat Donovan, as hereinafter shall appear.

And now they come to Tom Hogan's. A large force of police range themselves in front of the house. The door is open, and Darby Ruadh enters, looking flurried and excited, as if he expected to be knocked down at any moment. He has never forgotten the lesson he received from Bessy Morris's father, and has ever since been very gentle in his way of doing business, particularly where women and children are concerned. Nancy Hogan is looking very pale, but so beautiful that for a moment Darby forgets everything else in his admiration of her. Her mother is sitting upon a stool, quite calm. The house is soon cleared, and mother and daughter walk out quietly. Darby is obliged to have recourse to the cotton pocket-handkerchief, he is so much affected. He thought he would have been obliged to use violence, and is quite moved to find Mrs. Hogan so reasonable and considerate. And now Tom Hogan himself walks into the yard, and *won't* see the police drawn up along the barn—that barn that is as good as Attorney Hanly's and better than Maurice Kearney's—nor the party of soldiers on the road. Nancy covers her golden hair with her cloak and shades her face from their gaze.

" God save you, Darby," Tom Hogan says quietly, as he walks towards the door.

Darby places his hand against Tom Hogan's breast, and keeps him back.

" I was fencin' that gap Attorney Hanly's cows broke through," Tom Hogan observes, " an' I'm goin' to my dinner."

Darby Ruadh pushes him out upon the road. The sheriff and sub-inspector exchange looks and shake their heads. Poor Tom Hogan has that imbecile smile upon his face which is sometimes seen on the face of a helpless drunkard.

" Good luck to you, Darby," he says, " an' let me in ; I must finish that job to-day, as I'll begin the ploughin' to-morrow. There's nothin' like early ploughin'."

Some of those around looked surprised ; but Darby Ruadh and Wat Corcoran understand the state of the case very well. They have had repeated negotiations with Tom Hogan to induce him to give up possession, but he laughed at them, as if it were a joke, and never lost an hour in the improvement of that little farm in which his "heart was stuck."

"Never lose a day, Darby, whatever work you have on hands. That's what stood to me always."

Poor Nancy could hold out no longer. She flung her arms round his neck, and kissed his worn, hollow cheeks over and over.

"O father! dear father!" she cried, "have courage."

"Courage!" he repeated, staring vacantly around him, "who could ever say that I hadn't courage? Hadn't I courage to build them houses? Faith, Nancy, I always had the courage at any rate."

"O father," she exclaimed, "don't you see what's after happening? Let us go away."

"What's afther happenin'?" he asked, with another vacant stare on the crowd around him. "Where's Jemmy?" he exclaimed suddenly, as his eye caught sight of the fixed bayonets and red uniforms behind him. "Where is Jemmy? Jemmy is the boy that wouldn't let any wan lay a hand on me."

And where *is* Jemmy?

He clutches his musket at the command to "charge!" and his shout—clear and thrilling as when the ball was struck to the goal and Knocknagow had won—mingles with the wild hurrah that rises even above the cannon's roar. The general, surrounded by his staff, watches anxiously for what is to follow. The result of the battle hangs upon that charge. For a moment the bayonets flash in the hot sun, as they rush through the storm of iron hail that tears through their ranks; and then friend and foe are lost in a thick, white cloud, and the thunder is hushed. And, as the white cloud rolls away, the general's eyes flash fire, as, raising himself in his stirrups, and flinging his arm wildly above his head, he shouts— "Magnificent Tipperary!"

The day is won! England is victorious!

There is hot Tipperary blood gushing out upon the thirsty plain; and where the fight was deadliest, Jemmy Hogan lies mangled and bleeding. But there is one company of his regiment which has not shared in the glories of that famous victory. It is drawn up with fixed bayonets before his father's door at old Knocknagow; while the house in which Jemmy Hogan was born is being levelled with the ground!

Magnificent Tipperary!

Tom Hogan looks wildly around him now. He is startled by a loud crashing sound that seemed to come from the yard. It was the first crush of the crow-bar through the wall of the dear old home. And it went right through Tom Hogan's heart, and broke it!

Tom Carey, the carpenter, caught the poor old man in his arms as he fell senseless to the ground.

"Let us bring him up to my house, Tom," said Mat Donovan, "till he comes to himse'f."

"Wouldn't it be betther," returned Tom Carey, "to bring him down, as they're all goin' to stop wud me for a start, an' have him settled in the bed before he sees any more uv what's goin' on?"

"You're right, Tom," said Mat; "that's the best way."

They lifted poor Tom Hogan upon their shoulders, and bore him away, followed by his wife and daughter, weeping bitterly, but silently.

Half of Knocknagow is swept from the face of the earth. There is one more house, a little higher up the hill, to be pulled down, and then the day's work will be completed. 'Tis easily done. The walls are of clay, and the roof of sedge from the bog; and nothing to be thrown out but an old wooden bedstead with a slanting roof like a house, a table and block of bogwood, a pot and an old gallon, two white plates and a yellow jug. The mule's crib and the antediluvian elk's horns are fixtures, and he must seek for them among the ruins to-morrow if he wants them.

But he does not want them. He is not thinking of them, or of anything else belonging to him; or of himself. He is out in the bog "cutting a sod." He has found a smooth, soft patch of green among the heath, and carefully marking out what he required—having measured the length and breadth with his feet—he commences cutting it with his spade; rolling it up like a thick carpet as he goes on. Heeling his car close to it, he gets in the roll of greensward with some difficulty, using his spade as a lever. And then, after looking at the brown, spongy turf, which he has stripped of its emerald covering, he lies down at full length upon it, with

his face upon his arms, and wishes with all his heart that a
sod might grow over him. For the long-dreaded calamity
has come at last. Norah Lahy is dead.

This is Tuesday. On Sunday morning Honor Lahy sent
for him. He had only left the old house with the steep roof
an hour or two before, to prepare for Mass—having spent
the whole night sitting in the chimney corner, on the bench,
where he used to sit and play " Auld Lang Syne " for her.
And now he is prepared for the worst as he softly opens her
room door.

Mary Kearney is reading the Litany ; and Nelly Donovan
kneels behind her, kissing a pair of embroidered slippers, upon
which her tears are falling thick and fast. Norah has " left "
her slippers to Nelly Donovan. Honor Lahy stands at the
head of the bed, watching, watching. A faint smile ripples
for an instant over the dying girl's lips, and the poor mother,
bending down, holds her ear close to them ; and then turning quickly round sees that Billy Heffernan is standing inside the door. Norah wishes Billy Heffernan to lay his hand
upon her forehead, and keep it there. Mary Kearney
whispers to her sister Ellie, who leaves the room, and soon
returns with the " blessed candle " ; and as she has left the
door open, Phil Lahy is seen kneeling outside. His wife
beckons to him—poor Norah's lips have again moved—and
he stands up and timidly approaches the bed, as if he feared
to be reproached for all the sorrow he had caused her. But
he is welcomed with a fond, fond look. And dropping upon
his knees, Phil Lahy forms the resolution to make a promise
that shall never be broken or evaded ; a promise that *she*
never asked him to make, because (he used to say) she knew
his constituiton required " a little nourishment " ; but he
knows now that it was because she feared he would not have
the strength to keep it.

Mary places the lighted candle in the dying girl's hand,
keeping the wasted fingers closed upon it.

" I b'lieve she is gone," said Honor, in a low tone, and
with a look of the most intense anguish. " O Norah,
Norah, are you gone from me at last ?" But the eyelids
quivered, and again the lips trembled for a moment, and
then settled into a smile of heavenly sweetness. The smile
brightened over the whole face, as if a sunbeam had fallen

upon it. At the moment the old linnet in the window began to sing; and they all thought that her soul lingered to listen to the low sweet song that had so often made her glad.

As the song of the linnet ceased, her bosom heaved once; and Norah Lahy was among her kindred angels.

Father M'Mahon "himself" came to say Mass the day of the funeral. And how his heart was torn to see the ruined homes of Tipperary, on every side, as he dismounted from his horse under the beech-tree. And when the wail of the outcasts was heard amid the crash of falling roof-trees and the tramp of armed men, Honor Lahy said she was glad her darling was gone before that sorrowful day; "for 'tis she'd be sorry to see the neighbours in trouble." But in spite of all their trouble they attended her wake; and many stood round her grave who had to lie by the cold ditch-side that night, or, with burning hearts, bend their steps to the hated poorhouse.

The grave was filled up, and the clay heaped over it and beaten into shape by Mat Donovan and Tom Maher. Then Mat went to a corner of the churchyard to get some green sods to cover it; but Billy Heffernan touched him upon the shoulder, and Mat went to the mule's car and thrust the handle of his spade through the roll of greensward from the bog; and Billy, taking hold of the end of the spade handle, they carry the sod, and lay it gently on one end of the grave. Then it is unrolled, and the cold clay is wrapped in a mantle of green. Poor Honor Lahy felt happy, and thought her darling's sleep would be sweeter for that fresh green mantle.

"Would I doubt you, Billy!" she murmured, wiping the tears from her hot eyes.

Then the people knelt down, and offered up the customary short prayer; and the churchyard was deserted except by four mourners.

"Billy," said Phil Lahy, "she got you to take the pledge?"

"She did," he replied; "God knows what might become uv me on'y for her."

"Well, she never axed me to do that; because she couldn't find id in her heart to be hard on me, Billy. But I'll promise her now." He knelt down at the foot of the grave and took off his hat. His wife thought to interrupt him, but he motioned her back. "Norah, I promise you," said he ; and then got up from his knees.

Billy Heffernan lingered at the stile, and looked back.

"Come, Billy," said Nelly Donovan, "you may as well come——" She was going to say " home, ' but checked herself. Billy Heffernan had no home.

"Nelly," returned Billy Heffernan, "I was dead fond uv her."

"Every wan was fond uv her," said Nelly Donovan, putting her arm in his and drawing him away.

There was not a roof for miles around under which her name was not mentioned, tenderly and sorrowfully. And the tears sprang into the eyes of many a poor exile far away, on coming to the words, "Norah Lahy is dead," in the letter from home. But, perhaps, nothing spoken of her was more truly pathetic, or showed more clearly how much they all missed her, than a remark of Barney Brodherick's, as he sat by the turf fire that roared up the wide chimney in Maurice Kearney's kitchen.

"Ah ! poor Norah !" exclaimed Barney, raising his head from his knees, upon which it had been resting for a full hour before. "Ah ! poor Norah—she'll never sit in a chair again."

"Now, Anne," said Hugh Kearney, encircling his sister's waist with his arm, and bending over her, half playfully, and half seriously—"is not this rather a sudden resolution you have taken, to go to the convent at once ? You really ought to reflect for a long time before you take so serious a step."

"It is not a sudden notion," she replied. "I am a long time thinking of it."

"But is there any particular reason that makes you wish to go just now ?"

"Nothing, I trust and believe, but a sense of duty and the love of God," she answered calmly and firmly.

"Oh, I'll say no more," he replied, feeling somewhat awe-struck. "But you don't know how much we all shall miss you, and particularly Mary."

"Oh ! I know it very well, Hugh," she exclaimed, the tears streaming down her cheeks ; and, as she flung her arms round his neck, he felt her heart swell as if it were bursting. There was a knock at the door, and he was called out.

Mat Donovan was standing at the little gate.

"I came in by the stile," said Mat, "as I'd rather not meet the boys an' girls. But I couldn't bring myse'f to go wudout seein' Billy Heffernan. Nothin' 'd plase him but to put up some soart of a shed on his own turbary an' sleep in the bog, where, he says, he can feel himse'f independent. I'm runnin' over the short cut to him; an' will you tell Barney to have the ass an' car ready about eleven o'clock, an' we can slip away."

"Very well, Mat, I'll see that Barney is ready. I need not tell you that I am sorry to part with you."

"Say no more, sir," returned Mat, grasping his hand. "An' if my mother or Nelly is in want of a friend, I know you'll be a friend to 'em."

Before Hugh could reply, he crossed the little garden and disappeared behind the laurels. The emigrant girl's words, when she ran in to take her leave of them that stormy winter night, "God be wud you, Mat, 'tis many's the time we danced together at the Bush," occurred to him; and looking carefully around to see that he was not observed, he pressed his lips to the trunk of the old hawthorn tree. "Ah!" said he, "the grass is growin' all around id already; an', I'm afeard, 'tis long till 'twill feel a light foot again. God be wud ould times; 'tis terrible to think uv the change."

The night was not very dark, and, as he crossed the road near where the hook-nosed steed came to grief, he encountered Mr. Beresford Pender and Darby Ruadh.

"Is that Donovan? I'd like to know what brings you here at this hour of the night?" exclaimed Beresford in his big voice; but he seized Darby Ruadh by the arm, and got behind him.

"I don't see what id is to you," returned Mat; "but, if you want to know, I'm goin' down to look for Billy Heffernan at his own turbary. I b'lieve you know he hasn't a house now."

Billy Heffernan was not at the place; and, after waiting for some time, leaning against the bank where poor Mick Brien had his dream, that never-to-be-forgotten night, when Bessy Morris sat for an hour in the little old chair, and he accompanied her home as far as the little stream where Billy Heffernan's mule always stopped to drink, Mat retraced his steps by the short cut to his own house. He found Barney, with his donkey and cart, at the door ; and, after placing a deal box in the cart, he waved his hand and desired him to drive on.

He came up with the cart at the hill near Phil Morris's, and Barney was surprised to see him turn towards the wooden gate under the old hawthorns, and rest his forehead upon it. His last parting with Bessy was not one which he could remember with pleasure, and now he longed for a kind word at least. Bessy had received him with studied coldness, and as he was walking away with a heavy heart, through the little boreen, Peg Brady overtook him, and placed an open letter in his hand. He read it without knowing what he was doing till he came to the signature, when he started and read it over again. When Peg saw the colour fade from his cheek, she got frightened, and said that there might be some mistake.

"No, Peg, no," said he, returning her the letter. "But 'tisn't right, I think, to be showin' a girl's letter that way."

"I'll give id back to him," returned Peg. "I on'y wanted to have a laugh."

Mat Donovan looked around him, seeming quite bewildered, like a man that had lost his way.

"Sure, why wouldn't she meet him, or any wan else she'd like to meet," he said. "But to be sayin' she hated the sight uv him, an' that he was mane and cowardly to be talkin' uv her as he was ! I never thought Bessy had the two ways in her before."

Peg Brady wished that Mat would give up thinking of Bessy Morris. She didn't like to see him " making a fool of himself." But in the matter of the letter she feared she had gone too far. And, in fact, if it were not for that letter Mat Donovan would in all probability never have been able to make up his mind to go to America. It was a short note to the dragoon, telling him she would meet him at the hour and place appointed, and couched in rather friendly terms. But Peg—who with Kit Cummins had got up a little party of sympathisers with the dragoon, who pronounced Bessy's treatment of him " a shame "—suppressed the fact that the letter was an old one, written when she was in Dublin.

" Ah ! Bessy !" he thought, " you had no right to thrate me that way ; for well you knew—though I never tould you so—that I'd lay down my life for you."

" Is id tired you are, Mat ?" Barney asked. " If id is, sit up. Don't be afeard uv Bobby ; for, be herrins, I'd keep up to the mail coach every fut uv the way."

" No, Barney, no. I'd rather walk. Fire away !"

And Mat Donovan twirled his stick, and drew himself up to his full height, and stepped out, as if his heart were as light as a feather.

CHAPTER LX.

BURGLARY AND ROBBERY.—MAT DONOVAN A PRISONER.—
BARNEY DISAPPEARS.—MR. SOMERFIELD AND ATTORNEY
HANLY APPLY FOR LEASES, AND OLD ISAAC DREADS THE
CONSEQUENCES.

MR. SAM SOMERFIELD, J.P., with two policemen on his car, drove furiously up to Wellington Lodge. Other magistrates arrived soon after, and in the course of an hour or so quite a little army of police were on the spot. Mr. Beresford Pender described, in a tremendous voice, the particulars of a most daring outrage which had occurred the night before. Wellington Lodge had been entered by a band of armed men. Two of them tied Mr. Isaac Pender with ropes, and carried away all the money he had in the house. The robbers were so disguised, the old gentleman could not recognise them, but he had his suspicions, particularly of the tall man, who held a pistol to his head while another was breaking open the desk in which he kept his money. And most unfortunately he had a considerable sum just received from Maurice Kearney and other tenants of Sir Garrett Butler. The police were sent to scour the country in all directions ; and by some chance the cover of a letter directed to Mr. Pender was found on the brink of a deep, square hole in the bog. Beresford re- membered immediately that he had met Mat Donovan near that place at an unseasonable hour the night before. The bog-hole was drained, and the box in which the money was kept was found at the bottom, empty and with the lock broken. The man who handed up the box, feeling something hard under his feet, thrust his hand down into the soft mould, and held up a long gun, to the great astonishment of Mr. Beresford Pender and Darby Ruadh. It was at once recognised as Maurice Kearney's, for whom a policeman was immediately dispatched. Mr. Kearney scratched his head, and in reply to questions put to him by the magistrates, said the gun usually hung in the kitchen, and was seldom taken down except to shoot crows ; that his son the doctor broke the stock during the hard frost at Christmas, and that he gave the gun to Wattletoes to bring to Mat Donovan to be repaired, as he, Mat Donovan, could do it as well as a gunsmith. That's the last he saw of the gun.

" Where is Mat Donovan ?" Mr. Somerfield asked.

To the surprise of all present, Hugh Kearney said he believed Mat Donovan was gone to America. He had been seen late the night before in the bog. The whole affair looked very suspicious, the magistrates said. Then it was asked where was the person called Wattletoes ? He had gone with Mat Donovan as far as Waterford. The magistrates exchanged looks, and retired to consult as to what should be done. The country was in a very bad state.

On the evening of the following day, a policeman led Bobby and his blue cart up to Maurice Kearney's hall-door. The whole family ran out greatly surprised, and under the impression that poor Barney was a prisoner and in jail. But the policeman informed them that the ass was found tied to a post on the quay of Waterford, and that Barney could not be found, or any intelligence of him learned. This was still more astonishing, and Hugh began to feel really uneasy. But his mother consoled herself with the reflection that in all probability Barney was in hot pursuit of a Punch-and-Judy while the police were searching for him.

"What do you think, Hugh ?" Mary asked anxiously.

I really believe there is a plot of some kind," he replied, " But as yet I can't imagine what the object of it may be."

The next Saturday, Billy Heffernan was plodding behind his mule after selling the last pen'orth of his creel of turf, when a hand was laid upon his shoulder. It was the dragoon, whom Billy had often met since the night he mistook his burnished helmet for a crock of gold at old Phil Morris's ; and whom he had come to despise very heartily.

" How are ye all in Knocknagow ?" he asked, with a mean, shame-faced look, as if he felt he was despised, and deserved to be.

" All well, so far as what's left uv us," Billy observed.

" Will you tell Kit Cummins that I'll be out before to-morrow week ; I'm only waiting for a new suit of clothes to be made." He was dressed in plain clothes now, and not at all the fine, soldierly-looking fellow he was when Billy Heffernan first made his acquaintance.

" Kit was at the safe side of the road," returned Billy ; " so she's there yet. I'll tell her. Yo-up ! Kit." And he walked on as if he wished to get rid of the ex-dragoon. He pulled up the collar of his ratteen riding-coat to shelter himself from the rain, which a keen wind was driving straight in his face. " Begob," muttered Billy Heffernan, as he breathed upon the tips of his numbed fingers—the weather being un-usually cold for the season of the year—" begob, when they wor makin' the winther, they forgot to put these days in id."

" God save you, Billy."

He started, and opened his eyes in mute amazement.

It was Mat Donovan, handcuffed between half-a-dozen policemen, who as well as their prisoner were dripping wet and covered with mud after a long march. Billy left his mule to shift for herself, and ran back after them.

" Let me spake to him," said he to the constable, implor-ingly.

" What do you want to say to him ?"

" Well," he replied, holding his head close to the con-stable's ear, as he walked by his side, " just to say a word about a girl he's fond uv."

" Halt," cried the constable, who happened to be fond of a girl himself. " Let us stand in the shelter for a minnit to draw our breath. Come now, say what you have to say at once."

But poor Billy Heffernan was so overcome when his eyes rested on the iron handcuffs round his friend's wrists, he could say nothing at all.

" They tell me, Billy," said Mat, in a mild, sad tone, " that I'm charged wud robbery. I was taken in Liverpool."

" So we heard last night," returned Billy.

" But, Billy, do any uv the neighbours suspect me ?"

" The divil a wan," Billy answered with animation. " I was in at ould Phil's yisterday, an' if you hear the way Bessy spoke uv you. She said she'd depind her life on you, and that you wor the sowl uv honour."

" Did she, Billy ?" rejoined Mat Donovan—and his eyes glistened. " Remember me to all the neighbours ; an' tell my mother an' Nelly not to fret. There's some mistake that I can't make out. It must be because I happened to have a few hot words wud ould Pender that they pitched on me."

" But, Mat, where did Barney go ?"

" Didn't he go home ?" Mat asked in surprise. " I parted wud him on the quay uv Waterford just as the steamer was startin', an' I tould him to make no delay."

" There's no account uv him, high or low," returned Billy.

" Begor, that's quare !" Mat exclaimed. " I hope no harm is afther happenin' to poor Barney."

" She'd depend her life on me," said Mat Donovan to himself, as he lay down upon his bed in Clonmel jail. And he was certainly a happier man that night than he would have been if he had not met Billy Heffernan and his mule on the road.

When brought before a magistrate, Mat Donovan was startled by the weight of circumstantial evidence against him. He declared that Barney had never brought the gun to him ; and that he and Barney travelled together to Waterford the night of the robbery. Hugh Kearney told how Mat had called on him about nine o'clock that night and said he was going to the bog to see Billy Heffernan. And Nelly Donovan swore that her brother intended leaving for America the Sunday before the sheriff came out, but that he remained to attend Norah Lahy's funeral. These circumstances were in his favour, but the mysterious disappearance of Barney Brodherick, the magistrate said, was a most suspicious circumstance, and he must send the case for trial at the next assizes. So poor Mat Donovan was marched back to his cold cell, the magistrate, at the suggestion of the Crown prosecutor, refusing to admit him to bail. He could not conceal from himself that he stood in great danger of being transported as a robber and a housebreaker unless Barney Brodherick could be found. He knew, however, that he had a good friend in Hugh Kearney, who would leave nothing undone to get him out of the meshes of the law. And Bessy Morris had written him such a kind letter, he was almost thankful that he had come back to Ireland, even as a prisoner.

But those Tipperary homes—those that the crowbar has spared—among which we have, perhaps, lingered too long and too lovingly for the reader's patience, are gloomy enough now. Poor Honor Lahy can find little comfort even in Phil's eloquence, though he is always sober and industrious. There is a deeper shade of sadness in Mrs. Donovan's sad face ; and Nelly's ringing laugh is never heard now. She even stops her wheel sometimes, and sits down to cry over a pair of embroidered slippers. Billy Heffernan comes over now and again from his hut in the bog, and sits on the bench in the corner. He is every day saying he will " take courage," and begin to play his flute again ; but week after week passes, and he has not yet ventured to blow a single note. Nelly's mind is very much troubled on his account. She is afraid that when the flood rises, Billy Heffernan and his mule will inevitably be drowned in the bog. Billy assures her that the water was never yet known to cover the particular spot upon which he has erected his domicile ; but he admits that coming in and going out will be " no joke " after a heavy fall of rain.

Kit Cummins is mute ; and her next-door neighbour has been known to sit on the ground inside her own threshold, with her back against the open door, for hours together, and so oppressed by the unaccustomed silence, that after finishing a "round" of her knitting, her hands would drop down languidly by her side, as, sighing deeply, she muttered under her teeth, " Gir-r-r-out, you bla'gard," and fixed her eyes vacantly upon the pig crunching Kit Cummins's stirabout-stick in the dung-hole outside the door. The ring of Jack Delany's anvil is only heard by fits and starts ; and Brum-magem's face is so black that he must have discontinued the Sunday ablution in the quarry for some time. Tom Hogan is dying at Tom Carey the carpenter's, whom he used to look down upon as a " tradesman," who was " no match for a farmer's daughter." Nancy nurses him tenderly; and Tom Carey never hints at his old love for her, even by a look; but Nancy thinks of it often, and sometimes says to herself that Ned Brophy's love was not "the right love."

Old Phil Morris is becoming more and more cynical, and will talk crossly even to Bessy, and ask her what ails her, and why she looks so miserable. Even Peg Brady is unhappy, and resolves to ease her mind by telling Mat Donovan the truth about the letter; for her conscience told her that if it were not for her jealousy and duplicity, Mat would not have left for America at all, and would not be now a prisoner in the jail of Clonmel, in danger of being transported for life. Mary Kearney is doing her best to be strong; but since Norah Lahy's death the struggle is harder than it used to be; and when she thinks of her light-hearted sister going into a convent, she can scarcely suppress a cry of pain. There is a rumour, too, that Arthur O'Connor is going to be married to some rich lady who fell in love with him in Paris. And Mary sees the traces of care growing deeper and deeper in her brother Hugh's face, and fears that her father's affairs must be becoming more embarrassed. Ellie is at school with Grace, and Mary often thinks how Grace's presence would brighten up the old cottage—and how much it wanted brightening up now. Maurice Kearney, however, appears as jovial as ever; and the only weight on Mrs. Kearney's mind is the fate of poor Barney, who, she fears, must have fallen into the river at Waterford, or met with some other equally untimely end. "Unless, indeed," she would add, "he has turned ballad-singer or showman himself." And Barney's mistress derived great consolation from the hope that he had permanently attached himself to a Punch-and-Judy.

Attorney Hanly has got possession of one hundred and fifty acres of land adjoining Castleview, at one pound an acre. Besides Tom Hogan's little farm, for which Tom Hogan paid two pounds, some fifty acres, including Mat Donovan's "garden," and four or five other small holdings of from five to ten acres, are in pretty good heart. But the rest is so poor and exhausted, that Mr. Hanly does not consider that he has got much of a bargain after all. He can, however, make it all as good as Tom Hogan's, by deep-draining, and liming, and fencing, and manuring, as Tom Hogan did. But Mr. Hanly is a shrewd man of business, and he knows to do this would cost several thousand pounds; and, when 'twas all done, he knows also that the rent could be raised on him, as 'twas raised on Tom Hogan; or he could, like Tom Hogan, be turned out altogether. So he won't mind the draining until he has got a long lease. His lease of Castleview will expire the same time as Maurice Kearney's lease of Ballinaclash, and as Attorney Hanly looks upon his handsome house, and his groves and meadows, he begins to feel uneasy and dissatisfied. So he has had a good deal of talk latterly with old Isaac; and it has been suggested to Sir Garrett Butler that he ought to give a new lease of the whole farm to Mr. Hanly, who would then expend a large sum of money in improvements, and would not object to paying a reasonable fine. It happened that, at the same time, Mr. Sam Somerfield, J.P., applied for a new lease of Woodlands. And in both cases the arguments brought forward to show that long leases would prove advantageous both to the landlord and the tenant were so convincing, that the old baronet, with all his simplicity and want of experience, could not help wondering why his agent had always warned him against giving leases to his tenants—particularly to Maurice Kearney—and pointed to the practice and example of this same Mr. Sam Somerfield in support of his assertion that leases would be ruinous to the landlord's interests.

"And why does he ask me to give a lease to Mr. Hanly now?" the landlord thought. "Why should it be for my interest to withhold leases from all the rest, if it be for my interest to give a lease to him? And why does Mr. Somerfield urge me so strongly to give him a lease, though he considered it a crime for landlords to give leases to their tenants, and I understand has quite done away with leases on the estate over which he is agent? 'Tis very strange. There must be something wrong. I'll write to Mr. Pender, and say I cannot give the lease till I make further inquiries."

Old Isaac shambled about in a state of distraction, and had a severe attack of midges, when he read this letter. But Beresford was not at all sorry: for if Attorney Hanly and Mr. Somerfield had got leases, he could not see what excuse there would be for refusing to renew Maurice Kearney's lease.

And Mr. Beresford Pender had set his heart upon getting possession of Ballinaclash by hook or by crook. One obstacle was removed; Mr. Lowe—who, he feared, might do something to defeat his scheme—was gone to India. If Hugh Kearney were out of the way now, all would be right. Maurice Kearney, he suspected, was in debt; and if he were unexpectedly pounced upon for a year's rent he would never recover the blow, and could be put out even without waiting for the expiration of the lease. But old Isaac regretted that he had urged the landlord to give Attorney Hanly a lease.

"I'm afraid," old Isaac muttered, "Sir Garrett will take some notion into his head. I'm sorry now I ever disturbed Tom Hogan. Carey the carpenter stopped me on the road when his funeral was passing, and said, before all the people, that the coffin was his work, but that my work was in the coffin. A farmer dare not talk to a gentleman that way. But these tradesmen are very insolent. Phil Lahy the tailor never puts his hand to his hat for me. And look at that old Phil Morris. I never like to see his eye on me. 'Tis these fellows that destroy the country. Only for them the farmers would submit to anything."

"Donovan is sure to be transported," Beresford observed.

"I don't see what good that will do," returned his father, "unless Sir Garrett will make some allowance, when he sees it was as his agent I was robbed. I never liked that business. I'd rather keep out of such things, unless when something is to be gained."

"Slap at Kearney now for a year's rent—distrain his stock and he'll be smashed," said Beresford. "I'm told he's in debt, and has a thrashing machine at work night and day, and selling off his corn, though prices are low."

"His brother or some one might pay the rent for him," returned the old agent; "and then we'd be doing him good instead of harm."

"He owes his brother money," rejoined Beresford, "and there's no danger. The brother knows he has no hold of his place, and I'm told he always said he was a fool to expend so much money in improvements."

"Well, Dr. Kiely might interfere. He is a dangerous man, and if he thought Kearney was harshly treated he'd never stop till he got Sir Garrett to look into things. The creditors want the timber on Woodlands to be sold, and if matters are stirred at all something unpleasant may happen. But if Sir Garrett remains abroad, I think there is no danger."

" 'Tis reported Kiely's son has some notion of Miss Kearney," said Beresford.

" Well, that's only another reason why we should be cautious," replied his father, " and the longer he's let run the easier 'twill be to manage him."

" No surrender !" muttered Mr. Beresford Pender down in his chest, as he walked away to have an imaginary conversation with the " colonel," and invent a few new oaths.

CHAPTER LXI.

BARNEY IS CAPTURED—HIS ACCOUNT OF HIMSELF.—MAT THE THRASHER IN CLONMEL JAIL, AND THE BIG DRUM SILENT.

IT is Christmas Day again. But the day has dawned, for the first time within the memory of the oldest inhabitant, without the windows in the old town of Kilthubber being set dancing by the famous Knocknagow drum. The drum is silent and forgotten over Mat Donovan's dresser ; and Mat is a prisoner, awaiting his trial, in Clonmel jail. But even if the drum were banged, as of old, at the Bush, behind Maurice Kearney's, loud enough to awaken the Seven Sleepers, how few would have rallied to the call, compared with that day twelvemonth, when Mr. Lowe and his host followed the procession over the snow-covered road ? For in spite of Father Hannigan's encouraging assurance that the landlords thereabouts were not exterminators, like some he could name, the crowbar *has* done its work at Knocknagow. Brummagem made an attempt to collect some boys to hunt the wren in the afternoon ; but so few came, and so little heart did they put into it, that Mary Kearney thought it was one of the most melancholy sights she ever beheld. It reminded her of poor Mat Donovan and Barney ; and she thought of

Mr. Lowe, and Richard, and Grace, and how happy they all
were last Christmas. She remembered the tracks in the
snow, and how Arthur O'Connor had stood, for hours perhaps,
in the garden ; and even yet he did not know that she had
not received his note in time, and " what must he think of
her ?" She leant back in her chair with a sigh of pain. She
asked herself what business she had in the world, and would
it not be better for her and every one else if she were at rest.
As her head touched the back of the chair, she started, and
a faint blush stole over her pale cheeks.

"Oh," she exclaimed—drawing back the window curtain,
that she might have a view of the old castle and the little
ruined church near it—"'tis a shame for me !" And Mary
gazed towards the churchyard with her hand resting on the
back of the chair. It was a straw chair. It was Norah
Lahy's straw chair—which poor Norah had left to her
idolised friend. And how could she sit in that chair and
not be strong ?

She joined her father and mother and Hugh at dinner with
a smiling, happy face. But still there was a gloom over
the little circle—it was such a contrast to all the other happy
Christmases they had known ; and it was a relief to them all
when a servant came in to say that Billy Heffernan was in
the kitchen, and wanted to see Mr. Hugh, as he was going to
drive Mrs. Donovan and Nelly to Clonmel in the morning to
visit Mat in jail.

They found Mat quite calm, and prepared for the worst.
But a pang shot through his mother's heart when she saw how
thin and pale he had grown. He had lived so long in the open
air, and led so active a life, imprisonment was telling fearfully
upon his strong frame. At times, too, his heart would sink
at the thought that he must stand before the public gaze
accused—perhaps convicted—of a cowardly and disgraceful
crime. But his mother's sad face told him, more plainly than
words, to be a man, no matter what might happen ; while
Nelly, in spite of all her wild ways, utterly broke down, and
was supported out of the prison, crying and sobbing violently,
by Billy Heffernan. They told him all the news, and spoke
of all his old friends—except one. He longed to hear of *her*,
and yet her name was never once mentioned. He did not
ask for her—partly because he dreaded to hear something

unpleasant, and partly because he thought she would rather not be talked of by him. But he felt there was a want of sympathy with him on his sister's part when she never told him a word about Bessy. She spoke about every one she cared much for herself; and because she did not care much for Bessy Morris, she quite forgot that Mat cared more for her than for all the world. And to sympathise with him in this would, he felt, be a greater proof of affection than the greatest sacrifices his sister could have made for him. She told him, over and over, what a good friend Billy Heffernan was to them, and how he would drive them to Clonmel again the day of the trial; and Mat was truly glad to hear this. But why did she not speak one word of his darling Bessy? Why did she not *love* her for his sake? Billy Heffernan told him he had a letter from Hugh Kearney to his attorney, and that nothing would be left undone to prove his innocence.

" I'm sure uv that," said Mat. " I'd depend my life on him. And how is ould Phil Morris, Billy?"

" As sound as a bell, as he says himse'f," returned Billy. " I called in——"

" Time is up," said the turnkey. And Mat Donovan was alone again in that dreary cell.

Ah, if Nelly Donovan had " called in " to old Phil Morris's, and brought one kind word from Bessy, how much better it would have been for her brother than all her sobs and tears!

A week or two after the visit to the jail, Billy Heffernan stopped his mule opposite the little thatched house, where, exactly a year before, he sold the twopence-worth of turf while waiting for room to pass through the loads of corn that blocked up the street, after leaving the dragoon behind him on the road. The woman of the house had become a regular customer since, and even when she did not want a supply of turf, Billy often stopped to have a chat with her. While they were talking this morning, he observed a crowd at the corner of the street, around a yellow painted van, built on the plan of those houses upon wheels in which a tall lady and a dwarf are usually to be seen, but small enough to be drawn by a single donkey. Along one side were two rows of lenses, like burning glasses, the under row low enough for the smallest urchin to peep through, and the upper sufficiently high for a full-grown man to view the

wonders inside without stooping inconveniently. A green
baize curtain hung from a frame in front of the glasses, and
was drawn over the spectators who paid their half-pence, to
shut them in from the gaze of the crowd. The showman had
a loud voice, and in a monotonous sing-song tone he solemnly
announced to the public that he was there by order of her
Gracious Majesty, Queen Victoria, to exhibit his panorama
for the instruction of her Irish subjects, especially the warmhearted people of gallant Tipperary. He then commenced
letting down his pictures one by one by means of strings with
brass curtain-rings attached to them, desiring his patrons
to " look to the right " and " look to the left," and they
would see " Napoleon Bonaparte mounted on a grey horse,"
and " Solomon's Temple," and various other wonders, too
numerous to mention here ; always finishing his description
of a battle by asking them did they not " hear the cannons
roaring."

" Don't you hear the cannons roaring ?" he exclaimed, as
Billy Heffernan pushed his way quietly through the crowd,
and stood close to the orator.

" Oh, I do," responded a voice from under the green baize
curtain, in accents of the profoundest wonder.

The showman, surprised and delighted by so strong a
testimony to the excellence of his exhibition, fought the
battle of Waterloo over again, and again asked, " don't you
hear the cannons roaring ?"

" Oh, I do !" responded the voice again, in a tone of still
deeper wonder and profounder awe.

There was a broad grin on every face in the crowd, except
Billy Heffernan's—he not being much given to mirth. And
of course the showman himself could not for a moment so
far forget the dignity of his mission as to allow his features
to relax into a smile.

" Don't you hear the cannons roaring ?" he repeated, casting
a look of severe reproof upon his audience, to rebuke them
for their levity.

" Oh, I do !" responded the voice.

The curtain was drawn back, and Billy Heffernan started,
and, with eyes and mouth wide open, stared at the face,
radiant with more than human felicity, revealed to his
astonished gaze.

"For God 'lmighty sake," gasped Billy Heffernan, "is id yourse'f, Barney?"

"Begob id is, Billy," replied Barney, with a grin of intenser delight—if that were possible to a man who had been just viewing Solomon's Temple, and listening to the cannons roaring at the battle of Waterloo.

"Barney," said Billy Heffernan, "'twas reported you wor dead."

"Billy," returned Barney—laying his hand on his arm, and suddenly becoming very grave—"don't b'lieve a word uv id."

Billy Heffernan never took his eyes off him for an instant, apparently dreading that if he did Barney might vanish,

> "Like him the sprite,
> Whom maids by night
> Oft meet in glen that's haunted."

Heeling his car suddenly at the door of the thatched house, he threw the load upon the ground.

"Oh, what are you doin'?" cried the woman of the house. "I don't want any turf to-day. An' sure if I did idse'f, I couldn't afford to buy a whole load together."

"Never mind," returned Billy Heffernan, excitedly, "you can pay me by degrees." And collaring Barney, he pushed him into the car, putting up the hind part of the creel and fastening it upon him as he would upon a pig of lively propensities.

"Yo-up! Kit!" And away they went.

Kit, in the whole course of her life, never made the journey from Clonmel to Knocknagow in such quick time. The news flew like wildfire that the prodigal had returned, and was safely caged in Billy Heffernan's creel; and men, women, and children rushed out to see him and to speak to him, before they had reached Mat Donovan's. But Billy Heffernan begged of them to keep back, as his mind would not be easy till he had delivered up his charge to Hugh Kearney, who, he hoped and trusted, would find means to secure him, at least till after Mat Donovan's trial. So the crowd retired, except Phil Lahy, who walked behind the creel as solemnly as if he were following Barney to his last resting-place. The truant looked frightened as they approached the house, and showed decided symptoms of a desire to bolt, till he saw his mistress throw up her arms in surprise, and heard her exclaim, " O poor Barney ! did you come at last ?" And the long unheard " Wattletoes," in his master's well-remembered voice, satisfied him that it was old times again, and no mistake.

So that Barney could not keep in a " hurroo !" of exultation, which took rather the shape of a screech, as he flung up his left arm and assaulted himself with the heel of his right foot, in a manner which, from any foot but his own, would have been at least insulting. And, then and there, Barney performed one of Callaghan's most difficult and complicated steps, with a look of intense gravity, which deepened into a scowl, as he finished by clapping his foot upon the ground with all his force, remaining motionless as a statue in that position for half a minute, and then suddenly breaking into another screech, and assaulting himself with his heel again. Barney then favoured all present, jointly and severally, with his old grin ; and Tom Maher exclaimed, " Good again, Barney !" which seemed to be the meed for which Barney had been labouring, and without which he would have considered his efforts thrown away ; for Barney took off his hat and drew his sleeve across his forehead, with the look of a man who had done his duty, thoroughly satisfied with Tom Maher's " Good again."

" And now, Barney," said Phil Lahy, " will you be good enough to give an explanation of your disappearance, and where and how you spent your time, since you parted with Mat Donovan on the deck of the Liverpool steamer in the harbour of Waterford ?" And having thus delivered himself, Phil cast a " gentlemen-of-the-jury " look around upon his audience.

Barney seemed quite taken aback, and evidently feared that his troubles were before him after all.

" Wait till he gets something to eat first," said Mrs. Kearney. " I suppose he's famished with the hunger. Go to the kitchen, Barney, and I'll desire them to get you your dinner."

" Would I doubt you, ma'am !" exclaimed Barney, brightening up again. " Thundher-an'-turf, Miss Ellie, is id yourse'f at all ? Begor, Miss Mary, she'll shortly be able to ate a tuppenny loaf over your head. An' Masther Willie ! och. Masther

Willie, if you see the fine pup I had stole for you, but I couldn't brin' him wud me. Four months ould, an' as big as a calf. He'd be as big as Bobby. I see his father an' mother wud my own eyes dhrawin' tember tin mile o' ground. But bad luck to id, I couldn't brin' him."

"And where did you find him, Billy?" Mrs. Kearney asked.

"Lookin' at a peep-show, ma'am," returned Billy Heffernan.

"Oh, that was the peep-show!" exclaimed Barney. "I never see the likes uv id. I'd rather give a shillin' to get wan look at id than to spind a shillin' at a races."

"What did you see in it, Barney?" his master asked.

"The whole world," returned Barney, with a look of wonder.

"But tell us what you saw," continued his master, hugging himself in the excess of his glee. "Tell us what you saw in the peep-show."

"Look to the right," exclaimed Barney, in the solemn tones of the showman, "and you'll see Solomon's Temple— mounted on a grey horse." And his master immediately ran into the house to order a good dinner to be set before Barney Brodherick.

"Begob, Phil," Barney answered, when he had smacked his lips and wiped his mouth after the Ballinaclash bacon, "'tis all like a dhrame to me; but I don't much care as Bobby came home safe, as that was what was throublin' me." And Barney did look contented, and in a very happy frame of mind.

"But tell us where you went to and what kept you away so long."

"Well, whin the steamer dhrove off wud Mat, I felt so down-hearted I didn't know what to do wud myse'f. An' as Bobby wanted a rest, I walked up an' down lookin' at the ships. There was wan big wan full uv people, an' the sailors shoutin' an' singin' an' pullin' ropes, an' women an' childher roarin' an' bawlin' for the bare life, till you wouldn't know where you wor standin' 'Is that Barney?' says some wan out from the middle uv 'em. An' who was id but a b'y from Ballingarry side that challenged Mat Donovan to rise a weight wan day at the colliery; an' begob he put Mat to the

pin uv his collar the same day. So out he comes an' pulls
me in on the deck ; an' who the blazes did I see sittin' fur-
ninst me but Patherson the piper playin' away for the bare
life. Thin three or four more fellows that wor in the habit uv
comin' to the dance at the Bush med at me, an' you'd think
they'd shake the hand off uv me. The divil a wan uv 'em
that hadn't a bottle, an' I should take a small dhrop out uv
every wan uv 'em for the sake uv ould times, as they said.
Thin nothin' 'd do but I should dance a bout ; an' Patherson changed the ' Exile of Eryin' to ' Tatthered Jack Walsh
while you'd be lookin' about you. Well, Phil, you know
that's wan of Callaghan's doubles, an' if I didn't show 'em
what dancin' was, my name isn't Barney. But some way or
other some wan knocked up agin me, an' my fut slipped on
the boords, an' down I fell."

Here Barney scratched his head and fell into a reverie.

" Well ?" said Phil Lahy. " What happened you when you
fell ?"

" That's what I'm thryin' to make out, Phil," returned
Barney, " but I can't. Barrin' that I suppose I forgot to
get up ; for whin I kem to myse'f there I was ondher a hape
uv canvas, an' Patherson lyin' o' top uv me gruntin' like an'
ould sow. 'Twasn't long any way till a couple of sailors
pulled us out, an' whin I stood up the divil a stand I could
stand no more thin a calf afore his mother licks him. So
there I was spinnin' about thryin' to studdy myse'f, when the
flure slanted down, for all the world like as if a cart heeled
an' you standin' in id, an' I was pitched head foremost, an' was
d—n near dhrivin' my head through the captain's stummuck.
' Where's your passage-ticket ?' says he, shoutin' out loud ;
for you couldn't hear your ears wud the wind, and the say
dashin' up agin the sides uv the ship, till you'd think we wor
goin' to be swollied afore you could bless yourse'f. ' Where's
your ticket ?' says the captain again, seein' that I had my arms
twisted round a rope, an' I houldin' on for the bare life.
' Arra, what 'd I be doin' wud a passage-ticket ?' says I,
' whin I'm not goin' anywhere.' ' Come, my good fellow,'
says he, ' I want none of your humbuggin'. Hand me your
ticket an' go below.' ' I'm not a coddy at all,' says I. ' Let
me go look afther me little ass.' ' He's a stole-away,' says
the captain, turnin' to the mate. ' That's what they'll say

at home,' says I, ' an' if you don't let me out, Bobby'll be a
stole-away, too, God help me,' says I. ' An' where do you
want to go ?' says the captain, an' I see he couldn't help
laughin' ' Good luck to you, captain,' says I, ' an' let me
out on the quay uv Watherford, an' that's all I'll ax,' says I.
' We have another here,' says the mate, pintin' to Patherson,
' rowlin' hether an' over on the broad of his back.' ' That's
the piper,' said the captain. ' What are we to do wud 'em ?'
' Let me out, sir,' says I, ' or I'll have no business to show my
face to the misthress,' says I. ' You're fifty miles from
Watherford,' says he, ' an' I suspect this is a schame uv yours
to chate me,' says he. Wud that the b'y from Ballingarry
came up a step-laddher out uv a place they call the hoult—
an' the divil's own hoult the same place is—an' he explained
all to the captain, an' said I'd be handy about the cookin',
an' as for the piper, if the weather cleared up, he'd give 'em
a tune, an' keep 'em alive. An' that's the way myse'f an'
Patherson went to New-found-land. We wor home together,
too, an' he wanted to keep up the partnership, we did so
well in St. John's, he playin' an' I dancin'. But, good luck
to you, Phil, an' let me out to see Bobby, an' I'll tell you
all another time."

"Just tell me, Barney," said Hugh, who had been listening unobserved to the latter part of his narration, " what did
you do with the gun you were desired to bring to Mat
Donovan, to have the stock mended ?"

"Oh, for God's sake, Misther Hugh," Barney exclaimed—
showing such decided symptoms of a desire to run away, that
Billy Heffernan closed the door and placed his back against
it—" don't get me into a hobble about the gun, an' I afther
goin' through such hardship. Let me go see Bobby an' my
poor ould mother. Sure I'm bad enough, God help me."

"I don't want to get you into any trouble about it," said
Hugh. " But, by telling the truth, you will get your friend
Mat Donovan out of trouble. Why did you not bring the
gun to him, and where did you bring it ?"

"'Twas all on account uv Peg Brady," Barney answered,
moodily. " An' see all the throuble I brought on myse'f for
wan slob uv a kiss."

"Well, tell me how it happened."

"I see her goin' home by the short-cut, sir," returned

Barney, looking the very picture of repentance, " an' wint across to meet her, thinkin' id 'd be a fine thing to let her see me wud a fire-lock on my shoulder. An' thin I wint to help her over the double-ditch above the forth. An' as I was comin' back I hear the beagles givin' tongue, an' the hare wint poppin' through the nine-acre field, and was makin' for the furze over Raheen. Thin the hounds come on, keepin' on the thrale elegant, and the fust man I see toppin' the double-ditch was yourse'f, and the huntsman after you. So I stuck the gun into a brake uv briers, an' cut off to see the fun ; an' the divil a wan uv me ever thought uv the gun till the day uv the hurlin', whin Father M'Mahon tould me 'twas in Billy Heffernan's bog-hole ; and what use would id be for me to go look for id in a hole that's as deep as the top uv the house ?"

" Did he tell you who put it in that hole ?" Hugh asked.

" Not a word, sir," Barney replied, " on'y that 'twas there."

" All right, Barney," said Hugh. " You may go see Bobby and your mother as soon as you like now. Let him out, Billy ; he won't run away again, never fear," he added, on observing Billy Heffernan's look of alarm.

" Be my sowl, 'tis runnin' enough I'm afther gettin'," returned Barney. " An' that I may never die in sin if ever I put a fut on a ship again, anyway. Will I ride Bobby to see my mother, Misther Hugh ?"

The permission was granted, and in a few minutes Barney passed by the side of Knocknagow that was left, at full gallop ; in his excitement either not seeing or not heeding Kit Cummins, who ran to her door holding up a bottle and glass invitingly ; nor even seeming to notice Peg Brady, who, with the dragoon, stood behind her.

CHAPTER LXII.

SAD NEWS FROM BALLINACLASH.

ANOTHER year has elapsed, and Grace has never once visited the old cottage. She shrinks from it now, as she shrank from Norah Lahy's pale face. Yet she feels that Norah Lahy has done her good, and is glad to think that she won the love of the poor sick girl; for Mary Kearney mentioned in her letters that Norah had spoken affectionately of her to the last. Grace says to herself that she ought to spend some time with Mary in her now lonely home—that it "would be right"; and, as in Norah Lahy's case, she feels it would have done her good. But she has such troops of pleasant acquaintances now, and so many invitations to all sorts of parties, and is so admired and flattered, that she scarcely has time even to think of her old friends. She is reminded of them this morning by a letter from Mary. Mary tells her they are all well; that Anne writes from her convent in her old, cheerful way, but that Ellie did not come home at Christmas; that there was a letter from the Cape from Richard, who was delighted with the voyage. (He had gone as surgeon in an Australian vessel.)

"Billy Heffernan's house in the bog," the letter went on to say, "was swept away by the flood after the heavy rains; and he was barely able to save himself and his mule from drowning. But he is now hard at work building another house, as Mr. Lloyd has given him a lease for ever of twenty acres of his bog, for the yearly rent of a creel of turf; and though my father says a single sod would be too much for it, Billy thinks himself quite independent, and says he has an estate while grass grows and water runs, and no landlord can turn him out. Whether grass can be made to grow on the 'estate,' however, is doubtful. Nelly Donovan has given her heart to Billy Heffernan; but his heart, I really think, is in Norah Lahy's grave. And Mat, too, loves not wisely, but too well; and has become quite a grave and thoughtful character, devoting all the time he can spare to reading. Old Phil Morris is dead, and Bessy is gone to live with her aunt in Dublin. She had been very unhappy on account of the unkind things people used to say of her; and that foolish dragoon, encouraged, it is said, by Peg Brady, kept persecuting her to the last. Peg is our dairy-maid now; and she has confessed, with a flood of tears, that she deceived Mat Donovan about a letter of Bessy's, and is sorry she had not the courage to tell the truth before Bessy went away. As I have said so much of the ' course of true love ' running in the usual way in this part of the globe, I must tell you that a little circumstance which accidentally came under my notice the other day has convinced me that your friend, ' *Fionn Macool*,' is, after all, in love with somebody; but, for the life of me, I cannot guess who she may be, though I could tell you the colour of her hair. Strange to say, I thought of Bessy Morris, but—though you will say that is just what might be expected from an ' *oddity* '—I am sure it is not she. Might it be Miss Delany? He praised her beauty and agreeable manners more than ever I heard him praise any one else. But, take my word for it, Hugh is *gone* about somebody, as sure as the sun is at this moment sinking down behind the poplar trees on the hill—which trees always remind me of you and Bessy Morris, and all the chat we used to have about her father, and her anxiety to find him and live with him in their old home, after all his wanderings. That's what made me like Bessy, and I never could believe her heartless, as she had the name of being.

" The Messrs. Pender are carrying things with a high hand. Poor Father M'Mahon is heart-broken at the sufferings of the people. The poor-house is crowded, and the number of deaths is fearful. Last Sunday, when requesting the prayers of the congregation in the usual way for the repose of the souls of those who died during the week, the list was so long that poor Father M'Mahon stopped in the middle of it, exclaiming with a heart-piercing cry, ' O my poor people! my poor people!' and then turned round and prostrated himself at the foot of the altar convulsed with grief, and could not go on reading the list of deaths for a long time. Then he got into a rage and denounced the government as a ' damnable government.' I was quite frightened at the excitement of the people. Some faces were quite white, and others almost *black*. But a very affecting incident turned their anger into pity, though one would think it ought only to incense them all the more against their rulers. When he resumed the reading of the list, a woman shrieked out and fell senseless upon the floor. She was one of the paupers in the auxiliary workhouse, who are marched to the parish chapel every Sunday, as the chapel in the regular workhouse is too small even to accommodate the inmates of that house. This poor woman was only admitted the week before with her husband and children, from whom, according to their infamous rules, she was at once separated. She now heard her husband's name read from the altar, and with a wild shriek of agony fell down, and was borne senseless out of the chapel. They did not even take the trouble to inform her that her husband was dead ! Were human beings ever treated before as our poor people are treated ? I often wondered at the almost wild looks of the paupers while the list of deaths was being read. But I understand it now ! Oh ! I must drive away the thought of such barbarous cruelty, and not distress you with such pictures of human suffering. But perhaps it is well to think of these things sometimes, Grace, and pray to God to alleviate the misery around us. I do my best to keep up my spirits. I sit in poor Norah's chair every evening till the light in Mat Donovan's window reminds me to go down and read the newspaper or play a tune for my father, while mammá is making her favourite slim-cake for tea. Hugh, as usual, is nearly always in his own room, where I spend an occasional hour with him. He is, however, becoming amiable, and comes out of his den when our Castleview friends make their appearance. I am always glad to see them, and they cheer us up a good deal. Miss Lloyd scarcely recognises them now, and maybe she doesn't *get* it from Rose, with whom Johnny Wilson is again 'the white-headed boy.' Can you make out this mystery about Hugh as you did the tracks in the snow ?

" Ah, we had not so merry a Christmas as that since ! But I can't realise that idea of the poet you used to quote about a ' sorrow's crown of sorrow.' I like to remember ' happier things,' and would say with our own bard—

" ' Long, long be my heart with such memories filled.'

I take my walk nearly every evening. Great news of Tommy
Lahy ! His uncle, who is very rich, has adopted him. He is
in college, and from his likeness he must be a fine fellow.
Do you remember his laughing blue eyes and luxuriant curls ?
Fancy Tommy Lahy coming home a polished gentleman to
us. Would he have any chance of *you* ? It would be quite
romantic. I'm glad I have one more pleasant item to relieve
the gloom of this tiresome letter. Nancy Hogan is married
to Tom Carey, the carpenter, and they are as happy as the
day is long. Tell me all about your great ball. I am all
anxious to know whether it is the white or the pink you have
decided on ; but as you will have decided before you can get
this, I won't give you my opinion, though you say you would
be guided by it. Of course you will be the belle, as Eva
would have been the beauty. How I should like to go to
her profession ; but I fear it will be impossible for me to
leave home. Mr. Lloyd says still he will never love again.
It is a great loss to Edmund that he is not at home, as you
have such pleasant parties. I am so thankful to you to give
me such graphic descriptions of them. Edmund writes to
me sometimes. He and Arthur O'Connor will soon come to
spend a few days with Father Carroll, and they all promise
to pay us a visit. How glad I'd be if you would come. The
light is fading. I'll take to *thinking* now, till Nelly Donovan
lights her candle. Good-bye, dearest Grace, and believe me
ever your affectionate friend,

" MARY KEARNEY."

Grace was by no means unmoved by the passages in this
letter in which Mary glanced at the sufferings of her poor
neighbours, and the sad change that had come over Knocknagow, where, Grace used to say, the idea must have been
suggested to her favourite poet :—

> " You'd swear they knew no other mood
>   But mirth and love in Tipperary."

But that allusion to Hugh and Miss Delany put her into a
brown study. Could it be that matters had gone so far between him and Minnie Delany ? He had only met her once,
but Grace now remembered he was quite " taken up with
her," and scarcely took any notice of herself. Grace was
angry, and angry for being angry. For, what was it to her ?

The arrival of the dress for the ball—which fitted to perfection, and looked even more becoming than she expected—put everything else out of her head for an hour or two. Then, as she sat down to take breath, after trying the effect of all her ornaments, strange to say, she found herself thinking of Tommy Lahy, an educated gentleman, handsome and rich—perhaps famous—crossing the wide ocean to lay all his wealth and laurels at her feet. But then it occurred to her that the moustache with which, in fancy, she had adorned his lip was not yet a reality, and Tommy Lahy was dismissed contemptuously.

When dressed for the ball she went, as was her custom, to her father's study, in order that he might see her in all her glory. She was startled, on entering, to see a man standing alone at the table wrapped in a great-coat. It was Hugh Kearney. For a moment surprise kept her from giving him her hand, which she did give at last without speaking. He almost hesitated to touch the dainty glove, for he was wet and travel-stained, the rain glistening upon his face and beard. She thought the dark eyes glistened, too—and she was not mistaken. How immeasurable seemed the distance between them at that moment! She was so bright and so beautiful, so fitted for the sunshine, that to draw her towards him, into the gloom that hung over his pathway, even if he could do so, would (he thought) be almost a crime.

Recovering from her first surprise, she became quite formal, almost haughty in her manner, as she sat upon a chair, at the opposite side of the table from him, and said :—

" I had a letter from Mary to-day, and was glad to see by it that ye were all well."

This was a relief to him ; as he feared she might ask a question which he would have found some difficulty in answering.

" I'll be back in a moment," said the doctor, entering hastily with a letter in his hand. " O Grace !"—Hugh made a sign and the doctor checked himself. " You are already dressed for the ball," he added ; " I see you are determined to be early in the field."

" Mrs. D—— is to call for me," said she, laughing as she left the room.

" I don't like to bring you out such a night as this," said Hugh, " unless you think it absolutely necessary. Dr. Cusack assured me there was no immediate danger."

" Well, I prefer going at once," returned Dr. Kiely. " Will you have some refreshment ?"

" No, thank you. I had something at the hotel. And I have no time to lose," he added, looking at his watch.

" Well, I hope you will succeed in the object of your journey. If not, don't forget to let me know. Good night."

As Hugh Kearney sat upon the top of the mail-coach, regardless of the cold rain dashing into his face, he could wish that the night and his journey were a year long. It galled his proud spirit to think that he was going to *beg*. It would be easier for him to die. But he thought of his father and mother, and his sister, his beautiful and noble sister, and for their sakes he resolved to make any and every sacrifice consistent with honour. He bowed his head and covered his face with his hands as the thought occurred to him that he might never see his mother alive again. " And if I fail in my mission," he said to himself, " I could almost wish it may be so. She would feel the blow more keenly than any of us, when the first gust of the storm has almost killed her."

He was roused by the loud bray of the guard's horn, and, on looking up, saw a crowd of vehicles blocking up the road in front of a suburban mansion, from the windows of which the light streamed out upon the throng of smoking horses and shouting drivers, as they struggled and jostled one another to get out of the way of the mail-coach. Hugh remembered it was at this house the ball was to which Grace was going, and fancied he caught a glimpse of her crossing the hall as the coach plunged into the darkness.

" There's a ball there, sir," said the guard behind him, who thought he meant to inquire what it all meant ; for Hugh had waved his hand towards the lighted windows.

But the action was an involuntary " Farewell."

Grace was not there, however. She ran down stairs on hearing Mrs. D——'s carriage stop at the door, and meeting her father in the hall wrapped in his cloak, she asked where he was going.

" To Ballinaclash," he replied. " Mrs. Kearney got suddenly ill this morning."

" Why did not Hugh tell me ? "

" Well, he saw you dressed for the party, and did not like to spoil your enjoyment. He is going to Dublin by the night coach."

She paused for a moment, looking bewildered, and then hurried to the hall-door, where a servant was waiting to hold an umbrella over her while she got into the carriage. Her father looked sad, and shook his head, as he turned into his study for a parcel he had forgotten. Mrs. D——'s carriage was rolling up the street as he came out, but to his surprise Grace met him in the hall.

" I have told Mrs. D—— of Mrs. Kearney's illness," said she, in a low, firm voice. " And now will you let me go with you ? I'll be ready in ten minutes."

" It is a cold, wet night, for so long a drive," he replied.

" Oh, no matter. Do let me go."

" Well, then, lose no time."

She flew up the stairs, and there was no sadness in his look now, and no shaking of the head, as he gazed after her, with all a father's love and pride.

The tears welled into Willie Kearney's eyes when Hugh shook him by the hand in his uncle's warehouse.

" I hope you find Willie a good boy ? " said Hugh.

" No better, no better," returned his uncle. " He'll be a first-rate business man."

" Well, Hugh," said the merchant, when he had explained the business upon which he had come, " it is a sad business. But I must tell you plainly I cannot do what you require. It would be only throwing good money after bad, and I owe a duty to my own children. Your father was always careless and improvident, and I often told him he was a fool to expend so much upon his farms when he had no sufficient security. I lent him money before, which I never expect to be paid. And you know I never got a penny of what I was entitled to by my father's will. I left it all to them, and depended on my own exertions. And now I ask you is it just to expect more than that from me, particularly in so hopeless a business ? "

" I agree with every word you say," Hugh replied. " I'd cut off my hand rather than ask it for myself. But I can't bear the thought of seeing them ruined. And if the rent, now due, were paid, I do believe it possible, by care and economy, to pay you after a little time. I'll pledge you my honour I'll do my best."

After a long pause, his uncle filled a cheque, and handed it to him.

" It is not much more than half the sum you want," said he, " but I cannot give you more. And mind, it is to you, and not to your father, I am giving it. You won't go back without coming out to see us ? Your cousins would be most happy to meet you."

" Oh, I cannot lose an hour," replied Hugh. " Good-bye." And after shaking hands warmly with the sturdy merchant, who had some of his father's brusqueness in his manner, he hurried out of the office, his heart somewhat lightened of its load.

" Dr. Kiely will do the rest," said he, as he hurried through the crowded streets. " And if my poor mother has rallied, with God's help, all will be well."

While Hugh Kearney was picturing Grace whirling among the dancers at the ball, she was hurrying to his mother's bedside.

The second day after, she and Mary were sitting together in the well-remembered little room up in the steep roof of the old cottage. Mrs. Kearney was out of danger, but it was feared she would never wholly recover the effects of the shock she had got. The cause of the shock was kept a secret from Grace ; and she candidly told Mary that this made her feel uneasy and uncomfortable, for she could not imagine what motive there could be for concealing the circumstance, whatever it was, from her. Mary flushed scarlet as she answered—

" Well, it is very foolish to be making a mystery of it. But I believe people always feel ashamed under such circumstances ; though I scarcely know why they should. The fact is, we were all startled the other morning to find all our cattle, and sheep, and horses, and, in fact, all we had, seized upon by the agent for rent, and driven away to pound. When poor mamma heard the bailiffs shouting, and saw what had happened, she fell down in a fit, and we feared for some time she was dying. But, thank God, it is not so bad, and if I saw any hope of her being reconciled I'd be happy."

"I don't see anything to be ashamed of," said Grace.

"And yet," Mary replied, "people who would fawn upon us yesterday would not know us to-day. And if Hugh cannot prevail upon my uncle to advance the money to release the cattle before they are canted, I don't know what the end will be. How well I can now understand what the poor people suffer in being driven from their homes every day. I love the very stones of this old place," she murmured, with the tears in her eyes, as she leant out of the window, and looked round the garden, and out over the fields, and down to the little brook, along whose banks she and her brothers and sisters used to spend the long summer days in their happy childhood. And must they leave it all now to strangers, perhaps, who never heard their very names? Her father was standing on the "new ditch," looking towards that part of his farm which was a quagmire some years before, and she guessed what his thoughts were.

"It was very good of you to come to us, Grace," said she. "No one can cheer my father like you."

"Ah, I ought to have come long ago," Grace replied with a sigh.

"Better late than never," returned Mary, cheerfully. "And here is somebody else who wants you to comfort him. I really think he will change his mind, and give you Eva's place in his heart."

Grace laughed as Mr. Lloyd rode by on his grey horse; and then looked grave.

"Oh, here are the Hanlys," she exclaimed, brightening up; "and the pony coming on quite gaily, and head foremost. I suppose we must go down. By-the-by, Mary, what about——" She stopped in the middle of her question, which was suggested by Rose Hanly's curls, which fell over her shoulders in ringlets that might almost rival those in which Mr. Lloyd's heart got so hopelessly entangled the night he distinguished himself as a poet.

"What were you going to say?" Mary asked.

"Oh, nothing. Let us go down to them."

Grace looked very often at Rose's curls during the next half-hour; and when she and Mary were again alone, she was about asking for an explanation of that passage in her letter about Hugh's being in love. But, strange to say, she could not bring herself to ask so simple a question.

Mrs. Kearney was reclining in her arm-chair, propped up with pillows.

" I think, Mary," said she, " I hear the sheep."

Mary thought it was only fancy, and merely replied that the evening was very fine and calm.

" And the cows," she added.

Mary looked anxiously at Grace, for she feared her mother's mind was beginning to wander.

But just then Jim Dunn was heard shouting to Tom Maher ; and Tom Maher shouting to Barney Brodherick ; and Barney hallooing to no one in particular—but in a general way, and for his own private amusement. Mary and Grace ran to the window ; and there were the sheep already spread over the lawn, smelling at the grass, and snatching a hasty nibble ; and then holding up their noses in the air, and looking all round on the groves, and the lime-trees, and the elms, and the old cottage itself, as if a dim notion had got into their foolish heads that they had seen all that before. Then the cows and the heifers and the yearlings came rushing through the gate like a routed army ; but after a little while subsided into tranquillity, and began to low softly in response to Attorney Hanly's herd, which Joe Russell was driving to their stalls from Tom Hogan's meadow. And, to crown all, Bobby rushed through the open gate, and made straight for the house at a hand-gallop, twisting his neck into every possible position, and kicking up his heels in a most extraordinary fashion, till he came close under the window, and suddenly stood stock still. And raising his head as high as possible in the air, Bobby brayed so long and loud, that Mrs. Kearney and Mary and Grace were fain to stop their ears. Then Grace laughed her old ringing laugh ; and when Barney, suddenly remembering that " the misthress was sick," stopped Bobby's music by clapping his " caubeen " over Bobby's upturned nose, Mary laughed quite as heartily as Grace. And poor Mrs. Kearney smiled, and fancied she was quite well again ; and could almost persuade herself that the shock she got the morning everything was seized and driven away, and the stillness and desolation of the place ever since, were only the effects of a troubled dream.

Dr. Kiely assured them the accustomed sights and sounds about the house would tend greatly to Mrs. Kearney's recovery. And after his second tumbler Maurice was himself again, and abused old Isaac Pender and his hopeful son in so superlative and original a manner that Grace laughed as much as she did that Christmas Day we first made her acquaintance, when, between her gravity and her vivacity, Mr. Lowe did not know whether to call her a woman or a child.

Hugh sat at the end of the table, with his hand on the head of his favourite pointer. Grace thought, as his dark eyes rested upon her, without seeming to see her, that she never saw him look so sad. Could it be that what Mary alluded to in her letter had anything to do with it ?

He was looking into the future—the near future, and not the distant, as was his wont. The blow that he feared must fall, was only delayed. The lease would soon expire ; and were they to be ejected like Tom Hogan, or the rent raised ? In either case certain ruin would be the result. Then, he was in debt ; and until his uncle and Dr. Kiely were paid, he could never have an easy mind. And how were they to be paid ? There was only one way ; and it was when he thought of this, that Grace saw a deeper shade of sadness come into his dark eyes as they involuntarily dwelt upon her.

Maurice Kearney's " surprises " were exactly in his old style, and had for Grace the double charm of freshness— after the artificial manner of life she had for some time been accustomed to—and of recalling her merry childhood. She was asked to sing, too ; and the songs and the old tunes recalled the dance and the hurling, and Billy Heffernan and his flute, and Mat Donovan and the famous drum, and the stalwart youths and blooming maidens around the Bush on Sunday evenings, when

> " You'd swear they knew no other mood
> But mirth and love in Tipperary."

Ah, the cattle and the sheep could be brought back to Maurice Kearney's fields. But can *these* be ever brought back ?

CHAPTER LXIII.

EJECTED.—THE BAILIFFS IN THE OLD COTTAGE.—BILLY
HEFFERNAN PLAYS "AULD LANG SYNE" AGAIN, AND THE
OLD LINNET SINGS IN THE MOONLIGHT.

HUGH KEARNEY is in Australia, toiling to make money He
is resolved to pay the debt due to his uncle, and that for
which his generous friend, Dr. Kiely, is responsible. He is
determined, too, to have a home for his father and mother
and sisters, if they should require it. But he does not know
that they require it even now. Sir Garrett Butler made a
feeble effort to inquire into the condition of his tenantry and
the conduct of his agent, but his health or his energy failed,
and he relapsed into his former habits.

" He can't live long," said Mr. Beresford Pender to his
worthy father. " Mrs. Lowe mentioned that the doctors
ordered him to Italy, so we may as well slap at Kearney at
once. He will be likely to follow his son to Australia ; and
'twill be a matter of importance to have possession of the
place whatever happens."

Old Isaac had nothing to object against this, and legal
proceedings were forthwith taken against Maurice Kearney.
He had been careful to keep his rent paid up since the seizure
of his stock for the arrears ; but that was no use now, and
he was ejected for non-title. He had to sell off his cattle
and sheep at a ruinous sacrifice ; but when the sheriff came
to hand over the possession of his houses and lands to the
agent, Mrs. Kearney was so dangerously ill that it was found
necessary to allow them to remain in the house till she was
sufficiently recovered to be removed, or, what seemed more
likely, till she was borne to her last peaceful home in the
churchyard near the old castle.

Mrs. Kearney was slowly recovering. But they dreaded
to tell her that the sheep whose bleating she listened to were
not her own, but Mr. Beresford Pender's. The tears sprang
into Mary's eyes as she looked into the little garden, and saw

a sow with her numerous progeny lying upon one of the flower beds. There was a rude straw shed, also, erected near the rustic seat, which was broken and laid across the entrance, to keep in half-a-dozen calves, whose heads were thrust under it, as if they had been caught there, and could not by any possibility be pulled back again.

" I think, Mary," said Mrs. Kearney, " as the day is so fine, I'll sit out in the garden for a while. I know it would do me good."

" Oh, I'm sure it will," returned Mary, eagerly. " I'll get your shawl. You'll find, if you only take courage, you are much stronger than you think."

She induced the invalid, instead of going to the garden, to walk in the lawn in the shelter of the fir-grove. After a turn or two they sat down on the trunk of a fallen tree, and nearly an hour passed unheeded, as they listened to the cawing of the rooks, and the thousand dreamy sounds of the summer noon.

Mary saw her mother's face brighten as she looked round on the dear old place, and her heart sank within her as she thought the time had now come when the truth must be told—that it was no longer theirs, and they must soon leave it for ever.

" Oh," thought Mary, as she watched her mother's brightening looks, " how are we to break it to her ? I fear it will kill her. May God direct us for the best."

Her father had taken a house in Kilthubber ; and at her request a good deal of the furniture of the cottage was removed to it. She heard Beresford Pender ask him when he was to get possession of *his* house, and she wished that her father should not be exposed to such insults any longer than it was absolutely necessary. That very day she had persuaded him to go into town, and superintend the fitting-up of the new house. She dreaded Mr. Beresford Pender's brutal insolence ; and now that her mother was sufficiently recovered to leave her room, a visit from that gentleman might be expected at any moment.

" I was dreaming of Hugh last night," said Mrs. Kearney, " and of my poor Uncle Dan, God rest his soul. I hope it was not a bad dream. Mr. Butler—that is Sir Garrett now— came in with his ebony flute under his arm, and, strange to

say, Hugh clenched his fist and was going to knock him
down, till my Uncle Dan caught him by the arm. Then,
my Uncle Dan got his violin, and he and Mr. Butler played
the " Coulin " together. I never heard such heavenly music,"
said Mrs. Kearney, holding her hands together, and turning
up her eyes to the cloudless sky. " I'm sure it can't be a
bad dream. Grace ran in and flung her arms about Hugh,
and he looked surprised ! Then a whole lot of ladies and
gentlemen took hands and began to dance. You were dressed
in white and Ellie in blue, and ye were the beautifullest
of them all. But that Barney," add d Mrs. Kearney,
indignantly, " wouldn't stop dancing and prancing in and
out among them all, and jumping upon chairs, and standing
on his head, and kicking his feet about, till my mind was
confused, and I couldn't make head or tail of it. But I
know it wasn't a bad dream, for the music continued even
after that young Hanly roared, and poor Miss Lloyd was
tumbled head over heels. Then Richard began to kick
Beresford Pender—poor Richard was always too hasty,"
sighed Mrs. Kearney, pathetically—" and there was nothing
but uproar and confusion. But the ' Coulin ' could be heard
through it all ; and that's what makes me think it was not
a bad dream, at any rate."

Mary laughed as she pinned her mother's shawl more
comfortably about her, and said it was she herself who was
playing the " Coulin " last night, but she touched the keys
so lightly, she thought the sound could not reach her mother's
room.

" I think you may as well come in and have your broth
now," said she.

" You may as well bring it to me here, Mary," her mother
replied. " 'Tis such a beautiful day, and this is such a nice
place to rest."

" Oh, very well," returned Mary, " I'll go for it."

She walked quickly back to the house, in better spirits
than she had known for a long time. She thanked God that
her mother was so much stronger than ever she hoped to
see her again.

" If she knew that we must go, and could be reconciled to
it, I'd feel quite happy," she thought, as she pushed against
the hall-door, which she had left unlatched when coming out.

But the door was fastened, and she knocked loudly, as the old housekeeper's ears were not of the sharpest, and there was no one else in the house. There was no response to her knocking, and she went round to the back-door, a little annoyed, as she expected to encounter some of Mr. Pender's people, who occupied one of the out-offices. To her surprise the back-door also was fastened, and on looking round she started and seemed quite bewildered ! Chairs, tables, bedsteads, and household furniture of every kind, were strewn in heaps about the yard. The truth at once flashed upon her ; advantage had been taken of her mother's going out to get possession of the house. The discovery almost took away her breath ; but indignation at so cowardly a trick gave her strength, and she walked boldly to the office occupied by Pender's bailiffs and servants. That, too, was locked, and she asked aloud was there any one within. There was no reply ; and the silence and desolation of the place filled her with an oppressive sense of fear. But this was only for a moment. All her anxiety was for her mother.

"Oh," said she, covering her face with her hands, "it will kill her. If Ellie were at home, or even if I had Judy— but I know they have purposely contrived some plan to get the poor old woman out of the way—I might be able to do something." She was on the point of giving way to despair, when her eye rested on Norah Lahy's chair. Snatching it up between her hands she hurried back to her mother.

"The broth is not ready, mamma," said she, "and Judy is gone somewhere. You'd be tired sitting on that hard tree, so I brought you this chair."

"Oh, 'tisn't strong enough for me," said her mother, "I'm too heavy for it."

"Oh, 'tis quite strong. It was Mat Donovan made it, and there is a wooden frame inside the straw. You'll find is very comfortable ; I was often thinking of bringing it to your room."

"Well, bring it down to the hedge. I saw a wasp going into a hole at the root of this tree, and I suppose there is a nest there. I'm always afraid of wasps since my Uncle Dan got the sting in the eye-brow, and it swelled up till you'd think he hadn't an eye in his head. That's why I was always against keeping bees ; though Mrs. Donovan tells me

not one in her house ever got a sting, but one Mat got when
he grabbed at a bee that got entangled in Bessy Morris's hair.
Oh, I declare 'tis a very nice chair. I think I'll stay out till
your father comes home, and he'll be surprised. He said he
only wanted to see Wat Murphy about some sheep he bought,
so I suppose he won't be long."

The allusion to Mrs. Donovan suggested to Mary that the
best thing she could do was to get Nelly to assist her. Mat,
she knew, was with her father fitting up the house in
town.

Nelly and her mother were quite startled when Miss
Kearney told them what had happened. Nelly's first suggestion was to " choke " old Isaac without a moment's loss
of time. But, remembering that this summary proceeding
was not practicable just then, old Isaac not being in the way,
she let down her apron—which she had tucked up as if the
choking business were to be done on the spot—and became
more calm.

" Sure I can break in the doore, Miss," said Nelly.

" Oh, no," returned Mary, and she could not help smiling,
" that would not do. Darby Ruadh and the rest of them are
in the house, I am sure. I think the best thing we could do
is to get mamma over here, until my father comes with the
car And if she can bear the shock, Mrs. Donovan could
talk to her about old times, and that would cheer her. But
she is not strong enough to walk."

" I'll run over for Billy and the mule," exclaimed Nelly,
flinging her cloak on her shoulders. " He's at the big dhrain
to-day—an' sure 'tis at the same dhrain he is every day
a'most for the last twelvemonth."

As Nelly was starting off to the bog for Billy Heffernan,
the old housekeeper came in, vowing vengeance against
" that limb uv the divil," Darby Ruadh, who had told her
that Honor Lahy wanted her in all haste, and off she ran,
and never " cried crack " till she reached the " barrack,"
and found Honor did not want her at all.

" Never mind, Judy," said Mary, soothingly. " Anything
such people would do need not surprise you. Come with
me now, as I may want you."

Mary was quite alarmed to find Mr. Beresford Pender
standing in front of her mother's chair, while his father

shuffled up and down behind him, rubbing his face. But, to her surprise, instead of bullying and insulting her mother, the worthy pair were bowing to her with every sign of the most profound respect, and assuring her how much they regretted that she had been put to even the slightest inconvenience, while poor Mrs. Kearney looked from one to the other quite bewildered.

" 'Twas all a mistake, Miss Kearney," said Beresford, turning to Mary. " The rascals acted without my orders. But I am after telling them to leave the house, and the furniture will be put back again at wance."

" What is it, Mary ? " Mrs. Kearney asked, faintly.

" Something the bailiffs have been doing, I believe," she replied. " But it appears it was a mistake."

" Making another seizure ? " returned her mother, with a frightened look. And Mary, thinking she was going to swoon, put her arms round her, assuring her again it was all a mistake.

" All a mistake, Mrs. Kearney," said Beresford.

" All a mistake, Mrs. Kearney," old Isaac repeated.

" Good morning, Mrs. Kearney," said Beresford, with a low bow.

" Good morning, Mrs. Kearney," said old Isaac, with another low bow.

Though somewhat reassured by their obsequiousness, Mrs. Kearney was alarmed, and said she feared they were " bent on some villainy."

Billy Heffernan's services were not required. But Nelly Donovan's appearance in his lonely house that day, he afterwards confessed, first put the thought into his mind, that it would be pleasant, after all, to have some one to welcome him home on summer evenings and winter nights. And that same night, as Kit sat winking at the moon, after a luxurious tumble on a heap of dry turf dust, the remains of last year's rick, certain sounds reached her ears to which she had been so long unaccustomed, that she wakened up and switched her tail three several times. And though, except the tail, not a muscle moved, it was quite evident that Kit was going through a series of very wild gambols in her own mind. Her master, for the first time since Norah Lahy's death, took down his flute from the elk's horns upon which it hung, and played

" Auld Lang Syne." Then, putting back the flute, he went out and paced up and down through the rushes, feeling uneasy and excited. Was he going to forget her, he asked himself. And if she knew his thoughts would she not reproach him with her dark eyes ? But then he recalled her words the evening he ran to tell her that Mat Donovan was not killed by the falling of the hay-rick, and remembered how fond she always was of Nelly. He felt he could not sleep in the state of mind he was in ; and instead of going to bed at once, he thought he might as well walk over to Honor Lahy's for his usual supply of meal.

" God save all here ! " said Billy Heffernan ; " 'tis a fine night."

" God save you kindly, Billy ! " returned Honor and Phil together ; " sit down." They were sitting near the window, watching the moon as it peeped over the beech-tree. Billy sat down in his old place on the bench. And as the moon rose higher and higher above the tree, the light fell on the place where Norah used to sit, and the thought occurred to each of them that she was looking at them now.

" God save ye," said another voice, in a low, subdued tone, " 'tis a beautiful night." It was Nelly Donovan, who sat down exactly where Norah used to sit, and, resting her chin on her hand, gazed up at the moon, with a softness in her eyes that Billy Heffernan had never noticed in them before. The dreamy sadness of their looks changed suddenly to astonishment. The old linnet began to sing that low sweet song of his ; though his voice had never before been heard except in the day-time.

Honor Lahy made the Sign of the Cross, evidently viewing the incident in a supernatural light.

" There's somethin' goin' to happen that Norah ⁻'d be glad uv," said she.

And as Billy Heffernan continued to look into Nelly Donovan's eyes, he remembered still more distinctly what Norah had said about his leading so lonely a life, without one to care for him.

" There is Mat," said Phil. " I'll run out and ask him is there any news."

" Somethin' is up," was Mat's reply. " 'Tis reported the Penders forged Sir Garrett's name to a bill in the bank. I don't say 'tis thrue, for I met Darby Ruadh with his coat off, runnin' to hire a car; an' he wouldn't tell me where he was goin' if they wor makin' off. But there's somethin' up."

This rumour created great excitement; and the few of old Isaac's victims who still remained in the country indulged in wild hopes that the day of retribution had come. Among these, we need scarcely say, was Maurice Kearney, who hoped that if the agent were proved to be a knave, the landlord would not only give him back the possession of his farms, but compensate him for the injury he had suffered. And, though by no means so sanguine as her father, even Mary felt a presentiment that brighter and happier days were at hand, when she looked from her window next morning, and missed the sow and the calves from the little garden, and saw that all Mr. Beresford Pender's flocks and herds had disappeared from the fields.

CHAPTER LXIV.

A CONSPIRACY.—THE " COULIN."—MISS LLOYD WANTS TO KNOW ALL ABOUT IT.—VISIONS OF HAPPY DAYS.

" Come, Arthur, let us have a walk," said Edmund Kiely.

" Where shall we go?" Arthur O'Connor asked, laying down his book.

" Oh, to the Priest's Walk," replied Edmund. " That is the best place to see the sun setting behind the castle."

" If you don't hurry, the sun will be gone down," Father Carroll observed, looking, not towards the setting sun, but in quite an opposite direction, towards the turn of the road, where a car had just come in view.

It was evident that his reverence and Edmund were deep in some conspiracy, of which Arthur was to be kept in ignorance. But, quite unsuspicious of the plotting of his friends, he drew on his gloves and followed Edmund towards the river.

He looked stronger and happier now than when last he

stepped over those moss-covered stones. But, though his face lights up now and then, its prevailing expression is gloomy.

"Strange to say," Edmund remarked, "I have not yet got rid of the feeling that we are destined to be rivals."

"And what reason have you for thinking so ?"

"No reason ; it is only a feeling."

Their eyes met, and in both there was a look of suspicion.

"A very foolish feeling," Arthur observed, after a pause.

They passed beyond the Priest's Walk, and into the pleasure-grounds near the castle ; and Arthur stopped short as a strain of low, sweet music fell upon his ear.

"I thought these people were away on the Continent," said he.

Edmund did not reply. He was watching the play of his friend's features, which changed from indifference to surprise, and then softened into melancholy.

"That air reminds you of something," said Edmund.

"Well, it does," returned Arthur O'Connor, and his pale cheek became crimson for an instant.

"Of the day you heard it in Tramore ?"

"Yes."

Edmund dropped into a rustic seat near him, looking quite miserable.

"I suppose it can't be helped ! " he exclaimed at last. "And the sooner 'tis over the better. But it is a bitter drop in the cup which I thought would be unmixed bliss."

"Is it raving you are ?" Arthur asked.

"Now, Arthur, you know you are thinking of her ! "

"Thinking of whom ? "

"The person of whom that air has reminded you."

"Well, suppose that is the fact," returned Arthur, reddening again, "what then ? "

"'Tis a most extraordinary fatality," said Edmund, quite distressed. "Though you only saw her that one time."

"You are most certainly taking leave of your wits," returned Arthur. "Of course I saw her often since."

"You never told me that," exclaimed Edmund, looking up in surprise. "And she never gave me the least hint of it."

"Why, you saw me in her company repeatedly yourself," Arthur replied, looking as if he were really anxious on the score of his friend's sanity. "Perhaps Father Carroll's whiskey is too much for you?"

"My dear Arthur," cried Edmund Kiely, springing to his feet, "I have been making a fool of myself. It is not of the same person we are thinking at all. Let us go back. It is getting late, and Father Carroll may think we have been spirited away by some one of the numerous supernatural visitants who haunt the Priest's Walk after nightfall, if Mrs. Hayes is to be believed."

The candles were lighted in the priest's parlour when they reached the cottage. Arthur O'Connor stood still, looking quite bewildered, when he opened the parlour door, and saw the most gloriously beautiful girl he had ever beheld standing before him and smiling through her tears. She advanced as if she found it impossible to restrain herself, and clasped his hand in hers, while the big tears that sprang into her eyes when she first looked at him rolled down her cheeks. He looked to Edmund for an explanation, but that gentleman only rubbed his hands gleefully, evidently enjoying his friend's bewilderment.

"She is gloriously beautiful," thought Arthur, as he surveyed her splendid figure, and then looked inquiringly into her dark lustrous eyes.

"You don't remember me," she said in a clear, musical voice.

"I must have seen you before," he replied; "but I can't recollect when or where."

An old man, with long white hair and slightly bent figure, advanced from behind Father Cleary's high-backed arm-chair, where he had been standing unobserved by Arthur, and stood beside the lovely girl, holding an ebony flute in the hollow of his left arm, and looking at Arthur with a plaintive smile.

"I remember now," said Arthur, appearing more bewildered than ever, as the old gentleman shook him by the hand. At this the tears sprang into the young lady's eyes again, and then she and Edmund exchanged looks and laughed.

But all the laughing was not to be on Edmund's side, and he looked almost as astonished as Arthur, when Father Carroll led forward another lovely girl, of the mild and statuesque and not of the glowing sort like the first, who now caught her by the hand; though it was plain they had met that evening before. It was the first time that she and Arthur had met for years; but each read in the eyes of the other what the reader must have guessed by this time.

"My dear Miss Kearney," exclaimed the dark beauty, "how much I regret I did not know who you were that day at the seaside. And to think that the young abbé, as I have always called him, was my own cousin! It is like a romance. I never heard the 'Coulin' since that I did not think of both of you."

"I know now," said Edmund, "of whom the Coulin reminded you."

"Yes, and I have some faint notion of what you were driving at," returned Arthur. "But who is she?"

Before he could answer, Edmund felt a little hand glide into his, and turning round, he caught his sister Grace in his arms.

Father Carroll looked on, rubbing his hands in silence, and congratulating himself upon the success of his part of the plot, when Mrs. Hayes came in and whispered some words to him. He went to the white-haired old gentleman, who, buried in the high-backed armchair, seemed to be quite unconscious of what was going on around him, and started as if from a dream when the priest addressed him.

"Tell the servant to come in," said Father Carroll.

Mrs. Hayes withdrew, and a liveried functionary immediately appeared, looking so solemn and dignified that Grace asked Mary in a whisper, was he the bishop.

"Did I not tell you that I could not see that person?" said the old gentleman.

"Yes, sir," returned the dignified personage, with a slight bow, and turning his toes more out, "but when I saw he was determined to come over after you I thought it right to come and tell you." But the dignified functionary said nothing of the half-crown in the pocket of his plush breeches.

"You may as well see him," said Father Carroll.

"Very well," returned the old man, with a helpless sigh, as if he were quite incapable of thinking for himself.

The servant retired; and when the door was again opened, the ladies were startled to see Mr. Beresford Pender rush in and fling himself upon his knees.

" Mercy, mercy, Sir Garrett ! " he blubbered. " Don't transport me."

" I have nothing to do with it ; you must see my lawyer," returned Sir Garrett Butler, trying to push back his chair, which was already against the wall.

" I'll be transported, I'll be transported—Ooch ! whoo ! hoo ! " And Mr Beresford Pender burst into a hideous howl.

" I can do nothing. I have allowed myself to be deceived too long," said the baronet more firmly. " I fear I have much to answer for, for all the wrong that has been done in my name.

" 'Tis forgery, 'tis forgery," cried Beresford, looking one after another into the faces around him. " Mercy, Miss Butler, mercy ! " he blubbered, dragging himself across the room on his knees, causing the young lady to take refuge behind a chair, as he was about prostrating himself at her feet.

" 'Tis all my father's fault ; 'tis all my father's fault," he whined, dragging himself back again to where the baronet sat ; " I'm innocent, I'm innocent, Sir Garrett. Ooh ! hoo ! whoo ! "

" Do you see the face at the window ? " Grace asked in a whisper. " Who can it be ? "

" Perhaps some one who has been attracted by all this roaring," returned Mary. " 'Tis a woman's face."

" Yes ; and she has contrived to convert her nose into a badly baked pancake against the glass—oh, my goodness, the window is broken ! " Grace exclaimed, as the face vanished, and the broken glass fell upon the floor. But Mr. Pender's howls for mercy prevented any one else from noticing the accident.

" I think you had better withdraw," Father Carroll suggested, " or stand up at least." But it was no use. Beresford howled and blubbered, till there was nothing for it but to eject him by force. Edmund and Arthur advanced for that purpose, but both shrank in disgust from touching the grovelling creature, and Tom Doherty was called in. Tom quietly flung Mr. Pender on the broad of his back, and was pulling him away, when an assistant appeared upon the scene in the person of our friend Barney Brodherick, who jumped between Beresford's legs, and catching a shin in each hand, like the shafts of a wheelbarrow, started off round the table—that being easier than a short turn—and swept out through the door with such speed, that Tom Doherty was left standing on the spot where his prisoner was snatched from him, staring in utter bewilderment, till Beresford resumed his roaring—which the celerity of his exit had silenced— outside the hall-door. Then Tom Doherty walked out, scratching his head as if even still he thought the affair rather puzzling.

"Begob, Barney," said he, "you made short work uv him."

"The divil a thing I'd rather be doin' thin whalin' him," returned Barney. "But I'll never sthrike a man down."

"Don't lay a hand on him," muttered a gruff voice; and Barney was pushed rudely aside, coming violently into collision with a female, who at the moment ran round the corner of the house.

"Oh, my gracious!" she screamed, grasping at Barney as both tumbled to the ground.

"D——n your sowl, let me go," muttered Barney, "an' I'll smash every eye in his head."

"Can't you tell me what it is all about?" she gasped, panting for breath, and fastening her hands in Barney's shirt front like the claws of a kite.

"Where's his hat?" Darby Ruadh asked, after pulling his master to his feet.

Mrs. Hayes flung out the hat from the hall.

"Come away out uv this," Darby continued. "Didn't I tell you there was no use comin' here? An' you know you have no time to lose."

Barney forced open the claws that held him in a spasmodic clutch, and was rushing headlong to take instant vengeance for the insult he had received, when he was stopped by Tom Doherty.

"Never mind him, Barney," said Tom, "come an' finish your supper an' tell us about that letther from Misther Hugh. I'm glad he's doin' well."

"Dear Mr. Pender," exclaimed a voice, just as Beresford had got into the covered car that was waiting for him on the road, "do tell me what it was all about."

"Blast your eyes," Darby Ruadh whispered into his master's

ear, " now is your time ; you'll never have a betther chance.
Tell you all about id ? " he continued, turning to the lady.
" Av coorse. An' why not ? Here, come in here, an' I'm the
b'y that can tell you all about id." And he lifted her into
the car and told the driver to drive on.

" Oh, don't drive on—— "

" Never mind. We'll let you down at the gate. Sure I
knew you wor at the major's. An' glad I was whin the
butler towld me Miss Isabella an' the captain wor well, an'
doin' well, in Ingy, an' that they wor shortly expected home.
'Twas the wondher uv the world whin the captain married
Miss Isabella instead uv you, until we larned how it was,
an' that you refused him."

" Dear Mr. Pender, don't squeeze me so hard. And please
take care of my nose or 'twill begin to bleed again."

" Can't you talk ? " muttered Darby. " Wan'd think you
hadn't a word in your gob."

" No surrender," said Beresford.

" Oh, please, don't," she said faintly. " I hope we have
not passed the gate."

" An' you want to know all about id," continued Darby.

" Oh, yes. What was it all about ? And why was he
shouting so dreadfully ? "

" Faith an' sure no blame for him to shout, whin that ould
rascal wanted to make him marry his daughter in spite uv
him. ' No,' says Misther Beresford, ' I'll never marry a
woman but the wan that I always had the love in my heart
for,' says Misther Beresford ; ' though 'tis little she suspects
it,' says he. ' So for God 'lmighty sake, Sir Garrett Butler,'
says Misther Beresford, ' don't ax me.' Wasn't that enough
to make any man roar ? "

" Oh, 'twas dreadful ! "

" ' I'll die like the mules, Darby,' says Misther Beresford
to me, ' if I don't get the on'y wan I ever loved,' says he."

" Don't hold me so tight, please," said the lady.

" Don't blame him, Miss," returned Darby. " 'Tis little
you know all he's afther goin' through on your account."

" On *my* account ! "

" Oh, bedad I'm afther lettin' the cat out uv the bag,"
exclaimed Darby. " After he warnin' me never to tell a
word uv id to man or mortal."

"Oh, I'm sure we have passed the gate," said the lady.

"Never mind, my darling," returned Beresford. "Don't you know that I'd die for you. No surrender is my motto." And they drove on—whither the young lady did not inquire.

"Only think, Miss Kearney, I once almost worshipped that man as the most valiant of heroes," said Miss Butler, when Beresford's howling had ceased. She looked and spoke so piteously that Edmund burst into a loud laugh. "Indeed yes," she continued. "My aunt Lowe used to show me his letters. Cousin Henry was in the country at the time, and we thought you all—particularly your eldest brother—very bad people indeed. But Mr. Pender was in my eyes a most gallant and chivalrous gentleman."

"Yes, he and my friend, the abbé, were my only dangerous rivals," said Edmund.

"And to think the abbé was my cousin!" added Miss Butler, with a beaming look at Arthur; "and that he knew my beloved mother. And that we should meet in this old cottage where she was married. Did you ever read of anything more romantic in a book?"

"Really, Edmund," Grace observed, "you ought to make it the subject of a drama or a novel. It has every requisite for it."

"Except the sensational," said Edmund.

"Oh, that could be easily managed. Suppose you have her fall from the cliffs, when you were in pursuit of her along the shore, into the angry, roaring waters. Her shrieks bring her father to the spot. He gazes down into the deep, dark whirlpool, with a gesture and a cry of anguish and despair. She is seen to rise for a moment to the surface, and is again engulfed in the remorseless waves. He is about flinging himself after her, in the madness and agony of the moment, when you appear. You plunge boldly into the roaring, raging, seething surges, and, diving to the bottom, you are not seen for—say a minute and a half—which will be an age, of course, to the agonized spectators."

"You have given me only one spectator," Edmund interrupted.

"Oh, I am thinking of the readers—or the pit, boxes, and gallery."

"Well, I bring her up of course," said Edmund.

"Not the first time, I think," returned Grace, seriously. "You must keep them on the rack. You should dive at least three times before you bring her up. Then, with one arm encircling her waist, you buffet the mad waves with the other, and, after a desperate struggle, reach the dark, beetling rock that towers above you—as high as you please—and as you cling to it, a huge fragment gives way and falls with a crash like thunder into the whirling billows. You are lost. But no ; again you are seen buffeting the waves, but instead of struggling against the receding tide, you are borne out to sea, and raising your arm aloft, while you rise and sink upon the heaving billows, and the lightning flashes through the frowning sky above you, you shout for help. The hardy fishermen hear your cry. A boat is launched. They pull vigorously through the foaming surf—and so on. Nothing is easier than the sensational, to my mind. You might bring in a shark or two if you liked, and be met by a mad bull on the way home, or something of that sort."

"And then, I suppose, it would all end in half a dozen happy marriages ? " said Father Carroll, laughing.

"As it is likely to do in reality," returned Grace, "at least with a couple of happy marriages."

Mary blushed, and looked so distressed that Grace was sorry for what she had said.

"We'll send for Mr. Lowe, who, of course, will be a rich nabob, and give Grace to him," said Edmund.

"And I suppose," Arthur remarked, "Mr. Beresford Pender will be the villain of your novel ? "

"Oh, not at all," replied Grace ; "he would not make even a respectable villain."

"You used to say Hugh Kearney would make an excellent brigand," said her brother.

"Papa had a letter from him lately," returned Grace, looking grave. "He has had a severe attack of illness, but was recovering."

"I fear he means to settle down permanently in Australia," said Mary. "He wishes to have Willie brought home, but he says he would rather be a merchant than a farmer."

"I hoped to have Hugh for a neighbour," Edmund remarked, "and if he does not come home it will be a sore disappointment to me. But, after the turn things have taken now, I am sure you can prevail on him to come home."

" It was the ase of that poor man Tom Hogan that first opened my eyes," said Sir Garrett. " If it were not for that, more wrong would have been done in my name. But I'm glad Mr. Kearney has escaped."

" But how did you become acquainted with Sir Garrett Butler ? " Arthur asked, turning to Edmund.

" Oh, when you hear it all, it will be an interesting story," he replied. " You know the beginning of it in the old flute-player. The very day you left for Paris, Annie saw me, and sent a servant to learn my name in Kingstown ; but I didn't know who she was for a long time after. I'll tell you all another time. We must see them home now. Will you venture to go back by the Priest's Walk ? "

" Oh, certainly," Miss Butler replied. " It will be delightful in the moonlight."

" Was it Sir Garrett's flute we heard in the evening ? " Arthur asked.

" Yes, that was a plan of mine," replied Edmund. " I wanted to know would it remind you of the incident in Tramore. By George, I little thought what good reason you had for remembering it," he added, glancing at Mary " I was quite frightened at the thought that it was of Annie you were thinking. It is as Grace says, really like a novel. And if I should think of founding a story on it, what ought it to be called ? "

" I think the ' Coulin ' would be a suitable title," returned Grace.

" Is Flaherty the piper alive, and in the country ? " Sir Garrett asked.

" Oh, yes," replied Father Carroll. " I met him lately at Father M'Mahon's."

" I am very glad," rejoined the baronet. " I must have him at Woodlands. It was he first inspired me with a love of our native music."

" Cousin Henry told me about him," said Miss Butler. " He met him at a country wedding. Miss Lloyd reminded me of it to-day. She wants me to write to cousin Henry, and as much as say that she will go back with him to India if he comes for her, and that he will get twice as much money as Captain French got with her sister."

"Come, you must be off to bed," said Father Carroll. "Miss Butler will be sure to play the siren and these gentlemen won't be back for two hours yet."

"And why are you in such a hurry?" Mary asked.

"Simply, because I must sleep on the sofa," he answered, "and will have to say Mass at seven in the morning."

"Well, don't forget to close the shutters," said Grace. "There is a pane broken in the window."

Mary did not sleep much that night. She was too much agitated to be happy. Grace, too, was restless enough; but she is a "mystery"; and we must leave her to unravel herself.

"We are all quite alarmed about Miss Lloyd. She can't be found anywhere," said Miss Butler, who met Mary and Grace on their way home next morning. "They are afraid she followed us to Father Carroll's and fell into the river."

"No, Miss," answered Barney Brodherick, who was driving the car, "she went home be the road."

"How do you know?" Mary asked.

"Sure I see her, Miss," Barney answered, "cuttin' away as fast as her legs could carry her. She kem into the kitchen to put cobwebs to her nose."

"Cobwebs to her nose?"

"Yes, Miss, her nose was bleedin'. 'Twas gettin' the cobwebs that delayed me from goin' to help Tom to pull out Pendher."

"Why, Mary, it was she was at the window," exclaimed Grace.

"I must go tell them," said Miss Butler. "They are searching the deep pools in the river; and a messenger has been sent to her brother's."

Neither Mary nor Grace was disposed for talking on the way.

"Ah, that 'Good-bye' came from his heart," thought Grace as they passed the turn of the road that brought them in view of the cottage.

"Mary," she asked, "do you remember the day I came away from Ballinaclash with papa and Eva, and Richard and Mr. Lowe? It was the day old Mr. Somerfield died."

"Indeed I do," replied Mary. "I felt very lonely after you all. And you never came after, till mamma got ill. I used to think of that day as the last of the old 'happy days.'"

"The old happy days will come again," said Grace.

"I hope so," returned Mary. "Things look so bright now, I am almost frightened by the visions of happiness I have."

Maurice Kearney's voice was heard shouting to his workmen in his old style ; which so delighted Barney that he grinned from ear to ear, and made up his mind to earn a "ballyragging" as soon as possible for himself.

"My poor father !" said Mary. "It is dreadful to think how near he was to being driven for ever from those fields. And there is mamma superintending the feeding of the young turkeys. I really begin to hope she will be as strong as ever again."

"You will be as happy as ever," said Grace.

"I hope so. And yet there is one great drawback. I don't think I can ever be happy while Hugh is far away, and among strangers."

"Why did he go at all ?" Grace asked.

"Ah, you don't know him, or you would not ask. He went for our sake. He has all the old debts paid off. It is I that know what a sacrifice he has made. He is too generous, too noble."

The tears rushed into her eyes ; and Grace clasped her by the hand, and held it so tight that Mary looked at her in surprise. But Grace took no notice.

"Oh, you're home very early," said Mrs. Kearney. There's a letter for you, Mary, from Australia. I was so impatient, I'd open it, only for you are home so soon."

Mary jumped from the car, and ran into the house, followed by her mother and Grace ; all eager to know the contents of the letter from Australia.

CHAPTER LXV.

MAT DONOVAN FOLLOWS GRACE'S ADVICE ; BUT BESSY MORRIS
IS GONE.—HONOR AND PHIL LAHY IN THEIR NEW HOME.

A YOUNG merchant jumped from an omnibus opposite the
General Post Office, and, after glancing at his watch, hurried
down Sackville Street with the air of a man who had no time
to spare. Before he had got half-way down the street, however, he stopped short, after passing a tall, broad-shouldered
countryman, who was standing opposite a shop window.
There was something in the fine manly figure of the countryman that might well have arrested anyone's attention ; and
the young merchant smiled on observing how intent he
seemed in examining the newest styles in bonnets and artificial
flowers. He touched the rustic connoisseur upon the shoulder
with the end of his umbrella ; and, after a start, and a look
of surprise, there was a warm shake-hands, and mutual
expressions of pleasure at the meeting.

" How are they all at home ? " the young merchant asked.

" All well, sir," was the reply. " 'Tis younger your father
is gettin'. I'm afther sellin' two fine stall-fed fat cows for
him—I didn't see betther at the market. An' faith, Wat
Murphy'll have an argument against us ; for when all
expenses are paid, 'twon't be a crown a head more than
Wat offered. I sold a fine lot of bullocks for Mr. Kiely ;
no betther. But he spares no expense in buyin' the best
stock ; an' Woodlands is as good fattenin' land as there's
in the county."

" I saw in the papers that they had an increase in the
family at Woodlands, and that it is a son this time."

" So they had, sir. But they wor all sure you'd be down
to the christenin' at Docthor O'Connor's."

" Well, I was not able to go. How is my mother now ? "

" She's very sthrong, then ; on'y for the lowness o' sperits.
But Miss Ellie can get great good uv her ; an' when Miss

Grace happens to be at Docthor O'Connor's or at Woodlands she'll send for her, an' the misthress 'll be as gay as a lark in less than no time."

" Come down to the warehouse with me," said the young merchant. " I want to know all about everybody."

The countryman looked once more at the window, the display of flowers and feathers seeming to possess some extraordinary attraction for him, and, after glancing up and down the street, as if he would fain linger where he was, could he only find a reasonable excuse, walked on with the young merchant.

" I had my mind made up to call to see ye," said he, " as I have the day to myse'f till the six o'clock thrain."

" This is Mat Donovan, sir," said Willie Kearney to his uncle, when they reached the warehouse.

" Oh, how are you ? " said the merchant. " I hope all friends in Tipperary are well."

" All as well as you could wish, sir," Mat answered.

" I was very much interested in your case," Mr. Kearney observed, " that time you were charged with robbing old Pender. Hugh wrote to me about it, and I was glad to have it in my power to be of some use to you."

" I had good friends, sir," returned Mat. " But I suppose you heard ould Isaac confessed before he died that it was Beresford an' Darby Ruadh that took the money in ordher to have an excuse for robbin' Sir Garrett Butler, God rest his sowl."

" Why didn't Sir Garrett follow up the prosecution against them ? " the merchant asked. " I was hoping they would be both transported."

" Well, when Beresford made off, the ould father confessed all, an' gave up some uv the plunder, an' as he was so near his end, they left him so."

" Where is the son now ? "

" In Queensland, or somewhere off in that direction," replied Mat. " We heard nothin' about him since Misther Lloyd paid the two thousand pound. An' faith, Misther Bob'd be in the coorts like Sam Somerfield and the rest uv the landlords down there, on'y that Tom Ryan and Ned Brophy, an' a few more uv the tenants, made up the money an' lent it to him. He was just afther payin' his other sister's fortune to Captain French, when Beresford's attorney slapped at him. The tenants 'd be sorry to lose Misther Bob, an' these new landlords are such screws. Every wan was sorry for poor Major French, an' his fine place went for nothin'. But do you think will Misther Hugh ever come home, sir ? "

" I think he will. I have written to him to say it would be for his own interest as well as for the interest of the whole family."

" We're sure uv him so," Mat replied with a delighted look. " Whatever is for their good he'll do id. Many's the good turn I knew Hugh to do ; an' 'tis little talk 'd be about id."

" Hugh Kearney is a man," said the merchant.

" He wouldn't be his father's son if he wasn't a good fellow," returned Mat.

" He's worth a ship-load of his father," exclaimed the merchant.

" Come this way, Mat," said Willie, showing him into his office. " You have not told me half the news yet. Has Barney that thrush's nest with which he used to cheat me, still ? "

" He coaxed a bull-dog pup from Wat Murphy's son wud the same nest a few weeks ago," returned Mat. " Wat came out an' there was the divil's row. Peg Brady was rearin' the pup wud the calves unknownst to any wan, till Wat came out for him, an' said he wouldn't give him for the best fat sheep your father had. We expect that Peg and Barney'll be married shortly."

" I had a letter from Tommy Lahy lately," said Willie, " and he reminded me of Barney, and all the old neighbours."

'' I'm tould, like yourself, sir, his uncle is afther takin' him into partnership."

" Yes ; their house is one of the most respectable firms in Boston. It was about an order for Irish linen he wrote to me."

" 'Twas no later than last Sunday," returned Mat, " that the schoolmaster remarked, after readin' Phil's speech, that yourse'f an' Tommy Lahy wor the two innocentest boys he ever initiated into the sciences, as he said ; that ye wor no way crafty, an' could be chated out of your marvels wud the greatest facility, an' your castle-tops came in for the most hannels; an' now ye are the two richest men belongin' to the parish."

"What's that you said about a speech?"

"Wan that Phil Lahy made at a great Temperance meetin'," Mat answered. "An' the divil a finer speech was made there. He sent the paper to Billy Heffernan. An' sure I remember when Phil an' Billy wor the two greatest dhrunkards in Knocknagow, except Jack Cummins, that used to bate his wife, an' that's what Phil never done; an' Billy had no wan to bate but his mule. But it was poor Norah done id all."

" "I often think of Norah," said Willie. " I knew her chair in Mary's room the moment I saw it."

"An' Nelly has her slippers," returned Mat, " hangin' at each side of the crucifix at the head of her bed, wud her beads in wan an' a bit of palm in th' other. An' if you go into the churchyard uv a Lady Day in harvest you won't be long lookin' for Norah's grave, for not an inch uv id that won't have a flower on id. Nelly an' Billy dhresses the grave every Patthern-day as sure as the sun shines. But didn't Tommy say anything about his father an' mother?"

"Yes; he said they were well; but that his mother was always pining for home. I have no doubt it is that grave you mention that makes her wish for home."

"Poor Honor! she was the heart an' sowl uv a good woman."

"Tom asked how the mocking-bird he sent Ellie was going on."

"He's a fine singin' bird," replied Mat solemnly. "She sent him over to Billy Heffernan's to have Nelly take care uv him while she was at the wather wud Mrs. O'Connor and Mrs. Kiely, an' he picked up the whistle uv the plovers an' the curlews, so that he'd bother you sometimes. He frightens the life out uv Mrs. Kearney when he screeches like a hawk. She says he's not right; an' faith my mother has the same notion, an' thinks the lads in the forth has somethin' to do wud him. But is that Lory Hanly wud the bag?" Mat asked, looking through the window.

"Yes; he's going to the Four Courts. I suppose you know he is a barrister. He is getting on very well,"

" Oh, I know, sir. He was cheered in Clonmel afther gainin' the law for a poor man the landlord thought to turn out. That was a fine letther against the land laws his father wrote in the papers. An' 'twas a hard case to be turned out uv his place afther all he lost by id, for no raison but because the new landlord wanted to have a residence on his property. But the divil a word he had to say that poor Tom Hogan hadn't to say ; an' id come out whin ould Isaac was dyin' that Hanly bribed him to put out Tom Hogan an' give the farm to himse'f."

" It appears he did not see the injustice of the law till it came to his own turn to feel it," said Willie. " His daughter is married to a Mr. Wilson, a friend of mine."

" Maybe 'tis Johnny Wilson, that was in the bank ? " Mat asked.

" The same," returned Willie, " and you will be likely to have him in Kilthubber, as manager of the same bank soon. His wife is very anxious to go there, as she and Mrs. O'Connor were great friends."

" So they wor," said Mat. " An' the other sister was a grand girl."

" Yes, she is still to the good, and looked upon as a great beauty."

" I'll have a bag-full uv news for Miss Grace," said Mat. " But I must run an' get a letther uv credit for this money, as I don't like to have so large a sum about me. But I'll call in again on my way to the railway."

After getting the letter of credit, Mat Donovan made straight for the same window where we found him a few hours before, and which had bloomed into brighter and more varied splendour in the meantime, as if the flowers there displayed were alive and real and felt the influence of the sun. But this would scarcely be enough to account for the absorbing interest Mat Donovan seemed to take in that shop-window. Could it be that he wanted to make a purchase ? It would seem so, for, after deliberating with himself for some minutes, he walked into the shop. But then he seemed to have forgotten what brought him there, and looked a little puzzled and embarrassed.

" What can I do for you ? " asked a smiling young lady inside the counter, surveying him with a look of kindly encouragement.

Mat looked about him, and, after a long pause, asked for
" a ribbon to put in a bonnet." The ribbons were displayed,
and one selected and neatly folded in white paper ; and
seeing that the young lady laughed in spite of herself Mat,
as he put the parcel in his pocket, thought fit to set her
right and remove an erroneous impression, by remarking
carelessly that it was for a sister of his, who was as fond
of ribbons as ever she was, though she had " three or four
childher at her heels." But Mat evidently wanted something else, and, in reply to the question whether she could
do anything else for him, he told her to show him a broad,
thick ribbon.

" 'Tis for an ould woman's cap—for my mother I want
id," said Mat Donovan. And the young lady inside the
counter did not laugh now, but rather looked pensive and
melancholy. Perhaps she, too, had an old mother in some
Munster valley, who wore a broad ribbon over her cap.
This purchase was folded up and paid for, too ; but still
Mat Donovan lingered.

" I think you are from Tipperary," said the young girl.

" Well, I am," he replied. " Though I don't know how
people can know I'm a Tip. But you are right ; I am from
Tipperary."

" So am I," said she.

" Well," returned Mat, resting his elbow on the counter,
" I was tould a neighbour uv mine was employed in this
establishment, an' if so, I'd like to see her before I go home,
as some uv her relations would be glad to hear how she is."

" What's her name ? "

Mat Donovan rubbed his hand over his face, which made
him look quite flushed, and, after making several unsuccessful attempts to pick up a very diminutive pin from the
counter, answered, " Bessy Morris."

" Yes ; she is here ; but I didn't see her for the last week.
I'll inquire." And after much delay, and sending up and
down stairs, Mat Donovan walked out with Bessy Morris's
address written on a slip of paper.

After many turnings and windings, and inquiries, Mat
Donovan found himself in an out-of-the-way street in a very
poor neighbourhood.

" Number seven," said he, glancing at the paper. " It must

be the small house, wud the hall-doore. An', sure enough,
thim white curtains is what I'd expect to see wherever Bessy
'd be. 'Tis a clane, snug little house, though there's nothin'
but dirt an' poverty all around id.''

His hand trembled and his heart fluttered, like a very
coward, as he knocked at the door. Several minutes passed
before it was opened, and he had his hand on the knocker
again, when it occurred to him that the house was so small
it was impossible that the first knock was not heard ; and he
waited for another minute. At last the door was opened,
and Bessy Morris stood before him. She was very pale and
thin, but as captivating as ever. But how calm and collected she was ; and not in the least surprised to see him !
And though he felt the pressure of her hand, his reception,
he thought, was very cold indeed, considering how long it
was since they had met before. But he did not know that
she had seen him from the window, and sat down and covered
her face with her hands for a moment ; and then ran to the
glass, and hurriedly arranged her hair, and tied a ribbon
round her neck, before she opened the door. He walked in
and sat down, and replied to all her questions about her
friends in the country. And then she told him how her
aunt's only son, who was a sailor, had been drowned not long
before, on one of the American lakes, and she feared his
mother would never recover the shock the intelligence of his
death caused her.

" She has been so very ill for the last week," said Bessy,
" that I am obliged to stay with her continually. If she
does not get better soon, I must try and procure some work
that I can do in the house."

" An' how do you get your health yourse'f ? " Mat asked.

" Well, indeed, pretty well ; but I am a little worn-out
now. I am very glad to hear that your mother and Nelly
are so well."

" Will we ever have a chance of seein' you in Knocknagow
again ? " he asked, with his old smile.

She shook her head sadly, but made no reply. But a
dreamy look came into her eyes, as if she were thinking of
the days that were gone.

" I needn't tell you that we'd be all glad to see you," he
said.

" I don't know that, Mat," she replied with another sad shake of the head.

" Don't know id ! " rejoined Mat Donovan ; and his broad chest heaved—but he could say no more.

" Are you as fond of songs and music as ever, Mat ? " she asked, as he stood up, and held out his hand to say good-bye.

" Well, I am, then," he replied. " Miss Grace of'en plays a tune for me, an' so does Miss Ellie. But nun uv 'em can touch Mrs. Kiely. I never hear the like of her ! "

She handed him a little book, and, turning over the leaves, he said, " This is an elegant song-book."

" Keep it for my sake," returned Bessy, with her old winning smile, as she clasped his hand with energy, and hurried back on hearing her aunt's voice, calling to her.

The next day Mat Donovan was at Woodlands with the price of the cattle he had sold for Edmund Kiely. Grace brought him in as usual to play some of his favourite airs for him.

" Do you remember the day of Ned Brophy's wedding, Mat," said she, " when you asked me to play that tune for you ? "

" I do, well, Miss," he replied.

" Mr. Kearney wanted you to win a wife with a fortune," she continued. " But now that you are making money so fast as a cattle dealer, why do you not get married ? "

" I was asked the same question in Dublin about yourse'f, Miss," returned Mat, " an' I couldn't answer id."

" Who asked you ? "

" Bessy Morris," he answered. " She warned me not to forget to remember her to you and Mrs. O'Connor, an' how ye used to have many a talk in the little room in the cottage."

" So we used," returned Grace, thoughtfully. " I remember the day she told me the legend of Fionn Macool and the Beauty Race. Is Bessy herself married yet ? "

" No, Miss," he replied. " She's not married."

Grace's fingers ran carelessly over the keys, as she watched Mat Donovan from the corners of her eyes. He had covered his face with both hands and leant forward on the table near which he was sitting.

" I used to say long ago that you were fond of Bessy,' said she. " Now, tell me candidly, was I not right ?"

" You wor right, Miss," he answered, unhesitatingly ; for there was something in her manner that invited confidence, and he sorely needed sympathy. She went on questioning him with so much tact and delicacy, that she got the history of Mat Donovan's " whole course of love " from him, even from the time when he used to toss the cherries over the hedge to Bessy Morris, on her way from school.

" Mat," said Grace, " you should have told her."

" I was too poor, Miss," he replied. " An' seein' so many respectable young fellows about her, I thought id would be no use. An' besides, though she was always nice and friendly, she never cared much about me."

" Take my advice, Mat, and tell her ; and you'll find you are mistaken."

" Do you think so, Miss ?" he asked eagerly.

" It is *impossible*," returned Grace, with emphasis, " that she could be indifferent to such love as yours."

" In the name uv God," said Mat Donovan, after a long pause, " I'll take your advice."

Before many weeks had elapsed, Mat Donovan stood again at the door of the small house in the out-of-the-way street. He knocked with a firm hand this time, and there was no fluttering of the heart as on the former occasion ; for he had his mind made up for the worst. But there was no answer to his summons.

" She must be out," he thought, " an' maybe the ould woman is keepin' the bed still, an' I believe they have no wan in the house but themselves." He glanced at the windows, and it immediately occurred to him that the white curtains were gone, and then he saw that the shutters were closed.

" She's dead," said a woman, who came to the door of the next house, and found him looking at the windows.

" Dead !" he exclaimed—and the colour flew from his cheek—" who is dead ?"

" The old woman," was the reply ; "an' she had the beautifulest coffin I ever seen leavin' the street. They wor dacent people."

" An' the young woman ?" he asked, drawing a long breath.

"Well, I don't know where she's gone ; but she left for good the day after the funeral."

He hurried to the shop in Sackville Street, but could only learn from the proprietress that Bessy Morris had given notice that she could not return to her employment there ; for which they were very sorry, as she was an excellent work-woman.

"Might there be e'er a comrade girl uv hers in the house, ma'am, that could tell me anything about her ?" poor Mat asked in his bewilderment.

Inquiries were made, and a young girl came down to the shop and told him that Bessy was a particular friend of hers.

"An' could you tell me where she is ?" he asked.

"She's gone to America," was the reply.

"To America !" he repeated, in so despairing a tone that the young woman raised her eyes to his face, and said :

"You are Mat Donovan ?"

"Well, that is my name," he replied absently.

"She was thinking of writing to you," returned the young woman.

"Was Bessy thinkin' of writin' to me ?"

"Yes ; but she changed her mind. She was thinking, too, of writing to Mrs. Dr. O'Connor, somewhere in the county Clare, I think, but she didn't know the address."

"I thought I tould her we had Docthor O'Connor, in Kilthubber since Father Carroll got the parish," replied Mat. "But how long is she gone ?"

"She only left for Liverpool on Monday. The name of the ship she was to go by was the ' Ohio.' I was with her getting her passage ticket at the agent's."

"Where was that ?" he asked eagerly.

"Eden Quay," she replied, " but I forget the number."

The agent told him that unless some delay occurred, he would have no chance of catching the " Ohio " in Liverpool, as she was to have sailed that same day. But there *was* a chance, and next morning, in the grey dawn, Mat Donovan was hurrying along the docks of Liverpool, staring at the forest of masts, and looking round for some one who could tell him whether the " Ohio " had yet sailed for America.

"The ' Ohio ' ?" replied a sailor who was returning to his

vessel, evidently after being up all night. " Yes. she sailed for New York at four o'clock last evening."

Bessy Morris was gone !

" But sure 'tis long ago she was gone from me," he thought, as he rested his elbows on a pile of timber, and gazed at a vessel in the offing. " When is id that she wasn't gone from me ? An' for all that, I feel as if she was never out uv my sight till now, that she is gone for ever. He stood there like a man in a dream, he did not know how long, till the noise around him, and the lading and unlading of the vessels commenced, roused him, and turning from the busy scene he strolled listlessly into an unfrequented street, and wandered on, on, merely wishing to pass away the time, and to be alone, till one o'clock, when the steamer was to leave for Dublin.

" Lend me a hand, if you plaze," said a man, with a heavy trunk on his shoulder, in an accent which placed it beyond all doubt that the speaker was a Munsterman. The trunk was laid upon the pavement, and the man dived into an arched doorway, pulling off his hat and making the Sign of the Cross. Mat looked up at the building, and saw that it was a Catholic church. He entered, and kneeling in front of the altar, offered up a short prayer. As he rose from his knees, his attention was attracted by a young girl coming out of one of the confessionals. She knelt, or rather flung herself down upon the stone floor, and with hands clasped almost convulsively, raised her streaming eyes to the picture of the Crucifixion, over the altar. Her pale face told a tale of suffering, and misery, and sore temptation, which there was no mistaking.

" My God !" thought Mat Donovan, " maybe that's the way Bessy will be, afther landin' in a sthrange counthry, wudout a friend, an' maybe sick an' penniless. Oh, if I could on'y do somethin' for her ; if I could know that she was well an' happy, I'd be satisfied." Acting on the impulse of the moment, he walked towards the priest, who, after looking up and down the church, and seeing no other penitent requiring his ministry, was on his way to the sacristy. On seeing Mat approaching, he went back to the confessional.

" 'Tis to ax your advice I want, sir," said Mat. " Bein' an Irishman an' a sthranger in this place, I'd like to get your

advice about somethin' that's throublin' my mind very much."
And he told his story from beginning to end ; and how " she
was always in his mind," and how he never thought of any
one else as he used to think of her—though he never expected she'd be anything to him more than a friend—they
being neighbours and neighbours' children. And now what
ought he do ? He wouldn't mind crossing over to America
for her sake no more than he'd mind crossing the street. And
did his reverence think he ought to go ?

" I don't like to give an opinion in such a case," replied
the priest. " You should not forget your mother and your
sister, and it may be the young woman would not respond to
your feelings, and might not require your assistance. But
on the other hand she may, and probably will have to encounter severe trials, alone and friendless among strangers,
and you might be the means of saving her."

" That's id," Mat interrupted, fairly sobbing aloud, as he
glanced at the poor girl on her knees. " 'Twould break my
heart."

" In the name of God, then," continued the priest, " do as
your heart prompts you. You seem to be a sensible man, not
likely to act rashly or from a light motive. And at the
worst it will be a consolation to you to think that you did
your best for her. And it might be a source of much pain
to you, if any misfortune happened to the young woman
to think that you might have saved her and neglected to
do so."

" Thank you, sir," replied Mat. " Your advice is good."

He left the church a happier man than he had been for
many a day before. On passing a small print-shop within a
few doors of the church, the well-known portrait of Daniel
O'Connell, " the man of the people," caught his eye, and Mat
stopped short, feeling as if he had met an old friend. And,
while looking into the " Liberator's " face with a smile almost
as full of humour and pathos as his own, the writing materials
displayed for sale in the window reminded him of the
necessity of communicating his intention of going to America
to his mother.

" Miss Grace is the best," said he, after pondering over the
matter for some time. " I'll tell her as well as I can, an'
lave id to herse'f to tell my mother, and there's no danger but

she'll manage id all right," So he wrote to Grace that he would start by the first ship leaving Liverpool for the United States—which the man in the print-shop informed him was the " Erin " for Boston—in pursuit of Bessy Morris.

Mat Donovan counted the hours as the good ship sped upon her way across the great ocean. Never before did he think the days and the nights so long—not even when he lay a prisoner in the jail of Clonmel. The vessel was crowded with Irish emigrants, and many an " o'er-true tale " of suffering and wrong did he listen to during the voyage. But as they neared the free shores of America, every face brightened, and the outcasts felt as if they had seen the end of their trials and sorrows. Alas ! too many of them had the worst of their trials and sorrows yet before them. But it was only now Mat Donovan began to see how difficult, how almost hopeless, was the enterprise he had embarked in. He had no clue whatever by which he could hope to trace Bessy Morris. And his heart died within him at the thought that he might spend a life-time wandering through the cities of the great Republic, sailing up and down its mighty rivers, or travelling over its wild and lonely prairies, without finding her.

" Where am I to go or what am I to do ?" he said to himself as he stood alone on one of the principal streets of Boston. Suddenly he remembered Tommy Lahy, and it was like a ray of hope to think that he had at least a friend at hand to consult with. He had no difficulty in finding the extensive concern in which Tommy was now junior partner. But when in answer to his inquiries he was told Mr. Lahy had sailed for Europe only two weeks before, Mat felt more disheartened than ever.

" Can I see his uncle ?" he asked, recovering from his disappointment.

" Yes, come this way," replied the clerk.

The merchant received him civilly, and when Mat told him he was from Knocknagow, and asked, as Mr. Lahy was gone to Europe, could he see his father and mother, they being old friends and neighbours, the merchant replied of course he could, and very glad, he was sure, they would be to see him. " As for Mrs. Lahy—who, I suppose you know, is my sister—we can't make her feel at home in this country at all," he continued. " But she is more contented since

Tom has got a house in the country, where she can keep a cow and fowl, and grow potatoes and cabbages. It is only about a mile outside the city, and you will have no trouble in finding it."

Following the directions given him by the merchant, Mat soon found himself at the door of a handsome house in the suburbs. He knocked, and the door was opened by a smart-looking young woman, who looked inquiringly into his face.

" Is Mrs. Lahy wudin ?" he asked.

" O Mat Donovan !" she exclaimed, the moment she heard his voice ; and catching him by both hands she pulled him in ; and Mat found himself sitting in a nicely furnished room before he had recovered from his surprise.

" Is id yourse'f, Judy ?" he asked, looking round the room and wondering why it felt so hot, seeing that there was no fire—the stove being an " institution " with which Mat had yet to become acquainted.

It was the same Judy Connell who had caused such dire confusion, by forgetting to shut the door behind her, in Mat Donovan's kitchen, that windy winter's night long ago, when she ran in to " take her leave of them."

Judy told him that Mrs. and Mr. Lahy would be in soon. They had only gone to visit a poor woman whose husband had broken his arm by a fall from a scaffolding. Mrs. Lahy was always finding out poor families in distress. Judy herself had a situation in one of the principal hotels in the city, but she always felt unhappy among such crowds of strangers, and so she asked Mrs. Lahy to take her, and now her mind was easier than ever it was since she came to America. Mrs. Lahy was like a mother to her ; and besides, she had the same wages she was getting at the hotel, which was a great advantage, as she was able to send as much as ever home to her poor old father—besides feeling so comfortable and happy.

And Judy ran on with astonishing volubility, asking in-numerable questions, and answering them all herself. Her intimate knowledge of everything concerning her present neighbours was amazing ; but Mat opened his eyes in wonder when she detailed minutely and correctly every important event that had occurred in the parish of Kilthubber, since the day she left it down to the eviction of the Hennessys, which happened only three weeks before, and the election of poor-law guardians for the division of Knocknagow, on the head of which several black eyes were given and received in the city of Boston.

Here Mat managed to edge in a word, as Judy's voice subsided into an inarticulate murmur—she having caught her poll-comb between her teeth, while twisting up her hair, which had suddenly fallen down—and assured her that the election in question passed off quite peaceably at home, Mr. Kearney having nearly all the votes. The new landlord, who lived in Attorney Hanly's handsome house, set up a candidate in opposition to Maurice Kearney, but got no one to vote for him but his own tenants, who were few and far between. So that Mat Donovan was greatly astonished to hear that there had been a fight on account of the election of a poor-law guardian for Knocknagow in the city of Boston ; and managed to say so before Judy Connell's tongue had room to go on again.

" Here they are," she exclaimed, sticking the comb in her poll, and running to open the door.

And how Mrs. Lahy raised her hands in wonder, and welcomed Mat Donovan, as if he had dropped down from the sky !

Mrs. Kearney going to second Mass on an Easter Sunday was never a more respectable-looking woman than Honor Lahy, Mat thought. But she was the same Honor Lahy still, for all that. And as for Phil, dressed as he was in a suit of superfine broadcloth, and carrying a varnished walking-stick in his gloved hand—why, only for the shirt-collar, which was as high and as stiff as ever, Mat Donovan would not have believed his own eyes, that *that* old gentleman ever made a blue body-coat with gilt buttons for him.

" I'm glad to see you, Mat," said Honor. " Proud an' happy I am to see you sittin' in that chair. But ye're all lavin' Ireland—all lavin' the ould sod. 'Tis of'en I said to mese'f, when my heart used to be breakin', thinkin' how lonesome the ould place was—'tis of'en I said Knocknagow was not gone all out so long as Mat Donovan was there. I used to think uv yourse'f an' your mother standin' in your nice little garden, an' lookin' down to the beech-tree, an' thinkin' of them that was far away ; an' of poor Norah ; an'

maybe takin' a walk to the churchyard uv a Sunday evenin'
an' offering up a prayer at her grave. I always knew," continued Mrs. Lahy, who was quite as well-informed as her
handmaiden of all that had passed in her native place since
she left it, " I always knew Miss Mary an' Billy Heffernan
would have luck. I knew heaven would reward them for
all their kindness to my sufferin' angel. An' glad I am
that they are well an' doin' well. An' I know they'll all be
glad to see Tommy, for he promised me faithfully he wouldn't
come back wudout payin' a visit to the ould place ; an' sure
'tis well to have any wan at all left there to welcome him
after the scourgin' the counthry got." And Honor buried
her face in her hands and wept silently.

They were all silent for some minutes. Mat wished to say
something, but did not know how to begin. Phil tapped the
lid of his silver snuff-box, and took a pinch. And as for Judy
Connell, she seemed to have run down like a clock, and could
do nothing but stare at the window, and pant for breath.

" Ye're all lavin' Ireland," Honor repeated, as if to herself.

" If they are," Phil observed, " it is because the invader
won't allow them to live there. The Celts are gone with a
vengeance, says the London *Times*. An' the English Viceroy
tells us that Providence intended Ireland to be the fruitful mother of flocks and herds. That is why our people are
hunted like noxious animals, to perish in the ditchside, or
in the poorhouse. That is why the floating coffins are crossing the stormy Atlantic, dropping Irish corpses to the
sharks along the way, and flinging tens of thousands of living
skeletons on the shores of this free country. That is why
the last sound in the dying mother's ears is the tooth of the
lean dog crunching through the bones of her infant——"

" O Phil, Phil, stop !" his wife cried ; " 'tis too terrible to
listen to."

" Woman, it is true," he replied. " And England—whose
duty it was not to allow a single man, woman, or child to
die of hunger—when this glorious Republic offered to send
food to the starving Irish if England would send her
idle war-ships to carry it—England refused, and let the
people starve, and now shouts in triumph that the Celts are
gone with a vengeance. But mark my words," continued

Phil Lahy, rising to his feet, and gracefully extending his right arm, while the left rested on the back of his chair— " a day of retribution will come—

> " ' The nations have fallen, but thou still art young.
> Thy sún is but rising, while others have set ;
> And, tho' slavery's cloud o'er the morning hath hung—
> The full noon of freedom will beam round thee yet.'

And I say, Mat Donovan, if you could live in tolerable comfort at home, you had no right to desert your country."

" Well, I'm not desertin' Ireland," replied Mat. " I didn't come to this counthry wud the intention of remainin'."

They all looked at him in surprise ; and, after some hesitation, he told them the object of his voyage, adding that he feared he'd have his journey for nothing.

Judy Connell mentioned some twenty or thirty different places, to which, for one reason or another, Bessy Morris would be likely to go. But, after reflecting for a minute or two, Phil Lahy said :

" Lave it all to me, Mat, an' I'll manage it. Don't think of a wild-goose chase all over the States. It would be madness. Stop here for a few days with us and rest yourself. An' I'll get a few lines in the papers that'll be sure to come under her notice wherever she is. I needn't give her name in full if you like. But a few lines under the head of ' Information Wanted ' will be sure to make all right. So make your mind aisy, an' let us have a walk while supper is gettin' ready, an' we'll drop in to the editor, who is a particular friend of mine."

" That's a good advice, Mat," Honor observed, eagerly. " You'd be only losin' your time an' your money for nothin' if you went huntin' about the counthry. An' twill do us all good to have a long talk about ould times. So make up your mind and stay for a week or two wud us, an' you may depend on Phil that he'll find Bessy even if he was to go to the bishop himse'f."

It was so agreed ; and Judy Connell and her mistress—if we may use the word—set about the supper, and so astonished Mat Donovan by the display he found spread out before him on his return from the city, that he was afterwards heard to declare that he " didn't know what he was aitin'."

About ten days after, Mat Donovan found himself in the

sitting-room of a private house on the shore of one of the great lakes " out West." He had inquired for Bessy Morris, and was shown into this room.

" This is a grand house," said he to himself. " I never see such a lot of big lookin'-glasses. I wondher is id in service she is ? I thought she'd be more likely to go on as she was in Dublin. But sure she might be employed that way here, too, I suppose."

The door opened, and Bessy Morris stood before him ! She looked surprised, quite startled, indeed, on seeing him. Then her eyes sparkled, and the blood mounted up to her forehead ; and with the old winning smile, she advanced and gave him her hand.

" My goodness, Mat !" said she, " what a surprise it is to see you so soon. When did you come to America ?"

" I on'y landed in Boston the week before last," he replied.

" Well, will wonders never cease ?" returned Bessy.

A pretty little girl here came into the room, and Bessy desired her go and shake hands with an old friend of hers from Ireland. And as she glanced up into his face, Mat said to himself that she was the " dead image " of the little girl to whom he used to toss the cherries over the hedge, once upon a time.

" I will be back to dinner at the usual hour," said a gentleman, who advanced a step or two into the room. " I'm in a hurry, as I ought to be at the store before now."

" This is Mat Donovan," said Bessy.

" I'm glad to see you," returned the gentleman, shaking hands with him. " You have done well to come out West. Irish emigrants make a mistake by remaining in the towns and cities, when they ought to try at once and fix themselves in permanent homes in the country. Of course you will keep him for dinner, Bessy. We'll have a long talk, and I'll be glad to give you all the assistance I can. Good-bye for the present."

He hurried away, and Mat looked inquiringly at Bessy.

" Don't you know he is my father ?" she asked. " He was unsuccessful for a long time after coming to America. Then he was told that I had died when a mere child, and he put off writing to his father from year to year, till he thought the old man must be dead too ; and having married again, he never wrote to Ireland till, reading the account of the loss of the vessel in which my aunt's son was a sailor, he learned her address from a letter found upon my cousin's body when it was washed ashore. And this prompted him to write to my aunt. The letter only arrived the day before her death ; and in my impatience to meet my long-lost father, I lost no time in coming to him. He is very well off, quite rich indeed, and I have every reason to be satisfied with his reception of me. The little girl is his youngest child."

" God knows, I'm glad uv id !" exclaimed Mat Donovan, drawing a long breath. " I was afeard you might be wudout a friend, an' maybe in bad health ; for you didn't look sthrong at all that day I called to see you."

" I suffered a good deal while my aunt was sick," replied Bessy. " No one knows all I have gone through since poor grandfather's death. But, thank God, it is over. And so far as my father is concerned, my most sanguine hopes have been more than realised. I am the mistress of his house, and he says he must make up in the future for his neglect in the past. I am very glad to think that he can be of service to you, Mat, if you settle down in this part of the country."

" I'm not goin' to stay," returned Mat. " 'Twouldn't do to lave my poor mother. An', as Phil Lahy says, no man ought to lave Ireland but the man that can't help id."

She looked at him in unfeigned astonishment ; and Mat became quite confused, and regretted that he had said so much.

" You did not come to America with the intention of remaining ?" she asked.

" No, I never had any notion of stayin' in America," he answered absently. " God be wud you," he added, rising and holding out his hand.

She placed both her hands in his, and continuing to look earnestly into his face, said :

" But you will come back and see my father again ?"

" Well, maybe I would," he replied with a sorrowful smile, as he clasped her hands tenderly between his. " An' when-ever you think uv ould times, an' the ould neighbours, I hope you'll remember that Mat Donovan uv Knocknagow was your friend, ever an' always, Bessy. Ay,' he added, gulping down his emotion, " a friend that'd shed the last dhrop uv his blood for you."

He rushed out of the house, leaving Bessy standing in the middle of the room, as if she were spell-bound.

" Call him back, Fanny," she said hurriedly to her little sister. " Tell him I want to speak one word to him."

The child overtook Mat Donovan before he had gone many yards from the house, and brought him back.

" Mat," said Bessy Morris, speaking calmly and thought-fully, " was it you got the advertisement in the paper ? I thought it might be a girl I knew in Dublin, who came out last summer."

" Well, id was," he answered.

" And you came to America for nothing else but to find me ?"

" I thought you might want a friend," he stammered.

" And you are going back again ?" she continued, coming close to him, and laying her hand on his arm, just as she laid the same hand on the sleeve of the blue body-coat in Ned Brophy's barn.

" What else would I do ?" he answered, sadly.

" And have you nothing else to say to me ?" she asked, dropping her eyes.

" O Bessy, don't talk to me that way," returned Mat, reproachfully. " Where would be the use of sayin' more ?"

She moved closer to him, and leant her head against his broad chest, which heaved almost convulsively as she did so.

" Mat," she murmured, " I will go with you."

" Go wud me !" he repeated, with a start.

" And be your wife," she added, in a whisper that thrilled through his whole frame, making him feel faint and dizzy.

" Do you know what you're sayin' ?" he asked, recovering himself.

" I do, well," Bessy replied.

" Look around you," he continued. " An' then think uv the poor thatched cabin on the hill uv Knocknagow."

" I *have* thought of it," she replied. " I have often thought of that poor cabin, as you call it, and felt that if ever it was my lot to know happiness in this world, it is in that poor cabin I would find it."

Both his arms were round her now, and he held her to his breast.

"God bless Miss Grace," said he; "'twas she advised me to tell you all."

"What did she say?" Bessy asked.

"She said that you couldn't be indifferent to such love as mine," Mat answered, with his old smile.

"And she was right," returned Bessy.

"But are you sure, Bessy, this is no sudden notion that you might be sorry for?" he asked anxiously.

"As sure as that I am alive," she answered.

"Oh, you must let me go out to have a walk in the open air," Mat exclaimed. "My heart is too full; I'm smotherin'." He hurried out to wander by the shore of the lake, and think over his great happiness, and thank God for it.

"And so, Bessy," exclaimed her little sister, who had been a wondering spectator of the foregoing scene, "you're going to marry a greenhorn. Though Colonel Shiel admires you so much, and wants you to go to the hop with him."

"Yes, I am going to marry a greenhorn," returned Bessy, catching the child up in her arms and kissing her. "And who knows but you will come to see me to dear old Ireland yet; and find me in a pretty thatched cottage, with a fine old cherry-tree in the garden, and lots of beehives; and such a dear, kind old mother to take care of them."

"Yes, that will be nice. I shall go to Ireland to see you," returned the child, placing a hand on each of Bessy's cheeks and looking into her eyes. "I shall like the thatched cottage and the beehives very much."

"And you will like the greenhorn, too, I am sure."

"Yes, I think so. But it was so foolish for such a big fellow to be crying like a child."

"Was he crying, Fanny?"

"Indeed yes. When I overtook him at the end of the block he was crying. I'm sure he felt real bad. And now you are crying, too," added the child.

"It is because I am so happy, Fanny," Bessy replied. "I am so happy that I will go now and kneel down and pray to God to make me worthy of the love of that big, foolish greenhorn."

"I guess you Irish must be always praying."

"It is good to pray, Fanny."

"Yes, of course, once in a while. But have you got two
cents? Thank you. I'll go right away to the candy-store;
and if I meet the greenhorn I'll give him some, and tell him
to be a good boy and stop crying, and sister Bessy will marry
him."

"Well, there he is under the trees," returned Bessy,
laughing. "And remind him that twelve o'clock is our
dinner hour."

CHAPTER LXVI.

ONLY A WOMAN'S HAIR.—MORE WEDDINGS THAN ONE.—A
HEART AS "BIG AS SLIEVENAMON."—BEAUTIFUL IRELAND.
—THE SORT OF A WIFE THAT BARNEY GOT.

"POSITIVELY, Mary," exclaimed Grace, "Tommy Lahy—as
I suppose we may still call him between ourselves—is about
the nicest fellow I ever met."

"And your old weakness for nice fellows is as strong as
ever, I dare say," returned Mrs. O'Connor, smiling.

"A *strong* weakness!" rejoined Grace; "that's not bad.
But, really, he is so handsome, and so manly and intelligent——"

"And rich," Mary added.

"Well, of course that is worth counting, too. Even papa
says he never met a more intelligent young man. It is really
a treat to talk to him."

"Yes, I have noticed that you think so," returned Mary.
"Ye seem to like each other's society very well, indeed. But
is he in the toils in downright earnest?"

"No," she replied, shaking her head; "he does not seem
to be very susceptible."

"And what am I to think of that handsome and expensive
ring on your finger?"

"Nothing; only that he admires me."

"And suppose he more than admired you, how would it
be?"

" Well, though I scarcely ever knew any one else so much
to my taste in every way," returned Grace thoughtfully, " I
believe I could not love him. In fact I sometimes think I
have no heart. And only for papa I'd follow Eva."

" There was a time," said Mary, " when I used to say the
same of myself."

Grace bent her head, to hide the blush which she felt
stealing into her face, and, walking to the window, seemed to
take great interest in the movements of the magpies in the
elm-tree. Perhaps she was thinking of the evening long ago,
when Tommy Lahy peeped into the magpie's nest before
throwing down Mat Donovan's coat, after he had emerged
from under the fallen hayrick.

" I suppose," she observed, " you know we are to have
Kathleen Hanly at Woodlands to-night, and Lory. I never
can call him anything but Lory. He protests he admires
me as much as ever, and if I only have patience till he gets his
silk gown, he will lay that coveted garment at my feet."

" I am very glad to have Rose for a neighbour," said Mary.
" I always liked her, and was delighted when Mr. Wilson was
appointed manager of the bank."

" Johnny Wilson, an' you love me," returned Grace ; " let
us speak of them all as we used to do in the old times. I
wonder does Adonis think of Kathleen still ? I was greatly
amused by Mrs. Captain French's account of the tiger hunt.
Only to think that Richard and Mr. Lowe—or let me say
Adonis and Apollo—figured so conspicuously in it ! It is a
pity Mr. Lloyd was not with them."

" Hugh was very sorry," Mary observed, " that Richard
should go into the army. Arthur has written to him, strongly
recommending him to come home. But I really fear he
would not be contented."

" He might if he could retain the uniform," rejoined
Grace. " He came to see me—or rather to let me see him—
before he went away. And if ever mortal man soared into
the seventh heaven upon a pair of epaulettes, that man was
Surgeon Richard Kearney, of the —th Lancers. I asked him
did he think Annie handsome, and he only stared at me. He
could think of nothing but his new uniform."

" Hugh was greatly struck by Annie," Mary observed.
" He says she is the most splendid woman he ever saw."

"Yes, she does strike people at first ; but it wears off after a while."

"Edmund does not think so," returned Mary.

"Well, no ; he is as enthusiastic as ever. But Edmund is essentially an enthusiast. He is half out of his wits, he is so glad to have Hugh at home. I pity the poor snipe and partridges."

"Why don't you apply the same rule to Hugh as to the others, and call him Fionn Macool ?" Mary asked. "Do you remember giving him that name ?"

"Indeed, yes," returned Grace, pensively. "And how distinctly I remember the day in your room when Bessy Morris said I could not have given him a grander name, though I by no means meant to be complimentary. Were you frightened, Mary, when you saw him so awfully thin and worn ? I thought he had only come home to die. But papa said he would be as strong as ever again. And he is wonderfully improved during the last few weeks."

Mary clasped her hands together, and turned her mild blue eyes upwards, but made no reply.

"But where is he now ?" Grace asked.

"Writing in his own room," Mary replied. "He has little Grace with him. He is very fond of little Grace."

"Oh, between little Grace's prattle, and her mother's singing," returned Grace, with a frown, "he has no time to devote to other people."

"I'll go tell him what you say," rejoined Mary, laughing.

"You have kept the old writing desk during all your wanderings," she observed, on entering Hugh's room.

"Yes," he replied ; "I have brought it with me everywhere."

"Oh ! and you have kept this, too ?" she exclaimed, opening a loosely folded paper she had carelessly taken from the desk.

"Yes, of course," he replied, smiling, on seeing what she had discovered.

"And is it really somebody's that you care for ?"

"Well, it is," he replied, gravely ; but he reddened immediately, and would have recalled the words if he could.

"And can't you tell me who it is ? Do I know her ?"

"Oh, you must ask no more questions," he replied, snatching at the paper,

But she was too quick for him, and carried it off in triumph.

"Here is that mysterious lock of hair," said Mary to Grace, who was still standing at the window, gazing at the mountains. "Can you unravel the mystery, as you did that of the tracks in the snow?"

"I can't imagine who it can be," she said, after looking for a moment at the tress of hair.

"He admits it is somebody he really cares for," said Mary.

Grace scrutinised the hair again, and as her own hair fell down on her hand while she did so, Mary observed:

"It is very like your own. But what is that written on the paper?"

Grace looked sharply at the half-obliterated pencilling, and said, "Oh, yes. 'Only a woman's hair'—Swift, you know—

> "'The passioned tremble of the heart
>   That ripples in the little line—
>   "Only a woman's hair."'

But he has made a change which is by no means an improvement. He has—'Only a *girl's* hair.'"

"There is something else written under it," said Mary.

"Yes, it is the date. 'January 9, 18—.'"

The words swam before her eyes, and she fell senseless upon the floor. Mary caught her up, and placed her upon a low chair, by the side of which she had fallen. She was about to cry out for assistance when Grace's bosom heaved, and her eyes opened.

"Oh, what has happened to you?" Mary asked anxiously.

"O Mary," she replied as if she were just awaking from a deep sleep, "it is my hair."

Mary could only look the surprise she felt.

"Do you remember," continued Grace, "when Mr. Lowe was here, the day Mat Donovan asked me to play the air of the song he was to sing at Ned Brophy's wedding? It was the same day that Lory Hanly brought me the jay."

"Yes, I remember," returned Mary. "But what has that to do with it?"

"Look at the date on the paper," said Grace, closing her eyes.

"It is the very same day," replied Mary.

" And don't you remember," continued Grace, keeping her eyes still closed, " how I cut off a lock of Hugh's hair with your scissors, and he caught me and cut off some of mine ?"

" Yes, I recollect it all now," Mary answered, looking troubled. " I trust in goodness that I have done no harm."

" And he has kept it all the time," Grace thought. " He has always *loved* me !"

" This is Grace's hair, Hugh," said Mary, on coming into his room again.

" Well, it is," he replied, as if the earnestness of her manner had surprised him into the admission.

" O Hugh," said she, looking anxiously at him, " I never thought of this. I will bring her up."

" I fear you have been making me ridiculous," he exclaimed, getting between her and the door.

She told him what had just occurred in the parlour ; and so great was Hugh Kearney's astonishment, that for the moment he felt no other emotion. But when Mary asked him would she go for Grace, he seemed much agitated.

" Yes," he answered, with a motion of his hand towards the door. He paced up and down the room two or three times, and then sat down again at the table where he had been writing, looking quite unmoved ; save for that light, half fire and half softness, that swam in his dark eyes. Grace came in, and those dark eyes met hers. She crossed the room with a measured step, and laid her hand on his shoulder, still looking into his eyes. There was no need for words.

" I don't know what to say," said he at last. " But Grace, when did you first think of me ?"

" I don't know," she replied. " I think always."

" There must really be a mystery in these things, Grace. I never hoped such happiness would ever be mine. Did you know how much I always loved you ?"

"Well, I didn't *know*—but, somehow, I believed it."

They were silent again for a long time ; and Grace recalled Bessy Morris's words, " If a ship were sinking with you, or a lion rushing to devour you, wouldn't you feel safe if his arm were around you ?" Yes, she felt it was so.

" Wonders will never cease," exclaimed Mary, flinging the door open. " Fionn Macool can make himself agreeable,

Do you forget that we are all invited to a great ball at Woodlands in honour of Fionn's safe return from the Antipodes ?"

Grace, for once in her life, would have forgiven the great ball. But she resolved to make herself as " killing " as possible ; for it was rather provoking that Mrs. Kiely so dazzled her guests on such occasions, that even a certain young lady, who was generally admitted to possess some attractions of her own, was quite thrown into the shade at Woodlands.

" That dark dress becomes you admirably, Mary," said she. " And Ellie looks downright lovely in white. There is something faun-like about her. But which of these shall I wear ?"

" Ask Hugh's opinion," returned Mary.

" Yes, Ellie ; ask him which would he prefer."

" He doesn't care which," said Ellie, after consulting Hugh on this important matter, " as neither is green."

" I like green, but green does not like me," returned Grace. " I must leave that to Annie."

" Here is Arthur," said Mary, rather impatiently. " Decide at once ; we have no time to lose. Even mamma has all her bows pinned on to her entire satisfaction."

" Yes, but she had no difficulty in deciding on the colours," Grace replied. " Her Uncle Dan settled that long ago. I only wish his worthy nephew—or grandnephew—would do the same for me. But I will have my revenge, and dance all night with Lory."

" What will your papa say, when he knows ?" Mary asked, as they drove up the avenue at Woodlands.

" He will like it," Grace answered, emphatically.

And he did like it. And said—and said truly—that there was no man to whom he would rather entrust his daughter's happiness than to Hugh Kearney. And yet the patriotic Dr. Kiely felt disappointed, though he strove to hide it even from himself. For, in spite of his theories, he cherished the hope of seeing his darling Grace the wife of a descendant of one of those Norman freebooters, who " came to divide, to dishonour," and to whose ill-omened advent none knew better than the learned and patriotic doctor how to trace all the woes of unhappy Ireland. " But then," he would say in his grand way, " some of them became more Irish than the Irish themselves."

Is it necessary to add, that there was a wedding soon after ?

Grace wished to have the ceremony performed by Father Carroll, as it was he married Arthur O'Connor and Mary, and Edmund and his dark-eyed bride. But the democratic Dr. Kiely dearly liked *eclat ;* and Grace had the honour of being married by a bishop. And never did priest or bishop, or cardinal or Pope of Rome, hold his hand over a brighter or a happier little bride.

But there were more weddings than one.

" Mat Donovan and Bessy Morris !" the astute reader exclaims.

Of course. But a child would have guessed that.

And the tall pedlar, who never passed the way without taking a draught from the pail under the little window, opened his eyes in wonder on seeing a neat square farmyard, with barn, dairy, cow-house, and all other requisites, behind the little thatched house, to which two rooms with good-sized windows had been added. The tall pedlar, as he re-placed the cup on the little window, rubbed his cuff across his grey beard, and hoped it was not all the work of the " good people," and would not have vanished into thin air before he came his next round—as happened to his own knowledge to a snug little place one side of Holycross Abbey. And the tall pedlar, swinging off his heavy pack, and sitting on the corner of the table, gave a full and true account of how he had been hospitably received in the snug little house before-mentioned, one fine summer evening, and awoke next morning by the side of a furze bush, without a house, or the sign of a house, within miles of him. At which Mrs. Donovan the elder blessed herself many times, and devoutly thanked Providence that *her* house was not one side of Holycross Abbey—though nearer to an imaginary straight line between Maurice Kearney's fort and the quarry than she could have wished.

The little boarded parlour, with its papered walls and American clock on the chimney-piece, was just what Grace had fancied as suitable for Bessy Morris. There was a book-shelf, too, with a goodly number of volumes arrayed upon it, which caused Mr. Bob Lloyd to stare the first time he saw it, and furnished Mrs. Ned Brophy with a subject for much scornful laughter. Whenever Ned did not make his appearance in due time on the nights of market-days, he was pretty sure to be found by Mat Donovan's fireside. And as he meekly obeyed the order to " get up out of that," and staggered homeward, Ned invariably protested that his libations during the day did not exceed " a couple uv tumblers uv porther." But we fear this did not always save him from a whack of his own blackthorn across the shoulders.

Old Mrs. Donovan, however, preferred the kitchen with its snow-white dresser and shining pewter—not forgetting the old spinning-wheel and the straw-bottom chairs—as, indeed, did Mat himself, and Bessy, too. And as for Billy Heffernan, he protested that his flute became quite hoarse whenever he attempted a tune in the parlour. And when he took his place on the bench, with his back against the partition, Nelly always thought of the night when she made the discovery that Billy loved Norah Lahy ; and how, after the first pang of jealousy, she loved Norah herself better than ever. Yes, Bessy Morris and Mat Donovan were married ; and that dear, kind old mother's sad face had a moonlight sort of smile in it for ever after. But lest Mat should get credit for more than he deserves, we feel bound to admit that if Bessy's father had not behaved so handsomely, he could not have built the out-offices quite so soon ; nor would he have the ten acres at the other side of the road.

But there were more weddings than two.

" Where is that fellow ?" Mrs. Kearney asked, fretfully. " I can never find him when I want him."

No one seemed to pay particular attention to Mrs. Kearney's grievance. There was a car at the hall-door, with Mary and Grace on one side, and Mrs. Edmund Kiely—about whose feet Hugh was elaborately wrapping the rug—on the other.

" She is the only handsome woman," Mary observed, " that I ever knew Hugh to care about."

" Thank you," returned Grace.

" Did you send him anywhere ?" Mrs. Kearney asked from the door-step—addressing her husband, who was pointing out a defect in the horse's shoeing to the servant.

" Yes," he answered, at last. " I sent him to count the sheep."

"And you knew I wanted to send him to town," returned Mrs. Kearney reproachfully.

"He ought to be back an hour ago," Maurice answered. "But I suppose he fell into the quarry and broke his neck; or was attacked by the bull in the clover-field. Get that shoe taken off," he added, turning to the servant, as if the broken neck or the attack by the bull were a matter of little consequence compared with Edmund Kiely's chestnut going lame.

Mrs. Kearney was quite alarmed; but to her great relief Barney Brodherick was seen tearing across the lawn mounted on Bobby, who snorted and flung his heels in the air at every prick of the "spur-sauleen" with which the heel of one of the rider's brogues was armed. Flinging himself from his steed, Barney hurried up to his master.

"Are the sheep all there?" he asked.

"Begob I have 'em all in my hat, sir," Barney answered.

Mary's laugh was almost as ringing and quite as musical as Grace's—but Mrs. Kiely only looked astonished, with all her great black eyes—as Barney carefully scooped a fistful of sloes out of his hat, and presented them to his master, who commenced to count them with a look of intense gravity.

"They're all right," said he, flinging away the sloes, and looking quite satisfied.

"She's after consintin', sir," said Barney with a grin.

"Oh, very good," returned his master. "One fool makes many."

"But," continued Barney, rubbing his poll, "if Miss Grace 'd put in a good word for us, I know Father Carroll wouldn't be hard on us, an' he gettin' so many jobs all uv a slap."

"What is it, Barney?" Grace asked.

"Goin' to be married, Miss," Barney answered, looking very solemn. "An' if you would tell him to do id as chape as he could, I know he'd do anything for you—an' not to be too hard wud the questions. I have my prayers as pat as A B; an' what more do a poor man want? An' I'm purty good at the seven deadly sins, an' know what is mathrimony, now, since Miss Ellie put id into my head," Barney added with increasing seriousness.

"And so, Ellie, you have been putting matrimony into Barney's head?" said Grace, turning to Ellie, who was romping on the grass with two of Mary's children.

"Yes," she replied, throwing her hair back from her face; "because, when he went to get married last winter, the priest sent him away. He asked him, ' What is matrimony ?' and Barney answered, ' The marriage money ' ; and so Father Carroll refused to marry him till he had learned his catechism."

"An' damn hard work I had makin' up the same marriage-money," returned Barney, with an injured look. " An' whin I had id, 'tis little I thought I'd be throubled wud any other money."

"And what sort of a wife are you going to get ?" Mrs. Kiely asked, turning round and bending her black eyes on the odd figure before her.

"A good labourin'-man uv a wife, ma'am," Barney answered readily. " Peg Brady."

And so Barney and Peg Brady added one more to the "jobs," which happened to be neither few nor far between that season—though very like " angels' visits " to Father Carroll's mind, notwithstanding. But one more of these "jobs" concerns us too intimately to be passed over.

Do you recollect the still, summer day when the glad tidings that Norah Lahy was sitting out under the beech-tree ran like wildfire from end to end of Knocknagow ? And how, while Miss Kearney stopped to talk to Norah, a shy young girl ran into the house to talk to the old linnet ? And how she was caught in a motherly embrace as she jumped down from the chair ?

Well, that same shy girl was clasped to the same motherly heart in the pretty house where Mat Donovan was so warmly welcomed and hospitably entertained, near the city of Boston, a few months before.

"Oh, the villain of the world !" exclaimed Honor Lahy, "never to tell me a word about it ! He said 'twas goin' to see the Pope he was."

"And so I did go to see the Pope," said Mr. Tom Lahy, laughing.

"Oh, yes, Mrs. Lahy," Ellie added, " we were in Rome, and saw His Holiness. I have a beads blessed by himself for you. And we have got our portraits painted, and have a great many other things that you will like."

"Don't talk to me about anything but yourself"

returned Honor, with another hug. " Oh, did I ever think my poor ould heart would ever feel the joy that's swellin' id up this minute as big as Slievenamon ? Glory be to God for all His mercies ! Wondhers will never cease. But, O my darlin' Ellie, will I ever again kneel down on the green grave in the ould churchyard where my own darlin' is sleepin' —at home in beautiful Ireland ?"

" You will," Phil Lahy answered, emphatically. " There are bright days in store for beautiful Ireland, as you call her, and as she deserves to be called. There is a spirit growing up among the outcast children of beautiful Ireland that will yet cause another English monarch to exclaim, ' Cursed be the laws that deprived me of such subjects.' The long night of her sorrow is drawing to a close. And, with God's blessing, we'll all be in beautiful Ireland again."

" You are right, father," returned the fine young Irish-American. " We will never forget old Ireland."

But, however glad we are to have to record these happy events, we have not the least notion of attempting a description of them. To our mind, Ned Brophy's wedding was worth them all put together—including the bishop, whose presence so turned Mrs. Kearney's head that she all but cut the O'Shaughnessys for a whole month after. To be sure, Father Hannigan was at Ellie's wedding, and did something to make it like a wedding. For, if the truth must be told, the " grandeur " of the whole affair weighed heavily on the spirits of all present. Father Hannigan came all the way from his mountain parish where he was looked upon by his flock as an oracle in all matters, whether spiritual or temporal—and gave them the news of the week, with his own comments, from the altar every Sunday, after the last gospel. Not one newspaper, except his own—and a single copy of the *Weekly Catholic Illuminator*, which two policemen and a process-server jointly subscribed for—ever found its way into Father Hannigan's parish. And yet, we grieve to say, his parish supplied the London *Times* with more than one text for an article upon the well-worn theme of agrarian crime in Ireland. But Father Hannigan had a habit of addressing any member of his flock, against whom he happened to have a complaint to make, by name, in a manner that was very trying to the nerves of the congregation, and kept them upon the rack until he had come down from the altar, each dreading to hear his or her own name blurted out by the preacher at any moment. Hugh Kearney, who visited Father Hannigan the Sunday before his marriage, had an opportunity of witnessing this, when, as he rose from his knees at the conclusion of the Mass, he was startled by the words :—

" Mrs. Morrissy, why don't you send your daughter to the chapel to teach the children their catechism ? 'Twould become her better than dancing ' Follow me down to Carlow,' over there at Bosheenacorriga."

" She'll come every other Sunday, sir," returned Mrs. Morrissy, with a reproachful look at a young girl who knelt next Hugh, and whose burning cheeks told all too plainly that she was the delinquent who preferred the dance at Bosheenacorriga to teaching the catechism to the children in the chapel.

" If ever a man died of a broken heart it was poor Father M'Mahon !" was Father Hannigan's remark, as he and Hugh came to the turn of the road near Mat Donovan's. " Knocknagow killed him. He never raised his head after. And 'tis a terrible change, sure enough," he added, as he turned round in the gig, and looked down the hill. " 'Tis a terrible change. And 'tis hard to know where 'twill stop, or what will be the end of it. Ye had a narrow escape yourselves. Only for the new lease Sir Garrett gave you before the property was sold ye'd be in a bad way. There's nothing like security."

" That's true," Hugh observed. " And those new landlords are raising the rents to the last shilling the land will make. They look upon their purchases solely from a commercial point of view, and I fear many of them will prove harder masters than their predecessors."

" How is Edmund Kiely getting on with Woodlands ?" Father Hannigan asked.

" Oh, first-rate," returned Hugh. " He is becoming a capital farmer. But he may thank Mat Donovan, who is his right-hand man."

" 'Twas a great consolation to the old baronet to die in the home of his ancestors," the priest observed. " But I believe he could not have saved it from the wreck, only for the

doctor's money. But I believe the doctor had the best of
the bargain after all. What is he going to give yourself ?"

" Oh, I never spoke of such a thing," Hugh replied, looking
displeased.

" Oh, when the money is there, I don't see why you
shouldn't get it," returned Father Hannigan. " I'll talk to
Kiely about it."

" I request that you will not," said Hugh. " It would be
most disagreeable to me."

" Well, very well—I won't mind it. And, indeed, I believe
there's no occasion. He won't forget Grace, I'll be bound.
But are we going to have Flaherty ?"

" Yes," Hugh answered, laughing at the abruptness with
which his reverend friend changed the subject ; " he
promised to come."

And Mr. Flaherty kept his promise. And, though the
crimson-velvet bag was somewhat faded, not so was his
music, which was as brilliant as ever. Indeed, when, at
Father Hannigan's request, he commenced to play the
" Coulin," there was a little scene which surprised many
persons present. Mrs. Edmund Kiely could not control her
emotion ; and, pressing her face against her husband's breast,
she sobbed aloud, and was so overcome by her feelings, that
Mrs. O'Connor, who was, perhaps, as deeply moved as herself—though you would never guess it by looking at her—
led her impulsive friend from the room ; the blind musician,
as they glided by, raising his head with that listening
expression, as if an invisible spirit were whispering to him
what was going on.

Arthur and Edmund followed them out after a little while.

" Really, Annie, you surprise me," said Edmund.

" I couldn't help it, Edmund. It brought poor papa so
vividly to my mind. The night is very fine. Let us walk
for awhile——"

" I object," said Arthur, touching her shoulder with
the tips of his fingers. So they remained standing at the
window.

" I believe," said Mary, after a silence of several minutes,
as she raised her blue eyes to the clear sky, " I believe there
is no happiness in this world without a shadow upon it."

" And what shadow do you see now ?" Arthur asked.

" Poor Ellie, so far away," she replied sadly.

" She is a happy girl," remarked Arthur.

" Yes, I hope and believe so."

" And surely Grace is happy," Edmund observed.

" Ye'd be talking of happiness," exclaimed Maurice Kearney, who had come into the room unobserved, and somewhat startled them by the abruptness of his address. " Ye'd be talking of happiness. Wattletoes and Peg Whack "—Mr. Kearney had a genius for nicknames—" are the happiest pair in Europe. Come, Mrs. Kiely ; you must come in and give us a song."

CHAPTER LXVII.

GOOD-BYE.—THE OLD ROOM.—MRS. HEFFERNAN'S TROUBLES. " MAGNIFICENT TIPPERARY."—A GLEAM OF SUNSHINE.— BUT KNOCKNAGOW IS GONE.

WE have not counted the years as they stole away like visions of the night. What need to count them ? They were here, and they are gone ! And now we must say good-bye—and sad enough it is to be obliged to say it. God be praised ! we see truth, and trust, and thankfulness in the eyes raised to ours, and no shadow of reproach at all. And, God be praised again, there are tears in those eyes, and we feel the clasp of a slender hand ! But with this the reader has not much to do ; so we shall only add—may his or her good-byes, when they must be said, be all like this one.

But, whatever other changes the years have brought, the little room up in the steep roof of the old cottage is much the same as when Barney Brodherick threw Arthur O'Connor letter into the window in the ivied gable long ago. It is still called " Mary's room," and sometimes " mamma's room " by two lovely little ladies, who live almost entirely at the cottage, and for whose behoof the little room has been turned into a nursery. There is an old straw-chair there, which the little ladies regard with something like awe, as they talk in whispers of the poor sick girl who was

so good and so patient, and who gave the straw-chair to
their mamma when she was dying. These two little ladies
are their grandmamma's pets ; and even " dressing dinners "
is not half so important a matter now in Mrs. Kearney's eyes
as it used to be. But they have been observed, latterly,
feeling their noses carefully, and climbing upon chairs to look
at them in the glass ; for people are continually telling
them that the said noses are " out of joint " since the arrival
of the plump little stranger in the cradle ; and they wonder
much how that can be, seeing that the plump little stranger
never touched their noses at all, but, on the contrary, seems
to devote most of his waking hours to vigorously thumping
his own nose with his dimpled little fist, which, fortunately
for him, has no knuckles, and therefore cannot hurt him
very much. The nose, his grandmother avers, is her Uncle
Dan's ; and the rose-bud of a mouth—that is never done
blowing bubbles—his aunt Mary's ; and the double chin, his
grandfather's " all over." " And," Mrs. Kearney would continue, " he'll have his father's eye-brows." " And his mother's
cheek," Hugh added, one day. At which Grace laughed, and
shook her fist at him.

And who so happy as Grace ! For a while there was one
little vexation that used to put her into a scolding humour.
Hugh was as great a stay-at-home as ever ; and Grace was
as fond of a dance as ever. There was a round of very pleasant little parties at Christmas-time among their acquaintances, to not one of which Hugh could be induced to go—
except to Woodlands. He was ready enough to go *there*,
Grace said. And when her father was at Woodlands on these
occasions, and he and Hugh and Edmund discussed literary
or political subjects—with Dr. Arthur O'Connor to contradict everybody and object to everything—for Arthur was
nothing if not critical—Grace used to say it came fully up
to her idea of what refined and intellectual society ought to
be. And the old mansion, and the ancestral trees outside—
for the timber at Woodlands was not all cut down—and a
certain high-born air in the hostess, were not altogether lost
sight of ; though Grace's notions about the " upper ten " were
considerably modified since the time she used to edify Mary
with her views as to what an aristocracy ought to be.

But though Hugh would go nowhere but to Woodlands,

he wished her to go, saying that her account of all that happened would be better than being there himself. And this was quite true. But equally true was it that Hugh Kearney found it very pleasant to be alone with his books of an evening, reading and thinking. Yet, let the page or the vision be never so fascinating, the moment he heard her voice or her footstep, his heart leaped to welcome her.

One night Grace was home earlier than usual. She drew a chair close to his, and Hugh shut his book, prepared to listen to a lively description of Mrs. O'Shaughnessy's party. But to his surprise Grace remained silent and thoughtful. He looked anxiously at her, fearing that she might be ill. But there was no sign of illness in that bright, bewitching face ; for, though thoughtful, it was bright, and to him, at least, it was bewitching in all moods. It was pleasant, too, to look at her dressed in such perfect taste.

" But why does she not begin to talk ?" Hugh asked himself.

Not a word ; she only leant against his arm, and gazed into the fire.

" Do you remember the time when Mr. Lowe was here ?" she said at last, without moving, and still gazing into the fire.

" I remember it quite well," he replied. " Indeed, I have been thinking of him and Richard to-night. It is a strange coincidence that they should be together again in another quarter of the globe."

" This very night," continued Grace, still gazing into the fire—" I can't think of the year just now, but it was this very night—they were in this room. Richard sat in the old arm-chair, and Mr. Lowe was standing there with his elbow on the chimney-piece. Do you remember ?"

" Yes ; they used to come in here to smoke."

" Richard asked you whether you thought a person could love more than once." Here Grace seemed lost in thought for some minutes. " And you said yes," she continued, as if unconscious of the pause ; " that a person might really love more than once ; but that you believed it was the fate of some to love one as they never could love another. Do you remember ?"

" Not exactly. But I dare say I said so, for I have always thought so."

" Do you think so still ?"

" Yes, I certainly do."

" And you said, if it ever happened that a man or a woman could never love but once, it was when two spirits rushed together in this way, and were parted by death or some other cause that did not involve blame to either.

" That has been a theory of mine," Hugh replied.

" Is it still ?"

" Well, yes. It is," he answered, thoughtfully.

She was silent again, gazing into the fire.

" Hugh."

He bent over her, and looked into her eyes.

" Tell me——"

" What am I to tell you ?" he asked, smiling ; for she had relapsed into silence.

" Was it of *me* you were thinking when you said that ?" She bent back her head, and raised her eyes to his with a confident smile.

He was on the point of answering seriously " Yes," when he recollected himself, and, leaning back in his chair, laughed heartily.

She looked up in surprise, and even appeared troubled.

" Why do you laugh ?" she asked.

" Just remember how old were you at that time," he replied.

" Ah, no matter," said Grace ; " can't you say it was of me you were thinking ?"

" Well, perhaps I had some sort of a prevision of what was to come—

' And now I find the fancy true,
And fairer than the vision made it.'

But how did you remember all this ?"

" I don't know. I was passing the door while you were saying it. I didn't mind it at all at the time, but it occurred to me afterwards. That and Bessy Morris's story about the Beauty Race, and Fionn Macool, and ' the one little girl that he'd rather have than any of them,' were constantly in my mind."

" How much I owe Bessy Morris," said Hugh, half laughingly, half dreamily, laying his hand upon her head. " She and Mat Donovan are the happiest couple in all Tipperary this moment."

"No; not the happiest," said Grace. "I sometimes fear we are too happy, Hugh."

"Not too happy, so long as we do not forget the Giver."

She made no reply, but continued gazing into the fire.

"Now, Grace, do you think I can allow this? Where is the use in your being home early if you stay up this way? Here, drink this while 'tis hot. I thought you were in bed an hour ago."

It was Mrs. Kearney, who roused them from their dreaming a full half-hour after Hugh had last spoken. She came into the room with a posset for Grace; who, Mrs. Kearney would have it, required all sorts of nursing just then.

This was in the winter—the "dreary winter" some people call it. But no one in that old cottage ever thought of calling it "dreary."

It is now autumn, towards the end of September.

"I can't help feeling a little discontented," said Grace. "Whenever Edmund makes his appearance Hugh is never home till long after nightfall. And if they chance to go near Woodlands, I may give him up till eleven o'clock or later."

"What would you do if you were like me?" Mary asked.

"Well, I suppose," Grace replied, "I'd console myself with the idea that we were getting rich. Arthur seems to have great practice."

"Practice enough," returned Mary. "But scarlet-runners are more plenty than fees."

"What are they?"

"I thought you knew everything. They are the red dispensary tickets which require the medical officer to attend at the residence of the patient. Arthur said this morning, when he saw those young ladies in the garden, that if times did not mend, he did not know what to do with them. But I told him he need not give them fortunes at any rate." And Mary's mild eyes beamed with all a mother's pride as she looked into the garden where her two lovely little girls were playing among the formal flower-beds.

"You meant that, like their mother, they would require no fortune."

" Yes," Mary replied innocently. But seeing Grace beginning to laugh, she added with spirit—" I *am* proud that I had no fortune. But, on the other hand," she continued, somewhat sadly, " I wish I had ten thousand pounds."

" Well," returned Grace, thoughtfully, " I have not that to be proud of. But I think I may be quite sure my fortune did not influence Hugh, even in the slightest degree. On the contrary, the very fortune I was always wishing to have might have been a bar to my happiness. I think if I were poor Hugh would not have concealed his love for me as he did. It is appalling to think I might never have known it only for an accident. And it would have been a just judgment to punish me for my mercenary notions."

" I remember I used to be shocked at your notions," returned Mary. " But I knew you would see things in a different light, if once your heart was touched. But look at mamma with the children. Oh, here is Arthur !" she exclaimed with a start of delight. " I did not think he'd be back for hours."

" Yes, he knows that stile behind the laurels," Grace observed. " But where are those shots from ? If we could intercept the sportsmen before they get to Woodlands it would be well."

" I see them," said Mary. " They are in Billy Heffernan's turnips. Let us all walk round by the village, and they will see us when we reach the bridge."

Dr. O'Connor agreed to this arrangement ; and, after a glass of wine, and a kiss from each of his little daughters, went with Mary and Grace to prevent Hugh's escape to Woodlands.

Old Mrs. Donovan was among her bee-hives ; and it was pleasant to catch a glimpse of her white cap and her sad tranquil face through an opening in the clipped hedge. Mary always liked to see old Mrs. Donovan whenever she passed by the neat little thatched house. Grace liked a chat with young Mrs. Donovan ; they were congenial spirits. And so, perhaps, were Mary and old Mrs. Donovan.

" Aren't you afraid to have the child so near the bees ?" Grace asked.

" I am, then, and very uneasy," Bessy replied. " But his grandmother only laughs at me."

" Oh, he's a tremendous big fellow," Grace exclaimed, as she lifted Mat the Thrasher's son and heir up in her arms. " I thought my young Maurice was a ' bully,' as Barney calls him. But this lad is once and a half as heavy."

" Mat says he'll be a stone-thrower," returned Bessy, laughing, as she took the infant athlete from Grace's arms, and laid him upon the ground ; to roll and tumble, or lie still upon his chest, or his back, or to make short excursions upon all-fours—ever and anon stopping suddenly, propped up by his fat arms, to stare at a white head of cabbage with all his eyes—at his own sweet will.

" Do you ever wish to live at the Three Trees now ?" Grace asked. " Oh, never," returned Bessy. " Mat wanted to take the farm when my father sent us some money ; but I would not let him."

" Is it the same place ?" said Mary, sadly, as she looked down the hill. There was a low stone wall at each side of the road, the mortar of which looked very new and unpleasant to the eye. Perhaps the mortar looked all the more fresh because of the dark stones that seemed to thrust themselves through it here and there, in order that the traveller might read the story of quenched hearths and scattered households in their soot-browned faces. An odd tree, a perch or two in from the road, marked the boundary of a " haggart " ; for where an ash or an elm sheltered the peasant's cabin the tree was allowed to stand. The beech-tree escaped in this way ; and the pointed gable of Phil Lahy's old house, now roofless and crumbling to decay, seemed to regard the change wrought by the rule of the Stranger with a grim smile—such as Phil himself might have worn while emptying the vials of his sarcasm upon the head of "that poor crawler," Tom Hogan. No smiling faces now as they went on ; no children's voices ; no ringing of the anvil. Mary even regretted Kit Cummins's shrewish tongue, and the next-door neighbour's " G-ir-r-rout, you bla'guard —of which she was reminded by seeing a cat run across the road, and over the wall at the other side, pursued by a small red terrier that always accompanied Grace in her walks.

" It is an awful change," Mary observed.

" It really is," returned Grace. " I thought of it when you said we would go through *the village*."

" And think of the happy crowd that used to follow the big drum to the Bush," continued Mary. " And where are they all now ? Not one, I may say, left."

" There is one melancholy relic of the crowd you speak of," Grace observed, pointing to a man in the field a little further down.

" And what a handsome young fellow he was !"

" And for what is he rolling that stone from the wall into the field ?" Arthur asked.

" Surely," said Mary, " it cannot be that he is in Mr. Cummins's employment ? Though it was not he ruined them."

She alluded to the purchaser of a portion of Sir Garrett Butler's property—a brother of the redoubtable Kit Cummins, who had made a fortune by a peculiar mode of dealing with the struggling farmers in hard times. And it may be mentioned that Mr. Cummins's conduct as a landlord completely upset Maurice Kearney's favourite theory about " good Catholics," for Mr. Cummins was a most exemplary Catholic. And Billy Heffernan was hopelessly bewildered on the subject of " gentlemen," when he remembered that Kit Cummins's brother was a magistrate and a landlord, and, in fact, as great a man as ever Sam Somerfield was, to say nothing of Bob Lloyd, or Beresford Pender.

" There they are," Grace exclaimed ; " and if you don't stop them before they cross the road, we won't see them again for the day."

Arthur hurried on in pursuit of the two sportsmen, followed more slowly by Mary and Grace. He got within hailing distance on the bog-road, and when they heard his shout to them, they changed their course and came towards him.

Grace could see nothing but Hugh for some time, but Mary had eyes for other objects. Observing a goodly crowd around a stack of oats in the next field, and hearing the words, " Norah, throw up that bruckish to me," she laughed and made her way to them. It was Nelly Donovan, or we should rather say, Mrs. Billy Heffernan, and her whole family—from Norah, a black-eyed gipsy of nine years, to the " bruckish," of about the same number of months. Their mother, who was kneeling on the stack, the top of which

Billy Heffernan had just taken to the barn in his mule's car, wanted to give the " bruckish " his afternoon draught, while waiting till his father returned for the next load. But Norah found some difficulty in lifting him so high, and Mrs. O'Connor laughingly came to her assistance.

" This is the third fat boy I have taken in my arms to-day," she observed, as she pressed the bruckish against her bosom. " I'll begin to feel quite jealous and discontented ; everybody has boys except myself."

" Faith, then, maybe 'tis too many uv 'em you'll have yet, ma'am," replied Nelly, pulling up the child with one hand. " There's more bother wud wan uv 'em than a house-full of girls. Look at that fellow beyand now, an' nothin' will do him but to ketch a hoult uv that heifer be the tail ; an' wan kick from her would knock the daylights out uv him. Run, Norah, an' brin' him over here. Oh !" cried Mrs. Billy Heffernan, at the top of her voice, " look at him, look at him !"

The heifer had set off at full speed, the young hopeful holding on to the tail, till, the pace becoming too fast for him, he was flung headlong upon his face and hands—the stubbles scarifying his sun-burnt visage till it looked like a tulip.

" Lord help us !" exclaimed his mother, flinging the infant on the oat sheaves, and tumbling herself off the stack. But remembering, before she had run many yards, that the olive branch on the stack would be sure to creep out to the edge and fall down directly on his skull, thereby breaking his neck or causing concussion of the brain, Nelly ran back and pulled him from his couch ; and letting him drop upon the stubbles almost with as much violence as if he had descended on his own hook, but in a less dangerous position than upon the crown of his head. She was starting off again, when a great flock of geese, coming along the car-track, gabbling and picking up the oats that had been shaken from the load, attracted her attention ; and as it occurred to her that the old gander, who was of a vicious and misanthropic turn of mind, might take a fancy to the bruckish's eyes, Mrs. Heffernan looked wildly from one to the other of her olive-branches, quite at a loss how to proceed ; but, seeing that the elder had got upon his legs, and was now swinging from the tail of the mule's car, never minding his scratched countenance, Mrs. Heffernan heaved a sigh of relief.

" 'Tis little you know what bother they are, ma'am," said she, twisting up her abundant black hair, which had fallen about her shoulders. " When Mister Hugh an' Misther Kiely fired at the birds in the turnips a while ago, that fellow was makin' off over the ditch to get himse'f shot. An' there he is now, an' if the rope chances to get round his neck, he'll get himse'f hung. An' look at his father walkin' on, an' never lookin' back, or throublin' his head about him. This is the way my heart do be broke from ·mornin' till night. No, ma'am ; 'tis harder to rear wan boy than twenty girls."

" You'll have twenty barrels to the acre here, Bill," Hugh Kearney observed, looking round at the stacks, after feeling the weight of a sheaf of the oats.

" About that, sir," returned Billy, in his old solemn way. " You're a wonderful man," continued Hugh. " This is the very spot Richard stood in the day he left the leg of his trousers in the bog-hole ; and look at that crop of oats !"

" And all because the land is his own for ever," observed Dr. O'Connor.

" While grass grows an' wather runs, sir," rejoined Billy Heffernan. " Misther Lloyd laughed at me whin I axed a lase for ever of such a spot. But Sam Somerfield wanted him to go to law wud me an' break the lase whin he see the good I was gettin' uv id. He said 'twas a bad example to the counthry, an' that 'twould put dangerous notions into the people's minds. An' there is Sam himse'f wudout a sod of ground now ; an' Misther Bob is there yet."

" 'Tis really remarkable," Hugh observed, " that Bob Lloyd is the only landlord for miles around here who has escaped the Incumbered Estates Court."

" Because his tinants had the land for the value, an' long lases," returned Billy. " An' they wor always able to meet their rints, and to make up money for him whin he was in a hoult. An' there is Yallow Sam, that hunted every tinant he had, an' I'm tould his property was sould agin' ' t'other day for three times as much as it was bought for the first time."

" That's a fact," said Edmund. " And it does look a little hard, that, after all their· devotion to England, this law should have been introduced just when the value of landed property was at the lowest ebb. In fact, it looks very like robbery."

" The Irish landlords were encouraged to exterminate the people," said Dr. O'Connor, " and when the work was done, many of themselves were exterminated. England cares just as little for them as for the people."

" Mr. Somerfield's friends, however," Hugh remarked, " did not quite forget his services. You know he is a stipendiary magistrate."

" He whined frightfully," said Edmund, " at being obliged to give up Woodlands. It is strange that the most callous and merciless tyrants are the most abject hounds when it comes to their own turn to meet the fate which it was their glory to inflict on others. Poor Sir Garrett might have been moved to give him a lease only for those gables." And Edmund pointed to several gables that stood like large headstones, scattered over a great sheep-walk along the side of a hill within view of where they stood. Mr. Somerfield had left a solitary gable standing, of every roof-tree he had swept from the face of the land, and these he was wont to point to with the pride of an Indian warrior displaying the scalps of his foes.

" If we had the bogs itse'f," said Billy Heffernan, " some uv us at any rate might do some good. But they'd rather lave 'em to the cranes than give 'em to the Christians. What have I but the fag-end uv a bog ? An' begor, I wouldn't give id this minute for the best farm in the parish wudout security."

" You are right," said Hugh Kearney.

" 'Tis of'en I thought uv ould Phil Morris's words," continued Billy Heffernan, " that there was nothin' like security to give a man courage. Look at Mat Donovan, an' becase he had them few perches that his grandfather fenced in betune the two roads, when 'twas on'y a hape uv stones an' a lough uv wather, an' see how he kep' his grip. An' Tom Hogan an' the rest uv 'em swep' away like that," added Billy, taking a handful of chaff from the bottom of his cart and letting it fly with the wind. " Wo ! Kit ! Come, Nelly, up wud you on that butt uv a stack an' throw me the shaves. 'Twill be tight enough on us to have id all in afore nightfall.'

" No more shooting to-day," said Grace, putting her arm in her husband's. " Arthur and Mary are staying for dinner ; so, march ! "

Two gentlemen on horseback pulled up suddenly as they were passing " Tom Hogan's gate," as it was still called.

" That is Mr. Lloyd," said Grace. " But who is that with him ? "

" I don't know," Hugh replied. " They are calling to some one."

It was to the man who had rolled the stone into the field. He raised his head listlessly, on hearing Mr. Lloyd's voice, and looked towards the gate, as if waiting to know what he wanted. He had been sitting on the stone with his face buried in his hands, and must have remained motionless for some time, as the sheep were grazing quite close to him, one or two looking curiously at him, and almost touching him with their noses. But the moment he observed Mr. Lloyd's companion, he stood up quickly, and, after touching his cap, dropped his arms by his side and stood at attention.

" How are you, Hogan ? " said the gentleman.

" I hope you're well, captain," was the reply.

" What fancy have you taken to sitting there ? " Mr. Lloyd asked. " We saw you from the top of the hill, and didn't know what to make of you till we came to the gate here."

Jemmy Hogan's eyes moistened ; but his cheek flushed, and he seemed ashamed of being detected in giving way to such weakness.

" 'Twas a foolish notion," he replied at last, smiling somewhat grimly.

" I was going to ask you why you rolled that heavy stone into the field," said Dr. O'Connor, for they had all come up by this time, and were shaking hands with the two horsemen.

Jemmy Hogan walked, or rather stumped, to the gate— for he had a wooden leg—before he replied. He grasped the top of the gate, and rested his forehead upon his hands, just as his father had done the night he told Phil Lahy that " his heart was stuck " in that little farm.

" He is fainting," Mary observed in an anxious whisper to her husband, who approached the gate, and asked the young man if he were ill.

" No, sir," he answered, recovering himself ; " I'm not to say very strong, but I'm not ill."

His lips were quite pale, and his yellow cheeks looked hollow and worn. What a contrast to the handsome youth who leaped to Mat Donovan's side at the words, " Come here, Jemmy Hogan," that Sunday long ago in Maurice Kearney's kiln-field, when Tom Cuddehy's desertion of his party changed the hurling of the " two sides " into what Phil Lahy called a " promiscuous match !"

" You exerted yourself too much rolling that heavy stone," said the doctor.

" No, sir, no ; 'twasn't that," returned Jemmy Hogan. " I was tryin' could I make out the exact spot where the ould house stood. An' then I took a fancy to sit down where I used to sit when I was a little boy, in the corner beside my mother. So I rowled over that stone an' sot on id, till I thought I felt the hate uv the fire an' my mother's hand on my head. I b'lieve 'twas the breath uv the sheep that made me think I felt the hate ; for I was someway half asleep. An' when the thruth came back sudden on me, an' I see the grass an' the sheep, instead uv the blazin' fire an' my mother's smile, id gave me a change, I b'lieve," said Jemmy Hogan, as he took off his cap and wiped the drops of perspiration from his forehead.

" O Arthur !" Mary exclaimed, as, overcome by her emotion, she rested her forehead against his shoulder, " it is awful !"

Grace grasped Hugh's arm with both her hands, and fixed her eyes pityingly on Jemmy Hogan's face, but did not speak.

Captain French's horse, at the moment, began to plunge violently, and the ladies were about running down the road in their terror, when they saw a wild-looking cow running towards them.

" Stop her !" was shouted in a loud voice, but in a manner which would lead to the belief that the speaker considered the party at Tom Hogan's gate were there for the special purpose of stopping runaway cows. Hugh disengaged himself from the little hands that clutched his arm so firmly, and, going a few yards to meet the cow, brought her to a stand with little difficulty.

" I'm afther buyin' her from Mat Donovan," said Wat
Murphy the butcher, in a quiet way, " an' she turned at the
cross and med off for home. I was thryin' to buy another
from him, but he's axin' too much."

" She's a nice cow," Hugh remarked, " and in good condition."

Mat himself appeared at this juncture, and at the same
time his wife was seen running down the hill to meet him.
But, on seeing the gentleman on horseback, she stopped short
and turned back again. She had been wondering what was
keeping Mat out so long beyond his usual dinner-hour, but
Wat Murphy and the cow was a sufficient explanation, and
she hastened home, blushing at being observed by the gentlemen.

" Why," said the captain, " that is the girl poor Sergeant
Baxter lost his senses about."

" She is Mat Donovan's wife now,' returned Mr. Lloyd.

" Well, Mat," said the captain, " I can never have a cast
of a sledge with you again."

" I'm sorry for it, sir," Mat replied ; and his heart smote
him for having beaten the captain that day in the kiln-field.
" I'm sorry for it, sir," he repeated, looking at him, almost
with the tears in his eyes. For Captain French had only
one arm now.

" Do you have a hurling still ?" he asked. " We got some
smart fellows from about here."

" The hurlers are gone," replied Mat, looking around upon
the great pasture fields with scarcely a house within view.

" By George," said the captain, " if this sort of thing goes
on, there will be an end of ' magnificent Tipperary ' in the
English army "

" I was just going to remark," Edmund Kiely observed,
"that you and Jemmy Hogan would make a very suggestive
picture in illustration of that same ' magnificent Tipperary.' "

" How is that ?" Captain French asked.

" Why," Edmund replied, " he has come home with one leg,
after shedding his blood in the service of England, to find the
sheep grazing on his father's heath. And you come home
with one arm, to find a stranger in your father's halls."

" An' his property sowld for one-sixth uv the value," added
Wat Murphy, who was a privileged person. " The divil's

cure to the landlords. An Irish Parliament wouldn't thrate 'em that way. An' still they're agin their counthry."

" By G—," the captain muttered, absently, as if he were talking to himself, " that's just what they tell me my poor father said when he was dying of a broken heart."

" Come and dine with us," said Bob Lloyd to Edmund— for the rest of the party had moved on towards home. " We have a leg of mutton, and everything elegant."

" I'm after promising Mrs. Kearney to take an early dinner with her," returned Edmund. " And, by the way, I must send a messenger to tell my wife, or she will think I have been swallowed up in a bog-hole."

" Not shot from behind a hedge ?" the captain observed.

" No," Edmund answered, as he walked on to overtake his friends. " She is too long now in Tipperary for nonsense of that sort."

They had stopped to wait for him at Mat Donovan's clipped hedge.

" What is the matter with you ?" Arthur O'Connor asked, seeing the tears in his wife's mild eyes.

" It is such a sad picture," she replied, looking along the lonely road. " So different from what it used to be."

" There are gleams of sunshine in it," he answered.

" Where are they ?"

He pointed to Billy Heffernan and his wife and children, in the cornfield, which, a few years before, was a profitless moor.

" It is an omen," said Hugh Kearney. " The Irish people will *never* be rooted out of Ireland. Cromwell could not do it ; the butchers of Elizabeth could not do it."

" But there is a more deadly system at work now," returned the doctor. " The country is silently bleeding to death."

" Not to death," rejoined Hugh Kearney. " Those of her people who are forced to fly are not lost to Ireland. And those who cling to her are advancing in knowledge and intelligence. The people are becoming an educated and a thinking people. When Billy Heffernan's sons grow to manhood, they will in many respects be different men from their father."

" And would you say *he* will be a superior man to his father ?" Grace asked, pointing over the clipped hedge.

Mat Donovan stood under the cherry-tree, holding the
young " stone-thrower " high up among the branches, while
his mother glanced up at him—with the identical smile of
the little Bessy Morris of old, when she used to glance at the
cherries on her way from school ; and his grandmother
clapped her hands to attract the attention of the delighted
youngster, who crowed and kicked and plunged so vigorously
that Mat declared 'twas like holding a little bull.

" Yes," said Hugh, in reply to Grace's question, " he, too,
will be ahead of his father—at least of what his father was
in his early youth. For Mat is now a really intelligent man,
and is adding to his stock of knowledge every day."

" That is another gleam of sunshine," said Mary, her face
lighted up now, and her eyes almost dancing with pleasure,
as she contemplated the group under the cherry tree.

And when she turned to the dear old cottage, and saw the
blue smoke gliding up above its sheltering trees, and her
father, hale and ruddy, coming to meet them, and her mother
at the door, " wondering " what was keeping them so long,
and her own fair children gambolling upon the soft grass,
and her generous brother with his bright little wife clinging
so lovingly to him—that was a gleam—nay, a very flood— of
sunshine, too. And in Mary's home and in her heart there
was sunshine, bright, warm, and unclouded.

" Whack !" Maurice Kearney called out, " didn't I tell you
never to milk that cow without putting the spancel on her ?"

" O father, why don't you call her by her right name ?"
said Mary, appearing a little shocked.

" You may call her Mrs. Barney Brodherick if you like,"
returned Maurice Kearney, " but I'll call her Whack."

Grace and Mary sat in the drawing-room, feeling somewhat lonely, they could not tell why, when they were startled
by a ringing knock at the hall-door, which was quickly followed by a ringing laugh, and Mrs. Edmund Kiely had
administered a kiss and a hug to each, before they could
recover from their surprise. Of course it was just like her to
set off for Ballinaclash, when Barney announced to her that
Edmund was staying there for dinner. She flung her cloak
on one chair, and her hat on another ; and not a soul under
the old cottage roof—from Barney sucking his " dudheen "
in the kitchen chimney-corner, to young Maurice, blowing

bubbles and thumping Uncle Dan's nose in his cradle in the nursery—that did not feel the influence of her presence. Old Maurice rubbed his hands and shrugged his shoulders in a perfect ecstasy of delight, and lost no time in asking her to play his favourite tunes and sing his favourite songs— which she did till the tears ran down his cheeks.

And the old cottage was " filled with music " ; and their hearts overflowed with deep and tranquil happiness.

Mary saw the light shine out from Mat Donovan's little window, and thought of the dream of the Past from which it had awakened her long ago, as she sat there in the cold moonlight. And what a bright future was in store for her after all !

There was another dreamer awakened by the light from Mat Donovan's window that same moonlight night. And now, almost from the very spot where he lay in the black, lonesome moor, the light from Mat Donovan's window is seen by a happy household, basking in the ruddy glow of a bog-wood fire. The change is like what we read of in fairy tales. If poor Mick Brien could revisit the glimpses of the moon, he could scarcely believe that it was the dreary spot where he lay for hours meditating a deed of blood.

" Come," says Nelly, " I promised Bessy we'd go up to-night. An' brin' the flute."

Billy Heffernan took down his hat from the elk's horns and meekly obeyed.

" I'll go," exclaimed young Matty Heffernan, independently.

" No, you won't," returned his mother. " Stay wud Norah, an' help her to mind your little brothers. Give him the fife," she added, on seeing Matty showing symptoms of rebellion.

" I'll go see grandmother," he persisted. " She'll give me honey."

" You can stay all day o' Sunday at your grandmother's," said Nelly. " But you must stop an' mind the house to-night. An' there is the fife, an' you can play till you're tired."

" Well, Billy," said Mat Donovan, " did you hear any sthrange news yestherday ?"

" Not a word," he replied. " But I never see a town that's

gone like Clo'mel. I remember when I could hardly get
through the streets wud loads uv corn ; an' now there's
nothin' doin' there. The mills nearly all idle, an' the stores
an' half the shops shut up. 'Twas well Phil Morris used to
say 'twas the corn made a town uv Clo'mel."

"Nelly, you must bring in the kettle and fill out the tea,"
said Bessy. "This fellow won't go to sleep for me."

Nelly prepared the tea, of which all present partook, except Billy Heffernan, before whom his mother-in-law placed
a huge mug of milk.

"Have you the flute ?" Mat asked, as the American clock
on the chimney-piece struck eight.

"Let us come out to the kitchen," returned Billy
Heffernan.

"Arthur, stop for a moment," said Mary, an hour later,
as they reached the top of the hill on their way home.
"Can it be that Annie's voice could reach this ? The drawing-room windows are open, and I really think I can hear
her singing."

Dr. O'Connor reined in the horse, and listened with some
curiosity.

"Oh, it is from Mat Donovan's," Mary observed. "And
I am much mistaken if it is not Billy Heffernan's old flute."

"Why," said Arthur, when they had driven on a little
further, "there is nothing but music to-night. Do you hear
the fife from Billy Heffernan's own house, too !"

"It is very pleasant," returned Mary. "Thank God, there
are happy homes in Tipperary still ! But "—she added,
sadly, as she turned round, and looked along the two low
whitish walls that reached from " the cross " to Mat Donovan's
—" but KNOCKNAGOW IS GONE !"

THE END.

S P A
_ _ _   W²

P _ T C H